LIONS OF THE DESERT

A TRUE STORY OF WWII HEROES IN NORTH AFRICA

VOLUME FOUR OF THE WORLD WAR TWO SERIES

SAMUEL MARQUIS

MOUNT SOPRIS PUBLISHING

PRAISE FOR SAMUEL MARQUIS

**#1 *Denver Post* Bestselling Author
Kirkus Reviews Book of the Year Winner
Foreword Reviews Book of the Year Winner
Independent Publisher Book Awards Winner
Readers' Favorite Book Awards Winner
Beverly Hills Books Awards Winner
National Indie Excellence Book Awards Winner
Next Generation Indie Book Awards Winner
American Book Fest-USA Best Book Award-Winning Finalist
Colorado Book Awards Award-Winning Finalist**

"*The Coalition* has a lot of good action and suspense, an unusual female assassin, and the potential to be another *The Day After Tomorrow* [the runaway bestseller by Allan Folsom]."
—James Patterson, #1 *New York Times* Bestselling Author

"*Spies of the Midnight Sun* is not only a skillful, rapid-fire historical spy thriller, but also a fine source on one of the least-known and most heroic chapters of the Second World War."
—Kirkus Reviews

"Told through multiple viewpoints in a series of vivid scenes, *Lions of the Desert* is rather like a multi-character miniseries (a miniseries I'd love to see!)...Terrific storytelling."
—Historical Novel Society

"Marquis is a student of history, always creative, [and] never boring....A good comparison might be Tom Clancy."
—Military.com

"*Altar of Resistance* is a gripping and densely packed thriller dramatizing the Allied Italian campaign...reminiscent of Herman Wouk's *The Winds of War*."
—Kirkus Reviews

"Marquis grabs my attention right from the beginning and never lets go."
—Governor Roy R. Romer, 39th Governor of Colorado

"*The Coalition* starts with a bang, revs up its engines, and never stops until the explosive ending....Perfect for fans of James Patterson, David Baldacci, and Vince Flynn."
—Foreword Reviews

"Marquis writes quite well, but his real contribution with *Blackbeard: The Birth of America* is historical....An engrossing and historically grounded yarn."
—Kirkus Reviews

"In his novels *Blind Thrust* and *Cluster of Lies*, Samuel Marquis vividly combines the excitement of the best modern techno-thrillers, an education in geology, and a clarifying reminder that the choices each of us make have a profound impact on our precious planet."
—Ambassador Marc Grossman, Former U.S. Under Secretary of State and Co-Author of *Believers: Love and Death in Tehran*

"When I read a book about World War II these days, I look for something new...*Lions of the Desert* by Samuel Marquis delivered this in spectacular fashion. He has written another great book about the war that we should never forget."
—Ray Simmons for Readers' Favorite (5-Star Review)

"A simply riveting read from beginning to end, *Spies of the Midnight Sun* is impressively informed and informative, and a work of solidly researched history."
—Midwest Book Review

"In the richness of the texture of his material, Marquis far exceeds the stance of a mere raconteur and entertainer of the masses—he, in fact, becomes a public historian."
—Lois C. Henderson, Bookpleasures.com (Crime & Mystery) - 5-Star Review

"A combination of *The Great Escape*, *Public Enemies*, a genuine old-time Western, and a John Le Carré novel."
—BlueInk Review (for *Bodyguard of Deception*, Book 1 of WWII Series)

"*Cluster of Lies* has a twisty plot that grabs hold from the beginning and never let's go. A true page turner! I'm already looking forward to the next Joe Higheagle adventure."
—Robert Bailey, Author of *Legacy of Lies* and *The Final Reckoning*

"If you haven't tried a Samuel Marquis novel yet, *The Fourth Pularchek* is a good one to get introduced. The action is non-stop and gripping with no shortage of surprises. If you're already a fan of the award-winning novelist, this one won't disappoint."
—Dr. Wesley Britton, Bookpleasures.com (Crime & Mystery) - 5-Star Review

"Marquis is the new Follett, Silva, and Clancy rolled into one."
—Prof. J.R. Welch, Editor of *Dispatches from Fort Apache*

"Reminiscent of *The Day of the Jackal*...with a high level of authentic detail. Skyler is a convincing sniper, and also a nicely conflicted one."
—Donald Maass, Author of *The Emotional Craft of Fiction* (for *The Coalition*)

"Readers looking for an unapologetic historical action book should tear through this volume."
—Kirkus Reviews (for *Bodyguard of Deception*)

"Samuel Marquis picks up his World War II trilogy with *Altar of Resistance*, a well-researched and explosive ride through war-torn Rome with Nazis, booming battles, and intense cat-and-mouse chases....Grounded in historical fact but spiced up with thrilling imagination with the fate of the world in balance."
—Foreword Reviews

BY SAMUEL MARQUIS

WORLD WAR TWO SERIES

BODYGUARD OF DECEPTION
ALTAR OF RESISTANCE
SPIES OF THE MIDNIGHT
LIONS OF THE DESERT
SOLDIERS OF FREEDOM

NICK LASSITER-SKYLER INTERNATIONAL ESPIONAGE SERIES

THE DEVIL'S BRIGADE
THE COALITION
THE FOURTH PULARCHEK

JOE HIGHEAGLE ENVIRONMENTAL SLEUTH SERIES

BLIND THRUST
CLUSTER OF LIES

BLACKBEARD: THE BIRTH OF AMERICA

LIONS OF THE DESERT:

A TRUE STORY OF WWII HEROES IN NORTH AFRICA

VOLUME FOUR OF THE WORLD WAR TWO SERIES

SAMUEL MARQUIS

MOUNT SOPRIS PUBLISHING

LIONS OF THE DESERT
VOLUME FOUR OF THE WORLD WAR TWO SERIES
Copyright © 2019 by Samuel Marquis

This book is a work of fiction. Names, characters, places, government entities, intelligence agencies, religious and political organizations, corporations, and incidents are products of the author's imagination, or are used fictitiously, and are not to be construed as real. Any resemblance to actual events, locales, businesses, companies, organizations, or persons, living or dead, is entirely coincidental.

MOUNT SOPRIS PUBLISHING
Trade paper: ISBN 978-1-943593-25-5
Kindle eBook: ISBN 978-1-943593-26-2

All rights reserved. In accordance with the U.S. Copyright Act of 1976, the scanning, uploading, and electronic sharing of any part of this book without the permission of the publisher constitutes unlawful piracy and theft of the author's intellectual property. No part of this book may be used or reproduced in any manner whatsoever without written permission from the author, except in the case of brief quotations embodied in critical articles and reviews. Thank you for your support of author rights. For information email samuelmarquisbooks@gmail.com.

Second Mount Sopris Publishing premium printing: April 2020
Cover Design: Christian Fuenfhausen (http://cefdesign.com)
Formatting: Rik Hall (www.WildSeasFormatting.com)
Printed in the United States of America

To Order Samuel Marquis Books and Contact Samuel:
Visit Samuel Marquis's website, join his mailing list, learn about his forthcoming novels and book events, and order his books at www.samuelmarquisbooks.com. Please send all fan mail (including criticism) to samuelmarquisbooks@gmail.com. Thank you for your support!

ATTENTION: ORGANIZATIONS AND CORPORATIONS
Mount Sopris Publishing books may be purchased for educational, business, or sales promotional use. For information, please email the Special Markets Department at samuelmarquisbooks@gmail.com.

Dedication

To Colonel David Stirling (November 15, 1915—November 4, 1990), fellow Scotsman and iconoclast, as well as founder of the wonderfully irreverent, unconventional, and legendary Special Air Service (SAS) Brigade that gave Rommel and his vaunted *Afrika Korps* hell in North Africa during WWII.

LIONS OF THE DESERT:
A TRUE STORY OF WWII HEROES IN NORTH AFRICA

To me David Stirling was an inspiration and a hope. Of the SAS which owed its being to him, it is difficult to speak too highly—its services were, without exaggeration, invaluable. The courage, spirit and endurance of its leader and of the wonderful team he collected can seldom, if ever, have been equalled.
  —General Sir Claude Auchinleck, Commander in Chief of British Middle East Command

Rommel had gained the world's respect for his military genius. He was a legend, reminiscent of the more romantic, chivalrous days of old—and was a genuinely humane military officer. [T]he greatest desert fighting general of all time, [he] and his Afrika Korps were kicking the British's butt, pushing them back to Cairo. It became a case where the war might have been lost right there. He was ordered several times by Hitler to "Stand and Die." To fight to the last bullet, the last man. To execute and torture prisoners. He defied those orders.
  —Steven Pressfield, *Leaders with Character, Chivalry and Courage— Relics of the Past?*

[The true story behind Operation Condor and The English Patient] *is a dramatic story, with all of the essential elements of love, war, and a harsh landscape. It has gripped the imagination of writers and filmmakers since the Second World War. Before Michael Ondaatje's novel and film, it had inspired two best-selling novels: Ken Follett's* The Key to Rebecca *(1980) and Len Deighton's* City of Gold *(1992), [as well as several earlier first-hand] accounts written by the main protagonists. Entertaining and informative though these fictional and factual accounts are, none of them tell the real story [about] the notorious case of Rommel's spies in wartime Cairo. I think I can say, without a hint of exaggeration, that this is a different and far more dramatic story than we have been led to believe."*
  —Saul Kelly, *The Lost Oasis: The True Story Behind* The English Patient

As youngsters they went to war—some as volunteers, others as conscripts—with callous notions of King and Country on the one side, Volk und Führer on the other. The desert rapidly rendered them older, sadder and wiser. Many bear the visible legacy of the wounds they received in North Africa. All bear the subtler ravages of advancing age and harrowing recall. Theirs was a bitter and implacable war in which death came in many terrible ways. Yet men on both sides like to say it was a War Without Hate—Krieg ohne Hass, as Rommel himself described it. Soldier for soldier, it was fought with a regard for the rules of war unmatched on any other Second World War battle front.
  —John Bierman and Colin Smith, *The Battle of Alamein: Turning Point, World War II*

CAST OF HISTORICAL FIGURES

BRITISH-SCOTTISH-IRISH: SPECIAL AIR SERVICE COMMANDOS, ARMY OFFICERS, AND POLITICAL LEADERS

Captain-Lieutenant Colonel Archibald David Stirling: Founder of the British Special Air Service (SAS) and leader of the commando unit in North Africa; iconoclastic Scottish aristocrat and adventurer; nicknamed the "Phantom Major."
Major A.W. "Sammy" Sansom: Chief Field Security Officer, Corps of British Military Police in Cairo; fluent in English, Arabic, French, Italian, and Greek.
Lieutenant-Captain Robert Blair "Paddy" Mayne: Second-in-command and founding member of SAS; hard-drinking and hard-fighting Irishman; former rugby star, lawyer, and amateur boxer.
Lieutenant Fitzroy Maclean: intellectual, scholarly, and funny Scottish SAS officer; fluent in Italian, Russian, and German and competent in Greek and Latin.
Corporal-Sergeant John Murdoch Cooper: non-commissioned officer, gunner, driver, and unofficial quartermaster of SAS; former member of Scots Guards; nicknamed Johnny.
Peter Stirling: Diplomat serving in British embassy in Cairo; younger brother of David Stirling.
Captain Guy Bellairs: British officer stationed in Cairo; Hekmat Fahmy's British lover.
Randolph Frederick Edward Spencer-Churchill: Intelligence General Staff officer at British Middle East Headquarters and SAS officer; friend of David Stirling; son of British Prime Minister Sir Winston Churchill.
Field Marshal Sir Claude John Eyre Auchinleck: Scottish Commander-in-Chief of British Army Middle East from July 1941 to August 1942; nicknamed the "Auk."
Field Marshal Bernard Law Montgomery: Commander of the British Eighth Army in North Africa from August 1942 until the final Allied victory in Tunisia in May 1943; nicknamed Monty.

GERMANS: MILITARY OFFICERS AND INTELLIGENCE OPERATIVES

Major General-Field Marshal Johannes Erwin Eugen Rommel: Commander of the *Deutsches Afrika Korps* (DAK); nicknamed the "Desert Fox."
Major General Alfred Gause: Rommel's chief of staff from September 1941-May 1942 and August 1942.
General of the Cavalry Siegfried Westphal: Rommel's chief of operations (1a) from June 1941-May 1942 and September-November 1942.
Colonel Friedrich von Mellenthin: Rommel's chief intelligence officer (1c) from August 1941-May 1942 and chief of operations from June-August 1942.
Colonel Fritz Bayerlein: Rommel's chief of staff from June-July 1942 and December 1942-March 1943.
Captain Hans-Otto Behrendt: Rommel's chief intelligence officer (1c) from June-August 1942.
Lieutenant Wilfred Armbruster: Rommel's aide-de-camp.

Corporal Rolf Munninger: Rommel's personal clerk and fellow Schwabian.
Unteroffizier **Hellmut von Leipzig:** Rommel's driver.
Captain Count László Almasy: Hungarian aristocrat and desert explorer; Abwehr officer from 1940-1945; ·chief of the Almasy Commando (Operations Salam and Condor).
Lieutenant Johannes Eppler, a.k.a. Hussein Gaafar: German-Egyptian Abwehr spy and former lover of Egyptian belly dancer Hekmat Fahmy; recruited by Abwehr in 1941 for Operation Condor in spring 1942.
Lieutenant Heinrich Gerd Sandstette, a.k.a. Peter Muncaster: German Abwehr spy posing as American oilfield worker; recruited by Abwehr in 1941 for Operation Condor in spring 1942.

EGYPTIANS: ARMY OFFICERS AND CIVILIANS

Hekmat Fahmy: Famous Egyptian belly dancer and movie star; lover of British Captain Guy Bellairs and former lover of German-Egyptian Abwehr spy Johannes Eppler (Hussein Gaafar).
Captain Anwar el Sadat: Signals officer in Egyptian Army; militant Muslim, Egyptian nationalist, and key member of the pro-Axis, anti-British Free Officers' Movement within the Egyptian Army.
Captain Mourad Effat: Liaison officer with Egyptian Police; worked closely with Major Sansom of British Field Security Office.
Lieutenant Hassan Ezzet: Flight-Lieutenant in Egyptian Army, Coptic Egyptian nationalist and member of Free Officers' Movement.
King Farouk bin Fuad: King of Egypt and Sudan during WWII; anti-British and pro-Axis; strongly resented British domination of his country but was powerless to counter Great Britain's imperialistic presence.

AMERICANS: ARMY OFFICERS AND CIVILIANS

Colonel Bonner Fellers: U.S. military attaché in Cairo; called *Gute Quelle*, the *Good Source*, by Rommel for his accurate and detailed reports on British military operations, which German intelligence obtained word for word from having compromised the U.S. foreign service encryption Code 11, referred to as the "Black Code."
Momo Marriott: Prominent Cairo socialite; wife of Major General Sir John Marriott, daughter of American financier Otto Kahn, and mistress of Randolph Churchill.

LIONS OF THE DESERT: A TRUE STORY OF WWII HEROES IN NORTH AFRICA

VOLUME FOUR OF THE WORLD WAR TWO SERIES

TO THE READER

This is the story of the 1941-1942 Desert War in North Africa and Operation Condor, based on recently declassified British Secret MI6 files and U.S.-German Military Intelligence records. The Condor story has been told many times before—most famously in Michael Ondaatje's 1992 Booker Prize winning novel *The English Patient* and the 1996 Oscar-winning film of the same name—but until recently virtually every fictional and factual account has been historically inaccurate. The reason is simple: prior to the 2006 public declassification of large numbers of WWII government documents, the only historical records available to the general public were those written by the main protagonists, who had access to only limited information and were not privy to the larger military-intelligence picture. In addition, the historical record has conclusively shown that these participants, despite laying down a solid foundation of verifiable facts, have in a number of critical places distorted and embellished the Condor story to enhance their own role in history or embroider the story, making it difficult for subsequent researchers to separate fact from fiction.

The narrators of these early first-hand accounts included: Anwar el Sadat, the Egyptian Army officer, nationalist, and later President of Egypt (*Revolt on the Nile*, 1957); Johannes Eppler, the German spy in the Operation Condor affair (*Rommel Ruft Cairo*, 1960, later translated as *Operation Condor: Rommel's Spy*, 1977); Leonard Mosley, a British war correspondent in Cairo at the time of Operation Condor, who conducted extensive interviews of Eppler prior to the German spy penning his own version of events (*The Cat and the Mice*, 1958); and Major A.W. Sansom, the head of British Field Security in Cairo (*I Spied Spies*, 1965). While accurate in many respects and unquestionably entertaining, these subjective first-hand accounts have one fatal flaw in common: they exaggerate the espionage accomplishments of several of the key players in the Condor story and, consequently, draw conclusions that are not supported by reliable historical documents. Without access to the declassified materials and thus the bigger picture, subsequent writers on the subject—Anthony Cave Brown, *Bodyguard of Lies* (1976); David Mure, *Practice to Deceive* (1977) and *Master of Deception* (1980); Nigel West, *MI6* (1983); and Richard Deacon, *'C': A Biography of Sir Maurice Oldfield* (1985)—have fallen into the trap of relying heavily on the embellished accounts of the main protagonists. Following in a similar vein, the bestselling historical fiction novels by Ken Follett (*The Key to Rebecca*, 1980, made into a 1989

TV movie) and Len Deighton (*The City of Gold*, 1992) used both the original sources and the subsequent embellished works as the basis of their books, making for great entertainment but questionable historical accuracy with regard to the significant details of the North African campaign and Operation Condor.

As it turns out, the Condor story needs no embellishment. The real-life protagonists, while admittedly more prosaic than their highly fictionalized doppelgängers, are still fascinating in their own right. That is the goal of this work: to tell the real story—a story that has captivated the minds of authors, historians, and filmmakers for the past three-quarters of a century. It is told through the eyes of six of the main historical figures in Egypt and Libya at the time: Scottish Lieutenant Colonel David Stirling, founder and leader of the Special Air Service (SAS), a brigade of eccentric desert commandos that raided Axis aerodromes and supply lines; German Field Marshal Erwin Rommel, commander of the legendary *Afrika Korps*, who very nearly succeeded in driving the British out of Egypt; Egyptian Hekmat Fahmy, the renowned belly dancer, regarded as a Mata-Hari-like German agent in previous accounts but in fact a far more intriguing and ambiguous character in real life; Major A.W. "Sammy" Sansom, head of the British Field Security unit that hunted down Axis spies and pro-German Egyptian nationalists operating in Cairo; Johannes Eppler, aka Hussein Gaafar, the notorious German spy of Operation Condor whose real story is finally told; and Colonel Bonner Fellers, the U.S. military attaché in Cairo, who was privy to critical Allied secrets in the North African theater and inadvertently played an important role in intelligence-gathering activities for both sides in the campaign.

While recently declassified government files form the backbone of this book, the eyewitness accounts of Sansom, Eppler, Mosley, and Sadat have still proved useful—but only where supported by other eyewitness accounts, government records, or wireless decrypts. As David Mure, author of *Master of Deception*, states, "The Condor story has been told many times, always with new dimensions and variations; it is a tangled web indeed." But it doesn't have to be—not anymore. With the relevant WWII records now available, it is time the true story is told. With that in mind, I hope you enjoy this latest version of the timeless tale of WWII espionage, romance, and derring-do in the North African desert—with the knowledge that this time it is remarkably close to how it all really happened.

PART 1

CAIRO

CHAPTER 1

BRITISH MIDDLE EAST HEADQUARTERS
GARDEN CITY, CAIRO, EGYPT

JULY 9, 1941

FROM THE BACK SEAT OF A TAXI, Lieutenant David Stirling of the British 8 Commando studied the manned guard post outside General Army Headquarters, Middle East. It was a blisteringly hot midsummer morning, and the heat waves were already dancing across the street. Housed in a large block of commandeered flats surrounded by barbed wire, GHQ was tightly guarded by not only armed sentries at the main gate but by a perimeter foot patrol to keep out Axis spies.

How the bloody hell was he going to steal past the guards, sneak inside, and accomplish his mission when he stood out like a sore thumb at six feet six inches tall? Not only that but he could still barely walk due to his recent injuries.

For the past month, he had been recuperating in Cairo's Scottish General Hospital following a nearly fatal airplane jumping accident. His parachute had become stuck on the aircraft's tail section and was torn as he leaped into the slipstream, an unfortunate but common fate in paratroop operations in high desert winds and one that caused him to strike *terra firma* at an astounding velocity that temporarily blinded and paralyzed him, leaving the spine of the twenty-five-year-old, aristocratic Scots Guardsman damaged for life. But right now, he didn't care about his excruciating back pain, or that his legs were still so weak that he had to hobble about using crutches.

His sole concern was how to slip inside GHQ undetected.

Stirling's reason for stealth was simple: he was determined to put the memo inside his jacket pocket in the hands of one of two influential people: General Sir Claude Auchinleck, the newly appointed commander in chief of the British forces in the Middle East; or his immediate subordinate, Major General Neil Ritchie, deputy chief of general staff. The memo, entitled *"Case for the Retention of a Limited Number of Special Service Troops for Employment as Parachutists,"* had taken him the last month to prepare while recuperating from his parachuting injuries. The handwritten document provided a detailed plan on how to successfully attack vulnerable German aerodromes, fueling depots, and supply chains far behind the front lines. He was convinced that his proposal was precisely what was needed to help defeat Rommel and his seemingly unbeatable *Deutsches Afrika Korps*.

As a mere lieutenant—and an undistinguished one at that—he had no illusions that it would be easy to convince Auchinleck or Ritchie of the possibilities of his plan. But he knew that it would die a swift death if it was left in the hands of the unimaginative, by-the-book, mid-level staff officers at GHQ. He had to go to the top, or very near the top, if he was to have any chance of success. He was contemptuous of the stodgy British military bureaucracy, which he referred to as an unimaginative "freemasonry of mediocrity" and "layer upon layer of fossilized shit." In his view, the bureaucratic bean counters at GHQ were more concerned with upholding the military traditions of the last war and enforcing petty rules and regulations than in implementing the kind of innovative strategic thinking that would help win the new war in the desert. If his ideas on how to attack the Desert Fox's staging areas, air- and sea-ports, and overextended supply lines were to see the light of day, he would need to get his memo directly into the hands of the "Auk," Ritchie, or another high-ranking senior officer with authority before anyone lower in the hierarchy had a chance to squash it.

But first he had to sneak past the sentries and get inside the compound.

He took a deep breath to calm his nerves as he continued to study the procedure for entry. The sentries at the main gate were checking the passes of all visitors, except for the red-tabbed staff officers who appeared to be well-known to the guards. Stirling decided that his best chance was to bluff his way through the checkpoint, trying to garner sympathy as he hobbled up on his crutches.

Biting his lip to stem back his pain, he paid the driver, climbed gingerly out of the taxi, and bid him good day through the open passenger window. Adjusting his pair of crutches, he swung himself up to the main entrance of the headquarters compound wearing his battledress uniform with one pip on the shoulder and the insignia of No. 8 Commando on his sleeve. A stream of officers and staff personnel were shuffling through the gate, and the two sentries were carefully checking passes.

Adopting a benign and absent-minded expression as he neared the entrance, he smiled vaguely at the guard closest to him. He was halfway through the gate before the peremptory voice of the corporal halted him in his tracks.

"Sir. Your pass, please."

"Why yes, sorry." He patted his pockets, looking perplexed and mildly embarrassed. "Oh dear, I seem to have left it at the hospital. I have an urgent appointment with…well, I really can't say as it is top secret…but I'm sure it's okay. Can you possibly see fit to let me in?"

The corporal frowned, and Stirling could tell that his usual charm had flopped miserably. "No pass, no entry, sir. You'll have to go back to the hospital for it."

"But I've got an important appointment and I'm rather late on account of having to hobble about on these bloody crutches. You couldn't overlook it just this once?"

Again, he gave his most charming smile but the corporal was not open to persuasion.

"Sorry, sir, but you're going to have to return to the hospital and retrieve your pass. There can be no exceptions."

Firmly but politely, he took Stirling by the shoulders and turned him around, redirecting him to exit the premises.

"All right, I'll just step over here and catch my breath. It's awfully tiring with these bloody crutches."

"That's fine, Lieutenant. You rest easy by that tree and a taxi will be by in a moment."

He pointed to a large sycamore. Stirling hobbled a few yards away and leaned against the tree. Unable to accept defeat as an option, he continued to study the barbed-wire fence enclosing the compound for potential weaknesses. After a moment, he noticed a gap in the perimeter where the end post of the barbed-wire fence did not quite reach the corner of the guard house.

Hello. Might I be able to slip through the break in the wire next to the guard post?

It was as he was considering these machinations that he met with a stroke of luck. A pair of staff cars pulled up and several officers spilled out. The sentries quickly became preoccupied examining the passes of the visiting delegation.

Stirling looked again at the gap in the perimeter fence: he might never get a chance like this again and had to act fast.

This is it—you have to make your bloody move!

He felt his heart begin to beat wildly at the prospect of danger. Removing his crutches from under his arms and standing them against the tree, he slipped through the narrow gap and eased his way behind the wooden guard hut. With adrenaline flowing, he moved with astonishing adroitness, his long lean body knifing inside the compound just a few feet behind the preoccupied sentries. But a lancing pain shot through his lower back, his legs felt wobbly, and he was forced to slow down. Gritting his teeth, he struggled to walk as normally as possible but it took great effort. Shaking off the pain and ignoring his jelly legs, he hurried as fast as he could towards the asphalt path that led to the main building.

To his relief, he was able to mingle with the new visitors. Clasping his hands behind his back in a professorial manner, he pretended to engage the officer on his right in conversation as they headed up the pathway towards the headquarters building. Stooping his tall frame slightly and keeping his head down so as to appear inconspicuous, he mumbled some innocuous pleasantries and occasionally looked at his puzzled recipient. But when the party reached the bottom of the steps leading up to the main building, the others continued on and he was again left exposed. They were heading for some other part of the compound and he had to go inside.

Oh bloody hell, what do I do now?

He glanced back at the front gate. Luckily, the guards were facing towards the street, but all they had to do to spot him was turn around. Feeling a wave of panic, he turned abruptly and began climbing the steps to the main building. But the pain of lifting his feet the extra inches to ascend was excruciating and he was only able to negotiate the stairs by moving in a snail-paced half-crouch.

Don't stop now, he told himself despite the pain. *You're almost inside!*

When he reached the second to last step, he chanced a look over his shoulder. The guard on the right was gazing curiously towards the sycamore tree outside the compound. The corporal appeared to have noticed the abandoned crutches leaning against the trunk and was searching for the tall, dark-haired lieutenant to whom a moment earlier they had belonged. Searching the area, he proceeded to turn around and catch sight of Stirling's painful progress up the staircase.

"Hey, you, stop!" he cried in a heavy Cockney accent.

With an effort, Stirling made it to the top of the stairs, stooped his shoulders, and ducked inside the GHQ building.

"Someone stop that man!" he heard the corporal shout as the door closed behind him.

To the muffled sound of shuffling feet and agitated voices outside, he started for the nearest corridor. With the clock now desperately ticking, he knew there was not enough time to locate Auchinleck or Ritchie and he would have to dash into the office of the most senior officer he could find and plead his case. He stumbled around in the polished maze, lurching down one corridor and then another, until he came to a door marker that caught his eye: *Adjutant General*. Was that senior enough? He heard urgent voices down the hallway. There was no more time—the adjutant general would have to do.

He stepped quickly to the door. This was the moment of truth. Without an appointment or some sort of written authorization to call upon General Staff headquarters, he was likely to be turned away. But he had no other choice.

As he raised his hand to knock, he heard the corporal's agitated voice again, changed his mind, and burst straight into the office. Panting heavily from the effort of climbing the stairs and shambling down the hallway, he leaned back against the door and closed his eyes for a second. A voice quickly brought him back to reality.

"What in God's name are you doing?"

He opened his eyes. A short, plump major sat behind a wooden desk. He had stopped writing and was looking up at him in astonishment. But surprise swiftly turned to indignation as the senior officer noticed the single star on his shoulder. Equally stunned at his sudden change in circumstance, Stirling just stared back at him, unable to speak. Wearing his sharply creased and brightly buttoned uniform, the major was the very picture of bland HQ efficiency. *God, is there really a war going on?* wondered Stirling, suddenly conscious of his own crinkly, dirt-smudged battledress. He suddenly wished he had taken a little time to spruce up before he had left the hospital.

"Where are your bloody manners, Lieutenant? Have you never heard of knocking? What is it that you want?"

Wordlessly, he continued to look at the AG. He couldn't help but feel there was something familiar about the man, but he put the thought aside as he was unable to place him. A salute was clearly called for, but the maneuver would be difficult with his ailing back and he decided against it.

"By God, what's the matter with you, man? Why are you scrunched over like the Hunchback of Notre Dame?"

Ignoring the question, Stirling was finally able to find his voice. "Sir, I do apologize for bursting in. I have to speak with you most urgently."

The apology had no visible effect on the purple-faced major. "What the devil do you want? Get to the point, man!"

"I'm Lieutenant David Stirling of the Scots Guards, currently attached to 8 Commando," he began, and he quickly described how he had come to the Middle East with Layforce, the ad hoc military formation of the British Army consisting of several commando units under the command of Colonel Robert Laycock, after whom the force was named. Originally consisting of 2,000 men tasked with conducting raiding operations to disrupt Axis lines of communication in the Mediterranean, the unit had recently been disbanded with the German advances in North Africa and the Army's urgent need for replacements. With the preliminaries complete, Stirling then made his pitch: "I have some ideas as to how I can harass the German coastal defenses and supply depots. It will require only a few specially selected officers and men. I intend to prepare this unit for parachuting and explosives work before the next major offensive. Using a small command of handpicked troops, my force could parachute behind enemy lines and disable the whole of the German air force on the ground. I have my plan right here. Let me show you."

He started to take his handwritten memorandum from his pocket, but the major waved him off.

"Stirling? Ah, of course, Stirling! Don't you recognize me?"

"You do look familiar but I'm afraid I can't recall where from."

"Do you know why you don't remember me? And why, on the other hand, I remember you only too clearly?"

"No, sir, I'm afraid I don't know the answer to that either."

"Because in 1939, I was temporarily attached to the Scots Guards and gave a series of lectures to the Second Battalion at Pirbright on tactics. My name is Major Smith. It is a name that you will not soon forget, I can assure you."

He gulped. Now he remembered. If anyone was a freemason of mediocrity or fossilized shit, it was the pomposo Major Smith.

"When at Pirbright I came to question you, I found you in a deep sleep. The reason? Because I was told you made a habit of going to parties in London every night and not returning until dawn. Frankly, I regarded you even then as one of the least desirable officers in your regiment. I'm not at all surprised to find that you soon left and joined the first crackpot outfit you could find. Now you have the presumption to come to me and suggest that you be given your own private command, in charge of your own private strategy with your own private hand-picked men. In my whole military career, I've never heard such insolence. The answer is no, Lieutenant Stirling, a flat, unqualified no. And before you leave, let me say I'm sorry that you found your way to this office, for I assure you I will use my influence to see that you are posted to the battalion of your regiment now serving in the desert at the earliest possible moment. I am not sanguine about the advantage they will reap from your company, but in my report, I will recommend that drastic steps be taken to lick you into shape. Whatever lunatic idea you have, Stirling, you can forget it. My specific recommendations for your future will not include you getting even the smallest command. Good day to you—now get out!"

Not knowing what else to do, he stuffed his memo back in his pocket, gave an excruciatingly painful salute, and stepped resignedly towards the door. As he opened it and prepared to leave, the telephone on the adjutant general's desk rang and he heard the major gasp, "The sentry wants to make a complaint? Broke past the guard post? Send the sentry up here to my office immediately!"

Oh bloody hell, I'm blown!

He left Smith's office, hurrying unsteadily down the corridor. There was no point in retracing his steps. He was off the hook but his reprieve wouldn't last long. He walked down the hallway in as dignified a fashion his throbbing back and legs would allow, reading the signs on the doors as he progressed. He paused at a door marked D.C.G.S.

It was the office of General Ritchie, the deputy chief of General Staff, Middle East Forces.

Bingo! He knocked on the door and, before receiving an answer, stepped inside. Ritchie looked up from his desk with the same expression of startlement as Smith.

"Sir, I am Lieutenant David Stirling, Scots Guards. I apologize for bursting into your office without an appointment but there was no time to arrange it. I have a matter to bring to your attention which I believe to be most urgent. I have put together a plan for small-unit commando operations deep behind enemy lines that will greatly aid the war effort and help defeat Rommel here in North Africa."

"Rommel—you have a plan to defeat Rommel. I suppose this is my lucky day."

The note of sarcasm wasn't lost on Stirling, but he ignored it. "Yes, sir, indeed it is. I have prepared this for you and General Auchinleck."

He pulled the pencil-written memorandum from his pocket and started to hand it to Ritchie. The general took a moment to appraise him before taking the proffered document and motioning him to take a seat. It took great effort for Stirling to sit down without grimacing in agony, and even once seated he was forced to adopt an unusual posture with his legs locked together and back stooped at the waist. Ritchie began to read. Every now and then the DCGS's brow knitted into a frown, but he carefully perused the document for five full minutes without whispering a word. Stirling went over answers to potential questions in his head as he anxiously watched the general read over the document. All the time he kept his fingers crossed, but inside he had a sinking feeling that all his efforts would come to naught.

And then Ritchie surprised him.

"I must say, this may be just the sort of plan we're looking for," he said with a glint in his eye. "I will discuss it with the commander in chief and let you know our decision in the next day or so."

Unprepared for such a cut and dried response, Stirling did his best to hide his astonishment. "Why thank you, sir. That is most—"

"Your report will have to be studied in detail, mind you," Ritchie cut him off. "But I can see the merit in this. We have been looking at ways of tying up German manpower. I will discuss your proposal with General Auchinleck. You will be summoned when a decision has been made."

He could scarcely control his excitement. "Yes, sir."

"And just in case the C-in-C agrees to this, you ought to meet Major Smith, my AG branch officer."

"Major Smith?"

But Ritchie had already picked up the telephone and quickly summoned the major to his office. When he put down the receiver, the general looked back at Stirling and explained that Smith was the man who would have to work out the organizational side if the commander in chief decided to go ahead with the plan.

"Yes, General." He wondered how he was going to deal with Smith; he certainly couldn't allow the sniveling bastard to undercut his plan. But what preoccupied his thoughts even more was how he was going to manage to stand up again. Now that he had settled into his chair, he wasn't sure if he could even get up.

Smith appeared at the door with a firm knock. When he stepped into the room and saw the young lieutenant sitting in the general's armchair as if they were old friends, he was so taken aback he could find no words. Stirling smiled politely, welcoming him into the room. No doubt the major had just finished talking to the sentry and now in all likelihood Stirling would have charges brought against him for the security breach.

Ritchie said, "Major Smith, this is Lieutenant Stirling. He and I have been having a little chat about his proposal here."

"It pleases me to tell you, General, the major and I are old acquaintances," said Stirling without getting out of his chair. "Why we were chatting about old times only a few minutes ago."

"Oh really? Good, that will make things easier." Ritchie fixed his gaze on Smith. "Major, Stirling here has quite an interesting proposition for attacking the Germans behind enemy lines. It is just what we're looking for."

Stirling watched as Smith's eyes narrowed ever so slightly upon him. But the major offered no verbal protest. It took great effort on Stirling's part not to smile at his sudden change in fortune.

"If the plan is approved by the C-in-C, Major, you will be required to take action at very short notice," Ritchie went on. "Consequently, you should be prepared to assist the lieutenant here in any way you can."

Smith had to practically choke to get a response out. "Very well, sir."

"That will be all, gentlemen. You are dismissed."

The elation of having his plan up for serious consideration by the Auk sent a surge of electricity through Stirling's ravaged body, making him feel suddenly much stronger. He was able to lift himself up out of his chair without groaning in agony. But once he and Smith found themselves together in the corridor with the door closed behind them, the AG gave him a withering look.

"I will do my duty no matter how disagreeable," said Smith contemptuously. "But I trust, Stirling, you will not be expecting any favors."

"I wouldn't dream of it, Major. But you did hear General Ritchie. If my plan is approved, I am to have your complete support."

"Yes, and you shall have it. But I want you to know up front that I don't like you, and I don't like this special forces business of yours either. I will help solely because I have to—and that's it. As I said, you will get no favors from me or my branch. Now wait outside my office for the guard to escort you out the main gate."

He gave a little rebellious smile. "Yes, sir, Major, sir. I'll be in touch."

Smith waved his hand dismissively, flashed him a look of unconcealed disdain, stepped back into his office, and shut the door. Stirling waited for five minutes for his escort. As he was delivered back to the main gate, the corporal was in a more pleasant frame of mind.

"That was a clever move sneaking in like that," he said in his distinctive Cockney accent. "Don't get that amount of exercise very often. And I don't see the rules bent like that round here neither. Bully for you, sir."

"I don't like swanks any more than you do, Corporal. And I'm glad I could spice things up a bit and make your day more entertaining," said Stirling good-naturedly.

"I assume you will be needing your crutches back then, sir. I brought them inside the guard room."

"Why I don't believe I'll be needing them anymore. After my meeting with General Ritchie, I am suddenly feeling quite healthy. Quite healthy indeed."

CHAPTER 2

KIT KAT CLUB
IMBABAH, CAIRO

JULY 10, 1941

PEERING THROUGH THE BEADED STAGE CURTAIN, Hekmat Fahmy surveyed the audience she would soon be entertaining. The Egyptian capital in which she plied her craft—called *al-Qahira*, or The Victorious, since ancient times—was an Islamic city, which looked to the east. But it was home to not only a large Muslim population but a sizable minority of British, Greek, French, Armenian, and Italian nationals, Jews, and Christian Egyptians known as Coptics, and tonight's audience appeared to be just as eclectic as the city itself. There were few Muslims in the crowd, however, for *Raqs Sharqi*—Eastern Dance—was considered *haram* for the puritanical followers of Muhammad. Tonight's cosmopolitan patrons sat at their cozy dinner tables noisily chatting, puffing on hookahs, feasting on *molokhiya*, *ful medames*, and *kushari*, and sipping champagne, whiskey-and-soda, and gin fizzes beneath ceiling fans, as an army of pampering waiters wearing red felt *tarboosh* hats with silk tassels darted to and fro delivering food and drink.

While the British officers and their Empire counterparts were dressed in military uniform, lavish dinner jackets and evening gowns clung to the bodies of the wealthy Cairenes and European civilians, like silk sheets slung over priceless paintings. The jewelry at the throats, ears, and hands glittered in the pools of brilliance thrown down from the overhead chandeliers. These were the elite of Cairo, and here Hekmat Fahmy stood ready to entertain them in all their dazzling finery.

But she never danced for them. She danced only for herself.

While her legion of fans steadfastly maintained that she was still the most beautiful woman in all of Cairo, there were some in the fair city who claimed that, at the age of thirty-four, she no longer held that distinction though she was still quite ravishing. But what virtually no one disputed was that Hekmat Fahmy was the most intoxicating belly dancer in all of Europe, Africa, and the Middle East. Before the war, she had performed before large crowds in Budapest, Athens, Paris, Berlin, and Rome, and in her home country people came all the way from Alexandria and Assiut to watch her exotic dance routine. Seldom a night went by when the Continental Hotel rooftop garden, Madame Badia's Cabaret, or the Kit Kat Club wasn't packed wall to wall with her breathless, mostly male admirers.

She performed most often at the Kit Kat. It was her favorite venue and she usually did two shows a night, four nights per week. The two-story nightclub was on a sprawling houseboat moored along the western river bank of the Nile. Since the beginning of the war, the well-appointed yet surprisingly raucous cabaret had become a legendary center of debauchery. The doors, decks, and windows were made from precious wood that smelled like musk, and the splendid Nile vistas, river breezes, and shady riverbank gardens filled with flowers, creeping hyacinth, and guava trees made one forget about Cairo's teaming masses, noise, and airborne pollutants.

The club was reported to be full of spies and officers were warned to be discreet in front of the dancing girls, particularly the Hungarians. But Hekmat was no spy. Like many Cairenes, she was willing to pass on the latest gossip gleaned from British and Egyptian officers and diplomats, much as her colleagues on the belly dancing circuit did for financial considerations, but she was no Mata Hari.

Though she found the British occupying her homeland overbearing at times and considered herself a lukewarm Egyptian nationalist, she spent as much time among Brits as she did her own people and she bode foreigners no ill will. She just didn't want anyone but Egyptians running her country and longed to be rid, once and for all, of the stifling yoke of British imperial rule. At the same time, she hobnobbed routinely and mingled effortlessly with the British, French, Greek, and Armenian upper classes that dominated the Cairo and Alexandria social scenes along with the ruling Egyptian merchants, government officials, and royals. As the niece of famous Egyptian film actress, producer, and screenwriter Aziza Amir, she was too clever and cosmopolitan to go risking her career for Egyptian independence or anti-British sentiment when there was a world war going on and the police were arresting subversives, real or imagined, on a daily basis. It was because of the value she placed on her career that most of her friends were wealthy Europeans or Egyptians. It was for this same reason that she tended to avoid militant Muslims and outspoken Egyptian nationalists, and was a member of the orthodox Christian Church in Egypt.

All the same, she couldn't help but feel some resentment towards the occupying power. She was well aware that, behind closed doors, the British soldiers and civilians in Cairo pejoratively referred to her and her fellow Egyptians as "Wogs." Wog—which stood for Worthy Oriental Gentleman—was the slang term for any dark-skinned individual from the Orient, with distinctly racist connotations. During the course of the war, the derogatory word had become attached to anything unpopularly Egyptian, including "Wog prices," "Wog tarts," "Wog beer," and "Wog grub." With 150,000 British Commonwealth troops in the city—most of them drunk, bored, and randy—fistfights and other confrontations flared up frequently between the indigenous Wogs and the foreign invaders the "Tommies," who inexplicably considered themselves liberators.

While Egyptian women and children were rarely openly chastised, the Tommies wouldn't hesitate to beat up Egyptian men for even minor slights and engaged in puerile cruelty, like knocking off the fezzes of passersby or shoving them out of the way when walking the streets. Another favorite pastime was to sing along as the Egyptian national anthem was played in Cairo's movie houses, but with obscene lyrics. Egyptians got no compensation when the soldiers brawled in their cafés and bars and damaged their property, and the locals themselves were on occasion robbed or attacked in broad daylight with no repercussions to the occupiers. The Egyptians found the Australians the most loutish of the Empire troops, and King Farouk had insisted they be bivouacked far from the city to limit disturbances. That was just fine with Hekmat.

A drumroll began. The stage lights went off, and a silence descended upon the cabaret. Hekmat waited a full minute, allowing the anticipation to build, before parting her way through the beaded curtains.

She moved through the darkness as quietly as a scarab beetle to the center stage, where a bright spotlight picked her up and illuminated her. There, she threw her head back, raised her arms skyward, and gave an introductory bow. The crowd clapped and rewarded her with a rousing cheer.

It was her incandescent beauty as much as her unique ability to wriggle her torso on stage that made her the most beloved of belly dancers. She had a head of lustrous black hair, and luminescent green eyes inherited from a Circassian grandmother. Her nose was the delicate aristocratic beak found in ancient Egyptian paintings of Nile Delta women. Standing before her audience, she had the same dreamy face that could be seen on the bas-reliefs of the ancient dynasties of Upper Egypt. Her features were finely drawn yet lively, and her skin had a tawny color that was the perfect foil for her deep green eyes.

The music began—a pounding goblet-shaped drum accompanied by finger cymbals, a long-necked stringed lute, a flute, and a double clarinet—and she began to move. It was a fast *Malfuf* rhythm, often used by belly dancers to make a dramatic entry, and she glided across the stage to the propulsive rhythm of the drums and Oriental dance instruments.

Dom, tak-tak, dom, tak-tak.

At first, she moved her hips slowly, like the early stages of lovemaking, but two minutes into her routine she quickened her pace. Her arms and shoulders moved gracefully, like a gentle breeze coming in from the desert and rippling a dangling pennant. She dipped and thrust her hips and shook her ample breasts. But it was the movements of her lean but pleasantly soft stomach that captivated the audience.

Her motions were fluid and seductive, while at the same time she was able to shift her weight from leg to leg quite rapidly. She was a sensuous dancer with a number of unique movements in her repertoire, with each part of her body seeming to move independently of the rest. The crowd—including a number of elite British, French, and Greek women that ordinarily looked down their noses at Egyptians and their culture—was mesmerized.

She allowed herself a little smile. She was enjoying herself.

When she stepped down from the stage and began dancing amongst the tables, a coterie of British officers stood up from their seats, hoisted their glasses, and slurred a drunken but approving cheer. Her dance costume accentuated her voluptuous body. A successful film actress as well as a famous dancer, she wore a heavily beaded, sequined, and fringed halter top along with a low-slung, semi-transparent skirt with slits up to her hips, done in a risqué Hollywood style rather than the traditional Egyptian style. Along her waistline, she donned a hip scarf and belt with elaborate fringes and coins that she swirled and jingled with the coordinated movements of her legs and hips.

While her attire was straight out of *Arabian Nights,* her technique was Egyptian and incorporated little from other belly-dancing cultures. To her, the Egyptian style was the most structured and refined among all styles of Oriental dancing. It also had the most complicated dance steps and was the most unapologetically sensual.

As the cadence of the music quickened, she closed her eyes and entered an almost trance-like state, as did the audience watching her in rapturous silence and fascination. Her movements were faster and more repetitive now and the crowd could sense the coming climax. She went faster and faster until finally she stood writhing in the spotlight in a final great cataclysm. There was a thunderous crash of cymbals and a massive drumroll as she stood there shaking and quivering, and then suddenly it was over.

The room went totally silent for several seconds and she collapsed to the stage in a dramatic, choreographed move. Her legs folded beneath her body, knees apart, and her arms spread out away from her body like a Christ figure. She held the position for a moment before the stage light beam disappeared and all the lights went out.

The crowd leapt to its feet and roared with applause.

When the lights came back on, Hekmat Fahmy—the most celebrated belly dancer in all the world—had vanished.

CHAPTER 3

KIT KAT CLUB

JULY 10, 1941

DAVID STIRLING CLAPPED THUNDEROUSLY along with the rest of the crowd. He had never seen such a breathtaking stage performance, not even in the Parisian cabarets when he was a struggling artist living on the Left Bank before the war. He wanted to meet the renowned Hekmat Fahmy and congratulate her in person. She was utterly mesmerizing: the Egyptian goddess had cast quite a spell over him as he stood clapping breathlessly.

During the show, he had felt—as had every male member of the audience—that he was alone with her and she was dancing just for him. He knew it was nothing but a fantasy, but all the same it had seemed as if her on-stage writhings were not part of a rehearsed act but rather because she was driven to a state of sexual frenzy by her own lubricious body and uncontrollable sensuality.

He looked at his younger brother Peter, who worked as a diplomat at the British Embassy in Garden City.

"That was incredible," he exclaimed to him. "I've never seen anything like it. I don't know how she can do that with her body."

"I can only imagine how delectable she must be beneath the sheets. You'd like to give her a good rogering, wouldn't you, Brother?"

"Who wouldn't? She is the most alluring woman I've ever laid eyes on. But what I admire most about her is her mastery of her craft."

"She's said to be the very best. Would you like to meet her?"

His mouth fell open. "You know her?"

"Let's just say we run in the same social circles."

"Dear heavens, of course I'd be delighted to meet her."

"Good, then I shall arrange it."

His brother quickly flagged down a waiter, handed him an Egyptian ten-pound note, and informed him that they would like to visit with the exotic dancer in her dressing room. Five minutes later they were backstage with a fresh bottle of Veuve Clicquot Ponsardin champagne and three crystal flutes. Stirling chuckled inwardly as his brother smiled at him devilishly and rapped gently on the door: it was as if they had been transported back in time and were naughty schoolboys back in Scotland once again. A line of admirers, mostly British officers bearing bouquets of flowers and bottles of wine and champagne, began to form up behind them.

"Yes, who is it?" came the answer from behind the door.

"Peter Stirling from the British Embassy, my dear Hekmat. My brother David and I have come to pay our respects."

"Oh yes, Peter darling. Please come in."

"Peter darling?" chided David, and the two brothers giggled.

Wiping the schoolboy grins off their faces, they stepped inside the dressing room. Now wearing a diaphanous silk robe, Hekmat Fahmy was seated in a chair before a mirror removing her makeup. She turned away from the mirror and spun around slowly in her chair to greet them. At the sight of her, Stirling felt the same breathless sensation he had felt at the climax of her performance. He quickly closed the door for privacy, receiving envious stares from the growing crowd of admirers queuing up behind them.

"Hello, Peter," she said. "I take it you enjoyed the show."

"You were wonderful as always, my dear." He took her proffered hand and kissed it, then motioned towards his older brother. "David here was so impressed he insisted on meeting you. I do believe he's smitten."

Stirling couldn't help but blush as she turned her gaze upon him. "So, you are the illustrious older brother David? Peter's told me about you—you were a painter in Paris." She looked him over. "Wait, you look familiar. Have we met before?"

"I'm afraid not—I would have remembered. You are most enchanting." Bashfully and somewhat clumsily, he took her hand and kissed it.

"I'm afraid we didn't bring any flowers for you, but we do have champagne," said Peter. "We promise to be quick. You have a line of British officers waiting to fawn over you."

"Well, they can wait a few minutes. Please take a seat."

They sat down in the wooden chairs in front of her makeup table. As Peter poured them each a glass of champagne, Stirling took a moment to study the dancer. With her glossy black hair, bronze skin, arched nose, emerald-green eyes, and tall voluptuous body, Hekmat Fahmy was uncommonly beautiful. Her teeth were perfectly stacked and the color of ivory, providing an exquisite contrast to her coppery complexion. Looking at her, he realized he had never had a woman half as attractive share his bed. What made her so alluring was her expressive eyes, luminous dark skin, and magnificent figure. She could have been Cleopatra, and he wondered if she had Coptic bloodlines traceable back to the Pharaohs.

She touched him on the hand. "Now tell me about yourself, David. I can see by your uniform that you are a lieutenant, but what is it you do for the war effort?"

"He's a desert rat with the 8 Commando," blurted Peter before he could answer. "But, of course, that's top secret and you can't tell anyone."

"In that case, my lips are sealed." She smiled conspiratorially and looked at Stirling. "A commando? That sounds dangerous. Do you sneak behind enemy lines?"

"I'm afraid I'm not at liberty to say. Furthermore, I must apologize for my brother's lack of discretion. I suppose that's why he's a diplomat and not a soldier."

"Oh, come now old boy, there are no secrets here in Cairo," protested Peter with a good-natured tipsy slur, topping off his glass with champagne.

"I'm afraid your brother is right," said Hekmat. "Your fellow British GHQ staff officers are quite loose with their tongues. They spend far more time sharing the latest military gossip at the terrace bar of Shepheard's Hotel, and pillow talk with Egyptian and Hungarian princesses, than they do visiting the front lines. From your comrades in arms, all of Cairo knows what your General Auchinleck and his nemesis Rommel are up to before their own troops. But you seem like a smart fellow, so I'm sure that doesn't surprise you."

Stirling laughed. "Nothing surprises me about our languid military bureaucracy."

"David refers to GHQ as 'layer upon layer of fossilized shit' and the 'freemasonry of mediocrity.' Pardon the language."

Hekmat looked at David. "Oh my, you really don't like them."

"It's because they will never change. But when it comes to the Desert Fox, we all know that discretion is the better part of valor. After all, the chap is literally kicking our bloody asses. Therefore, to give us a fighting chance my lips must remain sealed."

"Very well. But in that case, I shall not be able to tell you any of *my* secrets."

"You have secrets?"

"I might. For instance, how do you know I'm not a German spy?"

"A spy for the Jerries?" snorted Peter. "Oh, you would never do that."

"Why not?"

"Because the Nazis have no sense of humor and exceedingly hideous taste in all things aesthetic—whereas you are positively exquisite on both counts. I know you, my dear Hekmat. You could never work for that vulgar lot. They don't know how to have any bloody fun."

"You're quite right, of course," she said, tossing back her head and laughing. "Then perhaps I am working for the British as a spy."

Stirling looked at her and they smiled at one another. *Possible but unlikely,* he thought. *And my brother's right, there's no way you're a spy for the Nazis.* But regardless of where her true loyalties lied, he was indeed smitten. He couldn't help but picture what her warm lips would taste like if he kissed her. Taking in her beautiful bronze skin, he was reminded again of the Egyptian Queen Cleopatra, sailing along the papyrus tree-lined banks of the Nile in her royal barge with a legion of servants attending to her every need.

"Peter is quite right," he said. "You are a national treasure here in the Land of the Pharaohs and would never throw your lot in with the Nazis. Not only would that be unspeakable, but they don't *deserve* you."

"Thank you, but I don't dance for the Germans, or for you British for that matter. I dance for *myself*."

"Well, the crowd seemed to enjoy the show immensely. Personally, I thought it was remarkable."

"Thank you. By the way, did you know that Eastern Dance is the oldest form of belly dancing?"

"No, I didn't know that. But I do know that the French refer to it as *danse du ventre*."

"That's a Western name. *Raqs Sharqi*—Eastern Dance—is the proper name. It has its roots in all ancient cultures from the Orient to India to here in North Africa. But probably the greatest misconception about belly dancing is that it is intended to entertain men. It was originally for women, you know."

"Interesting," said Peter. "I am told that you Egyptians are the very best belly dancers in the world. Judging from your show, David and I would have to agree."

"Egypt is the original homeland of Eastern Dance and we know how to do it best. *Raqs Sharqi* is in our blood. The Turks, Syrians, and Algerians learned it from us—though they would never admit it."

Stirling raised his champagne glass. "Let's have a toast then. To the Egyptians, the greatest dancers in the world."

"Here, here!" echoed his younger brother, and they tossed back their flutes. Of the two Stirling brothers, Peter was the bacchanalian party boy dedicated to living life to the fullest. He was considered witty, sophisticated, and extremely popular in Cairene social circles—in short, he was to savoir-faire what Shakespeare was to English drama. With his slow magisterial voice, he was equally at ease in a louche nightclub or an Embassy garden party and a magnet to many like-minded transient diplomats and officers from the finest English and Scottish families. His flat in the Garden City quarter of Cairo, opposite the British Embassy where he worked as a diplomat, was known for its wildly fun parties that raged deep into the night.

David said, "I'd like to also make a toast to you, Miss Fahmy. If you ever do become a spy, I do hope it is for His Majesty the King and not that bristly-mustached tyrant in Berlin. I do believe you alone could hypnotize my country into surrendering with your exotic dancing."

"Oh, you boys are so silly. You see a spy in every cabaret and on every street corner, don't you?"

"You think we're bad," said Peter, "you should see our prime minister. The word is he's obsessed with espionage from his experience during the Great War and reading spy novels."

"Is that so? Well, we can drink to spies if you want, but I would prefer to toast instead to the end of the war."

Stirling gave his usual shy smile. "But which side are you rooting for really, Miss Fahmy? I know you Egyptians want your independence desperately—and I must say I can't blame you. In fact, I respect you for it. But you must tell us the truth, for it is said that your King Farouk himself supports the Germans."

She took a moment before answering. "Farouk must walk a delicate line. Look what happened to Norway: it was neutral, too, but now the country is occupied by Nazi Germany and its king is living in England. That could be us if we are not careful. So, like many of my countrymen, I ultimately have no choice but to remain quietly in the background until it is certain which side is going to win and give us Egyptians the full independence we deserve. One must be practical during times of war if one wants to survive, or so Napoleon is reported to have said when he invaded Egypt in the last century."

"A most diplomatic answer," said Stirling.

"Or perhaps I am just being evasive," she said. "But you should know that I do very much prefer taking afternoon tea to eating *Braunschweiger*. On that note, I bid you good evening, gentlemen."

And with that, she gave a mischievous wink, turned back towards her mirror, and resumed taking off her makeup.

My God, thought Stirling. *What a woman!*

CHAPTER 4

BRITISH MIDDLE EAST HEADQUARTERS
GARDEN CITY

JULY 12, 1941

"WE'VE READ OVER YOUR BRIEF, LIEUTENANT. What we'd like to know is why you think this special unit of yours can get the job done better than 8 Commando? In short, what makes you believe your plan will work?"

The Auk was staring at him intently, and Stirling felt a stab of pain shoot through his still-injured back. A graduate from the Royal Military College at Sandhurst and long-time commander in chief of British forces in India, Auchinleck looked like a magnificent stag. Sitting there in his immaculately pressed uniform without even a hint of a sweat stain beneath his armpits, the brawny Scotsman also looked as though the Cairene heat was but a minor annoyance. General Ritchie, deputy chief of general staff, and Major General Eric Dorman-Smith, whom Stirling had heard was Auchinleck's resident Rasputin, brilliant yet quite mad and full of crackpot ideas, sat to the towering Auk's right.

He knew that the primary reason he had been granted an audience with the top brass here today was because of his family connections. Auchinleck was an old family friend of the Stirling's, and Ritchie had been grouse-shooting at the sprawling Stirling estate at Keir. Both were proud Scots, and both had fought in the First World War alongside his father, General Archibald Stirling.

Although Auchinleck had only recently taken over from General Wavell as C-in-C Middle East, he was already under considerable pressure from Churchill to make his presence felt by striking at Rommel. The ever-impatient PM was pressing for an offensive soon, arguing that the Reich's massive operations in Russia had greatly increased her difficulties in supplying the North African theater. He wanted British forces to attack as swiftly as possible. Thus far, the Auk had been able to resist the PM's badgering, claiming that he would not move against the Desert Fox until he was good and ready. But Stirling knew that no general could stand up to Churchill's incessant bullying indefinitely. Auchinleck had to show some progress soon or he would be out of a job.

"The reason my plan will work, sir," replied Stirling with more confidence than he felt inside, "is because the enemy is exceedingly vulnerable to attack along the line of his coastal communications and various transport parks, aerodromes, and other targets strung out along the coast. All my unit needs to wreak considerable havoc behind enemy lines is the element of surprise."

The three crinkly-faced generals looked at him skeptically but offered no rebuttal. "All right, Lieutenant Stirling," allowed the Auk, "please lay your full proposal out for us. We've read your brief, but we would like to hear it from the horse's mouth so to speak."

"Yes, sir. Well then, as I've made clear, my unit's greatest strength is its small size. In previous commando raids, the large number of troops employed on the one hand and the scale of equipment and facilities on the other, has prejudiced surprise beyond all possible compensating advantages in respect of the defensive and aggressive striking power afforded. There is great advantage to be gained in the fullest exploitation of surprise and of making the minimum demands on manpower and equipment. The application of this principle will mean, in effect, the employment of a small subunit to cover a target previously requiring four or five troops of a Commando, or roughly two hundred men. If an aerodrome or transport park is the objective of an operation, then the destruction of fifty aircraft or units of transport will be more easily accomplished by just one of my proposed subunits than a force of two hundred men. It follows that a hundred properly selected, trained, and equipped men, organized into these subunits, will be able to attack up to ten different objectives at the same time on the same night as compared to only one objective using the current Commando technique. A twenty-five-percent success rate in the former is equivalent to many times the maximum result in the latter."

"How do you propose you and your men reach your targets?"

"We will have to be so trained as to be capable of arriving on the scene of operation by every practicable method: by land, sea, or air."

"Your goal is to keep the enemy off balance then?"

"Yes, sir. Furthermore, the facilities for the lift must not be of a type valuable in tactical-scale operations. If in any particular operation a subunit is to be parachuted, it will have to be from an aircraft conveniently available without any modifications. If by sea, then the subunit will be transported either by submarine or caïques, and trained in the use of folboats. If by land, the unit will be trained either to infiltrate on foot or be carried within ten to fifteen miles of the target by another experienced unit."

"So your unit will act independently except for transport to and from the target areas?"

"Precisely. In fact, the unit must be responsible for its own training and operational planning and, therefore, the commander of the unit must operate directly under your orders as C-in-C."

"And why is that?" asked General Ritchie, looking unconvinced.

"It would be fatal for the proposed unit to be put under any existing branch or formation for administration for the simple reason that the head of any such branch or formation would have less experience than me or my successor in the strategic medium in which it is proposed to operate."

"Very well, Lieutenant," said Auchinleck. "How do you plan to deploy your forces during the forthcoming offensive?"

"As laid out in my brief, the targets for the November offensive are the enemy fighter and bomber landing grounds at the five forward airfields in the area of Gazala and Timimi in Libya."

"Yes, but how do you plan to do it?"

"In the night of D minus two, I propose that five sections of twelve men each be parachuted on to drop zones some ten miles south of the two objectives."

"I presume you'll use flares to aid the navigation to the drop zones," said General Dorman-Smith.

"Yes, sir. Then, after re-assembly at the drop zones, each section will spend the balance of night D minus two in getting to pre-arranged lying-up points from which they will observe the targets the next day. The following night, D minus one, each party will carry out its raid so as to arrive on the target at the same time."

"What about your explosive devices?" asked Auchinleck.

"Each party will carry a total of sixty incendiary-cum-explosive bombs equipped with two-hour, half-hour, and ten-minute time pencils in addition to a twelve-second fuse. The time pencils will be used on a time de-escalating basis to ensure virtually simultaneous detonation."

"And how do you plan on getting out of there?" asked Dorman-Smith.

"After the raid, each party will retire independently into the desert to a prearranged meeting place south of the Trig El Abd to rendezvous with a patrol of the Long Range Desert Group."

"Your very own desert taxi service," observed General Ritchie through an approving smile. The LRDG was a reconnaissance and raiding unit of the British Army founded in Egypt in 1940 by famous pre-war desert explorer and sand dune expert Major Ralph A. Bagnold. Stirling's plan was to use the existing outfit to shuttle his commandos about the desert for major sabotage operations behind enemy lines.

The conference room went silent as the three high-ranking British generals looked at one another and mulled things over. Then, with a decisive flourish, Auchinleck said, "I like your plan, Lieutenant Stirling. I like it because it is economical in manpower and equipment and, therefore, poses little risk to the overall campaign."

He could barely contain his excitement. "So you're granting my request and greenlighting the unit, sir?"

"Not only that young man, I'm promoting you to captain, effective immediately."

"Captain Stirling," said Ritchie. "It does rather have a ring to it."

"Indeed, it does," echoed the Auk. "Captain Stirling, you are hereby authorized to recruit six officers and sixty non-commissioned men and other ranks from the depot at Geneifa where the remnants of Layforce are encamped."

"Six officers and sixty men from Layforce? Why thank you, sir."

"Don't thank me, Captain. Just do your job and do it well."

"Where shall I set up my training camp?"

"In the Suez Canal Zone. You are to prepare your men for a raid on the advanced German airfields on the night preceding the major offensive in November."

"And who shall I report to?"

"As you specified in your memorandum, your unit will come under the direct authority of me as C-in-C. I assume that will be satisfactory."

"Yes, sir. I promise I won't let you down."

"Yes, I'd rather you didn't. Now about the name of your unit. We think we have something that dovetails nicely into our ongoing Middle East deception operations. Have you heard of the Special Air Service Brigade?"

"No, sir, I haven't."

"That's good because it doesn't actually exist. It's an invention of Colonel Clarke."

"Colonel Clarke? You mean Colonel Dudley Clarke?"

"So, you've heard of him?"

"Of course, sir. Everyone has. But I have not met him in person. He is said to be a military genius with a unique talent for deception and subterfuge—and a taste for theatricality."

"Yes, that sums up our Dudley quite nicely." Operating from the basement of a Cairo brothel, Clarke was responsible for strategic deception in the Middle East. This was the vital offshoot of military operations dedicated to concealing the truth from the Axis about the true size and firepower of the British Army in North Africa. His job was to make the Allied war machine seem far more formidable than it was.

"Your force shall be known as L Detachment of the Special Air Service Brigade," continued Auchinleck. "As I said, at present the SAS doesn't officially exist. Back in January, Colonel Clarke invented it to make the enemy believe that British parachute troops had arrived in the Middle East. The letter 'L' was selected to imply that detachments A to K were already in existence. Another ruse to fool the Jerries into overestimating our combat strength."

Ritchie nodded. "Clarke has planted fake photographs in Egyptian newspapers showing parachutists training in the desert, dropped dummy soldiers near the prisoner-of-war cages, and had two men in bogus uniforms wander around Egypt pretending to be SAS paratroopers. They're supposed to be convalescing from injuries sustained while parachuting. He's also had false documents identifying the SAS Brigade planted on known enemy spies and built dummy gliders, which have been left on airfields for the benefit of enemy air reconnaissance. The objective of the fake paratroop brigade is to fool the Italians into thinking that we might land airborne troops to assist the next attack. The aim is to soak up Italian forces by making them mount defenses against a nonexistent threat, inflate the apparent size of our forces, and corrupt enemy planning. Clarke's operation is code-named Abeam, and the bogus unit was given the invented name Special Air Service Brigade. Now you, Captain Stirling, will add to the deception. When the colonel caught wind yesterday that a real parachute unit was being prepared, he realized what a grand opportunity he had to bolster the deception. If your unit takes on the same name, he argued, it will reinforce the idea in the mind of the opposition that a full brigade of paratroopers is preparing for action. The colonel has promised to give you all the help he can if you will use the name of his bogus brigade of parachutists."

"I should very much like to assist Colonel Clarke's deception operation. He shall have my full support."

"And you shall have his. As L Detachment of the Special Air Service Brigade—until now a non-existent entity."

The Auk stood up, again looking like a magnificent stag, and extended his hand. This was the signal that the meeting was over.

"Whatever comes of your project, Stirling," he said, "your presence will greatly relieve Clarke's burden."

"With all due respect, sir, I'm hoping to do quite a bit more than that." He shook the general's hand then Ritchie's and Dorman-Smith's. "Trust me, I am going to make Jerry feel very uncomfortable."

"I am sure you will. Good luck, lad," and he was shown out and escorted by a staff officer to meet with the director of Military Information.

As they made their way down the hallway, he couldn't believe his good fortune. Had he really just met with the top brass of the Middle East command and gotten everything he had asked for? And yet it made sense. As the Auk had said, the plan was low risk but offered potentially high rewards, which was what generals always liked. It was cheap in terms of manpower and equipment, since the remnants of Layforce provided a ready pool of possible recruits, and unlike in previous commando operations the plan would not require the use of ships and complex naval cooperation. But most importantly, the attacks deep behind enemy lines could play an important role in hampering enemy airpower at a critical moment.

Upon meeting the director of Military Information, he thought he detected a faint note of hostility. He was glad his new authority stemmed directly from Auchinleck as C-in-C over the SAS. He then went to the adjutant general's department where he had to deal with his old foe, Major Smith. The major greeted him with pursed lips, to which Stirling responded with a firm handshake and a polite smile.

"I can't prevent you from recruiting the officers and enlisted men authorized by General Auchinleck," said the major. "But you may find the Q side a bit sticky."

"Are you telling me the quartermaster will refuse to give me the supplies I need?"

"No, I'm just telling you to lower your expectations. We've got Rommel knocking on our doorstep and can't be giving out supplies to just *anyone*."

Stirling tried not to let his irritation show on his face, but it wasn't easy. He had expected obstruction from the bureaucrats at GHQ, and especially Smith, but it was still hard to stomach. He suspected that the major had a friend at the quartermaster's department and had already briefed him on how to deal with his requests. When he was escorted to the quartermaster's office, he was not surprised, therefore, to find that the officer in charge regarded the supply difficulties as insurmountable.

"At the moment," said the captain responsible, "I'm afraid we can only lay our hands on two tents and not much else. There's a tremendous shortage, you know. We lost everything in Greece and Crete not to mention the recent setback here. Of course, we'll find the stuff in time, but I wouldn't count on anything for the next six months. You see most of it will have to come from England."

"Does it not occur to you that I am asking for very little in terms of supplies? We need weapons, transports, tents, and provisions for seventy men."

"Yes well, that's not my problem, is it?"

"But the operation is scheduled to take place in three months' time. Six months is too long."

The officer was adamant. "I see your problem, but there's nothing I can do about it. I'm snowed under with requests and everyone must take their turn."

"But I am authorized by General Auchinleck himself."

"Yes well, I'm afraid you still have to queue at Q. Sorry, old boy, but those are the rules."

He smiled at his little joke, and Stirling wanted to swat him across the face. But he held his temper. *I'll just have to pilfer supplies from another unit then,* he thought. *What matters most is the men, and I'll get them from Layforce.*

Leaving the building, he lit his tobacco pipe and headed on foot towards his brother Peter's nearby flat. It was infuriating that he would have to scrounge up supplies on his own, but at least he had his own unit and could strike out at the enemy. He was L Detachment of the SAS, by thunder, and was about to wreak havoc on Rommel's overextended supply line. *Or does "L" really stand for "Learner?"* he wondered jokingly.

He had to get a small nucleus together quickly. His first task would be to recruit Captain Jock Lewes, a talented Welshman that he wanted as his right-hand man, and to pull together a list of all the names he could remember from Layforce and the Scots Guards who might be interested in joining the new desert commando unit. The SAS was at least an embryo, and now that he had succeeded in creating it he would have to build it up and make sure the enterprise was successful. He could count on the enthusiastic support of Colonel Laycock, now that Layforce was no more, and on Dudley Clarke, who in return for getting some flesh and blood parachutists instead of bogus ones promised to use his extensive network of contacts to spread the word that Stirling was looking for recruits. Supplying the nascent outfit was going to be more problematic, but he would find a way to overcome the AG branch and that little shit Smith, who would for the foreseeable future persist in being unfailingly uncooperative. And until he recovered fully from his parachute injury, he urgently needed one or two leg-men to race about town and scrounge up whatever supplies they could manage to secure. He would make his brother's flat in Garden City the focal point for his activities.

But the most important thing in his mind, as he passed from under the shadow of the GHQ building into the crisp sunlight smoking his pipe, was the SAS was now born. There would be a well-trained force of Allied commandos operating in the North African desert and he would be in charge of them.

He thought of his dear mum Margaret back at Keir and his father Brigadier General Archibald Stirling who had passed away a decade earlier. He smiled with relish: despite the grueling war, the world suddenly seemed brimming with hope and possibility.

You're going to be very proud of me, Mum and Dad! I'm going to bring the great Desert Fox to his bloody knees!

CHAPTER 5

KIT KAT CLUB AND BROTHEL QUARTER, CAIRO

JULY 14, 1941

MAJOR ALFRED WILLIAM SANSOM, Chief of British Field Security in Cairo, surveyed the Kit Kat Club's broad expanse, searching for prying eyes and eavesdroppers among the officers and high-ranking diplomats in the room. Despite the many signs posted in the city warning His Majesty's troops that "Careless Talk Costs Lives," officers and enlisted men alike talked openly about military matters in the bars and clubs, especially after a few drinks. Sansom was well aware that there was no shortage of enemy spies listening in at all times. His job as a senior Defense Security Officer, or DSO, was not only to catch enemy agents but to prevent sensitive Allied military secrets from getting into their hands.

Yet Sansom hardly looked like a spy catcher. In fact, at only five foot five inches tall with a portly physique, he was not anyone's definition of the archetypal military policeman, nor was his bejowled face much to peek at. But he more than made up for his lack of looks and diminutive stature with his razor-sharp understanding of human nature and his dapper and elegant manner. His uniform always looked as if it were fresh from the tailor's; his moustache was trim; he smelled of expensive aftershave lotion and hair tonic; and, to give him the last touch of panache, he carried a slim switch-cane under his arm. Always well turned out, he resembled a young Hercule Poirot and was fluent in several languages, including Greek, Italian, French, and Arabic. The DSO, in fact, looked as if he had never heard a gun fired in anger in his life, but rather had spent his entire military career fighting a deft but hardly gallant war exclusively on paper.

Born in Egypt, he had spent most of his life in the country, having studied Arabic at Al-Azhar, the oldest Islamic university. He could pass for a native and often did, and sometimes in the field he liked to wear disguises. Tonight, for example, he donned dark sunglasses, a gray French Louis Vuitton civilian suit, and a crimson *tarboosh*.

In the summer of 1941, Cairo was a boiling cauldron of espionage, awash with refugees, smugglers, spies, hustlers, weapons dealers, deserters, and war profiteers—and tonight the Kit Kat Club was filled with many of the usual suspects. Up on stage Hekmat Fahmy was entertaining the cheering crowd, which bore an unusually large number of senior British officers from GHQ and on leave from the front. As always, the Egyptian belly dancer held the mostly male audience in rapture as she performed her exotic routine. Sansom usually spent two or three nights per month at the cabaret. He considered it the smartest nightclub in town and Hekmat Fahmy the most rousing of all the belly dancers. Both the club and its renowned performer were a magnet to officers on leave from the Western Desert and, therefore, the Kit Kat Club was the leading exchange for careless talk.

To assist in his job as Cairo's foremost spy catcher, Sansom had recruited informers from a wide variety of communities: Palestinian Jews, Greek Cypriots,

Lebanese Christians, desert Bedouins, and Sudanese were all on the British payroll. He had under his command a force of two thousand men to help him in his job of preserving security. They were a heterogeneous lot. The bulk of the force was composed of Egyptian policemen who had gone through a special training course in intelligence and had been drafted to Field Security. Working with them were Greeks, Yugoslavs, Turks, Armenians, Syrians, Iraqis, Israelis, and Kurds, plus a small, tight group of British non-commissioned officers who were fluent in German or French and at least one other language.

Through his network of paid informants, he kept a particular eye on Axis civilians and Arab nationalists. In spite of Churchill's directive calling for the Egyptian Government to inter Italian and German citizens, the Egyptians still allowed thousands of Italians and hundreds of Germans to walk around freely and, indeed, to act as suspiciously as they pleased. Much to his consternation, Sansom had to have unambiguous proof a person was a spy before he could have him or her interned, and confessions were virtually impossible to obtain.

He was constantly on the lookout for spies and security leaks among the usual big-city lowlife of crooks, deserters, prostitutes, extortionists, fences, gunrunners, and hashish dealers. While the madames of the brothels reported on the bedroom secrets and infidelities of the officer class, his network of paid informants kept him abreast of potential spies operating within his security fiefdom. He had an inside man at the central telephone exchange, who tipped him off about any unusual phone calls. Mac the barman at the Kit Kat Club, whose real name was Mahmoud, kept him informed of potential shady foreign characters and excessively loose-tongued British officers at the cabaret.

Major A.W. "Sammy" Sansom did not mind his fellow Tommies and Commonwealth troops having a good time at the clubs—after months of fighting at the front they had earned it—but too many of them got snot-slinging drunk and boasted how they were going to deal with the Huns when they returned from leave to their units. In the process, they sometimes gave away sensitive military information on troop deployments. He had found that officers were usually more discreet than other ranks, but higher risk because of their greater knowledge. Time and again, he would stumble upon officers from different units swapping information over a whiskey or glass of beer—and he would have to politely tell them to stop.

Again, his eyes swept the room, searching for signs of anyone suspicious or overly talkative. Looking around the cabaret, he saw eavesdropping potential spies and counterspies moving amongst the tables and jostling at the bar, sexy-looking sirens gazing admiringly at boastfully drunk officers and begging to be told their stories, and Mac the barkeep looking inscrutable while he doled out cocktails, watched, and listened. Accentuating the movie-set-like scene was a scantily-clad Hekmat Fahmy dancing up on stage to the boisterous cheers of two dozen British officers. She was a sight to behold and Sansom briefly wondered if she might herself be spying for the Germans. He considered the prospect unlikely: she was known to be quite cozy with high-ranking British officers and seemed to be too well connected with Cairo's British, French, and Greek elite to risk being an Axis spy.

Watching her perform her sexy gyrations up on the stage, he couldn't help but compare her to his wife Joan. But there was no comparison. He loved his wife dearly, but Hekmat Fahmy made her seem uncommonly pale, plump, dowdy, and, most of all, boring. Looking at the faces of the other men in the room, he could see that they were utterly mesmerized by her every movement and fantasizing about what it would be like to be alone with her. She was the most beautiful woman he had ever seen, of any nationality, and her movements were hypnotic.

When she finished her first performance of the night, Sansom lit a vile French Gauloises cigarette—he had run out of British Dunhill's, his favorite brand—and watched her return to her dressing room. *My God,* he thought, *look at how exquisitely she moves.* The symmetry of her body and her coordination were perfect. It was at that moment he overheard a group of British officers talking at a nearby table. They were red-faced and drunk and speaking very loudly about their recent ordeals in the desert against Rommel. Mac the bartender had overheard them, too; he made eye contact with Sansom and subtly nodded disapprovingly towards their table.

The spycatcher was up and out of his bar stool in an instant. He stepped over and tapped the most senior officer on the shoulder. The man was a captain with three stars on his dress uniform.

"Good evening, gentlemen," he said pleasantly. "I'd like to offer you a word of advice if I may. Unless you want the Germans to know everything you're talking about by the time you get back to the front, I suggest you change the subject of your conversation. Kindly refrain from discussing the war until you're safely back in your hotel rooms, although I can't guarantee there aren't microphones hidden there either. Why not just relax and forget the flipping war? What do you say, lads?"

They just looked at him, eyes narrow. "Who the bloody hell are you?" asked the captain.

"Major Sansom. I'm the chief of British Field Security here in Cairo, and I would appreciate it if you gents would talk about something else besides your recent adventures at the front. In fact, I'm going to have to insist."

"Why don't you bugger off," said a lieutenant. "You don't know what it's like out there going toe to toe against fucking Rommel."

"You're right, I don't, but that doesn't excuse you from having a loose tongue." He looked sharply at the captain. "I expect you and your men to be more careful what you say, that is unless you want me to contact the provost marshal. Do I make myself clear?"

A look of fear crossed the man's face and Sansom knew he would back down. Very few British officers dared resist him once he delivered his standard warning, but of course the worry was the ones he didn't overhear. Ironically, most of the officers he reprimanded for their security lapses regularly lectured their troops about careless talk before they went on leave. The only grain of comfort was that such men acted as unwitting decoys for enemy spies and informers. Most of the time when Sansom spotted a civilian edging nearer to indiscreet talkers, he had his men shadow them to their homes, which he immediately raided in conjunction with the Egyptian Police. But he hadn't observed anyone listening in on this particular group.

"All right, we'll keep our mouths shut," the captain said, making eye contact with his fellow officers at the table. "No need to threaten us, Major. We know you're just doing your job and we will obey your orders. Right, chaps?"

Several of the officers nodded.

"Enjoy the rest of your evening then."

He closed his bar tab with Mac, fetched his luxurious Hillman Minx officer's staff car, and returned to GHQ to make final preparations for tonight's scheduled sting operation in the brothel quarter of the city. A gang of Egyptian underworld figures had been luring drunken soldiers into the out-of-bounds area within the infamous red-light district, where British soldiers were not allowed for health and safety reasons, by promising them unusual sexual entertainment. The soldiers were apparently being led into a dark alley where they were attacked and robbed by four to six thugs. Besides the usual loot of money, watches, jewelry, and fountain pens, the gang always took their army paybooks. Army Book 64, popularly called the soldier's paybook, was the lower ranks' equivalent to an officer's identity card and the first requirement of every spy masquerading as a British soldier. With the large number of paybooks being stolen and the black-market price for the coveted books recently increasing from ten piasters to twenty-five, Sansom wanted to know who was buying paybooks on such an unprecedented scale. His goal was to put an end to the thievery altogether.

He navigated his Hillman Minx south alongside the Corniche—the lengthy tree-lined promenade that ran along the Nile River—before crossing first Zamalek Bridge and then Bulaq Bridge. The bridges served as the western and eastern gateways to Gezira Island and the borough of Zamalek, favored by Cairo's British denizens for its long straight boulevards lined with various types of palm trees and vine-covered pergolas. From Bulaq Bridge, he took Fuad el Awal through Bulaq until he reached Sharia el Malika Nazli. From there, he once again headed south, passing the Egyptian Museum and Kasr el Nil Barracks on the right, linking up with Sharia Kasr el Aini, and then passing the American University in Cairo, the Egyptian Parliament building, and the Palace of Princess Shevekiar on his left before reaching the spacious parking lot of GHQ in Garden City.

He held a 10 p.m. briefing with his staff and Captain Mourad Effat. He worked closely with the Egyptian police liaison officer, and he routinely had Effat and his men accompany him and his squad on major sting operations. Tonight the goal was to lay a trap for the gang of toughs, catch them in the act of armed robbery, and then have the Egyptian police interrogate them and find out what they were doing with the paybooks. Captain Bolton, the son of Lady Bolton of Jersey, had offered to act as a decoy. Dressed in the uniform of a private soldier, he would lurch around in the brothel quarter where the recent robberies had been committed, feigning drunkenness, while Sansom, Captain Effat, and three of Sansom's NCOs, all in plain clothes, lurked in the shadows to make the arrest.

At 10:32 p.m., they packed into Sansom's Hillman Minx and Effat's nimble little Fiat and drove to the brothel quarter. They took Sharia Kasr el Aini north before taking a right onto Sharia Khedive Ismail and then a left onto Sharia Ibrahim Pasha, heading north towards Clot Bey. After passing the Ezbekieh Gardens on the right and Cairo's most illustrious watering hole, Shepheard's Hotel, on their left, they soon entered the red-light district known as *Wagh El Birket*—the Face of the Lake. Here a salty freshwater lake had once existed in historical times.

In Cairo, mankind's oldest profession was in high demand due to the influx of more than 150,000 British Commonwealth troops stationed in and around the city. The infamous "brothel quarter," as the soldiers liked to call it, centered on the seedy quarter of Clot Bey to the north of Ezbekieh Gardens and along a main street called *Wesh al-Berka* that was known to the troops simply as the "Berka."

Berka was marked by official signs showing a black cross on a round white background designating that the area was out of bounds to Allied military personnel. By entering the area, the enlisted man or officer risked arrest by the MPs, but neither they, nor the threat of venereal disease, dissuaded those troops looking for intimate female companionship. It was frowned upon for officers to visit Berka's fleshpots, as it set a bad example to the men. If they contracted VD, most would swear that they had picked it up in a private house. Most officers were less streetwise than the enlisted men and carried more money and valuables; consequently, they were more likely to be mugged or robbed.

Parking their cars, they turned the decoy Captain Bolton loose, crammed into Sansom's car, and waited. The night air was redolent with the familiar smells of urban North Africa: a blend of exhaust fumes, overworked pack animals, cheap incense, and manure. The young uniformed officer stumbled convincingly down the street past the prostitute windows and drinking establishments, looking like a man who was seriously drunk. He had been well prepped about the gang's methods and managed to shake off several ordinary pimps and tarts before he fell in with two broad-shouldered Egyptian men wearing skull caps and *galabeyas*.

"There's our nefarious chaps," said Sansom to Captain Effat and Sergeant Gregory Bersos, one of his Greek NCOs. "I never expected it to be this easy."

"Hold on, Major Sammy," said Effat. "We don't know for sure those are our fellows."

"Well then, there's only one way to find out. Let's go."

He stepped from the Hillman Minx with Effat and his three NCOs just as Bolton started down the street with the two men, who were laughing along with him at some joke. Sansom and his team ducked into the shadows and followed in pursuit as the trio stepped into a narrow side street.

"Ah yes, the game is afoot," said Sansom to the team, feeling a sudden excitement in his veins, the thrill of the chase.

They dashed down the street after Bolton and his two shady cohorts. When they turned the corner, they saw them turn left into another narrow side street.

"I wonder what the devil they do with the stolen paybooks?" said Sansom as they continued to follow in pursuit from a safe distance.

"You can count on us to discover that once we've got the robbers in custody," said Effat grimly.

From what Sansom had seen of Egyptian police methods, he was inclined to agree with the captain. They continued following the three men, but it was not easy. Even though the city was not blacked out, the narrow streets of the brothel quarter were poorly lit, and they had to step carefully to avoid making noise. The shadows of Captain Bolton and his companions quickly faded into the distance, and they could follow only by the sound of their footsteps. Suddenly these ceased, and Sansom signalled to Effat and the others to stop.

They stood and waited, straining their ears. After a moment, they heard a murmur of voices, followed swiftly by a loud yell for help in the unmistakable upper-crust voice of Bolton.

"Let's go!" cried Sansom, pulling out his loaded pistol—an Enfield No. 2 Mark I .38-caliber revolver, the standard sidearm of the British Army.

Dashing around the corner, they found Bolton defending himself desperately against an attack by four large thugs. But when the robbers saw Sansom and his officers rushing onto the scene, they began to run in different directions.

Sansom zeroed in on the closest one. But rather than shoot the man with his gun, he took a flying leap at him, hoping to subdue him without firing a shot.

For his efforts, he was punched hard in the belly and knocked to the ground. He went down hard, his head striking the pavement. As he doubled up, he saw pinpoint stars and heard a shot fired. Out of the corner of his eye, he saw his assailant go down with a bullet wound to his arm. But Sansom was unable to engage in the fight. He lay dazed on the street as Effat blew his policeman's whistle and chased down the thugs with the rest of the squad.

Five minutes later, they had subdued the three robbers, who were handcuffed in a sitting position against a wall.

"What happened to the fourth man?" asked Sansom, still shaking away the cobwebs.

"He got away—the bastard," cursed Effat, and he smashed the butt of his pistol into the wounded arm of the thief who had attacked Sansom.

The man shrieked in agony. Effat told him to stop his whimpering or he would cut out his tongue. Then he helped the severely beaten Bolton to his feet and again blew his whistle. A pair of police patrols appeared quickly on the scene.

Sansom rubbed the back of his head. It hurt like hell and he knew he was going to have a terrible headache. "I believe I'm in even worse shape than you," he said to Bolton.

"Sorry about that, sir. But thanks for saving my bacon."

"Don't thank me, thank Captain Effat. I didn't do a bloody thing. But the main thing is we got most of them. Now we have to find out what they do with those bloody paybooks."

"We'll find that out when we question them at the station," said Effat with foreboding. "Don't worry, they'll talk. It may be the last thing they do, but they'll talk."

And with that, he smiled and delivered a sharp kick to the ribs of each of the three handcuffed attackers.

CHAPTER 6

MUSKI POLICE STATION AND EL AZHAR UNIVERSITY, CAIRO

JULY 15, 1941

AT THE POLICE STATION, Effat spoke in the polite tone of a maître d' at Shepheard's. "We're going to ask you some questions," he said to the three shackled Egyptian prisoners. Sansom was with him in the main interrogation room, along with Captain Bolton, Sergeant Bersos, and three Egyptian policemen. "I advise you to answer honestly. If you do, you will be able to return to your prison cell all in one piece to enjoy a plate of flavorless *koushari*. Are you ready, my friends?"

The prisoners squinted up at him defiantly and said nothing. Breaking them was going to be a challenge, Sansom could tell. Like the Egyptian nationalists in the Muslim Brotherhood and the Egyptian Army's Free Officers' Movement, common Cairo street thugs and other underworld figures were some of the toughest to crack during an interrogation. Effat nodded towards a work table containing a pair of truncheons, a wooden club taped with blood-stained cloth, a blindfold, a gag, a coil of binding rope, and a hand mirror. In the corner was a small oven with two sets of copper wires, which during interrogation were heated until red-hot and inserted beneath fingernails. Surveying the implements of torture before them, the prisoners' faces turned a shade whiter, Sansom noted.

"Let's start with the most important question, my friends," said Effat. "Who do you give the stolen soldier paybooks to? Who is paying you to do this?"

"We don't know anything about any paybooks," responded one of the Egyptians, a tall man who was the apparent leader of the criminal gang. His two cohorts said nothing.

"You do realize you're going to have to talk eventually," Effat went on in the tone of a threatening schoolmaster. "There is no avoiding it if you want to walk out of here under your own power. You can avoid needless suffering by telling us what we need to know. Do you understand?"

This time all three prisoners refused to answer and turned their eyes stubbornly into the floor. Sansom could see their individual minds working: How much can I lie and get away with? What minor information should I give up to make it appear as if I am cooperating? How long will I be able to hold out? As if reading their minds, Effat shook his head with disapproval and motioned to two of his men.

Suddenly, the three prisoners looked fearful.

"We don't know anything about any paybooks," blurted the tall leader, looking genuinely terrified as the policemen aggressively approached. "We just wanted the man's money."

"Then why did you steal his paybook?"

"We just grabbed everything in his pockets. I swear it's the truth."

"I don't believe you. I think you're lying," said Effat, and he motioned to his men, who had momentarily halted, to mete out the punishment. The officer in charge, a brawny Coptic, stepped forward with his rubber-covered truncheon and delivered several vicious blows to the leader's nose, drawing a cascade of blood. Two of the other policemen followed up with stiff blows to each of his ribs and knees, the left arm, and the back of the head. Sansom wasn't sure, but he thought he heard something crack when the arm was struck. The Egyptian screamed in agony and his two comrades gasped in horror, knowing they were next.

Sansom had observed the Egyptian Police interrogating suspects on several occasions before and they were almost always a bloodbath. Captain Effat's standard operating procedure to gain a confession was to attack a prisoner in the shins, knees, elbows, and other hard parts without striking the face or risking harming vital organs. That way, a prisoner could be interrogated indefinitely while under extreme agony without dislocating his jaw or damaging the brain, which could prevent obtaining any useful information and result in his accidental death. But tonight, the approach was more savage than usual. Already in the early stages of interrogation, Effat and his men were battering the prisoners all over their face and body remorselessly, inflicting considerable damage.

Effat waited for the screams to subside before addressing his victim once again. The leader's eyes darted left and right like a bird as he tried to determine which of the policemen would deliver the next blow, so he could brace himself for the impact.

"My friends," said Effat in a soothing voice. "It is time for you to avoid further needless suffering. Who are you getting the paybooks for? Just give us the name of your contact and answer our questions and this will all be over."

"We don't know what you're talking about," said one of the other prisoners defiantly.

"But of course, you do," said Effat, and he again signaled his pit bulls.

This time the officer in charge hit all of the victims in the face so hard that they fell off their stools. As they flailed about on the floor, Effat and his men kicked them several times in the ribs and beat them savagely with truncheons and brass knuckles. When the beating was finished, the three prisoners just lay there on the floor, groaning like wounded bears.

After calmly waiting a minute for the groaning to subside, Effat signaled his men to set the prisoners back on their stools. They had arrived in a battered condition at the Muski outpost a half hour earlier, but now their faces were reduced to a soggy pulp. They had to be either very tough, very scared, or very stupid to endure such physical abuse, and Sansom wondered how badly mangled they would be before they finally caved in and talked. He looked at the officer in charge, whom Effat had said on the way to the station was one of the toughest young policemen on the force. From his expression as he had smashed up their faces, Sansom could tell that the man enjoyed his work a bit too much. He was tempted to protest at the over-zealousness of Effat and his team, but was able to push his misgivings aside when the police captain whispered to him that it would not be much longer before the prisoners submitted and they had the answers they sought.

"My God, just look at yourselves," said Effat once the Egyptians were perched back on their stools. "You have to ask yourself if stubbornness is the right choice."

He grabbed the hand mirror from the table and held it in front of the three battered men, one at a time, so they could see themselves.

"An hour ago, when you were first caught, you were not half bad looking young men. But look at you now. No woman in their right mind would let you have her. Your faces already look like raw meat and we have only just begun. It is going to get a lot worse if you continue your defiance. Now talk. Who is your contact for the paybooks?"

"We already told you, we don't know what you're talking about," said the leader.

At Effat's command, the officer in charge picked up one of the heavy clubs taped with bloodied cloth and swung it several times like a baseball bat, striking all three prisoners repeatedly in the ribs.

The prisoners screamed in terror. Sansom looked at Captain Bolton and Sergeant Bersos and saw that they were as dismayed by the Egyptians' brutal methods as he was. But still, none of them uttered a word of protest.

Effat continued with the interrogation. "You are going to tell me the name of your friend that got away as well as your contractor for the paybooks. Now who are they? I want their names right now!"

"We told you we don't know, damn you!" cried one of the others.

Effat motioned the officer in charge. The pockmarked Egyptian stepped forward and smashed all three men in the ribs several times with the club.

"You know names and addresses. I need you to give them to us now or you will continue to suffer."

The prisoners moaned in pain but did not respond. One of them slumped off his stool unconscious. Two of Effat's men propped him back up onto the stool. Crippled and in agony, the victim was now unable to control his bowels. Urine poured down his pant leg and puddled onto the floor.

Captain Effat wrinkled his nose in disapproval. "Give me the name of your employer now or the suffering will continue all night long."

The prisoners remained silent.

Again, Effat motioned the officer in charge. This time he delivered hard blows to the shins and ribs of each prisoner with the club. The blows made sickening thudding noises and the victims screamed in agony.

Sansom winced. "I know that hurt badly," he said to the prisoner. "Just remember, only you can make the pain stop. Now please tell Captain Effat here what he wants to know because I don't think I can take much more of this."

"If we tell you, our boss will kill us," pleaded the leader.

"That's not our problem," said Effat harshly. "Now who you are working for? Tell us or the pain will continue."

"Come now, lads," said Sansom. "Don't you want to walk out of here under your own power? That has to be worth something."

When the prisoners didn't respond, Effat drove his fist into the leader's stomach, knocking the wind out of him. The officer in charge followed up with several blows to the legs and ribs of all three of them. The prisoners fell off their stools and passed out unconscious on the floor. Effat's men threw buckets of water on them until they came to again. But they still refused to talk, so they beat them again. When they still didn't talk, the officer in charge punched them in the nose with the brass knuckles. They passed out again and were revived with splashes of water and propped back up on their stools.

Effat stood above them. The prisoners, Sansom could tell, were very close to breaking. "It is time for you to stop this foolishness and tell us what we need to know," said the senior Egyptian officer. "Then the pain will stop."

"All right," said the leader through a mouthful of blood. "Please stop and we will tell you what you want to know. Just don't strike us anymore."

Sansom smiled sympathetically at the Egyptian. "Now that's more like it," he said. "Just tell us and we'll get you a doctor. Now who is the receiver of the stolen paybooks?"

"Mahmoud el Sharawani."

Sansom had heard of Mahmoud el Sharawani. The man was a notorious underworld figure whom the Cairo police had wanted to take down for quite some time. "Sharawani—you're quite certain?"

"Yes."

"Where can we find him?" asked Effat.

"He lives behind El Azhar University."

"Well done, old boy," said Sansom with a smile. "Now you will show us."

An hour later, the team quietly navigated the warren of narrow alleys behind the university and located el Sharawani's house. The officer in charge from the Muski outpost rolled down his car window and pointed his flashlight up at the dark house: it was a crumbling old villa and to Sansom it looked unoccupied. They stepped from the cars and held a quick conference. Sansom decided that the best approach would be to take el Sharawani, and whoever else might be inside with him, by surprise using overwhelming force. Effat and his Egyptian police team agreed.

After checking their weapons, they burst into the house. The officer in charge with the flashlight was out in front with Sansom and Effat right behind him.

The team was met with immediate resistance. The officer with the flashlight was knocked backwards by an unseen hand and then smashed hard with a chair. Charging past him, Sansom and the rest of the assault team lashed out at the still-invisible enemy. But in the pitch darkness, he and his men had no idea how many they were up against and they mistakenly swapped a few punches amongst themselves before Sergeant Bersos recovered the flashlight and they were able to overpower the three men in the room, one of whom proved to be Mahmoud el Sharawani.

They immediately cuffed him and the others and sat them down on the battered divan and chairs in the sitting room. Sergeant Bersos tried to turn on the lights but they didn't work and the only illumination in the room was still the flashlight.

"Mahmoud el Sharawani," said Sansom, as Bersos shined the light on him and the others. "You are in a lot of trouble, my Egyptian friend."

"What are you doing here? I have done nothing wrong so why have you invaded my home?"

"Done nothing wrong?" countered Effat sarcastically. "We'll see if that's true once we've searched the place."

"You have no right. Where is your warrant?"

"I'm afraid we don't need one, old boy," said Sansom. "As you might have noticed, there's a war going on and we are fully within our rights to arrest you and search the premises without a warrant."

Suddenly, the room exploded with gunfire, coming from above.

"Take cover!" cried Sansom.

He flattened himself onto the floor, rolled, and let loose with answering fire from his .38 in the direction of the shots, which appeared to have been fired as a warning volley to avoid injuring the nearby el Sharawani. But now as Sansom and his men scrambled for cover, both sides opened up with reckless abandon. The bullets hurled into the floor, walls, and furniture with terrifying force, causing prodigious destruction. In the commotion, Bersos stumbled and fell and the flashlight skittered across the floor. But luckily, the shots missed both the flashlight and the sergeant, who scrambled to pick it up and shone it in the direction of the firing. There, jammed between the top of a cupboard and the ceiling, Sansom saw a man holding a Thompson submachine gun.

"He's got a Tommy!" he cried. "Take him out!"

The concealed shooter let loose with another blast.

Sansom ducked behind the divan to avoid being hit before returning fire with his revolver. His ears were assaulted by the sound of splintering wood and breaking glass. It was then Bersos, who had tucked himself behind a large wooden chest, took careful aim and hit the shooter in the thigh.

"You got him!" cried Sansom.

The man howled in pain and anger and let loose with another burst.

"Take him now, men!" commanded Effat.

With stunning quickness, the officer in charge took a flying leap, grabbed the man by the lower leg, and yanked him down to the floor.

Two minutes later, they had subdued and handcuffed him. Sansom and Effat resumed the interrogation, while the Egyptian police captain's men searched the premises. The wounded man with the Tommy proved to be a Cypriot named Kyriakos Catzeflis, a deserter from the Army and the actual receiver of the paybooks. A cursory search promptly revealed a large number of stolen paybooks stashed inside the house—more than enough to have el Sharawani and Catzeflis convicted in Sansom's view—most of them from recent thefts.

"What do you do with the paybooks?" he asked Catzeflis. "Who buys them from you?"

"Fuck you!"

"That's not the answer I was looking for." He gestured towards Bersos and another tough-looking Greek NCO. "I'm turning you over to these two gentlemen. They speak your language even better than I do since they are Greek. Perhaps on the way back to the station, you will have better recall. For your sake I hope so."

Handing them over to Bersos, he drove back with Captain Effat and his men to the Muski outpost. Upon reaching the station, Sansom learned that due to the severity of Catzeflis's wound, he had agreed en route to give a full confession at the station without a hand being laid on him. Once Catzeflis had submitted to interrogation, Sansom had his wound dressed, gave him a cup of tea and a Gauloises, lit one up for himself, and repeated his first question.

"Who buys the paybooks from you, Kyriakos?"

"The king," said the Cypriot unexpectedly. "King Farouk, I mean."

Sansom smiled through a cloud of cigarette smoke. "I didn't bloody think you meant King George. I take it His Majesty is a friend of yours?"

"I've never met him personally," Catzeflis admitted, "but I've always delivered the paybooks to the Abdin Palace."

"That doesn't mean the king is behind it," pointed out Effat.

"No it doesn't," agreed Sansom. Then to Catzeflis. "So how do you know for sure the king is the one who buys them?" He suspected the Greek wasn't certain that the ultimate purchaser of the British paybooks was the Egyptian king. In fact, he thought it more likely that Catzeflis was mistaken and the king wasn't involved at all. More than likely, it was Farouk's right-hand men or servants who were breaking the law, and he knew of several high court officials who would be more than willing to give aid and comfort to the enemy. Farouk's Italians in particular could not be trusted. The young royal had inherited many Italian courtiers and servants from his father, King Fuad, who was very fond of Italians.

"You're either lying or spreading false rumors, Kyriakos. Now I'm going to ask you again, who is the specific contact that buys the paybooks from you?"

It took further prodding, but two minutes later Catzeflis proceeded to name a particular high-ranking officer of the Royal Household to whom the paybooks had been delivered, which elicited audible gasps from Effat and his men.

"You're sure that's the man," said Sansom, wanting to be certain before submitting his report to Army Intelligence. "You're not just trying to divert us from the real person responsible, or exact revenge on someone who has crossed you?"

"No, I told you who is behind it all. In the name of Allah, I speak the truth."

"Well then," said Sansom, taking a puff from his Gauloises. "I do believe this concludes the case for me." He looked at Effat. "I shall report my findings to Intelligence and wish them the best of luck. Goodnight and good luck, Captain. I'm off now then."

"Where are you going?"

"To bed. I need some sleep, old boy. It's been a long bloody night."

CHAPTER 7

PALAIS HINDU, HELIOPOLIS

SEPTEMBER 18, 1941

THOUGH SHE HAD BEEN A GUEST at Palais Hindu before, Hekmat Fahmy couldn't believe her eyes as she stepped inside the sumptuous palace built towards the end of the nineteenth century by Baron Édouard Louis Joseph Empain—Belgian industrialist, amateur Egyptologist, and founder of Heliopolis. The home was an homage to Louis XIV but with the exotic flavor of the Orient, sporting massive stone towers, lush green terraces, and decorative elephants, nymphs, and dragons; walls covered with thickly embroidered tapestries, Belgian mirrors, and fresco murals; massive gilded doors, marble balustrades, and parquet floors; and elaborately gilded and painted ceilings reminiscent of those of the Palace of Versailles. It now belonged to the prodigal son, Baron Jean Empain, who enjoyed throwing lavish, Great-Gatsbyesque parties for Cairo's elite along with his enchanting wife, the American cabaret dancer Rozell "Goldie" Rowland. Empain the Younger and the "showgirl" had met in a Cairo nightclub where she performed painted entirely in gold.

Standing in the foyer with her escort for the evening, Hekmat shook her head in amazement. "My God, it's like a museum," she said to Guy Bellairs, the British officer with whom she had recently become romantically involved and was living with her on her houseboat on the Nile. He looked dapper in his captain's uniform.

"You can say that again, my dear," he agreed. "Those works of art on the walls are priceless. I see a Gauguin and a Monet. Now let's get a drink, shall we?"

Taking her by the arm, he escorted her into the main ballroom towards the bar, where they ordered White Horse blended Scotch whiskey with soda. They began sipping their drinks while watching the crowd.

The room was filled with Cairo's finest glitterati: royals, diplomats, British and American military officers, Egyptian film stars, academic elites, journalists, foreign-dignitary refugees, business royalty, wealthy patrons of the arts, and land-owning *pashas* whose war profits from cotton and wheat in the fertile Nile River Valley were astronomical. They were all here, shimmering like precious diamonds in their most resplendent "formal" attire, as waiters in white jackets and crimson *tarbooshes* darted hither and yon with glasses of French Veuve Clicquot champagne and hors d'oeuvres of foie gras and chicken liver pâté, beluga and sevruga caviar, tomato and basil bruschetta, and Alsatian tarte flambée.

While the Maltese were being pounded by German bombers and British and Commonwealth troops were enduring the dangers and privations of the desert fighting Rommel, upper-crust Cairo enjoyed a life of luxury. It was as if those who ruled the fiefdom that was the City Victorious were in denial of the war raging in their own backyard. London and other European capitals might lie in ruins under endless aerial assault, but, insouciant in a world at war, the cosmopolitan Cairo elite—and members of the British military, diplomatic, and business hierarchy headquartered in the Egyptian capital—feasted lavishly, drunk copiously, and coupled with reckless abandon.

"Don't look," she said, "but there's Randolph Churchill, Momo Marriott, and Peter Stirling."

"The British prime minister's spoiled brat of a son, an American socialite, and a British diplomat—you don't say?" Bellairs swiveled his head and gawked at them. "Oh dear, that wasn't very subtle, was it?"

"No, it wasn't," she chided him, unable to restrain a little smile as she scanned the room. "I'm going to give you another chance. But this time you must control yourself." She glanced discreetly to their left. "Madame Capsalis and Colonel Fellers are talking over there."

"The wife of the Greek minister and the U.S. military attaché in Cairo, both married? How scandalous. Okay, this time I will definitely be more subtle." He craned his neck and waved at them.

Madame Capsalis looked at them with puzzlement before glancing away nervously—but the American Bonner Fellers recognized Hekmat and waved back enthusiastically. Nearby, the illustrious British society photographer Cecil Beaton snapped off several photographs of the blue-blood revelers at the party.

"The colonel's waving at you," observed Bellairs. "Do you know him?"

She smiled at the high-ranking American officer with access to the uppermost echelons of the British Middle East command. "Yes, Colonel Fellers is a regular at the Kit Kat Club, and at Momo Marriott's louche cocktail parties at the Turf Club."

"Good heavens, with half the Cairo male population pining for your attentions, I should thank my lucky stars I have you all to myself."

She pretended to reprimand him. "You won't any more if you don't stop waving like a madman." She took him by the arm and guided him towards the middle of the room. "Okay, I'm going to give you one last chance," she said. "There's King Farouk and Queen Farida talking to your ambassador, Sir Miles, and his wife Lady Lampson. Now be a good boy this time and show some discretion."

"Yes dear, I'll try."

This time he didn't do anything to embarrass her. They stood sipping their drinks and quietly watched the Egyptian king and queen exchange formal pleasantries with the British ambassador and his wife. Tall, well-built, and not yet the bloated caricature he would one day become, with the light hair and pale eyes so admired in the Orient, the twenty-one-year-old Farouk cut a dashing figure in his black silk dinner jacket and *tarboosh* set at a jaunty angle. His nineteen-year-old wife Farida standing next to him looked radiant in her *hotoze*, a Turkish headdress of white gauze which was still *de rigueur* for royal ladies. She was very popular in Egypt where she appeared in countless fashion magazines. Towering above her and Lady Lampson was Sir Miles, who stood an impressive six foot six and wore his standard gray frock coat with a spotted bow tie and silk topper. Dark, pretty, and Italian, Jacqueline Lampson barely came to her husband the ambassador's shoulder and wore a dress of silk ruffles and a picture hat.

"They say that the young king and Sir Miles don't much care for one another," commented Bellairs.

"That's because your ambassador is disrespectful. He refers to my king as 'the boy' not only in private circles but in public. It's quite rude."

"What are you talking about? Farouk *is* a boy—and a very coddled one at that."

"It's still disrespectful. You are guests in our country—you don't own Egypt—and Sir Miles should show our king the respect he deserves. Especially since he is only twenty-one and is still learning his way around the throne."

"He calls Sir Miles names too, you know."

That's true, she thought, as she studied the two couples. It was well known around Cairo that Farouk referred disparagingly to the British ambassador as "the Schoolmaster" and "*Gamoose Pasha,*" or "Water Buffalo Dignitary." Looking at Sir Miles, Hekmat realized that to her young king and the Egyptian people the avuncular Brit represented everything they hated most about the English: he was a ponderous, authoritarian, lecturing father-figure who symbolized a once-powerful British Empire now in decline. More than anyone else, he was the face of the foreign occupation her beloved country yearned to be rid of.

"I hear the royal marriage is under considerable strain due to Queen Farida's inability to produce a male heir," said Bellairs.

"They have two wonderful daughters and she is only nineteen and he twenty-one. I am sure they will have a son soon enough."

"It is said that he eats six hundred oysters a week. Such grotesque consumption may very well yield him a boy, but if he keeps it up he'll be as fat as a water buffalo by Christmas."

"That's just a made-up story. You British just like to make fun of him and call him a Wog."

"Come on, you have to admit he's eccentric. And he hasn't exactly endeared himself to *your* people with his lavish lifestyle while a war rages on, now has he?"

"If you're talking about his decision not to put out the lights at his palace in Alexandria, well I think it's a bad idea. He should obey the British blackout rules to keep people safe during German and Italian bombing runs. But as I said, he is young and still learning on the job."

"Sir Miles is still right though. He is a mere 'boy.'"

"That 'boy' as you call him stood up to your ambassador. He refused to intern his Italian servants at the palace following Mussolini's declaration of war on behalf of the Axis."

"Ah yes, what was it he said to Sir Miles with reference to Lady Lampson, who is Italian?"

"'I'll get rid of my Italians when you get rid of yours.'"

"Yes, I must admit that was a brilliant retort."

Hekmat smiled thinking back to the highly publicized incident. There had traditionally been a substantial Italian presence in Cairo, but when Mussolini declared war on the Allies, all Italian property in Egypt was sequestered and all Italian men interned, leaving their womenfolk to fend for themselves. Farouk had riled the British by refusing to allow his retinue of Italian servants to be interned and making the barbed reference to the ambassador's Italian wife. Sophisticated Cairenes loved to repeat the anecdote, and even some British officers had to admit that, for a Wog, Farouk had a sense of humor.

"I'll admit he's a feisty devil," said Bellairs, washing down the last of his

Alsatian tarte flambée with White Horse and soda. "But let's just hope he's not secretly working for the Nazis."

"Don't be ridiculous," she said. "Egypt is officially neutral, as you well know, despite the overwhelming presence of British troops in our country. That is our king and prime minister's doing. Sir Miles just doesn't like the fact that Egypt hasn't declared war on the Axis."

"Yes well, the ambassador feels that your prime minister, Hussein Sirri Pasha, should be more convincingly pro-British."

"Doesn't that defeat the point of official neutrality?"

"Now, look here. Great Britain has been a boon to your country and—"

She turned away from him and sipped her drink, not wanting to get into a full-blown argument. The truth was the wartime political situation in Egypt was complicated. Farouk and many Egyptians did indeed harbor certain Axis sympathies, but that was only because the British occupied their country and bossed them about like foot servants. Most of those in power rolled over for the occupiers and did their bidding because they knew Egypt was too weak to resist and was making money hand over fist from the growing imperial presence. In fact, Cairo enjoyed the distinction of being both a neutral capital and major base of military operations for the British—a paradox that rendered preposterous the government's May 1940 pronouncement of Cairo as an Open City and therefore immune to attack. Formally, Egypt was an independent country with a constitutional monarch, an appointed prime minister and representative parliament, and a seat at the League of Nations. But it was bound by a 1936 treaty that gave Britain the right to station troops on Egyptian soil to safeguard the Suez Canal and the crucial short route to India. So, in virtually all but name, the country was a British protectorate. Its actual status was revealed by the fact that, alone among the diplomatic corps, Lampson held the rank of ambassador while his peers were all either consuls or ministers.

The British could have pressured the Egyptian government to declare war on the Axis powers, but for the time being it seemed content that Egypt had broken off diplomatic relations with the enemy, interning adult German and Italian males and sequestering all Axis property. After all, the Tommies felt no need of Egypt's puny army and, given control of its railways, airports and seaports, and censorship powers over its newspapers and radio stations, the Brits were content so long as the pro-Axis inclinations of certain Egyptian politicians were suppressed.

That some among the Egyptian political class resented the British enough to be pro-Axis was hardly surprising. The British had been a dominating presence for generations, turning the largest Arab country into a quasi-colony. While the wealthy elite of Cairo and Alexandria got along well with the British, to the vast majority—especially the Islamists and the new generation of middle-class Egyptian Army officers—the Tommies were an unwanted intrusion. Furthermore, tensions had only grown since the outbreak of war had brought the working-class soldiery of Britain and the white Commonwealth to their shores.

At the same time, among the officers of the British military and administrative services and business community, there were many who felt a paternal affection for Egypt and its people. The public-school-educated officer class had the grace to hide its private contempt for the host nation under a cloak of gentlemanly politesse. But

Hekmat knew that in private most British, including her lover Captain Guy Bellairs, made little attempt to disguise their disdain for the "Worthy Oriental Gentleman."

"You're right, we shouldn't argue, my dear," said Bellairs, realizing he was getting himself into hot water. "Let's have a toast."

"To what?"

"To success against Rommel in the forthcoming campaign, whenever it may be."

"All right, I can toast to that," she said. "To Allied victory."

They raised their glasses.

"Wait, what are we drinking to?" asked a new voice in Arabic-laced English.

Hekmat looked up to see Egyptian Prince Abbas Halim, a bear of a man with a well-trimmed silver goatee. He had fought for the Germans in the First World War and was not shy about touting his admiration for Hitler. The British authorities did not approve of his pro-German sympathies, but had yet to find sufficient cause to have him interned for his unpopular political views. In the meantime, in fact, they enjoyed going to the cocktail parties he hosted with his charming wife Tahida Halim in Garden City. As the prince gave a slight bow and held aloft a flute of champagne, Hekmat noted that his face was red from drink.

"Why we're toasting to Allied victory," Bellairs said to him.

"Oh, I wouldn't be so sure about that with Rommel knocking on the gates of Cairo. He could be here any day now. But I'll drink to your toast." The prince then gave a mischievous look and raised his glass. "To victory then."

"To Allied victory," the British captain corrected him, and they clinked their glasses and sipped their drinks.

Despite the convivial atmosphere, Hekmat felt a new frisson of tension in the air with the unexpected arrival of the prince, who was well known in the Cairo royal and diplomatic community and closely watched by the Egyptian police and British counterintelligence. She noticed that several people were now looking at them and she felt uncomfortable.

"Now Hekmat, my dear friend," said Prince Abbas Halim with an obvious flair for the dramatic gesture. "How long have you and Captain Bellairs here been sleeping together?"

"Excuse me?" she said.

The prince reached out, touched her cheek, and began gently stroking it.

Her face crimsoned. "What are you doing? Please get your hands off me." She politely pushed his hand away and moved closer to her British lover.

For a moment, Bellairs was too stunned to speak. Then he seemed to recover his composure. "I say, I don't believe that's—"

"The way a gentleman treats a lady," she finished for him.

"Yes, quite so." Affronted, Bellairs stepped forward and shoved the prince hard in the chest. "Don't you have any manners, sir?"

"That's enough, Guy," said Hekmat. "We don't want to make a scene. I'm sure the prince didn't mean it."

"I think he bloody well did!" He again shoved the burly man hard in the chest, this time nearly making him topple over since he was so drunk. "Don't you ever talk to my lady friend like that again, you insufferable miscreant!"

Despite the packed ballroom, the harsh words echoed through the crowd like a gunshot, bringing the party to a sudden standstill. Bellairs retreated a half-step, stunned at his own boldness, as a collective gasp and murmur of voices went up from the guests closest to them. The still-life tableau stood frozen for a moment as Prince Abbas Halim's face reddened with naked fury from the public embarrassment. All around them people stopped talking and craned their necks to have a better view. As Bellairs struggled to regain his composure, Hekmat saw armed security men step forward quickly from three directions.

"My God, what have you done, Guy." She started to grab him by the elbow as the security men quickly closed the distance and were suddenly at their side.

It was in that instant an air raid siren sounded outside the palace.

"Good heavens, we're under attack!" cried someone, and the room turned instantly to pandemonium.

Hekmat dashed outside to the patio, with Bellairs fast behind her. There they looked up gaping-mouthed as a dozen German Junkers 52 bombers swept in from the southwest, screaming across the tops of the hangars of the RAF Almaza Aerodrome to the east. The sound of the shrieking air raid sirens mingled with the roar of the German bomber engines and clatter of antiaircraft machine guns. As the dark pewter sky lit up with flashes, she caught glimpses of the black Nazi crosses on the white backgrounds of the planes as they swooped towards the earth, dropping incendiary and explosive bombs that hurtled towards the ground like falling geese.

A series of tremendous explosions ripped through the British aerodrome and hangars along with the nearby troop barracks. The concussive blasts shook the palace as curious party guests continued to stumble outside onto the patio to have a look. Within seconds, one of the hangars and the adjacent barracks had turned to a raging inferno. The flames rose fifty feet into the air, the swelling black cloud mushrooming upwards like something out of Dante. She saw soldiers running to escape the flames, as the fire spread outward and began devouring the palm trees along the perimeter of the main building.

Has the world gone completely mad? she wondered.

Now a pair of nearby explosions rocked the palace, and Hekmat felt a wave of searing airborne heat. As smoke, debris, and a great quantity of dark dust enveloped the area around the explosions, the German bombers banked right, climbed to a higher altitude, and flew off to the northeast. It was then a pair of British nightfighters arrived on the scene to combat the bombers and their Focke-Wulf fighter escorts. She saw fluorescent-green tracer fire as the aircraft battled it out in a running dogfight. With their payloads dropped, the Germans were racing back to the safety of their Libyan airfields while the RAF was intent on stopping them. By now a crowd had gathered on the stone patio, all eyes fixed on the blazes on the ground and the running dogfight in the air to gasps of amazement.

Hekmat felt someone touch her by the arm.

Spinning around, she came face to face again with the prince, who was smiling at her and her British lover.

"Judging by what we just witnessed, the Desert Fox will be here soon," he said not to her but Bellairs. "I don't think you're going to be able to stop him, Tommy. But you are welcome to try."

And with that, he tipped his *tarboosh* jauntily and was gone.

CHAPTER 8

BRITISH MIDDLE EAST HEADQUARTERS
GARDEN CITY

JANUARY 3, 1942

"WELL, IF IT ISN'T THE 'BOY' STIRLING. Where do you think you're going?"

David Stirling tried not to let his surprise and irritation show on his face as he stepped up to the new GHQ sign-in desk, puffing his pipe. The desk was manned by a staff sergeant, and standing next to him going over paperwork was the newly appointed deputy chief of the general staff, A. F. Smith, who had recognized him. Why was he always having trouble with staff officers named Smith?

"I'm here to see the C-in-C," he replied with a pleasant smile.

Smith crossed his arms. "Back from the desert, are we, Stirling? Well, I'm afraid it will be quite impossible to see General Auchinleck. You see, he has a rather full plate today."

Stirling leaned his gangly frame forward and began filling out the sign-in sheet. "Yes, I am sure the general is quite busy. But nonetheless, he *is* expecting me."

Smith wrinkled his nose, as if he had caught a whiff of something malodorous—and not Stirling's pipe tobacco. "Be that as it may, Stirling, we must follow procedure. We can't very well allow just *anyone* to barge in here claiming to see the commander in chief, now can we? Now have a seat. Hopefully, we'll be with you in a few minutes."

"I don't see why I have to wait. Didn't you chaps see my signal stating that I had business with the C-in-C?"

Smith looked at the desk sergeant and smiled with malice. "No, I'm afraid we missed that one. Now do you really want to see the general with that"—he wrinkled his nose again—"growth on your face."

"Oh, you mean my beard. I'm sorry, but I didn't have time to—"

"You know the problem with you, Stirling. You want your little band of misfits to be totally independent. But in our *experience* this has proven unsatisfactory."

"But you don't have any experience with the SAS. So I don't know what 'experience' you could be referring to."

"It's quite wrong to have a number of little private armies. Why all you're doing is fighting your own personal war by your own self-made rules. That isn't very sporting, now is it?"

"All I care about is that we make the Jerries pay—and that we are doing."

"So it's *Who Dares Wins*, is it then?" sniffed Smith, making fun of the SAS motto that Stirling himself had come up with. The words were emblazoned on the cap badge he wore depicting a flaming sword of Excalibur, the legendary weapon of King Arthur. Technically, as a mere detachment, the unit was not entitled to such insignia, but Stirling wanted the SAS to have its own identity and openly flouted military protocol, insisting that his unit have its own badges and wings. The operational wings designed by Jock Lewes depicted the wings of a scarab beetle with a parachute. Any soldier who completed parachute training could wear the wings on his shoulder; after three missions, they could be sewn above the breast pocket. The cap badges and wings were held in reverence, the emblems of a private brotherhood, and were worn proudly by Stirling and his men.

"What, Smith, you don't like our humble insignia?" said Stirling, pointing to his cap with *Who Dares Wins* on the front.

"You're not a bloody regiment. You shouldn't be wearing that badge or wings."

"But General Auchinleck loves our insignia. Why I bumped into him on the steps of Shepheard's three weeks after we created them, and you know what he said?"

"No, but I'm sure you're going to tell me."

"He said, 'Good heavens, Stirling, what's that you have on?' I replied, "Our cap and operational wings, sir,' and I saluted smartly. To which he said, "Well, well, and very nice, too! Very nice, too!' So you see, Smitty Old Boy, the insignia of the Special Air Service has, you might say, received its official blessing."

The two were interrupted by a commanding voice. "Captain Stirling, what are you doing standing out here?"

He looked up to see Auchinleck standing in the open doorway. "My apologies, sir. I was just signing in."

"Well, come into my office at once. I've been expecting you. And by the way, I do much admire your luxurious beard. Why you could almost pass for a Bedouin."

"Yes, sir. Thank you, sir." He gave a triumphant wink to Smith, knocked the ashes of his pipe into the waste bin, and followed the general to his office, where he was offered a seat in front of the Auk's spacious desk. The brawny Scot launched in without preamble.

"I must congratulate you, Stirling. In the past two months, you have destroyed more than ninety enemy planes and made a major contribution to the war effort here in North Africa. Though the Germans have unfortunately gotten rather the better of us, Tobruk has nonetheless been relieved and Benghazi has been captured. You, young man, have played an important role in these achievements by attacking enemy airfields 'up front' so to speak. Well done—and I extend my thanks to your Lieutenants Paddy Mayne and Bill Fraser, whose recent exploits behind enemy lines I have been briefed about. Now I must ask you, what are your plans going forward?"

Stirling was taken aback. He knew that his unit had performed well during the recent offensive, but the SAS, as he and his men now referred to themselves rather than the more limited "L Detachment," had also had an inauspicious beginning and suffered several serious setbacks. The November parachute raid on five Timimi and Gazala airfields held in Axis hands had ended in disaster due to high winds, with only twenty-one of the original fifty-four commandos picked up by the Long Range Desert Group, or LRDG; and the unit had recently lost Jock Lewes—Stirling's right-hand man and inventor of the lightweight Lewes bomb—to a Stuka dive-bomber attack while returning to base from an unsuccessful raid on the Nofilia aerodrome. Despite these setbacks, he knew the SAS concept of striking deep behind enemy lines was a sound one. He just hadn't expected the Auk or anyone else at GHQ to understand let alone appreciate the strategic possibilities. Coming into the meeting, he'd feared that he was going to be given instructions or lectured about military strategy rather than invited by the C-in-C to expound on his theories.

"Well sir," he began in his typical unassuming tone, "with Benghazi once again in British hands, I believe that Rommel will now be forced to use Bouerat to harbor his fuel supplies. In my opinion, the enemy's storage depots are even more important targets now than before. I believe we can get into the port and blow up both the tankers and fuel dumps. We can and should hit more than airfields, sir."

"So it is to be Bouerat harbor then?"

"Yes, sir. We don't need to parachute in either. We are now working closely with the LRDG. They can deliver my SAS teams to any given point in the vicinity of a target with good security."

"Security is vital then?"

"Getting to the targets undetected is paramount to our success, regardless of whether the Jerries ramp up security. That is why we must remain under the radar and I must continue to report directly to you and you alone, sir. Furthermore, there must be no radio or written traffic regarding our movements and targets."

Auchinleck—a towering, larger-than-life figure even seated at his desk—blinked once, twice, but did not object. Stirling wanted the general to grasp the true strategic concept of what the SAS was all about, which meant that he had to grip the nettle with the man. He'd already taken a chance that the Auk would agree with him and set the wheels in motion with the LRDG. His problem now was men; he had lost dozens in the raids since November and the SAS ranks had yet to be replaced.

As if reading his mind, the general asked, "How many men do you think you will need?"

"About fifteen."

"Where do you propose that the Bouerat operation should be launched from?"

"Without a doubt, Jalo Oasis."

"Why Jalo?"

"There are good facilities there. It's one of the LRDG bases and is within an acceptable distance of the target. Anyway, our preparations are already in progress."

"Truly? And when do you think you might be ready?"

"If I can get back to Jalo by the tenth of January, I will be ready towards the end of the month. We have to strike when there is no moon if we are to go in with the minimum risk of detection. The best time seems to be about the twenty-fourth."

He watched as Auchinleck closed his eyes for a moment, mulling the operation over. "Fifteen is not enough men. I should think you will need more."

"If you say so, sir."

"You have the authority, as of now, to recruit up to six more officers and, let's say, a further forty men. Well done, Stirling, and from now you have the rank of major. Which, of course, may help a little with the quartermaster department."

"Excuse me, sir. Did you just promote me?"

"Yes, I did. You are hereby promoted to major, and your Lieutenant Paddy Mayne shall henceforth be a captain. And I am authorizing you to recruit an additional six officers and forty men."

"Thank you, sir. That's quite generous."

"I am also recommending the two of you for the Distinguished Service Order, and Lieutenant Fraser will be awarded the Military Cross."

The Auk stood up, signalling that the meeting was over. Stirling was stunned.

Was it really going to be this easy?

"I am going to give you extraordinary latitude, Major, in both the planning and execution of operations. You will maintain contact with HQ by radio, but there is no need to tell me exactly what you're doing at all times. Just keep me in the loop, so to speak, and let me know of your successes. Perhaps you can help keep the prime minister off my back."

He smiled. "Anything I can do to help, sir."

"I should also like to give you a copy of my official orders regarding our friend Rommel. It has to do with maintaining morale."

He plucked a sheath of paper from the tray on his desk and handed it to Stirling, who proceeded to read it.

TO: ALL COMMANDERS AND CHIEFS OF STAFF
FROM: HEADQUARTERS, B.T.E. AND M.E.F.

There exists a real danger that our friend Rommel is becoming a kind of magical or bogey-man to our troops, who are talking far too much about him. He is by no means a superman, although he is undoubtedly very energetic and able. Even if he were a superman, it would still be highly undesirable that our men should credit him with supernatural powers.

I wish you to dispel by all possible means the idea that Rommel represents something more than an ordinary German general. The important thing now is to see that we do not always talk of Rommel when we mean the enemy in Libya. We must refer to "the Germans" or the "Axis powers" or "the enemy" and not always keep harping on Rommel.

Please ensure that this order is put into immediate effect, and impress upon all Commanders that from a psychological point of view, it is a matter of the highest importance.

C.J. Auchinleck, General
Commander in Chief, M.E.F.

P.S. I am not jealous of Rommel.

When he was finished reading, Stirling had to suppress a smile. Good heavens, was the Auk really this insecure? Why his order made the German commander out to be some sort of Ares of the desert. Didn't the general understand that by issuing such an order he was only making the Desert Fox appear even more invincible?

"Thank you, sir. I will make sure my men are fully briefed regarding your order," he said convincingly, though he had no intention of doing any such thing. He would show his men the letter, of course, but only so they could have a good laugh.

"Carry on then, Major, and I wish you the best of luck."

"Thank you for this opportunity, sir. And don't worry, we'll continue to make Rommel *and* his Axis forces feel uncomfortable. Very uncomfortable indeed."

PART 2

THE DESERT FOX

CHAPTER 9

ER REGIMA TO BENGHAZI
CYRENAICA, LIBYA

JANUARY 28-29, 1942

HIS EYES SMARTING FROM ALKALI DUST AND SMOKE, Lieutenant General Erwin Rommel—commander of the *Deutsches Afrika Korps*—peered through his binoculars at the unfolding battle. Though of medium build, he stood tall atop Greif—his *Sonderkraftfahrzeug 250/3 leichter Funkpanzerwagen*—as the open-air half-track raced northward along with dozens of heavy German tanks and other armored fighting vehicles. He wore his regulation *feldgrau* uniform, a long greatcoat as protection against the dust, a light colorful scarf, and a peaked officer's cap. He was lean and sunburnished, like his men, with lips perpetually cracked and crow's-feet etched around eyes long accustomed to squinting through his Perspex sun and sand goggles. He had recovered the now-famous glasses from a captured British armored command vehicle in the spring of 1941 and was rarely seen or photographed these days without them.

Though the strain of months of battle had taken a heavy toll on his health and his body was covered with desert sores, he was in an energetic mood. Once again, his combined German and Italian *Panzerarmee* was on the move and the Tommies were retreating before him. Depending on which direction he looked, the battlefield stretching before him consisted of crested Libyan sand dunes the size of great ocean waves; tamarisk-covered spurs; craggy rocky hills; intricate wadis; and flat plains covered with huge boulders, lonely heaps of camel dung and scrub brush, and the occasional skeleton of a fallen soldier or goat.

On January 21, he had commenced his surprise attack against a thin armored British screen at Agedabia. Now on January 28, after six consecutive days of battle, his force had already destroyed or captured over 300 enemy tanks and AFVs and some 150 guns, as well as taken more than 1,000 prisoners, including part of General Ritchie's divisional headquarters. The British First Armored Division alone had been reduced to less than 50 tanks from 150. Following the heavy fighting northwest of Saunnu Oasis, Rommel halted the chase at the caravan stop of Msus, in the middle of the Cyrenaica bulge, as his fuel reserves were running dangerously low. After refueling, he resumed his advance over a broad front and now had the choice of striking east towards Mechili so as to threaten the Eighth Army's main supply route, or north through the Green Mountains to Benghazi and the coast.

He chose to feint towards Mechili while personally taking charge of the real thrust, to Benghazi. He was confident that his breakout had destroyed enough British artillery and armor to derail any offensive his adversaries might have planned. Unlike most generals, Rommel often led from the front with a complete disregard for his own personal safety, which made it exceedingly difficult on his staff. But his soldiers loved him for it and often cheered him on by waving their caps and weapons when he passed.

"Enemy tanks spotted ahead, *Generaloberst*!" cried Lieutenant Colonel Siegfried Westphal, his chief of operations 1a at Panzer Group HQ.

Rommel flicked away a sandfly and peered again through his Zeiss 10x50 field glasses: he had removed the eyecups so that he could look through them without taking off his desert goggles. "Where?" he snapped, his voice sharp and stentorian.

"Two miles, bearing north seventy degrees west!"

Focussing his binoculars, he spotted the enemy lurking in the shadows of a fractured limestone ridge. To their credit, the retreating Tommies had thrown up a dozen Mark IIs as a rear guard. The heaviest tank the British Army possessed at twenty-seven tons, the "Matilda" as the Mark II was affectionately known, was named after a popular feathered cartoon character because it moved about as elegantly as a waddling duck. Its top speed was six miles an hour over rough desert terrain and sixteen miles per hour on roads. Like all British tanks, its principal armament was a two-pounder cannon whose range and penetrating power left much to be desired; but what the Matilda may have lacked in firepower and speed, it more than made up for with its three-inch-thick armor plate, a hide impenetrable to all but the most powerful Axis tank and anti-tank gun, such as the lethal German 88.

"Take them out! Take them out now!" he commanded to his chief intelligence officer, Colonel Friedrich Wilhelm von Mellenthin, who immediately relayed the order to the other mobile units through his radio mouthpiece.

In a matter of seconds, the desert air was shattered by a thunderous roar and bright illuminating flashes against the sky as dozens of German Mark III Panzers and 88-mm cannons opened fire. Rommel felt the ground beneath his boots shudder and tremble; and he saw shock waves shimmering across the barren, rocky landscape like heat rising off the desert floor. A wall of fire appeared as the projectiles crashed into the turtle-like Matildas and nearby limestone ridge offering them partial concealment.

He watched as a pair of bright, fiery spumes erupted from three of the British tanks, as they were struck with direct hits from the powerful 88s. Most of his Panzers were equipped with short-barrelled, KwK 38 L/42 50-mm tank guns, with a small number possessing the older 37-mm main guns, and they had mixed success in penetrating the Matilda's thick armor. But the 88-mm anti-tank guns were getting the job done quite nicely, he noted with satisfaction.

"They need to hit them again—but this time harder!" he shouted to Westphal and von Mellenthin as he peered through his binoculars.

"Don't worry, they will!" replied Westphal. "That salient is not going to protect them for long!"

Westphal—who, in sharp contrast to the compact and direct Schwabian Rommel, was a tall Prussian with a dignified and slightly pompous air about him—proved correct. The anti-tank crews proceeded swiftly with the destruction of the pack of Matildas. For ten minutes, the roar of the shells on both sides was deafening. Then the noise died down as the British were forced to turn and run, leaving nine charred and burning tanks behind.

It was a complete rout and the subsequent pursuit attained a speed of 15 miles per hour as the defeated Tommies fled madly across the rough and spectacularly beautiful desert terrain. The enemy reeled from the massive coordinated attack across the line, which Rommel knew from radio intercepts and other intelligence sources Auchinleck and his subordinate field commander Ritchie had not expected.

Over the next two hours, the German anti-tank gunners worked in close support with the Panzers, using tactics that the British, with their rigid separation of different arms, had not mastered. The artillery crews leapfrogged from one vantage point to another, while the Panzers, stationary and hull down whenever possible, provided protective fire. Then the process was repeated with the 88s providing covering fire and the Panzers and armored support vehicles rolling towards the retreating enemy.

It was the kind of perfect *blitzkrieg* that the Desert Fox loved to deliver, and it proved a cruel baptism of fire for what he could tell was an unusually inexperienced British armored brigade. He almost felt sorry for the poor Tommies. Outnumbered and outfought at every turn thus far during the offensive, the British were being picked off in their tanks and other armored fighting vehicles before the spotters could tell where the enemy fire was coming from. Adding to the sense of confusion for the British was the sight of trucks full of their own badly maimed and wounded men and soldiers engulfed in flames as they scrambled out of their burning tanks, which panicked many of the support troops and made them bolt.

After a brief halt to confer with his HQ staff, Rommel continued his advance. Now riding along with him, his chief operations officer Westphal, his intelligence officer von Mellenthin, and his trusted driver, *Unteroffizier* Hellmut von Leipzig in his trademark bleached white cap, were Major General Alfred Gause, his forty-five-year-old chief of staff, and Rolf Munninger, his twenty-year-old personal clerk and fellow Schwabian. Rommel's full complement of staff officers drove in a caravan of forty-six vehicles, including several *Mammuts*—Mammoths—the huge British Dorchester 4x4 armored command vehicles his *Panzerarmee* had captured at Mechili seven months earlier. While on the move, Rommel split his time between his personal Mammoth staff car that he had affectionately named Moritz and his smaller half-track Greif, named for the mythical griffin with the body of a lion and head and wings of an eagle.

Always near his *Kampfstaffel*—his roving tactical HQ and armored close-protection detachment—were the trucks, half-tracks, and motorcycle sidecars of Captain Alfred Seebohm's 621st Radio Intercept Company. Seebohm's soldiers referred to themselves as the "circus" because of the unit's nondescript gaggle of buses and wireless lorries used to intercept enemy wireless signals. Many of these were commandeered civilian vehicles, and their non-military nature meant that Unit 621 looked quite unlike *Panzerarmee Afrika's* other frontline units.

Rommel relied heavily on the unit for intelligence. Each W/T operator has a "fist" as unique as his voice, and Seebohm and his German intercept operators had learned to recognize the various enemy radiomen across their front since the British typically failed to move around their operators, so each unit had a unique identifier. It didn't matter if the unit's coded call sign changed; the fist allowed the two to be linked. The intercept operators passed along what they heard to the company's evaluation center. During the past nine months, German thoroughness combined with British laxity had allowed Unit 621 to piece together the puzzle of who they were hearing. The analysts began to create a British order of battle, supplementing Rommel's other intelligence sources and giving him an edge in combat.

The German concept of operational command was to paint with a broad brush and not to give detailed orders below the level of unit commander. The approach, which had been proven successful time and again, was to allow the officer in charge to make tactical decisions since he was likely to have a much better understanding of how to carry out a given task. The British tended to do the opposite; few details were beneath the attention of their meticulous planners, an approach that tended to discourage changes of plan and stifle the ability to adapt in a timely manner to fast-moving events. After almost three years of war, Rommel and other German field commanders still found most British operations "sluggish" and "predictable."

By late afternoon of the 28th, Rommel had taken Er Regima and the Via Balbia, the coastal highway that ran all the way to Alexandria. Soon thereafter, he was knocking on the gates of Benghazi. Though he and his men were exhausted after six straight days of fighting, the *Panzerarmee's* morale could not have been higher. They had taken an enormous amount of booty: British water tankers; ration and supply trucks loaded with everything from tins of English biscuits, Ceylon tea, and pineapple to fine English linen; hundreds of drums of fuel; several large field guns; and more than thirty captured battle-worthy Valentine tanks. As they advanced, the Germans increasingly found themselves replacing broken-down vehicles with captured British transport, dining on much-prized British rations, and donning scraps of British uniform. One of the more popular items were British webbing belts. Slowly but inexorably, the Germans were turning into Tommies themselves as their replacement vehicles, petrol, rations, and clothing were all English.

The Desert Fox proceeded to split his army into three groups for the attack on Benghazi. A few armored vehicles, accompanied by enough trucks to kick up a sizeable column of dust, headed towards Mechili to make it look as if the main assault was heading in that direction. The bulk of the 90th Light Division and the Italian XX Corps were sent up the Via Balbia, to approach Benghazi from the south. Rommel led the third column—the fast, mobile assault column Gruppe Marcks, reinforced by his own *Kampfstaffel*, the 115th Panzergrenadier Regiment, and the 33rd Armored Recce Unit—northwest to try and cut the road east of Benghazi. Ritchie took the bait and ordered what remained of his battered 1st Division's armor to block Rommel's feint towards Mechili.

The three columns converged on Benghazi in the evening. The British were too weak to fight off the three-pronged assault and that night a large part of the garrison managed to escape to the east. By noon the following day, January 29, Benghazi fell to Rommel's main force. But even after all the success, the Desert Fox was surprised at his *Panzerarmee's* good fortune.

"I can't believe we've retaken the city. The offensive went like greased lightning," he said to Gause. They were sweeping up the coast road towards the Port of Benghazi in Greif. Up ahead loomed the shimmering twin domes of the Benghazi Cathedral in the Maydan El Catedraeya.

"Yes, but the advance will soon splutter to a halt because we have once again run out of petrol," pointed out the chief of staff pessimistically.

"But we got a week's worth of spare fuel from the Tommies. That's worth a lot."

"I agree," said Gause. "But if Kesselring and the *Comando Supremo* would just give us the supplies we need, there would be no stopping until we reached Cairo."

Rommel nodded. As commander in chief of Wehrmacht South, Field Marshal Albert Kesselring was in charge of making sure the Italian supreme command in Rome sent him the supplies he needed to keep up the pressure on the Eighth Army. But for more than six months now, Kesselring and the *Comando Supremo* had been letting him down and his tactical freedom had been limited accordingly.

The triumphant caravan continued towards the port. A light wind was blowing now and Benghazi's dirt-covered coastal roads and narrow streets were dusty. Rommel liked the feel of the breeze cuffing his face as he sped along the Via Balbia. In front of him, German soldiers clung to the decks of the massive Panzer IIs and IIIs and smattering of Panzer IVs with the short 75-mm howitzers at the head of the advance column. Making up the caravan's snake-like tail were more tanks, trucks, and footsloggers.

Over its 2,500-year history, the ancient Mediterranean seaport had been fiercely contested by Greeks, Spartans, Persians, Egyptians, Romans, Vandals, Arabs, Turks, Italians, and now British and Germans. The Italians had invaded in 1912, ruthlessly oppressing the locals and building a seafront of Italianate villas. Benghazi served as a showcase for Mussolini's imperialist vision, and on the eve of the war 20,000 Italians were living in the burgeoning colony with shops, restaurants, and a cinema. In February 1941, it had been captured from the Italians by the British in the first major Allied engagement of the Western Desert campaign. Two months later, the port was retaken by Rommel. It was seized back by the Allies on Christmas Eve, only to change hands once again weeks later as German forces swept eastward. A critical staging area in the see-saw war, Benghazi and its surrounding airfields had taken on strong symbolic, as well as strategic, significance. With Tobruk back in Allied hands, Benghazi was the principal supply port for the *Afrika Korps*, while the nearby airfields—Berka, Benina, Barce, Slonta, and Regima—were crucial to the Axis in the contest for air supremacy over the Mediterranean.

Although he had hardly slept in the past week, he felt a soaring feeling inside as he swept through the Cyrenaican capital that had changed hands so many times and no doubt would again. The last of the British defenders from the Indian Brigade had surrendered, and no organized resistance remained. Thousands of Libyans clogged the streets, waving their arms and chanting, "Heil Rommel! Heil Rommel!" The men were dressed in long white *galabeyas*, red and black *shashiyah* headdress, and large outer cloaks known as *jarid*, which they wrapped around their body and tied at the right shoulder like Roman togas. The women wore blouses embroidered with beads, baggy silk trousers, brightly colored cloth togas held together by silver brooches, headdresses embellished with pom-poms, and large pieces of gold or silver jewelry. They shouted and cheered as the cavalcade rolled up the street along the waterfront towards the port, while packs of children clambered aboard the Panzers, half-tracks, and radio trucks to catch a ride with the victorious new army that had swept into their city. The road quickly became so congested with cheering spectators—some offering palm dates, plates of couscous, freshly baked flatbread, and cups of black and green tea—that in places the traffic slowed to a crawl. Rommel was forced to detour to Omar Al Mukhtar Street that ran parallel to the coast road.

"They greet us as liberators," observed Westphal with a battle-weary smile.

"Yes, but they did the same to the British only a few months ago," said Rommel, taking in the spectacle. "Let's just hope the city stays in our hands for the duration of the war. We need both Bengazi and Tobruk as supply depots until we take Alexandria and Cairo."

"We're going to need a lot more tanks and petrol to make that a reality," said Gause.

The Desert Fox's face filled with resolve. "We will get there. And then we will seize the Suez. That's when we will have Tommy on the ropes."

They drove on to the Port of Benghazi. Stepping out of his command vehicle with his staff, he took a moment to stretch his legs and get his bearings as he surveyed the city and the shimmering blue water of the Gulf of Sirte. Dozens of German and Italian military supply ships, fishing and trading vessels, and oarboats were anchored in the harbor like little toy boats. The port was also littered with ships of various nationalities that had been sunk from aerial bombings. A few burnt vessels were piled up like whale bones in the shallows and along the white sandy beaches and jetties flanking the harbor proper.

Turning his head and looking back towards the desert from which he had just traveled after a week of furious fighting, he stared at the two large distinct domes of Benghazi Cathedral. Then he took in the rest of the city with the green hills of the Jebel Akhdar in the background. There were a variety of architectural styles in Benghazi, which reflected the number of times the city has changed hands throughout its history. Arab, Ottoman, and Italian rule had deeply influenced the different streetscapes, buildings, and quarters of the city—but the heavy bombing had given the city a generic, desolate, war-torn look. He looked back at the harbor. Although the port was useless for the moment due to all the bombing damage and the British decision to blow up stores to avoid supplies falling into German hands, he knew that Benghazi would provide him with a vast hoard of supplies and hundreds of vehicles with which to keep his army mobile.

As he stared out at the sea with the wind on his face, he felt the power of his victory, the sense that he was a part of history. But he also felt lonely. He thought of his wife Lucy, his son Manfred, and his illegitimate daughter Trudel from his 1912 affair with a young German girl, now deceased, named Walburgu Stemmer when he was betrothed to Lucie. He loved all of them dearly and wrote them often. He missed them terribly. As he stood there thinking of them, the words to *Lili Marlene* came to him.

He could hear the faint strains of the song about a lovesick German soldier floating on the salty air. The sad song made him remember back to the warmth of his wife's body, her womanly scent, the soothing reassurance of her voice. Yes, he missed his beloved Lucie, and his devoted son Manfred and daughter Trudel too. He loved waging war, the feeling that he was an integral part of the sweep of history, but he loved his family far more. Without them, he was nothing.

He looked up at the sky. The ball of sun was overhead, casting its radiant glow on the azure-blue water as the waves rolled lazily towards the lido to the west. The scenery fairly took his breath away. Even though he knew it was time to give new orders to his field commanders and resume the eastward push towards Mechili and the Egyptian border beyond, he couldn't help but take a moment to feel the power of the sea.

He felt the infinity of it all and the feeling of oneness inside. The blue water was a reassuring presence, like an old friend, reminding him that one day he would get to return home to his beloved family.

He bent down and picked up a clump of loamy soil next to a palm tree, sifting it through his fingers, watching the flour-like dust blow off in the breeze. The soil in Benghazi was a rich red color and very fine and clayey; its smell was redolent of the earth and had a power all its own. He realized that he would always remember this small moment: the lonesome tug he felt inside as he gazed out at the sweep of ocean with his victorious army at his side occupying the Libyan port city.

His peaceful reverie was broken by the voice of his chief of staff.

"Your orders, *Generaloberst*?" asked Gause.

"We will head east now and rejoin with the others. The first step will be to seize the coastal towns along the Via Balbia from here to Derna. The British will most likely set up a defensive line running from Gazala to Bir Hacheim. We will join them there shortly and wait."

"Wait?"

"For more tanks and petrol. Unfortunately, we have no other choice. The British will be out of commission for at least a month, perhaps two. They wouldn't dare counter-attack until then."

"And what about the Gialo Oasis?"

"The Italian XXI Corps will cover our southern flank."

At that moment, an Italian staff car drove up. A captain in a neatly pressed uniform that had not seen a lick of battle stepped out. He walked towards Rommel and his officers carrying a white envelope, clicked his boots together, and saluted.

"General," he announced in atrocious German as he handed him the envelope. "Il Duce sends his compliments." He saluted again.

With a contemptuous curl to his chapped lips, Rommel opened the envelope and read the message in silence.

After a minute, Westphal said, "What does it say?" He was standing next to Gause, von Mellenthin, and Munninger, who had drawn close out of curiosity.

Rommel couldn't help a smile. "It appears our good friend and ally Benito Mussolini wants me to launch an offensive to take Benghazi."

"What?" gasped Gause.

"Il Duce wants me to take Benghazi. Regrettably, I believe he's a little late to the party."

Gause and the others laughed, at first lightly then uproariously. Rommel turned towards the Italian captain, whose face had reddened with embarrassment.

"You can tell Il Duce that Benghazi has already been taken. And please make sure to give him my compliments."

With that, he and his staff piled back into Greif and set off to the east on the Via Balbia. Within an hour of his departure, his *Panzerarmee* had rounded up more than 1,000 prisoners, 6,000 tons of ammunition, 300 armored cars and other vehicles, and thousands of tons of British rations from the port city. Like so many legendary conquerors before him, the Desert Fox once again controlled Benghazi.

CHAPTER 10

ROMMEL *KAMPFSTAFFEL*
EAST OF MECHILI, CYRENAICA, LIBYA

APRIL 11, 1942

AFTER MAKING ONE LAST EFFORT to swipe away the eolian dust clinging to his greatcoat, Rommel pulled aside the wind flap of the HQ briefing room tent and stepped inside. The spring *khamsin* winds had been whipping up sandstorms of late, turning the desert into a choking fog, filling trenches, ruining food, and fraying tempers—especially that of the temperamental Desert Fox and his staff.

Seated around the conference room table were four members of the Abwehr, the German military intelligence service: Admiral Wilhelm Canaris, the white-haired chief of the Abwehr and top intelligence official of the German war machine; Count László Almasy, a Hungarian aristocrat and desert explorer with intimate knowledge of the Libyan and Egyptian frontier; and two of Almasy's junior officers, Johannes Eppler and Heinrich Gerd Sandstette, whom Rommel had been informed had been personally handpicked by Almasy for a new top secret mission to assist Panzer Army Africa in driving the British out of North Africa and seizing the Suez Canal. The operation—known as Operation Salam—would involve the insertion of the two German spies into British-held Egypt.

"Gentlemen, my apologies for being late for our final briefing, but I was busy at the front," said the Desert Fox as Canaris and the others stood up and saluted. He quickly surveyed the Abwehr chief. Known to his enemies as "Father Christmas" from his snow-white locks, the fifty-five-year-old Canaris was one of only a handful of officers with direct access to Hitler. For such a high-ranking officer, he was unusually soft-spoken and diminutive, with a height of just under five feet, four inches, which had nearly kept him out of the German Navy. For clothes, he wore a cheap jacket he had bought during his stopover in Madrid and a pair of shabby unpressed gray flannel trousers. Rommel smiled inwardly: he knew "the little admiral" revelled in wearing disguises, perhaps a throw-back to his pre-war career as a spy.

He strode quickly around the table and shook hands with Canaris and the other officers. Spread out before the group was a detailed, color-coded topographic map depicting Western North Africa from Tunisia to the Suez Canal. As they retook their seats, he quickly reiterated the purpose of the meeting, speaking to the assembled team comprising the Almasy Commando in his usual clipped manner, as if not a precious second of time could be wasted.

"As you are aware, gentlemen, your mission is critical to my drive to take Cairo and the Suez, for we may not get another chance." He looked directly at the two younger officers, Eppler and Sandstette. "We need information about the enemy's intentions as soon as practicable. That's why I need another network in Cairo." He now looked at Almasy. "How do you plan on slipping them into Egypt?"

The Hungarian took a moment to answer, collecting his thoughts. In 1932, the desert explorer and aviator had taken part in the expedition to find the legendary lost oasis of Zerzura—the Oasis of the Birds—with three British explorers; and he later went on to explore the Gilf Kebir plateau and the Great Egyptian Sand Sea through 1936, for which the Bedouin gave Almasy the nickname *Abu Romia*—Father of the Sands. He was a gangly, somewhat hideous man, even more shabbily dressed than Canaris, with a fat and pendulous nose, drooping shoulders, and a nervous bird-like manner. But the Abwehr adventurer and airman—who had thoroughly mapped the Libyan and Egyptian desert and been prominent in pre-war Cairo society—knew the contested North African frontier as well as Major Ralph Bagnold or anyone else in the British Long Range Desert Group, which made him a very dangerous man to the enemy. Rommel noted that the count certainly looked the part of the desert explorer: his skin was as tough and brown as old shoe leather.

Almasy pointed to the map. "Operation Salam will involve the infiltration of Lieutenants Eppler and Sandstette into Cairo by a 1,400-mile land route. We will travel via the Jalo Oasis to the Gilf Kebir plateau, bypassing the British LRDG base at Kufra, and then proceed east to the Kharga Oasis. Once we reach the oasis, the plan is to drop the two agents close to Assiut on the Nile. From there, they will make their own way to Cairo where they will transmit information using the radios they have brought with them to *Abteilung* I attached to the headquarters of your *Panzerarmee*. Once the agents have safely established their undercover base in Cairo, the transmission of intelligence will proceed under the codename of Operation Condor. We have assigned two of our best Abwehr wireless radio operators from Mamelin to be the points of contact with the two agents."

Rommel scratched his chin as he studied the map. "Who are the operators?"

"Lance Corporals Walter Aberle and Waldemar Weber," answered Canaris. "Aberle is the driver and Weber the W/T operator. The two Brandenburgers are Palestinian-born Germans. As Captain Almasy has indicated, they are two of our very best and have been specifically assigned to Operation Salam and Operation Condor from our fixed wireless communications center in Mamelin. The codename for Weber, who will receive and transmit all incoming and outgoing transmissions, is *Schildkroete*—Tortoise."

Here Canaris paused for a comment from Almasy, but the count had nothing to add so he asked the Desert Fox to tell them what specific intelligence he hoped to gain from the mission.

"The main thing I need in the coming weeks is a reliable unit in Egypt to convey by wireless detailed reports on the condition of the Eighth Army. I will need to know about their preparations for the occupation of important strategic and economic points, and notice of planned attacks and sabotage once my army enters the Nile Delta. In short, there are three things I need to know. First, where will the British make their main stand when I begin my final attack upon the Delta; second, what reinforcements, in men, tanks and guns, will they have received; and third, who will lead them? Success is absolutely essential. I don't know how much longer I can rely on my *Gute Quelle*—Good Source—in Cairo."

Canaris and Almasy, who knew to whom he was referring, nodded but Eppler and Sandstette looked at him with puzzlement. "What do you mean Good Source?" asked Eppler, who appeared to be the senior officer between the two spies.

"He's referring to Colonel Bonner Fellers, the U.S. military attaché in Cairo," said Canaris by way of explanation. "We've been able to read his radio traffic since October 1940. The U.S. Foreign Service uses what's called Encryption Code 11, colloquially known as the 'Black Code' from the color of its binding. It's the same code that Fellers uses. He has had access to the highest levels of the British Middle East HQ since his appointment to Egypt in 1941, which has made him privy to GHQ's most closely guarded secrets. But the supposedly impenetrable Black Code in which he has been transmitting his top secret information nightly to Washington has been broken. Even before America joined the war, Fellers had been granted privileged access to British planning. He's been a regular attendee at the staff conferences addressed by Auchinleck and his predecessors. He talks to British military and civilian headquarters' officials, reads top secret documents, and visits the battlefront on a regular basis. He is an incredibly valuable source. He composes long, very detailed, and highly accurate radiograms describing virtually everything he learns, encodes them, and files them with the Egyptian Telegraph Company for transmission across the Atlantic to Washington. His comprehensive reports form the basis of these daily dispatches to America. The High Command—and General Rommel here in particular—have found them invaluable. But as the general has pointed out, we cannot rely on the Good Source indefinitely."

The veteran desert explorer Almasy put in his two cents. "The problem is this source can dry up at any time. No military leader can tolerate a constant leakage of news to the enemy for any length of time. A trifling mistake, an indiscretion, a piece of treachery and the source will be closed. That is why we need you two to be the *generaloberst's* eyes and ears in Cairo."

"I understand," said Eppler. "How were we able to break the Americans' code in the first place?"

"We had help from the Italians," said Canaris. "They were able to extract a copy of the codebook from a safe in the U.S. Embassy in Rome one night in September 1941. This was three months before the Japanese attack on Pearl Harbor brought America into the war. General Cesare Ame, head of Mussolini's military intelligence branch, had duplicate keys to the embassy and two agents planted inside. One of them, Lori Gherardi, opened the ambassador's safe and noting the positions of the documents inside, carefully extracted the Black Code book. Two of his colleagues, waiting in a car outside, rushed it to military intelligence HQ, where it was photographed page by page before being returned and replaced by Gherardi, exactly as he had found it. The Americans never realized anything untoward had occurred, and the Italians were able to read Fellers's traffic to Washington from every U.S. station in Europe, the Middle East, and North Africa. Since the code book and cipher tables have been photographed and the book replaced, neither Gherardi's boss, Colonel Norman Fiske, nor the ambassador, William Phillips, have ever suspected Gherardi and he has continued in his job."

"The code was obtained from the Italians then?" asked Eppler.

"Indirectly," replied Canaris. "Mussolini refused to let us have a copy of the pilfered Black Code book. He did, however, authorize General Ame to let us have decodes of the messages from Fellers to Washington. Armed with these and assisted by Fellers's invariable habit of starting and ending his messages the same way, our cryptographers soon figured out how to break the code for themselves. When America entered the war in December 1941, Fellers graduated from trusted friend to indispensable ally with privileged access to even more sensitive information."

"Who does Fellers send the reports to?" asked Eppler.

"He reports directly to Colonel William Donovan, the chief of American intelligence, as well as the War Department's Military Intelligence Division," answered Canaris. "Furthermore, Fellers has informed Washington that select friendships have many times produced the information rather than the fact of his official position. He is something of an Anglophobe and has provided censorious assessments of British military strategy and tactics. Some at GHQ refer to him as 'Colonel Garrulous' because he seldom holds back from giving his opinion, even if it might be overly critical or offensive to his British allies. But most importantly, his reports are highly accurate. Apparently, due to Fellers's profound knowledge of the Middle East he has been recommended as a future commander in chief for Egypt. His reports are likely read by President Roosevelt, the head of American intelligence, and the Joint Chiefs of Staff."

"I call the intercepts my 'little Fellers's because they are so indispensable," said Rommel. "They always go crazy at Supreme Headquarters in Berlin when they get the latest telegrams from Cairo. Usually within two hours of receipt, Fellers's messages are decoded, translated, and on their way back to my field headquarters, where they keep me informed of British losses and often the precise whereabouts of British forces the night before. Typically, I get a complete run-down on British armored strength, including the number of tanks in working order, the number undergoing repair, the number available for action, and their whereabouts. I dread the day that I lose this intelligence source, but that is why it is imperative that I have you two in Cairo. My Good Source cannot last forever."

He looked pointedly at Eppler and Sandstette. They were nondescript in looks and dress, with only their peaked desert campaign caps identifying them as German soldiers. *Will they come through for me?* he wondered. All he could do was keep his fingers crossed. He was also counting on the two wireless men, Aberle and Weber, to do their jobs and do them well. Clear and unambiguous radio communications between the spies and W/T team were of paramount importance.

"Of course, there are no guarantees in such operations," said Canaris in a mollifying tone, "but these men are the best we have. Both have spent considerable years in the Middle East and speak English, French, and Arabic fluently. They have worked in the Army Topographical Department on maps. Both are experienced radio operators, having undergone training in Munich and the Abwehr wireless station at Berlin-Stansdorf."

Rommel kept his stern gaze fixed on the two young agents. Eppler had black hair, a square handsome face set on a small thin frame, a small moustache, and blue eyes. Sandstette was taller and also slim but with fair hair and an introspective look about him. They were both clearly of German ancestry. By his confident manner, Eppler was no doubt the leader between the two men.

"Tell me about yourselves. But make it quick—I must be at the airfield in an hour. I have a battlefield reconnaissance to perform."

"Yes, General," said Eppler obediently. "I was born in Alexandria in 1914. My father was a British officer and my mother German."

"I was told you had an Arabic name: Hussein Gaafar."

"That happened later. My mother Johanna married a wealthy Egyptian lawyer named Salah Gaafar. He adopted me as his son and gave me his last name."

"Where were you raised?"

"Germany from 1915 to 1931, at which time I was brought back to Egypt. My mother inherited a small hotel in Alexandria and became its manager. At that time, I had joint nationality and became fluent in Arabic, German, and English, which I learned while attending English-speaking schools in Alexandria and Heliopolis, including the Lycée Français. I subsequently became a merchant apprentice to a German national in Cairo. I stayed in Cairo until August 1937. While in Egypt I made numerous excursions into the desert. I later married a Danish woman named Sonia Eppler-Wallin and was in Germany and Denmark earning a living in a commercial enterprise until September 1940, when I was conscripted into the Army."

"What were your duties?"

"I served with a motor transport unit, then with a signals depot unit, and later with an interpreters' depot unit. I was later transferred to the Topographical Department of the OKW, where I checked maps of the parts of Africa I was familiar with." The OKW—*Oberkommando der Wehrmacht*—was the German Armed Forces High Command. "In the summer of 1941, I was transferred to the 15th Company of the 800th Brandenburger-Lehr Regiment, a special forces unit directly responsible to Admiral Canaris, and I have been with the Abwehr ever since. I know the Egyptian desert well, General."

"Are you Muslim?"

"No, I was baptized Roman Catholic as my mother came from the Catholic south of Germany. As a young man, I did make the pilgrimage to Mecca, but I have never been a devout Muslim. I find Islam to be too radical for my taste."

He now shifted his gaze to Sandstette. "What about you? What is your story?"

"I was born in Oldenburg in 1913—my father was a professor of chemistry—and I was educated and lived in Germany until 1930. In that year, I immigrated to West Africa and remained abroad until the outbreak of war."

"And you know Egypt and its customs?"

"Not really, sir. I have worked in several parts of the continent but not Egypt."

"Where exactly?"

"I worked my way around from old German Southwest Africa to South Africa and up to the former German protectorate of Tanganyika and British East Africa. I was arrested and interned by the British in Dar-es-Salam in 1939, but was repatriated to Germany in January 1940 as part of an exchange of German and British civilians. Like Lieutenant Eppler, I came under the wing of the Abwehr, and worked in the Army Topographical Department, correcting and translating maps of those parts of Africa which were known to me. I have been given a forged British passport in the name of Peter Muncaster—an American I met in East Africa—to be used once we reach Cairo for Operation Condor."

Rommel looked at them both. "And your wireless training? Are you truly as proficient as Admiral Canaris has suggested?"

"Yes, sir," said Eppler. "As the admiral has indicated, we both underwent extensive W/T training, first in Munich and then at the Abwehr wireless station at Berlin-Stansdorf. But Sandy is better than me, I must admit."

Rommel gave a satisfied grunt and the tent fell silent. Now that he had a better feel for the men, he felt more reassured. Nonetheless, he let his intense gaze linger a moment longer on them before he turned to Almasy and had him review the plan again in detail on the map of the desert. With a long bony finger, the count traced the route the Commando would be taking, around the British troop concentrations and across the Great Sand Sea into Egypt.

When the Hungarian was finished, the Desert Fox looked sharply at Eppler and Sandstette. "You have before you one of the most important operations of the war. I plan to be in Cairo before the end of the summer, and it is of vital importance that you provide me with the information I need. It will take courage, skill, and great effort. I know that the British Army in Egypt is dispirited and uncertain after the recent defeats, but they have not been destroyed. What they lack most is leadership, but Churchill will find his generals in due course. As I said before, I need to know who those new field commanders will be. I must have details of their plans: what forces they will use, what numbers of tanks, where they will make their main defensive line. I need to know, too, whether the Egyptian Army contains enough patriots to rise in revolt and help us once the fight for the Delta begins. This you must discover, Eppler, and it will not be easy."

"We shall do our best, General," said the German-Egyptian spy, to which his partner Sandstette gave a vigorous nod of agreement.

"That is good. But first you two must get there. And that"—he turned back to Almasy—"is your task. Do not attempt it if you think it will not succeed, because time is short and we do not want to waste any more valuable agents."

"I stake my life on the success of this mission, *Herr Generaloberst*," said the experienced Hungarian explorer, who before the war had worked closely with Bagnold and other British officers now in the LRDG that served as the desert taxi service for David Stirling and his SAS. "I shall deliver them to their destination. I know the routes. I know the water holes. I know the difficulties. Do not fear, I will deliver them safely to Cairo."

He allowed himself a little smile. "That's what I like to hear, Captain Almasy. But it is a bold plan. I hope you don't die in the damned desert for your efforts."

Again, the count pointed out his experience and said that the desert held no fears for him.

Rommel gave a fatalistic laugh. "Oh well, they say lunatics are usually lucky. Why shouldn't you be?"

"You can rely upon us to do everything required to achieve success, *Herr Generaloberst*," said the twenty-eight-year-old Eppler.

At this, Rommel bounced to his feet and gave a challenging snort. "I am sure you will do your best, youngster," he snapped. "But will that be enough to push the British out of North Africa if I somehow manage to lose my Good Source? Now that is the question, isn't it, young man?"

And with that, he shook hands with Canaris and each member of the Almasy Commando, bid them good luck, and drove to the airfield.

CHAPTER 11

BENGHAZI

MAY 21, 1942

WHEN STIRLING blasted around the corner and saw the red barricade light flashing in front of their path, he braked violently and crashed down through the gearbox, halting the "Blitz Buggy" just short of the wooden bar stretching across the road. An Italian sergeant with a submachine gun slung over his shoulder and a hand-held torch approached the car as a group of heavily armed guards looked on. If possible, Stirling hoped to bluff his way through the checkpoint and avoid a gun battle, but he had the uneasy feeling that was unlikely.

Driving with the commanding officer—CO—in the Ford V8 utility truck that had been transformed into a German staff car was his SAS team: Lieutenant Fitzroy Maclean, his third-in-command behind his hard-drinking friend and rival, the decorated Irishman Paddy Mayne; Gordon Alston, an intelligence officer who had spent three weeks in Benghazi during the latest British occupation; Sergeant Johnny Rose, a former manager of a branch of Woolworths and an expert mechanic, who had kept the Blitz Buggy running despite the harsh desert terrain; Corporal Johnny Cooper, a slightly built, boyish-faced former Scots Guardsman whose youthful appearance belied competence and resilience; and Captain Randolph Churchill, the corpulent, garrulous, and opinionated thirty-year-old son of the British prime minister whom Stirling, against his better judgement, had allowed to tag along when the battle-hardened Reg Seekings was injured on the journey from Siwa Oasis.

"All right, keep your weapons concealed and no sudden movements and we should get out of this alive," he said to his men. "Fitz will do the talking."

He pulled to a complete stop. The full-beam headlights of the Blitz Buggy now illuminated the Italians, who had tensed up at the SAS vehicle's approach and tightly gripped their weapons. In Stirling's view, he and his men presented nothing out of the ordinary. The Germans were always rushing around the desert at odd hours of the night and the Blitz Buggy looked authentic with its German look-alike paint and recognition insignia. However, Wehrmacht regulations specified that all cars driven at night should have dimmed lights to reduce the danger of aerial attack. But Stirling wanted his brights on to blind and disorient the Italians.

He quickly surveyed the enemy. The approaching sergeant was the only one armed with a submachine gun. Another Italian soldier with a bolt-action rifle stood some ten yards to the right of him. Three more, also carrying rifles, were keeping a close eye on him and his men from beside the guard hut. All had bayonets fixed.

Unfortunately, the Blitz Buggy was proving to be a liability. The vehicle made a high-pitched metallic screaming noise when driven at full speed and the Italians looked wary. Hours earlier, during a descent down a steep rocky incline into a wadi, its wheels had been knocked out of alignment and the bearings now protested at maximum volume. The whining noise, audible from a half mile away, only died away when the car came to a halt. Johnny Rose had tried to fix the car, but without success. Even if they managed to make it past the checkpoint, they wouldn't be able to make a stealthy approach into Benghazi. But they had no other option.

"Now stiffen up and act like Jerries," he said as the sentry stepped up cautiously to the vehicle.

"You mean act stupid?" joked Lieutenant Fitzroy Maclean, who like Stirling was a jokester and the scion of an ancient and warlike Scottish clan.

"No, I mean bossy, rude, and in a bloody hurry."

They all chuckled nervously. Stirling took a deep breath and rolled down the window. From the front passenger seat, Maclean spoke to the Italian sergeant in his native tongue. Tall, erect, with an angular face and dimpled chin, the thirty-one-year old Maclean had become a member of Parliament in order to obtain his release from the Foreign Office, and once in the House of Commons had promptly joined the army. He had been sent to the Middle East to take part in an adventurous "secret" organization, which was disbanded as soon as he arrived. That was when he ran into an old friend, Stirling's brother Peter, a former diplomatic colleague, and soon found himself the recipient of a warm invitation from David to join the SAS, which he promptly accepted. He had been Stirling's first official recruit.

"*Militari!*" snapped Maclean with a brusqueness befitting a Nazi officer.

Clutching his submachine gun, the Italian sergeant raised his torch and squinted back at them, scrutinizing them closely while the other armed guards drew closer to have a look inside the vehicle.

"*Staff officers, di stato maggiore!*" added Maclean sharply. "*Di fretto!*" In a hurry.

Stirling felt a bead of sweat trickle down his cheek as the moment seemed to go on and on with excruciating slowness. *Good heavens,* he thought, *are we really going to have to shoot our way out of this?*

"*Di fretto!*" bristled Maclean, this time with greater urgency.

Still, the Italian sergeant hesitated. The four other guards armed with rifles stepped away from the guard hut and closer to the vehicle with their drawn bayonets. Behind him, Stirling heard the ominous click of a safety catch being eased off the Tommy gun in the hands of the man behind him. The twin Vickers K machine guns mounted at the rear of the car had been taken down and hidden on the floor along with a spare can of petrol and the single Vickers gun at the front, so the team would have to make do with small arms and makeshift weapons if they got into a scrap.

Stirling made eye contact with two of the guards. For a split second, he thought that they might open fire on him and his men in the Blitz Buggy. But after an excruciating few seconds, the sergeant lifted the bar.

"You ought to get those dimmed," he said, pointing at the headlights.

"Yes, we'll see to it," responded Maclean in Italian.

The sergeant waved them through. Stirling breathed a sigh of relief and pressed his foot to the gas pedal, driving off. As the shrieking din of the wheels rose once more, he accelerated into the night towards Benghazi.

"This is absurd. We could hardly make more noise if we were a fire engine with a clanging bell," snorted Randolph Churchill, taking a nip of rum from his canteen.

They drove on down the road, but soon a new threat appeared as two German armored cars passed in the opposite direction. The cars stopped, turned around, and began to follow them into town. Stirling slowed down, inviting the cars to overtake them, but they, too, decelerated, and when he drove faster, they did the same.

"Bloody hell," he cursed. "I've no choice but to outrun them."

He hit the accelerator. The Ford V-8 engine roared and the Blitz Buggy tore through the night, hurtling into Benghazi at seventy miles per hour. When they reached the Arab quarter, he slammed on the brakes and shot around a corner onto a narrow side street to evade their pursuers.

That's when it happened.

A cacophony of air-raid sirens began shrieking into the night, accompanied by police whistles and shouting.

Now Alston—the young intelligence officer with twinkling eyes and a strong sense of adventure—yelled out directions: "Second on the right, that's right. No, you've passed it. Blast. Go on, and take the next turn instead."

Randolph Churchill and the others in the back held on for dear life as the Blitz Buggy slewed from side to side. They continued through the narrow streets, whipping around corners and making enough noise to raise the dead. Reaching what appeared to be a bombed-out cul-de-sac, Stirling turned in, braked, killed the engine, and switched off his headlights.

Then they waited.

As the anxious seconds ticked off, he wondered if the Italians at the roadblock or the Germans that had followed them had radioed ahead and alerted the authorities of their presence. Had they somehow walked into a trap, or were the air raid sirens an unfortunate coincidence? Since RAF attacks had been called off for the night due to the raid, an air attack was unlikely. But did that necessarily mean that he and his men had been detected, or could the siren be a coincidence? At the moment, all he knew for certain was that the Blitz Buggy, with its telltale screech, was a liability and would have to be abandoned. If he and his men managed to pull off their mission, they had no choice now but to leave Benghazi on foot for the rendezvous with the LRDG.

"We're going to have to hide the car and use the boats to take out our objectives," he said. "Let's unload them and get together our equipment."

Over the next fifteen minutes, they unloaded the two rubber dinghies from their kit bags, along with the explosives and machine guns. They had a small arsenal of Lewes bombs—incendiary and explosive devices consisting of mixed diesel oil and Nobel 808 plastic. The lightweight but lethal bombs were the brainchild of Lieutenant Jock Lewes, killed on patrol in December 1941, an exceptional officer Stirling sorely missed. Weighing slightly more than one pound, the bombs were unusually light yet powerful enough to destroy the aircraft on an enemy airfield. The only problem with Jock Lewes's clever invention was that the timing of the pencil-detonators was affected by extreme changes in temperature and moisture content, such as during hot desert or heavy rain conditions. In such cases, the devices sometimes exploded too early or failed to detonate at all.

Before setting out, Rose and Cooper placed a Lewes bomb with a half-hour time fuse beside the petrol tank of the no-longer-useful Blitz Buggy. With their preparations complete, the unit of six men set off into the Arab quarter in single file, heading for the docks led by Alston.

"Good heavens," exclaimed Randolph Churchill as they navigated their way towards the harbor. "I do believe the past half hour has been the most exciting time of my thus far unremarkable life."

"Yes well, please keep your voice down so you can live to tell your father about it someday," said Stirling. "He's going to want to hear all about the dash and derring-do of his prodigal son."

"I'll give it me best, old boy. After all, *Who Dares Wins*."

"Who Dares Wins!" echoed the group playfully.

They continued on through the European quarter, making for the port. Because of repeated attacks by the RAF, the city had a curfew and rigid black-out regulations. There was no movement and no light, and only the light breeze blowing in from the sea and lapping waves broke the silence. Along the route, they encountered numerous demolished buildings and bomb craters in the streets. Stepping through a breach in a wall, they walked down a street littered with blasted concrete blocks, rounded a side street, and ran straight into an armed Italian policeman standing under a streetlight. Once again, Maclean summoned his best Italian.

"What's all this noise?" he asked the uniformed member of the Carabinieri.

"Just another of those damned English air raids," said the Italian, who appeared to be either complacent or bored.

"Might it be that enemy forces are raiding the town?"

The policeman gave a dismissive snort. "No, there is no need to be nervous about that," he said. "Not with the British almost back on the Egyptian frontier."

"Thanks then," said Maclean. "Good night."

Stirling suppressed a gloating smile. The conversation with the Carabinieri, bizarre as it was, shed a different light on the situation. The sirens, it appeared, were simply responding to a false alarm, rather than warning of their arrival. Similarly, the pursuing cars had probably just been air-raid wardens trying to get them to dim their car lights. Which meant that they had not been compromised after all, the destruction of the Blitz Buggy was unnecessary, and the vehicle still represented their best means of escape. Moreover, the sirens had now fallen silent.

Stirling turned to Corporal Cooper. "Johnny, you'd better get back to the car and defuse the bomb before it goes off. We're going to need that noisy contraption to get out of town after all. We'll be right behind you."

"Aye, Major."

He dashed off. Ten precarious minutes later, he had managed to achieve his goal: defusing the explosive device, with less than three minutes left before it exploded. Once he had stuck the safety pin back into the time pencil, he was able to extract the detonator and throw it over a wall. With the bomb now defused, they left Churchill and Rose behind to find a place to conceal the car and set off again for the docks.

Having passed through the European quarter of white-stuccoed buildings, they found the harbor was wired-off and guarded. The wire perimeter surrounding the dock was ten feet high and double-strength. They cut a hole in the wire and slipped quietly down to the water's edge, careful to keep their distance from the sentries making their rounds. While Maclean and Cooper set to work inflating the rubber dinghy with a pair of bellows on the sliver of beach, Stirling headed off to reconnoiter the enemy vessels moored in the harbor.

Peering over a battered sea wall, he could make out several large ships at anchor. There was no moon, but the stars were brilliant. The shining surface of the harbor was like a sheet of quicksilver, and the black hulls of the ships seemed no more than a stone's throw away. Aerial photographs had confirmed a small strip of shingle, between the jetty and the harbor wall, ideal for launching the dinghies. The ships in the harbor would make viable targets if he and his team could reach them unobserved. They wouldn't have to paddle far, though he had hoped not to have to cross such a smooth expanse of open water to set the charges.

If two large ships could be mined and sunk at the harbor entrance, this would block the port, temporarily paralyzing Axis seaborne supply lines. Starving Rommel of food, fuel, and ammunition was a top SAS priority. Even if the impact was only short-term, the effect on German and Italian morale might be considerable. More troops would have to be deployed to defend the port, and the Desert Fox would be forced to look backwards defensively rather than forward towards Cairo.

Wrapping up his reconnaissance, he headed back to Maclean and Cooper to see how they were faring. Along the way, he ran into an Italian sentry but managed to slip past by mumbling unintelligibly in German and pushing him out of the way. When he reached the two men, he saw that they had been unable to inflate the rubber dinghies, which lay next to the sea wall like wilted flowers.

"You can't get bloody air into them?" he said to Maclean.

The Scot shook his head. "Since our wadi inspection they've been punctured."

A voice floated across the water. "*Chi va la?*"

Oh, bloody hell, what now? thought the CO, as he realized they had attracted the attention of one of the night watchman aboard one of the ships. He looked at Maclean. "Go ahead and answer him," he whispered.

"*Militari!*" shouted Maclean.

But the watchman remained unsatisfied. "What are you up to over there?"

"None of your damned business!"

To Stirling's surprise, that seemed to do the trick. But then they attracted yet more attention from a pair of night sentries aboard one of the other boats.

"Hey, what are you doing there?" one of them asked through the darkness.

"We are German officers, and we are growing very tired with being challenged!" roared Maclean. "Shut up and mind your own fucking business!"

Stirling couldn't believe their bad luck. It was growing light, and the sound of metal doors opening and slamming and excited voices from the ships revealed that their crews were now suspicious. Clearly, the mission would have to be scrapped. The men packed up the infuriating dinghies and headed back towards the perimeter.

As they neared the fence, a large African soldier wearing the uniform of the Italian Somaliland regiment stopped them. The sentry grunted, and by way of inquiry, prodded Maclean in the stomach with his bayonet.

"You bastard, get your hands off me!" snapped the lieutenant, and he launched into a flood of expletives in Italian.

It took Stirling a moment to realize that the sentry didn't understand a word of Italian as Maclean continued to berate him in a first-class impersonation of an irate and pompous German officer who has been interrupted in the performance of important duties by an insolent underling. The sentry, browbeaten, eventually lowered his bayonet and backed off with an expression of injured dignity. But as they filed off into the darkness, Stirling realized that the party had expanded; two more Italian sentries, alerted by the commotion and thinking some sort of drill was under way, had joined the line of men and fallen in at the back of the procession.

He could tell the situation was quickly spiraling out of control. If any real German soldiers showed up, they would be put before a firing squad. "My dear Fitzroy, I do believe it's time for you to extricate us from this imbroglio," he whispered to his Italian-speaking lieutenant.

"Don't worry, chaps, I've got us covered."

With surprising aplomb, he proceeded to lead the growing Anglo-Italian troop up to the gatehouse, accost the lone sentry, and indignantly demand to see the guard commander. A sleepy Italian sergeant emerged a few moments later, pulling on his trousers. The two Italian hangers-on, sensing trouble, melted back into the darkness as Maclean launched into a Hitler-like harangue.

"We are officers of the German General Staff and we have come here to test your security. Frankly, it is appalling. How is it that me and my party have been able to wander freely about the area without once being properly challenged or asked to produce our identity cards? Why we have been past this sentry four or five times"—he pointed to the nervous-looking guard standing next to him—"yet not once has he asked us for our ID. For all he knows, we might be English. We have brought great bags into the dock for a training exercise. How is he to know they are not full of explosives? It is a very bad show indeed. We have brought these materials in here, and now we are going to take them out. I will let you off this time, but you had better not let me catch you napping again. What's more"—he glanced disapprovingly again at the sentry, who winced—"you had better do something about smartening up your men's appearance. Do you understand, Sergeant?"

"My apologies! I will take care of the situation at once!"

"I trust you will! You may carry on then!"

Maclean turned stiffly on his heel and stalked out, with Stirling and the others following. The Italian sergeant saluted, and as they passed the sentry at the gate, the man made a stupendous effort and presented arms, almost falling over backwards in the process. Stirling couldn't help a little smile at Maclean's audacity. He was a magnificent actor and Stirling could tell he had reveled in the whole charade.

Dawn was breaking by the time the party had reassembled at the cul-de-sac with Churchill and Rose. The Blitz Buggy was now thoroughly camouflaged with rubble and planks inside the garage of a half-bombed house. Above the garage, up a rickety wooden outside staircase, Churchill had found a decrepit little flat that had long been abandoned and shuttered.

"I've christened it Number 10 Downing Street," said the chubby son of the prime minister ebulliently. "What do you think, Major? Will it do?"

Stirling glanced around. "Yes, it will do quite nicely. We'll hold up here for the day and make the attack tonight when it's dark again."

"But we don't have any boats," pointed out Maclean.

"We'll just have to improvise. Now let's get some sleep. It's been a long bloody night."

CHAPTER 12

BENGHAZI

MAY 21, 1942

"GREAT SCOT, THERE'S BLOODY GERMANS EVERYWHERE!"

Stirling was peering through the window shutters from the second floor of the abandoned flat along with Randolph Churchill. After catching a couple hours of sleep, the SAS team had awoken four hours earlier at 09:03 just as the town was stirring to life. Though exhausted from last night's high drama, the men spent the morning in high spirits and feeling as if they owned Benghazi. But now at midday, they no longer had only security-lax Italians to contend with but the *Afrika Korps*. The building opposite, it seemed, was some sort of German headquarters, with dispatch riders dashing in and out on motorcycles and staff cars, and fastidious-looking officers arriving and leaving as if on a vast movie set.

The abandoned apartment where they were hiding out, as it turned out, was not as secluded as it had seemed in last night's darkness. They had believed themselves to be in a deserted section of the town. However, it was now obvious that the Arabs only left Benghazi at night to avoid RAF attacks. They returned during daylight hours to sell, trade, and barter their goods. The noises of the city seeping through the shuttered windows and battered walls were loud. Stirling could hear the roar of German and Italian vehicles, the babble of Arabic, German, and Italian voices, and the drone of Axis aircraft coming and going from nearby airfields.

What would the enemy give, he wondered, *to know that they had the son of the British prime minister so easily within their grasp?*

"What do you propose we do?" asked Churchill in a low voice so they wouldn't be overheard by the elderly Arab couple that lived in the flat next door, or the children playing in the courtyard at the back of the house.

"There's nothing we can do—except wait until tonight when it's dark again," answered Stirling. "Then we'll hit them and hit them hard."

"But how? We have no boats."

"We can blow up the smaller vessels at the dock. Perhaps the torpedo boats."

Churchill smiled with relish. "Bible and sword, I'm looking forward to it. The Jerries won't know what hit them, eh?"

"I should think not." As he continued to scan the street below, Stirling suppressed a chuckle at Churchill's childlike exuberance, which was so much like his father. Captain Randolph Frederick Edward Spencer Churchill was an odd duck. Stirling considered him his friend and SAS brother-in-arms, but he also found him an annoyingly spoiled brat and cry-baby who was outspoken, ill-mannered, and often inebriated. The frustrated son had spent most of his life trying, and largely failing, to impress his illustrious father and was cruelly nicknamed "Randolph Hope and Glory" by his detractors, of whom there were many. But he was also clever, generous, and courageous, which was why Stirling tolerated his eccentricities.

Churchill had originally been dispatched to the Middle East with Stirling and

Layforce, and when the commando unit was disbanded he took over the propaganda section at Middle East GHQ. With reservations, Stirling had allowed him to join L Detachment, though he was hardly cut out for the rigors of desert warfare. On his first parachute jump, he struck the ground at an excessive speed because, in Stirling's curt assessment, "he was just too bloody fat." Later, after being endlessly badgered, Stirling reluctantly agreed to allow him to join the team for the Benghazi raid, but only as an "observer." He was not to take part in the action but remain with the vehicles at the LRDG rendezvous. But fate intervened. After Corporal Seekings was injured when a faulty detonator exploded in his hand, he had to be left behind at the rendezvous and Churchill was allowed to take his place on the raid.

Stirling had had an ulterior motive in inviting him along on the mission "to see the fun," as he put it. As a journalist by training, Randolph would report back to his powerful father on the daring qualities of the SAS. His presence on a successful raid would mean that the PM would get a first-hand account of the SAS in action even though it would probably be embellished in favor of his son. This alone could be important to the long-term survival of the unconventional unit. The more support Stirling could get for the SAS from high up, the better he would be able to circumvent the obstructive elements at GHQ. It was well known that Randolph and his father wrote each other frequently and that, in defiance of wartime security measures, the letters contained vivid accounts of sensitive ongoing operations. By keeping Randolph well informed and in the inner circle of the SAS, Stirling hoped that the prodigal son could exert influence over the prime minister, regaling him with tales of British derring-do in the desert with the ultimate goal of ensuring a favorable impression of the fledgling unit.

Gazing down the street, he spotted black-booted officers striding in and out of what appeared to be a Gestapo Headquarters. Could he and his team have picked a more risky place to lay low for the day than the bomb-ravaged dwelling they now found themselves? The midday heat was becoming unbearable and a hubbub of German, Italian, and Arabic rose from the street below. Any attempt to return to the Jebel would have to take place in the dark. The problem was waiting for nightfall was proving inordinately boring and nerve-racking.

Turning away from the shuttered window, he looked at his men spread out on the floor of the ramshackle room. They were only allowed to talk in whispers, something the voluble Churchill found virtually impossible. Randolph had passed the time by reading Frederick Scott Oliver's biography of American Founding Father Alexander Hamilton, while Maclean and the others had occupied themselves with tracking the movement of the sun across the room through the cracks in the windows and walls, as well as cleaning and oiling their weapons. Meanwhile, Johnny Rose had been working non-stop to repair the suspension of the Blitz Buggy in an effort to silence the squealing sounds. Not only were the men all restless and bored, they were growing hungry and thirsty. Since their overnight stay in Benghazi had not been anticipated, they had brought only a modest amount of food and water. They had already finished off their few tins of Bully beef and now only had their half-empty canteens and Alston's flask of rum with which to sustain themselves.

By half past one, Stirling could stand the waiting no longer. "I'm going for a stroll and a swim in the harbor," he announced, as casually as if he were heading to a London gentleman's club.

"Very well, but please tell me you're not going to go out there in that getup," teased Maclean, grinning at the sight of Stirling's attire of corduroy slacks, heavy desert boots, and polo-necked pullover, all of which was accentuated by his bushy black beard and towel draped around his neck.

"Are you saying I'm not dressed for the occasion?"

"Not in the least," said Alston, the intelligence officer.

"I must say, old boy," said Churchill, "we should probably say our goodbyes for this is surely the last we shall see of thee. To my eyes, you look absolutely English."

"All we can say then, T.E. Lawrence, is good luck," said Maclean. "We'll see you in heaven—but more likely it will be hell."

Stirling gave a mock fatalistic grin. "Thanks for the encouragement, chaps—well, I'm off then," and he headed out.

Descending the rickety stairs and stepping onto the street into the bright sunlight, he proceeded to make his way through the European quarter towards the waterfront as if he had been given the keys to the city by Ettore Bastico, the governor-general of Italian-occupied Libya, himself. He passed through several narrow streets, crossing Omar Al Mukhtar, and onto the wide thoroughfare of the Via Albia as he made his way towards the busy port. He did not walk close to the wire as he knew there would be sentry posts, but was able to take a back street which ran parallel to it. Every now and then he passed yawning craters where the RAF had dropped bombs wide of the mark. Most of the buildings were workshops and warehouses. Soon, he turned down one of the streets approaching the wire perimeter.

He had not gone more than a few yards further before he heard footsteps coming up fast behind him.

His heart lurched in his chest. Was it an enemy soldier or policeman? He ducked into a bombed-out doorway and stood perfectly still, drawing himself up against a wall.

He heard the sound of footsteps coming closer and held his breath.

Twenty feet, ten feet, five feet—and then suddenly the new interloper was right on top of him. He was a uniformed Italian captain.

But to Stirling's surprise, he just walked on down the street, as if late for an important appointment or perhaps a rendezvous with a *signorina*. Stirling blew out a sigh of relief.

He continued on to the waterfront. The water lapped gently against the pier and hungry stray cats seemed to be everywhere. He managed to steal his way through the wire, make his way around the breakwater, and sneak into the harbor through a breach, made by bombing, in the outside wall.

He spotted two German torpedo boats tied up at the dock. These could easily be bombed that evening on their way out of town and wouldn't require the use of the inflatable rafts. With the towel still wrapped around his head to make himself look Arabic, he snuck in for a closer look, taking cover behind a crane and pile of heavy bollards. He decided the two patrol boats moored to the quay would be worth taking out. He also managed to find out that, apart from the main gate leading through the wire, there was a side entrance with a guard post. But the sentry apparently had a section to patrol as no one seemed to be about.

Satisfied with his hour-long recce, he returned to the hideout without any further encounters. He was disappointed at the failure of the operation thus far, but at least they could take out a pair of enemy vessels. All the same, the situation was maddening. Three times now unworkable boats had frustrated his efforts: twice now in Bengazi and once in a training exercise on the Suez. On the other occasions, the responsibility belonged to the Special Boat Section, but this time it rested squarely with the SAS. So what had happened? Maclean and Alston had taken precautions; to make sure they were in working order, they had inflated the dinghies the previous afternoon hours before the expedition set off. Had they been exposed too long in the hot sun and somehow lost air? Or had they brushed against a treacherous blackthorn bush and been punctured? Maclean had wrapped them in heavy canvas before putting them in the car, so they couldn't have been damaged en route to Benghazi.

The worst part about it was he had proved once again that it was possible to reach Bengazi harbor. If he could only find a functional boat, he was convinced that a handful of men could do enormous damage. The biggest challenge he faced was getting the proper equipment and making sure it worked adequately. Whereas the Royal Navy and RAF experimented for months to find the right boats and dinghies for their particular needs, the SAS had no resources and was forced to improvise. The rubber dinghies were obviously not designed to be carried across precipitous ground or to be inflated in rough wadis. If anyone at GHQ took enough interest in the unit to equip it properly, he thought bitterly, the striking power of the SAS could be increased ten-fold.

He rejoined his team and told them his new plan to take out the German torpedo boats and then return to the Jebel LRDG rendezvous. At nightfall, they set off again for the harbor to set the explosives. Sergeant Rose had been working on the suspension and believed he had finally silenced the squealing Blitz Buggy, but after a few hundred yards the noise started up once more. Stirling parked at the roadside, and Rose slipped back underneath with his tools. Passersby barely spared them a glance.

"Thank heavens nothing arouses less sensation than people working on a car," commented Churchill from the rear seat after sneaking a nip of rum from his canteen. "No one has said a word to us."

Minutes later, Rose declared that the problem could not be fixed without a major overhaul. Determined not to come away empty-handed, Stirling insisted they continue as planned and blow up the two German vessels. It would be only a mild annoyance to the enemy, he realized, but they would come back again and make a more successful visit, especially since they had reconnoitered the town twice now and knew the precise layout of the harbor and its shipping.

When they reached the harbor, Stirling was pleased to find that the two motor torpedo boats were still tied up to the quayside. He parked the car near the waterfront. Rose and Cooper picked up two bombs each, and the small party of saboteurs walked down the main thoroughfare towards the dock, laughing and whistling, pretending to be soldiers on leave out for a relaxing evening.

But as they drew nearer, he realized that a sentry had been posted on the dockside. He couldn't believe his eyes and cursed their growing misfortune: the entire mission was turning into a comedy of errors. To make matters worse, as they approached the moored torpedo boats four Germans stood up inside them and looked inquiringly at the approaching group.

"Bloody hell," cursed Stirling. "I'm afraid that's the last straw, chaps. Say goodbye to Benghazi."

The team sauntered back to the car as nonchalantly as possible and drove off. After a few hundred yards, the comedy of errors became too much and all they could do was laugh over the sound of the screaming wheels.

Soon, they passed through the checkpoint they had negotiated the night before, in the opposite direction, in much the same way, and making much the same noise. Once again, Maclean negotiated the roadblock with the magic words.

"*Militari*," he declared crisply.

"What sort of *militari*?" asked the sentry, a little more inquisitive than his compatriot of the previous night.

"German staff officers."

"*Molto bene*." With a smile, he waved them on.

The Blitz Buggy and its exhausted occupants reached the rendezvous in the Jebel at daybreak, exactly twenty-four hours late. The Long Range Desert Group, assuming that the party had been captured or killed, were preparing to pull out. But Stirling and his team caught them just in time.

Just before hitting the road again, he patted Churchill on the back. "Well, old boy, what did you think?"

The son of the PM gave a weary smile through his dusty desert beard. "That, my good friend, was the longest twenty-four hours I've ever known!"

CHAPTER 13

SHEPHEARD'S HOTEL, CAIRO

MAY 23, 1942

"JUST WAIT TILL ROMMEL GETS TO SHEPHEARD'S—THAT'LL SLOW HIM UP!"

Though she had heard the joke before, Hekmat Fahmy chuckled along with its raconteur, Colonel Bonner Fellers, the U.S. military attaché in Cairo, and Captain Guy Bellairs, her British lover who had just returned from the front. The Brits liked to tell the joke over and over again to newcomers to the city, and seemed to enjoy making sarcastic comments about the conduct of the war in general, but this was the first time she had heard the joke told by an American. What made it funny was that there was a grain of truth to it: the grandest hotel in Cairo was indeed known for its slow service on the part of its Swiss, Egyptian, and Sudanese staff, including its world-famous bartender Joe. Despite a world war going on and men dying by the thousands in the Libyan desert, no one seemed to be in a hurry at Shepheard's. One would never have known that a few hundred miles to the west a dreadful war was raging like a sandstorm.

She and her companions were enjoying drinks on the hotel's famous terrace, set with wicker chairs and tables and commanding a lofty view of Ibrahim Pasha Street. Wartime austerity had taken none of the luster off the illustrious establishment, which for connoisseurs of dining and luxury still rivaled Paris' Ritz, Berlin's Adlon, and Rome's Grand Hotel. Founded in 1841, Shepheard's Hotel had provided a base camp for travellers journeying all over the Middle East, beginning with the earliest expeditions organized by Thomas Cook in the 1870s. The celebrated British explorer Henry Morton Stanley had stayed at the hotel, as had T. E. Lawrence, Theodore Roosevelt, King Faisal, and Winston Churchill.

Along with the Turf Club and Gezira Sporting Club, the hotel remained the preserve of well-to-do British officers posted in Egypt, but it was also the refuge of the ambassadors with letters plenipotentiary, Americans with fat purses, *pashas* and glamor girls of the Middle East, wealthy refugees from Greece and the Balkans, war correspondents, the civilian experts feeding the Allied war machine, and socialite spies on both sides. In the class-ridden British army, Shepheard's was off limits to enlisted men, most of whom were billeted in flea-infested suburban camps. With a nearly five-hundred-foot frontage and six stories, the hotel contained 400 rooms and 180 baths, and a great deal of care and money had gone into the Oriental rugs and tapestries, the silver service, the imported grouse, the Khartoum ducks, the vast wine cellars, and the lavish bedrooms with the service buttons and fifteen-foot ceilings.

The loquacious Fellers continued: "Look, I've got to tell you, I'm not the most popular fellow at the U.S. Embassy here in Cairo or back in Washington. They think I'm a defeatist, which I'm not at all. But I am a realist. Which is why I'm not going to stop saying what I think about the military situation. That's my job. The trouble is, Captain Bellairs, your British top brass are way too overconfident, which they've no right to be. Much of your gear is still inferior to the enemy's, and you are less well led. Too many of your senior officers are sitting on their asses at GHQ."

Looking at her lover, Hekmat saw his face redden. "Now look here, Colonel," Bellairs retorted angrily, "you bloody Yanks aren't even in the fight yet. You have no right to criticize us when you haven't gone toe to toe with Rommel."

Fellers waved his hand dismissively. His military tie was loose and a cigarette dangled lazily from his mouth, like a Hollywood movie star. The forty-five-year-old West Pointer came from an Illinois Quaker family, had attended the Quaker-affiliated Earlham College in Indiana, and had served in the Pacific under General MacArthur before the war.

"Hey, I'm just telling you what I've seen with my own eyes," he said in his usual direct fashion. "But you know what your problem is. You British have put Rommel on a pedestal and made him out to be some sort of Superman. Why even his nickname—the Desert Fox—is the creation of your British press, not the goddamn Germans. Goebbels just capitalized on the name for propaganda purposes."

Seeing that Guy was agitated and feeling the conversation was about to take an uncomfortable turn for the worse, Hekmat decided to try and put an end to it. "Must we argue about the war?" she posed with calculated rhetorical innocence. "It's such a lovely evening, and you two do know that you're on the same side, right?"

"Oh, we're not arguing," said Fellers good-naturedly, clinking his bourbon and soda against Bellairs's crystal flute of champagne as if they were having a friendly debate. "I'm just telling this young buck here the way things are."

Bellairs made a face, as if he had caught a whiff of something unpleasant. "The way things are? Are you bloody serious?"

"Yep kid, I'm telling it to you straight. Despite the fact that you have numerically superior forces, with tanks, planes, artillery, means of transport, and reserves of every kind, your army has twice failed to defeat the Axis forces in Libya. And the problem is, with the present command under Auchinleck and with most operations taken in a hit-or-miss fashion, America's Lend-Lease Program alone can't ensure victory. The Eighth Army has failed to maintain the morale of its troops. Not only that but its tactical conceptions are always wrong, it has neglected cooperation between the various arms, and its reactions to the lightning changes of the battlefield are always slow. Slower even than the service here at Shepheard's."

"All right, I'll grant you that the battle in the desert has been a bit of a cock-up, but Rommel is still five hundred bloody miles from Cairo."

"Yes, but for how long?" said Hekmat, sensing that Fellers was essentially correct and the seemingly invincible Desert Fox was poised to take the Suez because of British incompetence. In fact, just today she had heard an Egyptian taxi driver on the street say to a pair of British officers as they were disembarking from his cab, "Today, I drive you to Groppi's—tomorrow, you drive me!"

"Honestly, I'm not trying to pour salt in a wound," said Fellers. "I just think you limey boys are in over your heads. But don't worry, America and Generals Eisenhower and Patton are coming to the rescue just like the Lone Ranger."

"Oh, please. You Yanks do so love to thump your chests, don't you?"

"Look, I'm not trying to ruffle your feathers, Captain. I'm just being straight with you because I'm friends with Hekmat here."

"You should listen to him, Guy. He appears to know more about your own army's weaknesses than your own generals. Colonel Fellers, do you really think Rommel can take Cairo and the Suez?"

"Unfortunately, yes. His tank strength is now nearly equal to the British. Intelligence estimates suggest that Rommel's Panzer divisions may be brought up to full strength and that an Italian armored division may soon be sent to him as a reinforcement. These armored units, an additional small motorized force, together with the forces now in Cyrenaica, make possible the invasion of Egypt. But everything depends on the Red Army. If Hitler wants Egypt and feels he can divert a small force from his effort against the Russians, the British today have insufficient forces to stop him."

"But surely, it's not as bad as all that?" protested Bellairs.

"The present Libyan campaign has been costly because of poor execution. Such victories as are claimed are empty. It is estimated that the British have lost over 700 tanks and 15,000 troops. Simultaneous with Rommel moving closer to conquering the Middle East, strategic sea-lanes across the Atlantic, upon which Britain's survival depends, are under constant threat from U-boat attacks."

"It would seem, then, that the war hangs in the balance," said Hekmat.

"That is correct," said Fellers before taking a generous swig of his bourbon. "And at such pivotal moments, good intelligence can turn the hinge of fate."

"What about our battle strength relative to the enemy?" asked Bellairs, who now seemed to defer, at least slightly, to the higher-ranked officer who was obviously privy to much top-level military information at GHQ. "Are you saying that you believe we have insufficient strength in this theater?"

"At present, yes. But more important is the lack of leadership at the highest levels of command."

"What about our equipment? You really think it's inferior?"

"Unfortunately, no artillery you've got can match the German 88-millimeter gun. With regard to tanks, the new Grant M3 Medium Tank is as good an anything the Germans can field, with the exception of the Panzer IV Special. But your Eighth Army is in desperate need of more effective arms and armor across the board. The funny thing about the 88s is the U.S. War Department and your War Office turned the damned gun down before the war, as it has only a small shield to protect the crew and both of our countries thought it would prove too costly in men. As it outranges most other weapons and is very mobile, I think this was a huge mistake. Anyway, the Germans now have it in the desert where it is deadly. The Krauts also have a very good Fifth Column. Goebbels is goddamn relentless."

"So, what do you recommend since you seem to be the proverbial expert?"

"We need to get you more equipment. Sufficient bombers and fighters should be allotted to this theater by your War Ministry in London, and you need more Grant tanks and artillery pieces to counter those goddamn 88s."

Hekmat was intrigued by the discussion. She had never considered that making war could be so complex. She had thought that opposing armies simply marched towards one another and opened fire. But warfare was far more complicated than that, she realized. It required extensive logistical preparation just to feed the armies and move them from one place to another in the vast expanse of the desert.

"An American armored corps should also be sent here as a temporary security measure," Fellers went on. "The U.S. should also foster friendship with the Muslim world across North Africa and the Middle East."

"How so?" she asked.

"When our forces finally get over here, our government should arrange an understanding with the local governments. It will be important to establish friendly relations with the Muslims, especially in the postwar period. The Muslims possess more homogeneity and discernment than is generally supposed. They are far more of a force than the British realize. All Muslims feel the U.S. is the one country which is not imperialistic. Now is the golden opportunity for us to win Muslim friendship from Morocco to India. An American pledge for fair play at the peace table is all that is necessary to align these people as friends."

Bellairs was skeptical. "I think you Yanks overestimate your diplomatic aplomb. You really think the Arabic people will embrace you as liberators?"

"Yes, I do. But I'm not as sure about you British. I do believe the American Army will find the impossibility to work effectively in the same theater with your forces. You fellows have a field manual and position paper for everything—even going to the lavatory!"

Now Bellairs gritted his teeth. "Why if I wasn't a bloody gentleman, I swear I would—"

"All right, I've heard enough of your arguing, you two," Hekmat cut him off. "I'm going to the ladies' room—without a field manual. And when I come back, I want to dance with a real gentleman. At the moment, I question whether either of you squabbling schoolboys fit the bill."

She dashed off before they could get a word of surprise or protest in. Five minutes later, she had taken care of her business, but didn't want to return to the terrace just yet and so she went to the Moorish Hall. It was deliciously cool and lit by a dome of stained glass that hung resplendently above it. Guests sat in small groups in anti-macassared chairs around little octagonal tables. The ballroom featured lotus-topped pillars modelled on those of Karnak, which she found oppressive, as if she was in some sort of British Museum. From the Moorish Hall the great staircase swept upwards, flanked by two tall caryatids of ebony with magnificent breasts, which were sometimes subjected to humiliating indignities by drunken British officers.

From the Moorish Hall, she went and peered into the Long Bar. It was filled with uniformed officers and civilians in formal evening dress. The fact that women were not allowed in the Long Bar supposedly made its patrons notoriously indiscreet. Here those well-born few who had wangled commissions in the more romantic units—in espionage, counterespionage, or sabotage—traded tales of raids in the desert. It was said that anyone who wanted to find out the British order of battle for the next offensive had only to sit in the bar for a while and keep his ears open. Presiding over the Long Bar was Joe Scialom, a thirty-two-year-old Egyptian Jew of Italian heritage and trained chemist, whom she regarded as one of the best-informed people in Cairo along with Bonner Fellers. In fact, the renowned barman was so well informed that the Egyptian and British police suspected he was a spy because he served so many heads of state, generals, and journalists. Some thought the British authorities had planted the rumor Joe was a double agent to encourage discretion on the part of its officers. Joe fixed a potent house concoction called the "Suffering Bastard" that was the drink of choice for those returning to the front.

As she made her way down the hallway back towards the terrace, Hekmat took in the lavish surroundings. Everything about Shepheard's Hotel was manly, fraternal, and imposing in a stuffy British way. The opulent rooms spoke of the bibulous fellowship of the rich and powerful and preserved perfectly the monied grandeur of the British Empire. But she realized that she was not a part of that world—she was just the hired help that entertained the empire-builders.

She was suddenly gripped with raw emotion and felt like an outsider in her own country. She thought of all the whispered secrets that must have been overheard by the walls around her. She was a socialite who was on a first-name basis with most of the cosmopolitan elite of Cairo, yet she didn't feel like she belonged here at Shepheard's Hotel. To the British troops and expatriates that had taken over her country, she was ultimately nothing but an Egyptian Wog and alluring sex object, something excitingly exotic but still a second-class, dark-skinned caricature of lesser sophistication. She knew that the British elite looked down their noses and made fun of her behind closed doors.

And that bothered her. In fact, it filled her with simmering anger.

The common British perception was that Egypt's growing middle class and elites supported Nazi Germany and Fascist Italy because they were Egyptian patriots who hoped for an end to British imperialism at all costs. But Hekmat knew the situation was far more complicated than that. However, what could not be disputed was that the continuing British occupation of Egypt was a sensitive subject for most Egyptians, including King Farouk. Like many of her countrymen, she was growing increasingly tired of Great Britain's imperialistic attitudes and heavy-handed authoritarianism. In particular, the Egyptian people were still smarting over the February 4 ultimatum in which Sir Miles Lampson, the British ambassador, had forced Farouk to remove Egyptian Prime Minister Hussein Sirri Pasha and replace him with Mostapha el Nahhas Pasha, who was regarded as being more sufficiently pro-British. During the ordeal, Lampson had taken the drastic step of having British troops and tanks surround the Abdin Palace. He then stomped into the palace and demanded that Farouk remove the PM and replace him with Nahhas, the pro-Allied leader of the Wafd Party. At the threat of losing his throne, Farouk capitulated and Nahhas formed a government shortly thereafter. But the humiliation meted out to the king and the actions of the democratic Wafd in co-operating with the British and taking power cost support for both the British and Wafd among militant Arab nationalists, the Egyptian military, and even ordinary civilians, who viewed those in power as puppets to the powers of the West.

Now three months later, as Rommel pushed the British eastward across North Africa, an increasing percentage of the local population, especially the more nationalistic working class, was positively disposed towards Germany and Italy—but the middle and upper classes continued to back Great Britain, at least as the lesser of two evils. But Egyptians of all classes disliked the presence of, and occasional abuse by, the occupying British troops, and Egypt still remained officially neutral in the conflict. Like many of her countrymen, Hekmat favored

Britain and France over Germany and Italy in the current global struggle, but she put a premium on eventual Egyptian independence and the control of the Suez Canal by Egyptians rather than the British.

The idea that most Egyptians were quietly rooting for the Axis powers was based on the erroneous assumption that the enemies of the British must therefore be friends of Egypt. But in reality, she knew that the main Egyptian authorities, the democratic Wafd Party that supported the Allied forces, and the educated people of the country were all deeply afraid and suspicious of the German enemy just as she was. The middle and upper classes were willing to grudgingly accept the humiliation of King Farouk by Sir Miles and the appointment of a government whose leaders were pro-British because they saw Germany as more of a danger. But there were economic reasons for supporting the Allies as well. Although Egypt had not officially declared war on Nazi Germany, the Egyptian state supported the British in virtually everything it did. From her friend Peter Stirling and others, she had learned that more than 250,000 Egyptians were currently employed by the British as Rommel raced across the Libyan desert, mainly in military bases and camps. Real money was filling the pockets of the Egyptian work force on account of the British occupiers, and Hekmat knew that her own coffers had been overflowing since the beginning of the war.

In Egypt and elsewhere in the Middle East, it was the militant Muslims that were the biggest Nazi supporters. This was largely due to the widespread influence of Mohammed Amin al-Husseini, a Palestinian Arab nationalist and anti-Jewish and anti-British Muslim leader. Known as the Grand Mufti, Al-Husseini collaborated with Fascist Italy and Nazi Germany by making propagandistic radio broadcasts denouncing Jews and the Allies, and by helping the Nazis recruit Muslims for the Waffen-SS, thereby folding rabid antisemitism into Islamic fundamentalism, British anticolonialism, and Arab nationalism.

She returned to Guy and Fellers. They were now talking to socialite Momo Marriott, the wife of Major General Sir John Marriott and whispered paramour of Randolph Churchill. To be seen at her parties, in the company of generals, dignitaries, and celebrities, was to be at the heart of Cairo's wartime society.

"Hekmat, so good to see you," said Momo, looking stunning in her long red nails and beautifully cut clothes.

"Hello, Momo, you look wonderful," she replied, and she meant it.

"All right, before you two gals start up a new conversation, it's time to dance—and the captain and I aren't taking no for an answer," said Bonner Fellers. "Syd Lawrence and his jazz band are waiting for us on the garden patio."

"Then what are we waiting for? Let's get hopping!" exclaimed the good-natured Momo, who was said to never arise from bed before noon or miss a party.

"I just love American jazz!" gushed Hekmat, her rueful feelings drifting off in the gentle *tamsin* wind. "I don't have to wiggle my belly even a little bit!"

And with that, they all laughed, walked to the outdoor dancing garden behind the hotel, and danced up a storm. But deep down, she still had a nagging feeling.

When would she and her fellow Egyptians get their country back? And was it possible that the Germans were, perhaps, the better ones to deliver them their freedom?

CHAPTER 14

KHARGA OASIS, YABSA PASS, AND CAIRO, EGYPT

MAY 23, 1942

IN THE GLOW OF THE RISING SUN, the Almasy Commando drove through what German-Egyptian spy Johannes Eppler—alias Hussein Gaafar—regarded as one of the most beautiful places on earth: Kharga Oasis. On his right loomed the temple of Ibis; on his left the early Christian necropolis, Roman citadel, and small watch towers; and in between, luxurious green fields and great shady *lebah* trees and desert palms. After traveling more than 1,400 thirsty miles in nine days over dissected plateaus, soft sand dunes, and rocky ledges, Eppler eagerly awaited the end of Operation Salam and the beginning of Operation Condor, with its allure of an intoxicating nightlife in Cairo. Gazing out at the oasis, he couldn't help but feel a sense of destiny as he stood poised to return to the place of his youth in the vanguard of Rommel's muscular *Afrika Korps*.

Leaving the base camp south of Jalo on May 15, the Commando had headed south along the Palificata Track, struck the edge of the eolian dune country, skirting the vast Rebiana Sand Sea to the west, and took the route via Kufra Oasis and the Gilf Kebir towards Assiut. It was a risky route, as Kufra was in British hands and often tightly patrolled, but Almasy was convinced there was no better option. Driving in two Ford V8s and two Bedfords, the team travelling with the Hungarian count and Eppler included radio-operator Sandstette and three Brandenburg corporals: Munz, Woehrmann, and Koerper. Now, having driven over hundreds of miles of barren desert littered with the bleached white bones of humans and animals, the Salam men were poised to deliver the two German spies to their designated drop-off point just beyond Kharga Oasis. Their objective was to set up a wireless network in Cairo under the codenames "Max" and "Moritz," gather critical intelligence on the British Eighth Army by mingling with the local military population, and report on the enemy's strength and battle plans for the expected summer campaign.

They continued on the main dirt road heading north, driving past the early Christian tombs through the oasis. The well-maintained road took them along and across the railway embankment, past the old POW camp at Moharig, and up the steep corrugated Roman road which led through the Yabsa Pass. Leaving Woehrmann and Koerper in one car at Kilometer Stone 29, the remaining group struck east from the road until they encountered the old caravan track of Darb Arba'in. They followed the trail to the edge of the great limestone plateau overlooking Assiut on the Nile. Less than three miles below was the broad, verdant river valley with the large white city of Assiut and its countless *esbahs*—farmhouses—in the foreground and the silver glittering Nile in the distance.

"I think this is the place we want," said Almasy, and he let the Ford roll to a standstill, put on the handbrake, and lit a cigarette.

Eppler looked a dozen yards away at an Egyptian signpost shimmering in the desert sun. He couldn't quite make out the inscription on the sign, but the Hungarian explorer swiftly pulled the idling V8 forward for a closer look. Eppler strained his aching eyes and shouted out jubilantly to his exhausted brethren.

"Long live Frederick the Great! Jesus Christ, we've done it!"

It was a dramatic moment for the weary desert Commando as they read the words on the sign, written in both English and Arabic: DANGEROUS DESCENT: DRIVE IN BOTTOM GEAR.

"All right, lads, let's get a picture—and then I'm afraid I must be on my way," said Almasy.

Climbing quickly from their battered vehicles, they looked over the brow of the hill at the edge of the Egyptian Plateau overlooking Assiut. In the middle distance, in the heat haze, Eppler could see the outline of buildings; and beyond the glittering ribbon of light that was the reflection of the sun on the waters of the River Nile. They took turns taking photographs. In one shot, Eppler and Almasy stood side by side wearing their heavily sweat-stained *Afrika Korps* uniforms next to the sign. After the travails they had faced en route to their destination, it was a magnificent moment, and Eppler knew he would remember it for the rest of his life.

Then he and Sandstette—the two would be known by their chosen aliases of Hussein Gaafar and Peter Muncaster from this point on—took their suitcases out and changed out of their dusty military uniforms into their civilian clothes. Eppler wore a handsome business suit that a tailor in the Kasr el Nil in Cairo had made for him in 1939, and Muncaster a blazer and flannels he had bought in Dar-es-Salaam. Muncaster would pose as a Scandinavian-American oilfield worker who had been plying his trade in East Africa, for his English accent was distinctly trans-Atlantic. They carefully checked each other's papers and effects to ensure they both had all the little things a man carries about with him in his pockets that prove he is who he claims to be: Eppler's Middle East military pass, Egyptian driver's licence, Royal Automobile Club membership card, address book, torn cinema tickets, hotel bills, all of them collected from captured British officers; Muncaster's American passport, obtained for him by clever means by German agents in the U.S., and assorted bills and used tickets taken from enemy prisoners.

When they were finished, Almasy said, "That's it, lads. Let's keep the goodbyes short."

Solemnly, the Hungarian went over to Eppler and Sandstette and shook their hands. "Goodbye," he said to Eppler. "I wish you good luck."

"And safe travels to you back to Jalo," replied the spy.

Having now to make the return journey of 1,400 miles before the British caught wind of him, Almasy popped off the handbrake, turned his truck around, and set off with Munz back towards Jalo. The two newly minted spies he left behind stood peering over the edge of the escarpment looking down onto Assiut and the tannin-colored Nile beyond as Almasy drove around a bend in the wadi, the trailing dust cloud dispersing in the desert wind. It was a sobering yet exciting moment for the two German agents. They were now completely on their own and had to get to Cairo without being captured, despite the omnipresence of the British Army.

Salam was over—and Condor had now begun. They were spies in enemy territory, and if they were caught there was only one way in which it could end: before a firing squad. The possibility of such a fate had little effect on Eppler, who was naturally confident, outgoing, and sanguine. But Sandstette, who was a more cautious and introspective type, now appeared anxious and unsure of himself.

"All right, let's get going," said Eppler. "And remember, from now on, we speak nothing but English or Arabic."

Taking up a suitcase apiece, they began the walk down the hill towards the sleepy town three miles away and closer to danger. A mile and a half outside Assiut, they buried their German uniforms and one of their W/T sets in the sand between two hillocks, marking the spot with a pile of stones. Once they had buried the wireless, they set off again and quickly found that the road they were trudging along ran straight through a British Army camp.

"*Scheisse*, is this the end of the mission for us?" muttered Sandstette.

"No, it's nothing of the sort," replied Eppler. "Just relax. Our cover is sound, for only a lunatic would attempt to get to Cairo by the route we just took. No one will suspect us."

The two German spies continued down the road with suitcases in hand. Eppler couldn't help but feel ridiculously out of place, as if they were traveling door-to-door salesmen in a foreign land. But he said nothing, knowing that his partner had a less firm constitution. Soon, they came to a checkpoint manned by a British officer.

"Where in the devil's name have you chaps come from?"

Identifying the insignia on his uniform as that of major, Eppler stepped forward with an easy smile. "Good day, Major. Unfortunately, our car broke down back behind those hills," he said in fluid English as he pointed back behind them. "As we've managed to get this far, we should be grateful for a lift to the railway station. You see, we have to be in Cairo tomorrow on urgent business."

The major scrutinized him closely. "To the station? I can't do that without knowing who you are. We are not running a taxi service, you know."

He feigned innocence. "Yes, of course. Sometimes I forget there's a war going on. Let me introduce ourselves. This is my American friend Sandy. He wanted to see the desert before he returns to the States."

With this, Eppler pulled out his passport and tried his best to ignore his heart thumping against his chest in a turbulent rhythm.

"And I am Hussein Gaafar," he said, showing the British officer his documentation. "You've probably heard of my family in Cairo. My stepfather is Salah Gaafar, a well-known judge and very pro-British."

The major closely examined the passport then carefully reviewed Sandstette's paperwork in the name of American oilfield worker Peter Muncaster. When he was finished, he snapped the passports shut and handed them back with a polite smile on his face beneath his bushy red mustache.

"Glad to meet you, gents. Come on into the shade. We'll fix you up with a cold drink, and then we'll have a car take you up to the station."

Eppler breathed a sigh of relief and, glancing out of the corner of his eye, saw that Sandstette was deeply relieved as well. They had made it through their first checkpoint.

At the officer's mess, they drank a couple of marvellously cool whiskey and sodas and talked about the desert with a group of sunburnt Tommies, who were more than a little curious as to from whence they had come. They gave a location of their stranded car calculated to deceive any searchers for at least a couple of days and agreed heartily when several members of the mess told them they had been bloody idiots to attempt a desert trek without proper guides or a second car. The officers then fed their new guests lunch, capping their hospitality with cups of real coffee before driving them to the Assiut railway station. There, Eppler decided that it would be best to purchase their tickets right away before heading down to the *souk* to poke around. With the train not scheduled to leave for Cairo until the evening, there was plenty of time to wander around the town's marketplace.

"If you pricked me, I believe there would be no blood," said Sandstette as the driver disappeared out of sight and they stepped up to the ticket office.

"Just keep your wits about you. We still have to get to Cairo." He couldn't help but wonder if he and his comrade in arms were truly cut out for the spy business. But as they stepped up to the ticket window, he knew they had an even more pressing problem: how to get their suitcases safely into Cairo when they would be thoroughly searched by the British Security Police either on the train or upon arrival to the city. They were carrying thousands of pounds in British sterling and a smaller amount in Egyptian currency along with their primary 40-watt transmitter/receiver built for long-distance communications work—items which no one in their right mind but spies would be carrying. So what should they do about their suitcases?

He still didn't have an answer as he reserved two first-class seats on the late afternoon Luxor-Cairo express. He could send the leather cases as "Personal Luggage in Advance" but when it came to collecting them in Cairo, the Field Security inspectors would be certain to turn them inside out. Since luggage placed in the baggage van would inevitably be searched by the police, he and Sandstette had a serious problem to solve.

And then fate intervened.

While standing in the square outside the booking office, having left Sandstette to guard their suitcases, he came across four pitch-black Nubians propped up against the wall of the railway station, also waiting for the train to Cairo. The men explained that they hoped to obtain work in Cairo, and told him that they were tribesmen from Dangola. Suddenly, an idea came to Eppler. He considered Nubians to be unusually trustworthy, for not even the missionaries, for all their painstaking efforts, had succeeded in turning them into dishonest Africans. He told the youngest, who was about seventeen and called Mahmoud, that he was looking for a servant who would come to Cairo and keep house for him there.

"I am yours, *ja bey*," was the young Nubian's enthusiastic reply. "But how much?"

"I can offer you five pounds per month," said Eppler, knowing it was a fair offer but that common courtesy dictated that he haggle, or at least pretend to haggle, over the price if Mahmoud held out for more.

"Five pounds is most generous, *ja bey*, for all my family back in Dongola would pray for my health. However, should your generosity run to six pounds per month, why then, since Allah has made you a gift of all the wisdom of this world, the Prophet would this very day order you a divan from the heavenly carpenter, on which you should experience heavenly joys with three virgins, delivered fresh, each day."

The prospect of being blessed with three fresh—and naturally stunningly comely—virgins every day after his departure from the world, and of enjoying the delights of paradise with them, made him tip his head back and laugh uproariously.

"Three virgins! Why you, young lad, shall receive six pounds per month—or my name isn't Hussein Gaafar! Follow me!"

He led Mahmoud back onto the station platform where his partner was waiting with the luggage. Sandy's face evidenced instant surprise at the sight of the young Nubian, and even more startlement when Eppler gave the boy money for a third-class ticket and instructed him where to meet them at the Cairo train station. The boy duly picked up their bags, threw them onto his shoulders, and walked off to purchase his ticket.

"What the hell are you doing?" demanded Sandstette. "You just gave him our bags and we'll never see him again!"

"Relax. We absolutely will see him again and no British officer would bother to check on a Nubian."

"I'm afraid I don't share your optimism. And when we're blown, how do you propose to explain the loss of the suitcases when we get back to Berlin?"

"Trust me, this is going to work. You'll see when we get to Cairo. Our friend Mahmoud will have brought the bags through safely. But even if by some twist of fate he doesn't, we surely won't starve. Furthermore, whether we get back to Berlin or not depends on who wins the bloody war. So relax."

An hour later they caught the train. Arriving in Cairo that night they found their new servant Mahmoud of Dangola waiting for them outside the station with their suitcases precisely as planned.

"*Saida, ja bey*," he said to them as they came walking up. "British officer on train tried to open suitcases. I said you British officer and very angry type so he went away. Where we go now, *ja bey*?"

Eppler smiled the smile not of a spy, but of a good-time playboy.

"Why Shepheard's Hotel, old boy," he said in a mock British accent. "We need a bloody drink!"

"Very good, *ja bey*. And does my master have lady friend in Cairo to keep him comfortable at night?"

"No, but I did once love a young girl here. I have not seen her in years."

"*Ahlan wa Sahlan*. And what, may I ask, is her name?"

"Her name is Hekmat Fahmy. She is a belly dancer and said to still be one of the most beautiful women in all of Cairo."

"No, no, *ja bey*. I have heard of this famous woman and she is said to be one of most beautiful women in all the world! Do you have plans to visit her?"

"I don't know," he admitted, sneaking a glance at the smiling Sandstette. "The last time I saw her she was a touch angry with me."

CHAPTER 15

GEZIRA SPORTING CLUB
GEZIRA ISLAND, CAIRO

MAY 26, 1942

EXQUISITELY LAID OUT ON LAND given by the Egyptians to the British Army, the Gezira Sporting Club covered the entire southern end of Gezira Island with gardens, polo fields, a giant golf course, a horse racing track, cricket pitches, croquet lawns, and squash and tennis courts. The club did not cater exclusively to the British: many of its members were drawn from the richest and most Westernized Egyptian families, though they were outnumbered by English members. Horse racing and polo were its top attractions, but the club was also known for its sumptuous food and copious wine cellar. Built in 1938, the club house consisted of a square stuccoed building, painted cream and dark red, flanked by two wings angled around a comfortable dining terrace known as the Lido since it lay before a swimming pool.

Seated beneath the Lido's poolside awning awaiting lunch at 3:18 p.m. were Major Sammy Sansom and a senior officer in the Egyptian Army and paid informant codenamed Hussein. Sansom had ordered the braised beef tenderloin served on a bed of creamy roasted eggplant purée, while Hussein had opted for the fish *sayadiyah tajine* with a side dish of okra. They were both drinking White Horse and sodas and smoking Simon Arzt Egyptian cigarettes. Hussein was filling in the chief of the Field Security Office on the state of the Egyptian Free Officers' Movement, which was opposed to the continuing British presence in Egypt and waiting in the wings to rise up and support Rommel's Army if he invaded Egypt.

Of the same age, Sansom and Hussein had first met as schoolboys in Cairo and had become good friends through their mutual interest in tennis and squash. The son of a wealthy landowner and nephew of a political leader, Hussein had taken a commission in the Egyptian Cavalry. Over the years, they maintained their friendship and continued to socialize and play squash together. Since Sansom's posting in Cairo as chief of Field Security, they typically met once a fortnight at the Gezira Club, where they played a game of tennis or squash and chatted over drinks. They also attended official functions together at the Egyptian Army Officers' Club in Zamalek, where Hussein quietly pointed out officers whom he thought Sansom should keep an eye on. Because he was well-liked and friendly with a wide variety of people, no one ever suspected Hussein of being an informant for the British.

Sansom regarded his Egyptian friend as his most valuable asset and a true patriot, though he knew that the captain's own countrymen would likely regard him as a traitor. In Sansom's view, it was patriotism that led Hussein to give him information about his fellow Egyptian officers. He betrayed them because he genuinely believed his country would be worse off if Britain lost the war.

"You know Sammy, I may very well be the only pro-Allied officer left in the Egyptian Army after February 4," said Hussein, referring to Sir Miles's humiliation of Farouk the past winter when he forced him to replace Egyptian Prime Minister

Sirri Pasha with the more pro-British Nahhas Pasha, leader of the Wafd Party.

"Surely you are exaggerating," protested Sansom. "There must still be a sizable minority that supports our side."

"There are others like me," admitted Hussein, "but the numbers are dwindling. All the talk these days is of helping the Germans when they break through."

"I'm afraid that even my fellow officers are not immune to the Rommel myth. Why even Churchill himself proclaimed in his speech in the House of Commons this past January that Rommel was 'a very daring and skilful opponent' and 'across the havoc of war, a great general.'"

"But you won't have to fight off your fellow Brits if the Desert Fox takes Alexandria and Cairo."

"True enough," agreed Sansom. In his reports, he had long maintained that the Egyptian Army should be regarded as a potential fifth column—although too inefficient to be a dangerous one. The Army chief of staff, General Aziz el Masri, and the squadron leader of the Air Force, Hussein Zulficar Sabri, had been the highest-ranking officers with pro-Axis sympathies. But they had been dismissed from the armed services, and now most of the leaders of the clandestine anti-British faction that had filled the vacuum—the Free Officers' Movement—were unknown. From Hussein and his other informants, Sansom knew there were hundreds of Egyptian officers who were rabid nationalists that naively believed Axis victory would bring them independence. To prevent a general uprising, he had recommended that emergency plans be made for confinement to barracks, disarming, and even disbanding of all Egyptian forces. He had also suggested that officers should be classified according to their courage and initiative rather than their politics, since he believed most of them hoped for an Axis victory. But with the Desert War going badly for Great Britain, Sir Miles and the military higher-ups had not authorized mass arrests of suspected pro-Axis Egyptian officers, not wanting to further risk antagonizing the Army unless deemed absolutely necessary.

"Above all, you must keep your eye on the young ones," Hussein warned him. "They say least and plot most."

"Like Anwar el Sadat."

Hussein nodded. "It is the ones like him that will prove most dangerous to British interests in the coming weeks and months."

Sansom took a puff of his cigarette. He kept a "Subversive Elements" file with a separate dossier on each of the Egyptian Army officers whom he suspected might stir up trouble for the British occupying forces. Sometimes in the evenings, he would sit in his office with the dossiers spread in front of him, poring over the information and staring at the photographs, as if by sheer concentration he could discover which of the faces belonged to the leaders of the Free Officers' Movement. His prime suspect was a young Signals Unit officer with a sleepy look that came from his heavy-lidded eyes. His name was Anwar el Sadat, and he had been a frequent caller on the fiercely anti-British General el Masri as well as in contact with the Supreme Guide of the Muslim Brotherhood. Considering the German officer a paragon to be emulated, Sadat wore his hair cropped short and sported a swagger-stick and monocle. Sansom regarded him as particularly dangerous.

"Do you have Sadat under surveillance?" asked Hussein.

"Among others," replied Sansom, as a waiter appeared with another round of drinks for them both. "The problem is I hardly have enough men to do the job. Fortunately, even though there are more dissidents every day, they seem to be more concerned with conspiracy and minor acts of sabotage than having a long-term plan to achieve political power. But with Rommel poised to make a breakthrough into Egypt this spring that distinction is of little consequence. If he breaks the Gazala Line, that will be enough to mobilize the Officers' Movement and it will be all over for us, I'm afraid."

"I don't think Rommel will take Egypt. The Americans are backing you now."

"The bloody Yanks. But they don't even have a viable army pulled together yet."

"But more and more of their new tanks and aircraft are being supplied to your army every day. Mark my words, the Americans will eventually win the war for you British. All you have to do is sit back and watch them do it."

"You've been watching too many Hollywood movies, my friend. We've been fighting in the desert for more than two years now and the Americans haven't spilled a drop of blood. They will take a year, at least, to get up to speed."

"They'll catch on quicker than you think. Like Rommel and unlike you Tommies, they're able to adapt quickly to changing combat conditions."

"Oh Hussein, you cheeky bastard. I don't know why I put up with you."

"Because I bring you valuable intelligence. And right now, I am telling you that you should be more worried about German spies infiltrating Cairo and the loose tongues of your fellow British officers at GHQ than the Free Officers' Movement. As you say, they are too disorganized to pose a real threat."

"The question is how would the Germans sneak a spy, or team of spies, into Cairo?"

"That is easy. From the desert."

"All the way from Libya? Really?"

"With proper planning, it could be done."

"But with the position of the Gazala Line, they would have to travel through nearly fifteen hundred miles of barren wasteland. It is doubtful they could make it. And even if they did, their tracks would be picked up by the Long Range Desert Group. Then they would be captured."

"I wouldn't be so sure about that. The Germans have their own LRDG, you know, commanded by Captain Almasy."

"The Hungarian count?"

"He knows what he is doing. The Bedouin call him *Abu Romia*—Father of the Sands—for a reason."

"You seem to know an awful lot about the enemy, Hussein. Perhaps I shouldn't be so trusting and should keep an eye on you along with Sadat and the others? You might very well be a double agent, working both sides."

"As the Americans like to say, Sammy, that is a crock of shit. I am as loyal to the Allied cause as you, but that doesn't mean I like you being here in my country."

Sansom nodded: he knew that was true. He and his friend Hussein had had this discussion on many occasions. Though a member of the ruling class, what Hussein wanted most of all was to see his country purged of imperialism, feudalism, and corruption. He was deeply opposed to both the significant European presence in

Egypt and the rottenness of King Farouk, who pilfered a vast amount of wealth from his subjects and most of the time acted like a spoiled child. Hussein had told Sansom on many occasions how much he admired the British for their ideas of freedom and social justice, integrity, and democracy, but he also wanted them to clear out of Egypt. He shared the belief of many young Egyptian idealists that the British were the ones keeping Farouk on his throne and that political and social reform could not begin until the country had real democratic independence.

"The only difference between the members of the Free Officers' Movement and me," he said as he blew out a puff of cigarette smoke, "is that I think the Germans would be even worse. If I thought an Axis victory would mean Egyptian independence, I would be on their side. But I have read *Mein Kampf* and know what Hitler says about Aryans and non-Aryans. If Hitler wins the war, the world will be ruled by racialists, and we shall have permanent second-class citizenship and live in perpetual subjection. That's what the Free Officers don't understand."

"And yet, from what you've told me before, the young officers in the movement aren't particularly pro-Axis. They seem to be more anti-British."

"We all are. It is simply a matter of degree."

Although Hussein had spoken these exact words on more than once occasion, Sansom noted that this time he said it without smiling.

"These young men like Sadat have good reasons to feel frustrated, and I have sympathy for them. Whatever their motives, and I know they're mainly selfish, they want to do something to clean up the corruption in this country. Frankly, I wouldn't have told you about them if they hadn't originally looked to General el Masri for leadership. He is not nor has he ever been in the best interest of Egypt."

"I understand how you feel."

"But do you really? I like to think our present humiliation is only temporary. That's why I shall do all I can to help you win the war, even to the extent of informing against my misguided comrades. But after you British have won, I shall join them if it is necessary, and I expect it will be, in the struggle to kick you out."

"Well, until that day, let us drink to our solidarity." He raised his glass. "You are not only my most important informant, Hussein, but you are my dear, dear friend. That's why I always let you beat me at tennis and squash."

They clinked glasses and tossed back half their drinks in two hearty gulps. "You pompous English bastard—why I could beat you with my left hand."

"Indeed, you could. Ah, look our food has arrived."

They made another toast, finished their drinks, and each ordered another. Then Sansom pitched into his braised beef tenderloin and Hussein his fish *sayadiyah tajine* with gusto. After three games of tennis, they were both famished.

When they had finished their sumptuous meals and ordered deserts of *basbousa* topped with almonds and fresh cream, Sansom said, "Back to what we were discussing earlier. Do you really think the Germans could sneak a spy from the desert into Cairo in advance of Rommel's army?"

The Egyptian gave a knowing smile. "Yes, they could. In fact, Sammy, I wouldn't be surprised if they haven't done so already."

CHAPTER 16

SOUTH OF ALEXANDRIA, EGYPT

MAY 26, 1942

AS USUAL STIRLING—an exceptionally inattentive and dangerous driver—insisted on driving the Blitz Buggy himself. It was two minutes after midnight, and he and his four swashbuckling companions who had made it safely back from the Benghazi raid without a scratch were driving on the road from Alexandria to Cairo. With one hand on the wheel and quietly puffing away at his pipe, he was doing a cool 73 miles per hour as if he was undertaking a race on the Great North Road.

It was then disaster struck.

Seated in the front seat next to Stirling was Sergeant Rose. Packed into the back were Randolph Churchill, Fitzroy Maclean, and the celebrated journalist Arthur Merton, the correspondent of the *Daily Telegraph*, who had shared dinner with the SAS commandos back in Alexandria and asked Stirling for a lift back to Cairo. Merton was one of the most distinguished reporters covering the war, a veteran who had famously reported the discovery of Tutankhamen's tomb in 1922. Stirling, though he knew the celebrated war correspondent only slightly, had readily agreed to give him a ride. Exhausted from their long return trip through the desert, everyone but the CO had dozed off in their seats.

The moon was full and the visibility good through the headlights, but as Stirling took a sharp corner, tires squealing, he came suddenly upon a convoy of heavy military trucks. To his horror, he saw a lorry directly in their path, the tail end of a slow-moving convoy.

Breaking a fraction too late, he swerved to avoid hitting the lorry, but his rear wheel caught it as he tried to go around. The Blitz Buggy spun off the road, smashed into a sand bank, and somersaulted twice down an embankment.

Screams of surprise and terror rose into the night as the vehicle tumbled across the desert sand and rock. Stirling saw Rose, Maclean, and Churchill all fly out of the car as the Blitz Buggy pitched and rolled, and then he, too, was thrown from the vehicle.

He hit the ground with a heavy grunt, his hands out to break his fall. The force of the impact knocked the wind out of him and he felt his wrist hit something hard.

When the dust cleared, he scanned the wreckage. With the headlights illuminating the area around the crash, he saw that the truck had come to a halt upside down with the open top facing the desert floor. It was badly damaged. He felt blood trickling down his face as well as a throbbing pain in his head and wrist. But he was all in one piece and fully mobile.

He rose to his feet and called out to the others. "Is everyone all right?"

He heard a heavy groan and saw Randolph Churchill lying next to a patch of camel thorn. "I think I've broken my back. I don't think I can bloody move."

He kneeled down next to him. "Just stay put and hold on, my friend. We'll have you to a hospital in no time."

"My arm hurts like hell but I can walk," he heard Sergeant Rose say.

"What about the others?" Stirling asked him.

"I don't know. We'd better check on them."

He and Rose began searching the area as the driver from the lorry they had hit came onto the scene and military transports began pulling to the side of the road to offer assistance. Stirling quickly realized that everyone but Arthur Merton had been thrown clear and that the journalist was trapped beneath the vehicle.

It was then he smelled a pungent waft of petrol. They had to hurry and get Merton and the other injured parties out of the area. The fuel tank had obviously ruptured and he didn't want to take any risk that the car might explode.

"We've got to hurry, Johnny," he said to Rose. "That bloody tank could blow any second."

"Aye, Major."

With the help of the soldiers, one of whom fortuitously happened to be a medic, he and Rose managed to pull Merton out from beneath the open-topped car. He had suffered a major head injury and was unconscious. Maclean, too, had suffered head trauma and was out cold. But they were both alive, though just barely.

"We've got to get them to a hospital quickly, Major—or they might not make it," the medic said to him.

"Alexandria is closer than Cairo. Shouldn't we take them there?"

"Yes, that's what I would do."

"Alexandria it is then. Let's go—hurry now, chaps!"

Working swiftly but carefully since they didn't know the full extent of the injuries, the soldiers helped them load Merton, Maclean, and Churchill onto one of the lorries, and then drove all five men to the hospital. But unfortunately, Merton died along the way from his head injuries.

Stirling cursed himself for having killed the poor man, even if it had been an accident. He had been driving too fast and he damn well knew it.

At the hospital, he and the other survivors were treated for their injuries. Maclean had a broken arm and collarbone, a badly fractured skull, and was still unconscious. Randolph Churchill had three crushed vertebrae, was placed in an iron brace for his back, and would have to be invalided home. Rose's arm was broken in three places and he would be out for several weeks at least. Using one more of his nine lives, Stirling only had a cracked wrist bone. He and Rose were still in shock from the crash as they gathered around Churchill's hospital bed.

"I am so sorry," said Stirling, shaking his head in dismay. "It was my fault—I was going too bloody fast. I hope you two can forgive me."

"Oh, that's nonsense, it could have happened to anyone," protested Churchill, who, though heavily drugged-up, was still his usual garrulous self. "But I do have to say that thus far in the war, driving with you has proved far more dangerous than anything the Jerries have thrown my way."

"It certainly was for Mr. Merton," said Rose. "But in the end, it's really just a case of plain rotten luck."

"Yes, that's exactly what it is," snorted Churchill. "Just bloody bad luck."

All the same, Stirling felt miserable. The car accident and responsibility for the newspaperman's death had deeply shaken him, and the failure of the mission also gnawed at him. They had cheated death in Benghazi, only to find it on the road home, in a banal traffic accident. Following the aborted raid, they had driven across the desert and reached Siwa uneventfully, without losing a single man, but then fate had intervened. The car crash had been a horrifying end to a mission that had achieved nothing. Absolutely nothing. And now he was feeling guilty, ashamed, and angry with himself for failing Merton and his men. He had been ready to wipe out any number of enemies in uniform, and yet the first person he had killed, by mistake, was a civilian on his own side.

Damn you to hell, you careless bastard! How could you? How the bloody hell could you?

But the failure of the mission weighed heavily on his mind, too. He had now visited Benghazi twice without being caught, yet the operations had inflicted no damage on Axis shipping, no dent in enemy morale. Rommel's vital supply lines were undamaged, and the threat to the critical logistical supply island of British-held Malta by the Germans remained undiminished.

"Don't be so bloody hard on yourself, David," said Churchill, who had been watching him staring morosely off into space. "In wartime, people die. That's all."

"If that's supposed to make me feel better, it's not."

"Well, maybe this will. I should like to ask you a favor."

"A favor?"

"A favor that will be mutually beneficial for us both."

"That doesn't sound like much of a favor."

"Just hear me out, old boy. I would like your permission to write a secret and personal report on the raid to my father."

"And tell him what? How we failed in our mission and an innocent man was killed?"

"Dear me, no. I will simply tell him the truth. I know we didn't blow anything up, but your inestimable leadership in our foray into and out of Benghazi has most certainly filled us all with confidence for future operations. There is a silver lining in all this, if only you would see it."

Stirling scratched his chin thoughtfully and looked at Rose, whose expression seemed to say Churchill's idea wasn't a bad one. "Yes, I suppose we didn't come away empty-handed. From a reconnaissance standpoint, that is."

"And Fitzroy is, of course, worth his weight in gold. Why with him at my side I would be perfectly happy to spend a week in Rome battling Mussolini himself."

"You have a fanciful imagination, Randolph."

"Yes, indeed I do—but only half as much as my bloody father. You know this is precisely the sort of tale he adores: a secret mission deep behind enemy lines, replete with fast cars, brushes with death, narrow escapes, and British derring-do. To be perfectly honest, that the mission did not fully achieve its principal objective of the destruction of Axis war matériel is rather beside the point."

"And how will you portray yourself in the story."

"Well of course, I shall have to show some mettle, if only to preserve the family honor and keep my father off my back. He thinks I'm a nincompoop, and sometimes I am inclined to agree despite my prodigious ego. But the main thing I shall do is give a vivid account of the events that took place, stressing the daring and strategic value of the SAS and lavishing praise on both you and Lieutenant Maclean. I mean, you do want your little band of bearded rapscallions to grow, don't you? So, there you have it. What do you say, old boy?"

"I have to say it sounds like a good idea. But you can't make yourself out to be bloody Lord Nelson, Randolph."

"I wouldn't dream of it, old boy. But when it comes to your portrayal, and that of Maclean, I'm afraid I shall have to insist on a bit of artistic license."

"Artistic license?"

"Why of course. Just think of yourself as Gary Cooper in *Sergeant York*. Now that should do the trick quite nicely, wouldn't you say? And I promise, my father's going to absolutely love you."

CHAPTER 17

BIR HACHEIM
CYRENAICA, LIBYA

MAY 27-28, 1942

WITH THE FIRST STREAKS OF PRE-DAWN Rommel got his Panzers moving, just as a swarm of dive-bombing *Stukas*—the very embodiment of *Blitzkrieg*—screamed down upon the enemy from the sky, their terrifying sirens shrieking like doom itself in a tremolo of demonic sound. He had taken personal command of the *Afrika Korps* in the mobile advance, just as it was meeting the first screen of British armored cars south of Bir Hacheim. A signal flashed through *Panzerarmee Afrika*, coming in loud and clear through the radio headsets of the mobilized assault force and roving signals intelligence trucks: *"Rommel an der Spitze! Rommel an der Spitze!"*—Rommel is taking the point! Rommel is taking the point!

His carefully planned attack—*Fall Venezia*—was off to a promising start thanks to more than a month of crucial intercepted intelligence on the British Eighth Army's dispositions provided by his reliable Good Source, Lieutenant Colonel Bonner Fellers. The Desert Fox was rolling forward to conquer Egypt and punch through Palestine to join the German forces that, if everything went according to plan, would be driving down from Russia following the defeat of the Big Red Army. The intercepted messages from the U.S. military attaché in Cairo had informed him in stunning detail where the British had anchored their defensive line and the strength of their divisions.

Today's attack had been planned since April, and now Rommel personally commanded the German 21st Panzer, 15th Panzer, and 90th Light along with the formidable Italian Ariete Division. His tactics for the Gazala battle were to pin the British armor down with a feint frontal assault in the north where the Tommies were deeply dug in, while making his main armored thrust to the south around the desert, outflanking the British left in the area of Bir Hacheim. The British defenses consisted of a series of boxes separated by extensive minefields, with powerful artillery and infantry dug in to resist heavy air attacks. Using his proven combination of mobile tanks and 88s, he would severely maul the foreword elements and overrun the enemy's defensive boxes one by one, sowing confusion and panic. The end result would be to plant his main force firmly behind the British position and drive to Alexandria and then Cairo.

His *Funkpanzerwagen* command car and two signals vehicles came to a stop next to strip of camel thorn brush and a rocky ledge, its earthy tone transformed into pinkish yellow in the early morning light. A sandfly settled on his chiseled nose, and he brushed it away without thought. He peered through his binoculars at the unfolding battle. The British scout cars were scrambling to get out of the way of his advancing Panzers, and he thought to himself, *This is wonderful—the plan is working.* He thought of his wife back home in Germany and the letter that he had written her last night about his planned offensive. It read:

26 May 1942
Dearest Lu,
By the lime you get this letter you will have long ago heard from the Wehrmacht communiques about events here. We're launching a decisive attack today. It will be hard, but I have full confidence that my army will win it. After all, they all know what battle means. There is no need to tell you how I will go into it. I intend to demand of myself the same as I expect from each of my officers and men. My thoughts, especially in these hours of decision, are often with you.

"Look at them retreating before our eyes!" cried his chief of staff Gause.

"Come now, Alfred," Rommel mock-chided him. "The British never retreat—they *withdraw*!"

"Well, they are doing both now!" exclaimed Gause.

Brushing away another pesky sandfly from his face, the Desert Fox peered through his field glasses. With the morning air still somewhat cool, the flies were not out in force yet but would be swarming well before noon.

"I happen to subscribe to the opposite view, after the American Civil War General Sherman," he said.

"What did Sherman say?" asked his chief intelligence officer, Colonel Friedrich Wilhelm von Mellenthin, who was wearing his trademark circular goggles covered with a thin film of dust.

"When things are going badly at the rear, go to the front—things are always better up there!"

They laughed. "Yes, we all know you like to lead from the front, General," said Gause with good humor. "That is why you have an uncanny ability to be at the right place at the right time. But sometimes, I might add, at great risk to your own life."

"Not today—today I can sense only victory." He banged a gloved hand on the back of his driver's seat. "All right, let's go, Hellmut. We've got the Tommies on the run and I want to take Bir Hacheim by breakfast."

"*Jawohl, Herr Generaloberst,*" snapped *Unteroffizier* Hellmut von Leipzig, and he pressed his foot on the accelerator and quickly brought Greif up to a speed of twenty miles per hour.

The assault force roared over the camel-thorn-studded plain, the half-tracks and tanks in perfect formation, squealing and grinding along inexorably in a swirling cloud of dust and fine sand. They were moving so fast that many of the drivers had difficulty in maintaining contact with the vehicles ahead of them. The enemy minefields and decoys proved challenging obstacles to the advance in places, but two hours after daybreak the various formations making up his Panzer Army had achieved their first objective and he was feeling optimistic. Many of the supply dumps of British XXX Corps, for whom this area had acted as supply base, had fallen into his hands.

By midday the *Afrika Korps* had advanced more than 25 miles. But by then Ritchie had reacted and a furious battle developed, halting the German advance in its tracks, much to Rommel's consternation. The Panzer units ran headlong into the stout British 4th Armored Brigade on the enemy's left flank and were forced to slug it out with the 1st Armored Division. The division was no longer the hopelessly green unit he had so badly mauled back in January, and its tank crews fought like the seasoned veterans they now were. The British armor, operating under heavy artillery cover, poured into Rommel's columns and Panzer units. Fire and black smoke welled up from lorries and tanks, and he suffered serious tank losses. To his dismay, several of his columns broke into confusion and fled away to the southwest, grappling to escape the fearsome British artillery fire.

But the biggest problem was the large numbers of the enemy's new M-3 Grant tanks. All across his advancing front, his tank crews suffered a nasty shock when the tall-turreted and unfamiliar-looking behemoths began knocking out Panzers at ranges from which the German tanks couldn't begin to reply. This was his *Panzerarmee's* first experience with the new M-3 tanks given to the British by the Americans through their Lend-Lease program, and they immediately proved to be highly unpopular with the German tank crews and Rommel himself.

"Damnit, look at those things," he gasped. "They are as ugly as they are lethal."

"We need to move up our 88s and take them out," said Gause. "This can't go on like this."

"Indeed not," agreed Rommel.

His army's company and platoon tactics were superior to those of the British, which allowed his commanders to offset the disparity in firepower and protection, but he could ill afford the type of losses he was now sustaining. Thus far during the Desert War, his tanks and artillery pieces had outclassed anything the British could put in the field. His main *Panzerkampfvagen* was the Mark III, which carried a 50-mm main gun that was superior in terms of firepower and mechanical reliability to the 40-mm two-pounders mounted on British-made tanks. The new American M-3 Grant, however, was equipped with not only a lethal 75-mm cannon but also a thicker hide that at medium- to long-ranges rendered it all but impervious to the main guns of the Panzer IIIs and even IVs, save for the handful of the latter that were armed with longer-barreled, high-velocity 75-mm cannons. Its thick armor made it hard to knock out short of a direct hit from an 88-mm antiaircraft gun.

But as he studied the new enemy contraptions, looking for a way to destroy them, he began to realize that the Grant wasn't without its drawbacks. The 30-tonner stood nearly 10 feet tall, making it an easy target, and its 75-mm gun stuck into a sponson on the right front hull, which meant the gun could only engage targets to the front. On top of the vehicle was a second turret that could traverse to fire at targets to the flanks and rear, but it only contained a small 37-millimeter cannon.

The battle raged on until nightfall, by which time he realized that he was in genuine trouble. In a moment of clarity, he realized the cause of his failure: he had underestimated the strength of the British armored divisions. He had covered significant ground, destroyed a large number of enemy tanks, and taken thousands of prisoners, but at a devastating toll to his undermanned *Panzerarmee*—a Pyrrhic victory that negated his achievement. The advent of the new American Grant tank had torn great holes in his ranks, and his entire force now stood in precarious combat with a superior enemy.

When the sun set twenty-four hours later, on May 28th, Rommel knew he was in even greater trouble. Unlike during previous battles, the British had refused to become rattled and had vigorously counterattacked, backing his force and the Italian Ariete Division into a tactical and operational corner. He couldn't help but feel that he was on the brink of being undone by his own success. As he, Gause, and Westphal went over the ramifications, it was clear that he had advanced too far too fast, and that his supply lines had been cut behind him. Water was in critically short supply, his tanks were running on fumes, and food and ammunition were nearly exhausted. Not only that but General Crüwell's reconnaissance plane had been shot down and the general himself had been taken prisoner, which meant that Rommel was without the commander of his northern, mostly Italian attack force. To make matters worse, he had only intermittent contact with most of his army and was caught between two of Ritchie's fortified boxes—Sidi Muftah to the west, Knightsbridge to the east—a near-impenetrable minefield to the south, and four British armored brigades.

Knowing that his back was to the wall, he made his intentions clear to his staff as the sun sank low on the desert horizon. "Gentlemen, I regret to say that our only course of action is to concentrate the *Afrika Korps* in a central position, set up an all-round defensive perimeter, and re-establish our supply lines."

"I agree," said the Prussian Ia Westphal. "I'll send a party out to locate the missing supply convoys and guide them here. There are more than 1,500 truckloads—almost 3,000 tons of supplies—sitting somewhere to the southwest trying to get through. But unfortunately, they don't know where to go."

The Desert Fox shook his head emphatically. "No, I'm going to do it myself. If I can find them, I can lead them through the minefield by following the same route we took earlier."

Gause shook his head. "That is out of the question, General. The enemy is scattered all over between us and the convoy. You are of no value to our brave troops if you are killed or taken prisoner."

"He's right," said Westphal, also urging caution. "British reconnaissance patrols are everywhere."

He shook his head. "No, I'm going, damnit. Our troops need those supplies. There is enough petrol, ammunition, and rations for perhaps two days. That will be enough to sustain the offensive."

Gause and Westphal looked at one another with mutual exasperation. The two officers, his closest friends in the *Afrika Korps*, had surprisingly once been early detractors but were now his most trusted supporters. But they didn't like it when their commander led his army like the head of a small commando outfit instead of a senior officer a mere one rank below field marshal.

"You're not going to let us talk you out of this, are you Erwin?" said Gause.

"No, I'm not, gentlemen." He turned to his aide-de-camp, *Leutnant* Wilfred Armbruster. "Fire up Greif, Lieutenant, we're going on a little journey."

The young man—exhausted-looking in his soiled, sweat-soaked desert uniform—looked at him. "A journey, sir?"

"Yes, Wilfred. A little magic carpet ride through the desert for some much-needed supplies. Now let's go!"

CHAPTER 18

ROMMEL *KAMPFSTAFFEL*
BIR HACHEIM, CYRENAICA, LIBYA

MAY 29, 1942

THE NEXT MORNING AT FIRST LIGHT, before his usual early-morning coldwater shave, Rommel grabbed his field glasses and scanned the horizon to see what was happening on the field of battle. It was still and quiet with only a light breeze blowing in from the Great Sand Sea, but he knew the wind would pick up as the day progressed. The sky was periwinkle, the morning air still pleasantly cool enough to keep the sandflies at bay, and he could see for miles in every direction.

Last night, he had managed to find a route and guide the supply train past the British positions himself, the German and Italian trucks bumping and lurching through the dark behind his staff car. But he was now utterly exhausted. With dark circles beneath his eyes, he looked like he hadn't slept in a week. The reality was that during the past three days of heavy fighting he had been surviving on pure adrenaline and periodic thirty-minute catnaps in his staff car.

He knew it was not sustainable. At some point, he would have to take a leave from campaigning to convalesce back home in Germany. But first he had to win the battle for the Gazala Line, take Tobruk, and drive the British back into Egypt with their tails between their legs—though he was outmanned and outgunned with his back against the wall.

He adjusted the focus of his binoculars and pointed them in the direction of Tobruk. Near-sighted in one eye and far-sighted in the other, it took him a moment to get the proper setting. *Tobruk.* Along with vanquishing Ritchie's army that was his main objective. Not only was it of considerable strategic importance for its harbor well-suited for deep-water vessels, road network, and nearby airfields, but the immense political and cultural significance of Tobruk to the British made its capture of great psychological value. From intercepted Allied communications, he knew that Auchinleck was under tremendous pressure from Churchill to hold onto Tobruk at all costs.

In one week, or two at the most, you will be there, he told himself. *And then it is on to Cairo.*

He stepped into his HQ tent to shave. Having no shaving cream or mirror, he used soap and water on his face and a jagged shard of glass to see his image. By the time he had finished shaving the left side of his face, he heard the first volley of mortar fire explode through the camp. It was swiftly followed by several more.

With the ground shaking from the reverberations, his personal clerk Munninger dashed into the tent.

"We are under attack, *Herr Generaloberst*! We must leave now!"

"Take cover, you mean!"

"No, we must abandon this position! It is not just distant mortar fire—an LRDG mobile patrol is advancing rapidly and will be on us any second! We just received word from our spotters!"

"All right, let's go!"

They dashed out of the tent just as another shell exploded nearby, blowing up an armored car. His chief intelligence officer von Mellenthin was running towards them along with Gause.

"Quickly, we must get out of here!" yelled von Mellenthin. "Those are New Zealanders and they mean business!"

In a sudden barrage, four more mortar shells exploded twenty or thirty yards away. The concussion of the blast knocked him and his staff officers to the earth. When they arose and shook themselves off, Rommel realized that they would have been killed from the shrapnel if they hadn't been protected by the fleet of armored command and radio vehicles that had taken the brunt of the blasts.

They charged on towards the staff vehicles that hadn't been damaged from the mortar explosions. Now Rommel could see the enemy. They were sweeping in on trucks with mounted machine guns, a swarthy-faced bunch cloaked in desert headdresses like Bedouins. Out of all the British forces, he regarded the New Zealanders as the most formidable, seconded only by the gritty Australians. They opened up with a pair of Vickers machine guns, taking down a handful of men to his left as they scrambled for the staff cars.

Scheisse, how in the hell have the bastards taken us by total surprise!

As a clump of his soldiers returned fire, the enemy let loose with another concentrated fusillade, the white-hot bullets cutting down the low-lying camel thorn with a retching crash, kicking up shards of stone, and ripping up clods of dirt. He saw the two Brandenburgers, Lance Corporals Walter Aberle and Waldemar Weber, and other W/T operators from the Abwehr Signals Unit come under enemy fire as they made a mad dash for their mobile monitoring trucks. He had recruited the two radio operators—who had been assigned by the Abwehr to Almasy's Operation Salam and Condor—at the last minute to his mobile HQ from Mamelin because he was short of W/T operators and they seemed to be idle. Now that they were under heavy enemy fire and might very well be captured, that appeared to have been a very bad idea on his part. They were about to be cut off by one of the approaching LRDG vehicles with the mounted machine guns.

"Damnit, the New Zealanders could very well roll up our whole signals team!" cried the 1c von Mellenthin.

But Rommel was more worried about Aberle and Weber, who were a crucial element to the much-needed spy network he hoped to establish for his advance into Cairo.

"Hurry, get the hell out of here!" he cried to them, but they were too far away to hear him. He yelled out to the other radio men, but they were out of earshot too. He quickly realized that it didn't matter, for the New Zealanders were already closing in around Aberle and Weber and several of the other signals trucks, preventing them from escaping. Unfortunately, there was nothing more he could do to help them.

He and his men made a mad dash for the parked *Mammuts*—the mammoth-sized Dorchester 4x4 armored command vehicles captured from the British over a year earlier and now used by his staff. His legs churned like pistons from the adrenaline rush of literally running for his life as he closed the distance to ten feet to his personal armored staff car that he had affectionately named Moritz. The name was proudly and affectionately emblazoned on the front just above the fender headlamp and the *Deutsches Afrika Korps* palm symbol.

He saw another nearby trooper go down, this time from a hand grenade. The soldier's guts were blasted from his body in grotesque fashion, spattering against a short wall of piled desert stones like the spaghetti the Italian officers ate.

"Quickly, *Generaloberst*, before they cut us off too!" cried Gause.

Now his driver von Leipzig and two NCOs appeared on the scene along with his aide-de-camp Armbruster.

"You take Greif, we'll go in Moritz!" he snapped to them.

"*Jawohl, Herr Generaloberst!*"

He jumped inside the massive vehicle with Munninger, Gause, and von Mellenthin and called out to the others. The Iron Cross, First Class, at his throat bobbed with his movements.

"Follow us!" he cried. "*Los, los!*"

Quickly firing the engine and engaging the gears, Munninger drove off like a bat out of hell. A hailstorm of bullets crashed into the staff car as they raced through the desert in retreat. Rommel heard a whizzing sound and then a force upon his shoulder. *Damn, am I hit?* But as they sped off, he quickly realized that the bullet had only ripped through one of the epaulettes of his uniform jacket.

As they accelerated away from the chaotic scene and out of range of the attacking New Zealanders, he chanced a look over his shoulder. He could see Aberle and Weber, along with others from the Signals Unit, with their hands up being captured.

"Damnit, they've captured Aberle and Weber!" he said to von Mellenthin.

"No, it's even worse than that," said the intelligence officer. "Those damned New Zealanders will soon get their hands on their codebooks and other incriminating documents as well. All of their materials are in the signals truck."

Rommel shook his head in dismay. "This is a disaster."

"You're telling me," said von Mellenthin. "Once British intelligence interrogates them and sifts through everything, they're going to blow Operation Salam and Condor wide open."

"Are you telling me that Eppler and Sandstette are going to be compromised before they have even set foot in the city?"

"It looks that way. But I'm sure Canaris and Almasy have a backup plan."

"God, I hope so," said Rommel. "God, I hope so."

CHAPTER 19

ROMMEL *KAMPFSTAFFEL*-BRITISH POW CAGE
AND ITALIAN XX CORPS HQ
BIR HACHEIM, CYRENAICA, LIBYA

MAY 30, 1942

"WE HAVE THREE AVENUES OF ESCAPE OPEN TO US NOW. I urge you, *Herr Generaloberst*, to take advantage of this opportunity, fall back, and regroup."

Rommel's eyes lingered a moment on his chief of staff before returning to the large color-coded, topographic map on the table showing the current position of the enemy's boxes, minefields, and assembled tank units. He couldn't believe his bold offensive had slowed to a crawl after such promising early returns. His armored left hook was beginning to weaken through sheer lack of fuel, food, ammunition, and water, as the supply train he had escorted to the front himself two nights earlier was already nearly all used up. Ritchie's armor was now sufficiently organized to attack en masse and he would be hard pressed to hold the British in check without more sustenance for his *Panzerarmee*. A way had to be found to bring the much-needed supplies through the British minefields and around the two most bothersome Eighth Army boxes from which mobile raiding parties were constantly harassing his convoys: Bir Hacheim and Got el Ualeb, held by the British 150th Brigade.

"Please, sir," persisted Gause, "you must return the *Afrika Korps* and the Ariete Division to safe harbor. Even though our west-east supply routes have been re-established, General Crüwell has been captured and the Italian units in the north are making no headway. We have to regroup and fight another day."

The HQ tent went silent as Rommel pondered what to do next. It was then an officer stepped inside and informed him that a British major being held at the nearby POW cage had requested to see him regarding the treatment of his troops.

"We'll have to continue this later, gentlemen. For the time being, my standing orders are to hold our positions and not fall back," he said to Gause, Westphal, and his other staff officers.

"But, General," protested Gause, "we cannot sustain the—"

But it was just wasted breath as the Desert Fox was halfway out the tent. He proceeded quickly to the POW cage north of his headquarters' tent, a stone's throw from where his fleet of staff cars was parked. A crude rectangle of barbed wire had been laid out on the sandy and rocky desert floor to enclose hundreds of British soldiers, mostly from the 3rd Indian Cavalry that had been steamrolled by his Panzers. When he arrived at the guard tent just outside the wire, he found the British officer waiting for him in a dilapidated backrest, guarded by a pair of soldiers in lightweight desert camo uniforms.

He gave a quick salute. "You wanted to speak to me, Major?"

The tall, gaunt officer returned the salute with stiff British formality. "General Rommel," he began, "I am Major Archer-Shee, Third Indian Cavalry. As you must be aware, for the past two days, some six hundred of my men and I have been cooped up in this infernal cage with scarcely a drop of water. I am afraid I must formally protest our treatment."

"That is not true," countered Rommel. "Your men have been given water. In fact, it is precisely the same ration of water as me and my men: a half cup per day."

The major looked at him with surprise. "You…you have restricted yourself to only a half cup per day? A general?"

"Yes, as I said, I get only the same amount as my troops."

"Well, that may be well and good for you, sir, but dozens of my men have seen heavy action and are now very close to death from dehydration. A half cup per day is not adequate for men in such a state. They will soon die without more water."

"I am sorry about your men, Major. But as I said, you are getting exactly the same ration of water as the *Afrika Korps* and myself, half a cup. I'm afraid I have no more to offer you and your men at present until another convoy gets through."

Archer-Shee's eyes narrowed and he licked his severely chapped lips, as if struggling to maintain his composure. "You, sir, are in flagrant violation of the articles of the Hague and Geneva Conventions that protect military prisoners of war from abuse. If you cannot give your prisoners enough water, then you are bound by military honor to let us go."

"You want me to release you and your men?"

"Yes, General. By the articles of the Geneva Convention, that is indeed what you must do. Furthermore, if you don't have enough water, how do you expect to fight, let alone win? Your offensive is quite simply unsustainable."

Though he hated to admit, Rommel knew the major was right. But it was even worse than that. Not only did he not have enough water for his own army or his British POWs, he was very much on the brink of defeat and might have to surrender.

He looked the major in the eye. "I agree that we cannot go on like this," he said to Archer-Shee. "If we don't get another convoy through tonight I shall have to ask General Ritchie for terms. You can take a letter to him for me."

A raised eyebrow. "Are you quite serious?"

"Yes, and I will release you and your six hundred Indian prisoners. But I am telling you that you will have to head in a southwestern direction towards Bir Hacheim. A British patrol will pick you up and you can be evacuated from—"

"General!" he heard a voice call out. As he turned around, his aide-de-camp Armbruster rounded the corner and stepped into the tent.

"Yes, what is it, Lieutenant?"

"I must speak to you in private, General. It is urgent."

He turned back towards Archer-Shee. "If you'll excuse me, Major. And don't worry about your men—I promise they will be released shortly."

"I have your word on that."

"Yes, you do."

He followed Armbruster out the tent, stepping towards the parked vehicles until they were out of earshot of the British major. "What is it, Wilfred?"

"Field Marshal Kesselring is waiting for you at Italian Headquarters."

He felt as if he had been punched in the gut. "What?"

"He flew in on his Storch an hour ago."

Verdammt, this is all I need right now, my commanding officer to meddle in my affairs! But I have no choice. "All right, let's go," he said reluctantly.

Leaving Gause and his other senior staff behind, he set off with his driver Hellmut von Leipzig and Armbruster to the headquarters of the Italian XX Corps. Since they had to navigate their way through a British minefield, they rode in a *personenkraftwagen*, a lighter-weight cross-country passenger car, instead of the heavy-duty Moritz or Greif.

He found Kesselring and Major von Below, Hitler's adjutant, looking over a map of North Africa beneath a canvas awning set up next to a command car.

"Field Marshal," he said without preamble to the commander in chief of Wehrmacht South. "I was told you wanted to see me and came as fast as I could."

As the two men shook hands, Kesselring—who was known as "Uncle Albert" by his troops and "Smiling Albert" by the Allies for his wide, ever-present grin—gave his trademark smile. As Hitler's C-in-C South, the highly decorated Luftwaffe field marshal commanded all Axis air forces in the Mediterranean, reporting to Berlin from his headquarters in Rome. A pragmatist with an affable and naturally optimistic disposition, the fifty-six-year-old *Feldmaresciallo* worked reasonably well with the Italians and, like Rommel, was regarded by the Allies as a formidable opponent. He had served in the infantry during the Great War and in the *Reichswehr* before being transferred to the nascent Luftwaffe in 1934 and was no stranger to combat. His mission in North Africa, given to him personally by Hitler, was to see that the Desert Fox got his supplies, something Kesselring's predecessor, *Generalmajor* Stefan Frolich, had been unable or unwilling to do.

Most people accepted his constant air of bonhomie as genuine, but Rommel wasn't among them and considered "Smiling Albert's" sanguine manner a well-crafted act. The truth was the two had never warmed to one another, and the Desert Fox considered him a bit too ambitious. But more importantly, he didn't want the man looking over his shoulder and telling him what to do, and the same went for the Führer's man von Below. He couldn't help but feel that Kesselring's and von Below's sudden appearance at the front had the potential to be a distraction, which at this critical point of the offensive he most certainly did not need.

Pointing to the map, he gave a quick rundown of the military situation.

"This is the Gazala Line," he said, moving his index finger along the string of fortified boxes linked by minefields that ran from the coastal town of Gazala into the desert, stopping at Bir Hacheim—the Well of the Wise—some forty miles to the south and on the very edge of the Great Sand Sea. "We were able to flank the British around the southern end of the line and attack them from behind, but the attack has run out of steam." He now moved his finger to the north towards the coast. "In the north, the infantry assault by the Italian X and XXI Corps on the Gazala Line has penetrated as far as the main British positions and then come to a standstill in front of well-constructed defense works."

"Where is the *General der Panzertruppe* now?" asked Kesselring.

"Unfortunately, General Crüwell's plane was shot down and he has been taken prisoner. Even before that happened, he was unable to hold the Eighth Army facing him in place. Nor is he the only one of our generals to be put out of the fight today. General von Vaerst, commander of the 15th Panzer Division, was wounded earlier this morning and forced to leave the battlefield."

"What is your plan?"

"The British have now assembled their 2nd, 4th, and 22nd Armored Brigades and, with the 201st Guards Brigade, are throwing them in concentric counter-attacks against our front. In this situation, I believe it is far too hazardous to continue our attack to the north, as I had originally planned. The main thing now is to open up a secure supply route for our striking force, and I have, therefore, decided to move units of 90th Light Division and an element of the *Afrika Korps* against the minefields from the east. To cover this move, the remainder of the force must go over to the defensive on a shortened front. As soon as the penetration of the Gazala defenses has been made, I intend to cut off Bir Hacheim."

"The southern bastion of the British line?" asked Major von Below.

"Yes, right here," said Rommel, again pointing to the map. "The Free French at Bir Hacheim are fighting like pit bulls."

"Unusual for Frenchmen," said von Below disdainfully.

Rommel and Kesselring both shot him a glare. "Don't underestimate the French," said Kesselring. "They fight as hard and spill blood as good as any German. Who is their present commander?"

"The 1st Free French Brigade is commanded by Brigadier General Marie-Pierre Koenig," replied Rommel. "He has established a position extending a couple of square miles around an old Ottoman fort. The only British with him are the crews of six Bofors guns, reinforcing an antiaircraft unit of French Marines." Brushing away a pack of sandflies with his left hand, he again pointed to the map with his right. "As I have said, my initial infantry assaults have failed to capture this vital position, the southern pivot of the Gazala Line. I called for air support but it was insufficient to allow me to break the position."

"Your attack failed because of faulty coordination between the ground and air attacks. We will both have to do better in the future if we are to take Bir Hacheim."

"Going forward, I have made my plans on the assumption that, with strong German motorized forces standing south of the coast road, the British will not dare to use their armored formations to attack the Italians in the Gazala Line. A counter-attack by my Panzer divisions would put them between two fires. On the other hand, I am hoping that the presence of the Italian infantry in front of the 1st South African and 50th British Divisions will continue to persuade the overcautious British command to leave those formations complete in the Gazala Line."

"You consider it improbable that Ritchie will order these two infantry divisions to attack the Italian infantry corps without support from other formations?"

"Yes, that is what I am betting on. The British refuse to move without one-hundred-percent certainty. It's just not in their nature—and Ritchie is no exception."

"You believe the British mechanized brigades will continue to run up against your well-organized defensive front and use up their strength in the process?"

"Precisely, and my defense will have a maximum of elasticity and mobility."

"I would expect no less from you, Erwin." But then his eyes narrowed. "But you cannot go on like this."

Again, Rommel felt himself tense. "What do you mean, Field Marshal?"

"You cannot rush around the battlefield, racing about from unit to unit, crisis to crisis, always trying to be *an der Spitze*."

"One cannot lead an army from the rear, Field Marshal," he replied defensively.

"No, but you cannot run around like a chicken with its head cut off either, leading supply convoys, Panzer formations, and artillery units at your own whim. You must delegate those things to your staff."

"I don't trust what I don't see with my own eyes. If my army gets whipped in the field, it is my responsibility and no one else's."

"It is all our responsibility, Erwin, including the Italians. That is why I am here to voluntarily place myself and my staff at your disposal."

"You're placing yourself under my command? But you are senior to me."

"Yes, but the most important thing is to take some of the heavy burden from your shoulders and win this fight. And besides, someone has to replace Crüwell as *General der Panzertruppe*."

He studied the field marshal closely, trying to decipher if he was playing straight with him or if this was some sort of opportunistic move to take over his army. *No, he decided, he is a better man that that. You are just being distrustful.*

He gave a bow. "I would be honored, Field Marshal," he said, and he meant it.

But Kesselring wasn't finished. "I still must insist that you get a hold of yourself, your army, and the battle. This charging to and fro across the battlefield is accomplishing nothing. As your superior officer, do I make myself clear?"

Now that he had accepted the olive branch, Rommel knew he had no choice but to agree. Besides, he knew that in this case the man was right. He could not keep rushing about the desert trying to solve every problem that cropped up, like Hans Brinker the little Dutch boy trying to plug his finger in the dike to save the day.

"I understand and will do my best to resolve the situation," he said.

"Very well. Now how's your intelligence coming along? Are the intercepts from Colonel Fellers still proving useful?"

"Yes, my 'little Fellers's is still worth his weight in gold. I am receiving regular official reports regarding the Eighth Army's plans and intentions."

"It appears to me he still has *carte blanche* from the British to roam about and observe their operations. Would you agree?"

"I think he has access to as much information as Ritchie through the briefings he regularly attends at GHQ. His dispatches on unit strengths and positions, troop movements, convoys, reinforcements, supplies, and morale are concise and quite accurate based on our other confirmed sources of intelligence."

"The man's a gold mine. But the problem is such blessings cannot last."

"I know. That's why I've established my own spy network in Cairo. Or rather, the Abwehr has. They should be establishing radio contact with us any day now. Unfortunately, their controllers were captured yesterday, but I believe Captain Almasy has a backup plan for establishing wireless communications. He is the Hungarian count with intimate knowledge of the desert who was recently tasked with the special operation to infiltrate the agents into Egypt using captured British vehicles. He will be returning to base shortly."

"There is a team in Cairo? How many agents?"

"Two—Lieutenants Eppler and Sandstette. Operation Salam called for them to be delivered to the doorstep of the city by driving around the Great Sand Sea. I met with them two and a half weeks ago, shortly before their departure. Once they reach

Cairo and establish an alternative radio communication system, they will be operating under Operation Condor."

Kesselring made a disapproving face. "Personally, I don't much trust spies. In my experience, they aren't very reliable."

"I don't usually trust them either. But we had to give this a try. As you said, the British and Americans will likely discover in the not-too-distant future that we have broken the U.S. State Department's Black Code. Then I will no longer have my Good Source and will be out of luck. But the reality is, whatever advantage Fellers's intercepts provide are negated by our lack of petrol and ammunition."

To his credit, Kesselring didn't become defensive under the subtle rebuke that Rommel wasn't receiving adequate supplies, as sustaining the Desert Fox's army was a large part of Smiling Albert's responsibility. The ultimately responsible party, however, was the Italian *Comando Supremo* in Rome that had so often let them both down before. Rommel was painfully aware of the logistical situation he faced, but he had no choice but to rely on, primarily, the *Comando Supremo*, and secondarily, Kesselring and his Luftwaffe, to transport his supplies across the Mediterranean.

"We need to knock out Malta," said Kesselring. "Unfortunately, it appears to be recovering from the latest bombing and is providing a base for the British to attack our supply ships to Libya. I'm afraid that until we reduce the island to rubble, you will not be getting the supplies you would like to have to sustain your army."

"You do realize that if I had my petrol, we'd both be in Cairo right now."

"That is neither here nor there," said Kesselring, obviously not wanting to reopen their old argument. "In any case, you will have to take Tobruk first. That is your first and overarching objective. Once the port is taken, the tankers and other supply convoys can come directly to your front lines in Eastern Libya and Western Egypt, cutting out the long journey across the desert which consumes so much petrol."

"You and your *Panzerarmee* must work with what you've got, *Herr Generaloberst*," interjected the Nazi von Below, wiping a grain of sand from his immaculate staff uniform. "Now what of your other sources of intelligence?"

"I have also been receiving useful reports from Captain Seebohm and his 621st Radio Intercept Company. On several occasions, he has been able to place his aerial-tracking trucks right next to my command car and pass on translated versions of British radio messages even before being formally sent to OKW. My greatest fear is that I will lose both my 'little Fellers's and Seebohm. That is why having spies on the ground in Cairo is so important."

At that moment, Armbruster stepped beneath the awning. "I have an important message for you, General!"

"Give it to me." He snatched it from the aide-de-camp and quickly read it over.

"What is it? What does it say?" asked Kesselring.

"It's from General Ritchie to Auchinleck. He says, and I quote, 'Rommel on the run.' Auchinleck's reply is 'Bravo Eighth Army! Give him the coup de grâce.'"

Smiling Albert gave his trademark smile. "Well, Rommel, I am quite confident you know what to do about that."

"Indeed, I do," said the Desert Fox with an answering ghost of a smile. "And the Tommies are not going to like it one little bit."

CHAPTER 20

THE CAULDRON
BIR HACHEIM, CYRENAICA, LIBYA

JUNE 2, 1942

ROMMEL LOVED SOARING HIGH above the desert floor while performing aerial reconnaissance in his single-engine Fieseler Storch spotter-plane. It was one of the few times he was at war but without being at war and he felt as though Lu, Manfred, and Trudie were right there beside him—even though they were thousands of miles away in Germany. He often took over the controls from his NCO and flew the monoplane himself, skirting the northern edges of the Calanscio Sand Sea, Great Sand Sea, and Qattara Depression and the foam-fringed Libyan coastline, where horse-mounted warriors had fought countless epic battles over the millennia.

Though he had still not succeeded in destroying the British from the rear, he had planted his main force in the middle of their position in an area that, after three days of furious fighting, had become known as *der Hexenkessel*—the Cauldron. The battle for the Cauldron—in searing dusty winds that scorched the lungs and scoured skin and eyes until they were raw—was among the bloodiest he had taken part in since the commencement of his desert campaign.

The British had clearly hoped to keep him and his armor trapped in the Cauldron while they attacked in ever-decreasing circles, but one by one their defensive boxes were being attacked, overrun, and destroyed. Both sides had sustained enormous losses in the fighting, but Rommel was able to keep the various British counter-attacks at bay, with enough left over to attack the dug-in 150th Brigade at Got el Ualeb. Though the outcome of the battle for the Gazala Line was still uncertain, he could sense that the Eighth Army was on the verge of collapse from the inside and he would be able to continue rolling up the boxes, one by one, from south to north.

The 150th Brigade's box had surrendered yesterday on June 1, with 3,000 prisoners taken and over a hundred tanks and armored cars destroyed or captured and 124 artillery pieces seized. The Bir Hacheim box held by the Free French had been under attack from Stuka dive bombers and artillery, and his hope was that General Koenig would soon surrender as Brigadier Clive Haydon's 150th Brigade had done at Got el Ualeb. But the stalwart French were holding on fast.

He thought of poor Westphal and Gause. In a stunning reversal of fortune, his chief of operations and chief of staff had both been seriously wounded in two separate surprise British mortar attacks. They would have to go on sick leave in Italy. He couldn't help but feel the pain of two more grave losses, and dreaded having to do without his two top officers in the challenging days ahead. Both men had long been critical components of his staff because of their great knowledge, experience, and ability to make what he regarded as the right decision in his absence. They would be greatly missed.

Flying low to avoid deadly British Royal Air Force fighters, he banked the Storch left so he could take a closer look at the British boxes. His single-engine

Fieseler 156 V2 Storch observation and command plane was a light, spindly-legged aircraft used for short trips around the battlefield. The reconnaissance aircraft was well-adapted for takeoffs and landings on rough desert ground, but its effective range was only 235 miles before it needed to refuel. Upon his approach to the Bir Hacheim box held by the Free French, he was forced to dodge machine-gun and rifle fire from both British troops, and also from a battalion of Italian soldiers who failed to recognize his signature aircraft. But he was able to escape the hostile and friendly fire and make his way towards a makeshift runway.

It was nothing but a short, narrow strip of desert hastily cleared of heavy boulders, camel thorn, and smaller stones but it was well suited for his agile little monoplane. All the same, when he touched down he had the misfortune of striking a small boulder with his undercarriage that gave him and his NCO co-pilot a severe jolt. He brought the plane to a halt and hopped out just as Armbruster and his new chief of staff who had replaced Gause, Colonel Fritz Bayerlein, came running up.

"Captain Almasy has returned from the desert and is reporting in," said Bayerlein, who, though he had only been appointed to his new post yesterday when Gause and Westphal had been wounded, had been fully briefed on the LRDG raid by the New Zealanders.

"Oh Christ, I am going to have to tell him the bad news about Aberle and Weber."

"There's no avoiding it," said Bayerlein. "But hopefully Almasy has good news regarding Operation Salam, and Operation Condor can still be successfully completed."

"Let's hope so." He stumped across the sand towards his *Kampfstaffel* with the two officers in tow. Their calf-high leather boots kicked up puffs of dust that were instantly dispersed by the brisk desert wind. His HQ consisted of a pair of tents bracketed by two dozen staff vehicles and two signals trucks. At the entrance to his tent, sentries saluted as batteries rumbled and crackled in the near distance and the massive generators for the signals trucks hummed in a steady mechanical rhythm. The flap to his tent was open and he stepped inside, finding Almasy swatting away a pack of flies above his map table.

"Captain Almasy—you have returned safely," he said, taking off his greatcoat and tossing it on a battered foldup metal chair.

The Hungarian count looked up from the large map, saluted smartly, and took two steps towards him as Bayerlein and Armbruster looked on. It was obvious that he had come straight from the desert as a film of fine eolian dust still coated his face and uniform.

"*Herr Generaloberst*, Operation Salam successfully concluded—Operation Condor can now begin," he reported.

Rommel couldn't help but feel awkward and dreaded what he was about to say. But he decided that it was best to just come out with it.

"I'm afraid I have some bad news, Captain. News that you will undoubtedly find particularly troubling given the difficult journey you and your men have just made across the desert."

"What is it, General? What has happened?"

"I regret to have to tell you that the two Brandenburgers, Lance Corporals Aberle and Weber, have been captured by the enemy."

The gasp emitted from Almasy's mouth was audible throughout the entire tent. Rommel felt badly for him, but only for an instant as he had a more pressing matter on his mind: directing the assault on the Free French position along the southern end of the Gazala Line. The Hungarian stood there speechless for several seconds before speaking.

"But how could they have been captured? They were safe in the rear at Mamelin?"

"In late May, I brought them from Mamelin and attached them to my HQ Signals Unit?"

"But why?"

He hardly felt the need to justify himself in front of a mere captain, and a non-German to boot, but given the undoubtedly arduous, nearly 3,000-mile roundtrip journey the man had just undertaken, he felt he deserved an explanation.

"I was short of wireless operators and, unfortunately, Aberle and Weber were available and not being used. I thought they could wait for messages with my staff just as well as anywhere else and lend a hand. It was at the beginning of my offensive and I knew it would be for only a few days. But then they were captured by the LRDG. I barely escaped myself, with shaving soap still on my face."

Almasy made no reply, but Rommel could tell what he was thinking. *How could such a well-devised plan, upon which I have devoted such forethought, be compromised by a temporary need for more radio operators at the front!* The two men stood there in silence for what seemed forever, a long embarrassing moment for them both.

Then the desert explorer's expression changed, and Rommel could see that his mind was trying to gauge what the overall impact would be to Operation Condor.

"I am sorry, Captain. I know how much work you have put into Salam and Condor."

"Well, *Herr Generaloberst*, at least Operation Salam was a great success," he said, as if trying to find a silver lining. "I swear I could have taken a whole regiment with me to the Nile."

"What you did was a most remarkable achievement and is something we can keep in our back pocket for another day." He stepped forward and slapped him on the shoulder with soldierly bonhomie. "That's why I'm promoting you to major and recommending you for the Iron Cross. Both first and second class."

But Almasy still seemed upset. Rommel decided to try to make light of the situation. With a friendly laugh, he said, "I hope to arrive to Cairo soon with my whole army—and by a far shorter route than the one you and your agents took."

The Hungarian explorer's reply was laced with a hint of acidity. "*Herr Generaloberst*, our friends Eppler and Sandstette will certainly have prepared a villa there for you if the British haven't captured you in the meantime."

Knowing Almasy was upset, he pretended not to be offended by the remark. "I know that this is a troublesome setback, Captain, but does the fact that the two W/T operators have been captured mean that all is lost? I mean, what do you think will happen?"

"Before I can answer that question, during the LRDG attack, were Aberle and

Weber's Condor codebooks and documents captured along with them?"

"Unfortunately, yes."

"Then it would appear that the operation has been compromised and will have to be abandoned. Admiral Canaris will likely order that all messages from the agents in Cairo be ignored from now on."

"You're saying that the capture of the two Brandenburgers, along with their codebooks and other materials, means that for security reasons any messages coming from Eppler and Sandstette from Cairo will no longer be either confirmed or answered? Is that what you're telling me?"

"More than likely. But the admiral will have the final say. It all depends on whether he truly believes that their capture has irreparably jeopardized Operation Condor or not."

"Do they have a backup plan for establishing radio contact?"

"No, but they are trained operatives. They will come up with something."

"So not all hope is lost then?"

"No," said Almasy through clenched teeth. "But as you say, this is a serious setback."

CHAPTER 21

CONTINENTAL HOTEL, CAIRO

JUNE 4, 1942

JOHANNES EPPLER watched in quiet rapture as his former lover performed her *danse du ventre* for the packed audience on the Continental Hotel's famous rooftop garden. The German spy wondered if it was possible Hekmat Fahmy had somehow defied the aging process, for he was certain she had grown even more stunning since he had last seen her before the beginning of the war. Nursing a potent double White Horse and soda, he was seated at the illustrious rooftop bar with Sandstette, who was posing as the American oil field worker Peter Muncaster.

Her movements were exquisitely coordinated and graceful, and the crowd of British officers, Egyptian aristocrats, and European *glitterati* was showing its fulsome approval with vigorous cheering and hand-clapping. She was truly something special, and he could see that every man in the room was unable to tear his eyes away from her erotically twitching, lascivious abdomen. They were all fantasizing about a romp in bed with her. He couldn't help but feel a touch jealous, knowing there were so many men in Cairo that wanted her. But he gave his jealously no more thought. Out of all the men in attendance, he was the one who had once been intimate with her, having made splendid love to her on dozens of memorable occasions, though with the war going on their steamy love affair now seemed like a lifetime ago. There was no question in his mind that she was the best lover he had ever had, even better than his wife Sonia back in Denmark.

But right now, he had his sights set on her for another reason entirely: to recruit her for Operation Condor. She was very clever and on a first-name basis with the military and social elite of the city, both foreign and domestic. From what he had heard about her, she undoubtedly had access to a great wealth of information, though she was likely unaware of just how valuable it might be to the Axis war effort. But he would find a way to coax it out of her, just as he had once been able to coax her into his bedchambers.

While she continued to hold the audience in mesmeric rapture, he looked around the rooftop garden. Muted yellow light filtered down through the flowering shrubs lining the expansive terrace. The Continental was an ideal spot for espionage, being a favorite watering hole for officers at GHQ Middle East, as well as those on short leave from the front, many of whom could snatch a few pleasant hours in the company of lovely women. As at Shepheard's, the Turf Club, the Gezira Sporting Club, and the expensive restaurants and nightclubs in Cairo, the Continental was off limits to private soldiers, except on Monday afternoons when amateur concerts and shows were shown that enlisted men could attend. Eppler liked that the place was off limits to the rabble as he took in the sweet scent of a thousand roses in bloom, mingling with the French perfumes of brown- and white-skinned women.

He looked the crowd over from head to toe, looking for those who might be useful to his subterfuge. In addition to the British officers, there were stinking-rich

Egyptians, Greeks, and Armenians—who could have cared less about the war—making moves on assorted lovelies hung with precious jewels. Everyone who was anyone in Cairo was having fun here tonight, or at some elite establishment like the Continental. It might as well have been the Roaring Twenties in America, he thought, as he took in the scene of debauchery. The people all around him were "in" and fancied themselves as "belonging." Now if he and Sandstette could just take advantage of their loose tongues, he would reap a windfall on behalf of Rommel and his *Panzerarmee*.

Since their arrival and swift disappearance into the seedy districts of Cairo ten days earlier, they had engaged in one adventure or mishap after another. Initially, it had been a struggle just to find accommodations, but Eppler knew the city well and was quite resourceful. Late that first night, he had managed to find them quarters in a brothel, the Pension Nadia, for two nights. From there, they moved on to what they thought was a more respectable lodging that would serve as a permanent base of operations. The flat at No. 8 Sharia Boursa el Guedida belonged to Madame Therese Guillemet, a Frenchwoman married to an Egyptian. They rented the rooms for three months, paying seventy-five pounds rent in advance. But the flat soon proved unsuitable.

In an effort to establish contact with *Schildkroete* at Rommel's mobile HQ—the codename for the Abwehr *Abteilung* I W/T operator Weber—Sandstette had set up an aerial on the roof and sent out his call sign. But he received no reply and was unable to make radio contact through a "first-test" transmission to the Panzer Army's forward interception station. He concluded that he was sending a poor signal owing to the flat being surrounded by taller buildings. There was also the problem that the flat had once been the haunt of prostitutes—with the result that pimps, former clients, and Egyptian police were frequently at the door. Therese, the property owner, lived with them in the building and she herself had once been a prostitute and a madame. One day her former pimp, Albert Wahda, visited and recognized Eppler, whom he knew as Hussein Gaafar. Eppler explained away his absence from Cairo since 1937 by saying that he had been living at a farm in Assiut, which was the cover story he was telling everyone who knew him in his former life before the war. But it was clear to him and Sandstette that they had to leave the premises and find a better place to set up their base of operations.

Following the encounter with Wahda, Eppler immediately began looking for more suitable accommodation through people he met in the high-end watering holes and cabarets. He also hoped these contacts would lead to intelligence on the British order of battle and morale that might be of military value to Rommel. But the first priority was establishing radio contact with his army. With the two agents having just arrived in Cairo and still in the process of establishing their cover, they had no specific information to give *Schildkroete*, but it was important to establish the link, prior to preparing intelligence summaries. These were to be coded by reference to page and paragraph numbers in Daphne du Maurier's best-selling novel *Rebecca*, the code book chosen for the operation.

Another pressing priority for the two German agents was to exchange their British currency for Egyptian money. To their surprise upon arriving to the city, they had discovered that English sterling was not in general use in Egypt and that those found in possession of it could be arrested and imprisoned. They had three thousand British pounds in £5, £10, £20, and £50 notes and had little choice but to change the money out on the black market for half its value or less. Fortunately, they found willing takers, a few of whom were trustworthy, among the habitués of the Cairene nightclubs, cabarets, and bars. But the money changers they used took big cuts, and at the current rate of £20 per night they were spending in the nightclubs and fleshpots, they would burn through their money by mid-July.

Apart from the problems of communication and money, the agents were also having difficulty making useful local contacts. Their main contact was supposed to have been Mohamed Marnza, whom Eppler had known before the war, but they soon learned that he had been taken into detention. Another important contact was Egyptian Prince Abbas Halim, but the outspoken critic of the British and vocal supporter of Hitler's Reich was being closely watched due to his known pro-Axis sympathies and anti-colonial stance. There was also a Hungarian laybrother named Père Dimitriou at St. Thérèse's Church, but the agents had not been successful yet in getting in touch with him.

Up on the stage, Hekmat finished her performance with a writhing climax that brought the crowd to its feet. Eppler and Sandstette jumped up right along with them, clapping thunderously.

With the applause washing over them, he turned to Sandstette and said, "I need to talk to her. She could be of use to us."

"How is that?" asked his partner skeptically.

"She is on friendly terms with the British and knows everyone who is anyone in Cairo, including British officers from GHQ. I am told she receives dozens of letters of fanmail every week from her adoring officer fans. I'll be right back—I'm going to arrange it."

As Hekmat took a final bow and sashayed to her dressing room to change, he stepped towards the kitchen and had a word with Rossier, the headwaiter. Handing him a five-pound Egyptian note, he pretended that he didn't know the celebrated belly dancer and asked if he would introduce him to her. He did not give his name to Rossier, wanting to surprise her.

Ten minutes later, she reappeared on the rooftop garden, having changed out of her dancing attire into formal evening wear to talk with the members of the audience, which consisted mostly of officers in uniform. Eppler watched her closely, dazzled by her grace and beauty, as she exchanged polite kisses with smitten admirers and signed autographs. After a moment, Rossier gently pulled her away by the elbow and led her to his table.

Tossing back his third whiskey and soda, Eppler smiled inwardly. This was going to be fun.

ΨΨΨ

When they saw one another, Hekmat Fahmy couldn't believe her eyes. *No, it can't be him*, she told herself as the man she had once known as Hussein Gaafar rose up from his chair to greet her. Another man was seated next to him, and he, too, stood up to welcome her.

"Hello, Hekmat," said Eppler silkily, as Rossier melted back into the crowd.

For a moment, she was unable to speak. But there was no doubt she had come face to face with her former lover as he stepped forward into a ray of overhead light. It was Hussein Gaafar all right: medium height, on the thin side with narrow shoulders, a square handsome face, small mustache, and oceanic blue eyes, unusual among Egyptians but not unknown, even going back to the Pharaohs. But then she remembered that he wasn't actually Egyptian but rather British and German, though he had been raised by a prominent Egyptian stepfather when his mother married. He radiated the same supreme confidence and authority she recalled from their time as lovers and she suspected that he had to be in the military in some capacity. She wanted to say something, but her lips refused to move. How long had it been? Four years? Five? August of '37 so nearly five years.

My God, has it been that long?

"What's the matter, cat got your tongue?" he quipped good-naturedly. "Or are you just not happy to see your old paramour?"

People were now looking at them. She could feel their eyes heavily upon her, wondering how she knew this man. She felt a jumble of emotions, but what she experienced most of all were all the old amorous feelings. They came rushing back to her in a gushing torrent.

"Hello, Hussein," she said simply.

His blue eyes lit up with a gentle glow. "I must say you look even more fabulous than the last time I saw you," he said. "My apologies for not getting in touch with you sooner. It has been far too long."

She gave him a sharp look. "As I recall, you walked out on me."

His face instantly reddened and there was an awkward moment between the three of them. He struggled to find the words. "I...I didn't walk out on you. Something came up and I had to go away for a while."

"Awhile? It's been nearly five years, Hussein."

"Yes, I...I'm sorry about that. In fact, I'm sorry about everything."

She saw sincerity in his eyes, but the words still echoed painfully. He looked down, pensively, and she knew that he, too, was feeling five years of emotion welling up inside him. She thought of how the relationship had ended. Though there might be a perfectly logical explanation why he had just up and left five years ago, she knew that she would not be able to fully forgive him. One day he had been courting her—and the next he was gone. She secretly hoped there had been important extenuating circumstances and their relationship hadn't ended abruptly simply because he had decided to go elsewhere. *Did I somehow drive him off?* she wondered guiltily.

"I'm sorry, Hussein," she said. "I shouldn't have brought up the past like that, especially in front of your friend, who must at this moment wondering what he has just walked into. Why don't you introduce me?"

"Yes, yes, of course," said Eppler with obvious relief. "This is my American friend Peter Muncaster. He's an oilfield man."

"Hello, Peter," she said.

"Enchanted to make your acquaintance," he said, and he reached out, took her by the hand, and kissed it as if she were a princess.

"Well, well, it's good to see we still have some gentlemen in this town," she said with a smile.

Eppler motioned her to a chair. "Here, please sit down and have a drink with us. You must be thirsty after your dancing."

He summoned Rossier and ordered a bottle of Veuve Clicquot champagne for the table, which was promptly delivered along with three crystal flutes. As Rossier filled their glasses, Hekmat took a moment to study Hussein Gaafar and Peter Muncaster, who, unbeknownst to her, were well-trained German spies named Johannes Eppler and Heinrich Gerd Sandstette. In her eyes, her old lover looked as dapper as she had remembered him. A man who enjoyed the finer things in life, he had always been a stylish dresser. He wore a handsome cream-colored jacket, gray trousers, and open-necked shirt that a businessman might wear. His friend Muncaster wore a dark-blue, striped suit and was tall, strongly-built, and clean-shaven, with fair hair and blue eyes.

"Let's have a toast," said Eppler. "To the most magnificent performer of *danse du ventre* in all of Cairo, indeed the whole world."

"And to old friends," she added.

They clinked glasses and sipped their champagne. As the bubbly settled into their stomachs, she asked, "So, Hussein, what brings you to Cairo? Are you working on behalf of the war effort?"

"Not directly. I have been living and working on my stepfather's large farm in Assiut. He has passed away and there is a lot of work to be done."

"I am sorry to hear Salah has passed away."

"You remember his name. Impressive."

"Of course I remember him—and your mother Johanna too. You had me over for dinner many times. Do you not remember?"

"Indeed I do. Those were wonderful times."

They fell into a momentary silence. He glanced around the rooftop, and she couldn't help but feel that he seemed a touch nervous, as if searching for prying eyes.

"It's funny," he said. "Returning here to Cairo, it almost seems as if there isn't even a war going on. If not for the presence of so many British soldiers, you would never suspect that a few hundred miles to the west a dreadful war is raging in Libya."

She looked at him glumly. "But unfortunately, there is a war on and it is killing men by the tens of thousands."

"Yes, but it doesn't involve me—and it doesn't involve you either. It is Europe's war, though they have invaded our beloved country. Although I can see that for you, business is booming. I have been told—and now have seen with my own eyes—how popular you are with the British officers. They can't get enough of you."

"Yes well, a single girl has to do something to pay the bills—without having to lie flat on her back." She took a sip of champagne. "By the way, where are you two staying?"

At this, he and Muncaster exchanged nervous glances, and she couldn't help but feel that something was going on. But what? Were they really just visiting the city, or were they in fact black marketeers or informers of some kind? Or could they possibly be military spies? If so, were they working for the British or Germans?

"We are staying in a flat at Sharia Boursa el Guedida."

"I know that place. That is not a good part of town. Why would you want to stay there?"

"The British officers have taken all the good lodgings in town. We were unable to find other suitable accommodations," said Sandstette by way of explanation. "But we are looking for a new place."

"Yes, quite so," said Eppler. "Any place you might recommend? You always had exceptional taste."

"I live on a *dahabia* on the Nile in Agouza. I like it there and you might too. There are many houseboats on the river that would serve as excellent lodgings for the two of you."

"That sounds delightful. Might you be able to help us in that regard?"

"I might. Why don't you come back here on Saturday night and we can talk some more. I am giving a show that night. Now I'm afraid I must mingle with the crowd and visit with my admirers. If you gentlemen will excuse me."

"There's no rest for the beautiful and talented, I can see that," said Eppler good-naturedly.

"As I said, a girl has to make a living, especially in wartime."

"You were wonderful, Miss Fahmy," said Sandstette. "I look forward to seeing you on Saturday night."

"Me too," said Eppler with a playful grin. "But I have to be careful because I can already see myself falling head over heels for you again."

"I'm sorry, Hussein, but you already had your chance. I'm afraid this ship has sailed."

"That may be, but after seeing you again in the flesh, I am not sure that I can give up on trying to win over your affections," he said, and she could tell he meant it. "You have carved out a special place in my heart."

"And you have in mine as well," she said, and she, too, meant it. "I'll see you two on Saturday. Perhaps then I might be able to help you find more suitable accommodations."

Eppler reached out and gently touched her hand; she felt a little tingle. "Good night, Hekmat," he said. "And thank you for visiting with us."

"Good night to you too," she said pleasantly. But as she mingled once again with her fans on the rooftop garden, she couldn't help but wonder what Hussein Gaafar's and Peter Muncaster's game was.

CHAPTER 22

BRITISH MIDDLE EAST HEADQUARTERS
GARDEN CITY

JUNE 4, 1942

STARING OUT HIS OFFICE WINDOW on the second floor, Sansom thought of Hekmat Fahmy. While making love to Joan last night, he had pictured the Egyptian belly dancer's smooth bronze face and exquisitely supple body and had become intensely aroused. His poor wife thought that she was the cause of his wild passion and had cuddled up to him afterwards and whispered in his ear like a smitten teenager, and he had felt terribly guilty about it ever since. All morning long, he had hardly been able to concentrate and his work was suffering because of it. The truth was not only did he feel ashamed but he couldn't get the nubile belly dancer out of his mind.

After two more minutes of procrastination mingled with fantasy, he forced himself away from the window and returned to work. His cluttered desk was piled high with case files, memorandums, and dossiers; the latest issues of *The London Times*; the English-language dailies *The Egyptian Mail*, printed in the morning, and *The Egyptian Gazette* appearing in the evening; and the popular Arabic-language daily *Ruz al-Yusuf* and weekly *Al-Ithnayn Wa Al-Dunya*, both approved by the British occupiers. Farouk's acceptance of the British ultimatum of February 4 had marked the end of Egypt's neutrality—but only tacitly since the king still refused to declare war on the Axis Powers—but the acceptance of a democratic Wafd government under Nahhas Pasha had doubled Sansom's work load. While Egypt finally became a legitimate ally for the first time since the outbreak of war, one of the new prime minister's first actions was to set up a committee to deal with the internment of Italian and German nationals—which led to a plethora of arrests and interrogations along with a growing pile of paperwork.

Sammy Sansom and his team at the Field Security Service were at full stretch, both understaffed and overworked. The problem was not only the large number of suspects they had to track down, detain, and question but that the information they obtained was generally trivial and those who came forward had ulterior motives and were less than honest. Spouses betrayed spouses that cheated on them or that they wanted to be rid of. Businessmen tried to get their business partners interned so that they could keep the profits for themselves. Other denunciations came in from competitors. Sansom was amazed at the lengths people would go. Only this morning, he had informed his staff with a combination of disgust and amusement: "Another faithless wife offered to let me sleep with her every Friday if I locked up her Italian husband, who happened to be a loyal member of the anti-fascist group that helped us compile the lists." All of these relatively harmless suspects had to be housed at the Italian school at Boulac.

But a large portion of his time was also being directed at keeping the Free Officers' Movement and other militant Egyptian nationalists under close observation. He had learned that Anwar el Sadat, still a lieutenant in the Signals Unit, and a group of like-minded officers had penned a treaty ready to place before Rommel, stating that the German commander could count on them and their resistance movement. Furthermore, Sadat was reportedly already in contact with Axis forces, according to Sansom's multifarious sources, who had proved right more often than wrong. He was so concerned with Sadat that he had put one of his best men, Sergeant Wilson, on the job to watch the sleepy-eyed signals officer.

Stifling a yawn, he lit up a Dunhill and began flipping through the pages of another interrogation report of an Italian internee. It was then he heard a timid knock on his office door.

"Yes, come in," he said.

The door opened and in stepped Captain Bolton carrying two sheets of paper. "I've got something for you, sir."

"Good Captain, because I was about to fall bloody asleep. What is it?"

"Actually, sir, I'm not quite sure what to make of it. That's why I came to you."

Gesturing him to the sleek brown leather chair in front of his desk, he tapped the ashes of his burning cigarette into the ashtray on his desk next to the black-and-white photograph of his wife. "All right then, let's hear what you've got."

"Yes, sir. It appears that Bletchley Park and MI8's Y Section have identified a potential spy operation in our midst."

"What the devil are you talking about?"

Bolton handed him the sheets of paper, both inscribed at the top with a "Most Secret" marking in red ink. The young captain then began describing the summary of the decrypted radio communications while Sansom read the written text. The brief summary report was signed by Colonel G.J. Jenkins, Defense Security Officer with the Security Intelligence Middle East (SIME) in Cairo, a separate department from Sansom's Field Security Wing.

Though Sansom had access to intercepted and decrypted German wireless communications, he was not high up enough to be privy to Ultra or Most Secret Sources and was, therefore, given condensed summaries that omitted how certain intelligence had been obtained. Most Secret Sources was the official name of the Ultra top secret radio intercept system British intelligence had at its disposal, since the Allies had cracked the German Enigma code in 1940 and were able to read all German radio traffic at Bletchley Park, the location of British decoding efforts in Europe. The Government Code and Cipher School was hidden deep in the Buckinghamshire countryside, monitoring and decoding German military radio communications as if reading the enemy's mail. Thus, the British knew virtually every move Kesselring and Rommel were planning to make in the Mediterranean theater of operations before events happened.

Ultra served as a critical counterbalance to Bonner Fellers's intercepted communiques and the British Eighth Army's sloppy radio transmission protocols at the front lines. Thanks to slack Eighth Army wireless procedures and the brilliance of Captain Alfred Seebohm, Rommel's Wireless Reconnaissance Unit 621 continued to routinely eavesdrop upon British radio communications. In fact, Unit 621 had been snatching a steady flow of high-grade tactical intelligence out of the airwaves, including information on the British order of battle. But Ultra—which allowed the Allies to read every shred of German radio traffic—was still far more far-reaching and valuable than any intelligence coup the Germans had made, including the penetration of the U.S. Black Code.

Bolton said, "It seems that a German Commando successfully crossed the Libyan Desert and made its way to the outskirts of Assiut in late May, before making a return journey back to Tripoli."

"Yes, I can see it here. Operation Salam, commanded by the Hungarian count and desert explorer Captain Almasy of the Abwehr. But it doesn't say anything about the purpose of the expedition."

"Doesn't it mean, sir, that Almasy himself is on a secret mission to Cairo?"

"I think you're reading too much between the lines, Captain. It says nothing to that effect here."

"But it does mention him by name."

"Yes, that's true." He read the DSO summary one more time while puffing on his cigarette. "Bloody hell, it says here that the communication was intercepted on May 25. That's two weeks ago."

"We can thank the Long Range Shepheard's Group for that, sir," replied Bolton, referring to the nickname bestowed upon British staff officers who spent most of their time propping up the bars in clubs and hotels like Shepheard's. "It's too bad. No doubt we've missed an opportunity to deploy a unit to intercept Almasy."

"Yes well, at least they're on it now. It says here that the LRDG and Sudan Defense Force sent out patrols yesterday looking for him. Furthermore, apparently Captain Ken Lazarus's patrol found Almasy's fresh tracks at Wadi el Aqaba."

"Where is that again, sir?"

"It's the main route through the Gilf Kebir." He continued looking over the brief. "It also says here that they mined the track and set up an observation post, but Almasy was long gone."

"It's a bugger, sir. But it still appears we could have a spy in our midst, wouldn't you agree?"

"Unfortunately, we don't know that for certain. In fact, we don't know much of anything except Almasy is on the prowl. It may very well have been merely a scouting expedition and no spy was delivered."

"Or spies. There could be more than one, right sir?"

"Quite correct, Wilson. But to know one way or the other, we're going to need more information. A lot more bloody information. Now good day, Captain. Come see me again when you've got more."

And with that he cast an irritated glance at the huge pile of paperwork on his desk, stamped out his cigarette in his ashtray, and quickly lit another.

CHAPTER 23

PETER STIRLING FLAT
13 SHARIA IBRAHIM PASHA NAGUIB
GARDEN CITY

JUNE 4, 1942

AT HALF PAST FOUR, Stirling left the barbed-wire-enclosed GHQ building and walked down Sharia Ibrahim Pasha Naguib towards his brother's flat. Though the *khamsin* season had ended, it was still unusually hot for early June and sweat clung to his khaki officer's uniform. His meeting with the director of military operations and senior staff officers had gone reasonably well. But he was still rankled that many of them considered the SAS a band of bearded ruffians and saboteurs rather than an important military force in its own right—despite the fact that for the past nine months his unit had proven itself time and again.

During the meeting, he was told that a British convoy of merchant ships would run the Mediterranean gauntlet during the middle of June to try and relieve Malta. What could he and his outfit do behind enemy lines to reduce enemy attacks from the air? He promised the military planners that in twenty-four hours he would return to GHQ with a detailed plan that would help rescue the beleaguered British colony.

He continued strolling down the street, wincing ever so slightly. Unfortunately, his broken wrist, bound in a plaster cast, and his back were giving him a spot of trouble. But walking made him feel better. He also still suffered from what the doctors described as a "stress disorder" over the car accident; he still could not forgive himself for accidentally killing the celebrated journalist Arthur Merton and for the serious injuries to Randolph Churchill and Fitzroy Maclean. Five minutes later, he reached his brother's flat, located directly across from the British Embassy where Peter worked.

From the outside it wasn't much to look at. But inside was a spacious three-bedroom, two-bathroom apartment. Stirling stayed at the flat whenever he was in town for meetings at GHQ following desert raids, and he had turned it into his own SAS headquarters—with Peter's blessing. He had set up shop here partly because it was more comfortable than GHQ, but mostly because it gave him greater privacy and he was less likely to be interfered with by bureaucratic busybodies. The talk of Cairo, his brother's lodgings were frequently the scene of debauched revelry. They served as not only the unofficial HQ of the burgeoning SAS but a banquet hall, temporary barracks, spare equipment storage center, and dead-letter box. Cluttered with topographic maps, guns, papers, empty bottles, full ashtrays—and, in 1941 during a particularly drunken night of revelry, a recalcitrant donkey they had hauled up the stairs—the flat was presided over not by Peter or David Stirling, or their eldest brother Bill of the Special Operations Executive who also spent considerable time there between operations, but by a resourceful Egyptian butler and sufragi named Mohamed Aboudi.

A plump, Luxor-born Egyptian, "Mo," as he was known by the Stirlings and their friends, had stripped the English language to its bare essentials, but his word was sacrosanct. Serving in the role of majordomo, barman, unofficial quartermaster, and first line of defense against authority, he possessed an uncanny talent for simultaneously mixing pink gins, arranging wild parties, obtaining ammunition and vehicle spare parts, answering the telephone, and tidying up after the irreverent brothers. But before Mo would render service to any of Peter's friends, it was necessary for him to like them. He liked David, and consequently had proven to be a far more successful military aide-de-camp than anyone the army could have given Stirling. He was discreet and David used him to liaise directly with GHQ to chase down ammunition, rations, and other necessary equipment for the SAS.

He was also adept at patching up the walls and calming the neighbors, after the Stirlings and their friends had staged late-night revolver-shooting competitions in the sitting room, kitchen, or dining room. To hide the bullet holes from the nosy landlord, Mo would re-hang framed cut-outs of King George VI and Queen Elizabeth over them as temporary concealment. It was generally agreed in Cairo that Mo would do anything to protect the brothers and was the true ruler of the Stirling fiefdom at 13 Sharia Ibrahim Pasha Naguib.

When David knocked on the door to his brother's apartment, he was instantly vetted by Mo.

"Who is it?"

"David, back from the dead at GHQ."

"Yes, you come in."

"Thank you, Mo, my good man."

He stepped inside. They smiled at one another. With fondness, Stirling remembered back to the time Mo had openly admitted that he loved the brothers most of all because they were great landowners in what he called "Scotchland" and because David had served in the "Scotchguards."

"Where's my brother?" Stirling politely asked.

"They shooting again. I told them not to but they not listen."

Shaking his head with amusement, Stirling headed into the flat. It looked more like a college fraternity house than the home of an important diplomat. The sitting room sofas were a nondescript gray, dotted with cigarette burns, and stained with a grimy black line at head level. New photographs of the British king and queen cut from magazines had been glued to the walls only this morning—to hide the marks of last night's indoor revolver practice. On a table in the hall was a pile of letters, addressed to officers who might be dead, or in prison camps, or coming back at any moment. In the corridor leading to the bedrooms and bathroom was a telephone, the wall above it gray with doodles and scribbled telephone numbers. The bathroom was piled high with uniform cases, captured German ammunition, and a pair of elephant tusks; while SAS bedrolls and kit-bags were strewn about the bedrooms.

He went onto the kitchen, where he found Peter and his SAS second-in-command, Captain Paddy Mayne, setting up targets on the wall for a shooting competition.

"Ah yes, the prodigal older brother returns," said Peter. "How was your meeting with the Long Range Shepheard's Group?"

"Yes, how was your meeting, David old boy?" echoed Paddy Mayne sardonically and with a hint of competitive fire. A huge shaggy-bearded man from Northern Ireland, Mayne was a hard drinker and aspiring writer with a tendency towards fisticuffs and violence. He had been a rugby player of international fame before the war and looked it. For his actions at the Wadi Tamet raid last December—where he had destroyed fourteen aircraft and several petrol dumps—he had been awarded the Distinguished Service Order. His brave actions had helped keep the SAS in existence following the failure of the disastrous initial raid behind enemy lines at the Axis airfields of Timimi and Gazala during gale-force winds. For that and his unquestioned competence in special operations, Stirling was indebted to him, though they still clashed and competed excessively with schoolboy stubbornness from time to time.

"It was interesting," replied Stirling, with characteristic understatement and vagueness. "Who's winning the shooting competition?"

"We haven't started yet," said Peter. "But I don't know why we even bother. I'm the best shot."

"Hardly, Brother," said Stirling. "That would be me."

"No, I'm a better shot than the both of you put together," said Mayne. "But we're going to have to postpone this friendly little competition until you've given me a full debriefing, Major." He set down his pistol on the kitchen table.

"Right-eo," said Peter. "I'll have Mo bring us a round of gin fizzes. To the military planning room then, gents."

David smiled; his younger brother might as well have been a member of the SAS since he was privy to as much information on its inner workings as any officer in the unit. He knew this was the price for using Peter's flat as his own personal Middle East HQ. As Peter shuffled off to find Mo, Stirling and Mayne stepped into the spare bedroom that had been converted into an office. It was high-ceilinged and spacious, with a table at the window covered with maps, charts, intelligence reports, and aerial photographs. In the corner were a pair of SAS bedrolls and kit-bags belonging to NCOs Johnny Cooper and Reg Seekings, whom Stirling was becoming increasingly reliant on for logistical planning.

The two officers looked down at the map of North Africa and the Mediterranean on the table.

"Here's the Gazala Line where the heaviest fighting is going on," said Stirling, pointing to the map. "Our objective in the campaign is to attack the airfields in Cyrenaica behind the line to relieve the pressure on Malta."

"Malta? Not Tobruk?"

"Both actually, but Malta is the more pressing matter at present. With every passing day, the plight of the besieged island is growing more ominous and it is becoming increasingly difficult to supply. Apparently, they are hanging on by a slender thread. In the moonless period of mid-June, two convoys are to set out from Alexandria and Gibraltar to try to reach Malta with vital supplies. Churchill believes that it would be a disaster of the first magnitude if the island is taken and probably fatal in the long run to the defense of the Nile Delta. So while Ritchie and Auchinleck duke it out with Rommel along the Gazala Line, GHQ wants us to hit the airfields behind his line to limit the Luftwaffe's attacks on Malta."

Always one to rise to a challenge, Paddy Mayne beamed with excitement. "It would nice to stick it to Jerry in a big, big way. How many airfields do you want to hit this time?"

"That's just it—I want this to be our most sweeping op to date. I want to simultaneously raid six airfields around Benghazi on the night of June 13 and hit a seventh airfield on Crete the same night." He traced his fingers across the map from Northern Libya to the huge Greek island. "We'll have to go to Crete by submarine. For the others, it's the LRDG taxi service."

"I wish we had our own vehicles."

"We'll get them eventually. But for now, we have to use the LRDG."

They talked some more and then Peter reappeared with Mo, who was carrying a tray of cocktails.

"Oh, how delightful, Mo," said David, taking a gin fizz. "Thank you so much."

"Drink and stop Nazis," said the servant-factotum. "They no friend of Egypt."

They all laughed. "Don't worry, Mo, we'll get the bastards, all right," roared Paddy Mayne, and he proceeded to down half his gin fizz.

"Good, only good Nazi is dead Nazi. I go shopping for groceries now—you make own refreshments from here on out," said Mo, and he finished doling out the drinks and shuffled off.

Peter took a sip of his gin fizz and stared down at the map. "All right, what plan are you two rascals cooking up now?"

"We're going to attack seven airfields simultaneously from Benghazi to Crete and cause Jerry all kinds of trouble," said David, pointing to the map.

"Oh, how wonderful. When are the attacks going to take place?"

"Nine days from now on June 13th. That's the next dark period, though not completely moonless. We'll have seven patrols committed to seven different target airfields. Oh and by the way, we're going to save Malta."

"Malta? Like knights in shining armor—I absolutely fucking love it."

ΨΨΨ

Over the next eight hours, Stirling and Paddy Mayne worked out the details. The next morning, Stirling was back at GHQ with a detailed plan. As he and Mayne had discussed, they would send seven patrols to raid seven separate airfields on the night of June 13th and 14th. The patrols would operate in four different areas: two airfields in the Benghazi sector; three more in the vicinity of Derna, a coastal town about one hundred miles west of Tobruk; one at Barce airfield which lay sixty miles east of Benghazi; and the seventh on Heraklion aerodrome in Crete.

This time the operation would include French SAS troops. A contingent of fifty-two Free French paratroopers under the command of Colonel Georges Berge had become available to him in the spring and Stirling intended to put them to use and make sure they felt part of the team. The Frenchmen were "tough cases" who had escaped Nazi-occupied France and trained as parachutists in Britain. They were itching for an opportunity to take the fight to the Germans, and were more than willing to do so under any established Allied command. Thankfully, most of the British officers had at least a smattering of French, and a few of the French parachutists spoke English; even so, to avoid communication problems, it was agreed that smaller fighting units would be composed of one nationality or the other, while still operating under Stirling's overall command. Ordinarily, mixing French and British soldiers might be a recipe for friction, but Stirling had found that in actual practice the relations were quite agreeable, though the forces teased each other endlessly.

The French had not taken part in any operations up until now and Stirling believed that they were ready to make a major contribution to the SAS. In fact, he wanted this to be mainly their show. Therefore, out of seven patrols, six would be led by Commander Berge and his Frenchmen. He not only wanted to rest and retrain some of his own men, but he felt that the French had been kept in a state of uncertainty and anticipation for far too long. Making the current operation primarily a French op would be crucial for the long-term integration of the two nationalities. Commander Berge would lead the Crete raid; Lieutenant Jordan, his second-in-command, would take three French patrols to Derna Martuba; Lieutenant Andre Zirnheld, another French officer, would tackle Barce, and Lieutenant Jaquier would travel with Stirling and Paddy Mayne to the Benghazi area where they would launch a triple operation.

Each raiding party would not number more than five men. Maps, transport, and timetables would be studied closely, while GHQ Intelligence kept the planners informed of critical last-minute developments. The airfields were the most critical objectives, but they would also be the most difficult to reach without detection. Stirling and Mayne left much of the administrative work to Johnny Cooper and Reg Seekings, both of whom had recently been promoted to the rank of sergeant. Stirling found them dependable, and even though they were opposites in temperament, they seemed to have an intuitive rapport between them and knack for collaborative problem-solving. While Cooper and Seekings would assemble the necessary rations, weapons, camouflage, and ammunition, he and Mayne decided to have Mike Sadler calculate distances and petrol requirements to make sure they could reach their objectives and still get back to their desert base.

After the briefing at GHQ, Stirling returned back to his brother's flat, which was already abuzz with activity in preparation for the assault just nine days away. Supplies were calculated and issued; the latest intelligence reports and aerial photographs were reviewed in intimate detail; and travel routes were determined. On the face of it, he knew his plan was a masterpiece of simplicity. But the devil was in the details, and he and Mayne knew the unexpected problems they would encounter in the field had not even been remotely considered.

But they had to move—and move smartly they would.

CHAPTER 24

CONTINENTAL HOTEL, CAIRO

JUNE 6, 1942

HEKMAT PERFORMED TWO SHOWS on Saturday night. She was introduced both times by an attractive platinum-blonde American in a long chiffon dress, who rounded off the first performance with a solo dance. This she began with the words, "And now, introducing myself—Betty to you—in a beguine straight from the faraway Island of Martinique that you're going to absolutely adore!" Hekmat and the other dancing girls, as well as her fans in the audience, knew her as "Betty-To-You" on account of her standard introduction. Hekmat's second performance was followed by a pair of Hungarian acrobats and a Mr. Cardman who did card tricks, though not very well. After changing into formal evening wear after her second show, she made her way perfunctorily through the crowd, doling out polite cheek-kisses and signing autographs.

Eventually, she made her way to see Eppler, posing as the Egyptian Hussein Gaafar, and Sandstette, masquerading as the American Peter Muncaster, at their table, where she had a drink and talked with them for a while. Sitting with them was Albert Wahda, whom Hekmat did not know. Unbeknownst to her, the pimp had latched onto the two German spies for easy money, acting as a messenger and gofer. Eppler informed her that he and his American friend had moved out of Madame Guillemet's lodgings at Sharia Boursa el Guedida and wondered if they could stay on her *dahabia* on the Nile just for one night, to which she kindly consented. Just before midnight, she left the Continental with the three men and drove in her luxurious silver Cadillac 90 Town Car through town to the Bahr el-Ama section of the Nile where her houseboat was moored between el-Guezira and the western bank.

Parking the car along the Shariah el-Nil within sight of a white lookout-tower that stood like an exclamation mark, they strode up the street and then towards the river to her houseboat. The Agouza district of Cairo, situated along the Bahr el-Ama arm of the Nile, was a newly developed area with attractive new villas; East and West had taken the upper hand in Cairo by turns over the centuries and the eclectic architecture reflected the complex history of the city's occupation from the Caesars to the Ottomans to the French and now the British.

Walking up the gangway leading to the houseboat, they stepped under the massive awning and then belowdecks, where Hekmat served each of them a drink and gave them a tour. The air inside the houseboat was pleasantly cool from the breezes coming off the river. It was a very attractive *dahabia*, with a large sundeck, an elegant stateroom and dining room, a hand-carved mahogany bar, and two plush bedrooms with large beds and silken mosquito nets below the bulkheads. Her furnishings were a mix of Egyptian and British styles. The gossamer curtains at the windows, elegant divans, and other attractive cover materials and furniture had been chosen with great taste by Hekmat herself.

During the tour, she showed them the bedroom where they would sleep and had them store their belongings inside the room alongside those of her lover, Captain Guy Bellairs, whom she informed them had returned to the fighting at the front. She noted that her former lover Hussein looked a touch disappointed when she mentioned that she had another lover—and a British officer at that—but he seemed to get over it quickly.

"I must say this is quite swanky," said Eppler as they returned to the stateroom, drinks in hand, and took their seats on the comfortable divans with silk pillows.

"I'm glad you like it," she replied.

"By the way, when will your boyfriend be back? I hope there's no chance of him popping in later tonight while we're sleeping." He looked at Muncaster, who was grinning. "Peter and I shouldn't like to have an angry British officer after us."

"Guy was called away quite suddenly and didn't say when he'd be back. But from what I hear, the battle at the Gazala Line is fierce right now and is not expected to end anytime soon."

"Yes, I heard that Rommel has turned the British flank at Bir Hacheim and they are fighting in a place called 'the Cauldron.' The fighting's said to be some of the bloodiest of the war."

"If that's the case, I hope Guy's not there," she said with genuine concern. "He's a captain so I imagine he will be in the thick of it. But his fate is in God's hands."

"You really do love him, don't you?"

She looked at Muncaster and Albert Wahda, who were both smiling. She didn't particularly like them and certainly didn't want them to hear about her private life.

"Yes, I love Guy. He takes me out and makes me laugh and buys me pretty things. But he is still a snob—like most British officers stationed here in Egypt." She leaned forward in her seat, fixing him with a resolute gaze. "But let's not talk about me—let's talk about you. Where did you go when you abandoned me all those years ago? When was it, back in August of '37?"

"That's quite right—you have a good memory."

"Are you going to answer my question?"

"I took a job with a shipping firm that found my knowledge of German useful. I was based in Alexandria and Port Said. I also ran a small cotton business in Alexandria."

She had the sneaky suspicion he wasn't telling her the complete truth, but rather than challenge him she tried to look intrigued. "And when did you quit that job and go to work on your father's farm?"

"About a year ago."

"You said your father passed away?"

"Yes, seven months ago." Prior to his death, Salah Gaafar had been a retired Egyptian judge and farm owner. "My mother told me about it. I visited her the other day."

"Where does she live now?"

"Old Town Cairo. Her address is Sharia Masr al Khadina 10."

Hekmat was impressed. "That is a good place to live: very affluent."

"I visited her at home. I spoke to her for a long time but my stepbrother Hassan was out. Peter and I could stay with her, but I didn't want to impose."

"That is probably for the best as I have found a place for you two."

Eppler's eyes lit up. "You have? Where?"

She noted that Muncaster, too, practically jumped up from his seat. "Yes, where?" he asked.

"It is a *dahabia* right here in Agouza, only a two-minute walk away near the Egyptian Benevolent Hospital. Houseboat Number 10. The owner is Mohamed Badr Awab. I didn't speak with him—I just saw the 'For Rent' sign out front. You can contact him tomorrow and make the necessary arrangements."

"That is wonderful news, Hekmat," said Eppler.

"How much is it?" asked Sandstette.

"I believe the sign said fifteen pounds per month with a forty-pound deposit, but you will probably be able to talk him down. I have been inside the houseboat before and it is well-furnished and roomy, with an elegant stateroom and a great sundeck complete with a mahogany bar. You will be able to entertain many young lady friends there, I imagine."

Eppler gave a mischievous grin and clutched his chest. "Ah, but my heart is reserved for you, my dear Hekmat."

"As I told you before, you had your chance. I have another man now and he happens to be a British officer. And just so you know, your *dahabia* is next to another British officer."

Sandstette gave a look of surprise. "The houseboat is next to where a British officer lives?"

"Is that a problem?"

Eppler laughed. "No, of course it is not a problem. It is perfect. We know we will be safe if we have a British officer living next to us. What is his name?"

"Major Smith. He's with the Intelligence Corps."

"I feel safer already," said Eppler.

She detected a note of sarcasm and, once again, wondered what kind of game her former lover and his American friend were up to. And what were they doing hanging out with a low-life like Albert Wahda? The man had to be an underworld figure of some sort. It was all very puzzling and she didn't want to get mixed up in anything. But she told herself it was just for one night.

She rose up from her chair. "I'm going to bed," she said. "Please don't wake me before ten."

"We wouldn't dream of it," said Eppler. "Right, lads?"

Sandstette and Wahda nodded in agreement.

"And be sure not to tamper with Guy's things. He's very fussy about his belongings."

Eppler smiled. "We wouldn't dream of that either, my dear," he said.

"Good night then," she said.

"Goodnight, my darling Hekmat, and thanks again for your hospitality."

ψψψ

Later that night, when Hekmat Fahmy was fast asleep, Eppler and Sandstette awoke from the spare room and, ignoring her warning, proceeded to go through Captain Bellairs's personal gear while the pimp and money changer Wahda snored up on the deck beneath the awning. They swiftly discovered that the British officer had left behind a briefcase containing personal and military papers. They thought they had hit the jackpot when they found a pair of maps showing troop dispositions in Tripoli and the defenses of Tobruk, until they realized that they were Italian maps dating prior to the British occupation in 1941.

Eppler knew that if Hekmat had known about their rummaging through her lover's belongings, she would have been furious. Which is why he didn't whisper a word to her. She never suspected their subterfuge, and fortuitously the next day he and Sandstette got their coveted houseboat.

The two agents looked it over thoroughly, and everything they saw satisfied them that the *dahabia* was the ideal solution to their problems. Sandstette found a well-camouflaged hiding place for the transmitter under a radiogram, and the aerials on deck were unlikely to attract attention. The houseboat was equipped with two ladders leading belowdecks, which would allow the spies to escape in a hurry should the authorities close in on them. The sundeck and well-stocked mahogany bar were just as good as advertised, and Eppler was pleased to see that belowdecks the boat was furnished to a near exotic degree, with soft divans and gossamer curtains just like Hekmat's. And they even managed to talk the owner down to a price of £12 a month for the boat with a £30 deposit.

Later that night, at precisely midnight, Sandstette attempted to raise the Germans with his radio, using his *Rebecca* codebook and the call sign "HGS" at 14,430 kilocycles. When the wireless transmission was complete, he and Eppler stood by and waited to hear "HWB" in reply from *Schildkroete*—Lance Corporal Weber—at Rommel's mobile HQ.

But once again, the reply never came.

CHAPTER 25

RIGEL RIDGE AND KNIGHTSBRIDGE BOX
CYRENAICA, LIBYA

JUNE 13, 1942

"WHERE ARE MY 'GOOD SOURCE' DECRYPTS, DAMNIT!" snapped Rommel, staring through his field glasses as his Panzer column advanced inexorably towards the 2nd Scots Guards position on Rigel Ridge. His caravan of staff vehicles and signals trucks had come to a momentary halt along an outcrop of vuggy limestone. He had mauled the Free French and El Adem box defensive boxes, the southern and central anchors of the Gazala Line, while his tanks lunged ahead to roll up the British defensive boxes to the north and, where possible, outflank the enemy. Standing with him atop his *Mammut* Moritz were his new chief of staff Colonel Fritz Bayerlein, a forty-three-year-old career soldier from Würzburg; his liaison officer Lieutenant Wischmann; his clerk Munninger; and his driver von Leipzig.

Wischmann looked at him sheepishly. "I don't know, sir. The decrypts should be here any minute."

"I need them now—not an hour from now! We are about to attack!"

"*Jawohl, General!* I'll see what I can do!"

The young liaison officer jumped down from the command vehicle and dashed to the signals truck. Rommel cursed under his breath. During the past two weeks of fighting at Bir Hacheim, the Cauldron, and other pressure points along the Gazala Line, he had become increasingly reliant on the daily Cairo decrypts from his liaison officer. In some cases, he was able to read *Gute Quelle's* secret reports two hours after Fellers signed off transmission. The details supplied unwittingly by the American military attaché had for the past six months given the Desert Fox a massive advantage in the strategic and tactical decisions of Ritchie and Auchinleck; and in the recent see-saw battle he had become so dependent on his Good Source that he would delay his own troop deployments until he had received Wischmann's decrypts. In fact, he was becoming increasingly irked when Fellers's transmissions were not delivered by his morning breakfast.

Five minutes later, the liaison officer reappeared, but was unfortunately still empty-handed. Rommel shook his head in disgust and ordered his *Kampfstaffel* forward, leading the *Afrika Korps* north in the direction of Tobruk. Once in position with the Knightsbridge box on his left and Rigel Ridge to the north, he gave the personal order to attack.

"Forward Panzers!" he roared, waving his arm forward like a catapult.

After being routed in the field, the British armor and infantry were trying to regroup at the Knightsbridge box and the nearby ridge. Here the Scots Guards, supported by South African anti-tank gunners, did their best to hold him and his *Panzerarmee* at bay and bar his passage to Tobruk. They put up stout resistance and the enemy's 6th Battery delivered fierce artillery fire to delay his tanks from overtaking the position, but they could not hold out for long. His Panzers lay hull-down on the ridge with 50-mm anti-tank guns on the ground between them and the enemy, which engaged his armor with open sights. Supported by a lethal screen of 88s, his tanks maintained devastating armor-piercing machine-gun fire on the 6th Battery until all eight of the enemy's big guns were put out of action.

Once the batteries were silenced, he commanded his Panzers to approach cautiously and take the surviving battery personnel prisoners. Surrendering soldiers stepped out of caves, pill boxes, trenches, and from behind rocky outcrops with their hands in the air. Driving through the smoldering wasteland, he was moved by the stalwart resistance of the outnumbered enemy. It looked to him as if well over half the artillery detachments had been killed or wounded, including the battery commander and most of the officers. Almost every gun had the body of a Scots Guardsman drooped across the shoulder piece or slumped over the breech. Several men were still crouching in slit trenches with rifles, having been engaging the enemy even after their guns had been put out of action. He saw an officer lying on his face, his finger still gripped tightly around the trigger of a Bren gun.

My God, he thought, *they seem to have served their country even in death.* Inwardly, he saluted them.

He called for von Leipzig to bring the giant *Mammut* to a halt and studied the remaining British position to the south. The Knightsbridge box was his next objective. The remnants of the Scots Guards were retreating down into the box and it was too late to cut them off. But he knew it wasn't much of a sanctuary. The ground was too level, and once his Panzers were on top of the enemy, they would be finished. There would be nothing between his army and Tobruk.

"We have them on the ropes now," he said to Bayerlein, who was also staring down at the entrenched British position. "Give the order to bring every gun we have to bear upon that box."

"Yes, General," replied the colonel.

"These Scots and the South Africans have fought bravely. But they suffer from poor leadership at the top. This, combined with the British rigid lack of mobility, is their downfall. It's why we will overrun them and destroy their armor, either today or during their retreat tonight."

"Retreat? Are you certain?"

"They will use the cover of the sandstorm." He pointed to the south, where a brown curtain of windblown sand seemed to be gathering force. The Libyans called the towering storms *el-ghibli*. Originating from hot, dry, usually southeasterly dust-bearing winds, they occurred throughout the year but were most prevalent in spring and early summer. Greatly feared by the Bedouin and other desert dwellers of North Africa, they could last for days, make life miserable, and completely change the landscape in a matter of hours by moving vast quantities of eolian sand.

"How much time do we have, sir, before it is upon us?" asked Munninger.

"Maybe two or three hours. But I think it will get worse towards nightfall."

"It does seem to be growing," agreed Bayerlein, reaching for his radio handset.

At that moment, airplanes appeared from the northwest. It was a squadron of Stuka dive bombers. The pilots came in low, sirens screaming, and delivered their armor-piercing 500- and 1,000-pound bombs, ignoring the formidable screen of flak thrown up by the British guns. Within minutes, the Germans unleashed a reign of terror, scoring a dozen direct hits on enemy tanks and artillery and leaving the Knightsbridge box a smoking ruin.

And then another wave rushed in, but this time British fighters swooped in to intercept them from the northeast. The Luftwaffe pilots banked hard to the east to escape the nimble Hurricanes and suddenly the Stukas were heading straight towards Rommel and his staff caravan with the British hot on their tail.

He knew in that terrible moment that he and his men were in trouble.

"They're coming this way! Take cover!" he cried, and they jumped from the command vehicle and dove into the trenches abandoned by the enemy.

With a top speed of less than 250 mph, Stuka dive bombers were easy targets, for a half-decent shot from a Hurricane or even a slower Kittyhawk could knock them down from the sky. As they took cover, the Stukas, lame ducks that they were, raced right over his *Kampfstaffel* and dropped their bombs to increase their speed and make their escape. The friendly-fire explosions ripped through the sand and rock and brought a violent shudder to the ridge. The British fighters managed to take down one of the Stukas but then two Messerschmitts appeared on the scene and opened fire on the Hurricanes, bailing the dive bombers out of trouble.

"Is everyone all right?" asked Rommel when the planes had passed and the cloud of smoke and dust had cleared.

Bayerlein answered affirmatively and was echoed by Wischmann, Munninger, and von Leipzig, who had once again miraculously managed to avoid even a scratch.

"Good. Let's get out of here before they come back. The Tommies would like nothing more than to wipe out our *Kampfstaffel*."

They climbed back into Moritz and took off in a hurry, heading down from the heights into the broad plain below. Along the way, he received his daily intercepted report from Fellers in Cairo.

He was ecstatic.

He knew he was pounding the British into submission, but he now had precise figures to back it up. According to the reliable U.S. military attaché, Ritchie had only around 100 tanks left in running order, which for the first time was fewer than he had himself. To Rommel, it seemed almost unthinkable that the current battle—which had begun so disastrously for him 17 days earlier—was now his for the taking. All the same, the British were like a wounded lion. It was clear that there would be heavy fighting in the days ahead as they struggled to hold on to the Acroma position to keep a retreat road open along the Via Balbia for their troops.

At the same time, Rommel knew that he had lost heavily as well. True, by the end of the day he was likely to have a superiority of more than two to one in tanks fit for action; and being in possession of the battlefield, he would be able to continue to recover and repair many of his damaged tanks, while Ritchie was under so much pressure he could not. But he was not out of the woods yet and the resilient Tommies could be counted on to fight hard to the bitter end.

He charged on towards the battlefield. The fighting was in full throttle, his Panzers advancing while his anti-tank guns took out the enemy artillery and armor. Though the sandstorm had not yet hit, the pall of dust above the Knightsbridge box was thick from the shells and bombs crashing upon the hand-dug slit-trenches.

While the fighting raged on, he acted rapidly on intelligence obtained from British radio traffic intercepts from Seebohm and his 621st Wireless Reconnaissance Unit.

By late afternoon, the Knightsbridge box was surrounded, the British tank strength had been reduced from 300 tanks to 70, and his army had established armor superiority and a dominating line of positions, posing a severe threat to cutting off the enemy on the Gazala Line. From one of Seebohm's radio intercepts, he learned that the British soldiers were already calling the debacle "Black Saturday."

"Ritchie has no choice but to abandon the position now," he said as his tanks and infantry edged closer to the box. "Unless he wants to lose more good infantry."

"That seems to be exactly what is happening," said Bayerlein, standing next to him in the command vehicle as they stared through their binoculars. "Look, they are sending up smoke now to cover their withdrawal."

A strong force of Matilda tanks had arrived and the British were slipping away under a cloud of smoke, just as the sandstorm struck Rigel Ridge to the northeast and Knightsbridge. The Desert Fox saw plainly that the British had no cover from anti-tank fire; indeed, in preparation for the breakout, the commander was moving his tanks forwards and backwards a few hundred yards, trying to confuse him. But it was the sandstorm that saved the day for the Tommies. It was as if nature had intervened to bail them out, and Rommel, despite the fact that he wanted to vanquish the enemy with the full weight of his *Panzerarmee*, couldn't help but feel as if divine providence had come to their rescue.

"Shouldn't we chase after them and destroy them, sir?" asked Bayerlein.

"No, let them go." He watched as the British stole away against a backdrop of darkened sky from the smoke and the menacing *ghibli* sweeping in from the south. "*Krieg Ohne Hass*, Colonel. War Without Hate is how we fight here in North Africa. We have a code." But that was as much sentimentality as the Desert Fox could muster, and he again smacked his hand against the side of the command vehicle, directing von Leipzig to get moving again.

They drove through the southeastern edge of the vacated box. His eyes stinging with smoke, dust, and fatigue, he took in the devastation all around. It was as if a child had thrown a tantrum and tossed his toys all over a room. He saw upturned guns, trucks, and tanks everywhere—many of them still burning. His expression was stony-faced, but inside he felt the Tommies' pain and suffering. They were brave lads, all right, the cream of Britain and its vast but crumbling Empire.

"I have never seen so many dead Englishmen before," observed his young, fellow Schwabian clerk Munninger in disbelief.

"Don't worry," said Rommel. "If we are to win Africa, you will get used to it."

"I almost feel bad for them. They were quite brave," said Bayerlein ruefully.

"Like lions of the desert," agreed the Desert Fox. "Like lions of the desert."

They continued through the wilderness of devastation. Evidence of the British defeat could be seen in all directions. Vast quantities of destroyed and hastily discarded weapons lay all around them. Burnt-out vehicles stood black and empty in the desert sand. Whole convoys of undamaged British lorries had fallen into his hands, many of which his hard-working salvage and mechanical repair squads were already repairing to bring back into service.

As he moved through the battlefield, a captain came rushing up to him in an armored car. "*Generaloberst, Generaloberst!*"

"Yes, what is it?" cried Rommel as he had his driver bring Moritz to a halt.

"I have something for you, sir. When we overran the 150th Infantry Brigade, we captured many documents."

"So?"

"Among the captured documents, we found a copy of an order issued to the 4th Armored Brigade, directing that no food or water be given to captured German or Italian soldiers until they've first been interrogated by British intelligence officers."

"But that's a direct contravention of the Hague Conventions," growled Rommel angrily. "My God, so much for war without hate."

"I thought you should know what the British are up to, sir," said the officer.

"Yes, Captain, I appreciate your bringing this to my attention." He turned to his chief of staff. "Colonel Bayerlein, I hereby instruct you to inform Captain Seebohm and the Signals Section to send a message, in the clear, stating that all British prisoners of war in custody are to be deprived of food and water indefinitely, or until such time as Eighth Army's order is rescinded. Do I make myself clear?"

"Yes, sir," and he jumped to the radio.

Ten minutes later, the sandstorm hit them in full force. Rommel set up his headquarters not far from the Knightsbridge battle site and Rigel Ridge. By 21:00, he was informed from Bayerlein that he had an urgent message from the Führer. With his full staff present, he read over the message. In an order dated June 13, 1942, he was commanded by Hitler to immediately annihilate any and all German political refugees and Jews attached to the Free French forces or any other British units. The Free French at Bir Hacheim consisted of nearly 4,000 troops drawn mainly from France's colonial possessions: Africans from Senegal, Pacific islanders, and Foreign Legionnaires, including German-Jewish leftists whose politics made them wanted men by Hitler and the Reich. Where the refugees escaped being killed in battle, commanded Hitler, they were to be shot out of hand "unless they have to be temporarily retained for the extraction of information." The Führer explicitly forbade the order from being passed on in writing.

Rommel just shook his head in disgust. "This is not how the *Afrika Korps* fights," he said to his officers. "We know what to do with this, don't we gentlemen?"

He crumpled the order and threw it onto the ground. To shoot prisoners or execute or persecute Jews went against his practice of encouraging the enemy to surrender by cultivating a reputation for magnanimity.

But there was more to it than that: he knew it was goddamn wrong.

Two hours later, he listened to a radio broadcast out of Cairo, also in the clear, announcing that the Eighth Army's order refusing water to German and Italian POWs had been rescinded. He was satisfied. Both sides had up to this point fought a clean, almost exemplary, war: atrocities and brutality, which were taken for granted in the Balkans and on the Russian Front, had no place in the Desert Fox's war here in the Libyan desert. Nor would he countenance their introduction by either the British, whom he knew for a fact knew better, or Hitler, whom he admired but knew did not. He recognized that slippery slope for what it was, and refused to take the first step down it—or allow his foes or his Führer to do the same.

CHAPTER 26

JEBEL FOOTHILLS AND BENINA AIRFIELD
BENGHAZI, CYRENAICA, LIBYA

JUNE 13, 1942

AT HALF PAST MIDNIGHT, Stirling peered down from the Jebel escarpment at the target through his binoculars. The Benina airfield was the main repair base for Axis fighters and bombers, and supported all the coastal airfields by supplying airframes, engines, wings, and other spare parts. Below in the faint illumination he could make out a number of large hangars and workshops where the airframes were fitted with new engines. He could also see the runway used by pilots to take off from and test the finished products before they were sent to combat airfields closer to the front. He smiled inwardly: in two hours' time the whole airfield would be blown to kingdom come.

Acting as CO of the entire SAS attack force, his small subunit consisted of himself and Sergeants Johnny Cooper and Reg Seekings. Seekings was a scrappy former amateur boxing champion, blind in one eye and not very bright, who his SAS cohorts compared to "a bad-tempered dog, snarling and scowling." But the two-hundred pounder had one asset that set him apart: he had no compunction about the shedding of blood, whether in the boxing ring or on the battlefield. Consequently, he excelled at the brutal style of commando fighting that many men didn't have the stomach for, which in Stirling's view made him supremely valuable.

The overall attack plan was still the same as what he and Paddy Mayne had worked out in Cairo: six separate SAS subunits would simultaneously raid six airfields around Benghazi while a seventh party would be transported to Crete by submarine to attack the airfield at Heraklion. For Stirling, getting greenlighted by GHQ and completing the planning and equipping of multiple simultaneous missions had proven a daunting logistical enterprise, especially following so swiftly on the heels of his last foray into Benghazi and his recovery from his traumatic car accident. Though he was able to delegate much of the administrative work to the redoubtable Cooper and Seekings, the job had taken a heavy toll on him with his ongoing health problems. These included not just his broken wrist and post-traumatic stress from the car accident but increasingly severe desert sores and debilitating migraines—both of which he unwisely ignored against the orders of the new medical officer attached to the SAS, Dr. Malcolm Pleydell of the Royal Army Medical Corps.

The goal of the raids was simple: to destroy as much of the enemy airpower as possible in a single day, and thereby help ensure that Allied convoys got through to embattled Malta.

They had been anxiously hiding out for more than twelve hours, taking turns while two of them napped and the third kept an eye on the airfield a mile away—all the while swatting away endless waves of pesky sandflies. During the day, the panorama below had been so peaceful that it had almost seemed to Stirling as if a war wasn't even going on. In the distance, the low, white buildings of Benghazi sparkled in the hot June sun and created silhouettes which formed a quilted patchwork against the blue backdrop of the Mediterranean. The scene of tranquillity was made complete by the groups of brightly dressed Arab women in red, yellow, and green skirts and headdresses working in the fields alongside Bedouin shepherd boys urging their flocks not to stray and a steady trickle of Arabs with heavily loaded donkeys along the road. All in all, during the day it had been like a picture postcard, and if not for the fact they were deep behind enemy lines and swarmed by disease-carrying sandflies, they might have actually enjoyed themselves.

Using his flashlight, Stirling looked again at his watch. The raids at the six Libyan airfields were not scheduled for another half hour, at 02:00 hours, so he decided to regale his two companions with a lecture on the art of deerstalking in his native Scottish Highlands. He hoped to make them relaxed before they crept down onto Benina airfield.

"The key, chaps," he told them, "is to stay downwind of the stag at all times, use all available camouflage, and move with sufficient stealth that the quarry never sees you coming. Above all, the hunter should never take a shot unless certain of a kill, for anything else is unsporting."

He went on to describe the intricate details of the patient stalk: how he had lain flat for hours on end in the cold, dew-covered heather at his family's estate at Keir; the long, circling crawls to stay downwind of the quarry; and the camouflage methods and the critical eyes of the expert ghillies. For a half hour, Cooper and Seekings sat mesmerized listening to the lecture until Stirling looked at his watch and said, "Right then, chaps—ready to go."

Gathering up their equipment, they picked their way carefully down the escarpment and stole onto the airfield. They followed a track along the plain, each man carrying twenty Lewes bombs. There was no wire, and the guards were on the far side near the hangars.

But as soon as they stepped onto the grounds, they heard the roar of incoming aircraft overhead and came to a halt. Stirling concluded that they must be German aircraft and not RAF since GHQ knew that the SAS raids were taking place tonight and had promised to keep away from the area. But suddenly the sky lit up from multiple explosions and the ground began shaking like an earth tremor.

"Those are ours. But what the hell do they think they're doing?" bristled Stirling.

"That's GHQ for you," observed Cooper sarcastically above the din.

They watched in stupefaction as the bombs continued to strike wide of the planes on the ground as well as the large hangars, workshops, and fueling areas. A minute later, the Allied bombers began flying away, having hit not a single target of value.

"Not what I'd call very good shooting," said Seekings. "Just enough to put everyone on the alert."

"My thoughts exactly," said Stirling. "But we have a job to do so let's get going."

They went first to the two aircraft parked on the field. It took them two minutes to place bombs on the pair of Messerschmitt twin-engine Me-110s. They attached one-hour fuses, which Stirling anticipated would give them time to complete the rest of their work. Then they stole to the long line of hangars and workshops. But as they neared the first of three large hangars, they heard a footfall across the pavement.

"Hold on!" whispered Stirling, and they instantly froze in the shadows.

Sentries were patrolling nearby. To the right, a dim light came from one of the hangars, and not far from it another faint glow indicated what looked like a guardroom. Stirling waited for the sentries to walk past and for the footsteps to fade away altogether before motioning Cooper and Seekings to follow him.

They quickly made their way to the first hangar. Stirling fumbled in the darkness for the catch to the large rolling doors. He found it and pulled it just enough to allow them to squeeze through. The noise of the rollers seemed to echo over the airfield, but thankfully the sentries didn't appear to have heard the commotion.

The hangar contained a Messerschmitt, a pair of Stukas, machinery, and heavy repair tools. In the darkness, it was difficult to move through the maze of equipment without stumbling over something. Seekings stood guard by the door with his Tommy gun, while Stirling and Cooper began planting the Lewes bombs.

But five minutes in, Seekings suddenly hissed to them to freeze. The sentries were making their rounds again.

Stirling and Cooper stood in their tracks in the darkness until the footsteps died away. It seemed an eternity but was only a couple minutes.

"Good heavens, that was close," said the SAS commander when the danger had passed. "We'd better hurry up."

They quickly placed several more bombs on the planes and machinery before moving on to the next hangar. This one had lights on inside and the door was partly open. In the far corner, a working-lamp shined brightly and four German mechanics were bent over a piece of machinery. Not far away stood a half-dismantled Junkers 52 transport plane.

This time Stirling instructed Cooper and Seekings to stay by the door and keep watch while he crept up and planted a bomb on the plane. He stayed close to the shadowy wall. When he reached the JU 52, he was only five yards from where the Germans were working. Feeling his heart beating in his chest in a turbulent rhythm, he swiftly attached his explosive device and looked around for other targets.

He had passed two elaborate pieces of airplane machinery just inside the entrance. Retracing his footsteps, he was able to locate them and he planted two more Lewes bombs. Then he rejoined Cooper and Seekings.

They navigated their way noiselessly to the third and final hangar. Once again, they rolled back the huge door and squeezed through the crack. The hangar was packed with two intact JU 52s, spare parts, and thirty to forty large wooden crates—which they discovered were filled with spanking new aircraft engines. This time he had Seekings keep watch by the door while he and Cooper put bombs on the planes, then they turned to the long rows of crates. They worked hard for twenty minutes and were just completing their task when Seekings again alerted them that the guard had returned.

"Get down! He's coming back!"

Stirling flattened himself against the shadowy wall ten feet away from Cooper as they listened to the tramp of approaching feet. He held his breath. He didn't want to be caught inside the hangars, for they had begun to use half-hour fuses to synchronize the explosions.

The footsteps came closer.

They had to seek better cover. Motioning Cooper to follow him, he stepped away quietly from the wall and they hid behind a stack of crated engines in front of the building.

It was then he realized that the guard was being changed.

Over the next five minutes, the twenty men who were relieved marched past and went into the guardroom thirty yards away. Unbeknownst to Stirling and Cooper, Seekings was just moving out from behind the crates when another sentry came upon them from the opposite direction. When Seekings took cover again, he and Stirling nearly crashed into one another.

"What the bloody hell are you doing?" snapped the CO in a low voice.

"There's another bogie," whispered Seekings, and he pointed the sentry out to him.

They waited breathlessly until he passed. Once he was out of sight, Stirling and Cooper returned to setting the explosives, placing bombs on each of the six crates while Seekings kept a lookout and covered them with his Thompson submachine gun.

But as Stirling and Cooper were setting the Lewes devices on the last two crates, Seekings gave another warning hiss. The second sentry was almost upon them again, but this time Stirling didn't hear Seekings or the approaching footsteps. Luckily, the sentry accidentally knocked against a box, making a loud noise, and Stirling dropped to the ground.

With the sentry only feet away, he lay totally still, his heart thundering in his chest. But somehow the German didn't spot him, and after a minute, the soldier turned and marched away.

Stirling blew out a huge sigh of relief.

The trio quickly huddled up again. With all the charges set, they were prepared to make their escape when Stirling looked again at the guardhouse set apart from the hangars. He thought of Paddy Mayne's actions at the Wadi Tamet raid last December, where the Irishman had destroyed fourteen aircraft and several petrol dumps, in the process winning the Distinguished Service Order and helping keep the SAS in existence following the failure of the first SAS raid behind enemy lines. With his competitive juices flowing along with a rush of battle blood, he wanted desperately to do something to equal his second-in-command and rival. Though he loathed pomposo swanks with a passion, he wanted to make a final dramatic statement before they left the airfield, something that would impress Paddy.

"Before we go, chaps, I say we give the Jerries something to remember us by. How about a crack at that guardroom?"

The bare-knuckle brawler Seekings was all for it. "Bloody good idea, Major."

They crept up to the guardhouse. While Cooper and Seekings stood watch for unaccounted-for sentries and ready to provide covering fire, Stirling pulled the pin out of a grenade, threw open the door, and tossed it inside the room. Inside were the twenty Germans who had just come off guard duty. Their commanding officer was sitting at a desk making out his report at a small table.

"Here catch and share this among you!" shouted Stirling, taking the Germans completely by surprise.

The horrified officer caught the grenade and screamed, "*Nein, nein!*"

"*Ja, ja!*" replied Stirling, and he quickly jerked out the pin of another grenade, threw the grenade inside, slammed the door, and ran like hell along with his two stunned NCOs.

The two explosions, one right after the other, shattered the guardhouse as the trio cut through the darkness and made for the airfield perimeter and the escarpment beyond. As they reached the base of the slope, the Lewes bombs began to go off inside the hangars. Coming to a halt near a gun emplacement, Stirling stuffed his last bomb up the breech, which was still warm from the earlier air raid. Now the entire aerodrome ignited in multiple brilliant bursts of bright white-yellow flame and mushroom clouds of smoke.

The two Messerschmitts on the field and the Junkers in the hangars began to burn. The heat from the fire became so intense that it quickly set off one of the Messerschmitt's 20-mm cannons, sending brightly colored tracers shooting across the runways. It was like a fantastic fireworks display. The flames were soon licking the high roofs of the hangars, and the entire airfield turned into an inferno due to all the air fuel, oil, and lubricants stored on-site. Knowing that the conflagration would be able to be observed for miles, Stirling hoped that Paddy Mayne was watching the fires from Berka.

The scene of destruction gave him great satisfaction. But it was not the success of the raid itself that pleased him most; it was the fact that it had been accomplished by only three men carrying sixty lightweight Lewes bombs. It was now beyond a doubt that a few well-trained soldiers could achieve more devastating results by surprise and stealth than could a whole regiment by the usual commando methods or even air raids. More than any other operation thus far, this one convinced him that forces of SAS men, roaming along Rommel's flank and sneaking in to strike at precisely the right moment, could have a serious effect on the course of the war.

They started off again, climbing up the escarpment. But by the time they were halfway to the top, Stirling was forced to come to a halt. He felt as if his head had been stuck in a vise and he was about to vomit. It was one of his sudden and crippling migraines, brought about no doubt by the stress of the raid and the violent explosions and bursts of light in the night sky.

"What's happening? Why are we stopping?" asked Cooper.

"I'm terribly sorry, chaps, but I'm afraid I'm having one of—"

Before he could finish, his eyes rolled in his head and he collapsed onto the rocky ground.

"Good heavens! Major, are you all right?" cried Cooper.

"I…I'll be…"

"He's having one of his spells," said Seekings. "Come on, we're going to have to carry him."

Stirling was only half conscious as they pulled him gently to his feet and half-carried, half-pulled him up the escarpment. The journey back up to the top was excruciatingly difficult for the two men in the dark, especially given their CO's lanky six-foot-six frame and his being half-blinded. But to stop on the low ground of the plains below would be to invite discovery.

When they reached the top, Cooper and Seekings helped him into a covered position to catch his breath and recover his senses. The trio was fortunate to find refuge close to their observation point of the day before, and Seekings went in search of water. He located a well they had used previously, filled up their canteens, and returned to the overlook. The cold, fresh water and an hour of rest had a recuperative effect upon Stirling: he began to feel better and his migraine slowly subsided.

As he came to his senses, he couldn't help but feel guilty for killing the Germans at the guardhouse. He knew that Paddy Mayne and Seekings, and quite possibly Cooper as well, would regard what he had done at the guardhouse as nothing but a professional act of war, but he thought differently. Two hours earlier, he had been giving a lecture on the ethics of stalking deer. Now he had just killed and injured perhaps as many as twenty human beings in a surprise attack that may have been justifiable as an act of war but was hardly sporting.

He knew there was an unwritten code of honor in the Desert War held by both sides. Prisoners did not expect to be put to the sword or treated much worse than the soldiers of the capturing side. Though there was still massive killing and occasional acts of cruelty, the conflict in North Africa to date had been unusually clean, with none of the barbarity of the Eastern Front where the influence of the Nazi SS and the brutal Russians, who would often shoot down their own troops if they retreated, was pervasive. Stirling couldn't help but feel dishonorable and that the episode would haunt him for the rest of his life.

Taking another sip of water, he brought voice to his inner turmoil as he recovered from his migraine.

"I feel badly for killing those Germans," he said quietly. "What I did was wrong."

Seekings the pugilist, quick to anger and just as quick with his fists, scoffed at the notion. "No need to apologize, sir. I thought it was poetry in motion, I did."

"No, it was wrong. It was a silly show of bravado."

Cooper said nothing and just listened.

"In a fair fight, I know I would shoot to kill with the same zeal as the next man, but down there on that airfield was not what that was. To be honest, it seemed close to murder."

"Don't let your conscience get the better of you, sir," said Seekings. "In this war, it's either them or us. You shouldn't be so hard on yourself."

"I'm afraid I can't agree with you, Sergeant. The other thing which made it silly was that if the grenades hadn't gone off, I would have alerted the whole damned camp to our presence. They could very well have mobilized quickly enough to search the hangars and save a few planes."

"It's over now, sir," said Cooper. "You can't beat yourself up over it. And besides, as Reg said, it's ultimately them or us. The Jerries have taken quite a few of our good men, sir. Jock Lewes, for one, didn't deserve to die any more than those men did. And yet he's gone."

They're just trying to make me feel better, he thought, and he spoke no more about the guardhouse.

By noon the next day, the trio arrived back at the LRDG rendezvous and were once again sipping the familiar concoction which had become habitual on the safe return of a patrol: tea heavily laced with rum.

CHAPTER 27

JEBEL BASECAMP AND BENINA ROAD
CYRENAICA, LIBYA

JUNE 14-15, 1942

AT THE JEBEL BASECAMP on Sunday afternoon June 14, Stirling was able to get detailed reports on the attacks against the string of enemy aerodromes in the Benghazi sector and Crete. The simultaneous operations by his unconventional army on the seven different targets had been conducted under seven distinct COs over land and sea, with multiple vehicles, various weapons, and soldiers from several different countries. Not surprisingly, the degree of success had been variable as well, with the French contingent and Paddy Mayne's Commando having run into severe difficulties. But in the end, dozens of enemy planes had been destroyed in the combined raids, the Axis airfields had been distracted at a key moment, and large numbers of enemy troops had been tied down dealing with the threat.

Stirling had always prided himself with being "non-swanks," but after Mayne had described his rough treatment at the hands of the enemy he couldn't resist the temptation to be a bit pomposo about his success at Benina.

"It's a bit of a change to see my fires lighting up the sky instead of yours," he said to his second-in-command.

"How many hangars did you get?" asked Paddy Mayne.

"All three—the lot," he replied with satisfaction. "In fact, they ought to still be burning. JU 52s make first-rate kindling. You wouldn't care to take a look at the debris, would you?"

Mayne's eyes glittered with cool challenge. "Why not? If we got hold of a car, we could drive right into Benghazi and shoot up some stuff along the road. I don't like the idea of leaving this place with your aerodrome burning and nothing for me to show for my efforts."

"I can understand your predicament. It will be fun to go and see if the bits and pieces are still burning."

"More importantly, I want to make sure you're not exaggerating."

Stirling smiled at the gentlemanly provocation. He knew that the two of them together were a dangerous combination, for they aroused a competitive fire in one another that made them take foolhardy risks, which of course came under the heading of "having a bit of fun." Just like last night at the guardhouse, he was letting his competitiveness with Mayne and youthful bravado get the better of him, but he couldn't back down now, not after laying out the challenge.

But he also knew their rivalry served a purpose: it helped him overcome his own fear and sense of inferiority compared to the rough-and-tumble Irishman, who took out Hitler's finest with genuine relish and without a hint of regret. The truth was that while Stirling did his best to appear intrepid at all times, he often struggled with his own fear and felt the need to prove his courage under enemy fire. The fear of appearing wanting or fearful in front of Mayne was greater than the fear itself.

"The first thing we need is transportation," said Mayne.

Stirling nodded; it was a good suggestion. "I'll take care of it," he said.

He went immediately to see Robin Gurdon, the patrol leader of the Long Range Desert Group. The SAS still relied on the LRDG for transport to and from the enemy airfields. But the LRDG trucks were not supposed to be used for offensive action and could technically only be used to convey passengers back and forth between base and the agreed-upon rendezvous. Fortunately, Gurdon was not a man that stuck too closely to protocol and enjoyed a good adventure.

"I say Robin, it would be most advantageous if I could borrow a Long Range truck for the evening. What do you think? Can you help me out?"

Gurdon chuckled. "I suppose you and Paddy are cooking up something."

"Oh, it's nothing very much. I just want to show him what used to be Benina."

"And considering that, for the last twenty-four hours, the desert has been crawling with enemy patrols searching for you, you don't expect any trouble?"

"No, we're quite confident we can sneak in while Jerry's napping."

"Now listen, David. You can have the truck on one condition. You have to swear to bring it back in one piece."

"Oh, I swear," said Stirling. "I swear on behalf of me dear mum back at Keir."

ΨΨΨ

They set off the next morning in a brand-new Chevrolet truck borrowed from the LRDG, taking a team of five men with them.

Mayne drove the truck, Stirling rode shotgun, and the rest were in the back. The group included: Karl Kahane, an Austrian Jew who had spent twenty years in the German army before emigrating to Palestine in the late 1930s; the reliable and inseparable Cooper and Seekings; Bob Lilley, one of the oldest men in the SAS at nearly forty who had straggled back into the rendezvous after the failed attempt with Mayne at the Berka satellite airfield; and Corporal Storey. A Lewis machine gun was concealed beneath a tarpaulin in case things got hot.

They travelled all day without incident. Then, shortly after nightfall, they hit a roadblock on the Benina road, about ten miles from the airfield on the Benghazi plain. This time it was not a flimsy Italian barrier—but a newly built, fully fledged German roadblock with concrete and barbed wire strung across the road. As Mayne came to a stop, a German sergeant major emerged from the guardhouse, carrying a "potato-masher" hand grenade in one hand and a flashlight in the other. The NCO came over to the truck and flashed his light over it. Stirling could make out at least a dozen German soldiers standing in a semicircle with automatic weapons at the ready.

"Just our luck," he muttered. "All right, Karl, it's your show," he then said to Kahane.

The squat dark-haired Austrian Jew knew German military slang thoroughly. He had been recruited from the Special Interrogation Group, or SIG, a British Army unit of German-speaking Jewish volunteers from the British Mandate of Palestine. After the May raid on Benghazi, Stirling had decided it would be useful to have a German-speaking soldier in the ranks to bluff guards in case they were stopped. The commandos attached to SIG not only dressed, marched, and spoke like real German soldiers, they swore like them too.

Kahane didn't wait for the sentry to speak: "We're coming from the front. We haven't had a bath for weeks, and we're hungry. So cut out the formalities and let us through."

The sergeant major was unimpressed. "Password," he grunted.

Stirling felt a bead of sweat at his brow. Of course, they didn't know the bloody password.

But Kahane did know how to deliver a dressing down in fluent German military argot. "How the fuck do we know what the fucking password is? And don't ask for our identity cards either. They're lost and we've been fighting for the past seventy hours against these fucking Tommies. Our car was destroyed and we were lucky to capture this truck and get back at all. So hurry up and get that fucking gate open."

Still unconvinced, the German moved around to the driver's side, until he stood just three feet from the window. As he looked inside the vehicle, his face tightened with suspicion.

"Listen to me, you jackass. While all you guards have been sitting on your backsides in Benghazi, me and my comrades have been in the thick of things. As I told you, our car was destroyed and we were lucky to capture this British truck and get back at all. Now I don't have time to sit around arguing with blockheads like you, so open the fucking gate. And I mean right now!"

The German hesitated. It was then Stirling heard a clicking sound.

It was Paddy Mayne cocking his Colt revolver in his lap. The sergeant major heard the noise and knew exactly what it meant: he was a hair trigger away from a gun battle, in which he would be the first casualty. He had a split second to make up his mind. He knew they were British but if he gave his soldiers the alarm he would be a dead man. If he let them through he could telephone a warning ahead.

There was another clicking sound and another.

This was too much for the German: he shouted to one of his guards to raise the barrier.

Mayne drove quickly on. As they passed through the opening, Stirling pulled out his own pistol and kept an eagle eye on the grenade in the sergeant major's hand. They were carrying plenty of Lewes bombs in the Chevrolet and he meant to get the German before he could throw the grenade and blow them up. But they trundled through without incident and Mayne drove swiftly towards Benghazi.

But Stirling knew that the sergeant major was certain to radio ahead that enemy forces were approaching. Sure enough, four miles further on stood another guard post with half a dozen Italian soldiers drawn up across the road waving rifles.

"Drive through them!" commanded Stirling.

"I'd be delighted to!" answered Mayne with a feisty grin, and he stomped his foot on the gas pedal and accelerated towards the checkpoint, scattering the Italians. As the truck stormed through, Seekings swung up the Lewis gun shouting *"Tedeschi! Tedeschi!"*

The Italians jumped back and he opened up with the machine gun once they were through the opening. The enemy was now fully alerted, yet Stirling insisted they could not depart without leaving a calling card. But under the circumstances, it would be suicidal to drive into Benghazi, so they would have to content themselves with blowing up whatever they could find along the road.

They soon passed a cluster of buildings with a fuel filling station and depot. There were no sentries, and it was easy to plant the charges on the petrol storage tanks. Then they drove farther along to a village which boasted a roadhouse. There was a car park next to it with heavy lorries and trailers. While Stirling and Cooper busied themselves placing bombs with ten-minute fuses, Mayne and the others machine-gunned the building beside it. There was a camp next to it and they shot that up as well.

As they started off again, Mayne said, "I have to say this has been a delightful cross-country tour."

Stirling agreed, but he also believed they had had enough adventure behind enemy lines for one day. A half-hour had passed since they had gone through the German roadblock, and it was time to head for home. There were already shouts from the camp and poorly aimed machine guns firing into the darkness.

Since they could not go back along the road they decided to cut across the plain to the Wadi Qattara. The wadi started on the outskirts of Benghazi and ran parallel to the paved road. It was essential to cross it in order to reach the track on the other side, which offered the only alternative route up the escarpment. But the wadi was so rough it could only be crossed at the point marked on the map.

Stirling worked out the direction by compass while Mayne drove. The desert plain was incredibly bumpy, and the distance that had to be covered was at least five miles. Mayne was driving the Chevrolet with the lights off, when suddenly Stirling spotted another vehicle, a mile or two away with its headlights on, also navigating across the plain and apparently heading for the same point at the wadi.

"The bastards are trying to cut us off," said Stirling.

"Don't worry, I'll lose them," said Mayne.

He flicked on the headlights and went as fast as the truck would go. The Chevrolet rattled and thundered over the ground until it seemed as though every spring was broken. Stirling thought guiltily about Gurdon and his warning to bring the truck back in one piece. But he was more worried about getting himself and his team out alive, for he could tell the race was going to be touch and go. At one point, it looked to him as though the enemy vehicle was gaining on them. But Mayne just squinted with resolve and drove faster. Stirling and the other passengers were flung from one side to the other of the jolting truck. Within half a mile of the wadi, it was obvious that Mayne had narrowly pulled into the lead.

"You've got him, Paddy Boy," cried Stirling encouragingly.

As the truck approached the edge of the wadi, the enemy vehicle could not have been more than a quarter of a mile away. In the illumination of the headlights, they could now see that it was a German armored car. Though the going was too rough for either side to shoot accurately, Seekings and Cooper opened up with several warning bursts of tracer bullets.

The Germans returned fire.

In response, Mayne drove close to the edge of the ravine, searching for a safe way down.

"Look, off to the right! That's our spot!" cried Stirling from his shotgun seat.

Mayne swung the wheel and darted down the ravine. To Stirling's surprise, they had hit the crossing-place virtually dead on. As they disappeared over the edge and shuttled down the slope, the German pursuers pulled up at the lip of the descent and halted, fearful of an ambush.

"We've beaten those bastards, all right!" roared Paddy Mayne once they realized the Germans would go no further. "The race is over and we have won!"

A rousing cheer went up. "Who Dares Wins! Who Dares Wins!"

But maneuvering the truck up the other side of the steep gully and reaching the top of the escarpment proved more daunting. It took them three hours and several close calls, but once on top they knew they were fully in the clear. The surface seemed like glass compared with what they had been travelling over for the last hour. The men in the back began joking about their battered limbs, and Stirling pulled a flask of whiskey out of his knapsack and gave everyone a nip.

"By the way," said Mayne, "here we are on the way home and I forgot to look at those fires at Benina. Do you want to go back?"

Stirling and the others laughed. "You'd better just take my word for it, old boy."

It was a long drive back to the rendezvous. The men lolled drowsily against the sides of the truck, and Stirling started to doze off. But before he was fully asleep, he heard Lilley shout from the back: "Burning fuse! Hop out, quick!"

"He's right! Get the hell out!" echoed Seekings, who had smelled the fuse too.

Mayne didn't even have time to brake. The team scrambled out while the vehicle was still moving, and a split second later a deafening explosion shook the ground. The truck was blown to smithereens. The back had been full of explosives; apparently the ride across the plain had set off one of the time-pencils attached to a Lewes bomb. Lilley and Seekings had both smelled the burning fuse just in time.

Stirling surveyed the ruin along with Mayne and the others.

"My God," exclaimed Lilley. "What's left of our fine American truck you could put in a bloody haversack."

The patrol burst out with belly-splitting laughter and the men were unable to stop. Stirling laughed loudest of all when he again remembered back to his solemn promise to Gurdon to bring back the truck in one piece.

As the laughter subsided, the Austrian Jew Kahane looked at them as if they had all lost their senses. "You SAS men must be made of steel to be able to laugh at things like this," he said to the group. "Me, I am too fucking old."

They laughed even harder. When the laughter again died down, he added, "After being in the German Army, I had a poor opinion of the British when I first joined SIG. But since being with you fellows, I have changed my mind."

"How come?" asked Stirling.

"My experiences with the SAS have shown me the daring side of you British bastards. But not only have you lads changed my mind, you have convinced me that the Germans cannot possibly win this war."

"Why can't they?" asked Mayne.

"They can't laugh in the face of danger like you crazy sons of bitches!"

The group laughed uproariously once again before setting off on the long trek on foot. It was late afternoon of June 15th when an LRDG patrol picked them up and transported them back to the Jebel camp.

CHAPTER 28

TOBRUK, CYRENAICA, LIBYA

JUNE 21-22, 1942

STANDING ON A LIMESTONE ESCARPMENT south of Tobruk, Rommel peered down at the historic port city and surrounding coastal plain through his field glasses. The first streaks of dawn's pinkish light had turned to a muted yellow in the desert sky, and below the Mediterranean sparkled as the rising sun's rays touched the clear aquamarine waters. It was uncannily peaceful and he savored his quiet view from above. The light was just creeping slowly down the rocky ridges and barchan dunes, as a world that yesterday had been embroiled in war with screaming Stuka dive-bombers and thundering 88s now woke up to a momentary lull in the hostilities.

Against the morning chill, he wore his soldier's greatcoat with red lapel facings, gold buttons, and *'Afrika Korps'* stitched on the cuffs. A widow's peak stretched across his broad forehead, and the hair above his ears lay sleek as feathers. Hatless and with crow's-feet etched around eyes long accustomed to squinting through his desert goggles, he looked older than his fifty years. Though he may have appeared worn-out and ordinary to the casual observer, the glimmer of fierce determination on his chiseled face revealed someone larger than life, someone whose name would resonate through the ages for his military greatness—even if the cause for which he ultimately fought was a despicable one. In short, he looked every inch the unbeatable adversary that had consumed Churchill and rattled his generals. Here was an innovative offensive tactician every bit in the ranks of Hannibal, Alexander and Frederick the Great, and Napoleon—and here at this moment in history was also the one man who posed the greatest threat to the British Empire.

The commander of the Tobruk fortress, Major General Hendrik Klopper of the 2nd South African Infantry Division, had sent up a white surrender flag five minutes earlier. Last night, after two solid days of bombardment, the town, its prized harbor, and two-thirds of the fortress were captured by the *Afrika Korps*, but it took until morning for Klopper to realize that his situation was hopeless and send out his emissaries under white flag. Rommel was glad the fighting was over, even if only for a day, for he had been informed by his staff that last night his troops had been so exhausted that dozens of retreating British and South African soldiers cut off by his rapid advance had actually stepped over the bodies of his sleeping infantrymen and made their way back to friendly lines with scarcely anyone noticing them.

I still can't believe Tobruk in mine! he thought as he continued to stare through his binoculars at the concentric defenses ringing the legendary city. Klopper's garrison and the town proper were centered within a larger British-held area. The area was surrounded by a thirty-three-mile perimeter wire dotted with artillery strongpoints, machine-gun and anti-tank gun nests, and strategically-placed forts. But these fortifications that had given him so much trouble during his 241-day siege in 1941, during his advance through Cyrenaica from El Agheila in Operation

Sonnenblume, posed no threat to him now. The city of Tobruk—which during its history had served as an ancient Greek agricultural colony, Roman fortress, and a waystation along the coastal caravan route—was a wilderness of devastation not only from the furious Luftwaffe and artillery bombing of the past two days but from the long, drawn-out siege of '41.

His chief of staff appeared at his side. "Are you ready to go, sir?" asked Bayerlein.

He looked at the colonel and gave a rare smile. "Yes, I am ready to meet with General Klopper. I just wanted to look at the city from this vantage point one last time."

"It is a great day for the *Afrika Korps*, sir."

"Yes, yes, it is Fritz. But as always, I owe everything to my soldiers," he said, giving the credit for his stunning victory over the larger and better equipped British Eighth Army to the men that served under him. They had accepted every deprivation imposed upon them, including death, with steely resolve and discipline. God, did he love and admire them.

They headed for Moritz and departed for the city below with his caravan of staff cars and signals trucks. By 05:30 hours, they were driving through Tobruk proper, a prize that had eluded him for so long. Rommel noted that the devastation was much more dramatic up close than it had been gazing at it from afar at the top of the escarpment. Practically every building of the dismal place was either leveled or little more than a heap of rubble.

From the city, he drove off along the Via Balbia to the west. Along the way, a smattering of survivors from the 32nd British Army Tank Brigade offered their surrender to him and he was able to add thirty serviceable British tanks into his growing *Panzerarmee*. The route along the Via Balbia was, too, a picture of devastation. Vehicles stood in flames on either side of the broad roadway. Wherever he looked, he saw destruction. He was informed by von Mellenthin, who had taken over for Westphal as his chief of operations 1a, that Klopper had destroyed a large number of motorized vehicles, fueling facilities, and water storage tanks rather than allow them to fall into enemy hands, which infuriated Rommel since he now had a large number of prisoners whose welfare he was responsible for under the Hague and Geneva Conventions. Thousands of scraggly, grim-faced British and South African desert rats—now POWs—lined the road. How in the hell was he going to be able to supply them with water when the water tanks had been blown up?

But at least Tobruk's strong, naturally protected deep harbor was now in his hands. He regarded it as the best natural port in Northern Africa. Even if it was bombed, ships would still be able to anchor there and be safe from squalls, so the port could never be rendered wholly useless regardless of military bombardment. This was of critical importance, as Tobruk allowed him to reduce the length of his supply lines and continue to feed his desert warfare campaign, which would enable him to make his final push towards the Suez.

He set up his headquarters in the *Albergo Tobruk*, where he met with Klopper and accepted the South African's formal surrender. As part of the official capitulation, Rommel captured the entire 35,000-man garrison, taking 19,000 British, 13,400 South Africans, and 2,500 Indians as POWs, mostly base troops including sailors, along with a huge quantity of supplies. It was the second-largest British capitulation of the war thus far, after Singapore.

As the two officers tended to the details of the surrender at the historic hotel with their staffs, he learned that Klopper had been unprepared for his Panzer attack, which had come from an unexpected direction—the southeast. The general had thought it would come from the southwest, and had promised Ritchie and Auchinleck that he would hold until the last man and the last bullet. But the assault had happened too quickly and he had been unable to stave off defeat. Rommel almost felt sorry for the poor bastard. In a spirit of cooperation to ensure fair treatment for his troops, Klopper then said that he would do everything he could to maintain control over his men.

"Thank you for that," said Rommel, who, though typically a sore loser due to his competitive zeal, was magnanimous in victory. "To ensure a peaceful transition, I hereby instruct you to make yourself and your officers personally responsible for order among the prisoners, and to organize their maintenance from the captured stores." His eyes narrowed. "But I do have one bone to pick with you, General."

Klopper looked at him through slitted eyes. "And what is that?"

"I demand to know why you have allowed your motorized vehicles and your water and petrol facilities to be destroyed in the last twelve hours?"

The South African gave a little smile of defiance but said nothing.

"Are you really not going to answer my question?"

Still, Klopper refused to answer. He crossed his arms defiantly and took a sip of his brandy. Rommel had faced South Africans before: they were a stubborn lot.

"You do understand, General Klopper, that by destroying these critical facilities you have put me in an uncomfortable position."

"How so?"

"Your men will receive the same ration of water as mine—but only up to the point when my men start dropping like flies from sunstroke. Because of what you have done, your men may very well have to walk to Tripoli."

Klopper was up and out of his chair, his face flush with anger. "How dare you? My men are now prisoners of war and must be treated as such!"

"I will treat them in accordance with the Hague and Geneva accords. But not if I don't have enough water or transports for my own men because you have ill-advisedly destroyed the supplies of these precious resources."

"Do what you want with me, sir, but you have no right to treat my men in such a despicable fashion!"

Unable to control his temper, Rommel wagged a finger at him. "Don't you dare lecture me on morality! It is you who have put us in this desperate situation. Now I believe I am done talking to you, General. I have much to do. Now that Tobruk is once more in German hands, I plan on pushing what remains of your once-venerable Eighth Army back into Egypt."

"You may have won today, but we will drive you off this continent eventually—most likely sooner rather than later. Your supply lines are overextended, and it's only going to get worse the farther west you drive your Panzers."

"Perhaps, but I wouldn't bet against me. Now before I go, do you have any further requests of me? I do not want to be hard on your men who have fought so bravely, but when you destroy most of the water supplies, fueling terminals, and vehicles to keep them from my *Panzerarmee*, you are also hurting yourself. Do you not understand that?"

"My men will not march from here to Tripoli."

"Let's hope they don't have to. But I cannot guarantee they won't based on what you have done. Now is there any other request?"

"Yes, I ask that your men refrain from pillaging my men."

"We won't be staying around here long enough to do that. But my field security police have already been dispatched to prevent looting."

He knew he sounded far more certain than he was. The truth was he could never prevent some stealing on the part of his troops after a hard-fought campaign. While his soldiers were damned good fighters, they were also quite adept at pilfering from the defeated enemy. While everything belonging to civilians was left strictly alone, items previously the property of Eighth Army disappeared like snow in the Sahara—especially if it were food, alcohol, or tobacco.

"Do you have any other requests?"

"Yes, I would like to address my men. Where will you hold them?"

"We have set up a temporary POW cage in Derna."

"Take me there. I want to see it for myself."

"Very well, General. We have already begun to move some of your units there."

They quickly drove to the POW camp, Klopper following along with his chief of staff in their own car. As they neared the entrance, Rommel could see there was some sort of commotion taking place. The 2nd South African Division was being marched into captivity, and the unit's officers and NCOs appeared to be vigorously protesting to the German officers at the entrance.

"What the hell's going on?" he asked a captain who seemed to be in charge.

"The South African officers don't want to be in the same compound with the darkies, *Herr Generaloberst*," answered the officer.

Rommel wasn't sure he understood correctly. "What?"

"The white officers and NCOs among the South African Division are protesting, sir. They refuse to share the prisoner-of-war compound with their black soldiers. In their minds, the strict rules of apartheid should be maintained no matter what the circumstances. That's what they're telling me."

Klopper, who had realized what was going on, stepped out of his car. Rommel—at once both shocked and infuriated—waved him off, jumped down from Moritz, and grabbed a megaphone from an NCO barking out instructions to the new prisoners. Climbing back into his armored staff car, he shouted down through the megaphone to the prisoners refusing to enter the barbed-wire-ringed compound.

"Officers of the 2nd South African Division. It has been brought to my attention that you want to be housed in a separate POW compound from your black South African comrades. Since these brave men have fought beside you and endured the same privations as you these past months, I tell you now that you will not—I repeat, will not—be kept in separate compounds!"

A rumble of angry protest went up from the white officers and NCOs, making him even angrier.

"Listen to me, damn you! These black soldiers wear the same uniform as you and have fought alongside you with just as much bravery as yourselves. In my eyes, you are all the same, and will be treated as equals. As of this moment, this matter is closed. Do I make myself clear?"

This time there was a light murmur of grumbling but that was all. He had taken the wind out of their sails.

"I will say it one last time for those who are hard of hearing or don't listen well. Your request for separate housing for your white commissioned and non-commissioned officers versus your black South Africans I reject out of hand. I do this for the simple reason that these men of color are soldiers, too. They will be housed in the same POW cages and enjoy all the rights of any other prisoners of war. Now get inside that compound and don't test my patience any further!"

This time no one said a word. Shortly afterwards, he had a loudspeaker set up and allowed Klopper to address his fellow prisoners, but the garrison commander was heckled and booed and had to withdraw without delivering his message. Rommel was appalled that the South African's own men believed that he had sold out to the enemy when the odds had been stacked so heavily against him. Furthermore, Klopper's own British Eighth Army had abandoned him and his men for what his South African soldiers were already calling the "Gazala Gallup." But Rommel didn't interfere, considering it an Allied matter. Instead, he returned to his headquarters at the Hotel Tobruk and wrote a quick letter to his wife. It read:

21June 1942
Dearest Lu,
Tobruk! It was a wonderful battle. There's a lot going on in the fortress area. I must get a few hours' sleep now after all that's happened. How much I think of you.

ΨΨΨ

The next day—June 22, 1942—Rommel was promoted to *Generalfeldmarschall* for his victory, thus reaching the pinnacle of his military career. At fifty, he was the youngest man in the Army to attain Germany's highest military rank. In his own mind, he knew that his attack of June 20 on Tobruk was the second best battle he had directed, right behind his victory over the Italians at Monte Matajur during the Great War in 1918. Both were masterpieces and he was proud of them.

He had always been something of a showman, but from his humble Schwabian roots, he considered excessive pomp and ceremony to be pretentious, and he consequently made Orders of the Day the exception rather than the rule in *Panzerarmee Afrika*. Yet he also knew that there were certain moments in history when it was of paramount importance to acknowledge the sacrifice and achievement of the men serving under him—and the capture of Tobruk was one such occasion that demanded recognition for himself and his men. He knew that for every one of his beloved "Africans," June 21, 1942 would always be one of the high points of the Desert War and they would want something to remember it by. Accordingly, on June 22, he issued a special Order of the Day to his Panzer Army:

SOLDIERS!
The great battle in the Marmarica has been crowned by your quick conquest of

Tobruk. We have taken in all over 45,000 prisoners and destroyed or captured more than 1,000 armored fighting vehicles and nearly 400 guns. During the long hard struggle of the last four weeks, you have, through your incomparable courage and tenacity, dealt the enemy blow upon blow. Your spirit of attack has cost him the core of his field army, which was standing poised for an offensive. Above all, he has lost his powerful armor. My special congratulations to officers and men for this superb achievement.

Soldiers of the Panzer Army Afrika!

Now for the complete destruction of the enemy. We will not rest until we have shattered the last remnants of the British Eighth Army. During the days to come, I shall call on you for one more great effort to bring us to this final goal.

ROMMEL

Later that night, he celebrated in a typically restrained fashion. Sitting down to dine with Bayerlein at an actual dining table, he ate a can of pineapples and drank a small glass of well-watered whiskey from a bottle recently liberated from the enemy. After dinner, he became more somber. The entire rush of events ending in the fall of Tobruk and his promotion to field marshal seemed like a dream to him. It was then that he made a confession to his chief of staff, one that he would later repeat to his beloved wife.

"I would much rather the Führer had given me one more division than a promotion," he said to Bayerlein. "We're going to need every man and tank we can get our hands on to drive the British out of Egypt."

"What about Malta?"

"What about it?"

"Would it not be wise now for the *Panzerarmee* to pause and allow Kesselring to launch a combined airborne-naval operation against Malta to improve our logistics? Then, once that is done, we can resume the offensive."

"No offense, Fritz, but that argument ignores one key thing: there is a moral imperative to keep our victorious army in motion. And of course, you know how much I hate sitting around on the defensive. I don't want to become paralyzed by my own fears and lack of confidence like Ritchie and Auchinleck."

"Yes, I can see that we need to keep up the pressure while we have the enemy on the run. The word from our 'little Fellers's is that the British are likely to fall back all the way to Mersa Matruh, with a secondary defensive line running between El Alamein and the Qattara Depression if they cannot hold at Mersa Matruh."

"They won't be able to hold," said Rommel. "Which is why it will be further to the east where I will crush Eighth Army once and for all: at El Alamein!"

PART 3

THE FLAP AND OPERATION CONDOR

CHAPTER 29

TURF CLUB AND GROPPI'S, CAIRO

JUNE 28, 1942

"THAT was a swell party—but not as good as one of yours, Momo!"

Hekmat turned around at the same moment as her friend Momo Marriott, the wealthy American socialite, to see a smiling Bonner Fellers. The two women had been heading out of the Turf Club, where they had spent the last two hours gossiping about the terrible state of the war and taking afternoon tea. The Turf Club was a mostly British, all-male establishment at 32 Sharia Adly Pasha in Cairo's cosmopolitan West End—but it would not have looked out of place in St. James Street in London. Though foreigners and Egyptians were rarely admitted as members of the club, a small number of particularly influential personages had managed to be voted in since the beginning of the war, but women were still only allowed for special parties and holiday events.

Today the club had been buzzing with conversation. With Rommel pushing hard into Egypt and reportedly only a hundred miles from Alexandria, Egypt's two largest cities—Alexandria and Cairo—were in a state of agitation and uncertainty. The British aristocracy had already coined a name for it: with what Hekmat believed was characteristic understatement they were calling it "the flap."

"Ah, Colonel Fellers," said Momo, "I didn't even see you at the party."

"Unfortunately, I got pulled into one of the conference rooms with our British friends and couldn't get the hell out of there. If they don't get their act together—and I mean real quick—they are going to lose this goddamn war before our American doughboys even set foot overseas. I'm telling you, things are bad."

"Is the situation really that dreadful?" asked Hekmat.

"I don't mean to alarm you unnecessarily because I know your sweetheart, Captain Bellairs, is out there in the desert fighting this very minute. But the military situation…I'm telling you, it ain't pretty."

"Don't worry, you're not frightening me," she said stoically. "Guy's fate is in God's hands and all I can do is pray for him."

Momo took Fellers by the arm. "Dear heavens, Colonel, with all this war talk I'm afraid I have become flush with excitement. Now where are you off to?"

"I've got to get back to GHQ."

"Oh, no you're not. You're going to tell us your little secrets so we can prepare ourselves. Now come with us—and I'm not taking no for an answer."

"I told you, Momo darling, I just can't. I've got to get back to Garden City."

"Sorry, no chance, Colonel." Her bony little hand gripped him like an eagle talon. "You're coming with us to Groppi's and I'm buying. And that, sir, is final."

"Yes, you really should come with us," said Hekmat. "I need to know how worried I should be about Guy."

"Exactly," said Momo emphatically. "Now that you've scared the poor girl half to death—the least you can do is reassure her that everything's going to be okay.

And besides, I have some useful intelligence for *you*"—she gave a conspiratorial wink—"my fellow American friend and military attaché."

He perked up instantly. "You do?"

"You bet I do. Come now, let's get a taxi, shall we?"

"All right, but you'd better not be pulling my chain, Momo darling."

"Shame on you, Colonel. I wouldn't dream of anything so deplorable."

They laughed and walked down Sharia Adly Pasha, past Sephardi Synagogue, and went to the taxi queue. The heat was suffocating. There were two taxis parked along the curb, but the drivers had stepped out of their vehicles, laid out mats facing east towards Mecca, and begun to perform the afternoon prayer—*Asr*. The cab drivers wore long robes and turbans and had set their simple Arab sandals on their mats next to them. Touching their ears with their hands, they bowed, knelt down on their knees, and began a recitation while periodically bending over to touch their heads on the mat. Hekmat listened to their words in Arabic as they prayed.

"In the name of Allah, the Compassionate and Merciful. Praise be to God, Lord of the worlds, the Compassionate and Merciful, Master of the Day of Judgement. Thee we worship and from Thee we seek help. Guide us upon the straight path, the path of those whom Thou hast blessed, not of those who incur wrath, nor of those who are astray."

It was the *al-fatiha*, and though Hekmat was a Christian and not a Muslim, she knew the first chapter of the Quran and several other passages by heart. The brief passage was said to contain the essential message of Islam and was recited in daily prayer by millions of Muslims throughout the world.

When the two drivers had finished their prayer, they again bowed, rose to their feet, rolled up their mat, put their sandals back on, and returned to their taxis. Cairo taxis were a distinctive dark blue with white fenders to make them easily recognizable for Cairenes and foreigners alike in the city.

"I take you—where you go?" said the first driver in line.

"Groppi's at Midan Soliman Pasha," answered Momo. "*Allahu Akbar*," she added pleasantly.

The taxi driver smiled through dingy yellow teeth. "*Allahu Akbar*," he repeated after her with a vigorous head bob.

He then drove south towards Soliman Pasha Square. Along the way, they came across a traffic jam of cars, buses, motorcycles, horse-drawn carts and gharries, and people on foot from the many civilians already fleeing Cairo. The conveyances were packed with food, clothing, and furniture, and some people had strapped mattresses on the roofs of their vehicles. Those on foot shuffled past in steady streams pulling small hand carts or carrying heavy bags, many of them no doubt heading for the train station. Hekmat was stunned. Only two hours earlier, the traffic had been heavy but nothing to be overly concerned about. Now, however, Rommel's stunning desert victory and subsequent rapid advance seemed to have created a mild panic. Rolling down her car window, she asked several people where they were heading: most said they were seeking refuge in the Delta or as far away as Khartoum.

After a few blocks, the logjam lessened and they made it to Sharia Kasr El Nil and Soliman Pasha Square in good time. Upon their arrival to Groppi's, Hekmat watched with amusement as Bonner Fellers and Momo Marriott fought over who would pay the driver, but eventually the irrepressible heiress prevailed. As they stepped out onto the street, the driver again flashed his yellow dingy teeth and said, "What you think of this so-called flap? I say today I drive you to Groppi's—tomorrow you drive me!"

"Very funny, pal," said Fellers, and he slammed the door of the taxi.

"That was quite rude," said Momo. "I wish I hadn't given him such a good tip."

"You're telling me," agreed Fellers. "But let's not allow it to spoil our afternoon. Rommel's not taking Cairo, at least not anytime soon. At the moment, he doesn't have enough tanks or fuel and the RAF controls the skies."

"Then why is everyone panicking?" countered Momo.

"Because it's best to be prepared."

Hekmat wondered if her beloved city and country might not be better off with the Germans controlling the levers of power instead of the English. That's what her Muslim friends believed, but Guy and her European and Jewish friends disagreed. They said that Hitler was a fascist, racist pig who would enslave the entire country.

They walked inside Groppi's. Hekmat liked its art deco design with colorful mosaic tiles, rotunda style, high ceilings, and stately chandeliers. The entryway was filled with pastry cases boasting chocolates, petit-fours, cakes, and savory delicacies. The most famous café in Cairo was one of the few smart places open to everyone, although it was not cheap, and the clientele therefore tended to be mostly wealthy European refugees, Allied officers, and the elite of Egyptian society. As they were delivered to their table, Hekmat took in the fragrant smell of roasting French coffee and fresh pastries cooked in clarified butter. Established in 1909 by Swiss pastry chef and chocolatier Giacomo Groppi with the help of his son Achille, Groppi's now boasted two establishments in Cairo that were considered "the most celebrated tearooms this side of the Mediterranean."

"So, tell me the latest from headquarters, Colonel," said Momo to begin the conversation. "Of course, only what you're allowed to talk about. And then I'll tell you my little secret."

"The latest from GHQ is that the British don't know what they're doing. Despite the fact that for the past year they have had one and a half to two times as many men, tanks, transports, and planes as Rommel, the British Army has twice failed to defeat him in Libya. And with most operations taken in a piecemeal fashion, America's Lend-Lease Program alone cannot be counted on to ensure victory."

Hekmat was surprised. "But I thought you said the Germans would not be able to make it all the way to Cairo. They don't have enough tanks or fuel."

"It's true Rommel's forces are suffering from critical shortages. His soldiers are disease-ridden and weary, and he's operating at the end of a long and tenuous supply line, with shortages of water, food, fuel, and ammunition becoming acute and damaged armament irreplaceable. And it's also true that the British at Marsa Matruh are now much closer to their own supply depots, have air superiority, and are receiving large quantities of material and equipment. But Rommel is a goddamn magician and always seems to be able to pull a rabbit out of his hat."

"Is it that the British are incompetent then?" asked Hekmat.

"Their ordinary combat soldiers are tough as nails—it's their officers that have let them down. Ultimately, the Eighth Army has failed to maintain the morale of its troops. Not only that but most of the time their tactics are ill-conceived. But what I think hurts the British most is that they've neglected cooperation between the various arms and they react too slowly compared to Rommel."

"Coming from a staunch ally, that's strong condemnation," said Momo.

"Look, the British are our friends and I love them to death. But I don't like bumbling stupidity, wasted resources, or an inability to be flexible in combat. Hey, the Desert Fox does all these things so why can't the Auk?"

He seems to have a point, thought Hekmat. *How is it that Rommel can win great victories with less tanks and men than the British? It has to be leadership.*

"The bottom line is the British can't win the war without America's help. This is already being accomplished through Lend-Lease, but U.S. troops will also be arriving in the coming months to the Western theater, either here in the Mediterranean or in England. But you just can't squander precious resources."

A waiter appeared to take their orders. Hekmat opted for a caffè macchiato and petits fours glacé—an assortment of tiny cakes covered in fondant, small éclairs, and tartlets. Her Americans friends went for café au laits to drink and chocolate-covered dates and vanilla ice cream smothered in crème Chantilly. The elegantly dressed Greek waiter commended them on their selections, bowed, and disappeared.

"I wonder what will happen now that Auchinleck has relieved Ritchie of command of Eighth Army," said Momo.

"Even though the Auk has assumed command himself, I doubt it will change anything," said Fellers.

"I didn't know about the switch," said Hekmat. "When did it happen?"

"Three days ago. Tobruk is a disgrace and should never have taken place. Meanwhile, Rommel's bristling with energy and has been made a field marshal by Hitler. Auchinleck's going to have his hands full."

"Is there no way the British can stop him?" asked Hekmat.

"It's going to be tough. The only area where the British hold the edge is in air power. If not for that the Desert Fox would probably already be in Cairo by now."

"Well then," said Momo, "thank heavens for those flyboys in their Hurricanes and Spitfires."

"You can say that again. All I can tell you gals is that a numerically superior but demoralized army is on the run, while not 100 miles distant from Rommel lays the greatest strategic prize in all of North Africa."

Hekmat looked at him. "Alexandria?"

"Yes, ma'am. With 'Alex' in the bag, Cairo and the Suez Canal would be as good as taken. With the loss of the Suez, the entire British strategy for the Mediterranean comes crashing down. All because the British fighting soldier has been so poorly served by his senior officers. It's a damn shame. The good 'ol US of A is going to have to bail those poor Tommies out just like we did in 1917."

Again, Hekmat wondered if the Germans would make things worse or better if Rommel defeated the British and took Egypt. She still viewed the possible arrival of the Germans with a feeling of dread. At the same time, even though she had a British lover, she didn't love Great Britain or the British people. She didn't like that the Brits seemed to think they owned her country and that many of them considered her nothing but a "sexy Wog" who had no intrinsic value except to entertain British officers and diplomats. Compared to the enlightened and egalitarian French, Greeks, and non-fascist Italians, the British were condescending snobs. At the same time, she had to admit that the British occupation had been very good for her career. The Brits were good for business, fawning over her and filling her pockets with oodles of money, and she seriously doubted that the Germans would be such a soft touch.

Momo said, "All right, Colonel, you've been such a good sport, it's time to tell you my little secret. Or, should I say, secrets."

"I'm all ears, Momo darling."

"First off, the Hungarian desert explorer Count Almasy has been spotted in Cairo. People are saying he's spying for the Nazis."

Fellers laughed and waved his hand dismissively. "I heard that one too, Momo, and I don't believe a word of it."

"But it's true. The Long Range Desert Group found his tracks in the desert. They say he's on a secret mission to Cairo."

"And you have actual evidence of this?"

"He's been seen having drinks at several well-known watering-holes, including the Kit Kat Club and Continental."

"Who told you this?"

"Surely, Colonel, you can't expect me to reveal my sources. Let's just say it's someone high up in British counterintelligence."

"Momo my dear, you would make one hell of a spy, if you're not one already. Now what else do you have for me, Sugar Doll? I've got to tell you up front, I hope it's something better than the Almasy sighting."

"Indeed, it is. Have you heard of the Endozzi sisters?"

"No," replied Fellers. "Who are they?"

"Until quite recently, they worked at the Italian Legation."

"All right, you've perked my interest. What happened to them?"

"They were arrested yesterday by Major Sammy Sansom of British Field Security."

"Yeah, I know Sansom. What did he arrest them for?"

"Apparently, they hid a document in a cistern that they had prepared for Rommel's occupying force, and the major found it when he raided their flat."

"What kind of document?"

"It was a list detailing members of the Italian community in Cairo that are sympathetic to the British and those that are loyal to the Axis. They were planning to hand over the list to the Desert Fox if and when he takes the city."

Fellers laughed. "Good job by Sansom. Too bad he and David Stirling of the SAS aren't commanding the British Army. Then Egypt just might have a fighting chance of remaining in Allied hands."

"Oh, you are a devil, Bonner Fellers. Are you trying to scare us?"

"No ma'am, I just tell it like it is," he said with a cocksure smile.

Hekmat couldn't help but smile in return as their mouth-watering deserts and coffees arrived to the table. But inside she was genuinely worried: *What fate will befall me if Rommel and his Panzer Army take Cairo?*

CHAPTER 30

MISR RAILWAY STATION AND
BRITISH MIDDLE EAST HQ, CAIRO

JUNE 29, 1942

RACING IN behind the wheel of his Hillman Minx officer's staff car, Sansom ignored the Egyptian police officer waving for him to stop, drove into Misr Railway Station, and came to screeching halt before the crowded front entrance. Leaving a large placard that read *"Major A.W. Sansom, British Field Security"* on his dashboard, he jumped out of his car, swept past the famous sculpture by Mahmoud Mokhtar entitled *Nahdat Misr*—Egypt Awakening—and pushed his way through the sweltering crowd into the terminal.

With the flap turning from mild alarm to total panic and chaos in the past twenty-four hours, British wives and children were being evacuated to Palestine and the Sudan by the thousands. An hour earlier, when he had phoned his wife Joan to tell her to pack he discovered from his Egyptian valet that she had already left for the train station and was heading for Palestine. Instead of summoning his Egyptian driver, he had left GHQ immediately and driven his car himself to try and catch her before she left so he could give her a proper goodbye.

As part of Auchinleck's detailed contingency evacuation plan, he had been told that if Cairo fell he was to stay behind with a few handpicked Field Security men to carry out specified acts of sabotage, after which they were to lie low until British troops recaptured the city. He knew it would be dangerous, but a part of him relished the opportunity to stick it to the Jerries with a few well-placed bombs. When he had informed his Egyptian friends that he might be staying behind, several had told him that he could count on them for food and shelter if the Germans broke through to Cairo. He doubted that there would be a national resistance movement, but in the last twenty-four hours many Egyptians, and particularly those from the middle and upper classes, seemed to have reached the conclusion that they would be better off with Englishmen occupying their country than Nazis, which he found reassuring.

Bulling his way to the front of the line at one of the ticket windows, he asked the ticket salesman which platform the trains to Palestine were disembarking from. Platform 8, he discovered, leaving in two minutes.

He made a mad dash for the platform—but was too late. The train was racing down the track, a hundred yards away and gaining speed.

Bloody hell!

He kicked a dustbin. But that failed to satisfy him, so he tossed it onto the track. People gave him looks. He blubbered a half-hearted apology and returned to his car. Thankfully, it hadn't been vandalized or towed. His placard had produced the desired effect.

Thirty minutes later, he was back behind his paperwork-cluttered desk at GHQ—in an exceedingly foul mood. He had so much wanted to give his wife a proper send-off and was already missing her. He began reviewing files. By the time he had read through a dozen of them and stamped out his fifth cigarette of the day in the ashtray, a dapper-looking man in a fancy suit, silk tie, and bowler hat appeared at the open door. Without a word, the man strutted into his office as if he were King George himself. He carried a foldover leather satchel.

"Do you always walk into people's offices without knocking?" snorted Sansom.

"Hello there—I'm Bob," said the man laconically—without answering his question and with a seemingly intentional touch of mystery.

"I'm going to need more than that, Bob—if, in fact, that is your real name."

"Don't worry, it isn't. All I can tell you for now is that I work for MI6."

"Oh, so you're one of Cuthbert Bowly's boys," he said, referring to the head of Military Intelligence, Section 6, in Cairo with responsibility for the Middle East and Balkans. MI6 was the Secret Intelligence Service, or SIS, responsible for gathering intelligence outside Britain, while MI5 controlled counterespionage in the United Kingdom and throughout the Empire. While MI6's charter was to operate in all areas outside British territory, in actual practice the intelligence activities of the two covert agencies sometimes overlapped, which led to inevitable friction.

"Something like that," said Bob vaguely. "But more importantly, I'm here to help you. Just so you know, I have established good working relations here at GHQ, but like you chaps in Field Security, I am terribly overworked."

"Are you trying to garner my sympathy?"

"No, Major Sansom, but I am here to help you. Here, take a look at this."

He withdrew a copy of a book from his satchel and handed it to Sansom, who proceeded to look over the cover and flip through the first few pages.

"*Rebecca*, by Daphne du Maurier. And I suppose there's a point to all this?"

"Have you read it?"

"When it first came out a few years ago. But I actually preferred the film—I'm something of a Hitchcock aficionado. What's the significance?"

"I found the book when I was going through the possessions of two Abwehr wireless operators taken prisoner on May 29 when their forward Signals Unit was captured by the LRDG. Their names are Walter Aberle and Waldemar Weber. You haven't heard those names, have you by chance?"

"Can't say I have."

"The two Brandenburgers are Palestinian-born Germans. Aberle's the driver, Weber the W/T operator. Before their capture, they reported directly to *Abteilung* I, a small unit of six junior officers attached to the mobile HQ of *Panzerarmee Afrika* under G2 intelligence officer Major Max Zalling. Weber's W/T station is codenamed *Schildkroete*."

"Tortoise."

"Yes, that is the correct translation. Following their capture, they were briefly questioned at Eighth Army HQ before being hurried on to Cairo for a more thorough interrogation by intelligence officers."

"They were taken to the interrogation center at Maadi?"

"That's correct. At first, all they would give were their names and *Soldbuch* numbers, and throughout the process they remained pretty tight lipped. But what gave them up was what you have before you. You see, it was the only book they had with them. Oh, they had other reading materials—the usual Nazi magazines, newspapers, personal letters from home, and such—but that copy of *Rebecca* you're holding was the only English-language item among their possessions."

"Are you saying they were using it as a codebook?"

He nodded. "We weren't certain at first. It could have simply been a book captured from a British frontline unit and they were reading it. It was only when we interrogated them that we realized their knowledge of English literature was virtually nil and their English embarrassingly bad. So why would they possibly have an English language copy of a popular novel?"

"Where do you think they got it?"

"We've had a bit of luck there too. A forensic photographer from here at GHQ has worked out from the yellow dust jacket that the book was priced at fifty escudos." He point to the book. "You can see that that the Germans tried to remove the price, but without success."

"So you're telling me the book was bought in Portugal?"

"Right you are. And it just so happens that the wife of the German assistant military attaché in Portugal purchased six copies of the novel at an English language book shop in Estoril on April 3. This date happens to be only a week before Admiral Wilhelm Canaris traveled to North Africa via Spain to meet with Rommel. Coincidence? I think not."

"You're saying that the head of the Abwehr, having come to Africa via Spain, brought the six copies of *Rebecca* with him purchased by the wife of the German assistant military attaché in Portugal?"

"There's even more to it than that. Aberle and Weber also revealed that two German agents were delivered to the Nile by a Hungarian count and desert explorer named Captain Almasy of the Abwehr in late May."

"There have been whispers that Almasy himself is on a secret mission here in Cairo. Apparently, he has been spotted at several popular watering holes."

"No, it's not him—it's someone else. And there's two agents in Cairo, not one. Aberle and Weber said so under interrogation."

"The *Rebecca* codebook then is for these two Abwehr agents?"

"Precisely. Almasy brought them through the desert, but he is long gone and has returned to base. He's not here in Cairo—but his two operatives most certainly are."

"So the objective of their mission is to establish wireless contact with Aberle and Weber once they set up a base of operations in the city?"

"I believe that they've already commenced operations in Cairo. But obviously Aberle and Weber can no longer receive their transmissions as they have been captured. Were you aware that the radio monitoring section here at GHQ recently reported that a transmitter has been coming on air at precisely midnight, every night, for the past month?"

"The reports have been crossing my desk for the past week or so."

"Then you know from the reports that the location, or locations, of the midnight transmissions are, as of yet, unknown."

"Yes, but we do know they're coming from somewhere in the city."

"Whoever the radio operator that is using *Rebecca* as his code is, he has a unique 'fist.' He uses a single pattern and his signature is always the same."

"But as you've said, we still don't know precisely where he's transmitting from."

"No, but using *Rebecca*—or any book for that matter—as a spy code is fairly straightforward. Sentences are made using single words in the book, referred to by page numbers, line, and position in the line. The key is to change the page numbers every day. It's a secure method of communication—but only as long as no one else knows the title of the book. But that is no longer the case since the two Abwehr wireless men have been captured. The book is now basically a de-code manual. What I'd like to know is what the profile of the two spies might be?"

"They're probably German nationals with close knowledge of Egypt, or at least North Africa. They're obviously regarded by Canaris and Almasy as agents of sufficient importance that they have been provided with their own personal code and a special listening-unit to take the information they collect."

"With the listening unit—in the form of Aberle and Weber—rounded up, I would say then that the crucial task is to triangulate the transmitter's location here in the city."

"It would appear so. Who else knows about this?"

"Reports are passing through the Defense Security Office in Cairo, across the desk of Colonel Jenkins, and on to the War Office and MI5 in London."

"I haven't been copied."

"You are now." Bob withdrew a sheaf of papers with a cover sheet that read "Most Secret" in red ink, handed them to Sansom, took back the copy of *Rebecca*, and stuffed it back into his foldover satchel. Then he headed for the door, turning around just before reaching it.

"I'll be in touch," he said.

"I must say I'm looking forward to it," said Sansom, and he flipped open the Most Secret brief and began to read.

Five minutes later, he looked up thoughtfully and lit a vile French Gauloises cigarette since he had again run out of Dunhills. Things were beginning to click into place. The Germans were using *Rebecca* as a code manual and had planted two agents in Cairo to transmit in the agreed-upon code on the state of the British Army. Whoever the W/T operator was, he was not yet sending information because he was not getting acknowledgment; and suspecting he was being monitored, he was not about to make it easy for the enemy to locate his transmitter by broadcasting needlessly. With Aberle and Weber in captivity, the only listening post receiving the agents' transmissions was the GHQ monitoring unit right here in Cairo. But the current state of affairs was not going to last long. Eventually, the spies would realize that either something was wrong with their W/T set or no one was listening on the other end, most likely because Aberle and Weber had been captured. But surely they must have some other means to establish contact with their controllers, and even if not, the Germans were bound to answer from another station before long. Then the signals chaps at GHQ would jam the pirate, the Germans would tell their agents they were being jammed, and the agents would do a bunk.

In that case, Sansom—and his new friend Bob—would have nothing.

We've got to catch these devils, he thought, taking a puff from his cigarette. *And we must do it soon, before they figure out another way to get in contact with bloody Rommel.*

CHAPTER 31

EPPLER AND SANDSTETTE HOUSEBOAT
AGOUZA, CAIRO

JUNE 29, 1942

PARKING HER CADILLAC BY HER HOUSEBOAT, Hekmat rushed to Hussein Gaafar and Peter Muncaster's *dahabia* to tell them the shocking news. Earlier today, with Alexandria the first likely target for the *Afrika Korps*, Admiral Henry Harwood, commander of the British Mediterranean Fleet, had evacuated the entire fleet out of the city's port as Axis troops advanced towards El Alamein. The ships—which included the cruiser *HMS Dido*, seven destroyers, and the submarine depot ship *HMS Medway*—were said to be sailing for Port Said, Haifa, and perhaps Beirut. And then, to make matters worse, the Germans swiftly followed up with a massive air raid on the northern port city. With the loss of the protection of the Royal Navy and the Luftwaffe attacking without impunity, the European communities in Alexandria and Cairo felt abandoned and the flap had officially turned into a full-fledged panic, spreading across the Delta like wildfire. The BBC had only made matters worse by calling the ongoing battle between Rommel's and Auchinleck's forces around Mersa Matruh the "Battle for Egypt."

The news had so startled the citizens of the two cities that in a matter of hours shares had slumped on the stock exchange, property prices had dropped to pre-war levels, and people were now abandoning both cities in even greater droves for Palestine and the Sudan. British women and children were packing up what they could and joining the swarming crowds at the train station. Others were setting off across the Delta in cars crammed with as many earthly possessions as they could carry. People in both cities were already reportedly selling their properties and businesses at a loss before fleeing. Meanwhile, Egyptian shops and clubs in the city had already begun displaying decorations welcoming the German troops.

It was a terrifying time in Cairo—and an exciting one. But unlike the British, the Germans were an unknown quantity to Hekmat and, therefore, posed the greater threat. Many of her friends, though they viewed the British unfavorably or even disliked or hated them, considered them the lesser of two evils—and Hekmat tended to agree. In her view, given the harsh racial laws of Hitler and his senior Nazi officials, the Germans had to be considered a far more dangerous potential occupier.

As she neared the houseboat, she saw Hussein Gaafar swing in from the street at a hurried pace, walk up the gangway, step onto the deck, and descend the stairs belowdecks. He had an urgent look on his face and must have heard the news about the British fleet abandoning Alexandria and the Luftwaffe bombing. She was excited to talk to him about it. Picking up her pace, she quickly boarded the *dahabia*. But her enthusiasm was dampened by the sound of her former lover and Muncaster arguing from inside the boat. Though they were not shouting at one another, they were definitely quarreling.

You should probably just leave them alone, she thought, and she started to turn to walk away.

But then curiosity got the better of her.

Wanting to hear what they were arguing about, she stepped to the forward hatch to the stairs that led belowdecks. She could hear them but could not quite make out what they were saying. But with the *dahabia's* deck windows and portals wide open to allow the breeze to come in from the Nile, she had another way to eavesdrop. Looking around, she saw that there was no one on the decks of the nearby houseboats that could see her. There were two or three sailing vessels on the river and a pair of pedestrians walking along the riverwalk, but they were far away.

Ducking down to keep out of sight, she quietly crept along the port side of the houseboat to the edge of one of the open windows. The *dahabia* was sumptuously appointed. The furniture was chintz-covered and the woodwork painted pale green. There were hangings on the canvas walls with decorative Egyptian figure friezes. Between the two flights of steps which led to the upper deck was a long mahogany cabinet. On top of this stood a radio, and in the middle, sunk in, was a gramophone turntable and at each end a cupboard. She edged closer to the open port window. Listening carefully, she could hear every word now over the light croaking of the bullfrogs and the chirping cicadas in the sycamore trees along the banks of the Nile.

"...in turmoil. Foreign currency on the black market has dropped nearly fifty per cent in the past two days, damnit."

It was her old lover Gaafar talking. There was a tense silence, and then she heard Muncaster say in reply, "What the hell do you want me to do about it?"

"Well, you can start by hauling your ass out of bed and getting that damned radio to work. How do you expect us to communicate with Rommel's headquarters if we can't get the fucking radio to work?"

She felt the breath catch in her throat. *Rommel! My God, are they really Nazi spies?*

"Why don't you just fuck off!" snarled Muncaster. "And if you're so smart, why don't you get it to work? You've had wireless training too, you know."

"Don't be a whiner, you know you're better than me. Now get out of bed. How much did you have to drink last night?"

"No more than you and that Wog tart you brought back here. Talk about the pot calling the kettle black. You two were stumbling and drooling when you got back to the houseboat."

"Yes, but at least I was up and about at a reasonable hour trying to solve our money problems with Wahda and the Armenian," replied Gaafar, referring to their errand-boy, the money changer and pimp Albert Wahda, and the underworld figure Kevork Yirikian, whom Hekmat had not met. "But unfortunately, the exchange rate with all of this fucking flap business is only one-third. At this rate, we're going to run out of money in the next two or three weeks if we don't get back to German lines and get some more."

"But you're the one who said to spend like crazy as part of our playboy cover in the nightclubs," she heard Muncaster reply as he began putting on his clothes.

"Yes, but I didn't think we'd rack up bills of twenty pounds per night. We have to cut back."

"You have the gall to tell me that after that tart you bedded last night. How much did you spend on her?"

"You watch your tongue, damn you. We have to solve this situation together, not be at each other's throats."

"That's easy for you to say when you're the one who came charging in here accusing me."

"Okay, okay, I'm sorry. But right now, we have to take a deep breath and figure this situation out."

They fell into momentary silence. A twitch of shock passed across Hekmat's face. What had she stumbled into? A moment later, the bed squeaked, and she heard the sound of feet padding across the floor followed by the sound of Muncaster putting on his shoes. And then it struck her: *What would they do to me if they discovered I was listening?*

She realized she already knew the answer to that question: *They will kill you!*

Feeling her hands trembling ever so slightly, she moved further away from the window, not wanting them to see her. Muncaster resumed the conversation.

"I don't know what's wrong with the transmitter," he said to Gaafar. "I've been sending the messages to *Schildkroete* at precisely midnight almost every night since our arrival. But we've still received no response. I'm at my wit's end. I don't know what else could be wrong except that the transmitter is faulty."

"You don't think it could be because of the way you're tapping out the code?"

"Are you insinuating that I'm misusing the codebook?"

"Well, isn't it possible?"

"Possible yes, but I consider it highly unlikely."

Leaning forward to get a better view, she watched as Muncaster went to the mahogany cabinet where the radiogram was located. From beneath the radiogram, he withdrew a book with several sheets of paper stuffed inside it. It was a well-camouflaged hiding place. As Muncaster returned to the bed and sat back down, she could just make out the title of the book and the author's name: it was an English-language version of *Rebecca* by Daphne du Maurier. Hekmat had not read the book and knew nothing of the author. But having acted in several Egyptian films, she was an avid moviegoer and last year had seen the popular movie directed by Alfred Hitchcock and starring Laurence Olivier and Joan Fontaine, both of whom had been nominated for an Oscar for their performances. The book in Muncaster's hands had a distinctive yellow cover with red and black lettering, the author's name in black, the title in red, and the words "Famous Bestseller" on the front.

She heard a noise behind her, coming from the direction of the Egyptian Benevolent Hospital, but it was just a pair of Muslim women walking towards the river to wash their clothes. They posed no risk to her and didn't even look in her direction.

"So, you don't think something might have gone wrong at the other end. You think it's a faulty transmitter?" asked Gaafar, resuming the conversation.

"I don't know, but there's only one way to find out. We need to bring in an expert to check out the transmitter and make sure it's working properly."

"What about the aerial on deck?"

"No, we know from the major that it's in good working order."

Major Smith was Hekmat's friend, the officer in British Intelligence, who had unwittingly helped the two spies set up their aerial when they had first acquired the houseboat. A friendly neighbor living on a nearby houseboat, he had offered to help them when they were having trouble with the reception on their radiogram, and in almost no time he had a British signals officer from GHQ install a proper aerial that he claimed had a range of a thousand miles. Gaafar had boasted to her about how powerful it was.

Now she heard Muncaster again. He and Gaafar were now standing over by the mahogany cabinet with the radiogram. Muncaster pulled out what looked like a radio transmitter and receiver. "What do you want to do about this damned thing?"

"I don't know. It all makes me so angry," responded Eppler. "All I can say is this is a huge oversight by the Abwehr. Goddamned Canaris and Almasy. We should have been given some emergency means of communication with our controllers."

"Well, we didn't so we have to make due," said Muncaster. "What do you want to do?"

"We should get in touch with my stepbrother Hassan. He may be able to help."

"I thought you weren't sure you could trust him."

"No, I think he will be helpful. It's just that he's not my brother, he's only my stepbrother. Plus he was gone when I first met with my mother but she says that he's back in town again."

"Okay."

"Plus, the situation's changed. We've been unable to reach Rommel—either that or Weber's not responding—so we have to try something different."

"So how will you contact your stepbrother?"

"I'll write him and ask him to meet me at the Americaine Bar in Fouad el Awal. That's as safe a place as we can find."

"Are you sure you can trust him? And your mother for that matter? After all, she was married to a staunch British supporter."

"My stepfather's dead now. She wouldn't dare hurt her son. We can trust my mother and my stepbrother to help us."

"What about Hekmat?"

"I don't want to get her involved. At the same time, I hate myself for not being honest with her."

"You're still in love with her, aren't you?"

"A part of me will always love her. I should never have let her go."

It was a sweet thing to say and she felt a little rush of emotion. But as she did, she accidentally moved her hand and pressed it against the wall for support. But by shifting her position, the bracelet on her wrist made a little jingling noise.

Every muscle froze.

"What was that?" said Muncaster, and he looked alertly towards the open deck window.

She ducked down and flattened her body against the houseboat. Suddenly, her heart was pounding in her chest and she thought she would faint.

"I didn't hear anything," said Gaafar.

"I did. I think someone's out there."

She had to get the hell out of here. She looked at the gangway thirty feet away. *No, there's not enough time,* she told herself. *You have to pretend that you just showed up.*

With the athletic precision of the belly dancer that she was, she quickly crab-walked beneath the level of the windows and darted for the front door. She made it just in the nick of time as Gaafar and Muncaster—whom she knew were German spies but still did not know were named Eppler and Sandstette—came dashing out.

"Have you heard the news?" she blurted suddenly, hoping to take them by surprise. "The British Navy has pulled out of Alexandria, the Germans have bombed the city, and now people are fleeing by the thousands to the Delta and Palestine! What are we going to do if the Germans come?"

It was her best panicky woman routine, but she couldn't tell if she had actually fooled them. They scrutinized her for a long tense moment, as if trying to divine if she was telling the truth. She held her breath. And then, after what seemed like forever, Gaafar's face softened and he reached out and took her by the hand.

"Right now, I'm going to open a fine bottle of Cabernet Sauvignon and put together a little meal for us of flat bread and *ful medames*," he said. "The war can wait, my dear Hekmat—the war can wait."

CHAPTER 32

EAST OF EL DABA, EGYPT

JUNE 30, 1942

FROM THE TOP OF A BARCHAN SAND DUNE, Rommel stared at a cluster of burning Mark II Matildas in the foreground and, to the distant west, the regrouping British Army at the new El Alamein Line. Although he and his *Panzerarmee* were gripped with chronic shortages of petrol, food, transport, and almost everything else that mattered, it was good to see Tommy on the run and he was in high spirits. But time was of the essence. If he did not advance rapidly and break through at El Alamein in the coming days, his *blitzkrieg* would be unsustainable. Not only because of the formidable defensive terrain which favored Auchinleck, the growing strength of his defenses, and an expected infusion of American tanks and artillery pieces, but due to the haggard state of his own troops and overstretched supply line.

His men had been fighting for over a month with scarcely any pause to rest and refit—and it showed in the deep circles beneath their eyes, their tattered uniforms, and the fresh wounds and desert sores on their bodies. Like them, he rarely slept for five consecutive hours, lived mainly on adrenaline, and was not in good health. His personal physician that he rarely listened to told him he was suffering from a liver infection, a duodenal ulcer, low blood pressure, and desert sores. Meanwhile, his soldiers had taken a heavy toll from the high rate of dysentery and diarrhea which, along with hepatitis, seriously depleted his Panzer Army. But with Tommy on the run, there was no time for rest for him or his men. In fact, he had been in such a hurry to drive the British out of Egypt altogether that he hadn't even taken time to change out his shoulder badges on his uniform to those of his new rank of *Generalfeldmarschall*—two crossed batons.

At this stage in the war, the newly promoted and victorious Erwin Rommel was still pleased to serve his master Adolf Hitler. But he had always been and would always be the furthest thing from a rabid Nazi. Though before the war he had served on Hitler's personal escort battalion at the Führer's request and was the golden boy of the German leader and Propaganda Minister Joseph Goebbels, who considered him "the personification of the successful German soldier," he had never been a member of the National Socialist Party and did not trust the Nazis. In fact, even though he had long enjoyed a cordial relationship with Hitler, he had never been comfortable with National Socialism or Hitler's brown-shirted thugs that first rose to power in the late 1920s.

But while he was no Nazi, he was exceedingly naïve and blind to the growing evil of the regime he served. His fame as the Desert Fox was a boon to Nazi propaganda, and he happily cultivated this relationship. He frequently took photographs during his campaigns and distributed them to German magazines, while Goebbels sent film crews to follow him around to capture his victories for the hungry German masses back home. Because he regarded himself as nothing but a simple soldier and, for the time being, ingenuously believed that the Führer's and the Fatherland's goals were one and the same, he was somehow able to admire Hitler and slavishly do his and Goebbels's bidding while at the same time he despised the Nazis. In return, Hitler loved him like a favored son and promoted him at a dizzying pace even though he wasn't a National Socialist.

Though he didn't even know it about himself, he was a man whose earnest, simple convictions came at the price of being ignorant to the dirtier workings of the Third Reich. It was this dichotomy that on the one hand posited him as a genuine hero, a brilliant general, an ethical man, and a noble soldier who did not dirty himself with the crimes of the Nazis—and on the other as Hitler's pet, a tacit Nazi collaborator, and an officer who served his criminal government without questioning the essence of Nazi ideology. This schism he would not understand until the fall of 1944 when it was too late and Hitler had him killed.

With regard to the "Jewish Question," he had never felt the animosity towards the Jews of Europe that so many of his countrymen experienced, and in North Africa he was totally unaware of the atrocities taking place in Poland, Russia, and other occupied territories where the SS had a significant presence. He would not learn of Himmler's ongoing mobile SS death squads—*Einsatzgruppen*—and the even more heinous and far-reaching program of terror and murder that would reach its peak in 1944 and 1945 with the large-scale Nazi death camps and systematic "Final Solution" until after the Allied invasion on D-Day.

In North Africa, where there was no SS presence, he was far removed from the ongoing horrors transpiring in the occupied countries—and in any event, he didn't even know they were taking place. In his own eyes, therefore, all he could do was position himself to serve his country and limit the inhumanity in his own theater of operations. For him, *Krieg Ohne Hass*—War Without Hate—accomplished that noble if oxymoronic objective. He would never have considered that he was morally tainted because he fought for Hitler's Reich.

In his own moral universe, he was nothing but a simple soldier who loved his family and his country—and that was what he fought for.

ΨΨΨ

Peering through his Zeiss 10x50 field glasses, he studied the terrain and tried to imagine the forthcoming battle that would win him all of Egypt. He had surveyed this portion of the North African desert on two occasions in his little Storch scout plane and knew it well. Unfortunately, Auchinleck had already established a strong defensive position for his Eighth Army. It extended from the shores of the Mediterranean at the railway depot at El Alamein—with no right flank to turn and a siding that greatly simplified supply problems—to forty miles south at the northern cliffs of the Qattara Depression.

The 7,000-square-mile basin sank to almost 450 feet below sea level and was covered with impassable sand-encrusted saline lakes and marshes, tabletopped hills, and bizarre sand sculptures carved over the millennia by arid wind and wet rain. There were tracks through it, but it was hard going for camels, let alone tanks and wheeled vehicles. Between El Alamein and Qattara were three narrow ridges running parallel with the coast: Miteiriya, Ruweisat, and Alam el Halfa. The craggy,

8-mile long Ruweisat Ridge in particular was ideal for concealing large numbers of infantry guns and tanks. The ridge ran east-to-west, and had the natural effect of channeling any attack in its direction north or south of it, while any forces positioned on the ridge itself remained poised as a threat to the flank of such an attack.

Though Auchinleck's position had not been fully prepared due to the speed of the German *blitzkrieg*, Rommel could see that it was strong. The line consisted of a series of boxes similar to the Gazala Line. Astride the coastal road and railway, he could make out one box, which appeared to have been dug, mined, and at least partly wired. Fifteen miles to the south, closer to the Qattara Depression, was another box that blocked an east-west dirt road. He couldn't quite tell from his vantage point, but it looked as though the box had been dug but was not yet mined. And finally, just north of the Qattara escarpment, a third box stood on what looked like firm sand. Very little work had been done on this box, but every soldier who could lift a sandbag, swing a pickaxe, or lay a landmine was no doubt working to finish the fortifications. Behind the boxes, the Auk had positioned most of his remaining armor, and infantry and artillery were already deployed on the ridges.

All in all, what made the line far more formidable than the Gazala Line was the impassable Qattara Depression, which ensured that the Desert Fox would not be able to outflank the British to the south. But what caused him the most consternation was that more and more enemy tanks and guns were arriving at the front every day in an attempt to hold his *Panzerarmee* in check. From the latest intercepts, he had learned that a large shipment of new Sherman tanks and 105-mm M7 Priest self-propelled guns were expected to be delivered to Alexandria by September courtesy of the United States. Purported to be faster, more reliable, better armored, and just as heavily armed as most of his Panzers, the Sherman tank promised to be a gamechanger for the Eighth Army. Clearly, Auchinleck was determined to buy time with his defensive boxes and artillery sited on Ruweisat Ridge and other protective promontories until the arrival of the American weapons.

But what also troubled Rommel was that, despite being routed at Mersa Matruh during the past two days, Auchinleck was handling his forces with considerable skill. Tactically, he was far superior to Ritchie. The British, the Desert Fox knew, hadn't been soundly defeated at the Gazala Line, Tobruk, and Mersa Matruh due to a shortage of tanks, guns, troops, or the poor performance of the men in action, but to bad generalship, sluggishness, and indecisiveness. But now the Auk was in command. All in all, despite recent German successes, the towering Scot seemed to view the situation with decided coolness and was making sound defensive preparations. Which meant that breaking the Alamein Line was not going to be easy.

But it was going to be even harder, Rommel knew, now that he likely no longer had his "little fellers" to rely upon. Von Mellenthin and Captain Seebohm of 621 Company had notified him early this morning that the Americans had suddenly and mysteriously replaced their compromised Black Code with a new cipher and that Fellers had not sent his usual daily message. The U.S. military attaché always began his dispatches with the words MILID WASH for Military Intelligence Division, Washington, or AGWAR WASH for Adjutant General, War Department, as well as signed off with the word FELLERS so it was easy for the cryptanalysts to pick out his messages from the modest volume of radio traffic coming out of Cairo. Though it had yet to be confirmed, it appeared as if the British had somehow discovered that Fellers was the source of the leak in Cairo, had notified the Americans of their folly regarding the Black Code, and the Americans had changed the code. It was not clear yet exactly what had happened, but it seemed the Americans might be considering replacing Fellers or perhaps had already done so. Even worse, the Abwehr monitoring stations at Lauf in Germany, Berlin, Athens, and the nearby Signals Unit 621 had all been unable to crack the new code. Rommel couldn't believe it, but it was looking like his Good Source was no more—just when he needed him most to make his final push to destroy Eighth Army and take the Suez.

As the situation now stood, two out of his three primary intelligence assets had most likely been fatally compromised, he realized with dismay. The first—the spies Eppler and Sandstette along with their radio controllers Aberle and Weber—had been the first to be compromised. The capture of Aberle and Weber along with their signals trucks and codebooks had jeopardized Operation Condor before it had even begun, although Abwehr HQ in Berlin was still having its stations in Libya and Athens listen for transmissions from "Condor"—Eppler and Sandstette—in Cairo to try and establish contact with the spies. Berlin had ordered the stations to do so using the frequencies and call signs used by *Schildkroete*, the W/T operator Weber, whom the Abwehr knew had been captured by the British. But thus far, the spies and Abwehr listening posts that had replaced Weber had not been able to establish contact. But now with his Good Source seemingly vanished into thin air, Rommel knew his situation was actually even worse. The only definitive intelligence source he now had left was Captain Seebohm and his 100-strong Wireless Reconnaissance Unit 621—his last remaining secret ear into the enemy's communications.

Thankfully during their Gazala Gallop, the British were still failing to frequently change their unit radio codes and call-signs, displaying an unbelievable lack of battlefield radio discipline. They gave direct orders in the clear and pontificated on important military matters during combat, and his intelligence officers had been able to make significant conclusions regarding British plans, troop movements, and weaknesses from their lack of radio discretion. But even the outstanding Seebohm and his Unit 621 could not make up for the loss of *Gute Quelle* or the Cairo spies Eppler and Sandstette. Rommel knew he needed more intelligence sources not less if he was to succeed in his final push into Egypt.

He felt a presence at his side: it was von Mellenthin. *God, I hope he doesn't have more bad news.*

"The last of the enemy prisoners have been marched to the cage in Mersa Matruh," said his chief of operations 1a.

"Including the New Zealanders?" asked Rommel.

"Yes, sir. You know they should be shot for what they did to our men."

"No, they should not, damnit, and I don't want to hear any of my officers even suggesting such a thing. Do you hear me?"

"I do, *Herr Feldmarschall*, but I can tell you that there are still hard feelings over this incident."

"I am angry too. But we must maintain honor and discipline. We must uphold our end of the bargain and not retaliate in kind."

Von Mellenthin nodded, but Rommel could tell he didn't agree with him. The incident had happened two nights ago when the 2nd New Zealand Division had been encircled without armored support south of Mersa Matruh. The enemy had broken out in a night attack with fixed bayonets, yelling Haka war-cries. A German medical unit aid station had been directly in the path of the charging Kiwis and a number of German medical personnel and wounded soldiers that had bedded down for the night were killed in the rush, some shot, others bayoneted, while their trucks were set ablaze. As the New Zealanders rolled over the medical station, they thrust their bayonets into any human form on the ground, dead or alive. While a fortunate few managed to scramble out of their bedrolls and escape into the darkness, some of the German wounded were thrown onto the blazing trucks to burn alive or were bayonetted as they attempted to surrender. The New Zealanders were in such a state of frenzy that, in the darkness and confusion, many in the rear jabbed at their own wounded that had fallen in the first wave and several had to take cover to prevent being slaughtered by their own troops.

Rommel, who was nearly caught in the breakout himself, was furious when he learned of the incident and upbraided Brigadier George Clifton, the senior New Zealand POW officer, for the barbaric behavior of his troops, whom he considered "the elite of the British Army." Incensed, he threatened reprisals on captured New Zealanders if such practices continued. But the explosive situation was defused when Clifton apologized for the incident and pointed out that it had been a nighttime attack, lit only by muzzle and grenade flashes and the flames of the burning vehicles, and his men could not have known they were attacking a medical unit until it was too late. Rommel, who had seen his share of nighttime actions go awry, accepted Clifton's explanation, though it failed to explain why the frenzied Kiwis had thrown his wounded men into the flames and watched them burn alive.

Hearing the distant thrum of airplanes, he looked to the sky. At first, the sound was barely perceptible but slowly it grew, until he realized apprehensively what was coming. They were Curtiss P-40 Tomahawks—the lethal, American single-engine fighter-bombers supplied to the British that had been wreaking havoc on him lately. While the planes struggled against the Luftwaffe's superior Messerschmitt Bf 109 and Focke-Wulf Fw 190 at high altitudes, they could go toe-to-toe with any German fighter at low levels, and his troops loathed them like the plague.

"We need to take cover, sir," said von Mellenthin.

Rommel agreed, but the question was where. In additional to the fleet of vehicles making up his *Kampfstaffel*—his roving HQ and armored close-protection detachment—there was only the captured British ration store by the roadside, a pair of huts, the string of coastal dunes, and a single rocky outcrop.

They made for the scant protection of the outcrop.

The Tomahawks swooped down from above like a swarm of locusts. There were six of them, screaming in from the east, skimming the tops of the dunes as they skirted the edge of the Egyptian desert. From their low approach and aggressive-looking formation, there was no doubt they were gunning for his *Kampfstaffel*, and he wished he hadn't decided to take a roadside halt and scan the Alamein Line from the vulnerable top of a sand dune. And then to the west, he saw a pair of Focke-Wulf fighters with black swastikas and yellow trim on their tails and a Messerschmitt Bf 109-F flying in to intercept the British aircraft.

"There is hope for us yet, Friedrich," he said. "Look!"

"Unfortunately, the odds are three to one against."

"Nearly the same as the British versus us—and we have managed to prevail most every time. I think I like those odds."

The Tomahawks opened up with their machine guns and his forces on the ground returned antiaircraft fire. With machine guns rattling his ears and airplane engines roaring overhead, he looked down at his staff officers jumping from the line of parked staff cars, running out of the buildings, and scrambling for cover in the desert scrub and small depressions along the coast. He looked up again at the attacking planes and could now see their British markings. They were flying so low over the dunes that he swore they would clip the tops of them.

What happened next unfolded as if in slow motion. The Tomahawks began dropping whistling bombs into his fleet of vehicles on the coastal plain below. At the same time, the two German Focke-Wulf's intercepted the British planes and opened fire. For a brief instant, it was like some great pageant as the bombs plummeted downward through the air and the machine guns crackled and the nine engaged aircraft raced across the backdrop of blue sky, the men inside the flying machines rolling and turning desperately while heavily engaged in combat. The red tracer fire flew past like comets streaking across the heavens. It was so visceral and violent that up close it seemed surreal to him.

And yet, he loved it—this insane thing called war. Yes, he loved it.

He covered his ears and braced himself for the explosions. There were more than a dozen of them, one right after another. The detonations rocked the ground like an earth tremor. He saw three of his staff cars and one of the huts go up in flames and felt a wave of searing airborne heat from the blasts. The flames from the German vehicles rose twenty feet in the air in the foreground, the swelling black fuel clouds bending south in the light breeze and drifting towards him and away from the dreamily sparkling Mediterranean.

With their payloads dropped, the British fighter-bombers were racing back to the safety of their Egyptian airbases, while the Focke-Wulfs were intent on stopping them. The Tommies banked hard right towards the ocean, maintained their low altitude by nearly skimming across the waves, and flew off back to the south with the two German aircraft hot on their tail. He saw more tracer fire as the aircraft battled it out in a running dogfight. The planes worked their way east above the azure-blue littoral, following the jagged coastline, until he saw the Messerschmitt close in on two of the Tomahawks and take them down. The first clipped a coastal sand dune, losing part of its fuselage and a wing, and exploded in a burst of fire and smoke, while the second victim was clipped in the tail and dove into the sea like a gunshot hawk, a jet plume of fiery black smoke trailing behind.

When the planes had chased off the Tomahawks, they flew back towards the German line. He thought the sleek and speedy Messerschmitt looked particularly magnificent with its battle camo and black iron cross brandished across the fuselage. A cheer went up from his staff and hats were tossed in the air in celebration as the Messerschmitt and Focke-Wulfs roared by, their pilots saluting as they passed.

"Come on," he said to von Mellenthin, "we have to get the hell out of here before the British come back."

They dashed down the leeward side of the dune to the vehicles. Quickly assembling his officers, he told them that it wasn't safe here and they would be continuing briskly east towards the front. Leaving behind a medical team to look after the wounded, he jumped into his half-track Greif, which thankfully hadn't been hit, along with von Mellenthin, his clerk Munninger, and his driver von Leipzig. His chief of staff Bayerlein was scouting somewhere up ahead and he would have to reunite with him later.

The half-track tore off down the coast road. He was pleased to find that advance elements of his 15th Panzer Division had already reached a point close to El Alamein and that his troops were recovering large quantities of weapons, trucks, and fuel from the retreating Tommies. Up to 85 per cent of his transport now consisted of captured enemy tanks and other vehicles, and his men had managed to capture a powerful British 150-mm battery, which was put back into immediate action. While on his reconnaissance tour, he also came across a couple of lorries and a Russian 76-mm gun to add to his *Panzerarmee's* booty. One of the lorries was still fully loaded and there were cases of Tommy guns and rifles lying close by.

But as he sped off towards the Alamein front, in the back of his mind, he knew he was racing against time. His troops had always given their best effort, often performing like *Übermensch*—Supermen—and he had long enjoyed a superiority in his senior officers and of certain German weapons over their British counterparts. But the gap was closing, even if it seemed like he had the enemy on the run. Now there were already signs, in the new Allied tanks and anti-tank guns, of a coming qualitative superiority of Allied matériel. For that reason alone, it was essential to do everything possible to bring about a British collapse in Egypt before considerable shipments of arms could arrive from Britain and the United States.

That night, after driving far to the east through a violent sandstorm, he held a conference over the forthcoming attack on the Alamein Line with Bayerlein and several of his generals. Once his army had a full day to regroup following their breakneck advance, he would attack with his 15th and 21st Panzer Divisions, 90th Light Division, and other units two days hence on July 1.

It would be the Battle for Egypt that would settle the North African question once and for all.

He could almost taste the victory in his mouth. His beloved *Afrika Korps* was the best army in the war on either side he felt, and with his leadership—or, more importantly, with his example of being right there at the front with them, enduring the same hardships and dangers, at every turn—there seemed to be nothing they couldn't accomplish. With that in mind, before he went to bed, he decided to write a quick letter to his wife and tell her the good news of his most recent victory. He missed her and wished he could be in her loving arms.

30 June 1942
Dearest Lu,
Mersa Matruh fell yesterday, after which the Army moved on until late in the night. We're already 60 miles to the east. Less than 100 miles to Alexandria!

CHAPTER 33

BRITISH MIDDLE EAST HEADQUARTERS
GARDEN CITY

JULY 1, 1942

BONNER FELLERS stared glumly out the window of his third-floor office at GHQ overlooking the city. Although Auchinleck had won the eastward race by preparing stout defensive positions and making an about-turn to face Rommel at El Alamein, the Desert Fox was now only sixty-five goddamn miles west of Alexandria. Once he conquered Egypt, he would take Palestine, Syria, and the rich oil fields of Iraq and Persia, and join up with the German Army from the Eastern Front as it vanquished the Big Red Army and pushed southward from the Caucasus. From everything Fellers had seen of the British Army—and he had seen it as up-close as anyone and was privy to all of its top-level planning and operational details—the Auk would be lucky to hold out until late August.

What a disaster, he groaned inside, as he stared out at a world—and a British Eighth Army—in absolute turmoil. The streets were jammed with traffic and escaping people, and the train station was packed with women and children waiting to be taken to Palestine, Lebanon, and the Sudan. Beyond the fence line, Fellers saw cars and open-topped trucks, some carrying mattresses and furniture, grinding along Sharia Kasr Al Aini and Sharia Mansur and over Khedive Ismail Bridge spanning the Nile to the north. People were hurrying to get out of town before the Germans took control of the city and interned them in prisoner camps, rounded them up for labor or military conscription, or arrested them for anti-Nazi political views.

In the past three days, not only had there been a run on the banks but Egyptian civilians were fashioning swastika flags to hang from their windows and street mobs had begun openly taunting British troops with cries of "Advance Rommel!" Fellers found the attitude of the shopkeepers and even the shoeshine boys to be outright rude and almost gloating. This morning on his way to GHQ, he had seen an Italian flag prominently displayed in a shop window with a picture of Mussolini and King Victor Emmanuel on either side. All polite pretence that Egypt was a sovereign and independent country had long since been stripped away and many resentful Egyptians now believed their deliverance was at hand. As for the German prisoners of war, he had heard from some British officers that when they had driven past a POW cage, the captured soldiers were openly contemptuous, calling out: "You're just in time to see Rommel's victory march through Cairo!" and "More prisoners for the *Afrika Korps*!"

In response to the general panic, Lieutenant-General T.W. Corbett, Auchinleck's chief of general staff in overall charge in Cairo, ordered all officers to carry revolvers at all times and imposed an 8 p.m. to 7 a.m. curfew on central Cairo— without giving any explanation or reassurances to the civilian population. All this did, of course, was create more panic and ruined the capital's famous wartime night life. In fact, Fellers had heard that many British civilians and officers were more than happy to find a seat on the packed trains that left Cairo's central station daily for Palestine, Lebanon, and the Sudan, or on the planes that were flying to South Africa, rather than endure a city with no drinking or dancing.

Auchinleck had put together a contingency plan to ensure that the British Eighth Army survived even if it was driven out of Egypt altogether. Defenses were prepared in the Nile Delta and as far east as Palestine's Gaza Strip. Arrangements were even under way to ensure that sufficient Palestine pounds were available in the Mandate to pay the Eighth Army. Inevitably, such highly visible contingency plans sapped morale and contributed to an army desertion rate high enough to induce some senior officers to ask Auchinleck to consider restoring the death penalty, abolished in 1930, for desertion in the face of the enemy. He turned it down flat as undemocratic, knowing that during WWI very few of the more than 250 British soldiers executed for desertion or cowardice were officers. But the damage had been done.

The sense of panic was made only worse by the Royal Navy's decision to abandon its base at Alexandria and disperse the Mediterranean Fleet to Haifa and Beirut. With the harbor ominously empty, the nearby military and consular offices had begun burning their files, most European women and children had packed up and left, and the town appeared nearly completely deserted with few people on the streets and telephones ringing interminably in empty houses. Taking advantage of the chaos, Goebbels and his Reich propagandists were issuing radio broadcasts to Egyptian women: "Get out your party frocks, we're on our way!" Surreptitiously, shopkeepers made sure they had their photographs of Hitler and Rommel ready to slip into a frame, while their wives ran up red, white, and black bunting. Fellers had even heard reports that many households that rented rooms to officers who had left for the front were burning any incriminating British uniforms and photographs their lodgers had left behind.

All in all, the situation was bleak, and as he stared out the window at a city coming unraveled before his eyes, he couldn't help but wonder if somehow he—or more likely, his country—had unwittingly contributed to the disaster. Back in mid-May, officers from MI8, the British Signals Intelligence Service, had turned up at his office to review his security measures. He went over his procedures for filing his dispatches to Washington thoroughly with them and they had seemed satisfied. Furthermore, they didn't say anything about the U.S. Foreign Service Encryption Code 11, the Black Code, he routinely used for all his dispatches being broken. But at the time, he remembered having wondered why they were checking up on the cipher if there wasn't a problem. Was it possible that the Germans or Italians had somehow broken the code? In fact, the meeting with the Brits seemed to confirm the suspicions he had felt about the code back in February.

He had protested not once, but twice, to the State Department regarding the code. He had told them explicitly that he believed Code 11 had been compromised, but was told that it was secure and ordered to continue to use it over his objections. And then two days ago, he had been asked to make a change from the Black Code to a new code, the M-138 strip cipher, which he was told would defy all Abwehr *Chiffrilterabteilung's* efforts to crack. Though he had promptly agreed, he had again asked if the previous code had been broken, but no one would give him a straight answer. He felt fairly certain then that he had been right to begin with: the code had been compromised and he had most likely been a steady source of intelligence leakage for some time now because the damned State Department hadn't listened to him and changed the code back in February, when Rommel had begun his major push through Libya and into Egypt.

But he didn't know for sure because no one would tell him anything. All the same, he felt terrible as he stared out the window at the chaos that had overtaken Cairo. *Could my dispatches have aided Rommel in breaking the Gazala Line and taking Tobruk, or in the disaster with the British fleet at Malta?*

Malta. The British possession, situated just west of the principal Axis sea lane between Italy and North Africa, was critical to preventing Axis Mediterranean convoys from reaching Tobruk and other Libyan harbors. For the past two months, German and Italian aircraft had been pounding the little island, dropping some 9,000 tons of bombs in May and June alone. He remembered from his cables how clearly he had made it to Washington that the island was in a perilous position. In fact, he had predicted its surrender if the bombardment continued and supply convoys failed to reach it. In June, the British had decided to sail two convoys simultaneously from Alexandria in the east and Gibraltar in the west, respectively code-named *Vigorous* and *Harpoon*, in a full-scale attempt to relieve Malta. A vital part of the operation had been the neutralization of Axis ships and aircraft. Toward this end, the RAF had conducted air raids against key enemy bases and the SAS had attacked several airfields to destroy bombers before they could be flown against the convoys.

Shuffling through copies of the dispatches in his folder, he found the one he was looking for. Cable No. 11119 dated June 11, the same day the eastern convoy sailed from Alexandria, read:

"NIGHTS OF JUNE 12TH JUNE 13TH BRITISH SABOTAGE UNITS PLAN SIMULTANEOUS STICKER BOMB ATTACKS AGAINST AIRCRAFT ON 9 AXIS AERODROMES. PLANS TO REACH OBJECTIVES BY PARACHUTES AND LONG RANGE DESERT PATROL."

How had the convoys and David Stirling's SAS aerodrome attacks fared? He knew exactly how they had fared. During Operations *Harpoon* and *Vigorous*, German airplanes had delivered heavy attacks on both convoys. Only two of the supply ships for *Harpoon* from Gibraltar made it safely to Malta, while the *Vigorous* convoy from Alexandria had been forced to turn back after losing eleven vessels in the fleet. Meanwhile, the SAS had met stiff resistance at the German airfield outside Bizerte in Tunisia and during the submarine operation to Crete, where the Axis forces, it had been reported by the survivors, had seemed to be waiting for them. The Free French raiders that went into action behind the lines in Libya and on the island of Crete had been set upon by floodlights and machine guns and were slaughtered. But success had been achieved at several of the other airfields, including the one that Stirling himself had attacked. Was it possible that the raids were successful only where unwitting early warning was not received, was ignored, or was ineptly handled?

He didn't know the answer, but he intended to find out. All the same, he knew the security breach was hardly his fault. He was not responsible for the security of the Black Code. His mission was simply to report back to Washington using the officially designated code. It was not his mistake that he was not provided with a secure system. Furthermore, he had tried on two occasions to tell the State Department that their code was likely compromised and the bureaucratic bastards hadn't listened to him. He had also adhered strictly to communications security protocols. Until two days ago, his military code book had been held in a safe inside a room with a locked and barred steel door to which he held the sole key, and he had diligently reported breaks in cryptographic procedures back in February.

Putting away the file, he leaned back in his chair and sighed.

It was as he was going over it all in his mind that he saw a tall, gangly British officer standing in his open doorway.

He nearly jumped out of his chair.

It was David Stirling of the SAS! Wearing a full short-sleeved uniform and tie—it was said the major never relaxed his dress code whether going into battle or unwinding afterwards—he had a cast on one arm and desert sores on the other, some covered with bandages, others wide open and festering. Though smartly dressed in his officer's uniform, the man looked physically exhausted, and Fellers knew why. After returning in late June from his latest desert mission, he was quickly back in Cairo coordinating with GHQ and rounding up supplies for another.

Fellers knew David Stirling from his good friend, Lady Hermione Ranfurly, and from the major's diplomat brother, Peter Stirling who worked at the British embassy. In fact, he had shared drinks with all three of the Stirling brothers at one time or another, though he was not close friends with any one of them and knew Peter the best due to the legendary parties at his nearby flat. But like many military officers stationed in Cairo, he knew all about the legendary exploits of David Stirling and his SAS through the grapevine, though he had learned more about him from the detailed top secret briefings from Auchinleck's staff he regularly received. In spite of the fact that the special commando outfit had suffered a handful of unsuccessful or marginally successful raids, it had still managed to capture the imagination of the entire British Army for its resounding triumphs, and Major Stirling was becoming something of a celebrity.

"Yi'ya, David, what brings you up to my neck of the woods?" he said, quickly rounding his desk with an outstretched hand.

His gangly visitor spoke with a soft-spoken Scottish brogue and was the very picture of modesty. "Good morning, Colonel. I just wanted to come by and thank you."

Fellers couldn't help but give a double-take, though it was swiftly suppressed. "Thank me?" he said, still feeling guilty for the recent airfield disasters even though they were not his fault.

"For getting me and my men the war matériel we need. I am told, by reliable sources, that you are the man most responsible for getting us much-needed American supplies here in North Africa. Grant tanks, 105-mm guns, military jeeps, bombers and fighters, the list goes on. That's why I want to thank you. Plus, I know that you don't like bloody swanks any more than I do."

Fellers gave a wide grin. "If I had a drink, I'd goddamn drink to that."

"My men love our new four-wheel-drive jeeps. We just got twelve of them and are about to set off on a new mission and raise bloody hell with them."

"That's what I like to hear. Glad I could help. My argument to Roosevelt and the boys back in Washington has always been simple: more American help for our allies. And that means more American weapons and more American troops—and I mean right now. Tell me about your jeeps. They're beauties, aren't they?"

"I'm quite confident they're going to revolutionize our tactics. We've added bulletproof windscreens from Hurricane fighters. They're bloody marvelous. We've also modified the vehicles with water condensers to prevent overboiling, armor-plated radiators, camouflage paint, reinforced suspension, and extra fuel tanks."

"They sound like armored vehicles not jeeps. Rommel ought to be worried."

"I believe he's about to shit his bloody pants. Even with our add-ons, the jeeps are so nimble, they can handle virtually any desert terrain. We'll be able to approach our targets at night unseen."

"What kind of firepower have you equipped them with?"

"We've added Vickers K machine guns to several of the vehicles. They can fire up to 1,200 rounds per minute."

"Good Lord, none of the Germans airbases will be safe." *As long as the bastards haven't cracked the new cipher,* he thought, and once again he felt a touch guilty.

"The guns were originally intended for use on bombers to defend against fighter aircraft. We found a cache of them in an Alexandria warehouse and fitted them to three jeeps as an experiment. Two have twin guns bolted to the front, and the third carries four guns on two mountings, fore and aft."

"Sounds like you're about to kick Rommel's ass. I wish I could go along with you, Major."

"Well, Colonel, my men and I have you to thank for—"

He stopped right there as a commotion was heard outside the office. There were urgent voices and a great shuffling of feet. Fellers wondered what the hell was going on. Was it an air raid? But why was there no siren?

He looked at Stirling. "Something's afoot. We'd better take a gander."

"My thoughts exactly."

They went outside into the hallway and followed the flow of traffic until they came to a vantage point that looked out onto the back of the building. The military police had hauled out at least two dozen large, 40-gallon oil drums and appeared to be burning classified documents to keep them out of German hands. Flames billowed up from the drums and clouds of smoke and ash filled the air. But from a security viewpoint the burning was scarcely effective. Much of the paper was only lightly scorched before the hot air wafted it above the perimeter wall to flutter down onto the street outside. There the peanut- and bean-vendors, who normally fashioned their paper cones out of newsprint, were already exploiting a new packaging possibility using top secret military documents that the Germans would no doubt find quite useful if and when Rommel made his triumphal march into Cairo.

Fellers shook his head. "Jesus Christ, what a mess. I mean no disrespect, Major, but how is it that your army can't even manage to burn its own classified documents? Can they not get anything right?"

"It's not my bloody army," said Stirling emphatically. "This is exactly why I do things on my own. I answer only to General Auchinleck and, by God, I am going to keep it that way."

"That's good because whoever's running this show is a complete—"

"All right, all right, let's clear the hallways, shall we?" a new voice interjected.

They turned to see a pudgy, red-faced officer with heavy sweat stains on his uniform and carrying a swagger-stick.

"Everybody back to your offices and clean them out of all paperwork right this bloody minute! All documents are to be burned immediately and there are no—"

"By whose order?" protested Stirling.

"By the order of General Corbett! Now move along now! Back to your offices and get to work! Storage bins are being brought upstairs for you to use as we speak!"

Stirling shook his head in disgust. "Bloody Corbett. He's Auchinleck's chief of general staff."

Fellers chuckled. "Yes, I know. He's the one who this morning ordered all officers to carry firearms at all times and imposed the 8 p.m. curfew."

"Without telling anybody bloody why. What a swank."

"I didn't think the flap could get any worse, but Holy Toledo, how wrong I was."

"I'm out of here," said Stirling, and he held out his hand. "Colonel."

"Thanks, Major, for stopping by to thank me," said Fellers as they shook hands. "But crazy goddamn times, huh?"

"I'll say. Oh, by the way, we're having a little farewell party tonight at my brother's flat. It's something of a ritual we have on our last nights. Tomorrow, we leave for our forward patrol base camp at Qaret Tartura. Peter and I would both love it if you'd be our guest."

Funny how fate turns, thought Fellers. "Why sure, I'll be there. What time?"

"Nine o'clock."

"Sounds good." They started walking down the hallway. "You know, Major, if only you were running the show, the goddamn British Army would have driven Rommel and his Panzer Army off this godforsaken continent by now."

Stirling grinned bashfully. "That's very kind of you to say, Colonel," he said in his characteristic tone of modesty. "But I like my little outfit just the way it is."

CHAPTER 34

PETER STIRLING FLAT
13 SHARIA IBRAHIM PASHA NAGUIB
GARDEN CITY

JULY 1, 1942

WITH A PARTY RAGING AND COCKTAILS FLOWING FREELY, the Stirling flat looked like the least likely rendezvous point for a cutthroat, top secret military expedition.

The apartment was packed with SAS warriors making final field preparations and a multifarious assemblage of British, Egyptian, Greek, and American guests. David was at the front door having a heated argument with Mo about an important message he was supposed to have sent to GHQ. On the parlor sofa, Peter was holding court with Hekmat Fahmy and Momo Marriott over the blaring sound of a gramophone belting out Glenn Miller. He was telling the two women about how distressing his job had become recently with the flap since he was one of several officials responsible for allocating the four hundred seats on the daily train to Palestine. In the corner, a pair of smartly-dressed British officers representing the Long Range Shepheard's Group slacker set were discussing the racing form at the Gezira Race Track with a handful of Egyptian and Greek party girls, making comparisons to Sandown and Newmarket back home.

Meanwhile, in the spare bedroom Paddy Mayne stood peering over a map of the Qattara Depression, which formed the southern anchor of the Allied line that stretched northwards to the coast at El Alamein; and in the kitchen Cooper, Seekings, and a handful of other SAS men sat sprawled on the floor over maps of the desert, going over transportation, bearing, petrol, and ammunition requirements while cleaning their weapons. A few feet away putting together a delicious assortment of traditional Egyptian and continental European hors d'oeuvres was the house cook Mahmoud. He had trained under the fastidious gourmet and ex-prime minister Ali Maher Pasha, and had a predilection for hashish, of which the head housekeeper Mo strongly disapproved.

In the meantime, Rommel and his seemingly unstoppable *Panzerarmee* was only sixty-five miles from Alexandria.

"All right, please just take care of it," said David to Mo in a final fit of exasperation. "I'll check back with you shortly."

Before the resourceful factotum, whose full name was Mohamed Aboudi, could protest, Stirling turned away, walked down the hallway, and stepped into the spare bedroom where Paddy Mayne was still studying the map. The bedroom and bathroom next door were cluttered with weapons, ammunition, uniform cases, bedrolls, kit-bags, tents, and camp supplies.

"Everything all right with Mo?" asked Paddy Mayne.

Stirling frowned. "I'd rather not talk about it. Now where were we?"

"We were talking about whether our vehicles can make it over the salt crust if we're forced to take the southern route."

He pointed down at the large map on the table. Shaped like a huge pork chop, the Qattara Depression was filled with salt lakes and marshes representing the remnants of an ancient inland sea. There were two routes, a northern and a southern, which for centuries had been used by Arab traders and their camel trains, where jeeps and lighter-weight trucks, but not tanks, could cross the formidable feature. However, the thick salt crust was an unknown variable, even to the LRDG. In some places it could take considerable weight; in others, it would crack and a vehicle might slowly disappear into a saucer of quicksand.

"I'd like to avoid the crust if we can," said Stirling. "That's why I think we should infiltrate the enemy rear through the Allied line along the escarpment of the Depression. Here."

This time it was Stirling who pointed to the map, and they quietly lifted their Scotch and sodas and studied the topography represented on the drawing in silence. The overall plan, worked out during the past several days, was to raid six or seven airfields and the coast road in the early morning hours of June 8. This was to be coordinated with Auchinleck's planned offensive to regain the coastal ground as far west as Mersa Matruh. The main SAS force would be dispatched under the wing of the LRDG to meet with Stirling and Paddy Mayne north of the Qattara Depression, where the combined force would assemble in the launch area before striking northwest to hit the Desert Fox from the rear.

"All right, that will work," said Mayne, as a peal of laughter rose up from the main sitting room over the sound of Glenn Miller's rip-roaring Big Band jazz rhythms. "How are we going to divvy up the airfields? You can't just pick the easiest target for yourself."

"I wouldn't dream of it. You and I will command one group and hit all the airfields along the line of Fuka and Bagush here," he said, tracing his finger northwest across the map. "A second party, commanded by Schott and Warr, will raid Sidi Barrani. The last group will be led by George Jellicoe and Zirnheld. They'll attack the airfields in the area of El Daba here."

"How many total vehicles?"

"We'll have thirty-five this time."

"That's more on the ground than we've ever had before. That's going to create concealment problems with regard to tracks and leaguer positions."

"That's a definite risk, but we have no choice if we're to meet all of our objectives."

"What time will the attack be set for?"

"One in the morning. One week from today, on July 8, as planned."

"What about friendly fire?"

"There's nothing we can do about that either. For security reasons, our frontline troops won't be given advanced notice of our plan."

"Which means we'll be targets for both German and British aircraft."

"Unfortunately, but there it is."

"Are we going to brief the men beforehand regarding the targets?"

"Yes, but not until we're well into the desert."

They fell into silence, quietly sipping their cocktails and studying the map.

Stirling considered the plan. He would drive to main Army HQ in his staff car accompanied by Robin Gurdon of the Long Range Desert Group. Gurdon's job would be to take the SAS party to the rendezvous deep into the desert where they would meet the other LRDG patrol. Then the LDRG would escort the various parties to their targets. If everything went according to plan, while they were disrupting the enemy the Eighth Army would launch its counter-attack, with the objective of driving the enemy from Daba, Fuka, Bagush, and Mersa Matruh. If the commando teams could attack a half dozen airfields, destroy a large number of aircraft operating in the area, and interfere with enemy communications, the op would be of critical value to the overall offensive.

They were interrupted by a voice at the open doorway.

"All right, you two," said Peter Stirling. "That's enough shop talk for one evening. It's time to put away those bloody maps and mingle with my enchanting guests. And I just happen to have one of them right here."

Stepping into the open doorway was Hekmat Fahmy. Stirling's breath was taken away, and when he looked at Paddy Mayne, he saw that his was too. Stirling made no effort to cover up the map or aerial photographs on the table. Instead, he stepped forward and gave a formal bow.

"Hello, Hekmat," he said softly, feeling suddenly muddled in his head. *Dear heavens, I hope I don't get a bloody migraine,* he thought with dismay.

"Hello, David," she said silkily, and they shook hands.

She looked at Mayne. "And you must be the famous Paddy Mayne."

He was rendered totally speechless. The moment would have been embarrassing, but Peter stepped forward and said, "Paddy's Irish and gets tongue-tied from time to time. Me, on the other hand, I never have that problem."

That broke the ice and everyone laughed. At that moment, an even louder burst of laughter erupted from the sitting room, and Stirling could tell by the voices that some new guests had arrived, including the loquacious Bonner Fellers.

"Oh my, I know that voice. The party has truly begun," said Hekmat. She stepped towards Mayne. "Don't worry, I won't bite," she said. "It's an honor to finally meet you."

Stirling thought Mayne might actually faint. But then his brother swiftly jumped in to the rescue once again.

"Paddy's an aspiring writer," said Peter. "And he loves to read books. He blasts through at least one a week."

"Oh really," said Hekmat with what David could tell was genuine interest. "What are you reading now?"

"A book called *Sixty-Four, Ninety-Four*," replied Mayne bashfully. "It's the second book in *The Spanish Farm* trilogy by Ralph Hale Mottram."

"What's the book about?"

"The First World War. It depicts an oasis of calm and romance in the midst of a brutal war."

"Is that so? I must say you sound more like a literary romantic than a desert warrior, Paddy Mayne."

He smiled awkwardly. David felt sorry for him; the man had no idea how to even talk to a woman.

Peter said, "The trilogy is widely acknowledged as one of the great classics of World War One fiction. It's ranked alongside *All Quiet On The Western Front*, *Goodbye To All That*, and *The Secret Battle*. Marvelous stuff."

"As if we don't get enough war out here in the bloody desert fighting Rommel," said David. "And Brother, just so you know, that did sound a bit pomposo."

"Sorry, old boy. I must not be drunk enough yet."

They laughed again. When it subsided, Hekmat changed the subject.

"Peter has been telling me about his travails regarding the daily train to Palestine. It does seem as if the whole city is in turmoil."

"Completely bonkers," agreed Peter. "Everyone and their mother wants on, and people are literally fighting for spots. Of course, we give priority to women and children, and those who have 'helped us' and would, therefore, be in the so-called Axis black book. The state of panic is such that people are offering outrageous bribes to get themselves on the train. You wouldn't believe what lengths people will go to. Why just yesterday when I refused a bribe by one Greek gentleman, I was promptly offered the supplicant's wife."

"You can't be serious," said David.

"I am one hundred percent."

Paddy Mayne grinned. "What I'd like to know is did you take the bloke up on it?"

"Why of course not! My debauchery does have its limits, you know!"

They chuckled again as another round of laughter echoed from both the kitchen and sitting room. It appeared the whole apartment was bursting at the seams with good cheer.

Now Stirling felt Hekmat's eyes upon him. "Do you think Rommel will actually reach Cairo, David?" she asked him.

"Not if *we* can bloody help it," said Paddy Mayne.

"Spoken like a true defender of the realm," said Stirling.

Hekmat smiled. Her soft, moist lips glittered like a sapphire and David felt a little flutter in his chest.

"Coming from you, Captain Mayne, I definitely feel reassured," she said.

"Hey, hey! What the hell's going on here! Are you having your own private party or what?"

Stirling looked up to see Bonner Fellers with Momo Marriott on his arm, both of them bopping to the jazz music. His tie was loose, he clutched a fresh gin fizz in his hand, and a cigarette dangled lazily from his mouth. His complexion was already ruddy from drink, and Momo looked like she was tying one on as well. As always, she looked ravishing in her smart, beautifully cut French-style clothes, her long red nails, and deep red lipstick.

"Well, well, well, if it isn't our American friend, Bonner Fellers!" Peter welcomed him ebulliently. "I thought you'd never get here."

"Hey, what about me?" cried Momo. "What am I, chopped liver?"

"No, you are the life of the party as always, darling," said David.

Fellers was snapping his fingers to the backbeat of the music. "All right, it's time to put on a little Count Basie and get this party really rolling with some dancing!"

"Let's go, everyone! Into the other room and out on that dance floor!" seconded

Momo. "And for the next half-hour, there can be no talk of the war!"

"Yes, yes, I agree wholeheartedly!" cried Peter. "And it's my bloody flat so *I* make the bloody rules!"

Stirling chuckled and looked at Paddy Mayne, who was smiling from ear to ear.

"You're mine, David Stirling!" cried Momo, and she stepped forward and took him by the hand. Though inordinately shy and not much of a dancer, he could tell that she would brook no opposition so he readily submitted to her charms.

"And you, Hekmat!" roared Fellers. "You're all mine, Sugar Doll!"

She gave a radiant smile. "All right, but no funny stuff, you devilish Yankee!"

He stood ramrod straight and held up two fingers. "Scout's honor! Now let's roll! There's no one who does the jitterbug like you!"

"Not even Dearest Momo?" quipped Peter, feigning seriousness with cocktail in hand.

"Not even Momo, but it's not her fault! She just ain't no goddamn belly dancer!"

Roaring with laughter, they dashed into the other room to dance just as Mahmoud, smelling of hashish, brought forth a succulent plate of creamy anchoïade with crudités along with traditional Egyptian fare of *ta'ameya* and *dolmades*. Once they started shimmying about with the British officers and the Egyptian and Greek party girls, Stirling and the others were promptly joined by late-arriving Cairo elite—Baron Jean Empain and his rambunctious wife, the American cabaret dancer Rozell "Goldie" Rowland.

Despite the flap, the group danced up a storm to Glenn Miller, Count Basie, and Woody Herman, and the party didn't shut down until 3 a.m.

At the Stirling flat, it rarely did.

CHAPTER 35

BAGUSH AIRFIELD, CYRENAICA, LIBYA

JULY 7-8, 1942

AS THE BLITZ BUGGY ZOOMED OVER A RISE, Stirling spotted a column of armored vehicles travelling across his front, just over two miles away. He called an instant halt. He and Robin Gurdon—their LRDG guide whom he had identified as a possible third-in-command to take some of the load off himself and Paddy Mayne—climbed out and examined the column through their field glasses. Leading the largest SAS group with several vehicles, Stirling was heading for the Bagush and Fuka airfield areas. Here the plan was for the large party to split up, with two combined French and British patrols attacking the largest Fuka field, another patrol raiding the neighboring landing ground, and David and Paddy continuing on together to assault Bagush.

"Are they Jerries, sir?" asked Gurdon.

"There's definitely a German look about them," said Stirling. "Look at how they're bunched together. Although they do have British markings."

"Maybe it's one of our Jock columns."

Stirling considered a moment. "Jock" columns were not special commando forces like the SAS, but rather conventional British units in Auchinleck's army equipped with light armor and weapons. They were small scouting patrols sent in on occasion to do rapid, deep-penetration raids, usually designed to draw away the enemy's attention from the main attack along the front line. Was there such a column swanning about the desert, he wondered, that he had been told nothing about?

"You really think those idiots at GHQ wouldn't have bothered to let us know?" he posed rhetorically to the young officer. "Could they possibly be that stupid?"

"Unfortunately, yes," replied Gurdon. "But of course, the column could be Jerries with captured British material."

Stirling lit his pipe. "I don't think so. They're moving too fast. They'd be going slower with captured stuff. In any case, there's no way to know for sure until we're right on top of them. We'd better get moving."

Before they set off again, he huddled up with Mayne and the rest of the patrol. He quickly informed them that he didn't believe the column posed a danger, but that its presence had likely alerted sentries along the length of their attack line, thus depriving them of the element of surprise. "Which means from now on," he added with a final warning, "you must keep your eyes skinned for enemy aircraft and armored cars. Remember that we are targets for British as well as enemy planes, and if we are attacked and get separated you must all drive on towards the airfields. Also remember—nobody turns back. If we have to take evasive action, we must still head northward for our objectives."

Tapping out his pipe on the sole of his heavy boot, he gave his quick, shy smile. "It will be all right, chaps. But be on your toes. Now let's get moving."

After half an hour of driving, the group spotted three suspicious-looking trucks on the horizon, and shortly thereafter the camouflaged tents of an enemy camp silhouetted against the desert skyline. The column made a wide detour and did not reach the Fuka escarpment until 20:00 hours when dusk was fast approaching. Here, the large group broke up as planned to strike at the four targets.

Stirling and Mayne headed in the direction of Bagush aerodrome with nine men besides themselves, the Blitz Buggy and two of the rugged new American jeeps outfitted with Vickers K machine guns, and a three-ton truck filled with bombs, grenades, food, water, and spare parts. Bagush aerodrome was eighteen miles from the escarpment, and with the rough dissected terrain, it was 23:00 before they reached the coastal highway. Pausing to take their bearings, they reckoned that the target was another ten miles farther west. Stirling had been informed by GHQ Intelligence that a great deal of traffic moved along the road, and he decided to set up an ambush point about three-quarters of a mile short of the airfield to keep enemy vehicles from passing along the road while Mayne attacked the airfield.

The four vehicles drove along the coast road with their lights on. On either side, the desert stretched out like a black yawning void. They could smell the salty scent of the sea a half mile away, but there were no lights, not even Arab fires. Only an eerie emptiness.

David put his foot on the accelerator. He was in a hurry to get off the road and establish his ambush point before any enemy traffic passed him. Ordinarily, it wouldn't have mattered, but if the column they had spotted was a Jock column, the enemy might be alerted. He was anxious not to arouse suspicion before the team was ready. Twenty minutes later, he slowed the Blitz Buggy and turned off the road. Mayne followed in the jeep with the second jeep and the supply truck taking up the rear. The aerodrome bordered the road and was just over a mile away. Mayne's group, consisting of six commandos in addition himself, would steal in by foot, plant their bombs, and make their way back to the waiting vehicles. Then BOOM!

Stirling had Sergeants Cooper and Seekings as well as a private with him. He gave Mayne and his five men half an hour's grace before setting to work. It did not take long to establish a roadblock. Within ten minutes, they had rolled two good-sized boulders down a small slope at the far side of the road and placed them in the middle of the highway. Then they took up positions on both sides of the road with guns at the ready and waited. But after ten minutes had passed without a single vehicle, Seekings crossed the road to the CO's position.

"Doesn't look as though there's much activity tonight, sir."

"Yes, I can see that, Sergeant. But according to reliable army intel, heavy traffic passes constantly along the Bagush-Fuka road," he said sarcastically.

"Poor devils," said Seekings with mock sympathy. "They're like the weather chaps. They never quite get it right, do they, sir?"

"I'm afraid, Reg, those swanks at GHQ are not even half as accurate as the bloody weather forecasters. And that's saying something."

Over the next hour, they strained their ears for the sound of the detonations. But 01:00 came and still there was nothing. Stirling kept checking his watch. Soon it was fifteen minutes past zero hour and not a single explosion. *What the bloody hell has happened to Paddy?* Another twenty minutes passed and still silence. And then finally, there was a jet of light and a loud boom.

Stirling was jubilant and clutched his hand into a fist.

"There we go, Major," said Cooper jubilantly. "Now we can sit back and count them one by one."

Over the next forty minutes, Stirling counted twenty-two explosions. He watched with fascination as the flames leapt up into the sky. The scene looked like a series of campfires in a row. The light from the fires was so bright that in the darkness, the long line of burning planes looked much closer than a mile away.

"Captain Mayne seems to be in good form tonight, sir," observed Seekings. "And he seems to have gotten away without interference. No machine-gun fire or anything."

"Let's hope his luck continues," said Stirling, and he again looked nervously at his watch. Hopefully, Mayne and his men would make it back soon.

But it would take nearly an hour before the team returned. As Mayne came walking up, Stirling could see that he was angry. What had happened? He had expected him to be in a jubilant mood, as he usually was immediately after a successful raid, but he carried an unmistakable frown on his face and his body language seemed agitated. And why had it taken them so damned long?

"What is it? What's happened?" he asked him, knowing that it couldn't be that they had lost anyone because everyone was present and accounted for and not a single shot had been fired.

"We only got half of them. The bloody bombs wouldn't work," bristled Mayne. "Some bloody fuck put the primers in too soon."

"What?"

"The planes were well dispersed in clusters all around the perimeter. I divided the party into four groups, all of whom managed to infiltrate between the patrols without alerting anyone. We placed the bombs on the forty aircraft before withdrawing to the desert and waiting, half a mile away, to watch the results. But the explosions stopped after twenty or so. We couldn't believe our fucking eyes."

"So what happened to the charges?"

"Somehow they must have gotten damp. They had to have been primed too early and the lubricant in the charge seeped into the primer. I finally solved the mystery by examining one of the bombs in the sergeant's bag. The bloody primer was moist. I learned that it had been placed in the plastic twenty-four hours earlier instead of being put in, as it should have been, at the last minute. Whatever the hell happened, it was against my instructions—I'll tell you that. You should have seen those Jerry bastards running about frantically trying to put out the flames. They brought out fire-fighting apparatus but ran out of chemicals within five minutes, which is why some of the aircraft continued to blaze away. All in all, it was quite a sight, but too damned few planes were blown up. That's why I'm mad as hell."

"All right," said Stirling, trying to assuage him. "There's no point in holding an inquest now. It's too late. But all things considered, I'd say it was a resounding success. I counted twenty-two separate explosions."

"Yeah, but like I said, that bloody aerodrome was packed with at least forty planes. We left nearly half of the fucking things standing."

"Why did it take you so long? We were wondering what was happening."

"The sentries were on the ball. That's why it took us longer than usual to get onto the field. It's heavily patrolled by armed guards."

"So they were alerted to our presence? The column we saw was one of our own bloody Jock columns?"

"No question. Everyone's on the watch."

Stirling shook his head grimly. "That would explain why there's no traffic on this blinking road. Wait until I sink my teeth into those bastards at GHQ. I'm going to give them an earful."

"It's enough to break a man's heart," said Mayne. "Another twenty planes sitting there just asking for it."

Seeing his good mate, the Irish warrior and repressed writer, so disconsolate, Stirling wondered if something else might be able to be done. He hated to go home with the mission only half accomplished. After a moment's thought, a flash came to him.

"I've got an idea. Let's drive onto the field and shoot up the planes from our vehicles."

"Shoot them with the Vickers guns, sir?" asked Johnny Cooper.

"We've got eight of the beauties between us. After all, they're designed to shoot up aircraft."

Slowly, Paddy Mayne's eyes grew big as saucers and a mischievous smile took root on his heavily bearded face. "Now that's not a half bad idea," he said.

Stirling felt a sudden burst of rejuvenation; they had a real opportunity here and he wanted to take full advantage of it.

"All right, this is the way we'll do it," he said. "The truck will head for a point two miles beyond the aerodrome and wait for us. We'll drive the Blitz Buggy and two jeeps straight onto the field. We'll do a quick tour, knocking off as many planes as we can, then make for the truck."

The members of the patrol looked at one another. It was insanely bold, of course, but no one lodged an objection. In fact, it seemed a rather simple and sensible plan in its own peculiar way. Together, Stirling and Mayne selected two men to serve as front and rear gunners in the Blitz Buggy and two jeeps, while the rest departed in the truck to set up the rendezvous. After ten anxious minutes spent checking guns and ammunition, the raiding party took off for the still-burning Bagush Aerodrome with Stirling leading the way in the Blitz Buggy, Cooper manning the single Lewis gun alongside him, and another gunner sitting behind the twin Vickers guns in the rear. Grinning like a kid in a candy shop, the former rugby champion Paddy Mayne followed in his armed jeep with another jeep in his wake. Stirling could tell he was intent on finishing what he had started by inflicting maximum destruction.

They approached the field at the farthest point from the road. It was surprisingly quiet, with no sign of patrolling sentries. It looked as though the Germans had relaxed their watch, operating on the theory that when the horse has bolted there is not much point in locking the stable door.

Stirling stopped and held a final whispered conference. "Keep ten yards behind me," he said to Paddy. "I'll sweep right around the perimeter in the Buggy so that the jeeps can fire from the broadside." Then he turned to the gunners. "Remember to shoot low and aim at the petrol tanks. Right then, off we go."

They drove in yelping like Bedouins, unleashing a lethal curtain of gunfire. Still reeling from the initial assault, the defenders were not expecting another, let alone the bristling procession that now drove onto the airfield. Moving at fifteen miles per hour and spaced ten yards apart, the assault vehicles drove around the remaining planes, pouring out a devastating broadside at a combined rate of close to 10,000 rounds a minute. As each plane exploded, the fire illuminated the next. Cooper emptied three full magazines before his gun jammed. Designed for use in aircraft and therefore air-cooled, a Vickers fired from the ground could only accept a certain amount of ammunition down its throat before requiring a rest.

The operation took no more than five minutes, leaving behind a scene of destruction and confusion. The airfield was littered with burning planes and Germans scrambling about like ants from a stomped anthill. As he and his men retreated back into the darkness and safety of the desert, Stirling could see in his rear view mirror the conflagration from miles away. The repeated explosions continued to light up the skyline like summer lightning. He couldn't believe how easy it had been as they returned to the main road and headed back for the rendezvous with antiaircraft guns opening up behind them but failing to find their mark. They quickly found the waiting supply truck and drove furiously to the southeast, trying to put as much distance between themselves and the air patrols that would be out searching for them with dawn's first light.

When they reached the rally point eighty miles away the next afternoon, Stirling personally greeted the returning parties and totted up the scores, welcoming each of the five attacking forces as if they had just returned from an outing of golf. With Paddy's twenty-two and the second-round of fifteen at Bagush, he reckoned they had destroyed thirty-seven total aircraft on the raid. Unfortunately, George Jellicoe, the French officer Andre Zirnheld, and the members of the other commando units had not fared as well. In fact, Jellicoe and Zirnheld had only managed to blow up a truck and take three German prisoners.

But in Stirling's view, the most important thing the raid had proved was that there was a new way to play the commando game—and that was using American-made jeeps armed with rapid-fire, large-caliber Vickers machine guns suited for shooting down giant airplanes. All in all, he was delighted with his new technique, but he was also excited about the new freedom he had by having his own transport vehicles and navigators along with the ability to attack at will from a forward base. In short, the SAS, L Detachment, whatever one wanted to call it, was fast becoming what Stirling had always intended it to be: a small, independent army, capable of fighting a different sort of war.

A very different sort of war indeed.

CHAPTER 36

EZBEKIEH AND GARDEN CITY, CAIRO

JULY 8-9, 1942

IT WAS half past two in the morning when Sansom said goodnight to his driver, slid from his car, and headed towards his flat in the dim illumination of a pair of street lamps. He was returning home from his third raid of the night—exhausted, in uniform, and carrying his Enfield .38-caliber revolver in his shoulder holster.

With the flap still ongoing, he and his Field Security unit had been run ragged the past ten days with roundups of European suspects with Nazi sympathies, including the Endozzi Sisters. The Italian community had required the most thorough sorting out with Rommel knocking on the gates of the city. Sansom had locked up men and women who had previously convinced him of their innocence—and released a few who were scheduled for internment by the Germans. To his dismay, he was having to make several arrests per night and unable to do much else. Consequently, he had made hardly any headway in his investigations of the Egyptian Army and the Nazi spies that Almasy had slipped undetected into Cairo from the desert.

With all the arrests and interrogations, he and his police officers had been overwhelmed. Three nights ago, while trying to make an arrest, he was attacked by an Italian fascist who had escaped internment from Boulac. He and his Egyptian Police team caught up with the escapee in a bar and all hell broke loose. He suffered a black eye after being hit with a beer bottle, but he ended up getting his man.

As he turned into the block where he was now living alone since his wife had evacuated the city for Palestine, he heard faint cries for help in Arabic. Following the sound, he came upon six soldiers in desert-colored khaki uniforms attacking an Egyptian gharry. He could tell they were New Zealanders because they wore slouch hats that looked like Australian hats but with conical crowns. One of them had his hands around the driver's throat, while the others were trying to yank two terrified women from the back of the gharry.

What the devil? Don't tell me that they're going to rape them?

He felt his whole body go on high alert and couldn't believe his eyes. What kind of men would do such a thing? And then, once he drew a few steps closer, he realized how disgustingly drunk they were. They were deep into their cups, for even in the dim light it was obvious that the poor women were both well into middle age.

"You there! Stop that at once!" he shouted.

Six drunken heads turned, eyes narrow.

"Bugger off, you bloody fuck!" one of them slurred.

He stepped nearer. "I said stop that at once or you will be arrested!"

"Didn't you hear us?" snarled the one with his hands around the gharry driver's throat. "We said fuck off!"

"I will remind you that you are addressing an officer of the law and I am placing you all under arrest."

With a slightly trembling hand, he reached for his pistol. But just as he cleared his holster, out of the corner of his eye he caught a flash of movement in the shadows and was dealt a crushing blow to his face, just below his black eye from the Italian fascist escapee. The punch was so hard that it felt like his teeth would be knocked out, and he wondered if his attacker had a pair of brass knuckles.

He fell to the ground with a violent thud, landing on top of his revolver.

But as four of the New Zealanders swarmed him, he managed to blow his police whistle. The high-pitched sound shrieked into the night and the two women and the gharry driver began to scream.

"Help! Help!" they cried in Arabic.

"Shut up, the lot of you!" one of the inebriated Kiwis cried.

Sansom tried to blow the whistle again, but it was kicked out of his mouth. The soldiers then kicked and trampled him with their heavy army boots, delivering blows to his head, ribs, and back.

He struggled to rise to his feet, but was knocked down as more screams rose into the night from the Egyptians. He took two more violent blows to his head and was nearly losing consciousness when he heard one of the soldiers shout, "Get his fucking gun and shoot the bastard!"

With his life in mortal peril, he felt a sudden burst of desperation and shifted his body so that they could not get to his pistol wedged between his stomach and the pavement. He pressed his full weight down upon the weapon, knowing that if they managed to grab his gun he was finished.

"Give us the bloody gun, you shit!" one of the New Zealanders snarled.

But Sansom remained frozen in place as they kicked and punched him and tried to pull him to his feet. It was then he heard a pair of new voices and police whistles.

"Let's get the bloody hell out of here!" cried one of the soldiers. They dashed off into the darkness. A moment later, a porter and two policemen came running up. Sansom breathed a sigh of relief, but it hurt like hell just to take a breath.

"Thank…thank you, chaps," he managed to croak.

The police called an ambulance and he was taken to the hospital. He had two broken ribs and his face looked as if he had made an unsuccessful challenge for the world heavyweight championship. After staying at the hospital until eleven the next morning, he was discharged and went immediately to the Cairo District Commander, Brigadier Chrystal, who happened to be a New Zealander. Chrystal promptly ordered the commanding officer of the New Zealand base troops at Maadi camp to produce the culprits within twenty-four hours or else confine all troops to barracks for fifteen days.

Sansom went home to try and sleep, but was unable to. So he returned to his office and stared listlessly out the window until 5 o'clock in the afternoon when he received an intelligence memo. He read it over. The GHQ monitoring section had again picked up an unidentified transmitter in the Cairo area two nights ago and again last night. It had come on punctually at twelve midnight. Once again, it was broadcast in code—which he suspected was the *Rebecca* code he had discussed with the mysterious Bob—but so far its messages had been too brief to give the monitoring unit time to discover the location of the transmitter. Five minutes later Sergeant Major Harper, who had been working on the case with him and had already seen—and come to terms with—his extreme facial disfigurement from the New Zealanders, stepped into his office. Lighting up a fresh Dunhill, Sansom showed him the memo.

"What do you think?"

"At least our spy hasn't sent any intelligence of value," replied the sergeant major. "It's so short—there's just nothing here. Looks like nil reports to me."

"And you don't you think that's strange?"

"Why's that, sir?"

"With the desert fighting at crisis point and a security blackout on all military news, any German spy with contacts like Anwar el Sadat could not help but pick up information of interest to Rommel."

"I see what you mean, sir."

They fell into silence. Sansom's face and entire body hurt like hell so he took another morphine-derivative pain pill, washed it down with four fingers of twelve-year-old Scotch, took a long pull from his cigarette, and then looked at it appreciatively. He pulled out the intelligence report Bob had given him. The report from the monitoring unit described the unknown spy's first transmission and concluded that it was a simple station identification. The inference was that no acknowledgment was being received. The wireless experts had been given instructions to start jamming the transmissions as soon as any longer messages were sent, which Sansom knew would certainly not help him catch the spy.

At that moment, the telephone on his desk rang.

"Major Sansom."

"I'm a British officer and I'm at the Turf Club. There's a chap here who seems to me suspicious. A Rifle Brigade subaltern who's buying people drinks."

"To whom am I speaking?"

"Let's just keep the names out of it for the moment, shall we?"

Sansom wanted to protest but didn't. More importantly, did a junior officer buying drinks mean anything? Many of the suspicious persons brought to his attention were only leave-happy desert rats whooping it up.

"He's been here a few times before, and he always pays in English pound notes. Don't you find that odd, Major Sansom?"

Yes, I have to admit that is different.

"All right, I believe you. Thanks for the tip. Now I'd like to ask a favor."

"And what would that be?"

"Can you please try to keep him until I get there? I can be there in fifteen minutes."

"No, I'm afraid I'm not going to be your guinea pig. This bloke could be dangerous."

A clicking sound and the phone went silent.

"Damnit!" cried Sansom. He rushed to the Turf Club, but the subaltern had already gone and there was no sign of the caller. However, Peter the barman was there to fill in the details. He quickly described the man throwing around the British sterling and handed over several of the bills. The suspect had spent five English-pound notes and one fiver.

"Thank you," said Sansom. He ordered his standard fare—a White Horse Scotch and soda—and sat back and pondered a moment. Of course, there was nothing illegal in an officer paying in sterling, which any hotel or cabaret would accept. It was merely odd, for the British forces were all paid in Egyptian currency. Apart from a few notes, probably sent by relatives in letters, English money was hardly ever seen. The number of Rifle Corps subalterns who could possibly be in Cairo at any particular time was limited, and later that night back at GHQ his team was able to learn, based on a preliminary cross-check, that none of them answered Peter the barman's description of his mysterious customer's physical appearance. Which suggested that someone was indeed masquerading as a lieutenant in the Rifle Corps. It could be harmless—some soldier might have done it for a bet—but the spending of the British money made Sansom consider that possibility unlikely.

What then? A spy? But that also seemed an outlandish idea. Everyone knew that English notes were not normal currency in Egypt. Everyone also knew that officers bought their drinks with Egyptian money. It seemed unlikely that only the German Intelligence Service was ignorant of this.

Unlikely...but not impossible. While it was a platitude that one should not underrate the enemy's intelligence—it was just as important not to overrate it. The most plausible explanation of the affair seemed to be that the Jerries had made a colossal blunder of the most elementary kind. They had provided one of their agents with the wrong currency for the country in which he was operating.

Under the currency regulations in Egypt, English money was not changed by banks, but had to be taken personally to the British Army Paymaster. So the next morning, Sansom went to the Paymaster's office and spoke with a young Pay Corps officer to find out how much sterling had been coming in.

"As a matter of fact, I think there has been a bit more in the last couple of weeks," replied the young man, and he followed this with a quizzical, how-the-devil-did-you-know look. "Hang on a minute. I'll get the figures."

The figures showed that the increase was noticeable but not sensational.

"Actually, Major, it can vary quite a lot from one week to the next," the young officer then proceeded to point out. "Sometimes it's been even higher than this, and at other times it's dropped to almost nothing."

"Are you saying it could be a coincidence?" asked Sansom.

"I suppose I am, sir."

"Where has the money been coming from?"

"The usual places: Shepheard's, Groppi's, the Turf Club, Continental. Plus a few other cabarets and night-clubs. I can give you the details if you'd like, sir."

"Please do. And send me all future English notes you receive with details of their origin."

"Right-eo, Major. Glad I could be of service."

Sansom left and went back to GHQ. He had the feeling he was onto something, but doubted he could be dealing with one of the two spies that Almasy had slipped into Cairo from the desert. A German agent couldn't possibly fall into his lap that easily, could he? And even supposing German Intelligence was so incompetent as to provide its agents with British instead of Egyptian money, would an agent be dim-witted enough to openly spend it? Surely, once he realized that British money was not normal currency in Egypt he would try to change it unobtrusively rather than make himself conspicuous by always paying in sterling.

He called Sergeant Wilson and instructed him to find out the current rate for sterling on the black market. Two hours later, Wilson was standing in front of his desk.

"You just can't get rid of it—that's what I'm told," said the sergeant. "It's never been like this before. Apparently, none of the usual operators will touch sterling. They must think Rommel has got us licked."

Sansom had expected something like this. Obviously, black-market operators could not unload their sterling on the Army Paymaster, except indirectly and in comparatively small sums, so they had to hang onto it until some currency speculator wanted to buy it. Their exchange rate, therefore, depended to a large extent on the fortunes of the Desert War. The flap was now at its peak, and confidence in sterling had dropped to almost nothing. Sansom's question as to why an enemy spy would dare to use British currency in the watering holes and cabarets of Cairo was answered. The spy—whoever the bloke was—was presently in a bind and had the misfortune of being stuck with hundreds, perhaps even thousands, of British pounds in Cairo at a time when there was no easy way to dispose of it.

Slowly but surely, a smile began to overtake his ravaged face.

"What...what is it, sir? What is so funny?" asked Wilson.

He sat back in his chair and lit a Dunhill. "I was just thinking, Sergeant. If the suspect proves to be one of Almasy's spies, he has certainly gotten himself into quite a pickle. The irony is that he has no one but Erwin Rommel, the vaunted Desert Fox, to blame."

"To blame, sir?"

"Yes, Sergeant—for having been too successful in battle!"

CHAPTER 37

CAPTURED QATTARA BOX AND TEL EL EISA RIDGE, EGYPT

JULY 10, 1942

ROMMEL was half-asleep when he heard the sound.

It wasn't particularly loud, no more obtrusive than a roll of distant thunder or faint susurrus of wind, but it was enough to awaken him. He listened for a moment half-consciously, thinking he was just dreaming and hoping the noise would stop so he could roll over and go back to sleep. Having abandoned a captured bunker during the night because of sand fleas the British had left behind, he lay fully dressed in uniform in the back seat of Greif, wrapped in his greatcoat and covered with a wool blanket to keep himself warm against the nighttime desert chill. But he could tell something wasn't right and he wasn't dreaming. Sitting up, he wiped the slumber from his tired eyes, reached for his field glasses, and scanned to the north where he thought the sound had originated from.

Now he saw flashes of light against the sky and heard the dull roar of the sleepy moment before turn to a thunderous tremolo as British artillery opened up all along the northern Alamein Line. For more than a minute, he watched the distant flashes—strobing against the dawn one right after another—and soon realized that the massive artillery barrage was the opening salvo to a major ground attack.

Mein Gott, are the Tommies actually taking the offensive!

Suddenly, Bayerlein was at his side.

"It's the Sabratha Division, Field Marshal," the chief of staff said urgently. "They are under attack in their sector on both sides of the coast road. We just got word on the radio from Colonel von Mellenthin."

"Are there advancing ground forces?"

"Yes. The enemy seems to be concentrating in that area."

"So it is just the Italians under assault?"

"It appears so. But it has just begun so we don't know what British units are leading the attack."

Captain Behrendt, his chief intelligence officer, and Lieutenant Armbruster, his aide-de-camp, appeared along with two other officers. Rommel quickly gave Bayerlein and Behrendt orders.

"I want the *Kampfstaffel* and a combat group of the 15th Panzer Division ready to strike north to the battlefield in the next ten minutes, where I will personally direct operations. Our planned attack from Qaret el Abd scheduled for 06:00 must now be cancelled. Our striking force must go north to help plug the gap and we will be too weak here in the south to execute the thrust to the east. All right, let's move!"

With Greif in the lead, the mobile HQ headed north to the coast road in the area of Tel El Eisa Ridge. There he discovered that British artillery had blown the forward positions of the Italian Sabratha Division into oblivion. The enemy had followed up by sending forward the fresh 9th Australian Division, supported by British tanks. Already the Sabratha Division had been nearly annihilated and many of its batteries had been lost. It was obvious that Auchinleck had concentrated his surprise attack on the weak and vulnerable Italians, and the enemy was now in hot pursuit westwards after the fleeing infantrymen and artillerymen.

There would have been a serious danger the Australians would break through and destroy his supplies and break the line on either side of the coast road, he soon learned from Behrendt, if not for the quick thinking of von Mellenthin. As the senior officer at the tactical command post only a few miles behind the front, he had immediately driven forward to assess the situation when the firing had begun. When he saw hundreds of Italians running to the rear in panic, he signaled HQ and ordered it to organize for combat. The initial Australian attack was quickly halted in hand-to-hand fighting. And then, just as the tide was turned, a new German unit appeared on the battlefield. It was the 382nd Grenadier Regiment of the 164th Light Afrika Division. It had no vehicles, but marched directly into the battle and helped repulse the Australians. Minutes later, Rommel arrived to help stem the Allied advance, quickly dispatching the 15th Panzer Division forward to the battlefield. The attack was broken up, and the Australians and British tanks were only able to penetrate to within a mile and a half of the Panzer Army headquarters.

By noon, with disaster narrowly thwarted, Rommel received a full briefing from Bayerlein and Behrendt, who had interviewed combatants that had taken part in the engagement on both sides.

"It seems, sir, that most of the Italian battery commanders failed to fire upon the onrushing Australians and British tanks because they didn't have any orders," explained Behrendt. "The Italians left their line, many of them in panic. Making no attempt to defend themselves, they fled to the open desert, throwing away arms and ammunition as they ran."

"Thank God for von Mellenthin then," said Rommel, still livid that such a disaster had been allowed to happen.

"Not all of the Italians made a poor showing, sir," pointed out Bayerlein. "Major Rastrelli's and Captain Comi's men fought fiercely. As the Australians advanced upon their positions, they unleashed their massive 149-mm cannons as if they were machine guns. The guns became red-hot, and many of the handlers were burnt, but they didn't stop firing. When the smoke cleared, the area in front of them was deserted, except for blazing vehicles and heaps of dead Aussies."

Rommel nodded. Rastrelli, Comi, and their men had indeed fought bravely but, unfortunately, they such officers were the minority in the Italian Army in his view. He had seen with his own eyes that there were splendid Italian officers, like General Enea Navarini, commander of the XXI Italian Army Corps, for whom he held the highest regard. In fact, many of Italian generals and officers had won his admiration both as men and soldiers. But too often in battle the power of resistance of many of his Italian formations collapsed under even modest pressure from lack of leadership—and it was obvious the British were taking full advantage of it.

"There's no question now that Auchinleck is targeting our Italian units and will continue to do so," he said to his two subordinates.

"Are you worried they won't be able to hold their lines?" asked Bayerlein.

"After this morning, the conclusion is inescapable. Too much has been demanded of them by Italian standards and now the strain has become too great."

"What do you propose to do?" asked Behrendt.

"I think for the time being we're going to have to scrap any plans for any large-scale attacks. And we have no choice but to order every last German soldier out of his tent or rest camp up to the front. Given our lack of fuel, supplies, and armor along with the virtual default of a large proportion of our Italian fighting power, the situation is beginning to take on crisis proportions. Wouldn't you agree?"

With shoulders slumped, both staff officers nodded in the affirmative. "Unfortunately, sir, I have some more bad news," said Behrendt.

Rommel looked at the 1c sharply; he was already incensed and in no mood for even more bad news, but he had no choice. "Yes, Captain?"

"During this morning's attack, the Australians overran our Wireless Recon Unit 621. Unfortunately, Captain Seebohm was visiting his forward platoons at the time and he was captured along with seventy-three members of the intercept company, which has one hundred men. I am told he was seriously wounded."

He let out an audible gasp. "Seebohm? Are you sure?"

"Colonel von Mellenthin has confirmed it. Seebohm and most of his unit were either killed or captured along with their equipment and a large quantity of documents. The radio interception station was deployed as far forward as possible at Tel el Eisa Ridge, about a half mile from the front and three miles from El Alamein. The Australians came at them with Bren gun carriers, mortars, and anti-tank weapons and caught the unit completely by surprise. Though not heavily armed, they put up fierce resistance for over an hour while frantically trying to destroy documents, but they were eventually overrun. Unfortunately, Seebohm's second-in-command, Lieutenant Habel, and his adjutant, Lieutenant Herz, were captured as well. That's what we've been told."

Now Bayerlein spoke. "The thing is, sir, it could have been avoided."

He was flabbergasted. "Avoided?"

"Yes, sir. Seebohm didn't need to be so far forward. Apparently, he was reprimanded by some fussy colonel shortly after we took Mersa Matruh for not having his unit far enough forward during the fighting. Whoever the prick was, he obviously had no idea that the 621 was not a combat unit but a vital and irreplaceable intelligence-gathering operation. Unfortunately, the criticism, although unjustified, seems to have stung the diligent Seebohm and he moved closer to the front line."

"Are you saying that his position was far too far forward for safety?"

"It appears so. No doubt he figured that he could obtain better results from the top of that ridge."

He pointed to the east to the Tel el Eisa—the Hill of Jesus—two miles away. The long, rocky ridge was the most prominent feature in the area and Rommel could instantly see why Seebohm had deployed his radio interception station along the ridgeline. The signal reception would be clear all the way to Cairo.

"My God, what is happening?" wondered the Desert Fox aloud. The loss of the brilliant and always-dependable Seebohm and seventy-three of his experienced radio men, as well as the capture of their W/T equipment and documents, meant that the unit would have to be rebuilt from scratch. Now he no longer had the capability of eavesdropping on sensitive British radio communications and gaining a tactical edge by snatching a steady flow of high-grade tactical intelligence out of the airwaves. The capture of Unit 621 was a catastrophe with far-reaching consequences for *Panzerarmee Afrika*. Seebohm had been with Rommel since before the French campaign of 1940 and had played a decisive role at Gazala; losing him was not only a terrible loss militarily, but personally as he had known and liked the man.

"How badly injured is he?" he asked.

"Badly, I am told by the survivors," said Behrendt. "It is doubtful that he will live for long. Maybe not even long enough for interrogation. But I am told the Australians got their hands on two copies of the *Rebecca* codebooks."

"So the British now have four copies? The two they took when they overran Aberle and Weber—and now two more they have captured from 621?"

"It would appear so, sir," the intelligence officer said glumly.

"It appears then that there's no chance now for Eppler and Sandstette to get in touch with us."

"Our listening stations in Athens and Libya are still listening for them, but we shouldn't hold our breath. Now that the British Y Service radio recce units have four copies of the codebooks and all of Seebohm's written documents, it seems likely they will be able to read the Abwehr hand cipher."

"So Operation Condor is kaput."

"I would say so, Field Marshal. From the captured codes and documents, the British analysts will be able to tell from the captured cipher records that we have gained access to the Americans' Black Code. That is if they haven't done so already."

Rommel shook his head in resignation. He then looked skyward, as if by some miracle help might be coming his way from the heavens. "So our two agents in Cairo have been neutralized, my 'little Fellers's is no more, the Tommies have destroyed two battalions, our Italians are virtually useless, we are dangerously short of everything we actually need to win this battle in the desert, and our most vital Signals Unit has been extinguished as an operational unit. Given the situation we now find ourselves, gentlemen, do you see any good reason why we should go on fighting?" He gave a fatalistic grin. "That was a joke—I am not a defeatist. I am, however, a realist."

"*Ja*, we know you are, sir," said the two officers almost in unison.

He gave a heavy sigh. With crucial battles to break the Alamein Line coming up, he would now be forced to rely almost exclusively on air reconnaissance for intelligence. He could no longer count on his American gold-mine Bonner Fellers, his once-promising agents Eppler and Sandstette, or Seebohm and his miracle workers of his 621st Radio Intercept Company. They were all gone now. As he had told the two Cairo-bound agents before they had set off with Almasy into the desert, there were three critical pieces of intelligence that he needed to know in order to successfully take the Suez: "First, where will the British make their main stand when I begin my final attack upon the Delta; second, what reinforcements, in men, tanks and guns, will they have received; and third, who will lead them?"

Now, he had no answer to even one of these questions. Even worse, he was no better off than a blind man groping his way through the darkness.

CHAPTER 38

MADAME BADIA'S CABARET NEAR ENGLISH BRIDGE, GIZA CITY, AND EPPLER AND SANDSTETTE HOUSEBOAT AGOUZA, CAIRO

JULY 12, 1942

GERMAN SPY JOHANNES EPPLER—wearing a tailored blue European suit and posing as his Egyptian alter ego Hussein Gaafar—surveyed Madame Badia's Cabaret, looking for prying eyes, someone familiar or threatening amongst the crowd of mostly British officers. Up on stage was Cairo's newest and youngest belly-dancing sensation, Tahia Carioca, backed by a seven-piece orchestra. He was nursing a White Horse and soda with his stepbrother, Hassan Gaafar, who was working for him and Sandstette as a go-between.

The nightclub west of the Nile near English Bridge had become particularly popular with the British since Madame Badia had introduced comic anti-Nazi acts to her show to go along with her new fabulous belly dancer Tahia and a string of nubile chorus girls. A former singer, dancer, and stage actress herself, Badia Masabni had launched or promoted the careers of some of the most famous belly dancers and theater actresses in Cairo—including Hekmat Fahmy. The popular cabaret was filled with the usual mix of mostly affluent, gossipy, and boozy European and Egyptian clientele. Like most of the higher-end watering holes and theaters in Cairo, it was flooded with off-duty British officers and strictly off limits to the common soldiers of the Allied nations.

Seeing no one suspicious or intrusively watchful, Eppler turned his attention to Tahia Carioca. In her late-twenties, she was enormously talented, gorgeous, and younger than his beloved Hekmat, but he didn't think she could hold a candle to his former lover, whom he considered a far more refined and sensual dancer. All the same, as he watched her gyrations, he was entertained and cheered along with the crowd. A cocktail waitress came by the table. He ordered another drink for himself and his stepbrother and the waitress walked off.

He glanced at his wristwatch. It was after 10:30 p.m. and their contact Victor Hauer was late. Hauer was an Austrian who worked at the Swedish Legation in Cairo looking after the interests of Germans and Austrians in Egypt. Eppler had written to his stepbrother two weeks ago asking for his help and they had met soon thereafter at the Americaine Bar in Fouad el Awal. There Eppler, disguised in dark glasses, had picked up his brother and taken him back to his *dahabia*, where he had introduced him to Sandstette. Together, they explained their predicament: their transmitter needed repairs, perhaps a new quartz. Agreeing to help them, Hassan had contacted Hauer and arranged a meeting for tonight at Madame Badia's Cabaret. The plan was to take Hauer to the houseboat to show him their pirate radio and have him meet Sandstette.

But where could the Austrian be? He looked at his watch again: only a minute had passed but it felt like hours.

He looked around the room again. One of the British officers, a middle-aged lump of a man with captain's bars, was staring at him. He pretended not to see him and looked away. He didn't want to do anything to draw suspicion to himself or Hassan when they were waiting for another spy.

Or was he just being paranoid?

The truth was, over the past few days, he was becoming increasingly worried. He and Sandstette had been frequenting establishments other than the Kit Kat Club and Turf Club and engaging in liaisons with various women, in the hope they would make the sort of contacts who would not only provide them with information that would interest Rommel but also enable them to change their British currency out for Egyptian pounds. But they had met with little success and were becoming desperate. They had not known when they had slipped undetected into Egypt that sterling was not in use in the country and that those found in possession of it could be arrested and imprisoned. And now they had no choice but to change their money out on the black market at the current unfavorable exchange rate of only twenty-five percent.

To acquire intelligence, they had not only been bringing home a number of women to their houseboat, but recruited other Cairo good-time girls as paid purveyors of interesting pillow talk. Eppler had also been dressing up in khaki drill and going solo some nights without his partner at the Turf Club and other hot spots, passing himself off as a lieutenant in the Rifle Brigade. On the nights he went out to do some fishing on his own account, he had spent his British money freely at nightclubs frequented by British officers and kept his ears open. But he had, time and again, come up empty and was beginning to doubt his and Sandstette's abilities as spies. But even worse, he knew that their prodigal-spending ways could not last and their time was running out.

They were also growing increasingly concerned that they had done nothing to prove their worth to Almasy, Canaris, or Rommel. To assuage their guilt and build up a defense that would withstand at least cursory scrutiny, he and Sandstette had begun to make false entries into their independent journals to justify their actions in Cairo. Eppler could only hope that it would fool their superiors into thinking they had actually done useful espionage work—when all they had really done thus far was throw their money away on whiskey and women in the nightclubs and brothels. He was also worried about how they might steal out of the city undetected and return to Rommel's lines if they were forced to flee Cairo in a hurry.

"That's him, he's here," he heard his stepbrother say.

He turned to see a handsome, Aryan-looking gentlemen in his mid-thirties and wearing a sleek gray suit with a royal blue tie. He watched as Victor Hauer made a quick but thorough survey of the cabaret before walking over to their table. He looked and acted like the diplomat that he was, but he seemed to have a well-trained eye about him. Hassan had been able to pick up a few details on the street about him: he was born in Austria, had served in the Austrian Legation in Paris and Cairo before the war, and once the Germans invaded Poland, had transferred to the Swedish Legation in Section B, German Affairs, looking after Austrian and German internees and their families in Egypt.

Hassan quickly made the introductions over the loud orchestra and cheering audience, who were clearly enjoying the rousing Tahia Carioca. But he did not give his stepbrother's name nor did he reveal that they were siblings. "Herr Hauer, this is the man I was telling you about," he said.

"A pleasure to meet you at last—Captain Almasy sends his regards," said Eppler. "Thank you for meeting with me, but I'm afraid we must get going."

Hauer looked alarmed, his eyes darting around the room. "Is it not safe? Are we being watched?"

Eppler smiled reassuringly. "No, it's just a precaution. Come, let's get a taxi and go to my *dahabia*."

They quickly left, grabbed a waiting taxi outside the nightclub, and drove to Houseboat Number 10. After paying the driver, they walked up the gangway onto the sundeck complete with a bar made of mahogany. The city was blacked out for German air strikes, but there were still scattered pinpoints of light along the river. The streets of Cairo were loud both day and night with the rattling of tanks, half-tracks, and transports rolling up to the front. The British Tenth Army was on its way to the Land of the Pharaohs from Syria and Palestine, and other reinforcements for British and Commonwealth units were being hustled to the El Alamein front as swiftly as possible along with massive quantities of American and British weapons. Though in the past few days the flap had eased up and the curfew had been lifted due to a plethora of complaints from British officers unwilling to give up whoring and heavy drinking when on leave from the front, at least until Rommel and his Panzers were actually parading down Sharia Kasr El Aini, there was still a sense of urgency and significant military activity in the city.

Stepping inside the sumptuously appointed houseboat, Eppler poured everyone a Scotch and they sat down on the divans and chairs of the main stateroom.

Eppler spoke in German, "My partner and I are German officers in the Abwehr and we are having trouble with our transmitter. For reasons of security, we cannot give you our real names, but our codenames are Max and Moritz. We want to send a message to Rommel that we will be transmitting on a certain date at a specific time using a certain frequency. We would like you to help us either get our hands on a new transmitter unit, or the spare parts we would need to repair our unit or at least make it work properly. Alternatively, you could provide us with information as to the whereabouts of the Gestapo or Abwehr transmitter in Cairo that we have been told about. We could use this transmitter to send our message to Rommel's Signals Unit. Can you help us?"

"I may be able to help. It is my understanding that there is a wireless transmitter that has been stored in the basement of the Swedish consulate, apparently since 1937. It is supposed to have been left behind by the Germans and is not known by the Swedes."

"What kind, do you know?"

"I am told it is an American model, Hallicrafter I think. But I have never seen it so I am not sure."

To the surprise of everyone, Sandstette came walking into the room. Eppler realized he must have been out on the town and returned alone without his usual female companionship. Sandstette looked at him, then at Hauer and Hassan, and then back at him.

"What's going on?" the newcomer asked warily in English.

Eppler stood up. "This is Herr Hauer from—"

"Wait, I need to talk to you alone for a moment," Sandstette interrupted him.

"Yes, of course," said Eppler, though he was irritated at his comrade-in-arm's brusque demeanor in front of their new guest who was here, at grave risk to himself, to help them.

Sandstette went to the gramophone and turned it on so they could talk without being overheard. Eppler followed him.

"How do you know we can trust this man?" demanded Sandy as Marlene Dietrich's sexy, gravelly voice pumped out of the speakers.

"Because Almasy vouched for him," replied Eppler. "He works at the Swedish Legation in Section B, which handles German affairs."

"You didn't answer my question," snapped Sandstette.

"Everyone knows who he is, you fool. He looks after all the German and Austrian internees and their families in Egypt. More importantly, he is going to help us track down a new transmitter, quartz crystal, or other spare parts for the one we have. It's the only way we're going to get through to Rommel."

"All right, but you had better be sure about him. I don't want to die at the hands of a firing squad."

"Which one? Rommel's or Auchinleck's? We haven't discovered any intelligence worth reporting, remember? As things stand now, we're just as likely to be shot by our own as we are the fucking British. You should remember that when you make your next false journal entry."

"Fuck you."

"No, fuck you." He turned down the gramophone and smiled courteously at their guest and his stepbrother. "I apologize for the interruption, gentlemen. Now where were we?"

But Sandstette—whose real name and alias had not been revealed to Hauer—wasn't finished. He walked aggressively towards the Austrian and said, "If you betray us, we will get you for it. You should know that before you agree to help us."

But Hauer was not one to be bullied. "My loyalty to my fellow Germans and Austrians is beyond question. You can check with anyone."

Eppler gave a mollifying smile. "That's what I told him." He shot Sandstette a sharp look. "Now we've had enough delays. Let's get back to business. Now Sandy and I have collected solid information from Shepheard's, the Turf Club, the Continental, Groppi's, and other establishments. We've overheard conversations from British officers who drink too much. They've told us about reinforcements, new military equipment, morale, and the like. We have agents in Port Said and Suez, and in fact I have been to Suez quite recently performing reconnaissance. We've also given private soldiers a pound or two in return for information of conditions at the front and in the supply train."

"Yes, we've been directing Rommel's advance from Cairo with information," said Sandstette, picking up the line of prevarication and exaggeration, "but our transmitter has been on the blink for ten days or so and we fear that Rommel will think we have been caught."

Eppler nodded vigorously. "Which is why we need to get a new transmitter and we need to do it as soon as humanly possible."

"We were given three frequencies for transmission," explained Sandstette. "But because the transmitter broke down before we could inform our controllers at Rommel's HQ and go over the alternative frequencies, we are now without means of communication."

"Also," lied Eppler, "we believe our wireless messages may have on occasion been intercepted by the British Y Service. We exchanged spoof messages with them, we believe."

Hauer nodded. "I understand your situation, gentlemen, and will do my best to help you. I suggest Hassan and I meet on Tuesday at 2:30 p.m. at the Astra Milk Bar." He looked at Sandstette. "As I was telling your associate here, there is an American transmitter in the basement of the Swedish Consulate where I work. It was left behind by the Germans and is still unknown to the Swedes. Before the meeting, I will locate and examine the device and make a sketch of it."

"A sketch?" asked Eppler.

"To make sure it's a transmitter, I will make a drawing of the front panel and all the knobs. We should make sure it is the real thing before I go to all the trouble to borrow it, don't you think?"

"Yes, I will meet you at the Astra Milk Bar," said Hassan.

"Good, then it is settled," said Eppler. "Tuesday at 2:30 it is."

CHAPTER 39

EPPLER AND SANDSTETTE HOUSEBOAT
AGOUZA, CAIRO

JULY 14, 1942

"THERE'S NO USE LYING to me anymore—I know what you're up to."

"What is it that you think you know?"

"That you and your friend Peter Muncaster are Nazi spies—that's what."

There she had said it. Now she sat back and watched the reaction. Slowly but inexorably, the expression of Johannes Eppler—whom she still only knew by his Egyptian name of Hussein Gaafar—turned from startlement to a mixture of guilt, fear, and anger, then to one of pragmatic consideration as he seemed to calculate whether or not he should attempt to lie his way out of the entanglement he was in, and finally to something that appeared like acceptance, perhaps even resignation. But Hekmat Fahmy knew it might just be a ploy. As the anxious seconds ticked off, she stared directly at him with her deep, penetrating eyes, hoping to leave him no option but to come fully clean. After all, she knew him only too well, knew all his clever tricks, and had caught him red-handed. But of course, he was a spy and spies were trained to be damned good liars.

And then his expression changed one final time and he gave a guilty yet good-natured smile.

"All right, you've got me, you clever girl," he said with more than a little admiration and affection. Taking the bottle of Tuscan Cabernet Sauvignon from the side table, he refilled her glass then topped off his own. "So, what do we do now?"

She crossed her arms. "You tell me everything, starting from the beginning, and I don't report you to the police. That's the best you're going to get from me. You've deceived me all along since your return to Cairo and I'm not going to pretend I'm okay with it any longer."

"You would turn in your old boyfriend?"

"In a heartbeat. Now tell me what kind of mischief you've gotten yourself into? As I said, I know perfectly well you're spying for Rommel and that you and Peter are in a spot of trouble. You can't hide things from a woman, especially not someone who once shared your bed." She had decided not to reveal that two weeks ago she had eavesdropped on him and Sandstette nearly in this very spot and that was where she had discovered he was a spy.

"You were the best I ever had, you know," he said.

"Flattery won't get you anywhere, so you'd better start talking."

"But can I trust you not to tell anyone?"

"Yes, you can trust me. The British may occupy Egypt, but we are still officially a neutral country in this war so I am breaking no laws in simply listening to what you have to tell me. Your secrets are safe with me, but I will not accept you lying to me anymore. Is that understood?"

"Yes, I understand." He gave a little sigh of exasperation and they smiled at one another, like two opposing chess players. It was 11:56 p.m. on a Tuesday night and she had finished her second show of the evening at the Kit Kat forty minutes earlier. They were alone on the deck of his *dahabia*. Unbeknownst to Hekmat, Muncaster was belowdecks preparing to make his nightly radio transmission. It was a peaceful setting with the new moon and twinkling stars overhead of the blacked-out city. In the near distance, she could hear the groan of rumbling tanks and supply trucks threading their way through the streets of Cairo. Soon, they would turn north onto the great road to Alexandria.

"It is true Peter and I are German spies. We were delivered by truck from the Libyan desert and took the train to Cairo. Our assignment is to report on the British strength and military activity to Rommel, but we haven't even been able to get our transmitter working. Peter sends a wireless message out every night at midnight, but he's had no luck. It's always the same—he transmits our sending station's identification code but it is never acknowledged."

She already knew all this, of course, but did her best to look as though she was hearing it for the first time.

"What are your real names?"

"German intelligence knows me as Johannes Eppler, and Peter is really Heinrich Sandstette. We have both received extensive training by the Abwehr."

"So you have reported nothing to Rommel?"

"Not a single thing. We don't know if something's wrong with our wireless set, or if there's some problem on the other end on the part of our radio controller behind Rommel's line. But unfortunately, we have no backup plan, no other means to contact our controller."

"But aren't the Germans bound to answer from another station before long?"

"That's what we're hoping for. Then at least we would know what's going on. The British would likely jam our radio frequency, our controller or another station would tell us we were being jammed, and then we would have to get the hell out of Cairo or hide out until the coast was clear. But so far, nothing's happened."

"You don't have contacts in the city that can help you?" she then asked him innocently, though she already knew he had re-established contact with his mother and stepbrother.

"I have had problems with that too. Our best contact, Prince Abbas Halim, is under suspicion and being closely watched."

"I'm afraid it's even worse than that. Halim has been interned by the British."

"What?"

"Come now, you must have heard? It was in all the papers."

"No, I honestly didn't know."

She quickly relayed the story of how during the early days of the flap, the pompous bull-frog prince of the deposed Khedival family and vocal Nazi sympathizer was heard by dozens of people at the Muhammad Ali Club drinking a defiant toast to Rommel's health. "Now that the Desert Fox has gotten this far,' he is reported to have proclaimed, "let's hope he doesn't fall at the last fence!" The prince was interned three days later.

"What a mess," said Eppler. "We had intended to approach the prince through a servant at the Royal Automobile Club. Before the war this man was employed by

Dr. Schrumpf-Pierron, a well-known German resident and intelligence operative who is now in Libya. We have a letter of introduction from Schrumpf-Pierron, with which we were going to prove our bona fides to the servant, Mohamed Hamza. I knew Hamza before the war. But then we discovered that Hamza was in detention. I don't think I have to tell you that the situation is getting bleaker every day."

She nodded and they fell into silence. She stared off at Zamalek Bridge. The scent of jasmine was in the air and the night air was pleasantly warm but not hot. She realized that, despite herself, she was genuinely intrigued by her former lover's spying activities; it was like peering through a peephole into his life.

"Is there no one else that you have sought help from?" she asked him.

"There was also a Hungarian priest named Père Demetriou."

"Yes, I have heard of him. One of the Hungarian dancers at the club has mentioned him. He is at the Church of St. Theresa Shoubra."

"That's right. I was told he has a spare Abwehr wireless set left over from a failed operation." He held up his hands. "Look, I'm not sure I should be telling you all this. You do realize that if I am caught, I will be shot. And the same could very well happen to you."

"Not as long as I don't help you. There is no crime against knowing things. As I said, my country is not at war with either Britain or Germany."

"Yes, but the British and Egyptian police are arresting people every day and stuffing them in internment camps."

"Yes, but they are virtually all Germans, Italians, Austrians, or Hungarians. And most of these have been men, not women."

"There have been some Egyptians. Look what happened to Prince Halim."

"Yes, but he was shooting off his mouth. I understand that you are uneasy telling me all this," she said. "But the fact is, you now have me quite intrigued. Did you ever contact Father Demetriou?"

"We were going to, but were told that he may be being watched too."

"So the priest was a dead end?"

"Yes, but he did have close contacts with the Hungarian Legation, which was where he came across Almasy."

"But the Hungarian embassy is shut down since Hungary is allied with Germany."

"Yes, the Hungarians have closed down their interests and switched to the Swedish Legation. That's where Demetriou met a man named Victor Hauer, who is going to hopefully solve our radio problem. My stepbrother Hassan contacted him and we are working to get a new transmitter, or repair the one we have."

"Is Viktor German?"

"Austrian. He works at the Swedish Legation and looks after the interests of Germans and Austrians in Egypt."

She remembered when she had eavesdropped two weeks ago that he was going to get in touch with his stepbrother to help him solve their radio problems. She realized now that Hassan must have established contact with Hauer and now the Austrian diplomat was in the process of helping them.

"But my main worry right now isn't the radio," said Eppler. "It's running out of money and not having any intelligence information of value. I mean, things are so bad that Peter and I have been making false journal entries describing fictional visits to ports, supply depots, military barracks, and the like. But the truth is we've done nothing except fritter away our British sterling on cocktails and women these two months. Oh, and watching you dance. I have to say that you are even more delightful to watch than when I knew you before the war. In fact, I would say with conviction that there is no better performer of *danse du ventre* than you in all of Cairo—and believe me, Peter and I have seen every single dancer in the city these past two months, including Tahia Carioca. She's wonderful but no comparison to you, by the way. In any case, some spies we are, huh?"

He gave a self-deprecating laugh and she couldn't help but chuckle along with him. Even if she wanted to turn him in to the authorities, how could she? He and Sandstette had to be the two most bungling spies on either side. They were hardly worth throwing behind bars or putting before a firing squad.

"What are you going to do now?" she asked him, curious as to how he planned to get out of his predicament.

"If we stay here, we're going to run out of money or be caught. So even though we haven't achieved anything in Cairo, I believe we must somehow get back to the *Afrika Korps* to find out why we can't establish radio contact and get more money."

"How do you plan to do it?"

"That's what I don't know. But I am hoping that Herr Hauer can help us."

"And if he can't?"

He gave a fatalistic smile. "Then it's a blindfold and firing squad. But my biggest regret would be that I would never get to see you dance again."

Deeply touched, she finished her wine. "I have to get to bed—I have a busy day tomorrow. Performing two shows always wipes me out," she said. "And don't worry, I won't say anything to anyone. You told me the truth and that truth will not leave my lips for as long as I live."

He reached out and touched her hand. "I believe you," he said. "And again, I want you to know that you are the best I ever had. I was the luckiest man in the world when I was in your arms. I didn't know it then, but I know it now."

She felt not only flattered but vindicated, but she didn't want to make too big a show of it. "That's nice of you to say," she said with far more stoicism than she felt inside. "But right now, your top priority is your own survival. After all, if the British are anything, it is doggedly persistent. If you continue this game of yours, they *will* catch you."

"I know," he said sadly. "And then I'd never get to see you dance again."

CHAPTER 40

BRITISH MIDDLE EAST HEADQUARTERS
GARDEN CITY

JULY 21, 1942

WEARING HIS NEATLY CREASED UNIFORM, Major A.W. "Sammy" Sansom stared across the conference table at the humorless face of the MI6 senior intelligence officer he knew only as Bob. With the main conference room on the third floor occupied, they were forced to use a cramped room at the end of the hall. They sat at the far edge of the large conference table since it was cluttered and piled high with the records that hadn't been burned during the flap: thirty boxes containing case files, memorandums, dossiers, and the latest issues of *The Times* and the English-language dailies *The Egyptian Mail* and *The Egyptian Gazette*.

"It's been brought to my attention that you've set up a surveillance team to watch the movements of a certain chauffeured car and also a houseboat," said Bob without preamble to open the meeting. He then looked down at his leather-bound notebook. "A car with the Egyptian license plate number 14060, and Dahabia Number 10 in Agouza near the Egyptian Benevolent Hospital. Is that correct?"

Wary of the mysteriously well-informed Bob, Sansom hesitated before answering, trying to figure out what his game was. But he had no choice but to give an honest answer. "Yes, I've had a team keeping tabs on the car and the houseboat for the past three days."

"What's the name of the driver?"

"Ahmad."

"Full name?"

"The chauffeur's name is Mohamed Abdel Rahman Ahmad. Why do you ask?"

"I'll get to that in a moment. And the houseboat? Who lives on it?"

"Two men."

"Names."

"We don't know."

"You don't know their bloody names?"

"No."

"Are they renting?"

"Yes. The owner is Mohamed Badr Awab. We haven't questioned him because we don't want to raise any red flags. Same with the chauffeur."

"How many people do you have watching the houseboat?"

"Three. One of my NCOs is disguised as a beggar, and I have two more of my men waiting nearby to tail the visitors when they leave."

"What about the two men living on the boat?"

"We don't shadow them. We just keep an eye on them when they're on the boat. Now what is this all about, Bob?"

The pug-faced MI6 officer took out a silver flask, twisted the top, tilted back his head, and took a blast. He then offered the flask to Sansom, who shook his head and instead pulled out a *Sigarette Nazionali* seized from an Italian black-marketeer he had recently rounded up and interned. Lighting the cigarette with a silver, engraved Zippo lighter, he took a puff, looked at it appreciatively, and waited patiently for Bob to give him an answer.

"Before I tell you any more, you're going to have to swear to secrecy."

"Very well, consider it done: I swear on Lord Nelson's grave not to whisper a bloody word."

"You should also know that Colonel Jenkins instructed me to tell you that what I'm about to say to you has not been, nor will ever be, disclosed to our own police, except you, or the Egyptian authorities."

"I get the point, Bob. This is top secret and will remain so for me. Now what have you got?"

"Very well, we believe the two men are German spies," he said bluntly.

"How do you know?"

"On July 11, DSO Jenkins was informed by Dr. Radinger, one of his sources, that Viktor Hauer of the Swedish consulate had been in touch because he had received a telephone call from someone seeking his help. Dr. Radinger is a German-Jewish abortionist living in the city with ties to Germans, Austrians, and Swedes, among others, living in Cairo."

"Yes, I saw Colonel Jenkins report and we've been keeping an eye on Hauer. He's a German working at the Swedish Legation. He looks after the interests of German internees in Egypt."

"Actually, he's Austrian. In any case, it appears Hauer agreed to meet two Germans who had asked for passports and a Hallicrafter wireless transmitter that has been stored in the consulate's basement. As Hauer has known since 1939 that Dr. Radinger was an agent of the British, he asked him to act as an intermediary, and the result was that the DSO arranged for Hauer, whose precise diplomatic status is uncertain given the current state of affairs, to be abducted with his consent."

"You're telling me that Victor Hauer was kidnapped by us?"

"It took place last night as he left the Metro cinema. He was blindfolded and driven to the SIME villa at Maadi."

"Has he already been interrogated?"

"All day long. Jenkins plans to have his men pick it up again tomorrow. So far, he's described his background. He apparently served as an Austrian diplomat in Paris and married a woman from Alsace in Cairo in 1936. They have a five-year-old daughter who has returned with her mother to Europe and—"

"What's this got to do with my surveillance of the chauffeured car and houseboat?"

"I'm getting to that, Major—how about a modicum of patience, old boy?"

Sansom rolled his eyes. "All right, go ahead."

"Very well. Thus far during his interrogation, Hauer has confirmed that he was visited at the consulate on July 12 by a man named Hassan Gaafar."

"Who's Gaafar?"

"Nothing but a low-level gofer, it appears. But his father happens to have been an important man: a very pro-British Egyptian judge named Salah Gaafar. He passed away several months ago."

"You don't say. And what are Hauer and Hassan Gaafar up to?"

"As I said, they met at the Swedish consulate. Following their meeting, Hauer agreed to meet Gaafar again the same evening at Badia's Cabaret near English Bridge. They met there along with another man, a German-Egyptian, who didn't give Hauer his name. The three men talked there for a while and then took a taxi to a houseboat on the Nile. I presume you know what houseboat I am referring to?"

"*Dahabia* Number 10 in Agouza."

"The three men also met with another man—a tall German—on the houseboat. This man also didn't give his name and apparently threatened Hauer. This second German man is believed to currently live on the boat with the German-Egyptian. We believe they are both Abwehr spies."

"And this is all based on the interrogation of Hauer?"

"Not exactly. Our Austrian diplomat is just the tip of the iceberg. It seems that three days ago, or somewhere thereabouts, a German escapee from a civilian internment camp, one Kurt Siegel, was caught by British Field Security."

"Yes, I have been briefed on Siegel."

"Then you know that under interrogation he mentioned Viktor Hauer and spoke of a *dahabia* at Agouza where Siegel could find shelter with two Germans. I would have to say that Siegel fits in rather nicely with previous reports regarding mysterious happenings on the houseboat, wouldn't you? As well as reports about the movements of a certain car with the license plate 14060 driven by a moonlighting chauffeur named Mohamed Ahmad."

"All right, I can see that you and the DSO have been looking at this from the sharp end. What do you want from me?"

But Bob didn't answer. "A week ago, Victor Hauer made a second visit to the houseboat, accompanied by Hassan Gaafar. During this second visit, Hauer brought a large leather case with him—a rather important case as it turns out."

"What was in the case?"

"A radio transmitter. In fact, it was said to be an American wireless set that had been stored at the Swedish Legation."

"The Hallicrafter. So Hauer had access to it after all."

"Along with the wireless set he brought a Mauser pistol, ammunition, and detailed maps of Egypt. When he handed over the radio to the two operatives, you know what the tall German said in reply. He said that he had another transmitter buried five hundred kilometers away in Assiut. Hauer also said that in their messages they were known as Max and Moritz. You follow?"

A light went on in Sansom's head and now he understood the MI6 man's game. "Max and Moritz: those are the code names from the recent midnight broadcasts our surveillance vans have been trying to triangulate. Are you saying that these bastards living on Houseboat Number 10 are Almasy's spies that were driven through the Gilf Kebir?"

"Around it is more like it. And the answer is yes, I consider it a distinct possibility."

"But you don't know for certain."

"No, not for certain."

"Again, I must ask what you want from me?"

"It's not what I want. It's what Colonel Jenkins of SIME wants."

"And what does he want?"

"He wants you and your Field Security men to continue to keep an eye on the car and the houseboat, but don't arrest anyone or even think about launching a raid until the DSO gives the green light. You follow?"

"Of course, I bloody follow. Now what's the status of this Hauer? You said that you haven't gotten everything from him and he will be interrogated again tomorrow. Is he a cooperating witness that will continue to be under British protection?"

"Yes. Once he gave us his initial statement, Hauer's name was changed to Franz Muller and, at his request as he feared for his life from the Führer, he is in our protective custody. The plan is to transfer him to a POW camp in Palestine, where he will likely remain interned for the rest of the war."

"So you believe he is telling the truth?"

"Probably not all of it, but most. He also claimed to be acting as an intermediary for a group of Egyptian officers who had planned to block a British evacuation in the event that Rommel reaches Cairo. From what we understand their goal is to sabotage the bridges spanning the Nile and take heavy British casualties. But apparently they have no way of communicating with the Germans."

"We're watching General el Masri, Captain Anwar el Sadat, and others in the Egyptian Army Officers' Movement. I wouldn't be surprised if they know Hauer. We have files on all of them—and we will now on Hassan Gaafar as well. But these Germans living on the houseboat are new suspects."

"We don't know anything for certain yet. All we have is the surveillance of car 14660 and the chauffeur Mohammed, the detection of mysterious happenings on the houseboat, and the testimony of the escapee Siegel and the diplomat Hauer."

"That's not all you have. From the interrogation of Aberle and Weber, you know that Almasy's task was to shepherd two spies into Egypt equipped with the same ciphers and signals plan as that possessed by the two Brandenburgers."

"Yes, but that's all we know. So far it's all more alarming than useful."

"And too little to guide the DSO in the search for the spies."

"Precisely. Which is why we can't jump to the conclusion that there's a link between Aberle and Weber and the suspects on the houseboat, not without more evidence anyway."

"I see. So, to sum up, you don't have enough for an arrest and neither do I."

"Which is why we're both going to sit tight and continue to watch the car and houseboat until something breaks."

"And then what?'

Bob gave a bellicose smile. "Then we unleash the Giza Police and your British Field Security 259 Section, swoop down upon the houseboat, and bring all the bastards down—like bloody fucking dominoes."

"You're a hard man, aren't you Bob?"

"No, not really. I just don't like Nazi spies." And with that, the MI6 man pulled out his flask, took another snort, and grinned like a Cheshire cat.

CHAPTER 41

KUBEH GARDEN STATION, HELIOPOLIS

JULY 22-23, 1942

STEPPING OUT OF THE TAXI with his stepbrother, Eppler looked around for prying eyes and, seeing nothing suspicious, told the taxi to pull off to the side of the road and wait for them. Then he and Hassan walked over to the green icebox on the left-hand side from Kubeh Garden Station towards Heliopolis. They were here to meet with Egyptian Army Flight-Lieutenant Hassan Ezzet, whom Eppler hoped would be able to return him and Sandstette to Rommel's lines.

On Saturday July 18, prior to his British-staged abduction, Victor Hauer had, indirectly, set up the chain of events that had led to tonight's secret rendezvous. Hauer had put Eppler in touch with Fatma Amer, the Viennese wife of an Egyptian official who harbored Axis escapees and supported the Egyptian independence movement through her contacts with the pro-Nazi Egyptian Liberty Party. When he had met with her two nights ago, on July 21, she readily offered to help him and revealed that she was concerned that her efforts were not being properly recognized by Berlin. In return for offering him her assistance, she asked only that he put in a good word for her with the higher authorities at the appropriate time. To help Eppler return to German lines, she introduced him to Abdel Moneim Salama, a young relative of hers.

Salama took Eppler on foot to a coffee house in Giza, near the Abbas Bridge, and introduced him to the Egyptian Air Force officer Ezzet, a Copt who he said worked closely with a militant, up-and-coming Muslim captain in the Signals Unit of the Egyptian Army named Anwar el Sadat. Since the coffee house was crowded with some twenty Egyptian men in *mufti*, Eppler suggested that they talk in a less public place. Ezzet responded that they could talk quite openly at the café as all the patrons were loyal to the Egyptian nationalist cause. After Eppler had informed Ezzet of his and Sandstette's current plight, the flight-lieutenant wanted proof that they were who they said they were before he would be prepared to fly them back to Rommel. They eventually decided to meet again on the following night—July 22.

It was now the night of the appointed meeting and Eppler looked at his watch. It was 21:00 hours, the scheduled time of the rendezvous, but there was still no sign of Ezzet. And then, as if on cue, he was there at the open car window.

"We cannot talk here—I am being watched."

"What should we do?" asked Eppler.

"Go to the petrol station a half mile away near the Egyptian Army Hospital in Sharia Ismail Bey. Wait for me there."

"All right," said Eppler.

They drove to the station. Eppler paid the taxi driver his due fare plus a tip and instructed him to wait a little while longer. Twenty minutes after their arrival, a dark-brown, four-seat American luxury car slowly approached and pulled up next to them at the station. After instructing Hassan to return home in the taxi, Eppler quietly slipped into the vehicle. It was driven by Aziz el Masri Pasha, the pro-Axis former chief of staff of the Egyptian Army whom he had met last night, and sitting in the back seat were Hassan Ezzet and Captain Anwar el Sadat. They immediately tore off into the night towards Heliopolis, eventually pulling to a halt near Villa Baron Empain.

Taut with pent-up energy, Eppler could feel his leg shaking. How easy would it be for him to simply disappear on some desert backroad outside the city?

"We need proof that you are who you say you are," said el Masri. "Before Lieutenant Ezzet can fly you back to the safety of the German lines, he needs confirmation that you are truly a German and have come here from Libya."

"All I can do is show you where I am currently staying, my wireless set, and my German paybook. I can also introduce you to my radio operator and colleague Sandy."

Ezzet nodded along with el Masri. "All right, that will be satisfactory," said Ezzet. "The reason I need to be sure about your bona fides is because I have not had any news from my man Seoudi who flew over to the German lines two weeks ago."

"What was his mission?" asked Eppler.

"He had with him letters of introduction from me," answered el Masri for the flight-lieutenant. "And also codelists."

"He was to establish a wireless link with me," said Ezzet. "He had also taken with him more than a thousand aerial photos of military installations around Egypt."

Now the sleepy-eyed signals officer Sadat spoke up. "One of the targets our men photographed has already been bombed by the German Air Force," he boasted.

Eppler sensed that Sadat was something of a hothead. Nor were he or Ezzet the men in charge. From the conversation, it was clear that el Masri gave the orders to Ezzet and Sadat, and from them to Seoudi.

"So how do you propose getting me from Cairo to safely behind Rommel's lines at El Alamein?" he asked the trio of Egyptian army officers.

"We would most likely follow Seoudi's example and fly you from an emergency landing ground near the Pyramids, either Giza or more likely Sakkara."

"I see," said Eppler without much enthusiasm. For all he knew, Seoudi had been shot down and the same fate might very well await him.

They drove back to the petrol station. Along the way, Ezzet and Sadat continued to ask him leading questions to test whether he was telling the truth or not. Though he was nervous, he had no problem answering their questions since he had no reason to lie about Operation Condor. But he was evasive in some of his answers, not wanting them to know how desperate his and Sandstette's situation was becoming with their money problems and lack of success in obtaining valuable intelligence.

After el Masri dropped them off at the petrol station, Eppler, Sadat, and Ezzet walked to the main Heliopolis-Cairo road, near the Abbassia Barracks that had once been the base of the British Long Range Desert Group. From there, they took a taxi to the Kit Kat Club, picked up Sandstette, and drove to the houseboat. He and Sandstette were asked more questions along the way, and Eppler noted that the two officers seemed satisfied with their answers.

When they reached the *dahabia*, Ezzet paid off the taxi and Eppler looked around to make sure the coast was clear. The only person he saw was a middle-aged

Arab street vagrant in a blue-striped *galabeya* and well-worn leather sandals sitting cross-legged on the ground with his back leaning up against a palm tree. The beggar looked up incuriously as they walked past him towards Houseboat Number 10, and Eppler wrote him off as unimportant and certainly no threat. He led the group up the gangway and they went inside.

He and Sandstette had not cleaned up the stateroom or bedrooms in some time and the premises were a mess. Empty bottles of Scotch and wine lay on the side tables and a pair of women's panties had been left behind on the couch. The lingering fragrance of liquor, women's perfume, and hashish gave the houseboat a stagnant odor. As Eppler went to open a window, he heard Sadat grumble, "How can you live like this?"

He opened the window before turning around. Sadat stood frowning at him. He realized that the militant Muslim not only didn't approve of their carousing ways but was actually shocked by the riotous social life the German spies were enjoying.

"What do you care?" sniffed Eppler. "It's our houseboat, not yours."

"It's straight out of *One Thousand and One Nights*."

"Yes well, we happen to enjoy indolence, voluptuousness, and pleasure of the senses. I guess it's because we're German. You should try it sometime."

Sadat scoffed. "Don't be sarcastic with me. This dissolute atmosphere is no good. Have you young Nazis forgotten the delicate mission with which you have been entrusted?"

"No, we have not—and we are not Nazis," said Eppler emphatically. "Have you perhaps forgotten why we need your help?"

"No, I have not forgotten."

"That's enough arguing you two—we're all on the same side," interjected Ezzet. "Now before we take a look at your wireless, please show us your German paybooks so we can verify who you are."

"Yes, of course," said Eppler, and he and Sandstette each quickly produced a *Soldbuch zugleich Personalausweiss*—the official pocket-sized booklet carried by every enlisted man and officer in the German intelligence service, navy, infantry, and air force. The Germany Military *Soldbuch* was a condensed personnel file with data such as birth date, height, weight, parental information, blood group, vaccinations, eye examinations, but also information about pay, rank, military training, units, transfers, duties, and promotions.

Ezzet examined the two booklets quickly and nodded that everything was in order. But then Sadat grabbed them and made a big, cumbersome show of reviewing the *Soldbuchs* and cross-checking them against one another before curtly handing them back.

"All right, it appears you are who you say you are," he conceded. "Now let's take a look at those wireless sets."

Sandstette opened the mahogany cabinet containing the radiogram, rummaged around for a moment, and withdrew a pair of W/T transmitters. One was the set they had brought to Cairo with them from the desert with the Almasy Commando, and the second was the American set Victor Hauer had brought them from the Swedish Legation.

"I have not been able to establish a connection on the set we brought from

Libya," he said to Sadat, who for the moment seemed to have put aside his disapproval of the two Germans' bacchanalian lifestyle and began examining the primary wireless unit Almasy had given them, poking at knobs and checking the kilocycle frequency settings.

"What do you think happened when you transmitted?" asked Sadat as he probed the piece of equipment.

"I believe our receiving station—*Schildkroete*—and our wavelength have somehow been altered and that's why I haven't been able to get through to Rommel. I can use three wavelengths on the transmitter using these settings here." He pointed.

Nodding, Sadat toyed with the transmitter a moment longer before turning his attention to the American Hallicrafter W/T set provided by Hauer. "And this one?"

"I haven't figured out how to operate it," said Sandstette.

"We were planning on dropping the two sets overboard into the Nile tonight since they both seem to be worthless," said Eppler. "But perhaps you can do something with them and we should hold off."

"Don't do anything yet," said Sadat. "I can probably make use of the American set, at least, and you may have better luck with the other set in the future. It is best not to throw such equipment away."

"All right," said Eppler. "We won't then."

Ezzet said, "It appears that you two check out. Now I want to talk about what the next step is. I know an Egyptian in Zagazig—it's a town in the Nile Delta north of Cairo—who was in Germany for fifteen years and studied there. He came back to Egypt before the war and brought a wireless with him. He is in contact with the Germans. Give me a message and I will get him to send it for you."

"Yes, that sounds like a good idea."

"I'll write it," said Sandstette.

It took him a couple of minutes. While waiting, Eppler looked anxiously at his watch: it was after midnight. When Sandy was finished, he handed his note to Eppler, who quickly looked it over. The message would be transmitted to Major Seubert of Abwehr 1H West, the senior Abwehr officer responsible for Operation Condor whose codename was Angelo.

Please guarantee our existence. We are in mortal danger. Please use the wavelength No. 1 at 09:00 hours Tripoli time. Max and Moritz.

Eppler nodded. "That's fine." He folded up the message and handed it to Ezzet.

"I will see that the message is sent and will return to you with an answer from Angelo in six days' time."

"Very well." Eppler thought that it would take more like eight days, but he didn't tell Ezzet so. He was just relieved to have found a way to resume contact with Rommel.

"And one more thing," said Ezzet. "Make sure that you are on board the houseboat on the evenings of July 29, 30 and 31 so that you can receive the reply."

"I'm giving you my phone number in case you need to reach me," said Sadat.

"Yes, of course. Just give me a moment," said Eppler. He quickly grabbed his diary. Sadat recited the number and he jotted it down.

The German spies and Egyptian officers then said good night to one another. But the militant Sadat couldn't resist getting in one final dig as the two were leaving.

"You should clean this place up and focus more on winning the war for Germany, defeating the imperial British, and liberating our country than indulging in wine and women."

"And you should mind your own fucking business," said Eppler. "Otherwise, when my boss Rommel marches into Cairo, I will have to report to him that his Egyptian brothers were not very helpful."

At this, Sadat and Ezzet both gulped. "He didn't mean it—a thousand pardons," assuaged Ezzet, and he gave a little bow and shot his cohort a sharp look.

Summoning as much magnanimity as he could muster, Eppler saw them to the door. But he could not bring himself to bid adieu to Sadat, only Ezzet.

When they were gone, he turned to Sandstette and said, "What a fucking jerk! He's like Hitler Youth!"

"At least Ezzet seems to know what he's doing. All the same, I can't help but feel that this meeting may have been nothing but a waste of time."

"Well, we needed Sadat's expert opinion on the radios, and we got it, so from that standpoint I think it was mission accomplished."

"But why did the bastard have to be such a prick and go off in a huff like that?"

"He doesn't understand that this is the cover we've chosen. We're supposed to be carousing bachelors who support the Allies. In point of fact, I think we've given that impression quite nicely, don't you?"

"I most certainly do. It's none of Sadat's damned business what we do to maintain our cover, or what we do in our spare time."

"The bastard takes it for granted that a secret agent ought to live like a hermit. Oh well, we can't let it bother us. We have other far more important things to worry about. I don't care how things look to that Muslim—let's have a goddamn drink."

"Good idea," said Sandstette.

Eppler poured them each an outsize Scotch, four fingers of it, without soda and they were able to laugh about the incident. But soon the old familiar worries crept back into his mind. He was fed up with Condor: the operation was a fiasco. All they both wanted to do now was escape Cairo and return to Rommel's lines before their money ran out, they were captured, or the Desert Fox stormed into Cairo and discovered that they were total frauds. But Agent Condor would have been even more depressed if he had known his file as Johannes Eppler-Hussein Gaafar had already crossed Major Sansom's desk, along with the files of el Masri, Sadat, Ezzet, Hauer, and his stepbrother Hassan.

CHAPTER 42

KIT KAT CLUB
IMBABAH, CAIRO

JULY 23, 1942

THE FOLLOWING EVENING, Eppler and Sandstette strolled up to the Kit Kat Club's solid oak bar at half past eight. "Two White Horse and sodas!" said Eppler to Mac the bartender. "And make them bloody strong!" he added, slapping down a British five-pound note on the polished wood surface.

He hated to be spending sterling, but they had no choice. With the flap still ongoing, they were getting a horrible exchange rate on the black market but the nightclubs, restaurants, and cabarets were still taking British currency since soldiers receiving cash from home needed to be able to spend it somewhere.

A minute after he laid down his fiver, two young, tawny-skinned Egyptian party girls dressed in elegant evening wear, covered in jewelry, and smelling of French perfume came up to them. They were both strikingly attractive and exotic-looking, with dark highlights around their eyes that made Eppler think back to the days of the Pharaohs.

"*Fein el cocktail?*" asked the more voluptuous of the two in Arabic. Where is the party?"

"Right here, my lovelies," said Eppler with a big grin, also in fluid Arabic. "What are you two drinking?"

"Gin fizz," the curvaceous one replied, and she and her friend giggled. Miss Curvaceous would be his entertainment for the evening, he decided, and Sandy could have the other girl, not quite as much of a knockout but way above the standard fare. He waved down Mac, ordered two gin fizzes, and threw down another five-pound note on the bar.

After two months of carousing at practically every upscale nightclub in Cairo, he and Sandstette knew the drill. As long as a young woman on the Cairo club circuit was comely, or at least moderately attractive and interesting in some manner, she was not expected to pay for her own drinks or entertainment, and literally could go for months without paying for a single cocktail or her own dinner. If sociable, she could find herself out on the town seven nights a week for free with plenty to eat and drink, fine music, quality cabaret shows to entertain her—while the war raged on and men died by the tens of thousands in the desert. Eppler had discovered that not all girls managed to keep their heads in the face of such idolization, and some became so contemptuous of the men in the clubs that they referred to them as "meal tickets." But he and Sandstette rarely went for those types. More often than not, they struck gold with gorgeous and very willing Egyptian women to share their bed. It was a rare night indeed that they didn't end up having a wild night of fun and dancing out on the town with a pair of ravishing Egyptian beauties—followed by a wild romp under the covers on their stately Nile houseboat.

"What are your names?" asked Eppler as Mac delivered their drinks.

"I'm Nadia, and this is Jezebel," said the voluptuous one.

"Nadia and Jezebel," said Sandstette approvingly. "I like that."

Eppler quickly handed out the drinks. "Let's have a toast, ladies," he said, raising his cocktail glass.

"What shall we toast to?" asked Jezebel.

"Why to you two, of course. Nadia and Jezebel, we are at your disposal," he said with a devilish grin. "I am Hussein and my friend here is Sandy."

The young women looked at one another and giggled again. "All right, Hussein and Sandy," Nadia said. "To us girls then!"

"And to Hekmat Fahmy," said Eppler as they were about to tip back their heads and take a gulp. "She's about to take the stage."

"We know!" they cried in unison, bouncing on their feet. "Isn't she wonderful?"

"Oh yes, she is. In fact, I must say that we were quite the romantic couple back in the day. In fact, I was once madly in love with her. But then I had to go away."

"You really know her!" cried Nadia.

"Yes, I am proud to say I do."

"You're not playing with us, are you?"

"Now why would I do a thing like that?"

"Because you are a naughty boy."

"Well, you do have me there," he said. "But I am telling the truth because I do not lie about love. She was the best I ever had and I think about our time together every day. But alas, these days we are just good friends."

"Good," she said. "Then tonight I am all yours."

ΨΨΨ

With his usual watered-down drink from Mac in hand, Sansom scanned the bar for any suspicious-looking characters who might be spying for the Germans or assisting them by exchanging money, selling secrets, or engaging in some other illicit practice through connections to the underworld. Dressed in civilian clothes and posing as a shady Greek businessman, one of his more frequent covers, he had decided to spend the evening at the Kit Kat Club to see if any dud fivers were changing hands. The upscale club had a unique mixture of upstanding types and questionable characters. Known to be a haunt for spies, British officers were warned to be tight-lipped around the Hungarian dancing girls, and Sansom had months ago made the club out of bounds, which caused a furor with his fellow officers comprising the vast majority of the establishment's patrons, forcing him to swiftly reopen the establishment.

He and his team of Field Security officers had followed up on the Rifle Brigade subaltern case and had obtained a couple of promising leads, but still had no idea who the mysterious man was and what sort of game he was up to. Using Peter the Turf Club barman's description of the suspect, Sansom had thoroughly checked out the Rifle Brigade officers who could have been in Cairo at the time. He came up empty; however, while there were many reasons for someone to be masquerading as an officer, Sansom knew that spending such a substantial sum of out-of-circulation money pointed towards shady dealings, perhaps espionage. He still had trouble believing the Abwehr didn't know that the British forces in Egypt were almost invariably paid in Egyptian currency. But the only plausible explanation seemed to be that the Germans were genuinely in the dark: they were providing their Abwehr spies with the wrong currency for the country in which the luckless bastards were spying. And in the present case, whoever the man posing as a subaltern was, he was forced to spend British currency openly, as the rate of return on the black market was said to be twenty-five percent or less and dropping.

To catch their man, he had directed his team to watch out for English money spenders in bars and cabarets. He had warned them not to do anything that might put their quarry on guard, and he knew this would hamstring them somewhat, but his men were nonetheless working hard on the case. Unfortunately, they could not go around asking direct questions about the currency spending for fear that the fake subaltern would hear of it and be scared off. That was one reason why be believed his team was failing to obtain any major leads. Another reason was that he believed the man they were after had realized he was under suspicion at the Turf Club and had most likely gone underground ever since. Or perhaps he was still prowling the nightspots but was no longer wearing the uniform of a Rifle Brigadesman.

Since the money incident at the Turf Club, the most important lead Sansom had discovered was that the notes the fake subaltern had been supplied with were counterfeit. On July 9, the day after the incident, he had sent the money recovered by Peter the barman to Britain by plane to be checked out by experts at the Bank of England. The suspect had spent five English-pound notes and one fiver at the club. Working with British intelligence, the bank was able to trace the pound notes to deposits in neutral countries, including Switzerland and Spain. Furthermore, the bank was certain that the five-pound note was a forgery and product of the German government. As Sansom was soon to learn, the British Security Services were already aware that Germany was forging large quantities of foreign currency—including French francs, British pounds, and American dollars—but they were unable to give him any further details.

It seemed remarkable to Sansom that, if the suspect was indeed a German agent, he had been given not only the wrong currency but forged currency. This was an important revelation for it suggested that this was standard operating procedure within the Abwehr. But he still didn't know for sure whether he was dealing with an actual German agent or merely an underworld figure or shady opportunist who had come across a stash of British money. All the same, he believed the money would lead eventually to an arrest. On his office wall, he had posted a map of the city marked with pins where the forged bank notes had been spent, and he had ordered his staff to bring in anybody using sterling.

The flap offered the perfect cover. As large as the operation was, the lingering panic on the streets due to the dangerous proximity of Rommel and his army allowed him to take a large number of people into custody and interrogate them without raising undue suspicion. It was easy to pretend the increased scrutiny was simply a part of the security measures due to the flap. In the past ten days, he had roped in hundreds of people: British and Allied officers, pimps, money changers, and even shoeshine boys. Though he had been unable to find his man, he did manage to uncover a large number of people clearly involved in black-marketeering, drug-smuggling, robbery, and other crimes that were of interest to the Egyptian police, but unfortunately not to him. Out of the countless hours of questioning, he did not obtain a single decent clue.

He took a sip of his Scotch and soda. He always had Mac water down his mixed drinks when he was on duty at the club, so he was sober and sharp when he spied on people or if he had to make an arrest. As he looked up, he saw a man some distance down the bar laugh and light his cigarette with a British one-pound note.

"There are plenty more where that came from," the man said airily, in faultless Arabic.

Sansom's interest was instantly piqued. He discreetly studied the man for a moment. He was at the bar with a blond-haired companion and three cabaret girls. The two men appeared to be buying drinks freely and laughing and joking as if they were mildly drunk. Slipping on a pair of dark glasses, which were commonly worn by Egyptians in clubs even at night, he ordered a bottle of 1934 vintage Dom Pérignon from Mac and walked over and joined them at the bar.

"Will you help me drink this?" he asked in Arabic, feigning an intoxicated slur.

The cabaret girls quickly said they would. The two men indicated they were drinking whiskey, so he bought them a double each.

"You are celebrating?" asked the man who had money to burn. "Your birthday, perhaps?"

Sansom feigned an inebriated smile. The man seemed not to want his company, but was trying to be polite. "Just a good business deal," he whispered, trying to give the impression that he was either a black-marketeer or at least a shady businessman taking advantage of a war opportunity.

"Bravo for you."

"As a matter of fact," Sansom went on, in the manner of a carouser taking a stranger into his confidence, "it was a currency transaction but please don't tell anyone."

The man gave a conspiratorial grin. "I won't, I promise. Here, have another drink."

He reached for the champagne bottle and filled an empty flute. *Hmm, evidently the old boy thinks I might be worth getting to know, after all.* The party girls giggled and he filled their glasses, too, as well as one for the man's tall, blond-haired friend. Through his dark sunglasses, Sansom took in the scene. His mark might very well have been just another wealthy Egyptian with some spare British bills on hand. And yet...and yet there was something about the man and his companion that seemed vaguely suspicious. The war brought out all kinds of curiosities and inconsistencies in people, and it was sometimes hard to differentiate between whether someone was dirty or simply desperate. But this one seemed suspicious. Though the man's Arabic was perfect, he didn't look Egyptian or even Middle Eastern; his facial features and manner were European, which was enough to put Sansom on alert.

Soon the band struck up and they stopped talking while Hekmat Fahmy took the stage to rousing applause. She was a sight to behold and Sansom felt his breath taken away. It was on nights like this—when he got to drink and take in a show while playing the clever role of undercover detective—that he truly enjoyed his job.

Hekmat began to dance. He had seen her on countless occasions before tonight and was fascinated by her exquisite symmetry and coordination. She was sensual, yes, but she also seemed to be perfect with regard to the movement of her shoulders, the erection of her arms, the stance of her feet, and particularly the timing and movement of her stomach muscles. Keeping in time with the musical rhythm, she had an emotional impact on the audience that went far beyond mere dancing. Sansom was no expert on *danse du ventre*, but had been told by those who were that there were dancers who could stimulate and excite an audience of amateurs while leaving the expert cold. Hekmat Fahmy, he saw once again, had the gift of satisfying both kinds of aficionados.

As her convulsive belly dance approached its shuddering climax, Sansom looked at the men in the audience. To many of the officers, her long drawn-out gyrations and frenzied shuddering of her body accompanied by the frenetic clicking of her fingers was purely a simulation of sexual intercourse. But to the handful of Egyptian connoisseurs who watched her, he saw something far more subtle than this. They were plainly aware of the eroticism implicit in the dance, but they seemed to revel even more in the artistic genius than the sexuality. To them, she might as well have been an Olympic gymnast or circus acrobat.

Sansom could also see that his money-burning friend and his partner were particularly enjoying the show. They began clapping their hands rhythmically as she approached the climax. As the decisive moment came, he anticipated the general applause with a roar of lubricious appreciation when she reached her frenzied, shuddering portrayal of what appeared in Western eyes to be a woman in orgasm. Wanting to seem like one of the boys, Sansom clapped thunderously, roared his approval, and exchanged a few coarse clichés with his two new companions over a fresh round of drinks. He noted that his rowdiness was not wasted on the two men.

When the show ended, the money burner said, "Would you like an introduction to Miss Fahmy?"

Sansom felt himself involuntarily frown, but quickly caught himself and served up an approving nod accompanied by a smile. There was nothing in the world he wanted less, for he knew that Hekmat Fahmy must have seen him in the Kit Kat many times, in uniform as well as in civilian clothes. True, he had on dark glasses, as if he was nothing more than a clubby Egyptian, but it still seemed a shaky disguise. But he could not say no.

"I'd love to meet her, of course," he said.

To his horror, his host signalled vigorously from across the room for her to join them. She smiled and came over so swiftly that Sansom couldn't help but wonder who this new subject he had stumbled upon was. He knew that Hekmat Fahmy had been in Egyptian movies, including the recently released *Rabab*. Was this playboy perhaps an actor or producer of some sort?

"Here she comes. Please tell me your name so I can properly introduce you."

Sansom had to think quickly on his feet. "My name is Sawi—Ramsay Sawi. And what is your name?"

"My name is Hussein Gaafar."

He thought instantly of the suspect Hassan Gaafar who had made contact with Victor Hauer at the Swedish Legation and Lady Badia's Cabaret. Could the two somehow be related, or were the similar names merely a coincidence? But then he reminded himself that Gaafar was a fairly common surname in Egypt and it might mean nothing. All the same, his interest had been perked and he would now be on the alert.

"A pleasure to meet you, Hussein," he said, and they shook hands.

Now Gaafar's friend smiled, stepped forward, and introduced himself in English. "I'm Peter Muncaster," he said with a strong American accent.

Hekmat came walking up. Sansom noted that her face was still flush with color and she looked ravishing. He felt his brain suddenly become a little muddled in the presence of such an intoxicatingly beautiful woman, and for a fleeting instant he imagined himself alone with her. He thought of his wife Joan and felt a tad guilty for having such prurient thoughts.

"Hello, Hekmat my dear," said Gaafar ebulliently. "This is our new friend Ramsay Sawi." He leaned in close and whispered something in her ear that Sansom couldn't hear, and then she nodded in understanding, pulled away gently, and smiled pleasantly.

"I am pleased to meet you, Ramsay," she said, looking him directly in the eye. And then slowly, her expression changed.

Sansom felt something bad about to happen. He held his breath.

"Haven't I seen you in here before?" she asked.

It appeared she remembered him but thankfully didn't recall seeing him in uniform. "Yes, I have often seen you, each time more desirable than the last," he replied, and to underscore the point he gave a little bow.

Gaafar gave him a knowing smile. "We had to hold him back at the end of your dance," he said.

Sansom gave a little laugh. *Whoever you are, you're a clever bastard,* he thought. *But that wasn't very smart of you to use a fiver as a spill for your cigarette.* He figured Gaafar had decided he might be useful when he had said he dealt in currency, but the Egyptian had not mentioned it again. *Instead, he seems to be pretending that he likes me for who I am, as if he was amused by my boyish show of support at the end of the belly dance.*

Sansom also had the feeling that Gaafar had told Hekmat Fahmy to humor him. *Is that what he said to her when he whispered into her ear?*

They talked at the bar and drank for a while with Hekmat Fahmy while the young Egyptian party girls moved on to a group of dapper senior British officers with money to burn. Sansom could tell that he had fooled Gaafar and his friend Muncaster into thinking that he was a simple Egyptian money changer and opportunist. Furthermore, it soon became obvious that Gaafar was a close friend of the famous belly dancer, and from some of their remarks he realized they had known each other intimately in Cairo before the war.

"Why don't we all go to my houseboat for cocktails," suggested Hekmat after fifteen minutes of drinking and chatting.

"Why that's a splendid idea," said Gaafar. "What do you say, Ramsay?"

He couldn't help but feel he had an opportunity, but of exactly what he couldn't yet say. "Marvelous idea! Lead the way!"

CHAPTER 43

HEKMAT FAHMY HOUSEBOAT
AGOUZA, CAIRO

JULY 23-24, 1942

AS THEY WAITED FOR A TAXI, Hekmat looked at Major A.W. "Sammy" Sansom—who based on what Eppler had whispered into her ear, she had no reason to believe was anyone other than an Egyptian money changer named Ramsay Sawi—and wondered where she had seen him before. He indicated that he had seen her perform at the club on prior occasions and he was definitely familiar to her, but she was unable to recollect the specific time she had seen him before. The truth was there was nothing exceptional about him. He was unusually short, no more than five foot four she estimated, with ample love handles, a double chin, receding hairline, and bristly mustache with flickers of gray. It was solely because her former lover wanted her to be nice to the man that she was even acknowledging him right now.

After her former lover's confession on his *dahabia* the week before, Eppler had spoken with her again and made it clear how truly desperate his and Sandstette's situation was becoming. After nearly two months in Egypt, not only had they not established any useful contacts, their difficult financial situation had turned into a crisis. The money changers they were using were taking gigantic cuts of their sterling in exchange for Egyptian currency, and Eppler estimated they could last no longer than another week to ten days before they ran out of funds.

But to make matters worse, with Rommel advancing deep into Egypt, they were afraid he might reach Cairo before they had done anything to justify their existence. During the past week, they had been mixing in even more false entries recording fictitious espionage activities to embellish their real diary entries. Eppler told her about one where he claimed, falsely, that he had left Cairo for Suez and Port Said to arrange for agents in those ports to report all shipping and troop movements to him. He said the most important thing now was to pull together enough Egyptian money so that he could flee Cairo, rejoin Rommel's army, justify himself, find out why there had been no response to their radio signals, and get some more money. And then tonight, when he had whispered in her ear, he had told her that Ramsay Sawi was his ticket out of Cairo and begged her to help him by being especially nice to him and suggesting they all return to her luxurious houseboat.

A pair of blue and white taxis pulled up at the curb. She and Sawi slipped into the first while Eppler and Sandstette hopped into the second.

They drove the short distance to her *dahabia* on the west bank of the Nile. She allowed Sawi to sit close and put his arm around her. She gave a fake sigh as if this was bliss indeed. Though she wanted to resist, she didn't. She would do this one favor for her ex-lover and be the charming host, but she would not allow Sawi to do anything more than put his arm around her. At least he seemed a pleasant and harmless little man.

When they reached the houseboat, her guest paid the driver and she led him up the gangway just as the second car arrived. An Arab in ragged street clothes sat cross-legged with his back leaning against a nearby palm tree, but he seemed uninterested in them. Eppler and Sandstette spilled out drunkenly from their taxi, not even noticing the vagrant against the tree, and they all went inside the elegantly appointed stateroom. While she, Sawi, and Sandstette made themselves comfortable on the divan and chairs, Eppler went to the mahogany bar, poured drinks for everyone, turned on the radiogram as if he was at home, and handed out the cocktails. She could see his mind at work on how he was going to make his play with Sawi the money changer.

"Any more mail from your adoring fans?" he asked her.

She immediately saw his angle: it was to use her celebrity status to make Sawi feel comfortable so they could close a money exchange at a reasonable rate. "A few more letters—I haven't opened them," she responded casually. Then to Sawi. "I get a lot of letters from British officers. Too many actually."

"I can imagine," he said.

Eppler took one of her fan letters from the pile on the side table next to the bar and slit it open with a letter opener. It bothered her that he acted as if he owned the place, but she said nothing. Out of the envelope fell a photograph of a smiling British officer with a set of bad teeth. He picked it up, looked it over a moment, and began to read the letter.

"Why don't we dance," she suggested to Sawi.

"Why I'd be delighted," he replied.

They danced for a few minutes, which Hekmat had to admit was sort of fun. Sawi may not have been much to look at, but he was at least a jovial sort and not a half bad dancer. But at one point, he did something that struck her as curious. He seemed to be closely watching Eppler as he read through several of her fan mail letters. Then the song finished and Eppler refilled their glasses. Now that the money changer had had a couple of drinks and done a little dancing, she could tell that Eppler was ready to make his pitch.

"I have a friend who wants to change a bit of sterling," he said in a casual tone that did not fool her one bit.

"My advice is for him to do it officially," replied Sawi owlishly. "That way he'll get the full rate. On the free market it can hardly be changed at all at the moment."

"That's what my friend said," Eppler said smoothly. "I rather gather he doesn't want to change it officially, though. If there is another way, he is prepared to drop quite a lot on the exchange."

"I'm afraid I can't help personally, as I'm not touching sterling. But I, too, have a friend who might be able to solve such a problem."

She watched as Eppler nodded understandingly. Sandstette just sat there quietly sipping his drink and watching the proceedings.

"Have you any idea how much your friend wants changed?" asked Sawi.

"I think he said about ten thousand pounds," replied Eppler.

"I'll tell you what. I'll speak to him tomorrow and we can meet at the Kit Kat tomorrow night, let's say eight o'clock."

Eppler held up his glass in a toast. "Let's drink to it."

Hekmat felt an undercurrent of tension in the room with all this talk of black-market currency exchanges. She didn't want to get caught up in anything illegal, though at the Continental Hotel and Kit Kat Club where she most often danced, she couldn't help but rub elbows with many shady characters. However, they were usually rich, influential, and cosmopolitan.

"Oh dear, it seems as if we've run out," she suddenly heard Sandstette blurt out. He had tried to pour himself a drink of Scotch, but had found the bottle empty. "I'll go get some more."

Hekmat wondered why he was going to get more whiskey when she had an unopened bottle of the same brand at the back of her cocktail cabinet. But she said nothing.

"Where can you get it at this time of night?" asked Sawi.

"We live on another houseboat," explained Eppler. "It's just a ways downriver. He won't be long."

"Sounds wonderful."

She glanced at the clock on the wall: quarter to twelve. It suddenly dawned on her what Sandstette was up to. He was attempting their nightly radio transmission as he had been doing the other night when she was on their houseboat. Now she was definitely getting caught up in things. She looked at Sawi. Could he be trusted? Was he really what he seemed?

When Sandstette left, they sat and talked for a few minutes before the doorbell up on deck rang.

"I'll get it." She rose from the divan, answered the door, and came face to face with a short, dapper, slim, young Egyptian man in civilian clothes with heavily-lidded eyes. She had never met him before.

"Greetings, my name is Anwar el Sadat," he said. "I am looking for Hussein Gaafar. I am a friend of his."

She noticed that he seemed nervous, and she wondered how the newcomer Sadat fit into her former lover's puzzle. Perhaps he was another money changer and gofer like that foul man Albert Wahda.

"Hello, Anwar. Yes, he is here—please come inside," she said in a pleasantly accommodating voice, though she would have liked to have turned him away since she didn't know anything about him and wondered how he had known to show up at her door at midnight. Eppler must have said something to him about her nearby houseboat. She would have to talk to him about that, since she had made it clear to him that she didn't want to get involved in his espionage affairs. She was only ingratiating herself with the money changer Ramsay Sawi tonight because Eppler was desperate and, as his former lover, she felt sympathy for his plight.

"Thank you," said Sadat politely and he gave a slight bow.

He stepped inside the houseboat. Closing the door behind him, she led him into the stateroom. She felt anxious, realizing that she was now caught up in Eppler's espionage game with all these new shady characters coming around.

Well, she would do this last little favor for him and then she was done.

ΨΨΨ

Sansom looked at the man with Hekmat Fahmy, committing his face to instant memory as he had been trained to do. He had heard snippets of their conversation in Arabic but had been unable to make out what they were saying. But now, as he studied the smooth, brown face of the Egyptian, he had the vague feeling that he had seen him somewhere before. There was something familiar about the dark, sleepy-looking eyes.

"I came to look at your radio," the newcomer said to Hussein Gaafar without acknowledging Sansom. "I called at your houseboat, but there was no reply."

"Oh, thank you very much. Peter went over just a few minutes ago—you must have just missed him. I'll come with you."

He turned to Sansom.

"Ramsay, unfortunately our radio's been on the blink. We've been trying to get someone in here for days and it looks like we've finally gotten our chance. I'll only be gone a few minutes. You don't mind being left alone with Hekmat, do you?"

He gave a knowing, lecherous smile. Sansom glanced at Hekmat and saw that, fortunately, she hadn't seen it as she was rearranging a pair of magazines on the coffee table. He grinned back at Gaafar that he would be more than delighted to take good care of her while they were away. Meanwhile, his brain tried to work out what was going on. It seemed peculiar that anyone should come to look at a radio this time of night.

Pretending to drunkenly nurse his cocktail, he kept a discreet eye on the group and alert ear open as Hekmat saw them both to the door.

"Goodbye, Anwar," she said.

Anwar? That's his name?

And then it struck him. Could the Anwar exiting the houseboat, in fact, be none other than Anwar el Sadat, the sleepy-looking signals officer, the intimate of General Aziz el Masri and of Hassan el Banna, Supreme Guide of the Muslim Brotherhood, and now of his chivalrous but suspicious male host who was a friend of the famous Hekmat Fahmy, a man who lit his cigarettes with one-pound notes and read her doubtlessly indiscreet love letters from British officers in the desert? If the man was *that* Anwar, he looked different in person in his civilian clothes compared to the photograph of him in his Egyptian officer's uniform.

But was it really possible that all of these bad actors were interconnected? If they were then wasn't it possible that Hussein Gaafar and his tall friend with the American accent Muncaster were in fact the spies living on *Dahabia* Number 10? The same agents who had been delivered to Cairo by the Hungarian Count Almasy's desert taxi service that had been observed driving through Kharga Oasis on May 23 and 24? Furthermore, was it possible that Gaafar—or less likely, Muncaster, given his more restrained and introspective demeanor—was the mysterious British Rifle Brigade subaltern that had been making the rounds at the Turf Club and other watering holes in the city?

Great Scot, he wondered, *is it possible that after all this time the pieces of the jigsaw puzzle are beginning to click into place?*

He looked at his watch. It was just before midnight, the precise time that the radio monitoring section at GHQ had been consistently reporting a transmitter coming on air in the city, using a code. It was always the same, a sending station's identification which was not acknowledged. The transmissions had remained a puzzle to him until Bob at MI6 had showed him the copy of Du Maurier's *Rebecca* he had taken from Aberle and Weber's kit and revealed the important findings of their interrogations. So under this scenario, he reasoned, the two German spies were using *Rebecca* as a code manual and transmitting from Cairo on a nightly basis, but had not yet sent information because they were not getting acknowledgment. Furthermore, knowing that they were likely being monitored, they were not going to help the enemy locate their transmitter by broadcasting unnecessarily. With Aberle and Weber in captivity, the only place receiving the spies' transmissions was the GHQ monitoring unit in Cairo.

If all this were true, it would mean that Muncaster had invented the excuse about getting more whiskey in order to make his nightly broadcast. And if they were still not receiving acknowledgement of their transmissions, they must have come to the conclusion that something was wrong with their radio apparatus and that was why they had called upon Sadat. He had come by to look at their radio at midnight while it was being operated because he was a trained signals officer and because he was one of their contacts. And Gaafar was masquerading as a Rifle Corps subaltern at the Turf Club and was reading Hekmat Fahmy's fan mail to pick up any military indiscretions from admirers who had gone back to the front.

And then there was the famous belly dancer herself. Was it possible she was working for the Germans? At first, the idea seemed laughable. It was impossible to think of her as a latter-day Mata Hari. At the Kit Kat Club and Continental Hotel rooftop, he had seen her make so many unquestionably spontaneous gestures of goodwill towards an Eighth Army captain, whom she seemed to be romantically involved with, and dozens of other Army admirers requesting autographs. In a milieu where rumors abounded, as they did at the Kit Kat and other high-end nightclubs and cabarets frequented by British officers, he had never heard a murmur of suspicion whispered against her. She was also a very cultured and independent woman, a well-known and well-liked celebrity of means who socialized regularly with the elite of Cairo. Furthermore, he had never heard anything about her having strong political views, like those of el Masri, Sadat, and others who rallied around the cause of Egyptian independence. She was also known to be a Christian not a Muslim and was of Circassian lineage, which further distanced her from the more radical elements of Cairene society, those naively hoping for a German victory and British defeat that would usher in a new era of Egyptian independence.

He was torn from his thoughts of conspiracy as she returned from the front door. "How about another drink and another dance?" she asked.

The words were delivered pleasantly, but something in her eyes made him suspect that she was really doing it to please Hussein Gaafar. He wondered what kind of power he wielded over her. The Egyptian had admitted to knowing her intimately before the war, but they no longer seemed to be a couple. And yet, the bond was strong between them and she clearly felt a sense of loyalty to him. Egyptian woman were certainly not submissive—unless they were strict Muslims, of course, which dictated firm obedience in the name of Allah—but by her manner around Gaafar she seemed to be remarkably devoted to him.

"Are you sure you don't want to read your fan mail?" he asked, hoping that she might show him one or two letters so he could see what kind of a security leak he might be dealing with.

"Oh, that!" she laughed. "They're nice boys, those young British officers, but I have a boyfriend. His name is Guy Bellairs and he's a captain in the Eighth Army. He's not here, of course. I'm afraid he's away at the front fighting Rommel." She smiled. "But there's no harm in us dancing," she added, and she edged closer to him on the divan. "But before we do, you must take off those dark sunglasses. We aren't in a club any longer, you know."

Sansom realized he was in a pretty pickle. If he took off his dark glasses and she was able to see his eyes up close, she might very well recall having seen him in uniform at the Kit Kat Club. He had been to the club and watched her dance on so many occasions that he was stunned that he had been able to conceal his identity thus far. But no doubt with so many admiring men in uniform around her in the club, he must have been just another nameless face in the crowd. Perhaps she did have a faint recollection of seeing him, or at least someone like him in uniform, but it was probably the fact he spoke fluent Arabic that made her unsure of herself.

He took a big sip of his drink and laughed, hoping she wouldn't insist on him taking them of. At the same time, he couldn't help but feel that she expected him to make some sort of pass at her. *No doubt Gaafar, he thought, with his hopes of changing sterling through me, instructed her to humor me.* But what he didn't know was how far she was prepared to go.

"Come on, take off those silly glasses and let's dance. I want to look into your eyes."

As she reached over, the touch of her soft hands arrested his cerebral processes. Had she made him and was now toying with him? Or was she just being friendly and genuinely wanted to see his eyes? If he flatly refused to take off his sunglasses, he would no doubt arouse her suspicions, and that would make him an incompetent security officer. So instead, he pretended to be smashed.

He took another big gulp of his Scotch and, feigning drunkenness, staggered to his feet, as if he would be delighted to dance. He then gave a little wobble and expression of distress, pretending to suddenly be sick. It was not that hard to pull off; although he was only mildly intoxicated since Mac had given him watered-down drinks at the Kit Kat Club, it appeared he had been drinking nonstop since first meeting Gaafar and Muncaster at the club. He was tight enough to appear authentically drunk yet still pull off what he was about to do.

He staggered and lurched, then coughed, spluttered, and retched, trying so hard to sound as if he was about to vomit that he nearly did. He saw the revulsion on Hekmat Fahmy's face as she quickly directed him towards the lavatory. Once inside, he continued to make disgusting noises. Five minutes later, he came out wiping genuine sweat off his face, slumped down on a chair, and asked for a glass of cold water. She would surely not expect him to take off his glasses and get close to her after that, he reflected with a sense of relief but also a trace of regret, as he watched the movements of her perfectly-honed limbs when she walked over to the cocktail cabinet.

With her back turned, he snuck a peek at his watch: twenty-three past twelve. *Hmm, what is taking Gaafar, Muncaster, and Sadat so long?*

A thought that had been lurking in the back of his mind forced its way to the front: if these two were indeed Almasy's spies smuggled into Cairo and working with Sadat and the Free Officers' Movement, this might be the night when the Abwehr would get a new listening station into operation. If Sadat somehow managed to get their W/T set working properly, the spies would most likely send a long message, transmitting all the information they had collected during the time they had been off the air. The GHQ monitoring unit would, in turn, intercept the signal the moment it began and start jamming the airwaves. In response, the German listening station would inform the spies they were being jammed, while GHQ would desperately try to locate the transmitter while it was still operating.

Should I say I feel ill and rush off to the nearest telephone to ask our monitoring unit if a message just went out, and then raid the spies' houseboat if it did? Or should I wait a little longer? But he realized there could be a different reason for the delay: perhaps Sadat was taking apart the transmitter to try to find something wrong.

But before Sansom had reached a decision on what to do, they all came tromping back, Muncaster brandishing an unopened bottle of whiskey.

"Anwar says there's nothing wrong with the radio," Hussein told Hekmat.

Sadat nodded. "Yes, its fine," he said. "Now I must go. Good night."

The Egyptian signals officer looked and sounded a tad angry, and Sansom wondered what he might be mad about. Did he have some disagreement with Gaafar and Muncaster?

It didn't matter for it was time to go. He had uncovered a wealth of information, and needed to politely extricate himself from the lion's den before he was discovered. Pleading an alcohol-related sickness that he had almost persuaded himself was real, he bid everyone goodnight and confirmed his appointment to meet Gaafar the following evening at 8 p.m. at the Kit Kat Club to make a currency exchange.

He then left the houseboat, pretending not to notice the Arab with the black eyepatch, blue-striped *galabeya*, and well-worn leather sandals leaning against a tree just up the promenade—who happened to be one of his NCOs planted to keep an eye on the houseboat. From the river bank, he swiftly made his way to the nearest telephone and dialed up GHQ. He asked the signals monitoring unit what they had picked up this evening between midnight and half past the hour.

"Same as usual," he was told. "Nothing received or acknowledged."

That was good news, but it was still time to meet again with Bob. They needed to decide whether or not to move on the boat and roll up the spy network, before Gaafar and Muncaster decided that their luck had run out and it was time to abandon Cairo.

CHAPTER 44

BRITISH MIDDLE EAST HEADQUARTERS
GARDEN CITY

JULY 24, 1942

AT 09:08 THAT MORNING, Sansom once again found himself staring across a conference table at the humorless pug-face of the man who worked for the cloak-and-dagger Cuthbert Bowly, head of MI6 in Cairo responsible for the Middle East and Balkans. The conference table was packed with an eclectic group of senior SIME, MI6, and Field Security officers in addition to Sansom and Bob. Sansom was just finishing up bringing the group up to speed on the latest developments at the Kit Kat Club and on Houseboat Number 10 involving Hussein Gaafar, Peter Muncaster, Hekmat Fahmy, and Anwar el Sadat. The *dahabia* had been under surveillance for nearly a week now, and the question was should they swoop in and arrest the parties involved in the case, as it appeared likely, though not one-hundred-percent certain until confessions could be obtained, that Gaafar and Muncaster were the German spies that had been snuck into Cairo from the desert by Almasy.

"So there you have it, gentlemen," said Sansom in conclusion. "Do we raid the houseboat at once or give the spies more time to reveal their network more fully?"

Bob cleared his throat. "If you're going to raid it now, the sooner the better. Unless you can capture the code intact, which doesn't seem very likely, our chaps should have the maximum time possible for cracking it."

Sansom could see his point. British MI5 counterintelligence could turn the presence of the spies in Cairo to enormous advantage if they could broadcast false information to the Germans using their own chosen *Rebecca* code. But if they swooped in now, they might alert some of the key supporting players in Cairo that had assisted the two spies and be unable to arrest them.

"From my point of view, it would be better to postpone the raid for at least a few days," he said. "If I can have them shadowed and continue to have a watch kept on their houseboat, I'll be able to round up their contacts."

Bob frowned. "What if their transmission is acknowledged in the meantime? If we wait, there's a decent chance the Abwehr will reply to the agents' nightly transmission. They would tell the agents to abort since they know of Weber and Aberle's capture in May, and that the operation has been compromised."

"That is a possibility," allowed Sansom.

"Also, as soon as they receive acknowledgement, they'll start to broadcast all the information they've collected so far, which is already encoded, and we'll have to jam it. And, of course, their listening station will tell them they're being jammed."

"I think we have to take that chance. Now that we've identified where they are staying, at least it won't be difficult to stop them from getting away. If it's decided to postpone the raid, I'll undertake to have a squad standing by every night at twelve, ready to storm the houseboat at a moment's notice, so that even then we might catch them before they have time to destroy their codebook, papers, and such."

"How will your squad get the signal to raid?"

"I'll have a radio man with a receiver turned to the appropriate wavelength, so that if we're jammed he'll hear it right away."

"If that happens, we won't be able to plant anything on Jerry. Once he hears the jamming, he'll write the transmitter off."

Sansom shook his head. "You can't be certain that you'll crack the code in time if we raid now. With a little more time, I may be able to penetrate the houseboat and snatch the code."

The table fell silent. So far, Sansom and Bob had done all the talking, as they were the two with the most at stake if the operation blew up and they failed to roll up the spy network. As Sansom looked around the table at the other security officers, he knew that some fell into his camp and others into Bob's. But there were huge risks either way.

The debate continued for another two hours until it was decided to allow him and his Field Security team to hold off on the arrests for the time being and continue the surveillance. Meanwhile, the team would meet on a day-to-day basis to assess the status. Sansom proposed adding to the surveillance units already keeping an eye on the houseboat as well as beefing up the teams following the visitors when they left the boat and shadowing the two spies wherever they went. Before the meeting, he had directed his staff to look into the histories of Hussein Gaafar and Peter Muncaster, so he would have information regarding their backgrounds soon that might prove useful.

"All right, that's it then, chaps," said Bob. "For now, we hold off on raiding the houseboat and give the spies more rope to hang themselves. While a quick capture would give us more opportunity to examine the German codes, and we might find vital information on the boats and be able to broadcast misleading information to the Germans, having more time will allow us to round up more of the nest. So there we have it gentlemen. It's a trade-off."

"Indeed it is, but under the circumstances it is the best that can be done," said Sansom, and he returned to his office to get to work.

ΨΨΨ

For the next seven hours, he and his team pieced together the history of Hussein Gaafar and Peter Muncaster by putting together dossiers on both suspects. Sansom swiftly discovered that Gaafar's late stepfather, Salah Gaafar, the highly respected magistrate who had been friendly towards the British, had been totally unaware of his adopted son's wartime espionage activities. Indeed, he had not seen him since the outbreak of the war. This piece of information led Sansom's Field Security team to the discovery of the gap in Hussein Gaafar's life in Cairo, which had lasted from September 1939 through May 1942. Sansom also learned that Gaafar's mother was German, and a bit of research into the archives revealed that he had been baptized with the name Johannes Eppler. Sansom did not need to know any more than that.

Muncaster, on the other hand, remained a closed book. The United States authorities had never heard of him. Though Sansom found it hard to believe, he and his team were unable to find any evidence of his having been in Cairo before Eppler's recent return. Based upon the available evidence, he appeared to be the junior partner in the relationship, the radio technician rather than the boots-on-the-ground spy, and whether he was a renegade American or a German in disguise was ultimately unimportant. No doubt he had a real name and Muncaster was his alias, but Sansom's staff was unable to discover what it was.

That evening, he kept his 8 p.m. appointment with Eppler at the Kit Kat Club, and changed £100 into Egyptian currency for him at a reasonable discount. He promised he would try to change some more, and asked how he could get in touch with him.

"Through Hekmat," he said. "She's my neighbor, as you know."

Sansom had hoped for an invitation to the houseboat so he could reconnoiter it now that he knew of its significance, but perhaps that would come later. He returned to his office and quickly discovered that interesting reports were coming in about the various contacts Eppler had made in the city. Even allowing for the fact that Cairo was his home town, in the short time he had been back in the city he had established many contacts. There were money changers; prostitutes, party girls, and exotic dancers; doormen; taxi drivers and chauffeurs; bartenders; civilians; and even military officers who had come into contact with the German-Egyptian playboy who was making the rounds about town. His contacts even included two civilians employed at GHQ, both of whom had been carefully screened by Sansom and his unit. Among his other proven contacts were a number of Egyptian Police officers, his stepbrother Hassan Gaafar, and the Austrian diplomat Victor Hauer.

Sansom proceeded to order the discreet arrests of contacts that he thought might yield useful information through interrogation while in custody, and he also roped in those that seemed too dangerous to leave at liberty even a few more days. Not wanting to have any political snafus, he did not yet take any Egyptian Army officers like Anwar el Sadat into custody, and all arrests were made far from the houseboat, so that there was no reason for Eppler to connect them with himself.

He considered having the *dahabia* searched when Eppler and Muncaster were away from the boat, but decided against it because it was virtually impossible to search anything without leaving traces, and this would only put the spies on their guard. He couldn't imagine them going out and leaving their codebook lying around. Just after 10 p.m., as he was about to quit work and return home for the evening, two men in dark suits appeared at the door to his office.

It was Bob and Maurice Hohlman, who worked for the Jewish Agency in the city.

"Good evening, Major," said Bob pleasantly, holding a file in his hand.

"I'm going home, Bob. I'm bloody tired."

"I'm afraid not just yet, old boy. There's someone we want you to have a little chat with."

"Who?"

"A friend of ours. In fact, she's a very valuable friend. Her name is Yvette, and she, too, has uncovered our little spy network. She may have some useful information and we want you to talk to her."

"She was brought in for questioning a few hours ago after leaving Eppler's houseboat and works for me in Jewish affairs," said Hohlman. "The work we perform to root out Nazi spies and help our people find safe haven in Palestine is crucial to the war effort."

"It's not crucial to *my* war effort," said Sansom. "In fact, your agency, Mr. Hohlman, can at times be a formidable obstruction to my security efforts in the city."

"Just talk to her. That's all we ask."

"Very well, I'll talk to her tomorrow. But right now, I'm going home and getting some much-needed sleep."

Bob shook his head. "That's not going to work. You need to talk to her now."

"Says who?"

"Says the DSO Colonel Jenkins. If you'd care to ring him up, he will repeat what I just told you. But no doubt he'll be angry at you for pestering him."

Sansom shook his head with irritation. "You're a bastard, Bob. All right, get on with it then."

"I'm glad you see the situation in the proper light." He turned on a heel and stepped out the open door. "Yvette, if you'll please come inside. The major will see you now."

You little weasel, thought Sansom—*you had her there all along.* He heard the click of heels on the wooden floor and a young woman appeared in the doorway. She was young and pretty, although not in the same sensual way as Hekmat Fahmy he thought, and as he would soon learn, she was also very, very cool.

"Here's her file, Major." Bob stepped forward with a little smile and set down the file. "We'll be back in a few minutes to see how everything went. And please be polite. I wouldn't want to have to disclose to Colonel Jenkins any improprieties."

Oh sod off, he thought, though he knew he had no choice but to accede to his and Hohlman's request. He motioned the woman to sit in one of the chairs in front of his desk and took a moment to look over her dossier. She was listed as a French cabaret dancer named Yvette, but he saw that her true nationality was not French but Palestinian. She and another girl had gone to the spies' houseboat in the afternoon and stayed for several hours. There was no harm in that, but the security man who followed Yvette discovered she was also the occasional mistress of a high-ranking British Army officer. So she was hauled in for questioning, but refused to speak to anyone but Maurice Hohlman. It appeared that she had visited the houseboat on two or three prior occasions and had been intimate with Eppler.

"My time is very short," he told her as he looked up from her dossier. "You have five minutes, so you'd better talk fast."

"You will give me more than that, Major," she said assuredly. "And I have to tell you that I am not only a dancer but a professional spy."

"Yes, your boss Maurice just told me and it says so right here in your dossier. You are an agent for the Jewish underground."

"Yes, but after this affair I'm afraid I won't be of further use in Cairo."

"I would agree." Sansom was by no means unsympathetic towards the Zionist movement, and he appreciated that the Jews of the Middle East wanted to be ready to resume their struggle for a national home when the war was over, but he could not tolerate any private-enterprise security outfits in his territory. "Am I to take it your duties include going to bed with Nazis?" he asked with more of an edge to his voice than he had intended.

"To serve my cause, I will go to bed with anyone of importance, as you have doubtless discovered in reviewing my file. Should I withhold my body while my people are still without a home?"

"That sounds good dramatic stuff," he said, deliberately taunting her. "But suppose you cut this cackle and come to cases."

"Sometimes your path and ours lead in the same direction," she said. "We have to help you beat the Germans before we can resume our fight against you. Hussein Gaafar and Peter Muncaster are German spies, as you know, and that is why your men arrested me. I have been spying on them, too. I went to their houseboat because I suspected them. I saw their radio transmitter up close. It is hidden inside a big radiogram in the stateroom. Muncaster broadcast last night at twelve, but he did not get a reply. He and Gaafar were not happy about it this afternoon."

"Did you see any papers? Any written messages in codes?"

"I have seen Muncaster before carrying some papers when he was about to make a broadcast. Afterwards, he put them inside a book, which he placed under his pillow before he went to sleep."

"Do you remember the title of the book?"

"Yes, it was a novel with a Jewish name: *Rebecca*. It said it was a best seller on the front."

His view of her was softening. "Thank you, Yvette. Would you be kind enough to draw me a rough sketch of the interior of the houseboat, showing where the radiogram is and where the suspects sleep?"

"Are you going to raid the houseboat?"

"Perhaps."

"Yes, I will draw you a map. And please remember that I have told you all I have found out. I have told you freely, without pressure, and I did not ask for anything in return for the information, not even my freedom. Right?"

"That is correct."

"If you believe me, and I think you do, will you not let me help you further?"

"How could you do that?"

"They don't know I have been arrested. Set me free, let me get myself invited there for another night, and I'll try to steal the papers in the book."

She was obviously an adventurous young woman who enjoyed being a spy. "I'll consider the idea. But in the meantime, please draw me the map of their *dahabia*. When the time comes, it could be quite useful."

Bob suddenly reappeared. Sansom and Yvette both gave a start. *My God, was he listening in this whole time?* wondered Sansom with irritation. The mysterious Bob was beginning to grate on his nerves.

"I quite agree a map of the boat could be useful, but you're not going to believe what I just heard," said the MI6 officer, his face filled with urgency. "I just got off the phone with the DSO and he informed me, Major, that you're going to hit the houseboat tomorrow morning."

He was shocked. "Tomorrow morning? But I thought we were going to wait?"

"I'm afraid not, old boy. Jenkins says we've waited long enough. The plan is to hit them at dawn. Now Yvette, if you would be so kind as to draw my friend Sammy here that map of yours, I should be much obliged."

CHAPTER 45

EPPLER AND SANDSTETTE HOUSEBOAT
AGOUZA, CAIRO

JULY 25, 1942

SANSOM FELT A RIPPLE OF ANTICIPATION as his joint British Field Security and Egyptian Police team moved into final position. He looked at his watch: it was seven minutes to 05:00 and nearly an hour before dawn. With the target houseboat shrouded in semi-darkness beneath a waxing gibbous moon, his team assembled at the edge of a cluster of olive trees on the west bank of the Nile, while a squad of river police quietly paddled their launches towards the *dahabia* from beneath the shadows of Zamalek Bridge to cover any escape in that direction. Though he spent most of his time behind his cluttered desk, he felt most alive when he was out in the field, taking part in arrests and experiencing the rush of the occasional skirmish against a worthy adversary. But this raid was truly special: Eppler and Muncaster would be his first Nazi spies taken into custody.

Just out of sight of the houseboat, he gathered Captain Effat and the ten others comprising his raid team to go over the final plan of attack. As the group assembled, he thought of what the British Admiral Lord Nelson had once said: "Five minutes make the difference between victory and defeat." In this case, it was five minutes of final pre-raid planning that would hopefully make the difference. He wanted Eppler and Muncaster badly and had fantasies of blasting in like a sheriff with a posse in an American Western. But he knew that would be a mistake. He was dealing with one of the most unpredictable of all human enterprises—arresting cornered enemy agents in wartime—and he had to have a sound strategy if he was going to capture them without anyone getting hurt or killed.

"Remember why we are here, chaps," he said to the group. "We are going to seize two dangerous German spies. I want it to be a short, sharp, and successful operation. By that, I don't just mean that we simply capture them. I want them both alive, but I also don't want any of us to be harmed. We also want their radio transmitter, their codebook, and any other items of an espionage nature they have in their possession. Our ultimate goal is for them to talk, but bear in mind that they may be equipped with suicide tablets. But even if they decide to fight it out, no one is to shoot to kill. At all costs, I say again, I want these Nazi bastards alive."

Here he paused to gauge their readiness. The men looked at him with beady eyes in the pre-dawn darkness, their faces an odd palette of blood red and soot black in the shadows of the olive grove. After spending most of the war cooped up behind their interminably dull desks and arresting low-level Italian and Egyptian criminals, gossipy British officers, and brawling Australians and New Zealanders, they looked eager to take down some real German spies.

"There are two exit points on the boat," continued Sansom. "Captain Bolton, once we cross over the gangway, your team will maneuver across the deck to the south side and seal off escape from that direction. Sergeant Wilson, you and your men will come with me and Captain Effat's squad and hit them from the sundeck. Once my team is in position, Captain Effat will give them one—I repeat, one—chance to throw down their weapons and surrender. If they do not, we will break down the door and take them with overwhelming force. From our surveillance, we know they are alone with no women on board, so there should be no civilians if there is shooting. Hopefully, they will give themselves up without a fight. But I want to reiterate that it is critical to take them alive. GHQ needs to know who their contacts are in Cairo and everything else they know. This is it, men. When you hear Captain Effat order them to surrender, we will hit them from all sides, including from the river in the launches."

Again, he paused. "Any questions?"

No one spoke.

"All right, let's move!"

They darted through the trees with Sansom and Effat leading the way. The two officers carried American-made M1 Thompson .45-caliber submachine guns—whose inventor, General John T. Thompson, had ironically created the first hand-held machine gun to end the First World War that had led to the mass carnage of the Second. The other British and Egyptian senior officers, NCOs, and enlisted men carried Enfield Mark I .38-caliber revolvers and Enfield Mk I bolt-action repeating rifles, both standard weapons of the British Army. They crossed over the gangway and spread out all along the prow and stern of the houseboat. A handful of men carried flashlights, and in the illumination, Sansom could see the two launches that had come from Zamalek Bridge pulling alongside the boat. Thanks to Yvette's hand-drawn sketch of the houseboat, Sansom knew exactly where to go once inside the *dahabia*, and the flashlights would point out where the two spies were sleeping.

He took a deep breath.

This was it. In a matter of seconds, he would have his two Nazi spies in custody. The houseboat was surrounded, all possible escape routes sealed off. And beyond the front door lay the unsuspecting quarry.

He signaled Captain Effat to step forward and shout "Police! Open up!" in observance of the legal formalities.

Then Sammy Sansom took another deep breath to steel his nerves and clutched his Tommy gun. It felt supple and reassuring in his hands.

ΨΨΨ

Eppler lay awake thinking of Yvette.

He had rumbled her under the covers yesterday afternoon—twice in fact—and he couldn't get her out of his mind. He pictured her as if she was right there. Her eyes were doe-shaped and slanted, her mouth bloodred without a touch of make-up, and her eyebrows perfectly symmetrical arches. She had wonderful teeth, like those girls with frozen smiles in advertisements. Her hands were delicate and expressive, her hips shapely, and her breasts firm and pointed. Her long legs had driven him wild as he had mounted her from the front and back, and he remembered how her skin was soft to the touch and firm all over her body.

And only a few hours later, he had learned she was an enemy spy.

Albert Wahda had broken the news to him. The errand boy and money changer had claimed that Yvette had been overheard to say that Eppler was her lover and that her real employers were unlikely to work in his best interests. Wahda also said she was not a French cabaret dancer as she claimed, but an agent working for the militant Jewish "Stern Gang." Eppler found that hard to believe and doubted that the Jewish group could afford to dress her in the style she was accustomed to, for in the three weeks he had known her he had never seen her in the same outfit twice.

"A wardrobe like hers costs a lot of money," he had said to Wahda.

The money changer had laughed and told him the money came from the British.

But now, as Eppler lay awake thinking, it was all falling into place. A week ago when she had visited his *dahabia*, she had shown an inordinate interest in his radio setup. He remembered when he had gone below to fetch something and, halfway down he had looked around to see her. She was standing by the post above the radio cabinet that kept the sun awning up and next to which the aerial wire hung. Fortunately, she could not see the aerial because it was concealed above the awning, but it was clear that she was examining the wire to see where it led. When he had turned around and surprised her, she had pretended to be looking for a glass behind the bar, although she never drank alcohol in the morning. Moreover, she was well aware that everything non-alcoholic was kept in the refrigerator in the stern and could not be obtained from the front of the boat. Thinking back, he remembered the incident very clearly, and he couldn't help but wonder if she was perhaps working not only for the Jewish network but serving as an informer for British Field Security. If that was the case, she was a double agent.

Angry at himself, he gritted his teeth. *Damn that girl. I'm going to have to settle the score with her—and soon.*

He rolled over and looked at his clock. It was almost five and dawn would soon beckon. Despite his anger, he liked the intoxicating scent of jasmine coming from the garden hedge of a nearby villa. The room was pitch dark and the night still. Every now and then the quiet was broken by the croaking of bullfrogs and chirping of cicadas in the sycamore trees along the riverbank. But there was a great tranquility in the cool nighttime river air and he dozed back to sleep.

He wasn't sure how long he had been asleep when he heard the sound—all he knew was something wasn't right. He felt the sensation for only a second and then shot out of bed, wearing only his underwear, as if fired from a gun.

They're here!

He heard a barely perceptible splashing on the water, like fish jumping, but this was not the time of year when they jumped. A raid team must be approaching the boat from the river, and the police had wrapped their oars in rags in order to sneak up on the *dahabia* as quietly as possible. He could hear another group creeping up on the houseboat from the street.

There was no time to get dressed.

One option was to slip through a window into the water and swim past the neighboring *dahabias* to Hekmat's boat, but the police would be able to easily track him and Sandstette on foot from the riverbank while the team in the boat paddled after them and caught them. Their best chance then was to catch the raid team by surprise by suddenly throwing open the door, dashing past them to the gangway, running like hell onto land, and then losing them in the labyrinthine streets of the city. Hopefully, the authorities had not anticipated such a desperate move.

He crept into the main cabin on the side away from the river bank. He could hear whispering voices outside now. There must have been a small rowboat right under the window. He saw a shadow fill the frame. The figure hovered motionless for a moment, only to fall out of sight. Thankfully, whoever it was hadn't seen him and could not open the window since it was securely fastened.

Should I fetch my gun?

No, that would be crazy, he decided. The authorities would want to take him and Sandstette alive for they were of no use to them dead, but if they opened fire on the police they would not get far before being shot. They were greatly outnumbered and the raid team had surrounded the houseboat completely; the two of them would be riddled with bullets in a matter of seconds.

Now he heard footsteps and whispers on the deck.

His mind worked frantically to determine a way to escape. The only way to open the door was from the inside, and it was securely bolted with two heavy iron bars at the top and bottom. It would be impossible to force it open from the outside unless they bashed it down with some sort of battering ram or other heavy object.

Where was Sandy?

He had almost forgotten about him in the heat of the moment. He went down the passage to the concealed radio-transmitting cubicle and gently knocked.

"I heard them, too, and am coming," whispered Sandstette.

"Have you opened the hatch to let the river water in?" asked Eppler.

"Yes. They're going to have a hell of a job salvaging this tub. In a quarter of an hour she'll be at the bottom. You do the same."

"All right." He went amidships and lifted up the trapdoor they had sawed into the double-hull to hide the bung. As he knocked the bung out, water began to gurgle into the boat. With nervous fingers, he quickly replaced the trapdoor lid, shot the bolt back into position, and went to his room. Within a minute, water began trickling up between the floorboards.

Up on deck, he could hear footsteps and low voices as the raid team climbed on board from the stern and maneuvered for the stairs that led belowdecks. He felt his way to the door of the radio cubicle and opened it. In the dim light, he saw Sandy crawling out from the wall. He had fought his way through the partition, clad in nothing but his pyjama trousers, and was holding a flashlight.

Eppler had a sudden idea and returned to his room. On a chair near the open door lay two pairs of dirty black socks. He quickly grabbed them, rolled them up into two balls, and returned to his partner.

"Get behind me and shine your flashlight," he instructed him. "I'll open the forward door, hold these socks up to my mouth as if I'm pulling the pin from a grenade, and then throw them on deck. It's a long shot, but if they duck for cover, we can run past them and down the gangway."

"All right," agreed Sandstette. "Let's keep our fingers crossed."

They tip-toed towards the door. The water was well below the ankles but uniform across the floor of the houseboat. Eppler realized that it was going to take far longer than Sandy thought for the *dahabia* to sink to the bottom.

Slowly and cautiously, he lifted the steel bars out of their hasps and let them slip quietly into the rising water on the floor.

It was then he heard an Egyptian voice call out to him in English. "Police, surrender yourself and open up! We're coming in!"

Not so fast—I've got a little surprise for you, thought Eppler, clutching his dirty balled-up socks.

It wasn't much but it was all they had.

ΨΨΨ

Feeling his heart racing, Sansom stepped forward with the nose of his Tommy gun pointed at the front door. "Break it down!" he commanded.

While two of Effat's men trained their flashlights on the door, Sergeant Wilson stepped forward, lowered his shoulder, and made a run at the door like a rugby player. But to Sansom's surprise, before he struck it down the catch suddenly came unlocked, the door opened, and the NCO went flying through the open doorway, past two stunned figures, and then skidded across the wet floor. Sansom then watched in horror as the closest figure in the open doorway seemed to tear the pin out of pair of hand grenades and hurl them onto the deck.

"Look out—hand grenades!" he heard one of his men shout.

"Don't fire—duck!" cried Sansom, wanting to catch the pair alive.

He and his men flung themselves to the deck. He felt a soft object land on his back.

Dear Lord, have we been bluffed?

Someone snapped an interior light on, and he now saw Eppler—*good heavens, was he not wearing any trousers?*—start to make a mad dash across the deck while everyone was flat on the deck. But before he had taken his second step, a wiry British private and Effat standing by the door blocked his escape by sticking the barrels of their guns into his ribs.

"Stick 'em up, mate!" said the private in a Cockney accent.

"That's right!" said Sansom, rising to his feet. "Do as he says, or we'll fill you with holes before you make it halfway to that gangway!"

Wearing only a pair of undergarments, Eppler looked around at all the guns now pointed at him. Shaking his head in dismay, he slowly raised his arms in surrender.

One down, thought Sansom. *Now where is Muncaster?* He suddenly felt sick in the stomach as he realized that in the initial confusion the German wireless operator had somehow managed to sneak out of the cabin.

And then he saw him, making a dash for it across the deck.

"Halt, or we'll shoot!" he cried.

But Muncaster was swiftly overpowered by one of his NCOs and an Egyptian policeman.

"Wait, sir, I think he threw something over the side!" said the NCO. "I didn't hear any splash, though!"

"Question him and find out what it was!" He turned back to face Eppler, who was staring at him in his major's uniform, which he had not seen before since he only knew Sansom as a money changer in a European-cut suit.

"Why if it isn't the black-market currency king. I believe I owe you a drink, sir."

"And if it isn't the Kit Kat playboy who likes to light his cigarettes with British notes. I have some advice for you, young man."

"What's that?"

"You'd better talk, that is if you want to live."

His men were now playing the beams of their flashlights into the houseboat. He could see the water slowly rising and Eppler saw it too.

"Major," he said, "in ten minutes she will have settled on the bottom. There is no time to lose. We need to get off this boat."

"I'm afraid not." He stepped to the entrance. "Sergeant Wilson, take a detail and seal those bungholes, and I mean quickly." He turned to the spy again. "Herr Eppler, if you and your partner-in-espionage would be kind enough to show my men where the bungholes are located, Captain Effat and his Egyptian police will not break your legs. Do I make myself clear?"

Eppler looked warily at Effat, who squinted harshly. "Yes, I understand."

Effat and Wilson forced the spies belowdecks to plug the open holes.

"And when you're done, strip-search them," Sansom called out to them. "The rest of you, come with me. We need to find that codebook and radio."

He and his men began tearing the place to pieces. But they were unable to find either the *Rebecca* codebook or any coded messages. But the transmitter was where it was supposed to be, hidden in the capacious radiogram just as Yvette had said. Unfortunately, that was all they had. Sansom hoped it would be enough to prove that they were German spies if the two refused to talk.

The bungholes were quickly resealed and the ankle-deep water was no longer rising. But as his team continued their frantic search for the codebook, he saw Eppler and Muncaster exchange a little smile. It was then he realized what Muncaster had thrown overboard. *You bastards won't be smiling when they hang you.* He wondered if he should have allowed Yvette to try to steal the codebook as she had proposed. But perhaps the inquisitors at the Interrogation Center in Maadi would be able to persuade them to reveal the code and they wouldn't need the actual codebook.

It was at that moment—when these unsettling thoughts were beginning to give him a headache—that an Egyptian police sergeant came down from the deck.

"River police, sir. This landed in our launch when we came alongside."

Sansom could scarcely contain his excitement as the sergeant withdrew a copy of Daphne Du Maurier's *Rebecca* from his haversack and started to hand it to him. Eppler, still wearing only underwear, made a sudden grab for the book. Sansom sent him flying to the wet floor with a vicious back-hander to the face.

"Take them away!" he commanded to Bolton. Then to Effat and Wilson. "You two, come with me and bring along two men. We're going to the other boat."

Eppler looked puzzled. "The other boat? What other boat?"

"Why your belly dancer friend Hekmat Fahmy's, of course. She's one of your agents here in Cairo along with Anwar el Sadat and Victor Hauer."

He looked suddenly desperate. "You've got this all wrong—Hekmat's not part of this! She's just a friend, that's all!"

"We'll just have to see about that, won't we?" He squinted menacingly at Eppler. "And remember what I said. Take my tip and talk—if you want to live."

CHAPTER 46

HEKMAT FAHMY HOUSEBOAT
AGOUZA, CAIRO

JULY 25, 1942

YEARS LATER, when Hekmat Fahmy was an old woman reminiscing about her glorious time as the most beloved belly dancer in the world, she would think back to today, the worst day of her life, and wonder what had possessed her to rise from bed early and go out on her sundeck just before dawn. Since she normally worked until midnight, she usually slept in past ten, but not this morning. This morning she had heard unfamiliar noises coming from one of the houseboats to the north and wondered what was going on.

As she stepped onto the deck in her dressing gown, she found it was still dark though dawn was fast approaching and the air pleasantly cool. She scanned to the north where she thought she had heard the sounds, but she didn't see anything suspicious, and she no longer heard anything unusual beyond the lapping of water against her houseboat and the cicadas among the riverbank trees. To the east, a thin pink ribbon was just beginning to emerge above the Mokattam Hills. Soon it would be light and another cloudless blue sky would break over Cairo, and then tonight she would dance two shows before a thousand cheering fans and a propulsive orchestra. Though there was a savage war going on in the desert only a hundred miles away, she might as well have been living in Outer Mongolia as the fighting had virtually no effect on her day-to-day life.

Today, unbeknownst to her, that would all change.

She looked again in the direction of the sounds, but there was still nothing. She turned her face into the light wind blowing off the river, enjoying the salubrious coolness on her face. She could smell the heavy scent of jasmine from the hedges bordering the river to go along with the fragrance of roses in full bloom. Her thoughts turned to Guy. She missed him terribly and wondered if there was some way she could get in touch with him at the front. She remembered back to the vulnerability in his eyes just before they made love the night before he left to fight Rommel. She had realized in that moment how much she had cared for him, though she sometimes found his sense of British entitlement insufferable.

She hoped desperately that he hadn't been wounded or killed in the recent heavy fighting along the El Alamein Line. She thought of their times together strolling through Ezbekieh Gardens, sharing chocolate-covered dates and ice cream smothered in crème Chantilly at Groppi's, taking in shows at the Royal Opera House, making love in her sumptuous bed on her *dahabia*, and sipping cocktails on the terrace or dancing up a storm in the lush garden at Shepheard's. Yes, the past several months of romance with Captain Guy Bellairs of the British Fifth Army were some of the most precious moments of her life, a period of loving intimacy that made it seem as if there was no war going on at all. She felt a tide of emotion wash over her; this was the way she wanted to remember their relationship.

Somehow, she felt as though she was about to lose him. At the thought, tears came to her eyes. She also suddenly felt very old at age thirty-five. Realistically, how much longer could she be a dancer? Was it possible that she had already lived the best moments of her life and would never feel the joy of youth again? She stared out at the murky greenish-brown waters of the Nile, tears pouring from her eyes. There wasn't a damned thing she could do to stop them.

A moment later, she went downstairs to the lavatory to grab some tissues to wipe away the tears. It was then she heard a hard knock on the door.

The hostile urgency of the sound startled her.

She started from the lavatory to answer it, but before she had made it halfway to the front door it was battered down and a half dozen uniformed policeman stormed into the stateroom like a pack of ravenous desert jackals. She wanted to scream but her shock was so great no words came out.

And then she found her voice. "What are you doing? Get off my houseboat!"

The puffy-faced British officer out front looked at her severely. For a moment, she didn't recognize him, but then she knew.

It was Hussein Gaafar's friend, the Greek money changer from the other night, the one who had drank too much and nearly vomited all over her. She had been disgusted by the man, but why was he wearing a—

And then she understood.

He was not a money changer at all but an undercover policeman of some sort, a clever man who spoke Arabic as well as King Farouk himself.

"I said what are you doing here?" she demanded angrily. She remembered how badly he had wanted her, this little uniformed bureaucrat who now stood triumphantly before her as if he were the prime minister of Britain himself.

"Hello Hekmat, I'm here to arrest you—and I'm afraid I don't need a warrant."

"But I have not broken any laws," she protested. 'You must leave at once."

He gave a dismissive snort that was as close to saying "Bugger off!" as a snort could be—and she simultaneously loathed him and was impressed by his subterfuge. The other night he had fooled her, Eppler, Sandstette, and Sadat with his fabricated personae and impervious dark sunglasses. God, she wished she had never helped her former lover. A part of her had sensed it might lead to trouble like this.

"Search the premises," he snapped to a tall Egyptian officer. "The letters are next to the bar over there." He pointed. "I want every single one put into evidence."

"What are you doing?" she demanded. "Those are my personal letters."

He smiled harshly. "Not anymore, they're not. Now let's just calm down, shall we? While they do their work, let's sit down."

He motioned her towards the divan. He was a hard and calculating little man, she realized; the whole thing had been a setup from the beginning. "Who are you?" she asked. "What is your real name? It is obviously not Ramsay Sawi."

"My name is Major A.W. Sansom. I'm the head of British Field Security in Cairo, and to be perfectly honest, I do not take any pleasure in this."

He was a gentleman at least, though a treacherous one. "What do you want from me? As I told you, I have done nothing illegal."

He pulled out a pen and a small police notebook so he could take notes. "I'm afraid that's not quite the way we see it. Look, I'm going to be honest with you—

I'm going to have to turn you over to the Egyptian police for questioning."

"But why?"

"You know why. You have been linked to two dangerous German spies."

"You're talking about Hussein Gaafar and Peter Muncaster. But I don't know anything about them except that they're trying to change out their money."

"But you are plainly aware that currency exchanges are illegal."

"I have not been involved in any currency exchanges, and I didn't know they were German spies."

He began taking notes. "But you had your suspicions, correct?"

"No more than I had suspicions about you—and you turned out to be a policeman. I was only nice to Hussein because I used to be in love with him and know his mother and father."

"So you know Hussein Gaafar's mother Johanna is German then?"

"Yes, and I also know that his late father Salah Gaafar—who bestowed upon him his Arabic name—was a great supporter of the British before he passed away."

"I'm more interested in the German mother. You knew Hussein Gaafar was baptized as Johannes Eppler?"

"No, I didn't know that. Nor, as I have told you, did I know he was a spy."

They looked up as Effat and another officer brought forward a large cardboard box filled with fan mail letters and a leather suitcase. They opened the suitcase and spread out Bellairs's captain's uniform, a toiletry kit, and several maps.

"Who do these clothes and maps belong to?" asked Sansom.

"My British lover."

"Yes, you told me about him. What was his name again?"

"Captain Guy Bellairs. The uniform and maps belong to him."

"And where might your white knight in shining armor be at the moment?"

"Fighting at the front—unlike you."

He was writing vigorously now. "What did you tell Gaafar about him?"

"The truth, of course. You've got this all wrong. Whatever Hussein Gaafar did it has nothing to do with me. All I did was put him up on my houseboat for one night and help him get his own place to live. And that's the God's honest truth."

He studied her sharply for a moment then picked up a pair of letters and read through them as his men continued to thoroughly search the houseboat. She couldn't help but feel violated but was powerless to stop either Sansom or his men. Looking at the box filled with fan mail, she estimated that she must have received more than two or three hundred fan letters total from her admirers in the Eighth Army. Sometimes she received as many as a dozen in one week. Though she hadn't read all of them, she knew from the ones she had read that many were written from the front and contained shocking breaches of security, which she realized was why Eppler and Sansom were both so interested in them.

"I want my letters back," she said. "They are personal and you have no right to take them from me."

"I'm afraid they must be taken into evidence along with the uniform and maps."

"You're a cold-hearted bastard."

"I've been called worse. I am sorry but you, Miss Fahmy, have broken the law. That's why I am placing you under arrest."

"I have violated no Egyptian laws. It's not my fault if my British officer fans disclosed more than they should have about the war in the desert. I didn't ask them to write me, you know."

He stopped taking notes and flipped his notebook shut. "Yes, I understand that."

"What's going to happen to them?"

"Their indiscretions will no doubt be reported along with the names of the erring officers, and I imagine some rockets will be delivered as a result."

She shook her head in dismay. He had no right to place her under arrest. It was true she had overheard Eppler and he had later confided in her about the real reason he and Muncaster were in Cairo, but she had not changed money for them or helped them perform any espionage activities. She was not one-hundred-percent innocent, true, but in a city in which hundreds were breaking the law daily in far more serious ways her infractions were minor. Didn't the British have larger fish to fry?

But then she realized what Sansom was really here about: the fan letters and her close ties to Guy Bellairs. The British were irate and embarrassed that their officers may have given up secrets to an Egyptian linked to German agents. So, they would blame the Wog tart rather than their own indiscreet captains, majors, and brigadiers.

She felt a burst of anger. "What am I being charged with, damn you?"

"Conspiring against the security of the Egyptian Kingdom. That is treason against your king. Not only that but you have endangered the war effort of Egypt's ally, Great Britain."

"You can't be serious. That's a trumped-up charge if I've ever heard one. Egypt has not even declared war on Germany. I demand to see my barrister."

"You want a lawyer? In case you haven't noticed, there's a war going on. Barristers are not exactly popular these days."

"But I am no conspirator. I have always been sympathetic to the British cause."

The one called Captain Effat and a beefy British sergeant gave her skeptical, accusatory looks. She felt her face crimson with embarrassment, and it took all her self-control not to break down and cry.

"Where are you going to take me?" she asked, struggling to remain composed.

"The interrogation center at Maadi."

She was stunned. It seemed unthinkable that she was to be consigned to such an unjust fate when she had done nothing at all to betray either her native country or the British Empire, except allow her former lover and his friend—whom at the time she hadn't known were spies—to sleep on her houseboat for a single night and to help them find a houseboat to rent.

"Maadi? I have to go to Maadi?"

"I'm afraid so."

"You're making a big mistake," she said, feeling her lips trembling ever so slightly. "You can have those letters because they don't mean anything to me. They're just lonely and frightened boys who like to watch me dance and miss their sweethearts. What is the harm in making them happy for a few hours before they go off to die because of your stupid war?"

"There's no harm in that at all," said Sansom, with something approaching sympathy. "But unfortunately, it's not up for me to decide. Now it's time to go."

PART 4

THE PHANTOM MAJOR

CHAPTER 47

SIDI HANEISH AIRFIELD (FUKA LANDING GROUND 12)
NORTHWEST EGYPT

JULY 26, 1942

AS THE ASSAULT TEAM CAME TO A HALT, Stirling stared out from beneath a pregnant moon at the eerie desert landscape. The scudding clouds in the night sky cast weird shadows across the ground littered with burnt-out tanks, broken-down trucks, and the shapes of dead bodies sprawling where they had fallen. A light desert breeze brought the sour-sweet smell of the recent battle to his nose. They had crossed some seventy miles of desert, in the middle of the night, in a caravan of eighteen heavily armed American jeeps, with no headlights, an ancient map, and one supremely gifted twenty-two-year-old navigator named Mike Sadler in whom Stirling and his SAS commandos put all their trust.

"How close are we?" Stirling asked him as the two men peered into the gloom next to the lead jeep.

"By my reckoning, we're less than a mile short of the field," replied Sadler. "It's right in front of us."

"Really?"

"Yes, sir."

"All right then." And yet, it seemed impossible. There was no sign of life—only silence and vast emptiness. However, his faith in the young lieutenant's navigational skill was so absolute he accepted his verdict with no further question and ordered the men to move into line abreast. "Make sure you keep in formation until I give the signal for line astern," he added. "Right then, we're off, chaps."

The drivers revved their engines and one by one the jeeps pulled out. The assault caravan moved into line abreast with the vehicles spaced ten yards apart and resumed its northward trek. The going was slow in the soft churned-up sand and rough ground at the foot of the escarpment and it was difficult to maintain formation. All eighteen vehicles were fitted with lethal Vickers K machine guns, which were double-mounted and bolted to the front and rear. Along with the twenty new vehicles Stirling had managed to coax out of GHQ came ample supplies of water, rations, petrol, ammunition, explosives, spare parts, and several welcome luxuries: rum, tobacco, new pipes, sticky Turkish delight, and a pint of *eau de Cologne* in place of soap. He and his desert raiders might be unable to wash, but they would go into battle under a full moon well-scented.

According to air reconnaissance reports, the Sidi Baneish airfield—or Fuka Landing Ground 12—was the main Luftwaffe staging post for planes going to and from the front, with an abundance of aircraft at all times, especially Junkers 52s. The heavy transport planes were the mainstay of Rommel's supply system and he was known to have less of them than he required due to logistical shortages. The plan of attack—a tactical deviation from the normal SAS playbook and which Stirling had rehearsed days earlier—was a massed jeep assault. During the past two weeks, Rommel's eastward thrust toward Alexandria and Cairo had been halted, but the Eighth Army had sustained more than 13,000 casualties and the North African war was again reduced to a stalemate. Which in Stirling's view made it a perfect time to strike deep behind enemy lines—only this time using a blunter and noisier approach that would make a bold statement.

He drove the lead jeep and directly behind him in the number two spot was the navigator Sadler. Each vehicle had an officer or NCO driving, and a front and rear gunner. The gunners sat with their thumbs on the catch and weapons levelled in front of them. In Stirling's jeep were Cooper and Seekings as front and rear machine gunners.

Suddenly came a shock. A half a mile away the landscape exploded in a flood of artificial light. He was surprised at first but then quickly realized what was happening: the landing-strip lights had been switched on at Sidi Haneish and before him lay the flood-lit aerodrome. But had he and his men spotted? Even if they hadn't, with the floodlights now upon them the enemy would be able to open fire upon them as if it was broad daylight.

Then, above the noise of the grinding jeeps, he heard the deep-throated thunder of an incoming airplane engine.

Good Lord, is that a German bomber coming down to land?

"Why it's Brighton Beach, sir!" exclaimed Johnny Cooper from his shotgun seat next to the CO. "At least we know now that we've found our target!"

"Right on time and on the nose, Johnny!"

With the aircraft coming into land, it was a perfect cover for the attack, Stirling realized, though he was further away than he would have liked. He gave the signal and the eighteen jeeps rolled forward line astern, the four Vickers machine guns in each vehicle jostling over the uneven terrain and bristling with enough firepower to destroy an entire air force, which was exactly what he had in mind. He hit the accelerator and charged straight for the main runway, bathed in floodlight only a few hundred yards ahead.

At the distance of a rugby field, he fired the Verey light and the illuminated airfield turned to an explosion of phosphorescent green. His lead jeep opened fire: Cooper from the front, Seekings from the back just as the Luftwaffe bomber touched down and bumped along the asphalt tarmac. As the convoy smashed through the perimeter, sixty-eight guns followed suit and the fusillade erupted, sending the airfield's defenders scrambling for cover.

Stirling managed to follow a smooth piece of tarmac and turned in between the two long rows of neatly parked Messerschmitts, Stukas, Heinkels, and a large number of the important Junker 52s. The double line of jeeps rumbled forward at a brisk walking pace, laying down a blanket of strafing fire to left and right as the Vickers guns opened up from a range of fifty feet.

The enemy now turned off the landing lights, but the airfield was still illuminated by the Verey light. A cascade of red and white tracer poured onto the airfield followed by rasping and roaring machine-gun bullets. The jeeps maintained perfect formation with the Vickers guns making a terrible symphony. The belching fire mingled with the boom of igniting fuel and the crackle of exploding ammunition.

For Stirling, the cacophony represented the sound of victory, a tremendous *feu de joie.*

The first aircraft detonated with such force that it singed the eyebrows and eyelashes of the men in close proximity. But some planes took longer to catch fire than Stirling had imagined. One Stuka dive-bomber took thirty seconds before the interior of the aircraft suddenly glowed red and exploded into bits. Some planes did not just explode in the inferno, but seemed to crumble and disintegrate as the bullets ploughed into them. The Luftwaffe bomber was hit by a volley from the leading jeeps just as it touched down; the plane burst into flames and slewed to a stop.

The burning wreckage brilliantly lit up the aerodrome and Stirling could see German soldiers running about in the distance. In the glow, he spotted the shadows of other planes parked further out on the field. He made a mental note to go back for them when the first pass was completed.

"My God, it's like a duck shoot!" cried Johnny Cooper, gunsmoke spewing from his Vickers up front. "There's no way to miss!"

"Aye, it's a good day for sport!" roared Seekings in the rear of the jeep, blasting away through the smoke.

From somewhere, a German mortar shell whistled through the air. The shell exploded between the two lines of jeeps and the air was suddenly filled with mortar fire, the steady rap of a Breda gun, and a rattle of small arms fire. The defenders were fighting back. Another Breda gun began its slow tattoo and two more mortar shells blasted nearby. Stirling felt a blaze of heat pass across his face and the jeep came to a shuddering halt.

"Why won't it bloody go?" he demanded from Seekings.

"We haven't got an engine anymore!" the sergeant shouted back.

He realized that one of the Breda shells had passed through the cylinder head, missing his knees by inches. No one was hurt by the mortar shrapnel but the vehicle was put out of action. He shouted to the gunners to concentrate on the Breda post and signalled the jeep behind him to pick up him and his crew. Luckily, the Breda was firing from much the same position as the mortar and was using tracer, which pinpointed its position.

It was swiftly silenced.

The jeep behind them came to a halt to pick them up. As he, Cooper, and Seekings scrambled to board the vehicle, he saw a figure sitting motionless in the rear seat, his back curiously straight and head and shoulders resting on the guns.

"Bloody hell, Robson's dead," said Seekings.

Stirling saw that the twenty-one-year-old artilleryman had been shot through the head. He waved down the fleet of jeeps to halt and gave the order for the drivers to switch off their engines so they could hear his instructions. For a moment, there was an uncanny stillness save for the crackle and noise of the burning Luftwaffe airplanes.

"Johnny Robson's gone, chaps," he said. "Is everyone else okay?"

"Yeah, we're all right," answered Paddy Mayne, looking around. Several more chimed in too.

"How much ammo have you got left?"

"Two drums! One drum! Half a drum!" came the answers.

"Great Scot, you lads have certainly unloaded on the poor bastards, haven't you?

Now listen carefully. From here on out don't fire unless you're certain of a target. We're going to finish the circle, then move back and knock off the clump of planes on the perimeter. Then we'll beat it. All right, let's get on with it!"

The column quickly made the second pass around the perimeter, the lethal Vickers guns roaring and belching fire once again, picking off planes parked away from the main runway. A small dispersal area marked the completion of the circle, and they fired into tents and a few station buildings. Then they turned and headed for the shapes on the outskirts of the field, which proved to be a cluster of JU 52s. Once they had shot them up, Stirling gave the order to pull out. A second Verey light, this one red, soared upward to signal the general withdrawal.

But as they were moving off, he caught sight of a single surviving plane silhouetted against the night sky.

How did we miss that one?

Suddenly, he saw a bearded figure jump from one of the jeeps with bomb in hand and run up to the untouched bomber.

It was Paddy Mayne.

Stirling watched with amusement and pride as his second-in-command reached up high, placed the bomb in its engine, and ran back to his jeep.

Then the patrol took off once again. The jeeps, no longer in formation, hurtled for the gap in the fence and out into the open desert. Mike Sadler lingered at the southwest corner of the field, watching for any stragglers and photographing the burning wreckage as the Germans began towing any planes they might be able to salvage away.

Once in the open, a mile outside the perimeter, Stirling called a halt. Soon the enemy would regroup and come after them by ground and by plane to cut off their escape, and they needed to split up and make their way back in smaller groups to the rendezvous. They would cross to the west of the big track, with the telegraph poles running along it, which led from Bagush to Qara at the northwestern tip of the Qattara Depression. The jeeps split into groups of three or four vehicles and scattered south, with orders to find somewhere to lie up for the day, under camouflage, and then head for the rendezvous under cover of darkness.

"Well done, chaps," he said cheerily to close the quick conference, as if they had just enjoyed a good round of golf. "I'll see you back at base. Good luck!"

He hopped back into his jeep and tore off into the night. His party consisted of four jeeps, two badly damaged, and fourteen men, including the body of the dead gunner Johnny Robson. It was going to be a race to reach cover before first light. He drove fast over the flat, rocky ground with the Vickers guns swinging wildly as the vehicles jolted along their homeward journey.

He was very satisfied with the results of the raid. They had destroyed thirty-seven aircraft, mostly bombers and heavy transport planes. But deep inside he was torn up over the death of poor young Johnny—the latest casualty in his beloved band of unconventional warriors.

CHAPTER 48

SANYET EL MITEIRIYA (RUIN RIDGE)
NORTHWEST EGYPT

JULY 27, 1942

PEERING THROUGH HIS FIELD GLASSES, Rommel watched with a combination of satisfaction and sorrow as his Panzers vanquished the Australians. The last of the enemy holdouts clung like barnacles to the rocky hogback—known as Ruin Ridge from the ancient ruins on its crest—and he admired them for their stout resistance. After taking the position late last night from his 164th Light Afrika Division in a moonlit attack, the Western Australian 2/28th was almost completely cut off and surrounded by his German infantry and armor. Suffering heavy casualties, the majority of the enemy battalion—around 500 men—had been forced to surrender, but a hundred or so refused to give up or had lost contact with the rest of their brigade and weren't certain what to do.

"What a waste of fine infantry," he said to Colonel Bayerlein, standing alongside him in Greif. "The Aussies took the hill all right, but their British armor never showed up in support."

"We would never make such a mistake," said the chief of staff.

"No, we wouldn't," agreed Rommel. "The Australians are hot about it too."

From intercepted radio communications over the past year, the Desert Fox knew of the ongoing spat between the Australians and New Zealanders—commanded by Generals Morshead and Freyberg, respectively—and Auchinleck and his senior British commanders regarding tactical armor support. The Aussies and Kiwis had long been dissatisfied with the performance of the British armor. More often than not, the British tanks had difficulty coordinating with the infantry and they turned up at the wrong place at the wrong time—indeed if they turned up at all.

"Take me closer—I want to see our Panzers make the final push," he commanded his white-hatted driver, *Unteroffizier* Hellmut von Leipzig.

They drove to a small knob to the west of the hill. Now he could feel the percussions from the muzzle blasts from his Panzer Mark III's and IV's. They shook his body like a tuning fork. Towering clouds of smoke and dust blanketed the battlefield, brilliantly illuminated from within by bursting shells. He could make out the embattled Australians; they were dug in deep all along the ridge, desperately firing their Bren light machine guns against his approaching tanks and infantry. Once again, he couldn't help but admire them for their tenacity. German machine guns roared with return fire from positions along the flanks of Ruin Ridge. To Rommel, the scene looked like a meteor shower as hundreds of reddish-white tails of light, from both sides, streaked across the sky from tracer fire.

He felt the swoosh of a British projectile as it zoomed past his ears from a Matilda. A pair of Mark IV's armed with the massive 75-mm cannons instantly returned fire on the tank and it shuddered to a halt and burst into flames. Then the earth shook again as more Mark IV's opened up. Along the ridgeline, an eruption of flour-like rock dust spewed up from the ground, and men screamed in terror as they were pulverized by the blast.

When Rommel looked up, he saw an apparition that was as ghostly as it was grisly. An Australian's helmeted head had been blown completely off. He shook his head in dismay: the poor bastard had taken a direct hit. It reminded him of the Headless Horseman from *The Legend of Sleepy Hollow*; his mother had read the book to him when he was a boy along with the folk tales of the Brothers Grimm.

Now several more of his Panzers moved into position and unloaded with their terrible 50-mm and 75-mm guns, pinning the Australians down all along the spiny ridge. Despite the protection afforded by the rocky brow, he saw several men vanish into thin air in the lethal blasts. As the German tanks closed in on the battalion headquarters where a flag had been planted, a Bren gunner ran to an exposed position to open fire. His .303 bullets were useless against thick steel and he was shot down by one of the tanks. The battle had degenerated into a bloody mess and Rommel wished the Australians would surrender.

Thankfully they soon did. Peering through his field glasses, he saw a colonel stand up in his weapon-pit and wave his hands, signaling his battalion to end the hopeless struggle. Slowly, Australians began coming out of their foxholes with their hands up. But in the fading sunlight and with a brisk desert wind kicking up a dust cloud, many in the rear were able to escape.

Through the gaps in the smoke and dust, Rommel could see them picking their way through the pulverized outcrops of rock and scrabble, lugging their wounded over their shoulders and retreating pell-mell under the cover of a pair of Grant tanks. The Grants came under a lashing fire from the Mark III's as well as a handful of Panzer Mark IV's that were shooting towards the ridge. But as was so often the case in the Desert War, the Germans withheld their fire from the fleeing Australian footsoldiers, allowing them to escape and for the stretcher-bearers to dash into the open to evacuate the wounded. He estimated that over sixty men got away.

He nodded approvingly, proud of the restraint and integrity of his soldiers. *The enemy is beaten and the ridge is ours once again, but we did it with mercy.*

The tanks on both sides withdrew from the field, leaving the infantry to round up the remaining prisoners and dig in again.

"Let's go," he commanded von Leipzig. "I want to take a look from the top before the sun sets."

"*Jawohl, Herr Feldmarschall!*"

Within minutes, they had ascended the low, stony, east-west trending Ruin Ridge that looked like a scaly dinosaur's back. His troops were already marching the last of the Australian prisoners down the northwest flank and re-establishing the line by laying anti-tank mines and digging foxholes.

The area was devastated. Gaping holes were blown out of the stone wall ruins and large craters perforated the ground. There were bodies everywhere and the air was filled with the cries of the wounded. He made a rough count of the bodies strewn about the ridgeline: it had to be upwards of fifty with another fifty, dying or seriously wounded, among the blown-apart corpses and scattered body parts.

Looking at the carnage and pockmarked battlescape around him, Rommel shook his head in dismay. He had taken the ridge and would reform his broken line, but he had lost far too many good men doing it and the Australians had suffered terrible losses. The conflict in North Africa may have been War Without Hate, but it was still carnage on a massive, industrial scale with countless lives ended or destroyed forever from crippling wounds and mental trauma. Today had been no exception.

And tomorrow, the bloodletting would begin again.

ΨΨΨ

Five minutes later, as he was studying the battlefield, a *Mammut* drove up bearing Captain Hans-Otto Behrendt, his chief intelligence officer, and Lieutenant Wilfred Armbruster, his aide-de-camp. The last of the sun's dying rays slanted over the desert floor, turning the sky a resplendent orangish pink. It seemed surreal to witness such transcendent beauty and tranquility above a scene of such mass slaughter. He wondered how many brave warriors had shed their blood in battle on this very hill over the millennia. How many wives and loved ones had shed tears for those lost on this narrow strip of rock that bore the ruins of the ancients?

Behrendt hopped out and stepped up to him. "Field Marshal, I have intelligence on last night's airfield attacks," he said.

Wiping the sweat from his brow, Rommel took a seat on an outcrop of limestone embedded with a variety of marine fossils, including seashells from an ancient epeiric sea that had once covered what was now desert. "Tell me," he said laconically.

"As our recent intelligence indicates, the British have three commando groups that have been harassing us: the Long Range Desert Group, Popski's raiders, and Major David Stirling and the Special Air Service Brigade. Last night's attacks were performed by Stirling and the SAS. Berlin even has a name for him: they are calling him the Phantom Major."

"The Phantom Major? So it is the Desert Fox versus the Phantom Major. Who comes up with this crap?"

"Goebbels, most likely. Apparently, German radio bestowed the nickname on the shadowy commander of the band of marauding rogues in a recent broadcast."

Rommel waved his hand dismissively. "More than likely, the nickname is an invention of British propaganda."

"Whatever the case, the name has stuck and we're going to have to deal with him, as well as the other commando units wreaking havoc behind our lines. Our losses are adding up and starting to have a telling effect."

"How many planes did we lose in the attacks?"

"As many as fifty-five between all the airfields. Most of them Junkers transports, but also a number of Messerschmitts, Stukas, and Heinkels were lost."

"My God, I had no idea it was that many. Were all of the planes destroyed?"

"At least forty were blown up or are beyond repair. Twelve were only damaged and can be repaired or cannibalized for spare parts. But reports are still coming in."

He shook his head in dismay. The tales of British commandos slipping behind his lines, inflicting damage, and stealing back into the desert had spread in recent months. In the beginning, he had regarded the raids as hit-and-run affairs conducted by isolated groups, possibly supported by Bedouin raiders. Now he knew they were being carried out by multiple permanent military units, which were gradually increasing their striking power and might someday be included in the British order of battle. The forward base camps of the commando units were the Kufra Oasis near the Egyptian border, the Qattara Depression, and even well into Cyrenaica, where they caused considerable havoc and seriously disquieted the Italians. The raids tended to accompany major ground operations or air strikes during a new or waning moon, although last night's strike had for the first time been during a full moon.

"They are using American jeeps now armed with multiple Vickers guns," said Behrendt. "We were able to salvage one of their partially destroyed vehicles."

"Tell me about Stirling. What do we know about him?"

"Very little, I'm afraid. Most of what we know is from British POWs we've interrogated. He's attained something of a mythical status with this 'Phantom Major' moniker of his. He is not yet thirty, comes from Scottish nobility, and is a skinny but towering giant. He started his military career in the British 8th Commando and formed the SAS a little over a year ago. The formal name of his little band of misfits is L Detachment. They look and dress like swashbuckling desert fighters. They don't wear regulation uniforms. Most sport bushy beards and have adopted Arab headdresses or bandannas. They carry a variety of guns: Lugers, Berettas, Colts, you name it. They are highly irregular."

"A reflection of their commander no doubt."

"They come out of nowhere in the middle of the night. The Italians, in particular, are frightened to death of them. From the British regulars who have spoken of their exploits, they are bold, successful, and gleefully break all the rules. Word of their adventurous deeds has spread through the Cairo bars, brothels, and cabarets."

Rommel scratched his chin, thinking. He knew that the dramatic narrative of war was as important a weapon as guns and bullets, and at a time when the war in North Africa was going badly for Auchinleck and the British Eighth Army, it made sense that the enemy had made Stirling and his SAS desert rogues into heroes. Better than anyone, he—as the Desert Fox—knew that he and his beloved *Afrika Korps* possessed the same flavor of romance. He struck mortal fear into the British, who lionized him and his men and attributed superhuman feats to them both. No doubt Stirling and his desert swashbucklers were mindful of their own drama, adding a dash of exotic adventure and a reputation for indomitability during the past month of "the flap" when he had dominated the battlefield headlines. Just as he and his *Afrika Korps* had a psychological and theatrical role to play along with a military one in this strange War Without Hate in the North African desert, so did the clever Stirling and his band of nighttime marauders.

"What else can you tell me about him? There must be something."

"I can tell you two things. The first is that he *asks* his men to do things—he doesn't order subordinates about—and his men do the same. In the SAS, an officer has to earn the respect of the men under him. It is not given by virtue of rank."

Interesting, thought Rommel. In the class-conscious British Army, that was saying something. He recalled two amusing anecdotes following the fall of Tobruk and his capture of 35,000 Allied prisoners of war. When he had passed through one of the POW cages, he had stopped to talk to a band of captured junior British officers: "Gentlemen," he had said, "you have fought like lions but been led by donkeys." And then later, he had heard an interesting remark following the motion of censure against Churchill by the British Conservative Party following the defeat. A British newspaperman had quoted a House of Commons' member denouncing the class-ridden mentality of the British Army. "In this country," the politician had declared, "there is a taunt on everybody's lips that if Rommel had been in the British Army, he would still be a bloody sergeant!" To his credit, thought the Desert Fox, Stirling seemed to run a private army founded on the principle of leading by example and a meritocracy earned in battle, not by rank.

"What's the second thing?" asked Rommel.

"It appears our Phantom Major is actually a very shy and quiet type who insists that his men never boast about their exploits. As one regular army POW described it, Stirling insists that his men do 'no bragging or swanking' as he calls it."

Rommel nodded. The more he learned about this Stirling, the more he found himself intrigued by the young man. "That is interesting. Is there anything else?"

"No, that's it. But I will say that it doesn't matter that Stirling and the other members of the SAS are modest about their exploits outside their own ranks."

"Why is that?"

"Because everyone else brags for them. Even though British censorship precludes reporting on SAS operations, the tales of the unit's success have become a staple of the Cairo Eighth Army barroom chat, and a most effective recruiting tool. While the SAS are under strict orders never to boast of their achievements, they don't need to because others do it for them. The Phantom Major and his men are fast becoming the most romantic figures in the British Army and their exploits a mainstay of military morale."

"Well, as much as I am beginning to like young Stirling, we're going to have to change that."

"Yes, sir. We need to do a better job of tracking these raiders down by reconnaissance planes and destroying them through bombing and strafing when they return to their base camps. We have had some success harassing them by air and destroying their vehicles during their retreats through the desert, but we have yet to capture one of their parties or destroy them at their forward bases of operation. That goes for the LDRG and Popski's raiders as well."

Rommel shook his head. "We have to track them more aggressively by land. That's the best way to combat them."

"How do you plan to do that?"

"By organizing special ground units to hunt them down. Plus, we're going to have to make it harder for them to gain access to our airfields and other targets. We'll have to implement better countermeasures: erecting wire perimeter fences with lights, digging trenches around the aerodromes, mounting additional guards around the planes, and stationing armored cars at the gates of the airfields with powerful floodlights. These commandos must realize that it is increasingly difficult to slip undetected onto an airfield, so that's why they're driving in on jeeps with machine guns blazing. But in the future, we'll be ready for them."

"Are you saying we're going to lure them into a trap?"

"I don't think we have a choice, Hans—if we want to catch them."

CHAPTER 49

BRITISH SECURITY INTELLIGENCE MIDDLE EAST
INTERROGATION CENTER
MAADI, EGYPT

JULY 29, 1942

SITTING ON THE STEEL BENCH of her dirty, stench-ridden, crowded holding cell, Hekmat wondered how many years she would be imprisoned for doing nothing more than allowing her former lover and his cohort to stay one night on her houseboat and helping them find their own boat to live on. At the time, she hadn't known that Hussein Gaafar and Peter Muncaster were German spies. True, later she had technically failed to report the two Germans as spies, which made her susceptible to charges of treason, but since Egypt had not declared war on Nazi Germany or any of the other Axis powers she regarded this as a weak charge at best. Furthermore, in early- and mid-July during the height of the flap, many Egyptians had placed Nazi flags in their widows, hurled insults and thrown stones at British troops, and removed all traces of support for the occupying powers—but very few of these people beyond Prince Halim, an outspoken critic of the British and vocal supporter of the Reich, had been arrested.

So why was she sitting in a revolting prison cell like a common criminal when she had committed no real crime?

It all seemed like a bad nightmare—and she could never have foreseen that her contact with her old lover would lead to such a miserable fate. Her life had been turned upside down. The British authorities had refused her request for a lawyer, and there was no one to speak on her behalf. It seemed a fait accompli that she would be found by the Egyptian Court of Inquiry to be a traitor to her country. Even if she was by some miracle found not guilty of treason, her life as a professional dancer was likely finished. No one would want to associate with her now, especially not the owners of the Kit Kat Club and Continental. And her relationship with Guy was finished. She wondered if Sansom and his Field Security men had tracked him down at the front and interrogated him. Would he, too, be punished—or set scot-free because he was British and a public-school-educated officer from the ruling class?

She glanced around her ten-by-ten cell that she shared with six other female inmates. Like her, they were among those arrested for providing assistance to the enemy and had been brought in for questioning during the recent wave of police roundups. The prisons were overflowing with people—and she knew that many of them were, like her, innocent or at least guilty of only minor infractions. She and the other women—three Italians, one Hungarian, and two Egyptians—were not shackled with leg and wrist irons but the conditions in the prison were deplorable nonetheless. They were crammed into a single stiflingly hot cell with insect-infested mattresses, little in the way of light or comfort, and only rats for company. They were allowed outside to stretch their legs for no more than an hour per day. Their diet consisted of horrid tinned British Bully beef, which she didn't believe could possibly have come from a cow, boiled potatoes, moldy biscuits, and tainted water.

She went to the window and peered through the iron bars at the sentries. Armed with submachine guns, they stood in the guard towers at either end of the barracks. It was hard to believe that she was in prison and had not performed as a dancer for three days. How could she have allowed her life to come to this? Why hadn't she seen this coming? Why hadn't she done more to protect herself?

She heard a footfall outside the cell in the corridor followed by the jingle of a set of keys and the sound of the jail door opening. Two guards stepped into the cell. The older one, a dyspeptic-faced private with a huge paunch, grunted for her to follow them. They took her to a spartan interrogation room with a scratched brown table, metal folding chairs, and pictures on the walls of the pyramids of Giza, the Sphinx, the Salah El-Din Citadel, and the Khan el-Khalili. Seated at the table were two uniformed British officers who gazed at her as she walked in, and in the corner was a young female stenographer, also in uniform.

"I'm Major Dunston and this is Captain Shergold. Sit down," the older of the two men said pleasantly while his partner looked on sourly. He carried streaks of silver hair at his temples, spoke with an upper-class British accent, and was tall, gracile, immaculately dressed, and well-groomed. On his uniform was pinned a single medal and he smelled of strong cologne. She had danced for thousands of Brits just like him at Madame Badia's, the Kit Kat, and the Continental for the past three years. In contrast, his partner the major seemed to be his polar opposite: he was bald, corpulent, and ugly as sin, with a crush of fissures and pock marks lining his face and a nose that looked like it had been broken several times. Though he, too, was dressed in an officer's uniform, he was not as spit-polished and had a mean look about him. She could already tell that Major Dunston would play the role of the good cop and Captain Shergold the bad cop in the interrogation.

Taking a deep breath, she told herself to remain calm and just tell the truth. Or at least most of the truth, because she could under no circumstances admit that she knew about Eppler's and Sandstette's espionage activities. The main thing was she had not helped them in any way to obtain information or perform their role as spies.

She met the gaze of her two inquisitors, fighting the urge to scowl at them as she took her seat. She distrusted police under any circumstances, but in the current environment of paranoia and retribution against those that chose to defy the all-powerful British Empire, she was terrified of what fate might befall her.

"State your name and date of birth please," said Major Dunston, who was clearly the one in charge as he looked over her file in front of him.

"Hekmat Fahmy. I was born on November 24, 1907 in Cairo."

He proceeded to politely ask her a series of preliminary questions about her upbringing and a full list of her jobs before describing the nature of the crime for which she was being detained: treason through the aiding and abetting of Egypt's military enemy Nazi Germany as promulgated in the Egyptian General Civil Penal Code, specifically by "establishing, joining, taking an active part in or giving significant economic support to a party or an organization which operates for the benefit of the enemy."

When the major was finished with his opening remarks, he posed his first question. "Miss Fahmy, if you could please start out by telling us when you first began collaborating with the enemy?"

"I've never collaborated with the enemy."

He feigned a look of surprise. "Are you denying that you worked for German intelligence operatives Johannes Eppler and Heinrich Gerd Sandstette?"

"I have never worked for German intelligence and I don't know who those people you just named are."

"Perhaps you know Eppler as Hussein Gaafar, and Sandstette as Peter Muncaster?"

"Yes, those names I know. But I did not know they were spies."

"When did you first meet them?"

"On the Continental rooftop terrace."

"When?"

"In early June. I do not know what the date was. I was dancing that night and Hussein Gaafar asked me to join him at his table."

"And you joined this man even though you didn't know him? Do you make it a habit to go right over to any man that summons you to his table?"

She glared at him. "How dare you speak to me like that. I am an entertainer and it is my job to socialize with my fans. I sometimes sign autographs or have a drink with them after my shows."

"So I have heard. It appears that you are very popular with both British officers and German spies, Miss Fahmy. But we'll get to that in a minute. What did you do after Hussein Gaafar asked you to join him at his table?"

"Actually, he wasn't the one that asked me. It was the head waiter Rossier who told me that a man had requested me to come to his table."

"And you agreed even though you didn't know this man?"

"Yes, but as it turned out I did know him. From before the war."

"You knew Johannes Eppler, the German spy?"

"No, I knew Hussein Gaafar. He and I were…"

"Were what? Lovers?"

"Yes, but as I said it was before the war. I knew him as Hussein Gaafar. He came from a good Egyptian family—his father was a prominent judge and loyal supporter of Britain. He passed away several months ago."

"But his mother was German and you knew this. You also knew that Hussein Gaafar had been baptized as Johannes Eppler, a German name."

"I don't believe I did know that. And if I did, I didn't think anything of it. What I do know is that when we were together before the war he was Hussein Gaafar."

"When was this? When were the two of you romantically involved?"

She thought back. "It would have been the spring and summer of 1937. In August of that year, he left."

"To go where?"

"I don't know. All he told me was he had to break things off. At the time, I was very angry at him."

"But you forgave him and that's why you agreed to join his table at the Continental. And that's also why you agreed to spy for him, isn't it?"

"Don't try and put words in my mouth. You know perfectly well I am not a spy. There are hundreds of people that will vouch for me in Cairo—and most of them are very well-connected."

"We'll see about that. Now what happened next at the Continental after you joined Gaafar at his table?"

"We had a cocktail, talked for a while, and then I left. Oh, and he introduced me to his American friend, Peter Muncaster."

"You mean the German Hans Gerd Sandstette?"

"At the time I didn't know that was his name, nor did I know he was German. He told me that he was American and he spoke English quite well and with an American accent. I had no reason to doubt him."

The two interrogators stared at her through slitted crocodile eyes. Everything about them was unsympathetic, suspicious, quietly hostile. Were the bastards here to discover the truth or had they already made up their minds she was guilty?

Now the mean-looking one, Captain Shergold, took over the questioning. She felt her throat go dry. "What were you doing fraternizing with these German agents?" he asked accusingly.

"I wasn't frater—"

"Yes, you were—you just described it," he cut her off, his forehead crinkled and thick eyebrows knitted together in a dark scowl.

"We had a drink and talked, but I had no idea they were spies. As I said, Hussein Gaafar was an old flame of mine from before the war."

"If he was a former lover that you willingly visited at his table, you would have every reason to help him, wouldn't you?"

"No."

"But you did help him, didn't you?"

"What do you mean?"

He looked down at his notes. "I have it right here. You told Major Sansom of Field Security when you were arrested that you put Eppler and Sandstette up for a night on your houseboat."

"Yes, that's true. But that was a few days later. And, as I've already told you several times, I knew them only as Hussein Gaafar and Peter Muncaster, not as these other names you keep bringing up."

"And what about Albert Wahda? Did you put him up on your houseboat?"

"Yes, he was with the other two."

"How do you know Mr. Wahda?"

"I don't know him."

"So you're telling us you didn't know that Albert Wahda was an underworld figure when you allowed him to stay on your houseboat? I find that hard to believe."

"I told you I didn't know him. I only let him stay on the boat that night because he was a friend of Hussein's."

"You had no idea that he is a pimp, thief, and money changer?"

"No."

"Where did these men sleep on the *dahabia*?"

"Gaafar and Muncaster slept in the spare bedroom, Wahda on the sundeck."

Shergold ran a fat hand through his brilliantined hair, then frowned, his eyes narrow on her. "Did you sleep with any of them?" he asked. "Or perhaps all of them?"

"Of course not, you pig. How dare you talk to me like that?"

"You watch your tongue, you stupid Wog. Do you not understand the charges against you? We can have you locked up for the next decade and there's not a bloody thing you can do about it. So *we* will talk to you any damned way *we* please."

She wanted to fight back but bit her tongue, though she hated to back down from such a bully. "Yes, I understand," she said. "But I did not sleep with my former lover Hussein Gaafar or any of the others."

"All right, that's more like it," said Shergold. "Now who do you share the houseboat with? Or do you live alone?"

"From Major Sansom, you already know that I share the boat with a British officer and the spare bedroom belongs to him. So you can stop pretending that this is all new to you."

"What is the name of this British officer?"

"Captain Guy Bellairs. He is away at the front. I don't know what unit he is in."

"This…this Captain Bellairs…you claim he is your lover?"

"That is correct."

"So the trunk with the uniform and the civilian clothes taken into evidence by Major Sansom belong to him? Along with the smaller attaché case containing personal papers and maps?"

"I do not go through his belongings so I don't know what he keeps in the room."

"You're saying you had no idea what the contents of the trunk and attaché were? Even though they were both unlocked?"

"I don't go rummaging through people's belongings. Now how much longer do I have to submit to these questions?"

He scoffed. "We're just getting started," he said menacingly.

"But I don't belong here. I haven't done anything wrong."

"If you were innocent, you wouldn't be here."

He kept his gaze fixed on her with open contempt. At the same time, she could see by the salacious gleam in his eye that he wanted her. Over the past two years, she had learned that virtually all the British officers stationed in Cairo fantasized about having a dark-skinned beauty from the Near East do the things with them that their pasty-faced British wives and girlfriends would never do. They all wanted their own sleek-bodied Wog tart to do dirty little things with them, though they would rarely admit it and treated most Egyptians no better than dogs.

"You're telling us that you didn't show Gaafar or Muncaster the contents of the trunk or attaché?"

"No, I did not."

"But you must have known that there were maps in the case? Captain Bellairs must have shown them to you."

"No, he did not."

"You never saw a map of the defenses at Tobruk?"

"No, of course not."

"But you must have known that Gaafar and Muncaster would go through your lover's belongings?"

"Come on, how could I have known that?"

"We've confirmed that they took the opportunity to look them over. And yet, you did nothing to stop them. Why is that?"

"I already told you I know nothing of Guy's belongings."

Now Major Dunston leaned forward in his chair to take over the questioning again. "Would you like a cigarette or a cup of tea?" he asked. "You know we're not the Gestapo. We simply have to ask these questions. But we will be cross-checking everything you say, so you had better be above-board with us. Consider that fair warning. Now to carry on here, do you deny having any dealings with Hussein Gaafar and Muncaster of a military or espionage nature?"

"Yes, I deny helping them in any way."

"You're telling us these German spies never asked you to get them any maps or photographs of any kind, or to contact anyone on their behalf?"

"Yes, that is what I am saying and it is the truth."

"And you knew nothing about the espionage work they were engaged in?"

This was the decisive moment, for this was where she was most vulnerable. After all, she had overheard the two spies talking on their houseboat, and Eppler had later spilled his heart and confided in her on two separate occasions. Since she had never told him about her eavesdropping, she could only keep her fingers crossed that he had not confessed to the British authorities that he had told her about his and Muncaster's espionage activities. If she admitted she knew what they were doing in Cairo that would be tantamount to admitting that she had been working as one of their subagents.

"No," she said firmly, looking them both in the eye with the most sincere look she could muster, "I had no idea what kind of work they were engaged in. And it just never came up in conversation."

"But you must have had your suspicions based on Gaafar's German past?"

"No, I never knew anything and I never helped them in any way."

"But that's not true," Captain Shergold pressed her as he looked over his notes. "It says right here that you got them a houseboat to live on. That's what you told Major Sansom on the way to Maadi."

"Yes, I helped them find their *dahabia* to rent. They moved in the day after they spent the night on my boat. But I had nothing to do with the contract they signed."

"Did they show you the contract?"

"Yes. It was drawn up by Hussein Bey Raouf of Midan Lazoghi. The boat is owned by Mohamed Badr Awab, who owns several boats in Agouza, so Raouf must work for him."

"How much did they pay?" asked the major, tugging at the silver streaks of hair at his temples.

"As I recall, it was twelve pounds per month with a bonne-sortie of thirty Egyptian pounds."

Eyeing her skeptically, Shergold withdrew a sheet of paper and pushed it across to her. "The passage you see before you was recorded in Sandstette's diary. Would you please read it to us?"

She wanted to refuse, but knew they would just hold it against her and make things more difficult for her, so she relented. "It says, 'Hekmat has rendered us valuable service. Today I received the plans of the dug-outs and fortifications of Tobruk. This pile of material will have to be destroyed again—to Seulen. I dare not keep too much—the diary alone is enough of a worry.'"

"Well, what do have to say for yourself? You are clearly implicated in the spy ring."

She felt a wave of desperation. "But it's not true! I never gave them any plans of anything!"

"You're telling me that a lieutenant in the Abwehr—the German intelligence service—planted lies in his own journal. Why would he do that?"

"I don't know, but I swear I'm telling the truth!"

"I don't believe you, damnit! Now come clean! We know you are a Nazi spy!"

"No, I'm not—I'm telling the truth! I know nothing about any espionage, I swear. All I did was let them sleep on my houseboat, and offer to find them a place to live!"

"And I say you're a liar!"

The room snapped silent. The two men just stared at her, allowing the silence to cut like a knife. Did they really not believe what she was saying, or were they just trying to break her? Suddenly, she felt her life slipping away. A lump of despair clogged her throat and she knew her career as a professional dancer was finished. She was a traitor in the eyes of the British and it was doubtful she would survive this. The dismal thought tore her up inside; it was only with great effort that she was able to stem back tears.

Captain Shergold's harsh, stentorian voice snapped her back to reality. "It all just sounds too convenient," he sneered. "There's just no way you're innocent in all this. You're holding something back, I just know it. You're not telling us the bloody truth!"

She looked at Major Dunston. His expression seemed sympathetic, but she could tell that he was just pretending and playing his good-cop role.

"You really must tell us the truth, Miss Fahmy," he said, as if he actually cared about her interests. "If you don't, you will force the court to put you away for a very long time."

Tears came to her eyes as she realized she was in real trouble. The interrogation was not going how she had expected. There seemed to be nothing she could say to convince them of her innocence, or at least that her role was so minimal as to be not worth pursuing. How naive to have thought she could simply tell the truth about everything except what she had overheard from her former lover and what he had confided in her—and it would all be properly sorted out.

She felt herself being swept into a riptide. Somehow, she had to get in touch with some of her powerful friends or her lawyer. But she was being held at a military detention camp and subject to military law in time of war; it was unlikely that anyone could help her even if they wanted to. She was essentially without rights.

Shergold fixed her with a prosecutor's glare. "You'd better just stop with the lies, Little Miss Bellydancer, and tell us what really happened. Because we're going to go over it and over it and over it—until we get it bloody right!"

CHAPTER 50

WHITE HOUSE
WASHINGTON, D.C.

JULY 30, 1942

FOR BONNER FELLERS, the road to the White House was a circuitous one. To attend his scheduled meeting with the president, the former U.S. military attaché in Cairo had flown by military plane through four different countries, navigated via automobile countless paved and unpaved roads packed with military transports, cars, ox-carts, and donkeys, and been driven by taxi along Independence Avenue and north across the 15th Street Mall to the White House security checkpoint. Here the Secret Service directed the lifelong Republican through the southeast gate and into the august residence and place of work of staunch Democrat Franklin Delano Roosevelt, who had summoned him to the Oval Office to give a detailed briefing on the state of the war in North Africa.

Walking through the narrow corridors, the lieutenant colonel saw at once that the historic mansion was battened down for combat. Blackout curtains draped the windows, and skylights had been painted black. Every room in the old tinderbox was equipped with a bucket of sand and a shovel, along with folded gas masks. After patiently waiting in a small, vaulted antechamber for precisely twenty-two minutes, the wide solid-oak door to the Oval Office opened and he was led inside by an usher and a Secret Service agent.

As he entered the president's *sanctum sanctorum*, he felt his heart rapping against his chest. In the back of his mind, he had the uncomfortable feeling that his purpose here today was not to give a formal presentation on the military situation in North Africa, but to be sacked—in short, to be the scapegoat for the intelligence disaster of the compromised U.S. Code 11 and for becoming *persona non grata* with the British at GHQ in Cairo.

Sitting behind his desk in an armless wheelchair, a beaming FDR greeted him cordially. Few people even in America knew he had been wheelchair-bound for twenty-three of his sixty years on Earth. The president waved him towards an empty chair before the nineteenth-century Resolute desk that had been occupied by more than a dozen U.S. commanders in chief. White House carpenters had raised the desk six inches to accommodate the president's wheelchair, and when Fellers sat in the low leather chair opposite him, the desktop came almost to his shoulders. Behind the desk, two tasseled United States flags hung proudly from poles.

"So good of you to come, Colonel Fellers," said FDR with his signature cigarette in hand and the jaunty toss of his head that U.S. Army Chief of Staff George Marshall privately called the "cigarette-holder gesture."

The cordial greeting made Fellers feel more at ease, but he had been told that the president was always cordial—even with his bitterest enemies. "Thank you, sir," he replied. "It's great to be back home."

"I'm sure it is, Colonel," said Roosevelt, still holding out his burning cigarette in its Bakelite holder. Fellers could make out white teeth marks on the stem.

This being his first time in the Oval Office, he took a moment to take in the décor as he settled into his seat. The gray-green walls and office furnishings gave the room a nautical air, reflecting Roosevelt's lifelong love of the sea and sailing. On his spacious desk stood a brass paperweight shaped like a ship's capstan. The pennant he had designed for himself when he was assistant secretary of the navy was displayed on a smaller staff near the fireplace. On a stand at the end of his desk was an intricate reproduction of the USS *Constitution*, one of the many ship models in the president's collection. The only floor furnishing was an animal skin rug; the carpeting in the Oval Office had been removed to allow the president's wheelchair to move about more easily.

His desk was cluttered with an eclectic and somewhat comical assemblage of knick-knacks and mementos to go along with his telex machine, banker's oil lamp, mail pouch, and the latest copies of *The New York Times* and *Washington Post*. Feller's cast his eyes over several of the items, chuckling inwardly at some of them. There was a carved ivory elephant figurine and a billowy stuffed elephant that was said to be his favorite possession; a Missouri Mule figurine with the title "Missouri Mule Downs Ol' Man Depression"; a set of Scottish and West Highland terrier figurines mounted on magnets; a commemorative half-dollar coin; an Uncle Sam glass hat; and various donkey, pig, and ostrich figurines. The president seemed to be very fond of figurines, Fellers noted.

"Now please, Colonel, tell me about the war in the desert. I have heard so much—and yet I know oh so little."

"Well, sir, it's complicated."

"Undoubtedly. But I know that if anyone can make sense of it, it is General Donovan's handpicked man in Cairo. Do tell." He underscored the request—well, coming from the president, it was really a demand—with another jaunty smile.

Fellers took a moment to compose his thoughts. Maybe he had this all wrong and he wasn't in trouble. Though it seemed improbable after the cold-shoulder treatment Major General Russel Maxwell, the commander of the newly created U.S. Army Forces in the Middle East, and the British officers at GHQ, had given him just before he had left Cairo in mid-July.

"Mr. President, if I may speak frankly."

"Please do."

"I believe we need to send the British as many planes, tanks, and artillery pieces as we possibly can—and as fast as we can."

"Your reasoning, Colonel?"

"I am not convinced the British can hold Rommel off much longer, especially if he is reinforced and is able to overcome his supply problems."

"So, you are pessimistic as to the ability of the British to hold the Nile Delta and Suez Canal."

"That is correct, Mr. President."

"How long do you think the Eighth Army can hold out?"

"I estimate that Rommel will penetrate the British Line at El Alamein by the end of August. He is a wily and determined son of a bitch, sir."

Roosevelt chuckled, puffed thoughtfully on his cigarette, and lifted his head in the manner that some—especially his political enemies—inferred was arrogant but which simply allowed him to peer through his spectacles. "I have stripped three hundred brand new Sherman tanks from our newly outfitted U.S. 1st Armored Division and am sending them to the Eighth Army along with one hundred self-propelled Priest guns. If the British can't push Rommel back into Libya and retake Tobruk with that, then…well, let's just hope it doesn't come to that."

"If it was me, I would supply them with ten bombers a day too, sir. The war in the air is where the British are actually winning."

"Ten bombers a day, you say?"

"Yes, sir. That's what I believe. The Axis airfields and supply lines are taking a terrific pounding from combined airstrikes and commando attacks. The Special Air Service Brigade commanded by Major Stirling has made many successful raids deep behind enemy lines from the desert."

"Stirling, you say?"

"Yes, sir. If only he were the one in charge of the British Army, the Germans would have given up North Africa long ago. He's a master at improvisation. He's caused the Germans so much trouble, they've even given him a nickname."

"Oh, I love nicknames. What is it?"

"The Phantom Major."

"How delightful. The Phantom Major versus the Desert Fox. If only Stirling were a field marshal then it would truly be a clash of the titans."

"Yes, Mr. President."

Roosevelt stamped his cigarette out in the ashtray in his desk, pulled out another Camel from its pack, and stuffed it into his Bakelite holder with the teeth marks on the stem. He then lit it with a silver Ronson 1933 Princess lighter, which bore an art deco reverse etch image of him and had been given to him as a gift.

"I want to tell you something, Colonel Fellers," he said once he had the faggot lit. "Actually, a few things. But I'm afraid before I tell you, you must swear to secrecy."

"I swear on my grave, Mr. President."

"Good. Then I shall tell you and we shall never speak of it again. Do you understand?"

"Yes, Mr. President—I do."

"I have been fully briefed by General Strong and General Marshal on the broken Black Code situation in Cairo, of which you were an integral—"

"But Mr. President, I warned the State Department about the code way back in February!"

"Steady as she goes, Colonel Fellers. You must let me finish. I may be in a wheelchair, but the last time I checked I was still the commander in chief."

He gulped hard. "Yes, Mr. President. My humblest apology."

"Now it seems that the Germans have somehow managed to compromise our Foreign Service Code 11. The code you have been using as a cipher in your work as military attaché in Cairo. We don't know how they did it, or whether the Italians were in on it with them or not, but it doesn't matter now because we have changed the code. General Strong tells me that the Black Code has been replaced by the M-138 strip cipher, whatever that is. But the point is the Germans, and Rommel in particular, had access to every cable you sent from January of this year through June. Now before you get all in a lather, let me say that we know it wasn't your fault and that you were simply doing your duty. Our British allies, of course, don't agree. They think that you have demonstrated an appalling lack of radio discretion and discipline. Apparently, you always encoded your messages with the same markers: MILID WASH for the Military Intelligence Division, Washington, and AGWAR WASH for the Adjutant General, War Department, Washington. You also always signed them FELLERS. But that doesn't mean anything to me since it was the State Department, not you, whose code was so weak as to be easily penetrable. So you are not at fault, Colonel. In fact, I am promoting you and giving you a medal."

Fellers felt his jaw drop. "What did you just say? Did you just tell me you're promoting me and giving me a medal?"

"Yes, Colonel, and you deserve it. In your dispatches, you have demonstrated an uncanny ability to foresee military developments in the Middle East. Furthermore, your reports have been models of clarity, brevity, and accuracy. In short, your service to your country has been truly commendable."

Why do I feel more surprised than vindicated? "Uh, thank you, Mr. President."

"Now here is how this is all going to play out. Since your recall from Cairo, I am told General Strong has assigned you for temporary duty in the British Empire branch of the Military Intelligence Division here in Washington. Is that correct?"

"Yes, Mr. President."

"Well, you will continue in that role for the time being. But a month or two from now, you will be awarded the Distinguished Service Medal in recognition of your outstandingly prescient dispatches and you will be promoted to brigadier general. Furthermore, you will be reassigned once again, joining your old friend General MacArthur in the Pacific theater. Now how does that sound to you?"

Fellers was dumbstruck. "That…that sounds great, Mr. President."

"Wonderful, I am glad to hear it. Again, I'm sorry this all has to be so hush-hush. But I truly believe you have done your country a great service."

"I know my reports were accurate and detailed, Mr. President, but I must say they were highly critical of British generalship. How are you going to justify all this with our allies? When I left Cairo, I wasn't exactly on the Christmas card list of anyone at GHQ."

"You just let me worry about our British friends. I love Winston, but he still can't seem to realize that he's a nineteenth century colonist living in the twentieth century. The old order cannot last and neither can Britain's pre-eminence as the senior partner in our military alliance. America is the new kid on the block and we are going to have our say—once we've been properly blooded in North Africa that is."

"North Africa? Are you saying that there's going to be a joint American-British force in North Africa?"

"You didn't hear it from me. I will be making the announcement to my senior military advisors later tonight that North Africa is now our principal objective. And remember, your lips are sealed and this conversation never took place."

"Yes, sir. No one will hear a peep from me."

"Good to hear, good to hear. The funny thing about all this is that you—Great

Britain's staunchest critic who has unwittingly helped the enemy—have done more than anyone else come to Britain's aid in North Africa and ensure victory on the continent by Allied forces. The net effect of your reports has been to convince me that we need more American supplies and troops to help the British in the desert campaign."

"That's what I've been saying all along, sir."

"You'd be delighted to know that your military position on U.S. support for our British friends flies in the face of what the Joint Chiefs of Staff want to do. They, of course, want us to invade France first and view North Africa as a sideshow. But I don't agree with them, Colonel—I happen to agree with you."

He could hardly contain his excitement. "Goddamn, Mr. President, I don't know what to say. I am totally speechless."

Roosevelt pulled out a sheet of paper. "It just so happens I have a recent General Staff strategic assessment memo right here in front of me. This will amuse you. It reads, 'The Middle East should be held if possible, but its loss might prove to be a blessing in disguise. The British, once free of the tremendous drain upon their resources represented by Middle East requirements, might then be in a position to launch an effective offensive based on the British Isles, and directed against the enemy's citadel on the Continent.' Do you agree with that assessment, Colonel?"

"You know I don't, sir. I agree with your North Africa first strategy."

"Contrary to George Marshall and my other military advisors, it seems that you, me, and my new best friend Winston are the ones in agreement. Now I'm afraid I have to ask you one more thing. It's a small matter so I'm sure you'll have no problem with it."

"Whatever you want, sir. I am yours to command."

"Well Bonner, I know you're a registered Republican, but I need you to vote Democratic in this fall's midterm election. I'm told by my so-called experts that it's going to be a close one because our troops are sitting around doing nothing and voters are growing impatient with me, so I'm afraid I'm going to need you to vote for Democrats across the board in November. Do you think you can do that for me?"

"I mean…I suppose…"

The president tilted his head and gave a jaunty laugh. "I'm just pulling your leg, Colonel. Now if you'll excuse me, I must get ready for tonight's meeting with the military brass. And don't forget our secret pact."

Feeling a jolt of patriotism, he stood up and saluted. "I'll never forget our secret pact, Mr. President. As long as I goddamn live."

"Now that's what I like to hear." He rounded his desk in his wheelchair and ushered him out the door with a firm handshake and a hearty "Godspeed, Colonel Fellers—Godspeed."

Leaving the former U.S. military attaché in Cairo to wonder what in the hell had just happened.

CHAPTER 51

SAS FORWARD BASE CAMP
BIR EL QUSEIR, NORTHWEST EGYPT

AUGUST 2, 1942

STARING OUT AT THE LONELY DESERT LANDSCAPE, Stirling thought back to the funeral of Johnny Robson five days earlier. After the successful raid on the Sidi Haneish Airfield, he and fourteen others had taken refuge in a bowl-shaped depression at dawn to avoid detection by German scout planes. It was here—in the vast, arid emptiness where the SAS had been born—that the young artilleryman's body was placed under a blanket and he was laid in his final resting place.

It was a somber scene. The early morning light revealed a ragged-looking bunch in the scrub, standing gathered around a pathetic heap of sand and stones. The raid of the previous night had left many with thumping headaches, saliva that tasted of fuel, and inflamed eyes. Standing around the grave, they looked like vagabonds: their faces, hair, and beards were covered in a thick yellow-gray film of dust and clotted blood, and their open-necked battle dress and loose overcoats hung upon them like scarecrows.

Having fashioned a crude cross from an old ration box, they stood bareheaded and stared at the grave, each with his own thoughts. They had no prayer book so Stirling thought a moment of silence would be best. He had hardly known Robson, who had been one of the more recent arrivals, but for some reason the lad's death tore him up inside. Most of the other men hadn't known him either. He had just been a name, a cheery pink face and shock of ebony hair. And yet everyone was emotionally moved. For two minutes after Stirling's remarks, they stood in transcendent silence next to their solemn comrades, and for that two minutes in the lonesome desert there was dignity.

Amen, there was dignity.

He snapped back to reality as he heard footsteps coming up behind him. "Ah, here's our fearless leader—already deep in thought about the next operation."

It was Paddy Mayne, wearing a sardonic grin, and he had with him Dr. Malcolm Pleydell, the SAS doctor, and a bespectacled man in his late-twenties wearing a German officer's uniform with a red-cross armband. Stirling studied the curious-looking man with the aristocratic, scholarly air for a moment before looking back at Mayne, who he could tell was up to something.

"All right, who's your new friend, Paddy?" inquired Stirling. "The Count of Monte Cristo perhaps?"

The little man stepped forward eagerly and spoke in perfect, Teutonic-accented English. "Ah, a most wonderful book, by one of my favorites, Monsieur Alexander Dumas. Please allow me to formally introduce myself." He bowed and clicked his heels together. "Surgeon Captain Baron Markus von Lutterotti di Gazzolis und Langenthal at your service."

With regal bearing, he offered his hand. It took great effort for Stirling not to crack up as he took the proffered hand and shook it.

"That's some name—quite a mouthful. Can we call you something shorter?"

"Dr. Markus Lutterotti will do quite nicely, thank you. And I think it only appropriate for you to know that I am not German. I hail from South Tyrol, the German-speaking region of northern Italy. It was once part of the Austro-Hungarian Empire and annexed by the Italians after the First World War."

"Thank you for the history lesson."

"You are quite welcome."

"How did you manage to stumble into our little camp in the middle of nowhere?"

"He was captured by the LRDG," said Mayne. "He was taking a joyride over the desert in a Fieseler Storch reconnaissance plane and had just touched down to take a look at a pair of burned-out trucks when they came upon him and the pilot."

"It was most shocking, I must say," said Lutterotti. "They came out of nowhere in two trucks, painted a peculiar combination of pink and green and manned by shouting, bearded men wearing Arab headdresses. I thought they were a German patrol, albeit a very odd one. But when I stepped forward to greet them, the pilot and I were stopped dead by a deafening burst of gunfire. The gunners strafed the plane and then blew it to pieces with bombs. The whole thing was astonishing."

Stirling looked at Dr. Pleydell. "Where's the pilot?" he asked.

"Using the loo. He has a spot of stomach trouble."

"Don't worry," quickly added Mayne. "He's under guard."

Stirling nodded. "What made you decide to make a reconnaissance flight in the Storch?" he asked Lutterotti. "I mean, you're a doctor."

"Believe it or not, I wanted a break from the monotony of treating desert sores, heatstroke, dysentery, and the like. I don't know what I was thinking."

"Why did you think you could safely land?" asked Mayne.

"We didn't see any Allied troops and I wanted to inspect the desert at close quarters and stretch my legs. Me and the pilot climbed down, lit cigarettes, and set off to inspect the wrecks—when suddenly the two camouflaged vehicles came racing in driven by your wild-looking men. I must admit I nearly wet my pants."

They all laughed, Paddy Mayne the loudest. When the laughter subsided, Lutterotti continued with his description of the harrowing events.

"They planted bombs on the bullet-riddled Storch, bundled us into the back of one of the trucks, and drove off. I saw the plane explode as we sped away. It's crazy to think it was all for a joy cruise. I went up for pleasure, and it ended unhappily." He threw up his hands. "*C'est la guerre!*"

Stirling could tell that the earnest, bespectacled Austrian-Italian doctor was a good chap, but the question was what to do with him. Though he was quaintly amusing and well-mannered, he was still an enemy prisoner and would have to be treated as such.

"I guess it's your lucky day, Herr Lutterotti," said Mayne with a hint of menace. "Normally, we don't take prisoners."

"What do you do with them?"

"We usually line them up and shoot them. Right between the fucking eyes."

The doctor's eyes widened with fear, and Stirling shook his head. "No, we don't shoot anybody. He's just toying with you. But we do have to decide what the bloody hell to do with you."

"What do you propose?" asked Pleydell.

"I don't know. Usually, when we capture someone, we disarm them, briefly hold them, and then release them. But out here on the edge of the Sand Sea, simply abandoning Dr. Lutterotti here would be tantamount to killing him." He turned to the little man. "So perhaps instead I should offer you parole."

"Parole?"

"Yes, the ancient military convention under which a captive is left unguarded in return for a solemn promise not to escape."

Lutterotti smiled at this quaint suggestion. "I see. What would you do in my position?" he asked.

Stirling looked at Paddy Mayne. "I certainly wouldn't accept parole—and I know my bloodthirsty Irish friend here wouldn't either."

At this, Mayne gave a wry smile.

"Then nor shall I," declared Lutterotti flatly.

Stirling turned to Pleydell. "Well then, he's all yours, Malcolm," he said to his chief and only medical officer. "Along with the pilot when he finishes his business. You are under strict orders to keep both prisoners under close guard at all times."

"Yes, Major."

He turned back towards the prisoner. "Perhaps you can help Dr. Pleydell treat some of the patients. The infirmary is right over there." He pointed to the rendezvous' makeshift surgery center notched into a small cave, where the men came to be treated for desert sores and other ailments. Pleydell also busied himself with making studies of the local fauna of snakes, scorpions, gazelles, and the occasional howling jackal, and perhaps he could keep Lutterotti and the pilot occupied with camp hobbies like that as well.

"I must be going now, doctor. Now even though you haven't agreed to parole, I wouldn't try and escape if I were you. The desert can be deadly and inhospitable even for a Bedouin. I doubt you would get very far."

"I don't know, I might get further than you think."

"I seriously doubt it. But you are welcome to try."

Leaving Dr. Pleydell and Lutterotti, he and Paddy Mayne headed for the shade of a camouflaged lean-to. They had spent the morning checking their food, petrol, and ammunition stores and returned to those details. Their plan was to set up a new rendezvous thirty miles to the west and carry out raids from the new base location for several weeks. The current camp at Bir el Quseir was becoming too much of a risk. The heavy traffic of vehicles had left deep tracks in the sand around the wadi, visible to enemy spotter planes, and wireless reports from Cairo revealed that the Germans, in response to the Sidi Haneish raid, were sending out scouting patrols to intercept the raiding parties. Also, after nearly five weeks, the buildup of human waste in the latrine hole had attracted disgusting swarms of flies, and Pleydell had indicated a change of scenery would be good from a sanitary standpoint as well.

At noon, Stirling announced that they would be shifting the camp again to the new location thirty miles to the west before launching another series of raids on German supply lines. The targets, he promised, would be "very enticing."

After making the announcement, he and Mayne analyzed the intelligence reports coming over the wireless. Stirling felt more sanguine about the future of the SAS than ever before. During the last three weeks the detachment had destroyed over a hundred aircraft, the highest score ever achieved in a single month. For once everything appeared to be going without a hitch and it looked as though he would be able to stay in the desert indefinitely, on permanent offensive.

Then the axe fell.

Instead of the expected message announcing the arrival of supplies, a signal came from GHQ instructing him and his unit to return to Kabrit, and that from there he was to report to Cairo for further orders. A new operation, based on one of his ideas, was in the process of being planned and his presence was urgently required.

He was livid.

"Based on what bloody idea?" he roared to Paddy Mayne after showing him the wireless transmission. "Who the fuck do they think they are planning operations behind my back?"

Mayne took the order from him and read it over while Stirling continued to curse.

"Goddamnit, I am the planner of SAS operations, not some idiot from the Long Range Shepheard's Group dilly-dallying about at HQ? Jesus Christ, if they would only let us alone and keep us supplied we could do real damage in the next few weeks. They're buggering everything up, damn them. Well, I'm not going to take this crap—I'm going to fire back a strongly worded protest."

"Worth a shot, I suppose," said Mayne without much enthusiasm. "But I don't think you're going to change their minds. It looks to me as if the bastards have made their decision."

Together, they composed the response. Stirling pointed out that important targets were within his reach and if supported, not thwarted, he could paralyze Rommel's communications. He also threatened that if the SAS were to come under someone else's planning authority, he would refuse to carry out the orders under pain of court martial. They sent the response, requesting to be left to continue operations that were proving most effective, and then waited on tenterhooks for GHQ's reply back.

It came in less than an hour.

The tone was mollifying but firm. The proposed operation was of vital importance, the SAS was indispensable, and Stirling would be granted complete independence in the planning of the operation. Three transport planes of 216 Squadron would land on a nearby emergency strip and deliver sufficient fuel for the return of all vehicles to Kabrit, and would fly the bulk of the men home. A time schedule was given along with instructions for the lighting of flares.

"Complete independence!" cried Stirling as they read over the reply. "If that's what we had, we'd carry out a lightning raid on bloody GHQ!"

"You've got to calm down, man," said Mayne. "An order's an order, whether we like it or not. There's no use in fussing over it."

"Well, I don't happen to like this one, damnit!"

"I don't either, mate. But as that Dr. Lutterotti chap said, '*C'est la guerre!*'"

"Very funny. You're a bastard—you know that, don't you?"

"Aye, I already know that. So when do we leave?"

Stirling shook his head in disgust. "Damn them to hell. We'll set out after midnight—and we're taking those two German prisoners with us."

CHAPTER 52

BRITISH MIDDLE EAST HEADQUARTERS
GARDEN CITY

AUGUST 3, 1942

SITTING AT HIS DESK talking to Captain Bolton, Sansom heard an urgent knock on his door.

"Yes, come in!"

It was Sergeant Wilson and he looked excited. Sansom blew out a puff of smoke, stamped out his cigarette, and sat upright in his high-backed leather chair.

Last week after Eppler, Sandstette, and Hekmat Fahmy were arrested, he had promptly arrested several other people connected with the two German spies—including Eppler's brother Hassan Gaafar, the money changer Albert Wahda, and the Austrian Frau Fatma Amer and Egyptian Abdel Salama that had introduced the two spies to members of the Egyptian Free Officer's Movement. Sansom had put others under surveillance. Foremost among those being watched was Anwar el Sadat. He had assigned Wilson to keep Sadat under close observation and to investigate all of his contacts.

Yesterday, the sergeant had discovered that one of Sadat's closest contacts was a fellow Egyptian Army officer, Flight-Lieutenant Hassan Ezzet. What made the association unusual was that Ezzet was a Christian Copt and not a Muslim like Sadat. Under normal circumstances a Copt was unlikely to be friendly towards the Muslim Brotherhood or Free Officers' Movement, but these two men were obviously linked by their common antipathy towards the British Empire. In response to the discovered connection between the two Army officers, he had Wilson put a watch on Ezzet in addition to Sadat. During his surveillance, Wilson had already observed Ezzet trying to make friends with British soldiers. Sansom's overall goal was to bring both Sadat and Ezzet down—and with them the Officers' Movement.

But with the ongoing arrests related to the flap and the Condor case in full force, he was getting pulled in too many different directions at once and unable to make much headway in the investigation of the Egyptian Army. In fact, he had been run ragged the past several days with roundups of European suspects with Nazi sympathies and was in no mood for anyone wasting his time.

"By the look on your face, Sergeant, I can tell you have important news. Or is it just more bad news about the flap? Please don't tell me we've ceded Egypt to Rommel and his bloody Panzer Army."

"No, sir, that's not it at all," said Wilson.

"Then tell me some good news. Like you've got something on our Coptic friend, Flight-Lieutenant Ezzet. Is that what you're here to tell me?"

"No, sir, not exactly. I mean, yes, sort of. What I mean, sir, is take a look at this."

He stepped forward to his desk and handed him a sketch of a young, unusually attractive Arab woman.

"A smasher, isn't she, Major? I could fall for her in a big way."

Sansom failed to see what the drawing of a pretty girl had to do with Anwar el Sadat or Hassan Ezzet.

"You sound as if you've fallen for her already, Sergeant. What's going on?"

"Her name is Zahira Ezzet—she's the sister of Hassan Ezzet. I made contact with her and it seems she wants something."

Sansom was growing impatient; it was unlike Wilson to waste his time with trivialities. "Get to the bloody point, man!"

"Well, sir, she asked me for a plan of GHQ."

"You don't say."

"The drawing is mine, sir. I followed Lieutenant Ezzet into a café and—"

"What café?"

"Ahwa El-Fishawi. It's the most popular coffee shop in El-Hussein."

"Yes, I know of it."

"Well, I took a seat a few tables away from Ezzet. I ordered a *kanaka* of coffee and, rather ostentatiously, began to sketch a portrait of the lieutenant's companion. The girl was naturally flattered, and introductions were easy."

"What did they say?"

"At first, Ezzet wanted to know where I worked and what branch of the service I was in. He was in uniform and pretended to be very pro-British. Within five minutes, he asked if I knew my way round GHQ. Obviously, he wanted to make sure from the start that he was not wasting his time."

"What did you tell him?"

"That I knew it like the back of my hand."

Sansom looked at Bolton, who was nodding with approval.

Wilson continued: "At that point, Ezzet dropped the subject and invited me to his home. We had a meal together, and then he left me alone with his sister after dropping pretty broad remarks about being in our way. I gathered I was expected to make a pass at her—"

"Ah yes, the old honey trap," ribbed Sansom. "I'm sorry, Wilson, that you get all the lousy jobs."

"Yes, sir. Well, as it turns out she was pretty scared, but she pretended to be quite affectionate and then asked for this small favor of a plan of GHQ. I asked her why she wanted it, and she said she'd just like to see what it looked like. As a spy, she's obviously only a beginner and I told her I'd do what I could to help her."

Sansom withdrew a Dunhill from the half-empty pack on his desk, lit it with a silver lighter, and leaned back in his high-backed chair. He was impressed. With his talent in drawing, Sergeant Wilson was indeed a man of many parts. Sansom had known that he spent a good deal of time sitting outside cafés sketching street scenes while simultaneously collecting information on suspects—and obviously it was beginning to pay off. As an artist at work, the sergeant appeared oblivious to his surroundings, which gave him a degree of immunity against normal suspicions of eavesdropping. People around him tended to lower their guard, which allowed him to pick up confidential information.

"I think this is very heartening, Sergeant," said Sansom.

The young NCO looked confused. "What is, sir?"

"The fact that Ezzet and the Officers' Movement don't have a plan of GHQ already."

"I see your point, sir," commented Captain Bolton, who had remained quiet until now. "GHQ has always been our main security headache."

Sansom nodded. With so many people, including scores of civilians, coming and going all day, he had always been most worried about leakage at the top. The very fact of working at GHQ made people careless, and officers would exchange information over the internal telephone without a thought about the receptionists on the exchange. Most of them were young British women with the Auxiliary Territorial Service, or ATS, but quite a few were locally enlisted. And then there were the civilian employees. Sansom had made sure that they had been carefully vetted, but he knew that no security screening system in the world was foolproof. Most of the gate wardens were Cypriots or Maltese. Whenever possible, he had reinforced the civilians from his own uniformed sections, and he had changed the pass system as often as the higher-ups would permit. He had also made the inspection of passes something more than a formality, and instituted snap checks. But even with all of these precautions in place, he knew GHQ was still vulnerable.

"A job well done, Sergeant Wilson. Now I want you to write out a full report of this case so far and we'll take it to the C-in-C."

"And what do I do about the girl, sir?"

"Why you must keep up the pretense of a relationship and ask her to pay a sum of money. If she agrees, we shall have you make a dummy map and we will arrest all those involved and have them interned. But don't give in to the girl too easily or her brother the flight-lieutenant will be suspicious."

"Yes, sir."

"Thank you, gentlemen. You are dismissed."

They saluted and headed towards the door. As Wilson reached for the knob, Sansom brought the two men up short.

"Oh, one last thing, Sergeant."

"Yes, Major?"

"I expect you ought to get more than a few chaste kisses out of this operation. Wouldn't you agree?"

"I suppose so, sir."

"You're also going to have to put up with quite a lot of envious ribaldry from your fellow NCOs."

The young policeman grinned. "Oh, I'll find a way to manage, sir."

Sansom returned the smile. "I'm sure you will, Sergeant. I'm sure you will."

CHAPTER 53

BRITISH MIDDLE EAST HEADQUARTERS
GARDEN CITY

AUGUST 8, 1942

STIRLING COULDN'T BELIEVE THAT Lutterotti had escaped from under his nose. He had just pulled into the parking lot for his important meeting with the planners, the temperature was 110 degrees Fahrenheit, and the guards had just checked his credentials at the gate—and all he could think about was the sneaky little Tyrolean doctor who had made a fool out of him.

It had happened five nights ago when the team had left—or rather, had been ordered to leave—the Bir el Quseir base camp. In the early morning hours of August 2, shortly after the jeeps and trucks were loaded and the men stood around in the dark waiting for the order to move, the doctor had asked for permission to collect a blanket and moved to the rear of one of the trucks. A few minutes later someone said, "Where's the bloody doctor?" and Stirling realized that Lutterotti had tricked them and was gone. As the men searched among the lorries, it was soon discovered that the German pilot had vanished too.

Stirling immediately sent out search parties. They hunted for several hours for the two escaped prisoners but came up empty. It was then Paddy Mayne, wearing his usual sardonic grin, said in an attempt at levity, "They've only forty miles to walk before they make contact with their own side. Cheer up, David. The Jerries will have a full description of us by noon tomorrow. It's just as well we're leaving."

Though the incident had happened days earlier, Stirling still smarted. He couldn't help but feel violated, even though he may have given the doctor the idea to escape when he had told him that he himself would never accept parole. Lutterotti may have taken that as a challenge and decided to escape right then and there. But what nettled Stirling most was that the doctor had become friendly with Dr. Pleydell and the rest of the men, regularly taking afternoon tea, swapping stories, and singing *Lili Marlene* around the campfires at night, as well as lending a helping hand with Pleydell in his physician's duties. It had also turned out that George Jellicoe, one of Stirling's favorite SAS officers, had known Lutterotti's wife before the war and he and Jellicoe, too, had hit it off. In fact, everyone had liked the little Tyrolean—and yet he had planned out his escape in precise detail and made them look like fools. Shortly after the escape, Stirling had discovered that Lutterotti had been surreptitiously gathering tea for days, pouring the dregs from the cups into a water bottle he had kept hidden under a truck. By the night of his escape, it was estimated that he had more than a pint of liquid and had scrounged up a full bar of dark chocolate.

Stirling stepped from his jeep, walked inside GHQ, and was ushered to a large conference room for the meeting. He was not only annoyed at being torn away from his desert rendezvous but suspicious of the newest plan from the "freemasonry of mediocrity"—even if it was based on one of his previous plans. In fact, that made the prospect even more dangerous since it was likely that GHQ had taken his original concept and turned it into something untenable. He was willing to cooperate with anyone in achieving an objective, but it had always been understood that as far as the SAS was concerned, the choice of tactics was his alone. He had little faith in the planning staff; how could officers who had no experience in night raiding know the best way to employ his forces? He was also dog-tired and in a grouchy mood. Upon his return to Cairo, his returning group had crossed the Qattara Depression, and he had gotten little sleep and more than a few migraines during the grueling desert journey over the past few days.

As Stirling took his seat at the conference table, he saw a few familiar faces amongst the GHQ planners and some new ones as well. The conference table was packed with an eclectic group of men: the Director of Military Operations, Middle East, or DMO; representatives from both A and Q Branches; senior officers of the LRDG, RAF, and Royal Naval intelligence units; and several junior officers, including a military stenographer. Among those that Stirling knew and actually liked were two colorful chaps more than a dozen years older than him: Lieutenant Colonel Vladimir Peniakoff, the adventurer known as "Popski" who led an SAS-like detachment of desert raiders and organized Arab resistance behind enemy lines; and Colonel John Haselden, a pre-war Arabian traveller and expert on Arab languages and affairs who had successfully operated as a British agent for almost a year along the Cyrenaica coast. But as he exchanged friendly glances with the two men, he couldn't help but wonder if one of them was the culprit responsible for pilfering, and most likely repackaging, his previous plan.

And then his worst fears were confirmed as the DMO rose from his seat at the head of the table, made a few introductory remarks that only reaffirmed to Stirling that he truly was among "layer upon layer of fossilized shit" here at GHQ, and proceeded to turn the briefing over to Haselden. Over the next twenty minutes, Stirling was shocked to learn two things. The first was that as of this morning Churchill had replaced Sir Claude Auchinleck as C-in-C Middle East with General Harold Alexander, an unknown quantity who would now be the senior officer to whom Stirling would report. The second was that it was clear that the Arab expert Colonel Haselden was the one who had co-opted his plan. He listened with growing alarm as Haselden described an operation that was built on his original concept of a raid on Benghazi with naval support.

My God, he thought, *are the bastards really this bereft of creative ideas that they are using one of my throwaways?*

Back in July, he had casually revealed to Haselden how a small party of saboteurs could infiltrate Benghazi and destroy enemy shipping. The concept was based on what Stirling had learned from his three previously unsuccessful attempts in the Libyan port city—and that's all it was, a concept. As an added element, he had proposed that a small naval unit should accompany him and try to block the mouth of the harbor with a sunken ship. This last suggestion apparently had fired the imagination of Haselden and the other planners—and now the scheme had swollen beyond recognition. They had taken his modest preliminary concept built upon the small-scale SAS model and inflated it into a full-scale ground, naval, and air operation.

As Haselden and then another officer droned on, Stirling grew angrier and angrier. It was true, the GHQ planners seemed to finally grasp SAS ambitions—but with a total disregard for the tactics behind them and a lack of appreciation for the economy of scale that was crucial to success. This time instead of slipping into Benghazi with a tiny force, Stirling would lead an army of some 250 men, over half of whom were not SAS-trained, in a convoy of eighty vehicles across a thousand miles of desert. Once inside Benghazi, his orders were to "destroy everything in sight." A simultaneous seaborne raid would be launched against Tobruk by commandos and infantry. Meanwhile, the Sudan Defense Force, the British Army unit originally created to maintain the borders of Sudan, would attempt to retake Jalo Oasis from the Italians, and the LRDG would attack the airfield at Barce, sixty miles northwest of Benghazi. The Benghazi raid, code-named Bigamy, was a classic combined-operations commando raid: naval personnel would take part in order to commandeer ships in the harbor, and would sink some to block the entrance while the Allied POWs in the town would be liberated and armed.

On paper, the plan was simple. But Stirling knew in reality it was a bloated operation riddled with major flaws. It was a long way from his concept of small, highly mobile attack units operating by stealth. As inducement, the planners not only requested him to lead the Benghazi attack and offered him a pair of Honey tanks, but promised that, in the event of a successful operation, he would be given area command with the responsibility of destroying all enemy installations in Cyrenaica according to his own plans. He was further assured that the SAS would be expanded under his direction. But these seductive measures failed to convince him. It was obvious that he couldn't accept GHQ's word with any real confidence and he swiftly voiced his objections.

"Though I think we can all appreciate the serious thought that has gone into this plan," he said to the assembled senior officers, "I have to tell you all right now that this operation goes against every single principle of the SAS."

The Director of Military Operations frowned. "Can you please be more specific, Major?"

"By all means, General." He raised his gaunt six-foot-six frame from his chair. "First off, it has been planned by persons with no training or experience in our operations. Second, it is, at least in part, a tactical use of the SAS, which is not the proper procedure. I report to the C-in-C and no one else and the SAS is directed solely by me."

"But we are offering you free rein in the—"

"Third, I am expected to take completely untrained men with me, which is in itself a recipe for disaster. Finally, there is simply no way that surprise can be achieved with these sorts of numbers. I mean, you've said that my force alone would number in the region of 250 men, with 80 to 100 vehicles split between heavy support duties and armed jeeps. That, gentlemen, is not a stealth attack—it's a thundering herd. The Jerries will be alerted to our presence well before our arrival. They'll give us the red carpet treatment all right: they'll turn on the floodlights and open up with machine guns and mortars to welcome us."

Now Haselden was up on his feet. "Now just wait a minute here, Major, I don't think you're—"

"No, I'm giving this operation more of a fair look than it deserves. And I say that on top of all the objections I just gave, John, there is one I forgot to mention."

"And what is that?"

"With all due respect, Colonel, you're an intelligence officer not a commando. And yet, you are to command a taskforce that entails not only leading infantrymen but requires close co-operation with naval artillery and commandos—units and tactics that are quite unknown to you."

Out of the corner of his eye, Stirling saw a little smile from Popski, whose desert raiders were, like the SAS, garnering a reputation as a successful and disruptive commando unit, though on a smaller scale.

"All right, we've heard your objections, Major Stirling," said the DMO, jumping in as referee. "You two may sit down now." He shot them a patriarchal frown before addressing the entire room. "Gentlemen, I don't think I have to tell you that these raids could very well prove to be a turning point in the whole African campaign." He looked again at Stirling. "And as we've said, Major, if you are willing to offer your…cooperation…I can guarantee that all possibly influence, and pressure mind you, will be exerted to see that your command is expanded and extremely well-outfitted. Indeed, I can say, with a high degree of confidence, that if the operation comes off as hoped, the forces taking part in the Tobruk, Jalo, and Barce operations will come under your personal command and you will be given the job of systematically destroying all the supply dumps and installations in Cyrenaica." He kept his eyes fixed on him a moment longer before again looking around the room. "The planning meeting will be this afternoon at 02:00. All commanding officers are required to attend. If for some reason, you do not want to attend, you must voice your official objection now." Now he looked at Stirling. "Major?"

He gulped. Every instinct told him not to give into their blackmail. But success would lead to further expansion of the SAS and, unfortunately, the unit still had its detractors at GHQ. He had seen a memo back in July from the chief of staff to Auchinleck that disparagingly referred to the SAS as one of several "small raiding parties of the thug variety." And there was talk of downgrading the unit to a minor role if the counteroffensive planned for November was able to break the back of Rommel once and for all. It was true a large-scale assault on Benghazi might not be what the SAS had been created for, but success would ensure its continuation.

"I'll be at the meeting at 02:00," he said, and the preliminary briefing broke up.

ΨΨΨ

The atmosphere of the afternoon planning meeting in the DMO's office was tense from the start. Stirling knew that his objections to the ambitious operation were well-known, and he could tell by the stony faces that he was less popular than ever at GHQ. Once again, he made his misgivings known, though this time he was hoping that the planners would listen to his concerns and accommodate him, at least to some extent. But it was not to be. A red-faced air vice-marshal with Dundreary side-whiskers lost no time in making his own personal views known.

"This is a job for regular troops and not the colorful individualists which seem to have been attracted to the SAS," he said in response to Stirling's criticism of the proposed operation.

The major looked at the elder man with calm defiance. "The SAS is as well disciplined and led as any regular unit. But I agree this is not a job for us."

"I don't mean to say that your unit is not courageous, Major," said the AVM. "But I dare say that the word 'enthusiastic' better describes your band of desert ruffians than 'disciplined.' I believe that on the evidence I have seen in this headquarters some of the claims made by the SAS have been exaggerated."

Stirling shook his head. "If anything we have always underclaimed our results. If I, or one of my men, see an aircraft in flames we feel reasonably confident that it is on fire. If we see one explode, we feel equally confident that it cannot fly for at least some days. If we plant a bomb on an aircraft and see neither of those things, we make no assumption whatsoever and this is reflected in our reports."

The AVM stuck out his jaw in an intractable pose. "That is nonsense. Your claims are inflated and it must be tried and tested regular troops for Benghazi."

You insufferable old fool, he thought, feeling himself growing hot with anger. Considering that he had always taken great pains to underestimate his claims, the injustice was unbearable.

"What's that, Stirling, do you have something to say?"

Out of the corner of his eye, he spotted a heavy glass inkwell on the DMO's desk. Slowly, his hand moved towards the weapon, inching forward like a scorpion. But the DMO noticed the movement, as did the A Branch staff officer to Stirling's left. The DMO locked eyes with him and the officer reached out a restraining hand.

Stirling pulled his hand away.

But the air vice-marshal had also seen the movement and looked at him with astonishment. As he started to open his mouth in protest, the air commodore present for the meeting interjected to diffuse the tense situation.

"I believe Major Stirling is right," he said. "His unit has been phenomenally successful. In fact, I dare say that post-operation air photography has confirmed everything he has ever claimed. Even though he does not consider this to be an assignment appropriate for the SAS, and I can appreciate his reasoning, I am in favor of his taking the initiative in Benghazi if simply because he is the only commander we have available who has actually been there before. And on more than one occasion, I believe."

He turned to the Phantom Major inquisitively.

Stirling wanted to say something, wanted to tell them that they were numbskulls who still had no idea of what he and his men were all about, but there was no use even trying. The game was lost. If he refused to take on the operation, he would be replaced. And if he complained, he would sound like a bleating sheep and lose significant ground in his goal to make the SAS a permanent feature of the British order of battle. But he was a gambler and optimist, and in the back of his mind, he wondered if by some miracle he could actually pull the bloody op off.

An hour later, the meeting thankfully ended and Stirling walked downstairs and outside to his jeep. Deflated from the day's meetings and exhausted from his return trip to Cairo from the desert, he wanted to go to his brother's flat, take a long hot shower, and sleep for twenty-four hours. But he was stopped in the parking lot.

It was the legendary Popski.

"Well, that was an interesting day," said the commander of Number One

Demolition Squadron, colloquially known as "Popski's Private Army." A resolute-looking fellow with a strong Slavic nose and jaw, robust build, and twinkle in his eye, Popski had been born in Belgium to an affluent Jewish Russian émigré, attended Cambridge where he had studied mathematics, and fought for the French as an artillery gunner in the Great War.

Halting from getting into his jeep, Stirling shook his hand and smiled. "Bloody awful is more like it," he said with a twinkle in his eye like Popski's.

"You know why that air-vice marshal was all over you, don't you?"

"You mean it's not because he fancies us as a band of silly schoolboys playing with pop guns?"

"No, I just spoke with Brigadier Marriott. He says the reason that old bastard has a stick up his ass is because Marriott approached him recently with the suggestion that you be given the Distinguished Flying Cross."

"You're saying this is all about politics?"

"So it seems. You know what the air marshal said to Marriott when he made the suggestion to give you a medal? He said, 'What on earth would Stirling get a DFC for?' The fellow's not in the bloody Air Force.'"

"And what did Brigadier Marriott say?"

"He said, 'The reason he should receive it is because he's destroyed two hundred and fifty aircraft. That's more than any squadron of the RAF can boast. I think you ought to consider it.'" To which, the air marshal spluttered, 'How ridiculous!'"

"You're telling me that's why I caught the brunt of his displeasure at the conference?"

"That's correct, Major."

"What do you think of the operation?"

Popski smiled. "I think the planning rooms at Middle East HQ are not lacking in boyish enthusiasm."

"I quite agree—and at twenty-six, I'm the one who should be the reckless 'boy' not those bastards."

"They come up with the most convoluted schemes—because they all fantasize about being *the one* to put a stop to Rommel and his *Afrika Korps*. With a few hundred men, armed, it seems to me, with little more than peashooters, they think they're going to capture the whole of Cyrenaica from Benghazi to Tobruk and leave the enemy troops on the Alamein Line without a base in their rear. John Haselden, who's nearly my age, should know better."

"He does seem to show more youthful spirit than anyone."

"His scheme to drive into Tobruk with eighty men pretending to be British prisoners of war, carrying Tommy-guns hidden under their greatcoats is crazy. Absolutely crazy."

"So is his proposal to have the three trucks driven by German Jews in German uniforms, pretending to be German soldiers escorting the prisoners. How he believes they can slip past multiple check points and capture every single one of the coastal batteries is beyond me. And then, at dawn the next morning, the Royal Navy is supposed to land troops from two destroyers and several MTB's, seize and hold the port, and liberate four thousand prisoners. It's mind-boggling."

"After lunch, you know what happened? Haselden asked me to join his little party," admitted Popski.

"He did?"

"Yes, and when discussing the plan with him, I discovered that for ammunition and supplies, he's going to rely on what he can find in Tobruk."

"You've got be joking."

"He said to me, 'Don't be a fool, Colonel. There will be no difficulty. Tobruk is full of everything.' I decided then and there to keep away from Haselden's party and told him I would rather go to Derna with the LRDG, as I knew the country better."

"You're lucky you get to pick and choose. I am stuck with Benghazi."

"I don't envy you, my friend." He looked at his watch. "Sorry, but I've got to get going. Good luck, Stirling—you're going to need it."

"Yes, I bloody well know."

They shook hands again and parted ways. David drove to his brother's flat, parked his car on the street, grabbed his two bags, dragged himself up the stairs, and knocked on the door. He was looking forward to a good night's sleep in Peter's flat.

"Who there?" came the heavily-accented voice.

"It's me David, Mo."

"Ah, Master David!" and the door flew open.

"Good afternoon, Mo."

The factotum took his bags from him as he stepped inside the apartment. "I have good news for you," he said. "You invited to ambassador's residence for dinner."

"Sir Miles has invited me to dinner?"

"Yes, you and Lieutenant Maclean."

"What about my brother?" He had assumed he had been invited because Peter worked at the embassy and was close to Ambassador Lampson, but perhaps that wasn't the case.

"He not invited. Just you and Maclean."

"What's the occasion? Honestly, I think I'd rather get some sleep."

"Prime Minister Churchill is going to be there. That the occasion."

"You don't say." He realized that Randolph must have spoken to his father about the SAS in the manner he had hoped.

"I was also told that in addition to your prime minister, Generals Smuts and Alexander will be there."

"Well then, you'd better get out my brother's best evening attire. It will be a tad short in the legs, but it will have to do."

"Yes, Master David. Don't worry, I make you look very, very good."

Suddenly, he didn't feel tired at all. If he could have a word in private with Churchill, he could make his case and ensure the future of the SAS. He decided then and there that his first sortie in his marketing campaign would be tonight across a formal dinner table from the PM.

CHAPTER 54

ROMMEL *KAMPFSTAFFEL*
SOUTHERN ALAMEIN LINE, EGYPT

AUGUST 7, 1942

THE DAY BEFORE STIRLING'S ARRIVAL TO CAIRO on August 8, Rommel was surprised when his chief intelligence officer delivered Baron Markus von Lutterotti di Gazzolis und Langenthal to his tent for the first of several debriefings. The aristocratic surgeon and captain proceeded to recount to the field marshal and Rommel's 1c Captain Hans-Otto Behrendt about his harrowing return journey to German lines over nearly fifty miles of harsh desert landscape. Exhausted and sun-blistered from his four-day trek, the doctor had already been given food, water, and medication for heatstroke at the medical tent.

On the night of his escape, he and the Storch pilot had agreed to split up, to increase the chances that at least one of them might get away. The British would expect him to head north; instead, he walked to the western side of the camp, with his pint of liquid and bar of chocolate as his only sustenance for the long journey, before dashing away. He had run perhaps three hundred yards when the first flare went up behind him, bathing the ground in light, including a patch of scrub to his right. Lutterotti leapt into the bushes and lay still, panting. Back at camp, the entire SAS force had awoken and mobilized to hunt for the escaping Germans.

As Lutterotti lay in hiding, the search party fanned out and began scouring the surrounding area. But he quickly learned that hiding out in the desert and avoiding detection was easier than it seemed. In the darkness, the advantage lay with him and his fellow Luftwaffe escapee. After what seemed like an eternity but was only a couple of hours, the SAS called off the search. When Lutterotti heard the convoy depart, he quietly emerged from the undergrowth, took a sip of cold stale tea, and began walking towards the North Star.

He reckoned that on the first night he had covered no more than ten miles before the stars disappeared and the sun arose. He lay up all day, in the scanty shade of a camel thorn, with the desert stretching endlessly in all directions. Around midnight, the North Star reappeared, and Lutterotti set off once more. The second day was the worst: the heat was brutal. He began to lose track of time and to experience the first symptoms of heatstroke as he lay waiting for nightfall. The third night of walking, he knew, must be the last, one way or the other. He had no more tea, and the chocolate was long gone. Around dawn, he heard an animal in the darkness. "If that is a dog," he reflected, "then humans must be close by." He headed towards the noise. Three hours later, he was back in the German lines.

"You were incredibly stupid," said Rommel when the doctor had finished recounting his story. But then the Desert Fox's mouth curved into an admiring grin. "But the fact that you managed to get back is pretty impressive, *sehr anständig*."

"Thank you, *Herr Feldmarschall*."

"I want to know more about this Major Stirling and these SAS men of his. How long were you their prisoner?"

"I would say almost a week."

"Tell me about him. What's he like?"

"The truth, Captain Lutterotti, is we don't know much about him," Behrendt cut in. "We'd like you to fill in the blanks."

"Yes, of course. First off, I have to say that the SAS is a most unusual fighting unit."

"How so?" asked Rommel.

"Well, when you look at them, they seem to be nothing but a band of bearded ruffians. They are unkempt, ill-clothed, and full of profanity. It doesn't matter that they are a mixture of British, New Zealand, Free French, and Free Jewish-German troops. They have none of the spit and polish, or the bombast, that you see in regular British Army officers and their units. And yet, they are more gentlemanly and professional than their compatriots. They are an army unto themselves, following only the rules that they want to follow."

He found this both puzzling and intriguing. "What do you mean, Baron?"

"It's rather unusual, actually. The men treat their officers with a respect very different from the rote obedience required under traditional military discipline—both ours and the British."

"For example?"

"They are clearly not impressed by what an officer says, or by the way he says it. It is only what he does that counts."

"Interesting."

"Yes, I would say so. Major Stirling treats all his men with the same courtesy, never raising his voice or pulling rank. His authority seems to stem from the quiet certainty of one who is used to getting what he wants and knows how to ask for it."

"That is consistent with our intelligence," said Behrendt, looking over his dossier on the Phantom Major. "Though he comes from a wealthy royal Scottish family, he is reported to have been rebellious as a young man, especially during his early years in the British Army. However, though he is something of an iconoclast, he is very well connected. He is the son of Brigadier General Archibald Stirling, who served with distinction in the Great War and has close connections of friendship to Generals Auchinleck and Ritchie. The younger Stirling also apparently has a close friendship with Randolph Churchill, the British prime minister's son."

"Yes well, let's remember that wealth and privilege alone don't make a good battle commander," said Rommel, who, as the son of a humble school teacher and administrator born in the Kingdom of Württemberg, had been fighting prejudice from bombastic Prussian officers with "von" prefixes his entire military career. "I don't care about his upper-class upbringing. I want to know more about what makes the young man tick."

"I learned a lot about him from watching him, and also from Dr. Pleydell, the chief medical officer. There's a certain charm and personal modesty about Stirling, and he tends to flatter even subordinates. From what I've seen, I would have to say that his flowery form of expression disguises a hidden shyness. At the same time, he is a strong personality. Physically, however, the desert has taken a toll on him and he appears far from strong. Dr. Pleydell says the major suffers from migraines, infected desert sores, and a bad back from a parachute-jumping injury he suffered earlier in the war."

Rommel quietly nodded. He knew the feeling only too well. He had not only bad desert sores himself, but he had lately been suffering from frequent bouts of faintness. He had undergone a medical examination by his medical advisor Professor Horster, with whom he was on very good terms, and Horster had informed him that he was suffering from chronic stomach and intestinal catarrh and nasal diphtheria in addition to having circulation trouble. The professor and his chief of staff Gause had informed him that he was not in a fit condition to command the forthcoming offensive, but he was having none of it. What was he going to do, not fight? And who would replace him? The only one he would even contemplate commanding his troops would be General Guderian.

"Stirling's second-in-command is Captain Paddy Mayne," continued Lutterotti. "The two are like brothers—they seem to care deeply and respect one another, but they are fiercely competitive."

"What's this Mayne like?"

"He's a hulking figure—he literally dwarfs any chair he sits in. He drinks a lot, smokes all the time, and curses like a stable boy when he's angry though he usually says little. When he does speak, he seems determined to provoke. He told me to my face that he disapproved of the Red Cross, and described how, for every SAS man killed, he would kill a given number of Germans to wipe off the debt. He said to me that he likes killing Germans, and that when the opportunity presented itself there was no question of sparing the enemy. He said that he would neither ask for nor expect quarter in battle. To him, there are no rules except the death of the enemy."

"Are you sure he wasn't just trying to scare you?" he asked, unsure if he believed the doctor or not.

"He might have been trying to frighten me a little bit. But there's no doubt he enjoys killing. My every instinct tells me to save lives, Field Marshal, so I must confess I was taken aback by what he said. But he never harmed me in any way and was actually quite respectful. I just think that when he gets in the heat of battle, he takes pleasure in the slaughter. Fighting is in his blood—he thrives on it."

Rommel nodded, and he and Behrendt proceeded to ask more questions. Captain Lutterotti gave further detailed descriptions of the British desert raiders: their courteous commander, vehicles, weapons, camps, and rigorous adherence to the tradition of afternoon tea. For the Desert Fox and his chief intelligence officer, Major David Stirling and his hitherto shadowy British commando unit were coming into sharper focus.

When Lutterotti was finished with the briefing, Rommel gave the order to scour the desert in the area the SAS had just vacated. Now that he knew who and what he was dealing with, he was certain the Phantom Major's days were numbered.

CHAPTER 55

BRITISH EMBASSY
GARDEN CITY

AUGUST 8-9, 1942

AFTER shaving, bathing, and having Mo help him slip into his brother's undersized formal dinner attire, Stirling walked across the street to the British Embassy to unleash his charm offensive against Sir Winston Churchill.

He knew that his invitation to a private dinner with the prime minister was the result of Randolph Churchill's enthusiastic letters to his father describing the exploits of the SAS, especially the late May raid on Benghazi. Though the mission had not been the success Stirling had hoped for, it had proven that a small commando unit could sneak into the city and cause considerable havoc if properly equipped with explosives and small arms. Furthermore, they had obtained valuable reconnaissance on the layout of the town and key checkpoints for future operations. But by bringing Randolph along on the raid, he had achieved the most important part of his plan: getting an instrumental figure high up the military ladder to appreciate what the SAS was all about.

Convalescing from the post-raid car crash, clad in an iron brace for his back, Randolph had no doubt exaggerated the Benghazi raid and his own role in it, regaling his father with tales of British derring-do. But Stirling didn't care about a little artistic license. All that mattered was that Randolph had stressed the strategic value of the SAS. The fruitless raid in Benghazi was his first and last foray with the unit; his back injury was sufficiently severe for him to be invalided home. But Stirling knew he had made a vital contribution to the SAS—not with a gun or Lewes bomb, but through his pen. Winston Churchill had probably not even been aware of the Special Air Service's existence before he read his son's breathless account. But the story had obviously left an impression on the PM; otherwise, Stirling knew, he and Fitzroy Maclean would not have been invited to tonight's dinner party.

As he neared the embassy, a pair of hunter-green American Fords and a midnight-blue British Aston Martin 2-Liter pulled up. Guests in lavish evening attire spilled out of the cars. He had been to the official residence of Sir Miles and Lady Lampson on several prior occasions since Peter worked for the British ambassador, though never before in honor of a head of state. The spacious colonial house was built on the east floodbank of the Nile. It was protected from the sun by a wide-columned veranda on two stories and guarded by wrought iron railings adorned with the cypher of Queen Victoria. The front portico was flanked by stone lions, and in the back a verdant, well-manicured lawn spread from the terrace down to a low wall at the very edge of the mighty river.

At the front gate, he gave his credentials to a pair of armed guards. From there, he was led by a *tarboosh*-hatted attendant in white evening attire up the short flight of stairs leading up into the house and to a drawing room next to the main dining room. Along the way, he passed lofty rooms hung in silk damask and overflowing with antique chests and chairs Sir Miles had brought back from China, along with a priceless collection of Persian rugs.

He quickly scanned the room. He instantly spotted the prime minister: pink-faced, beaming, and ringed by high-ranking generals. He looked in ebullient form, wearing a bow tie and velvet "siren suit'—the military-style, one-piece boiler suit that he had somehow managed to make fashionable during the Battle of Britain. He now wore siren suits at home and abroad, especially when engaged in international diplomacy with his fellow Allies. He was talking to General Alexander, the newly arrived commander in chief who had replaced the Auk, and Field Marshal Jan Smuts, South Africa's prime minister and a member of the Imperial War Cabinet.

"Ah, there you are, Major," he heard a voice to his left say.

He turned to see the happy face of Lieutenant Maclean, fully recovered from the car crash in late May. "Hello, Fitz," he exclaimed. "Jolly good to see you."

"Likewise, Major."

They shook hands and Stirling studied him a moment. Fitzroy Maclean was one of his favorite officers, and he still felt guilty for nearly killing him during the accident. Maclean hadn't regained consciousness in the hospital until three days after the incident, with a broken arm and collarbone and a badly fractured skull. Looking at him, Stirling was glad to see that his fellow Scot and key lieutenant appeared to have made a full recovery and would soon be back in action. It would be good to have him back: not only was he resourceful and one of the bravest men in the British Army, he was fluent in Italian and German, which had come in handy during the previous Benghazi raid and would no doubt again in the forthcoming op.

"You look well," said Stirling. "Any lingering effects from…" His voice trailed off guiltily.

"No, sir, I'm in tip-top shape and ready to report for active duty. But you should know one thing."

"What is that, Lieutenant?"

"Your driving is the most dangerous thing in this bloody war!"

His eyes gleamed with convivial jest when he said it, and they both shared a laugh, but Stirling couldn't help but feel guilty. They hadn't suffered so much as a scratch at Benghazi, and yet had found disaster on the road home in a traffic disaster that had left a reporter dead and Randolph Churchill, Maclean, and Sergeant Rose badly injured and himself with a broken wrist. Though he and the other survivors had rarely spoken of the crash, he knew he had suffered from mild shock for some time afterwards. Seeing Maclean brought back the old feelings of guilt and shame.

A tray with flutes of champagne came by and they grabbed a pair of glasses each and promptly downed them. As they talked some more, Stirling put aside his guilty thoughts and soon found himself thinking back with fond recollection to the day he had recruited the tall, fellow Scotsman before him, who never failed to make him laugh. Maclean had been his first recruit, which had always made him special.

"Why not join the SAS?" Stirling had asked him that day in 1941. At the time, he hadn't known him well, having only met him briefly before the war.

"What is the bloody SAS?" asked Maclean.

"A good thing to be in," was Stirling's enigmatic answer.

"Sounds promising. I should be delighted to join."

Now back in the present, Stirling noticed a short man with a mustache closely watching them from across the room. "Why is that bloke eyeing us?" he asked Maclean. "Do you know him?"

"That's Major Sansom. I met him when I first arrived. He's the head of Field Security."

"Field Security, eh? Nosy little fellow, isn't he?"

"It's his job to be nosy. He's responsible for the prime minister during his visit here to Cairo."

"Well, he'd better not bollix that job," he said, and he waved at him from across the room.

Sansom waved back, smiled, and took a pull from his cigarette. Seven minutes later, at precisely 8:30 p.m., the guests took their seats with Churchill at the head of the dinner table. Stirling was seated between Lady Lampson and Momo Marriott, who had been invited, no doubt, to charm the Americans. In aggressively fostering a special relationship between Washington and Whitehall, the prime minister had made it no secret that the official British policy was to woo the United States to ensure a favorable outcome to the war that, thus far, Great Britain was losing badly.

With drink in hand, Churchill made the announcement that he was stopping off in Cairo on the way to Moscow for his first face-to-face meeting with Stalin, an encounter that he said his wife, Clementine, characterized as "a visit to the ogre in his den." Everyone laughed, and Churchill continued to hold forth while downing prodigious quantities of alcohol, yet appearing completely unimpaired, regaling his guests at the sprawling table with story after story in the exuberant manner of an overexcited schoolboy.

The menu for the evening was French-Italian Mediterranean. The first course consisted of a Bouillabaisse Provençal loaded with clams, lobster, and fish in a broth delicately flavored with fennel, onion, garlic, leeks, and licorice-flavored pastis. Stirling found it delightful and acknowledged to Lady Lampson that he hadn't tasted bouillabaisse remotely approaching tonight's splendid concoction since he had been a struggling artist in Paris. The soup was followed by two main courses: rosemary and garlic roast leg of lamb with a provençale blend of herbs and garlic, ample potatoes, and sautéed julienne of carrots; and a savory lobster thermidor in a creamy white wine sauce and topped with baked Parmesan cheese.

The dinner was so magnificent that Stirling couldn't help but feel a sense of unreality. Here a table had been set with the best silver and served with sumptuous food, with the British PM at the head of the feast, just fifty miles or so from the Allied front line. He knew he would long remember the images after the war: the long table, the shining silver, the decorations, the hum of voices, the prime minister all pink-faced, beaming, and resplendent yet quaintly comical in his one-piece siren suit. In the space of a few days, Stirling had gone from blowing up Junkers and Messerschmitts to dining with prime ministers and generals in evening dress.

After dinner, cigars were lit, brandy was poured, and Churchill challenged the South African PM, Field Marshal Smuts, to a game: who could recite more Shakespeare without stopping. Stirling and the other guests watched with amusement for a quarter of an hour until Smuts's brow began to furrow and he admitted he had run out of quotations. Churchill continued unstoppably for a minute longer before giving a wink to the guests to indicate that he was inventing the quotes and not reciting genuine verse at all, but rather a sort of mock-Shakespeare of his own extempore invention. Smuts quickly caught on to the charade and burst out with a good-spirited, "Touché! Touché!"

When the game came to a close, Sir Miles motioned to Stirling and Maclean and they were summoned over to accompany the prime minister in a stroll around the elegant embassy gardens.

"Ah, so this is the Phantom Major that has caused so much havoc with Rommel," said Churchill as they shook hands. "It seems my son Randolph isn't the only one talking about you. Judging by your *nom de guerre*, it is clear that even the Führer and his henchman Herr Goebbels have been fully briefed on your exploits."

"I love your motto *Who Dares Wins*," said Smuts. "Did you come up with that, Colonel?"

"Yes, sir," said Stirling, shaking his hand too. "I wanted something snappy."

"And here," said Churchill to the South African, "is the young man who has used the Mother of Parliaments as a public convenience." He tipped his head approvingly to his left at Fitzroy Maclean, who had used his election to the House of Commons as a ruse to get into the war. "Now, gentlemen, let's take a walk, shall we?"

"Sounds delightful," said Stirling. They bid Smuts and Sir Miles adieu and headed out to the spacious gardens flanking the Nile, followed by Sansom and a security detail that fanned out and maintained a discreet distance from the prime minister's group. A gentle breeze floated off the river and the warm night air smelled of sweet alyssum, roses, and jasmine. A waning crescent moon hung overhead like a thumbnail, and the North Star glimmered in the direction of Alexandria. Churchill popped out a seven-inch-long, Cuban "Pepin" Fernandez Rodriguez cigar and lit it with an engraved Zippo lighter. Despite his modest five-foot-eight-inch height and portly waistline from lack of exercise and excessive drink, his ruddy complexion, twinkling eyes, and natural exuberance made him look every inch the powerful statesman who had inspired millions during the Battle of Britain.

"Randolph speaks highly of you lads," he said as they reached a row of neatly trimmed hedges. "He has reported to me what original and enterprising officers you are, and how you, Major Stirling, think of the war in three-dimensional terms."

Stirling didn't know what to say. "Thank you, sir. Lieutenant Maclean and I are quite fond of Randolph."

"Yes, yes. Well, he's certainly not much of a soldier, but he writes quite well and has a good eye for talent. Now tell me about this Special Air Service you have created, Major Stirling. I need to know more about your tactics and your planned operations going forward under our new C-in-C General Alexander."

Stirling and Maclean looked at one another and smiled. While having cocktails in the drawing room, they had been officially warned by a senior GHQ staff officer that they should on no account discuss the impending attack on Benghazi with Churchill. When Stirling had asked why, the officer had told them that the PM was regarded by his staff as an inveterate gossip and security risk, with a habit of turning top secret information into amusing postprandial entertainment. When the officer had shuffled off, he and Maclean had, of course, decided to ignore the injunction.

For the next ten minutes, Stirling described the history of the SAS and gave the prime minister a preview of the planned Benghazi raid, with Maclean chiming in several times to underscore a particular point. Churchill listened intently as the two young officers described the unit's methods, successes, and plans for the future, insisting that what they had developed was a new way to wage war that had not reached its full potential. When Stirling outlined the Benghazi plan, to which Maclean was not yet privy, Churchill was delighted and pressed him closely about his planned tactics. He capped off the briefing by stating that he believed the unit, if used properly, could play an important role behind the lines in Occupied Europe at a later stage in the war, once the Americans had joined the Allied forces.

"I must admit, Prime Minister, that while we will without question give our blood and sweat to the forthcoming Benghazi operation, I have to in all honesty tell you that I do not consider this one of our classic roles."

"Why is that?"

"Because the operation is too big. Our success comes from stealth not the use of blunt force."

"The SAS—we're rather sneaky and cheeky, Prime Minister," said Maclean, adding a bit of his usual levity to the briefing.

Churchill looked at the two young men with a twinkle in his eye. "I see, gentlemen, I see. And I positively love it." And with that, they returned to the party, escorted by Sansom and his security detail.

ΨΨΨ

When Stirling stumbled back to his brother's flat later that night and flopped exhaustedly into bed, he knew the meeting with Churchill had gone well, but he still didn't know if he had won the PM over enough to ensure the long-term survival of the SAS. However, not in his most grandiose dreams could he have imagined the dramatic impact he, and Maclean in a supporting role, had made on the PM.

Unbeknownst to Stirling, seconds after he and Maclean had left the embassy, Churchill had rejoined Smuts in the embassy drawing room and recounted the SAS nighttime attacks deep behind enemy lines. The two young officers were precisely the type of adventurers the prime minister adored: swashbucklers, daredevils, and, above all, amateurs. He felt that the young major was a soldier after his own heart, he told Smuts, and he admitted that he was bowled over by the man and especially intrigued by the contrast between the twenty-six-year old's gentle demeanor and his ferocious pursuit of the enemy. He described Stirling's record in glowing terms and quoted the famous line from Lord Byron's *Don Juan*: "He was the mildest-mannered man that ever scuttled ship or cut a throat."

The next morning, Stirling was sitting with Peter in the drawing room of the flat—nursing a wicked hangover with a cup of tea, a croissant from Groppi's, three aspirin, and a shot of Scotch—when a note arrived at his brother's flat. From Sir Leslie Rowan, Churchill's private secretary, it read: "I have been asked by my chief to ask you to let me have, for him, without further delay, the short note for which he called on what you would advise should be done to concentrate and coordinate the work you are doing. I have been asked to make sure that this is in my hands today. I can be got at the embassy."

Focussing his bleary eyes, he read the note twice before handing it to his brother.

"Looks to me like you've won over the old boy," said Peter as he read the note. "Does this mean you're going to start wearing siren suits?"

"Very funny. The battle's not won yet. Churchill is clearly intrigued and wants to hear more. But I still have those idiots at GHQ to contend with. Not only that but this newest op is going to cull my herd and I have no control over that." He picked up a sheet of paper on the table. "May I use your typewriter?"

"Yes, of course. But what is that sheet of paper?"

"This?" He held it up innocently. "Oh, just before I left last night's party, I asked Churchill and Generals Alexander and Smuts to sign my little sheet of paper as a souvenir of the evening."

"What do you intend to do with it?"

"I don't know yet. All I know is that I have to write a letter posthaste to the PM outlining my plans for the SAS, and the signatures of the three most important men in Egypt are now in my possession."

"You're going to get into trouble, you know."

"I don't think so."

He rose from the couch, went into his brother's office, and set to work on the typewriter. In less than an hour, he had hammered out a two-page memo, headed "Top Secret," written so fast it included several spelling mistakes and missing words: "All existing Special Service Units in the Middle East be disbanded and selected personnel absorbed, as required, by L Detachment...Control to rest with the officer commanding L Detachment and not with any outside body...The planning of operations to remain as hitherto the prerogative of L Detachment."

As he was finishing up, his brother came in and he handed him the hastily drafted memorandum. "Quick, read this and tell me what you think."

Peter did just that. A minute later, he looked up with a smile on his face. "You've got bloody balls, Brother, I'll tell you that," he said. "You're proposing to take over all special forces, steal anyone you want from any unit in the British order of battle, and run operations as you see fit. Why not just call yourself Il Duce?"

"Sure, it's a power grab, pure and simple, but there's no other way to keep GHQ at bay. But most importantly, what I propose will increase versatility and resourcefulness with obvious advantages from the point of view of security."

"Yes, but the unstated implication is that the bureaucrats at headquarters are incompetent, interfering gossips. How do you think your new C-in-C Alexander will take that? You do realize that Auchinleck is gone and you no longer have an ally at the top of Eighth Army."

"Winston's the commander in chief. He's the only one I care about."

"Oh, so its Winston now, is it? You're on a first-name basis with the PM. Jolly good."

"Piss off, Brother." He stood up to leave. "I have to deliver this plan."

He went quickly to the embassy and delivered the document to Sir Leslie Rowan. Later in the day, he was summoned back to the embassy for further discussions with the prime minister, who he was told had very much enjoyed his plan. Stirling was so excited that he was beside himself. He quickly shaved, bathed, and dashed back across the street to the embassy. Running up the staircase, he cannoned into the bulky form of the PM himself.

"Oh, dear heavens, I am so sorry, sir," he apologized.

Churchill just chuckled. "Hmmph, the irresistible force meets the immovable object, eh?" he grunted. "Now let's talk over a drink, shall we?"

They went into the drawing room. A pair of Scotch and sodas appeared, and Churchill lit a cigar. The prime minister asked him to summarize his plans for the SAS based on what he had presented in the memo and what he may have left out but considered important, and then posed several questions. During this second meeting, Stirling again conveyed his conviction that the SAS had a positive and important role to play after the Desert War was won and the Allies made amphibious landings on Hitler's *Festung Europa*. He was looking to Sicily and Italy, the soft underbelly of Europe. His immediate problem was that the role of the SAS was not fully understood or appreciated by the senior commanders, and it was still only a detachment that could be disbanded at any time. However, he pointed out that if it were to become a properly constituted regiment, no one could deny it the continuing task in Europe and beyond.

"I like what you've presented here," said Churchill through a cloud of cigar smoke when he was finished. "I'd also like to ask a favor of you."

"A favor? Most certainly, Prime Minister."

"I wonder if you'd mind if I borrowed your phrase 'soft underbelly of Europe' to describe the campaign for Sicily and Italy."

"No, sir, I don't mind at all. By all means use it."

"I think is a very good hunter's expression and properly describes the vulnerable Mediterranean flank to which it will be applied."

"Yes well, I'm a stag hunter, sir. On my family's estate at Keir, we do a lot of hunting. It takes great cunning and patience to sneak up on a deer, you know."

"Yes, I'm sure it does. You're a good Scot, aren't you, Stirling?"

"Yes, sir. But I am at your service because you, sir, are a *very good* Englishman."

Churchill laughed, a deep throaty bellow, followed by a cough. He slammed back his drink, called out to the waiter standing by for another.

"The thing about war, Major, is it's not just about bombs and bullets—it's about capturing imaginations. That's why I get along so well with Franklin—er, President Roosevelt. We both understand the vital importance of perception in this conflict. You, young man, display just the right combination of daring and romance—and that is precisely why you are vital to our war efforts, both in working with our American allies and in fighting the Germans and Italians. That's why I think of you as something of a 'Scarlet Pimpernel.'"

"Are you referring to the hero of Baroness Orczy's novel of the same name?"

"Sir Percy Blakeney. A wealthy, foppish Englishman on the outside, but in reality a master of the secret undercover war. You, young man, are neither foppish nor an Englishman, but you are just the sort of hero we need to inject some panache into the North African war."

"I'm not sure I want to be a hero, sir. Really, I just want to be left alone to fight. We can cause Rommel great havoc and then do the same in Italy, France, and Germany when the war moves, as it inevitably will, into those theaters."

"Yes, and you shall. But right now, you are doing a wonderful job keeping the enemy off balance and rallying our troops. They don't call you the 'Phantom Major' for nothing. You, young man, are fast becoming a legend. Your *nom de guerre* is being freely used by the Germans and has been picked up by the British press."

"Yes, I know. Me mum back in Scotland, it seems, has been fighting her own battle with the newspapers."

"They've made her a target for their inquiries of your adventures?"

"Yes, sir. She wrote Peter and myself recently to tell me about it. Thankfully, she is very security conscious and hasn't told the newspaper reporters a bloody thing."

"So Mum's keeping mum. Bully for her."

"I have to admit that I derive a certain pleasure from all the 'Phantom Major' nonsense, as it shows we're really taking it to the enemy, making them hurt and all that. But I must say it doesn't make the battles with GHQ any easier."

"Why is that?"

"The Phantom Major tag merely serves to reinforce the private army image. It has the psychological effect of portraying the SAS as a product of North Africa to be shoved under the carpet when the ongoing campaign against Rommel is over. I still have not succeeded in getting the Long Range Shepheard's Group to understand that this is a new form of warfare we're developing, not a young man's whim."

"You let me worry about that, Major," said Churchill reassuringly. "What I see is a new weapon—a weapon that, if allowed to mature and grow, will be accepted as a permanent feature in the British Army order of battle."

"Thank you, sir. I appreciate that."

The meeting ended. Stirling bid the PM good luck with his meeting with Stalin and returned to his brother's apartment. Peter was getting ready to head out for the evening.

"All right, how did it go, Brother?" he asked.

"It went well, but there's one last thing I must do."

He went into his brother's office, grabbed the "souvenir" signed by two prime ministers and the new C-in-C Middle East, and began typing on the sheet of paper.

Peter was suspicious and had followed him into the room. "What in God's name are you doing?"

"Ensuring the future of the SAS." Above the signatures of Churchill, Alexander, and Smuts, he typed "Please give the bearer of this note every possible assistance." Then he handed the sheet to his brother, who quickly read it.

"You've got to be joking, Brother. This is a forged document."

Stirling smiled devilishly, thinking of the brave new world that the SAS would now enjoy with this single sheet of paper. Seekings and Cooper, the unofficial SAS quartermasters, would soon find that supplies, vehicles, weapons, and ammunition, up until now so difficult to secure, could be obtained simply by brandishing the note.

"You're telling me you have no qualms whatsoever about this blatant forgery," Peter persisted.

He shrugged. "Churchill's a staunch supporter of the unit now—so in a sense it's authentic."

Peter burst out laughing. "Oh, you are priceless, Brother. Bloody fucking priceless. Now let's go to Shepheard's—the drinks are on me!"

CHAPTER 56

CAFÉ EL-FISHAWI AND MUSKI POLICE STATION, CAIRO

AUGUST 12, 1942

SANSOM FELT his left leg twitch with excitement as the moment of the arrest drew near. He was sitting at a table at Café El-Fishawi drinking coffee and trying to act incognito with his surveillance team: Captain Mourad Effat, Sergeant Bersos, and two Egyptian policemen. He and the Greek Bersos had picked up the senior Egyptian police liaison officer and his two constables, all in plain clothes, at the Governorate only an hour earlier at 3 p.m. All he had told them was that they might shortly have to make an arrest. Sitting two tables away was his subordinate Sergeant Wilson and the target of the arrest, Flight-Lieutenant Hassan Ezzet, the Coptic Egyptian Army officer with ties to the Free Officers' Movement and Captain Anwar el Sadat.

Wilson had made the four o'clock appointment with Ezzet's sister to deliver a detailed map of GHQ, in return for one hundred Egyptian pounds. Ahwa El-Fishawi—the most popular coffee shop in the Muslim Mouski district a stone's throw from the tenth-century Mosque of el Azhar—was considered a safe haven for sensitive transactions of this sort. The sergeant had drawn the architecturally precise yet fictitious plan of GHQ himself and was about to hand it over, though the two sides still seemed to be negotiating. Sansom had insisted on having an imitation of a real map of the headquarters to ensure a conviction in court.

He had already taken Sadat and Aziz el Masri Pasha, the former chief of staff of the Egyptian army, into custody earlier this morning, leaving Ezzet as the only remaining suspect he had yet to arrest in the Condor case. From the interrogations of Eppler and Sandstette at Maadi, he knew that Ezzet, Sadat, and el Masri had all been part of the German espionage operation. Ezzet had been asked to fly Eppler back to the German lines; Sadat had offered to repair Eppler's radio and to transmit an emergency message if required; and el Masri, although he had not offered direct assistance to the spies, had held meetings with Eppler knowing full well he was an Abwehr agent. The trio had long been suspected of being Nazi sympathizers, and in the police search at Sadat's house a copy of *Mein Kampf* annotated in red ink had been found. But Sansom wanted more dirt on Ezzet, and perhaps his sister as well, and that was why he had given Sergeant Wilson more time to pursue the GHQ map angle involving Ezzet and his sister.

In all likelihood, Ezzet and Sadat would be court-martialled by a military tribunal headed by the Egyptian Army and either interned for the rest of the war or sent before a firing squad. In contrast, Eppler and Sandstette had been handed over to the British military authorities as prisoners of war, since during their arrest German military paybooks had been found on their houseboat. They had been interrogated for three straight days with little sleep from July 29 through 31. At first, they were recalcitrant. But gradually, as they realized how much was known of their movements and parent organization, they submitted to a full confession. They proved more than compliant. Not only did they implicate Sadat, Ezzet, and a large number of Egyptian co-conspirators, they even offered to appear as prosecution witnesses at their trials. The principal point which emerged was that, although they had been transmitting regularly in the agreed code and on the agreed frequency, they had no viable response from Abwehr headquarters. On one occasion they did manage to receive an answer, but since it didn't conform with their *Rebecca* code they decided it must be a trap by some British intercepting organization.

Sansom looked at Wilson. He could see that the sergeant was playing his part well. Ezzet was evidently reluctant to hand over the money until he knew the rolled-up paper in Wilson's hand really was a plan of GHQ. Wilson, on the other hand, was refusing to hand it over until Ezzet paid up. Finally, after what seemed like forever but was only an excruciatingly long minute, Ezzet risked a peek inside the roll. Satisfied, he handed over a cash envelope, which Wilson checked, then took the bogus plan. The two men shook hands and rose from their chairs.

Sansom took a deep breath to steady his nerves. Now was the critical moment to make the arrest. He didn't want to create a scene in the café, where Ezzet might have dangerous friends or associates, so he waited until the subject walked out of the café and onto the pavement.

"All right, let's go," he quietly commanded his men.

They moved smartly for the front door, with Wilson closing the distance behind them as agreed upon beforehand.

But they were not quick enough, Sansom realized. Ezzet the professional soldier was considerably brighter than his neophyte sister, for he had a huge American Chevrolet waiting for him with three Egyptian men in European attire inside. Unbeknownst to Sansom and his team, the car had pulled up and the door was thrown open as Ezzet had started to leave the café. In a few brisk strides, the Copt reached the vehicle and stepped inside.

"Bloody hell!" cried Sansom. "Quickly, after them!"

They dashed outside. But the car raced off, tires screeching, before he and his men had even reached the curb.

He looked around. He had parked his Hillman Minx and Effat his little Fiat two blocks away; they wouldn't have time to retrieve them if they wanted to catch Ezzet and his accomplices. But by a stroke of luck, a taxi stopped nearby to pick up a fare.

He dashed for the taxi just as a bearded man wearing a skull cap and *galabeya* was about to step into the back seat.

"Police business! Find another cab!" he cried to the bewildered and indignant Egyptian.

At the same time, Captain Effat and Sergeant Wilson rudely yanked the irate cabby out of his seat. Effat then jumped in behind the wheel while Sansom took the shotgun seat and Wilson, Sergeant Bersos, and one of the other Egyptian policemen climbed in the back of the large cab, leaving one of the Egyptians as the odd man out to fetch the police car and catch up.

"Now that's what I call first-class police work, gentlemen," said Sansom excitedly, "for no cabby on earth would risk damaging his vehicle by driving the way we're about to! Now step on it and catch that bloody Chevrolet!"

"I'd be delighted to!" said Effat. He stomped his foot onto the gas pedal and drove off in pursuit.

They raced down a pair of narrow, twisty side streets until they reached Gohar Al Kaed, a long thoroughfare between the stately Al-Hussein Mosque to the north and the even more magnificent Al-Azhar Mosque to the south. But as they made the right hand turn, Sansom realized they had already lost their prey.

"They couldn't have doubled back," said Effat. "They must be making for Mouski."

"You're sure?" asked Sansom.

"No, but it's the way I would go."

The Egyptian took a hard left on the next side street, the taxi screeching and burning rubber as they drove southwest towards Sharia el Mouski. As they passed the Mosque of Sultan Al-Ashraf Barsbay on their right, its marble façade and stained-glass windows glinting in the late June sunlight, Wilson spotted the green Chevrolet.

"There they are!" he cried.

Holding onto the leather hand grip, Sansom blew out a sigh of relief. *Good heavens, that was close!*

Effat raced after their quarry. But as they approached the next intersection, a group of pedestrian Muslim women began crossing the street. They wore long, loose cotton tunics that reached down to their knees, silk *salwar* pants under their tunics, and *khimar* headscarfs, which were veiled across their faces for modesty and to keep the sun off their heads. At the sight of the taxi barreling towards them, they scattered in panic and began loudly clucking their disapproval.

"Be careful, damnit!" he roared to Effat. "And that's an order!"

"You don't want me to lose them, do you?'

"No, but I don't want you to kill anyone either!"

They took a right onto Sharia el Mouski and, after a mile heading west down the wide paved roadway, they were able to close the gap with the Chevrolet. That was when Flight-Lieutenant Ezzet and his men started shooting at them. The Egyptians aimed low: they were apparently trying to shoot out the taxi's tires.

"In the name of Tutankhamun, shoot back, damnit!" yelled Sansom as Effat swerved the taxi left and right to avoid being hit. He and Wilson proceeded to roll down their car windows and open fire along with Sergeant Bersos.

But as they returned fire, the Chevrolet made a hard left turn, crossed over into the oncoming traffic, and began heading east back in the direction from which they had come. Now Sansom could see his adversaries up close. Ezzet and another man in a black suit were leaning out the windows of the vehicles to fire their pistols. With the wind flapping the collar of his suit jacket, the air force lieutenant looked fiercely determined as a spray of bullets ricocheted off the pavement and sides of the taxi. Another round of gunfire cut through the air, mingling with the roar of the revving engines, and then the Chevy was gone.

"After them, Captain!" cried Sansom.

Effat swerved left and jumped into the eastward-bound lane of Sharia el Mouski just as their quarry had done—except that the taxi was nearly crushed by an oncoming military transport. But by some miracle, the policeman was able to avoid the collision and race after the retreating Chevrolet. They caught up to the car again on the southeast side of the massive Al-Azhar Mosque, when the quarry again opened up with a thunderous explosion of gunfire. Erected during the Fatimid dynasty in 970 A.D., Al-Azhar was the first mosque established in the ancient metropolis that would become known as "the City of a Thousand Minarets."

Sansom and his men returned fire as the chase had now escalated into a full-fledged, roving gun battle. He saw one of the enemy take a round in the shoulder and fall back into the Chevrolet and then the enemy started to pull away. But both cars quickly came upon a traffic jam in the road as the Chevy tried to cross back over Sharia el Mouski.

Switching lanes and driving straight into the incoming traffic, Ezzet and his men were forced to zigzag dangerously through the myriad cars going in both directions. Weaving through the heavy traffic, they nearly bowled over a man pulling an ox cart and a pair of teenage lovers, who barely managed to dive out of the way at the crossing at Gohar Al Kaed.

The Chevrolet screamed on. With no option but to follow closely in its wake despite the crowded street, Effat kept a hot pursuit on its tail, both vehicles scattering cars and pedestrians in all directions.

"They're heading for the bazaar," cried Wilson.

"Christ, that's just what we need, innocent civilians to be hurt," said Sansom. "All the same stay on them! And no shooting until we get through!"

"Don't worry, Sammy, they won't get away," said Effat, his hands gripped tightly to the wheel and concentration nursed to the highest level.

They turned right on Al Mashad Al Husseini, left on Sekat Al Badstan, and drove through the Khan el Khalil bazaar. Originally built to serve as a mausoleum for the Fatimid royal family, the bazaar was originally part of the Great Eastern Fatimid Palace. A prosperous area within the Muslim quarter of Old Cairo, it now looked like a giant movie set with little shops, cafés, and street vendor stalls along a narrow street barely the width of two elephants. The streets were packed with Arabs in white robes, red *tarbooshes*, and sandals along with observant Muslims in skull caps and *galabeyas*, dark- and light-skinned soldiers in every kind of military uniform, and civilians of every nationality. Both residents and tourists alike came to Cairo's largest open-air market—or *souk* as it was known in Arabic—to buy faience beads, silver, alabaster, rugs, spices, perfumes, and Arabic food.

But today was not a good day to be out shopping at the bazaar as the honking Chevy sent people flying in all directions and knocked down stalls all down the narrow street. Following closely behind, Effat had better luck avoiding flattening the vendor stalls, but still managed to scatter men, women, and children, scaring them half to death.

And then they were out of the *souk* and found themselves once again in a hair-raising chase through the streets of the Muslim quarter all the way north to Kubeh Gardens, ending in a maze of alleys where Ezzet and his men finally abandoned their car and barricaded themselves in a house. Three minutes later, Sansom had scouted out the exterior of the building and determined that the front door was the only way in or out except for the windows. He quickly huddled up the team.

"All right, here's what we're going to do," he said. "Once we enter the house, I will give them one—I repeat, one—chance to throw down their weapons and surrender. If they do not, Sergeants Wilson and Bersos and I will provide heavy sustaining fire, while you, Captain Effat, and your man locate and engage the targets and keep them from escaping. Hopefully, if we bring enough firepower to bear, they will give themselves up without much of a fight."

The men looked at him with eager eyes in the late afternoon sunlight. Even though there was a war going on, it wasn't every day they got to take part in a gun battle in British-occupied Cairo.

"The leader Ezzet is the one we want. It is critical, therefore, that we take him alive, if possible. We want to be able to interrogate him and find out more about the Free Officers' Movement and Muslim Brotherhood. This is it, men. Stay low, keep moving, maintain a hot suppressing fire, and, no matter how bad it gets, don't be pulled into a bloody cross fire. The objective is to take them by surprise with overwhelming numbers and arrest them without loss of life. I repeat, I don't want to lose anyone so don't be sloppy."

Here he paused. "Any questions?"

No one spoke.

"Tally ho, we're off then!"

They bashed down the front door and charged inside the house. The world all around them exploded with gunfire before Sansom even had a chance to demand Ezzet's surrender.

How bloody rude! he thought as he flattened himself down onto the floor, rolled, and let loose with answering fire. The bullets hurled into the walls with terrifying force, causing massive destruction. The lethal burst came from deep in the interior of the house.

From a kneeling position, he delivered a fierce suppressing fire as Captain Effat and his policeman charged into the front parlor. Bullets continued to whine and snarl overhead, ripping through an Egyptian wall tapestry and dislodging splintery shards of wood, lath, and plaster.

He slid to his right. The storm of lead continued.

He, Wilson, and Bersos let loose with another blast of cover fire as Effat and his man did the same, pushing further into the room. The air quickly turned thick with gun smoke. He was answered by another blast of enemy fire, and he and the NCOs poured into them again. This time Ezzet and his men were forced to fall back, crouching and firing as they retreated, crab-like.

The shooting slackened for a moment on both sides. Listening closely, Sansom heard shuffling feet and voices speaking in Arabic. Were they still retreating or moving into offensive position?

And then from out of nowhere, he saw a flash of movement to his right. As he turned to face his attacker, he saw one of Ezzet's men clutching a wooden chair. Before he could fire, the chair swung at his head. But at the last second he was able to duck enough to receive only a glancing blow. Still, there was sufficient force to knock him to the floor. But thankfully, Wilson quickly managed to subdue the attacker by grabbing him in a chokehold and no serious damage was done.

Two minutes later, the firing stopped and Ezzet and the rest of his men stood before them in surrender with their hands up. Captain Effat and his Egyptian constable knocked Ezzet and his men face down onto the hard floor and jerked their hands behind their backs. A second later cuffs were slapped on them and each man was searched along with the house. Although the worthless plan of GHQ had been carefully preserved throughout the chase, Sansom was unable to find any incriminating documents in the house. To his dismay, he realized that Ezzet must have burned them.

Thirty minutes later, the prisoners had been booked and were undergoing interrogation at the Muski Police Station. But not even the most vigorous softening-up treatment by Effat and his Egyptian police could persuade Ezzet to reveal what he had intended to do with the bogus plan. Perhaps he was convinced that he would soon be liberated by the victorious Germans and suitably rewarded, or perhaps he counted on help from highly placed Egyptians. After an hour of interrogation, Sansom realized they weren't getting anywhere and left with Wilson and Bersos. Captain Effat and his men were ramping up the interrogation, using techniques that Sansom was not comfortable with but was not in a position to protest.

Once they left the room, he said to Wilson, "Are you sure that Ezzet's sister doesn't know any more about the affair?"

"Pretty sure," he replied.

"I wonder if it would be worthwhile for you to make up to her again and try to find out more about his contacts. What do you think?"

"She's not a tart, sir," the sergeant said with sudden anger. "You'll have to find someone else if you want that done. After today, she wouldn't let me near her anyway."

Seeing that the young man felt guilty for manipulating her, he let it go. "I agree, Sergeant. We've bagged enough criminals for one day.

"Sadat, Ezzet, and el Masri. That's quite a haul, sir," said Bersos.

"Yes, it is, and you two did a wonderful job. To show you my appreciation, I'd like to buy you both a drink."

"Where, sir?" asked Wilson.

"Why Shepheard's of course. I think we all could use a Suffering Bastard from our favorite barman Joe right about now."

CHAPTER 57

EGYPTIAN COURT OF INQUIRY, CAIRO

AUGUST 25, 1942

AS THE PRESIDING JUDGE prepared to deliver the court's final verdict, Hekmat Fahmy felt her hands trembling. Her future looked bleak. A month earlier she had been a leading citizen of Cairo, its most popular entertainer, and a loyal friend of the British Crown—now she was about to become a convicted felon who could very well find herself interned for the duration of the war or hung from the gallows for aiding and abetting Nazi spies.

She studied the faces of the presiding judge and his panel of assistant justices. They were a stern and solemn-looking lot—as was the British ambassador, the plump, stuffy-looking rascal with the receding hairline seated in the front row. As a Cairene celebrity, she had talked to Sir Miles at many glittery social events before today—yet right now he acted as if he had never laid eyes upon her before.

She looked at her mother and father seated in the mahogany-paneled gallery. Though they were here to support her, she couldn't help but feel ashamed in front of them, as if she had somehow failed them. Her mother gave her a little wave of reassurance and tried to put on a brave face, but Hekmat could tell she had been crying. The sight of the tears in her mother's eyes crushed her.

She next turned her gaze to Major A.W. Sansom. He sat next to the Egyptian Police Captain Effat that had arrested her. Sansom bore an easygoing expression on his face, as if he was at a cocktail party instead of a staid court proceeding where peoples' lives were on the line. She was still angry at him for his deception at the Kit Kat Club and on her houseboat, but mostly she felt guilty for being friendly to him in her efforts to help out Hussein Gaafar. It also irked her that he seemed to have the temerity to believe she had been genuinely interested in him—when she had simply been lending aid to an old lover and friend who was in desperate need of getting money so he could leave Cairo. Still, she had been foolish to have gotten mixed up with Hussein Gaafar again; that had been her biggest mistake.

She looked back at the judges—all men—who would decide her fate and the future of her life. They had patiently listened to testimony from more than a dozen individuals over the past thirteen days and were poised to render their decision.

Will they judge me fairly? she wondered. *Or did they make up their minds before the proceedings even began?*

She had made her case, convincingly she thought, that she had done nothing except allow Eppler and Sandstette to sleep on her houseboat for a single night and help them rent a houseboat of their own. She made it clear that she had not known at the time they were German spies, and that she had never assisted them in any of their espionage activities. Nor had she known that Albert Wahda, who had also slept on her boat, was involved in illicit money changing. It was true that she had eventually discovered on her own that her old lover was actually an Abwehr spy named Johannes Eppler and attempting to spy for Rommel's *Afrika Korps*—but the court did not know that. She had never disclosed that she had overheard Eppler and Sandstette talking about their espionage work on their houseboat or that Eppler had later confided his true reason for being in Cairo. Furthermore, as far as she could tell, Eppler had not spoken about taking her into his confidence since her British interrogators had not pursued the theme in their line of questioning.

So in the end, it was a moot point whether she knew anything or not about the spies' activities in Cairo. Knowing something was not the same as engaging in treasonous activities, especially since Egypt was technically not even at war with Nazi Germany. To her, it was paramount that her native country had not declared war on Hitler's Reich like England, the United States, the Soviet Union, and France, for it ensured that she was not bound by the same rules of conduct as the other Allied powers. Just because Sir Miles and his bossy British imperialists considered merely knowing information a crime punishable by internment or death, that did not make it so in her eyes.

As she continued to study the faces of the judges, she wondered if it was possible that she would get the rope. She shuddered at the thought of a public military hanging in front of her mother and father. It was too grim a fate to contemplate and one that one month ago she would not have believed was remotely possible.

Now the presiding judge spoke. His face was all sharp angles and his nose long and narrow like a knife blade. Looking at his stern visage, she had a terrible feeling that he would make an example out of her.

"Will the accused please stand!" he announced in a stentorian voice that echoed across the chamber.

Though the judge was Egyptian, he spoke with a strong English accent, as if he had been educated at Oxford or Cambridge. Hekmat had a sinking feeling. She felt a lump clot her throat as she stood up along with the ten or so accused. She looked at the others, what the court regarded as her fellow conspirators but which she considered to be people nothing like her. They were a collection of pro-Nazi idealists and petty criminals whom she would never come into contact with if not for the circus proceedings taking place today.

"You all stand here guilty of acts of treason against His Majesty the King of England and his close ally the King of Egypt—most by verdict of the panel of judges before you, others by confession. You all have been indicted based on the facts. It has been proven at this trial, even by unwilling witnesses, that you have engaged in treasonous activities. These are activities which God in His everlasting glory frowns upon and condemns. But more importantly, these are activities which you shall all pay for in fulfilment of the laws of the sovereign nation of Egypt."

This did not sound good at all. Hekmat felt tears coming to her eyes, but she held back. She did not want to appear weak in front of these bastards that had no right to pretend that she was anything but loyal to her country and Great Britain. If anything, she had done more than anyone in the courtroom to raise the morale of British officers on leave from the front. After all, they sent her letters by the hundreds telling her how much she and her dancing meant to them.

"As to the German spies—Johannes Eppler alias Hussein Gaafar and Hans Gerd Sandstette alias Peter Muncaster, with the codenames Max and Moritz—they do not fall into the jurisdiction of this Court of Inquiry. They are German prisoners of war and their fate will be decided under British military law in accordance with the wishes of His Majesty the King of England and Prime Minister Churchill.

"As to the Flight-Lieutenant Hassan Ezzet and Signals Captain Anwar el Sadat, their sentencing will be decided by the Egyptian Military authorities. They, too, do not fall under the jurisdiction of this court."

Now he turned his head to look at Hekmat and the others standing expectantly in the accused bench. A hushed silence fell over the courtroom. His eyes narrowed as he prepared to speak, and she felt a spinning sensation in her head. Suddenly, her ragged prison clothes felt terribly constricting.

"You all here before me know that the treasonous crimes you have committed are evil in themselves," he said, "and contrary to the light and law of nature, as well as the laws of God. General Aziz el Masri, Frau Doktor Amer, Abdel Salama, and Hassan Gaafar, brother of Johannes Eppler alias Hussein Gaafar—I hereby sentence you to internment in a detention camp, where you will be held and perform labor for the duration of the war."

The courtroom gave an audible gasp and several women began to cry. These were the mothers, wives, and daughters of el Masri and the others standing accused. But at least, she thought, they hadn't received the death penalty. She wondered if the judge was saving the death sentences for last. The terrifying thought made her want to shove aside one of the guards and run for her life from the courtroom.

"As to Father Père Demetriou," bellowed the presiding judge. "You stand accused of conspiring against Great Britain and its Egyptian ally by offering material aid to the enemy. It has come to the attention of the court that an Abwehr wireless transmitter was stored at the Church of St. Therese, Shoubra, where you serve as lay-brother. Although this device has not been located, this Court of Inquiry has discovered irrefutable evidence from several witnesses regarding your pro-Nazi views and treason against His Majesty the King's government and the sovereign nation of Egypt. Consequently, your punishment for this offence shall be deportation to Palestine."

The room fell silent. There was no one present to cry for the Hungarian priest whom Hekmat had learned was a close contact of the desert explorer and Abwehr agent Count Almasy.

"In the case of the chauffeur Mohamed Abdel Rahman Ahmad and the money changer Albert Wahda, the court finds the accused guilty of gross stupidity and impropriety, but cannot find sufficient grounds for internment or deportation. Therefore, you are free to go, but with a stern warning that you are, hereby and for the duration of the war, on probation. Any illegal act perpetrated by you will result in immediate arrest and imprisonment without trial. Do the subjects of this court proceeding understand?"

"Yes, honorable sir," said Wahda.

"Yes, Judge," echoed the chauffeur Ahmad.

The presiding judge nodded and now looked at Hekmat with a cold patrician eye. She felt a shudder down her spine. Why had she been saved for last? Glancing around the room, she saw that all the eyes in the courtroom were heavily upon her, especially among the British officers and diplomats in attendance. *My God*, she thought, *what have I done to draw the special ire of the judge and the courtroom?*

Then she saw her mother and father. They looked at her tenderly, but a moment later her mother couldn't help herself and broke down and started crying again. She wasn't loud, but her sniffles were audible in the cavernous, echoing courtroom.

"Hekmat Fahmy," said the judge. Here, to her shock and dismay, he paused as if to draw out the agonizing moment. A hushed silence fell over the courtroom, and she couldn't help but feel embarrassed and angry at being humiliatingly singled out and treated differently than the others. "Hekmat Fahmy," he repeated, "you have been found guilty of putting up the German spies Eppler and Sandstette on your houseboat, helping them find a boat to rent, and closely associating with them when they were engaged in illegal money-changing activities in the presence of Major Sansom. However, in lieu of your cooperation with the authorities, this Court of Inquiry is letting you off with a warning and you are free to go when these proceedings are completed." He wagged a long bony finger at her. "But make no mistake, you are hereby and for the duration of the war on probation, just like Mr. Ahmad and Mr. Wahda. As I made clear to them, any illegal act perpetrated by you will result in immediate arrest and imprisonment without trial. Is this understood?"

She was so relieved that for a moment she could hardly breathe. "Yes, your honor," she said, and she heard a murmur of approval from the crowd. So, there were many here rooting for her today after all.

"This concludes this Court of Inquiry." The judge reached for his gavel. "Is there any public official in this courtroom representing His Majesty the King of England who does not agree with this sentencing? If not, then this proceeding is adjourned."

A hum went around the courtroom and people looked at one another. Hekmat felt a flicker of trepidation. What was this? Why was the judge leaving the door open for someone to challenge the verdicts reached by the court? Or was the Egyptian court somehow being strong-armed by the British?

My God, she thought, *this could be a disaster.*

To her shock and dismay, Sir Miles Lampson cleared his throat and rose his ponderous frame from his front row seat. "If it pleases the court, I should like to say a few words."

Before the towering British ambassador, the judge suddenly looked meek and powerless. "Yes, Sir Miles. Please proceed," he said.

"Firstly," began Lampson, "I understand that Flight-Lieutenant Ezzet and Captain Anwar el Sadat are to be dealt with by the Egyptian military authorities. However, I should like to humbly impress upon this court and Egyptian Prime Minister Nahas Pasha that we, the British government, believe that the case should be pressed vigorously on espionage grounds regardless of any personal considerations or of consideration for the Egyptian Army. In short, it is the contention of my government that these two traitors should be executed and not merely cashiered and interned."

"I will pass on your recommendation to the Egyptian Army, Sir Miles," said the judge. "Is there anything else?"

Slowly, Lampson's gunmetal-gray eyes shifted in her direction, and Hekmat felt her heart flutter in her chest. *No, please, no,* she told herself, but she could tell that it was already too late.

"I am not here to challenge the court's decision in these sober matters," said Sir

Miles, his upper-class British accent mellifluous yet incisive like an axe. "But I must say that I do have one additional reservation."

"What is that, Sir Miles?"

"Ought the dancer Hekmat Fahmy be let out again? To consort, as in the past as this case has clearly shown, with erotic young British officers? I should think most assuredly not!"

A rumble of shock, perhaps even protest and indignation, suddenly filled the courtroom and the judge was forced to reach for his gavel and pound it into the table for order. After a tense moment, the room turned as silent as a tomb as everyone awaited the judge's final verdict. Hekmat felt as if her whole world was suddenly crumbling before her. A minute ago, she was a free woman—now, if the stodgy British Ambassador Sir Miles Lampson had his way, she would remain a prisoner in a cage. Suddenly, tears poured from her eyes, unbidden, and she could do nothing to stop them. In the gallery, she could see her father shaking his head in disbelief and her mother sobbing with her head in her hands.

"Well," snapped Sir Miles. "What does the court say to this in rendering its final decision?"

The Egyptian judge licked his lips and glanced discreetly around the courtroom. To Hekmat, he looked weak before the tall, erect, blustery diplomat who only six months earlier had bullied her king into backing down by surrounding his palace with tanks and giving him an ultimatum, in the process humiliating a whole nation and an invaluable ally in the war against the Axis.

"Well, Judge, the British government is waiting."

To Hekmat's surprise, instead of looking weak the presiding judge now looked resolute. He calmly took off his glasses and rubbed his eyes. Then he put them back on and looked out at the courtroom in silence for several seconds. It seemed to her like an eternity.

"My verdict stands, Sir Miles," he declared in a firm voice. "Hekmat Fahmy, you are hereby released from this courtroom and are free to go." He picked up his gavel and it came crashing down with a plangent thud. "This court is adjourned!"

With tears in her eyes, Hekmat dashed to her mother and father and the three of them embraced.

CHAPTER 58

MONTGOMERY'S TACTICAL HQ
BURGH EL ARAB, WEST OF ALAMEIN LINE,
NORTHWEST EGYPT

SEPTEMBER 23, 1942

AS STIRLING DROVE WEST along the coast road, he snuck occasional peeks out the window at the spectacular scenery. On his left, the serene desert landscape consisted of a series of barchan dunes, low-lying ridges, and clumps of palm trees dappled with shadows from the overhanging clouds; while on his right lay the sparkling azure-blue waters of the Mediterranean, with white-capped waves rolling onto sandy beaches stretching in both directions as far as the eye could see. The tranquil setting, coupled with the lack of Allied or Luftwaffe aircraft roaring overhead, made the war seem a long way off, if only for a brief respite.

Riding along with him for their meeting with General Bernard Montgomery, who had taken over as commander of the British Eighth Army on August 13, was Colonel Shan Hackett. GHQ had set up a new department know as G Raiding Force, and it was Hackett's job to coordinate Stirling's activities with the Army's forthcoming offensive and help him with supply. Today, they were visiting Monty's forward command post to try and obtain his permission to handpick recruits from the best regiments in Eighth Army. The SAS was under orders to strengthen its ranks quickly, and with raiding parties set to go into action in the coming weeks Stirling knew they would have to be composed of seasoned fighting men.

Despite his lingering health problems that he continued to ignore against the advice of Dr. Pleydell, Stirling was in a cheery mood. Operation Bigamy, the ill-advised mission in mid-September to destroy the harbor and storage facilities at Benghazi and raid Benina airfield in Libya, had been an unmitigated disaster just as he had predicted—and yet, in its aftermath, he had been promoted to lieutenant colonel and the SAS was granted full regimental status. A unit that had started with a fictitious name was now a formal element in the British order of battle and was approved to undergo a major expansion to 29 officers and 572 other ranks.

The Phantom Major was understandably proud—and completely stunned. But once he had a chance to think about it, he knew why his fate and that of the SAS had turned out favorably. A combination of Churchill's sponsorship, the legendary reputation of the SAS, and its track record of sabotage when properly deployed, coupled with a desire on the part of General Alexander to placate Stirling for the debacle of Operation Bigamy, had all come together to turn an abject failure into an improbable triumph. The new force would be divided into four squadrons: A Squadron, under the command of Paddy Mayne; B, commanded by Stirling himself; C, the French squadron; and D, the Special Boat Section.

At the age of twenty-six, Stirling had become the first British officer to create his own new regiment since the Lovat Scouts were raised by his own uncle in the Boer War nearly a half century before. It was not only an honor, but a tremendous victory for him and his men. It meant that SAS tactics had become an accepted part of the Allied war effort. It meant that his unit was a permanent institution. And it meant that he could recruit sufficient men to bring his strength up to full regimental status, which would triple the number in his ranks.

Despite the recognition he and his men now enjoyed, he was still kicking himself for having agreed to a plan which he knew up front was dead wrong. Operation Bigamy had departed from his concept of small, highly mobile units operating with stealth, with deleterious results. Rommel had definitely known he was coming: over a quarter of Stirling's force had been killed, wounded, or captured, and more than half his vehicles destroyed. Apart from diverting a number of enemy troops to defend Benghazi, the operation's impact was negligible. The simultaneous raid on Tobruk as part of Operation Agreement had proved even more disastrous. The whole affair was such a fiasco that when his battered men limped back into Cairo, they were mistaken for a grubby batch of newly captured German prisoners.

They soon arrived at Montgomery's headquarters, a series of camouflaged tents strung along the coast ten miles behind the Alamein Line. Stirling was pleased to see several spanking new American jeeps parked outside the general's trailer; at least the latest commander to take the reins of Eighth Army had the good sense to make use of first-rate equipment. Jumping out of their own jeep, they were received by Freddie de Guingand, Montgomery's chief of staff, and escorted inside the trailer. De Guingand was a friend of both Stirling and Hackett.

When Stirling first set eyes on Montgomery in his black beret set at a military angle, he felt as though he had stumbled across an underweight fighting bantam cock. But what struck him most was not that the new commander was uncommonly short for a general and scrappy-looking—all wiry sinew and strut—but the captivating nature of his piercing blue eyes. They were filled with ruthless determination. Here most assuredly was a tenacious soldier.

"Well, well, well, if it isn't the Phantom Major," said Monty brusquely and without preamble. "Now what is it that *you* want, Colonel?"

Stunned at the wrong-footed lack of polite preliminaries, Stirling's mouth fell open and words momentarily escaped him.

"Do I have to say it again, gentlemen. What are doing here?" repeated the little wiry bantam cock, looking sharply at both Stirling and Hackett. "I'm afraid my time is short so you had better get on with it. Please state your business."

Stirling was still taken aback, but he recovered quickly and launched into his speech. "Uh yes, General...the reason I am here is to offer my unit, the Special Air Service Division, to support Eighth Army in the coming offensive. We are prepared to make your job much easier by raiding Rommel's overextended supply lines and knocking out fuel dumps, ammunition depots, and airfields."

"Good, I could always use support in hitting Rommel behind his lines. I plan to defeat him by the end of October, you know."

"Marvelous, sir. Me and my men are looking forward to helping you do it, General. But to best support your offensive, I will need to recruit at least one hundred fifty first-class fighters from other regiments."

Montgomery fixed him with a bayonet stare. The HQ trailer went agonizingly quiet for several seconds before the general spoke.

"If I understand you correctly, Colonel Stirling, you want to take some of my men from me. Indeed my best men—my most desert-worthy, my most dependable, my most experienced men. I am proud of my men. I expect great things of them." Here he fixed his blue eyes crossly on him. "What makes you think, young man, that you can handle my men to greater advantage than I can handle them myself?"

Stirling felt himself becoming angry. What did this newcomer mean talking about *his* men? He had only arrived in the Middle East six weeks ago. But Stirling also realized he had made a major mistake in setting up a meeting before he knew what made the new commander of Eighth Army tick. Before today, all he had known about Montgomery was that he was a protégé of the new C-in-C Alexander, who had taken over for Auchinleck. He had looked upon him as merely another British general in a fairly long succession. Like many officers on both sides and taking into consideration Eighth Army's overall abysmal performance in the Middle East thus far, he took it for granted that Rommel was the only brilliant field commander in the North African theater. But clearly Monty was made of sterner stuff than his predecessors. Not only that but he seemed to be a rather prickly sort who had to be handled altogether in a different manner than the compliant Auk and Ritchie.

"I'm sorry, General, but I need to bring my regiment up to strength. I need experienced men or I won't be able to carry out my immediate plans. There just isn't enough time to train up raw recruits for the sort of offensive actions that will be most useful to Eighth Army."

"But I need experienced men too," pointed out Montgomery sarcastically. "How long will it take you to train fresh troops?"

"A couple of months. Whereas if I get seasoned men only three or four weeks."

"But I am planning to open my offensive in a fortnight. If I keep my experienced men myself, I can use them. If I give them to you, they won't be ready to play any part in the action."

There was a supercilious note in the general's voice and Stirling felt his vexation mounting. Now he realized another big mistake he had made in coming here today: he had underestimated this new kid on the block—this General Bernard Law Montgomery—badly. He had also overestimated his own importance now that he was a colonel and the SAS a full-blown regiment. Auchinleck had looked with an indulgent eye on the SAS's unconventional approach to warfare. It was painfully obvious that Monty was a different sort of general. He had not been grouse hunting at Keir, was averse to taking strategic risks, and did not like being told what to do by anyone, least of all by a young Scottish Turk with a taste for extreme adventure. The meeting was going badly and Stirling realized that somehow, he had to find a way to turn their first encounter into a positive one. At the moment, it was a disaster.

"Perhaps these seasoned men won't be ready for the next offensive," he said in a tone of appeasement, "but they'll be ready for the one after."

"But I don't intend to have one after. I intend the next offensive to be the last offensive. What's the matter with you, Colonel Stirling? Why are you smiling?"

"Nothing, sir, it's only that we heard the same thing from the last general—and the one before him." He looked at Hackett for support, but his partner just looked down into the floor, not wanting to get in the middle of the argument.

Now Monty gave Stirling a withering look.

"I'm sorry, Colonel, but the answer is no. A flat no. Frankly, your request strikes me as slightly arrogant. I am under the impression that you feel you know my business better than I do. You come here after a failure at Benghazi demanding the best I can give. In all honesty, Colonel Stirling, I am not inclined to associate myself with failure. And now I must be on my way. I'm sorry to disappoint you, but I prefer to keep *my* best men for *my* own use."

He couldn't believe his bad luck. In the past, he had always achieved his ends through a combination of charm and argument. Here was a general immune to both, and even more determined to get his own way than Stirling himself. Instead of cherry-picking prime recruits from veteran Middle East forces, Stirling knew he would now have to build up the expanded SAS with men from the Infantry Base Depot and General Jumbo Wilson's Palestine-Iraq Force, most of whom were without desert or combat experience. This, in turn, meant restructuring the force: most of the SAS veterans would now have to fight under Mayne in A Squadron, while Stirling's B Squadron, largely made up of new recruits, would have to undergo extensive training in Kabrit before going into action.

"Now Stirling, I'm lunching at Guards Brigade Headquarters. I shall be pleased if you and Colonel Hackett will lunch in the officers' mess as my guests, even though I can't be there. I'm sorry to disappoint you, Colonel Stirling, but I prefer to keep my best men for my own use. Good luck then."

And with that, the bantam cock turned on his heel and clomped out the trailer.

Stirling began to mutter curses under his breath at once. "Bloody failure at Benghazi...what about our fucking successes?"

"You've got to let it go, man," said Hackett, trying to calm him down. The stocky, pink-cheeked soldier had won a great reputation as a commander of the 4th Light Brigade and knew his way around curmudgeonly generals.

"I'm not inclined to associate myself with failure," Stirling sniffed sarcastically, mimicking Monty's high-pitched, nasally twine. "Jesus Christ, the whole point is to create havoc in Rommel's rear once the offensive begins—not to be training green troops! Damn that man!"

"Let's go get a drink and grab a bite to eat, shall we?" proposed Hackett, and he quickly steered him out the door and towards the officers' mess.

But Stirling was still fuming. He couldn't believe he was beaten. But Montgomery was adamant and it seemed nothing could persuade the new commander of Eighth Army to part with any of his desert-trained warriors. What this meant for Stirling was obvious: he would not be able to carry out a major operation for another two months. Of course, he could send the old hands of the SAS to make weekly attacks on a limited sector behind the enemy's lines, but that was no way to stick it to Rommel. Only concentrated raids against eighty or a hundred miles of communications, carried out unceasingly night after night, would have a profound effect on the Desert Fox's fortunes, he knew.

He and Hackett sat down at a table with three officers they didn't know. "Hello, chaps," he said pleasantly, concealing his irritation behind a polite mask. "This lunch is on Monty," he said. "Let's make it a grand one."

He signaled the mess waiter and asked what there was to drink. After being handed a list, he gave an extensive order of cocktails, wine, kummel—everything that could be procured.

"What are you doing?" asked Hackett.

"I hear the general's a teetotaller. I'm putting everything we drink on his bill. Perhaps it will make him look more human at the end of the month."

The officers laughed.

The lunch of Woolton vegetable pie and oily tinned Snoek fish from South Africa was bland and barely edible, but the three glasses of wine and single Scotch lifted Stirling's spirits. When lunch was over, Hackett remembered that he had left some papers in the general's trailer and the two men, a little tipsy, went back to fetch them. They found that Montgomery had already returned and was buried in paperwork at his desk. Freddie de Guingand, was also there and joined them outside the trailer once Hackett had gathered his leather attaché case.

"Your general has plenty of cock-sparrow assurance," Stirling said to the chief of staff. "If one could judge by talk, the war in Africa is as good as over. Unfortunately, we have to judge by results. And frankly, I'm skeptical. Unless you use the SAS, my bet is that the only way you'll ever beat Rommel is to have the Americans land in North Africa and smash him on a second front."

Still irked by Montgomery, he was only pulling de Guingand's leg and venting his frustration, but as soon as he saw the chief of staff's reaction to the mentioning of a U.S. North African landing, he knew he had stumbled onto something.

"Well, I'll be damned. So that's what we're bloody planning, is it?"

"For God's sake, David—hush up," warned de Guingand.

But Stirling couldn't resist teasing his friend. "I'm afraid, Freddie, you're going to have to put pressure on your general for us. We want men for our regiment. Good men. And he's being quite stubborn. We expect you to intervene for us. Otherwise, we might be forced to let slip about this U.S. landing business. Saying, of course, that we obtained this top secret information from Monty's indiscreet chief of staff."

"You're incorrigible, David. Of course, I'll try to help you. However, for the moment, I don't think you'll change the general's mind. But I promise I'll impress him with the SAS record and perhaps after the offensive he'll be more reasonable."

"Let's hope so, Freddie. Let's hope so."

They bid de Guingand goodbye and drove back to Cairo. Stirling was still angry as hell, but he knew he had no other choice but to make the best of the situation. He would have Paddy round up all the experienced men, put them in a squadron, and have them leave immediately for Kufra to set up their base on the edge of the Great Sand Sea. From there, they could carry out as many raids as possible against the Matruh railway line and the coast road. Meanwhile, he would finish the recruiting and get the training at Kabrit moving as swiftly as possible. Perhaps by the end of November the new men would be trained sufficiently to go into the field.

He could only hope they would be ready. Otherwise, he might be looking at another bloody fiasco like Operation Bigamy.

ψψψ

A few days after his contentious meeting with Stirling, Montgomery attended a dinner party, where he let his true feelings be known regarding the young Turk the Nazi propaganda artist Goebbels and the British newspapers were calling the

"Phantom Major." Stirling did not know it—and the irascible Monty was careful to conceal it—but the twenty-six-year-old lieutenant colonel had made a distinctive impression upon him. The new commander of the Eighth Army was bereft of social grace and stubborn as an ox, but he was also a clever military strategist, a solid judge of character, and a master of mechanized warfare who knew a promising young officer with a plan when he saw one. At the dinner party, Montgomery said something to Colonel Hackett and several other officers that, although patronizing, Stirling would have found surprising and that bode well for his growing desert regiment.

"The Boy Stirling is mad—quite, quite mad," exclaimed the general. "However, in war there is often a place for mad people. Now take this scheme of his. Penetrating miles behind the enemy lines. Attacking the coast road on a four-hundred-mile front. Who but the Boy Stirling could think up such a bloody plan? Yet if it comes off, I don't mind saying it could have a truly decisive effect on my forthcoming offensive."

Shortly after the dinner party, a delighted Hackett notified Stirling of what the new commander of the Eighth Army had said. "Army Commander feels your activities could have decisive effect on course of battle!"

To which Stirling—not one to be bullied or impressed by generals—gave his usual pithy reply: "Congratulate Army Commander on perspicacity."

PART 5

ALAMEIN

CHAPTER 59

EL ALAMEIN LINE, NORTHWEST EGYPT, AND SEMMERING, AUSTRIAN ALPS

OCTOBER 23-25, 1942

LATE IN THE EVENING of October 23, more than 900 artillery pieces of General Bernard Law Montgomery's British Eighth Army opened fire on the German line at El Alamein to launch Operation Lightfoot. The massive barrage of exploding shells, fired from everything from 25-pounder guns to massive 5.5-inch howitzers, was the most intense of the war so far, measured by volume of high explosives and rate of delivery. The Germans and Italians on the receiving end on the ground who were only deafened for life or suffered bleeding eardrums were the fortunate ones. The most vulnerable targets—including the 62nd Italian Infantry Regiment assaulted first—were vaporized in a matter of seconds.

The opening barrage, supported by Allied Air Force bombers, lasted a full twenty minutes and threw up great clouds of smoke and dust that hung thickly over the pill boxes, machine-gun nests, and minefields. A carefully calculated fire plan brought the rounds of all 900-plus guns onto the entire 40-mile front at the same moment. In the eerie silence that followed, specially trained infantry units climbed from their forward trenches and moved forward to clear paths through Axis minefields that had been nicknamed "the Devil's Garden." They carefully probed their way forward with man-portable mine detectors used in combat for the first time. Behind the minesweepers came four infantry divisions: their mission was to establish a bridgehead on the far side of the 5-mile deep minefields, through which more than 500 British tanks would rush in order to attack the Axis armored units from the rear.

Montgomery had withheld from making his offensive move until he had mustered overwhelming numerical superiority and was satisfied that his logistical base was properly organized. Unlike Rommel, the concepts of leading his men from the front, improvisation, and exploiting unexpected opportunities were alien to him. But what he did have was a massive superiority in manpower and especially war matériel—much of it as the direct results of Bonner Fellers's pessimistic but accurate appraisal of the British Eighth Army, which had spurred FDR to divert huge amounts of weapons and aircraft intended for U.S. troops and deliver them to Monty at El Alamein. Not only did the British general have 195,500 men under his command compared with the enemy's 104,000—he had 300 brand-new American Sherman tanks that were superior to Rommel's best armor, the Panzer IV, 246 American Grants, and 421 British Crusaders, bringing his total to 952. Meanwhile, Rommel had only 230 German tanks and 320 Italian, the latter of which were totally inadequate in armor and gunpowder.

Monty was confident the Eighth Army would win because even if its losses were greater than those of Rommel's *Panzerarmee*, it could afford them and the Germans could not. To the bristly yet brilliant commander who had injected a new *esprit de corps* into the Eighth Army, Operation Lightfoot was to be a battle of attrition. He had told war correspondents bluntly that it would be a "killing match" and that the Germans and Italians would undergo a "crumbling." The British armored attack would not be pressed until Eighth Army had methodically "crumbled" the enemy and Rommel was too weak to prevent a breakthrough.

The breakout from the stalemate at El Alamein took place one day before General Patton and his American force departed from the U.S. for what in two weeks' time would be the amphibious Allied landing in Morocco and Tunisia as part of Operation Torch. So far the war had provided only a series of British defeats, and the Empire was falling apart. Like Bonner Fellers who had been given unlimited access to witness the Eighth Army up close and personal as an observer, the British people were losing faith in their generals and in their army's ability to win anything at all, let alone a scrap of barren desert. Churchill had long shared their doubts, and with good reason: he had come dangerously close to losing support in the House of Commons and his government was under extreme scrutiny. The need was not just for a victory but for a resounding British victory. Churchill had been pressing hard for Rommel to be defeated in September and when Monty said he was not yet ready, Churchill had insisted on October.

Only then could the British Bulldog and his generals have their purely British victory before the Torch landings in November.

Torch was predominantly an American affair. Churchill and the War Office recognized that after Torch, America would quickly become the senior partner in the alliance. The defeat of Rommel at any time after Torch would be seen as the U.S. Army saving the British and that was unacceptable to Churchill and his commanders. The British needed to defeat Rommel before Torch. A successful offensive at El Alamein would accomplish that objective, but in case Monty somehow failed to deliver, the Torch landings two weeks later would force Rommel to fall back anyway and Cairo and the Suez Canal would not be lost. Operation Lightfoot preceded Torch because the British had to be seen to have defeated Rommel on their own account before the first American troops set foot in North Africa. Churchill and Montgomery were prepared to pay for the victory in the lives of British and Commonwealth soldiers as well as tanks, most of which were American and would simply be replaced with more American tanks.

There was an American corollary to this. Churchill may have needed a British victory to save his political career, but President Roosevelt knew that the American public had lost faith in Great Britain's ability to fight and win the war, and that they feared American troops would be forced to carry the load, which translated into fewer votes for his fellow Democrats in November. Therefore, FDR needed a British victory in the worst way too.

By the end of the battle's first day, the Germans and even some of the Italians had put up fierce resistance and the British attack seemed to have stalled. But both sides knew better. In raw numbers alone, the Eighth Army possessed a two-to-one superiority over *Panzerarmee Afrika*. When comparing British numbers to German, the situation was even more disparate: in manpower the British outnumbered the Germans six-to-one, in tanks by better than five-to-one. Montgomery literally had men and matériel to burn if necessary to achieve success. During the second day of the offensive on October 24, Montgomery's "crumbling" operations continued like blows from a sledgehammer. He never let up, constantly sending in new infantry formations, supported by tanks, airplanes, and artillery. The main assault that day was an infantry attack, supported by over 100 American Grant and Sherman tanks from the 1st Armored Division. Since he had been denied the quick victory he had hoped for in the original plan, the British commander decided to wear down the Panzer Army with unrelenting pressure. By the end of the day, the rout was on and it looked like his sermon to his troops calling on "the Lord mighty in battle" to give the British victory was not merely a hopeful prayer but a fait accompli.

By the evening of October 24, Rommel's Chief of Staff Colonel Westphal had seen enough and signaled Berlin that the long-expected British offensive had come and that if the *Panzerarmee* was to survive, it would need a miracle.

In short, it needed Rommel.

There was just one problem: he was recovering from his ill health in the Austrian Alps some 1,400 miles from the front at El Alamein.

ΨΨΨ

Rommel kissed his wife Lucie on the lips. They were soft and warm and for a blissful moment he felt like a schoolboy again. He was a not a sentimental man—in fact, he was far from it—but the past three weeks of mountain air, fresh food, rest and, most importantly, his lovely wife's presence at their villa at Semmering, he felt young and vigorously alive.

He had even coined a name for their intimate time together, spent with their beloved teenage son Manfred. He called them "our wonderful weeks."

His health had improved dramatically. He had not healed completely from the liver infection, ulcer, low blood pressure, and desert sores that had plagued him and worried his doctors throughout the past several months, but he was feeling much better. He and Lucie had made love last night and retired early, as was their habit at Semmering, and they had gone for an invigorating alpine hike holding hands with Manfred this morning by the lake.

After a year and a half of virtually non-stop warfare in the desert, he felt rejuvenated. His love for his wife and son had never been stronger, and he felt lucky to have them.

Prior to his recuperation in Austria, Rommel had left a quiet battle front at El Alamein and handed over command of his *Panzerarmee* to General Stumme on the morning of July 23. Then he flew to Rome. In the Eternal City, he held tempestuous meetings with Mussolini and the *Comando Supremo*, making it clear that he would need far greater supplies to sustain his army if he was to defeat Montgomery. From there, he flew to Berlin, where on September 30 he was the guest of honor at a formal reception and Hitler presented him with his *Feldmarschall's* baton. Later, in a conference with the Führer, he candidly informed him that he had to have a minimum of 35,000 tons of supplies a month—anything less and it would be impossible to halt the British offensive that he and Hitler both knew was coming. But *der Führer* wasn't listening. He bluntly informed the Desert Fox that when the *Afrika Korps* once again took the offensive—he made lavish promises of new Tiger tanks, *Nebelwerfer* rockets, tank destroyers, and the like—Rommel would sweep the British out of Egypt and deliver the Suez Canal into German hands.

Rommel was shaken. For the first time, he realized that these men in Berlin, who were responsible for directing a war in which Germany was fighting for survival, were disturbingly out of touch with the reality in North Africa. He found Göring even more foolish than Hitler. When he informed him that British fighter-bombers were wiping out his tanks with 40-mm shells provided by the Americans, the corpulent *Reichsmarschall* ludicrously countered: "That's completely impossible. The Americans only know how to make razor blades."

To which Rommel replied, "We could do with some of those razor blades, *Herr Reichsmarschall*."

When Göring continued to demur, Rommel produced one of the spent American-made 40-mm shells and laid it in front of the *Reichsmarschall*, who promptly fell silent. In that moment, the Desert Fox couldn't help but wonder if he was not fighting for a band of nincompoops—and it started with the bristly-mustached leader at the top who slept in until noon every day.

Unsettled by the events in Berlin, he hurried down to his villa in Semmering to be with his wife and son. Though taking his cure with his family under the watchful eye of Professor Horster, he couldn't help but fret about the situation in North Africa. He had arranged with General Stumme when he went on sick leave that in the event of a British offensive he would return to Africa and resume command. After all, he could hardly leave his troops to face Montgomery without him.

The telephone rang and was quickly brought to him. He looked at Lucie as he put it to his ear; she looked worried.

It was Field Marshall Wilhelm Keitel, chief of staff of the German Armed Forces High Command. He quickly informed Rommel that the British offensive at El Alamein had begun last night. The situation, Keitel said, was uncertain, but General Stumme was missing. Was Rommel prepared to return to North Africa if needed? The Führer preferred him not to cut short his convalescence, for he wanted his newest field marshal rested and in top form, but he did want him to be ready if the situation became critical. Rommel assured Keitel that he was ready to return to action, then waited anxiously with his wife at Wiener-Neustadt airport until midnight, when he took a personal call from Hitler. The Führer informed him that the fighting had escalated and asked if he would be willing to fly back to Egypt as soon as possible. He swiftly agreed.

"I hate to see you go," said Lucie when he told her the news.

There were tears in her eyes and the sight of them made him feel all muddled inside and yearning. "I know you do, and the last thing I want to do is leave you right now," he said, taking her in his arms. "But my men need me. They have laid down their lives for me and gone far beyond the call of duty on so many occasions. I cannot let them down."

"Yes, but I dread the thought that something might happen to you."

Suddenly, she lurched forward and kissed him on the lips. He felt a warm feeling envelope him, but also a crushing sadness. She leaned in close to him, willingly and desperately. After a moment, they pulled apart.

"I love you Lucie. I love you with all my heart," he said.

"I love you too," she said. "And that love will burn as brightly as a winter hearth forever. Forever."

In that vulnerable yet uplifting moment, he almost—*almost*—felt tears come to his own eyes. "Whatever happens, don't ever forget that I cherish you. I could not lead my men into battle without knowing that, when the guns have stopped and the smoke has cleared, I will once again be in your loving arms. I promise I shall return."

They kissed again. Then she gently pulled away and he carefully brushed away her tears with a gloved hand. He could feel the power of her emotions.

"Manfred is a good boy," he said. "And the goodness in his heart is because of you."

"And you," she said. "Our son adores you."

"He will make a fine man someday. It is my earnest hope that he becomes a great sportsman, hero, and mathematician."

"I know you have high hopes for him."

"Yes, I do." He took her in his arms again and squeezed her tight. "I won't let you, Manfred, or Germany down. And I promise I will live through this war."

"Good, that is what I want hear, my love," she said.

He gently wiped away another tear. "Please, I don't want you to cry."

"It's just that I don't want you to die," she said. "I couldn't bear it."

"Hush now, I'm not going to die. I'm going to make it. We…we're going to make it through this war. You, me, and Manfred. We're going to survive, and when it's all over, we're going to live a wonderful life together." He didn't mention his illegitimate daughter Trudel, but he was thinking of her as well.

"Yes, we will be together," she said. "But quite honestly, I just want it all to end. Too many have perished on both sides."

"Yes, far too many have died," he agreed. He kissed her goodbye one last time and without further delay boarded the awaiting plane for Rome. Here he discovered that, as he had feared, the *Comando Supremo* had made good on none of Mussolini's promises of adequate supply for the Axis troops in North Africa. He couldn't believe it: before he had even taken the field against Montgomery, his situation was desperate. He flew from Rome to Benghazi, knowing that he would fight the Second Battle of El Alamein with little hope of success. There were clearly no more laurels to be won in North Africa.

It was late in the day when Rommel arrived back at the front on October 25, but immediately upon arriving he had a signal sent out to every unit, hoping to shore up morale: "I have taken command of the army again—Rommel." All around his *Kampfstaffel*, heavy guns rumbled and cracked. Some of his own batteries were close. There was a constant ripple of flashes along the eastern horizon and the massive generators for the signals trucks hummed in their own mechanically reassuring way. Lucie, Manfred, and the crystalline lakes and pine-scented alpine forests of Semmering seemed a world away.

General von Thoma, who had taken temporary charge of the *Panzerarmee* when Spume's body was found dead, and Rommel's staff officers briefed him on the situation beneath an awning attached to Moritz. It turned out the battle was an even more desperate struggle than he had imagined. There was less than three days' supply of petrol for his entire *Panzerarmee*. The infantry units were beginning to take appalling casualties as the British attacks continued, and while the Panzers had begun local counterattacks the previous day, the fuel crisis prevented any large-scale riposte against Montgomery's armor. Making the situation worse, the RAF was operating with near-impunity over the rear areas of his army, specifically targeting German and Italian airfields, often dropping more than 100 tons of bombs in a single raid. The only positive was that Montgomery, like his predecessors Ritchie and Auchinleck, was naturally cautious unless he had overwhelming superiority at a specific point in the line, which Rommel knew meant that a concentrated attack or counter-attack could be successful. He realized that he had a remarkable tactical opportunity, one that had the potential to turn the entire battle in his favor despite Eighth Army's numerical superiority, but there simply wasn't sufficient petrol to make it a reality.

The briefing ended and he was alone with his staff. By temperament, he was not someone who fell prey to despair, but he began to feel something akin to it. The situation that now confronted him was every commanding general's worst nightmare: an operational and strategic situation so perilous that his only real option was to pick the least disastrous solution.

His officers were looking at him. "What are we going to do, Field Marshal?" asked Westphal.

He didn't answer at first. But then, after a moment of staring off at the shells exploding in the distance, he said, "Sometimes it is a disadvantage to have a military reputation. One is aware of one's limits, but others go on expecting miracles and put defeat down to deliberate obstinacy."

"Are you saying the situation is hopeless?"

"No, it is not hopeless but it is a tall order we face. The one thing we have going for us is the British have failed fully to exploit their surprise, the death of General Stumme, or the disruption of our communications from the initial bombardment. It's true they have severely dented the northern part of our defenses, but nowhere have they succeeded in driving a hole through it."

Westphal nodded. "Most of the British armor is still stuck behind the infantry. The few regiments which have managed to get a few tanks through…well, we have been able to pick them off as soon as they emerge from the gaps in the minefields."

"Once again, it seems the British have devised a way to squander numerical superiority in armor by serving it up in easily digestible pieces. But Montgomery is different than those that came before him. He is a hard, ruthless man, and he has shown some clever new tactics."

"But we can defeat him, can't we?"

His face was buried in the map. "I honestly don't know. But whatever we do, we will make that Englishman and his army pay a heavy price. A very heavy price."

CHAPTER 60

MONTGOMERY'S TACTICAL HQ
BURGH EL ARAB, WEST OF ALAMEIN LINE
NORTHWEST EGYPT

NOVEMBER 3, 1942

AS STIRLING headed towards the HQ trailer with Colonel Shan Hackett, he saw Montgomery talking with his senior officers. Stirling had met with the prickly commander on two occasions since his first disastrous meeting in late September, and the two now got along well enough. It seemed he had underestimated the tenacious general who was at this moment taking it to the Desert Fox. Monty wore a gray pullover and black tank beret—complete with his own rank badge and the badge of the Royal Tank regiment—that Stirling had not seen him dressed in before. The sound of exploding shells could be heard in the distance, like a roll of distant thunder.

Except for a week in a hospital bed in Cairo for treatment of his desert sores, Stirling had spent most of the past six weeks at the SAS training camp in Kabrit organizing the new men under his command. He was disappointed that his regiment had not been able to play a more important role in the ongoing Battle of Alamein that had captivated the attention of the entire world the past twelve days. However, Montgomery's refusal to allow him to recruit desert-trained soldiers left him no option but to take on green troops and try to whip them into shape as quickly as possible. Kabrit, which for weeks at a time had been deserted and forlorn, bristled with activity. Once again men were being put through gruelling night tests, marching thirty miles on a bottle of water, jumping from moving platforms, and experimenting with the latest explosives.

But the setback with Monty had not deterred him, and in fact since their inauspicious beginning he had won over not only the prickly new commander but scored victories with other higher-ups that were further augmenting the SAS. Churchill's enthusiasm for the regiment had been communicated to General Alexander and was especially bearing fruit. Aside from the recruits Stirling had gathered himself, and the French Squadron which had served with him for the past year, he was given command of the Special Boat Section, the remnants of the Middle East Commando, and a group of Greek volunteers known as the Greek Sacred Squadron. The total strength at his disposal was now over eight hundred men. And this was not all. His brother Bill had been given permission to raise a second SAS regiment which would leave shortly for North Africa and be brought up to full strength. When he confided this news to one of his fellow officers, the latter replied, "At last I know what 'SAS' stands for—Stirling and Stirling!'"

Freddie de Guingand, Montgomery's chief of staff, broke away from the general and the other officers and came walking up to them. "We're making the final push against Rommel—your meeting with Monty is going to have to wait for a few minutes," he said. "Here, let's take a look from the hill, shall we?" He pointed to the little rocky knob behind the trailer.

"You look terrible, Freddie," said Stirling.

"I know. I think I'm about to have a nervous breakdown. Monty's been driving me ragged with this offensive."

"Well, please don't have a breakdown until after we've talked with him, all right? It's important to get your priorities straight, old boy."

"Very funny, David."

They quickly climbed the little hill. Once at the top, they looked to the west at the battlefield through their binoculars. Smoke and dust covered large portions of the desert plateau and coastal plain, but through the gaps Stirling could make out British armor attacking the German positions. Swarms of British light bombers were blasting away at German 88-mm anti-tank and antiaircraft guns. He saw little mushroom clouds all along the ragged front line, which appeared to have been broken in at least two places. Even from his distant vantage point, it appeared that Monty truly had the vaunted Desert Fox on the run. After a year and a half of mostly crushing defeats at the hands of the wily German field marshal, it was almost impossible to believe.

"My God, Rommel's line is breaking up before our eyes," he said, giving voice to his thoughts. "To be honest, I wasn't sure if we'd ever see this day."

"Yes well, you can see it with your own eyes now," said de Guingand. "These past two days we've been delivering the coup de grâce: Operation Supercharge."

"Supercharge. Who came up with that one?"

"Monty did, but I have to give myself a bit of credit. I was talking to Generals McCreery and Richardson and we decided that it would be best to abandon the attack in the north and make it further south, where the line was defended by Rommel's weaker Italian divisions. A breakthrough there would enable us to swing north behind the Panzers. But when I went to tell this to Monty, he said, 'No, I won't have it.' Dick McCreery wanted to challenge Monty about it, but I knew that would never work so I told him what I would do. I said, 'Look I will go and talk to Monty about it again—but don't you, for goodness' sake, because if you do he won't do it. But if one can persuade him it's his own idea, so to speak, then I'm sure it's the right thing to do.'"

Stirling looked at Hackett; they were both amused. "So what happened?"

"I went back and had another go, and Monty did accept it. And then, the next morning he said to me that he was pleased that he had changed his plan and had decided to attack further to the south."

They all laughed. *That's typical Montgomery,* thought Stirling. *Stubbornly refusing a sound plan and then adopting it as his own!*

"You know you can never breathe a word of what I just told you to anyone, or I'll never let you within spitting distance of Monty again. Do I have your word, gentlemen?"

"Come on, Freddie, lighten up," said Hackett. "We won't tell anyone."

"Bible and sword, my lips are sealed," said Stirling. "So what are your losses so far?" he then asked, changing the subject, as a squadron of bombers roared overhead. He felt his hair stand on end as they screamed towards the cloud of smoke and dust hovering above the German lines like a dense bank of fog.

"We've lost over ten thousand so far," admitted de Guingand. "But the Jerries have lost at least twice that number. Our artillery and air attacks are turning them to mincemeat."

"What about tanks?"

"We've lost at least three hundred, Rommel around two hundred. But he can't replace them and we can. We still have more than six hundred tanks operational to his two hundred or so, many of which are the useless Italian tanks. We know from our intelligence sources that Rommel's on the ropes. The Italian navy has been unable to deliver enough supplies and reinforcements for him to hold the line. On October 26, we sunk the ammunition ship *Tergestea* and the tanker *Proserpina*. Two days later it was the tanker *Luisiana* and freighter *Tripolino*. Three Italian destroyers managed to sneak through the gauntlet into Tobruk harbor, but they are believed to have been carrying less than two hundred tons of supplies. Rommel can't hold out much longer. We've torn a two-mile-wide hole in his front line. But we've got to keep pushing because he hasn't surrendered or withdrawn from the field yet—and our time is running out."

Stirling looked at him. "What do you mean your time is running out? You mean because the Americans are coming."

"We shouldn't be talking about such things. It could get officers into trouble."

"Oh, stop this nonsense, Freddie," said Hackett. "Everyone knows the bloody Yanks are scheduled to arrive somewhere on the West or North African coast any day now. Why you act as if GHQ is the Secret Service when its as gossipy as a roomful of schoolboys. Good heavens, do you think we're stupid, old boy?"

De Guingand looked around, as if they were conspirators, and spoke in a low voice. "All right, I suppose there's no harm in telling you. Churchill wants the battle wrapped up before Operation Torch, the Anglo-American landings in Vichy-controlled North Africa scheduled for November 8."

"November 8?" exclaimed Stirling. "But that's only five days from now."

"Precisely, and with the Germans and Italians tied up here, there's no chance that they can muster any resistance to the landing. That's why Monty's been pushing so hard with Supercharge. We need a resounding British victory before the landings—otherwise, it will look as though the bloody Yanks are bailing us out."

"They have been bailing us out," pointed out Stirling, staring out at the battlefield littered with smoldering tanks and half-tracks. "Where do you think we've been getting our heavy-duty jeeps and a large number of our tanks, planes, and artillery pieces—China?"

"Yes, I can see your point, David. But someone has to drive those bloody tanks, fire those shells, and fly those planes, now don't they?"

They chuckled and paused to look out over the battlefield again. British artillery guns opened up as another squadron of RAF fighter-bombers screamed overhead and dropped hundreds of bombs. Stirling saw the little blossoms of fire and smoke as the enemy tanks burst into flames in the open desert. From a distance, it seemed almost poetic.

"We've heard that Churchill is putting a lot of pressure on your general," said Hackett.

"Monty's always known that Eighth Army would win the numbers game with the *Panzerarmee*. In a battle of attrition, time favors the stronger side and that's what Operation Lightfoot has been all about. Monty's been calling it a gradual 'crumbling.' But Winston has been most insistent and that's why we've had to step on the gas pedal with Supercharge. The prime minister is an impatient man, I must say. Oh wait, it looks like they're is ready for us." He pointed down to the trailer, where one of Montgomery's aides was waving up at them. "Let's go, chaps."

They dashed down the hill and into the trailer, where they found Montgomery standing over a huge map of North Africa on a table. Wearing his black beret, long-sleeved pullover that clung to his scrawny frame, and no insignia of rank, he looked more like a commando than a general. Stirling had learned more about the man since their first visit and had discovered that he had endured more than his fair share of tragedy, which at least partially explained his naturally fussy, insecure, and combative disposition. Growing up in Tasmania and later England, Montgomery's father Henry was a bishop who spent a great deal of time away from the family and his mother a cold disciplinarian who gave young Bernard and his siblings "constant" beatings, then ignored them most of the time as she performed the public duties of a bishop's wife. Maud Montgomery apparently had taken little active interest in the education of her children other than to have them taught by tutors brought from Britain. Stirling had discovered that despite his painful childhood, Montgomery's marriage to his wife Betty had been an extremely happy one—until tragedy struck. Three years before the war, while on holiday in Burnham-on-Sea, she suffered an insect bite which became infected, and she died in her husband's arms from septicaemia following amputation of her leg. The loss devastated Montgomery, who was then serving as a brigadier. But he insisted on throwing himself back into his work immediately after the funeral. After his wife's passing, his only familial connection was to his beloved son David, who he frequently wrote from the Alamein front. Because of the loveless environment he had endured growing up with a distant father and abusive mother, he refused to allow his fourteen-year-old son to have anything to do with his mother.

Montgomery stepped forward to greet them. "Good day, Colonel Stirling and Colonel Hackett," he said in a peppy voice. "I'm glad that Freddie was able to show you around. As I wrote my son, David, last night, I am enjoying this great battle against Rommel very much. In fact, I must say that thus far it has been a terrific party, a real solid and bloody killing match. Now, gentlemen, due to ongoing operations, I'm afraid I only have a few minutes to spare, so you'd better get on with it. What are your plans, Stirling, once I have hammered the final nail in Rommel's coffin and he is forced to withdraw into Libya, or perhaps even into Tunisia?"

Though once again taken aback by the stringy game-rooster of a man and his high-pitched nasally voice, Stirling was more prepared for this, his fourth visit with the Eighth Army commander, than his previous meetings. "Yes, General, sir," he began deferentially, "my plan is to provide support to your next offensive. Whether that takes place in Libya or Tunisia, I will send a force of about two hundred men, equipped with jeeps and trucks behind the enemy lines. These men will be divided into sixteen subsections. They will spread along a two-hundred-mile or more stretch of the coast road, depending on whether or not Rommel turns to make a stand and digs in or not. Each subsection will attack and mine the road every three days, which would mean four or five raids each night."

Montgomery nodded. "And your plan is to coordinate this with my new offensive?"

"Yes, sir. We would begin our attacks at the same time you launch offensive operations. Our goal will be to create sufficient havoc to prevent Rommel from using the coast road at night. Since this highway is the only road suitable for heavy lorries and armor, it ought to make his supply problems so intolerable that he will be forced to use the road by day. This will, in turn, allow the Royal Air Force to take a heavy toll on his retreating columns."

"I must say it sounds like a sound concept, Stirling. Prepare your plan and submit it to Colonel Hackett here. Shan's co-ordinating all raiding forces in the Middle East and if it meets his approval, it is likely that it will meet mine as well."

"Very good, General, and may I say what a splendid job you've done in winning this battle at Alamein."

"The battle is not won yet, Colonel Stirling. The enemy is breaking up but certainly not routed. The reports I just received indicate that Rommel is disengaging some of his infantry. His troops still hold the line across a broad front but his rearguard is expected to fall back next. I have just ordered more planes to bomb the retreating columns as they march."

At that moment, the distant sound of explosions shook the trailer.

"That's the enemy blowing up their ammunition dumps," said Monty with a gleam in his eye. "They are getting desperate. I have driven two armored wedges into Rommel and am in the process of passing three armored divisions through those places. These elements will soon be operating in the enemy's rear. Those portions of the enemy's armor that can get away are in full retreat. Those portions that are still facing our troops will be put in the bag soon enough. After very hard fighting, the Eighth Army and the Allied air forces will soon gain a complete victory. But we must not think that the party is over. We must keep up the pressure. We intend to hit this chap for six out of North Africa. And you can help me do that, Colonel Stirling."

"Yes, sir, me and my men will be pleased to join the party."

"Good, Stirling, that's what I like to hear. Now here's a copy of my Special Order of the Day for you and Colonel Hackett. I want you to have a copy to memorialize this magnificent day."

He reached onto the table, grabbed a sheet of paper, and handed it to Stirling. In that moment, Stirling realized that he was standing before a truly great military commander. Even with his superiority in troops and tanks compared to Rommel and supreme control of the skies by the RAF, he had to be given immense credit for turning around the fortunes of Eighth Army. Bragging, bluster, and theatrics of any sort by a commanding officer, particularly a new commanding officer, were usually greeted with a skeptical eye at best, derision at worst. Yet the self-aggrandizing and publicity-conscious Monty had succeeded where Auchinleck and the others before him—with the lone exception of General O'Connor who had driven the Italians out of Egypt—had not. He had molded an army low on morale and stung by defeat into a potent force that stood poised to defeat its foe in less than two months after he took over command. The men of the Eighth Army knew who had brought them to this redoubtable point where they were about to turn the tables on the Axis forces and drive them out of North Africa once and for all: his name was Monty.

Though the Tommies, South Africans, Australians, New Zealanders, and Indians would never fight for Monty the way that Rommel's "Africans" fought for him, now that they had tasted victory they would not lag far behind in the months to come, Stirling felt certain. Understandably, the British people were hungry for victories and victors to celebrate, and Churchill, Brooke, and Alexander would go to great lengths to show off how bold and wise they had been to select the underweight fighting bantam cock nicknamed "Monty" to command Eighth Army, thus ensuring that the seeds of his "legend" would fall on fertile ground. But it could not be denied that the man who was in the process of becoming "the victor of Alamein" had turned the situation around in North Africa and built up a formidable army that now knew how to win. From first-hand experience, Stirling knew that was worth a great deal. Indeed, he was eager that the SAS contribute to the winning streak in the months to come.

He and Hackett read over Monty's Special Order of the Day:

The present battle has now lasted twelve clays, during which the troops have fought so magnificently that the enemy is being worn down. He has reached the breaking point, and is trying to get his army away. The RAF is taking a heavy toll of his columns moving west on the main coast road. We have the chance of putting the whole Panzer Army in the bag, and we will do so.

When they finished reading the note and looked up, the general said, "That's it then. I bid you farewell, gentlemen. I must now set about regrouping the army in preparation for getting my armor through the minefields and into the enemy's rear."

"Good luck, sir," said Stirling, and he and Hackett gave crisp salutes.

Monty returned the salute and smiled thinly. "I don't believe in luck, Colonel Stirling. I believe in preparation—and the master plan must be written by the master himself. Now good day to you."

As Stirling headed to his jeep with Hackett, he couldn't help but smile. *Now we finally have a worthy field commander—it's about bloody time!*

CHAPTER 61

ROMMEL *KAMPFSTAFFEL*
DISINTEGRATING EL ALAMEIN LINE, NORTHWEST EGYPT

NOVEMBER 3-5, 1942

WHEN ROMMEL STEPPED DOWN from Moritz onto the desert hardpan and marched into his HQ tent, he saw immediately that something was wrong.

"An order from the Führer," said Westphal with a look of disgust on his face.

He could see that his chief of operations was deeply agitated. *My God, what could it be?* He took the message from him and read it over.

November 3, 1942
TO FIELD MARSHAL ROMMEL
It is with trusting confidence in your leadership and the courage of the German-Italian troops under your command that the German people and I are following the heroic struggle in Egypt. In the situation which you find yourself there can be no other thought but to stand fast, yield not a yard of ground and throw every gun and every man into the battle. Considerable air force reinforcements are being sent to Commander-in-Chief South. The Duce and the Comando Supremo are also making the utmost efforts to send you the means to continue the fight. Your enemy, despite his superiority, must also be at the end of his strength. It would not be the first time in history that a strong will has triumphed over the bigger battalions. As to your troops, you can show them no other road than that to victory or death.
ADOLF HITLER

When he was finished, he slumped into a chair and stared out the open flap of the tent. The sound of American 105-mm self-propelled Priest guns and drone of British Wellington and Albacore bombers rumbled in the distance. He was flabbergasted. For one of the rare times in his life, he had no idea what to do.

"We can't obey the order," said Westphal emphatically. "You know that, sir."

At first, he was unable to speak. But after a few seconds of intense thought, he gave his response. "I know I will probably regret this decision for the rest of my life, but I feel I have no choice but to obey. But first let me talk to General von Thoma."

He telephoned him and read Hitler's order to him over the phone. Then they talked for a long time. They tried to think of some way around the orders, but were unable to come up with anything since the words were unambiguous. Rommel did, however, hold firm that the order still allowed the *Afrika Korps* to maneuver. But they would still have to fight for every inch of ground and would not be able to put up a mobile defense. The troops would have to hold fast at their current positions until they had expended their ammunition. He then concluded by telling von Thoma that he was sorry, but this was the best that could be done for the time being.

When he hung up, Westphal was looking at him. "So that's it then. Even if this means the end of the *Afrika Korps*?"

"I have always insisted upon the unconditional obedience of my men. How can I deviate from this principle and disobey my Führer?"

"But as I said, if you obey that order, it will be the end of the army. Is that all we have fought for—to be wiped out by the stroke of a pen from a distant tyrant?"

"Watch your tongue, Siegfried. That kind of talk is treason."

"No, under the circumstances I would call it quite reasonable. The men are exhausted from twelve days of constant fighting. We have inadequate supplies of food, petrol, and ammunition and are faced by overwhelming enemy numbers on the ground and in the air. Our position here at El Alamein is untenable. If we withdraw now, we can possibly save the Italian infantry. If we stand and fight, then we have to accept the complete destruction of *Panzerarmee Afrika*."

He rubbed his head with his hands; he was as physically exhausted as his poor men. "You think I don't know that, Siegfried?"

"But our Wehrmacht tradition has always been for higher command echelons to accept that the commander on the spot has the best handle on the situation and, therefore, the freedom to make tactical and operational decisions."

"These are different times. I am sorry, but I am a soldier and a soldier must obey his orders. We now have it from the highest authority to defend our present position to the utmost. No one may abandon the field without my specific orders. The orders to withdraw to positions in the rear are hereby cancelled. Halt the retreat, command the army to fight to the last shot, and distribute hand grenades and machine guns to all members of the staff. I am sorry, General, but there is no way out of this."

Westphal's lip quivered ever so slightly. "Yes, *Herr Feldmarschall*."

Rommel rose wearily from his chair, went outside, climbed into Moritz, and pointed his binoculars towards the battle front. The stutter of machine guns echoed some distance away, and further to the north he saw artillery shells detonating in white puffs that reminded him of blooming white chrysanthemums. He knew this was a watershed moment: the magic that had thus far kept him spellbound by Hitler was no more. He had seen a hint of what was to come when he had visited the Führer in Berlin in late September, and now a line had been crossed and there was no going back. The unspoken bond between a soldier and his commander, he knew, was never that the commander will not ask the soldier to stand and die, but that he will never ask him to do so without serious justification; yet that was precisely what Hitler was immorally demanding of him and his men. The Führer was obliged to the officers and enlisted men of *Panzerarmee Afrika* to explain why he was insisting upon such a fate, if only to encourage them to sell their lives more dearly. But now Rommel knew moral obligation ran in only one direction for Hitler.

After fifteen minutes, he returned to the HQ tent and wrote a letter to his wife. It was short, fatalistic, and bitter.

November 3, 1942
Dearest Lu,
The battle still rages with unspent fury. I can no longer, or scarcely any longer, believe in its successful outcome. Berndt flies to the Führer today to report.
Enclosed 25,000 lire that I've saved.
What will become of us is in God's hands.

Hours later, he was still wrestling with his conscience regarding Hitler's "victory or death" missive as he paced back and forth outside his command tent with Major Elmar Warning, an officer on Westphal's staff. On the one hand, he was torn by his customary instinct to obey the orders of a superior; on the other, he was furious at the implications of Hitler's ill-advised directive. He had pledged obedience to the Führer, and he demanded the same from his own subordinates, so it seemed hypocritical to suddenly exempt himself from the same standard of conduct. And yet the order was not justifiable.

"What do you think? Should I disobey it?" he asked the tall, bald staff officer.

Warning looked at him thoughtfully and started to reply, but was cut off by the Desert Fox, who suddenly dismissed all doubt and made his decision.

"If we stay put here, then the army won't last three days. But do I have the right, as the commanding officer, or even as a soldier, to disobey an order? If I do obey the Führer's order, then there's the danger my own troops won't obey me!" He paused then blurted out, "My men's lives come first! The Führer is crazy!"

Warning nodded but said nothing. Ignited with passion, Rommel went on: "Warning, believe me, Hitler is the greatest criminal whom I know. He will fight not only to the last German soldier, but to the total destruction of Germany—in his own selfish interests!"

His mind made up, he stomped back into the command tent and issued new orders that were deliberately ambiguous. The 90th Light Division, along with the Pavia, Folgore, Trento, and Bologna Divisions, were ordered to stand fast, dig in, and resist the British armored advance for as long as possible, thus ostensibly satisfying Hitler's demand to "yield not a yard of ground." At the same time, he ordered the remaining German and Italian units to continue to fall back. Even then, he felt an overwhelming bitterness as he realized that, despite having scaled back his orders, many of his men would still die unnecessarily and even a supreme effort on their part could no longer change the outcome of the battle.

Uncertain as to whether he would survive the next twenty-four hours, he wrote a letter to Trudel just before going to sleep in Moritz.

Dearest Trudie:
The battle is coming to an end and I'm sorry to say it is not to our own profit. The enemy's strength is too strong and they are overwhelming us. It is in the hands of God whether my soldiers will survive. To you I send my heartfelt greetings and wish you and your family all the best for the future.
Your Uncle Erwin

ΨΨΨ

The next day, November 4, Rommel awoke to find that his military situation was deteriorating even faster than he had anticipated. His rearguard was crumbling and there was no point in pretending that he was making any real effort to comply with Hitler's "victory or death" directive. Late that morning, he sent one final pro forma request for permission to withdraw from El Alamein while at the same time doing his best to speed up the westward movement of the army. Soon after he issued the order, von Thoma appeared at his headquarters to report on the state of the *Afrika Korps*, pronounced Hitler's order madness, and drove back to what was left of his Panzer divisions. Fifteen minutes later, Field Marshal Kesselring appeared. The senior Wehrmacht commander in the Mediterranean and Rommel's direct superior had flown in from Rome. Still enraged by Hitler's order, the Desert Fox laid into him instantly.

"Have you seen this insane order? You do realize that it means certain death for most of my men."

Smiling Albert wasn't smiling. "I am not sure that—"

"It is probably the overly optimistic reports by your Luftwaffe officers—including you yourself—that has misled the Führer about the true situation at Alamein. Well, is that so?"

"No, it is not. My reports have been accurate. I have not exaggerated the difficulties you face."

"Then what is behind this crazy order? Why would Hitler do such a thing if he knows that we have no recourse except to save as much of the army as we can and live to fight another day?"

Kesselring sighed heavily. "Hitler is applying the tactical experience of the Russian Front to North Africa. That's the problem."

"You're saying he has not given any thought to the vast operational differences between the two?"

"Yes, that's exactly what I'm saying."

Rommel grudgingly agreed. "All right, I can see how that might be the case. But he still should have left the decision to me!"

"Look, I can understand your anger and—"

"No, I don't think you do! I am not going to obey this damned order!"

Kesselring looked at him with what appeared to be commiseration. "All right. In that case, perhaps there is a way we can circumvent it."

"Are you telling me that you will support my disobedience of a direct order from our Führer?"

"No, I am saying that perhaps Hitler's order does not have to be interpreted so literally. I am also saying that you, as the commander on the spot, should do what you think is right."

"As it turns out, I already have. But it would be best if you put in a word for me."

"Don't worry, I will."

ΨΨΨ

Smiling Albert was as good as his word. He made a personal telephone call to Hitler and that night the order was rescinded. But by then General von Thoma had been captured and the British 1st and 7th Armored Divisions had broken through the crumbling Italian rearguard. At the moment, the British armor was sweeping wide to the west, intent on turning north at some point to cut the coast road near Fuka and complete the entrapment of Rommel and his army. The Desert Fox realized that, with his front broken and the motorized enemy streaming into his rear, the decision to withdraw was now out of his hands. He swiftly issued orders for a full retreat of all forces.

But all he could do now was save the motorized part of his Panzer Army from destruction. He had already lost so much firepower as a result of the 24-hour postponement of the retreat that it was no longer possible for him to offer effective opposition to the British advance. Any vehicle that did not immediately reach the coast road and race westwards was lost, for the enemy followed his retreating army over a wide front and overran everything that came in its path.

And then, mercifully, on November 5 the early winter rains began and Montgomery became even more cautious in his pursuit. Allowing the Desert Fox to save enough of his *Panzerarmee* to survive and fight another day. But now the battle for North Africa would be fought in Tunisia—with Patton's 107,000-strong Anglo-American force of Operation Torch set to land in three days' time on November 8. And until Rommel received reinforcements and supplies, he had barely 5,000 men, 20 tanks, and 50 guns to face two armies, not one.

After more than three years of war, Second Alamein was the first indisputable victory over a German-led army, some three months before the even more momentous German surrender at Stalingrad. The Eighth Army's total casualties in killed, wounded, or missing were 13,500, or about 8 per cent, while the Germans lost 32,500 men, nearly a third of Rommel's army. However, though Churchill did not realize it yet, it was the last hurrah of the British Empire, as the United States would gradually yet forcefully exert its role as the dominant partner among the Western Allies.

In the meantime, Great Britain had its new hero. By the time Montgomery had taken Tobruk on November 12, he had received a knighthood and been made a full general. Forever after, he would be known as the "1st Viscount Montgomery of Alamein." "We have a new experience," proclaimed Churchill. "We have victory—a remarkable and definite victory!"

On Sunday, November 15, the church bells rang out all over Great Britain for the first time in three years, their peals relayed by the BBC Overseas Service in a special outside broadcast from Coventry Cathedral, where only the spire and bell tower had survived German bombs. "Did you hear them in Occupied Europe?" a proud radio commentator asked. "Did you hear them in Germany?"

The smoke and dust had hardly settled when the Army Film and Photographic Unit began putting together a documentary featuring Montgomery and the British Eighth Army, to be called *Desert Victory*. The film was a counter to the popular 1941 Nazi propaganda film featuring Rommel in the *blitzkrieg* of France and the Low Countries entitled *Victory in the West*. But as Churchill would say, the victory at El Alamein was not the end or even the beginning of the end of the war—but it was the end of the beginning of Nazi Germany's downfall.

CHAPTER 62

SOUTH OF GABÈS GAP, TUNISIA

JANUARY 22-23, 1943

IN THE GATHERING DUSK, Stirling didn't spot the two modified Junkers 88 reconnaissance aircraft on the horizon until it was too late. He immediately led the five camouflaged jeeps comprising his fourteen-man Tunisian attack force for cover. The planes swept in from the south, scouring the rock-strewn ground south of Gabès Gap, a natural bottleneck between the Mediterranean and the vast and impenetrable salt marshes to the west. It was north of the gap that Stirling wanted to join up with the British First Army, commanded by Lieutenant-General Kenneth Anderson, that had marched in from the west following the successful landings of Operation Torch in Morocco and Algeria.

The column had set off at sunrise on January 16 from their base camp at Bir Zelten, Libya, preceded by Captain Jordan and his French SAS unit. During the week-long journey, Stirling and his Arab-headdress-covered raiders had skirted the Great Eastern Sand Sea, stretching out from Algeria into Tunisia, and made a wide sweep south of Tripoli, through some of the most treacherous terrain the SAS had crossed thus far. Where the sands of the Sand Sea had taken the form of gigantic ocean rollers, the rutted desert waves along the Libyan-Tunisian border were short and choppy like a rough Mediterranean sea. As the convoy made its way northwest, often reduced to driving at no more than one mile an hour, word came over the radio that Tripoli had fallen to Montgomery. Later, as the men neared Gabès Gap along the Tunisian coast, the going became ever tougher, with boggy marshes and furrowed dunes alternating with steep, boulder-filled wadis. All traffic heading for the coast had to pass through the bottleneck of the Gap, which was only five miles wide at its narrowest point and crawling with Jerries.

Stirling hoped to link up with Anderson's First Army at its forward position at Gafsa in Northern Tunisia. There was a lot of ground still between the British Eighth and First Armies advancing from opposite directions, and to further the aims of the SAS, he wanted his commando force to be the first Eighth Army unit to make contact with the Torch forces.

To manipulate events to suit his purposes required more than the usual daring, so Stirling worked around two precepts. The first was that Monty had requested assistance west of Tripoli, and the second was that mapping and intelligence in the area of the Mareth Line had thus far been desultory at best. The Mareth Line was the string of fortifications built originally by France in the 1930s to defend Tunisia against Italian attacks from Libya, but which were now being used by Rommel and his *Panzerarmee*. Stirling put himself in a position to solve both problems simultaneously. To pull off the operation, he had decided upon a four-way split of the SAS: the French squadron commanded by Jordan would raid between Gabès and Sfax in Tunisia; Harry Poat would take a group to raid Tripoli in Libya and satisfy Montgomery's request; the third group, under Paddy Mayne, would operate along the Tunisian-Libyan border near the Mareth Line; and Stirling would move into northern Tunisia, conduct a detailed reconnaissance, and link up with the First Army. He knew that, unlike in Egypt and Libya, it would be a true journey into the unknown.

His fourteen-man force consisted of his expert navigator Mike Sadler, Cooper and Seekings, and an important newcomer: a thirty-one-year-old French sergeant, Freddie Taxis, who spoke Arabic. There was a strong likelihood they would encounter hostile local native tribesmen, and Stirling considered an interpreter to be essential for the patrol.

"Do you think they saw us, sir?" asked Cooper after the reconnaissance aircraft had made two passes.

"Unfortunately, yes," replied Stirling. "It's too late for them to attack us but they'll definitely alert the German ground forces in the Gap. Jordan must have bumped into the enemy, or begun his operations on the Gabès sector," he added, referring to the French SAS unit commanded by Captain Jordan that had left twelve hours before them.

"Are we going to hole up here?"

"No, we've got to keep moving. Once we cross the Gabès-Gafsa road, we'll be beyond the Jerry bottleneck and can lie up and get some sleep."

He passed along the command to the navigator, Mike Sadler, and the other vehicles and the convoy took off again. Although no one had taken any rest for forty-eight hours, he knew they had to press ahead and get through the Gap before morning. Unfortunately, the Germans already knew they were coming so they would have to move quickly.

To Stirling's dismay, the drive proved a nightmare of deep ravines and rocky tracks. One of the jeeps went into a bog and took several hours to extricate. However, they didn't encounter any enemy patrols, and by first light on January 23 they had reached the edge of the Gafsa tarmac road. Enemy traffic was running along it. They waited an hour until there was a brief lull before making a dash across the road and passing through the Gap. A mile or so farther on, a German armored division encamped by the roadside was in the process of waking up.

"We're going to bluff it, Johnny," he said. "Just look straight ahead."

As they passed the group of German soldiers drinking coffee in the morning sun, Cooper gave a friendly nod and the five vehicles drove straight on.

"Well done," said Stirling, as if they were taking a stroll through Edinburgh.

"Amazing," said Cooper. "Nobody challenged us and nobody shot at us. In fact, nobody did a bloody thing."

Stirling chuckled. "I think they were still half-asleep."

They drove on. Now they needed to get away from the coast road as quickly as possible, and find somewhere to hide out for the day. Two miles down the road, they stopped briefly to confer. Sadler thought it best to head for the foothills of the Jebel Tebaga, and Stirling agreed. Hopping back in the jeeps, they soon crossed another dirt road that was not marked on their maps, drove another twenty miles northward, and began passing through open country. A little farther on, Stirling spotted a long, narrow wadi dotted with bushes that seemed to offer perfect cover. With the patrol exhausted after more than thirty-six hours without sleep, he decided to hide there for the day. The jeeps were hurriedly camouflaged, and the men settled down to sleep, spreading out in the nooks and corners up and down the gully, many too tired even to remove their boots. It was a cold clear day and the men dropped asleep almost at once.

Before turning in, Cooper and Sadler climbed to the lip of the wadi to survey the road. Through binoculars, they saw a column of German troops halt and climb down from their vehicles. Carefully watching the enemy for a few minutes, they saw several trucks draw up and unload. They realized they must be near some sort of junction and quickly reported the interlopers to Stirling. He was unperturbed and insisted that the best thing they could do was to get some sleep like the others. After sleeping for the day, they would raid the Sousse road and railway that night, and it was important that the patrol was well rested.

That was the plan. But unfortunately, it did not turn out that way.

ΨΨΨ

Stirling wasn't sure how long he had been asleep when he felt the kick on his shin. He looked up through sleepy eyes to see a tubby, red-faced German officer pointing a Luger him.

Bloody hell, he thought miserably. *It's a Jerry and I'm not dreaming!*

He was sleeping in a shallow hillside cave next to Corporal McDermott, a tall thin Irishman, and as they awoke they looked at one another with puzzlement. The red-faced officer cocked his pistol and began to shout orders in a violent German staccato, his gun weaving dangerously.

Stirling chanced a glance at his watch: it was 03:06 in the afternoon.

The two men disentangled themselves from their sleeping bags, cautiously rose to their feet, and held up their hands. Stirling's experienced eyes took note of their pudgy captor's overexcited manner and unsteady hand. Obviously, he was new to North Africa and had most likely never fired a gun since basic training. If this was the opposition they had to contend with here in Tunisia, they might as well have been dealing with Italians and need not worry. They would be able to escape.

"*Los! Los!*" the German ordered nervously.

As they stepped forward, the German backed out of the cave, his gun still levelled at them, motioning them to follow him. Still backing up, he moved timorously down the wadi. Stirling and McDermott scowlingly advanced towards him, their eyes strained to any move that would give them the opportunity to make a break. The German marshalled them around a bend, where an overwhelming sight greeted Stirling and his comrade. There at the mouth of the wadi stood a force of some five hundred armed German soldiers and an armored personnel carrier blocking the exit from the narrow ravine. They were obviously engaged in the business of rounding up him and his men.

But how did they know we were even here?

All of a sudden, he heard shouting voices and gunfire. He turned to see Cooper and Sadler dashing up the rocky pinnacle, making a run for it along with the French interpreter Freddie Taxis.

"Run, you bastards, run!" he cried.

Thirty Germans armed with Schmeisser submachine guns and rifles tore after them, but Cooper, Sadler, and the Frenchman had a good head start and were clamoring quickly up the talus-strewn hill. They quickly made the hundred-yard climb and vanished out of sight.

But they were the only ones who got away. Stirling and the rest of the troop were captured without a fight, herded together, and searched. Their German captors did not find the tiny compass David was wearing as a button, nor the silk map of Africa sewn inside McDermott's coat. Most of the SAS were bootless. The officer in charge finally allowed one of Stirling's NCOs to hike back to the wadi with an escort and pick up personal belongings such as shoes, blankets, mess tins, and the like.

The eleven prisoners were led to a small hill about a hundred yards away and put under heavy guard. In the meantime, a patrol went through the wadi, pulling the camouflage off the jeeps, and collecting the weapons. The vehicles were driven out, and another squad of soldiers walked the length of the ravine spraying the area with machine-gun bullets to make sure no one was left behind. Stirling saw a German squad climb over the top and search the high ground a second time, shouting to each other and firing into any scrub which might serve as a hiding place. He prayed that they wouldn't find Sadler, Cooper, or Taxis.

While this was going on he pondered the best method of escape. His impulse was to make a break for it then and there, for the Germans looked green and poorly organized. But they were heavily armed and in the broad daylight the chances of stealing away were slim. It would be better to wait until dark to make an escape.

Two hours later, the Germans motioned Stirling and the other prisoners towards a lorry. Though the sun was sinking, the CO felt it was still too light to attempt escape. Eight armed guards stood in the back of the truck, and two rode in the driver's seat. When they had packed into the vehicle, it drove off in the middle of a convoy, bumping along a dirt road until it reached the coast road, then turned south. Soon thereafter night fell, and Stirling could no longer see his surroundings.

After driving south for almost two hours, they were ordered out of the trucks into what appeared to be a large garage and locked inside. Stirling reckoned they were somewhere near Medina. The room was empty save for a few benches against the wall and a couple of chairs by the door. It had an asphalt floor and windows so high that even he could not see out.

The guards were jubilant. Stirling guessed that they had been through the papers which they had found in his jeep, and had discovered the identity, and value, of him and the other captives. Soon thereafter, he learned that the Germans were a special Luftwaffe paratroop force, Company z.b.V. 250, sent out to track down the raiders and alerted to the presence of the SAS following a skirmish with the French Captain Jordan's troops the day before. To Stirling's further indignation, he learned that the tubby, red-faced German officer who had captured him and McDermott was the unit's dentist.

Soon one of the German officers, who spoke English, approached him and his men menacingly. "Don't be disappointed," he sneered, "if you get very little to eat. It would only be a waste of food, as we're going to shoot you. We have orders to execute all saboteurs, as an example to others who might be foolish enough to follow in your footsteps."

Stirling did not take him seriously and knew he and his men were merely being intimidated. Though the Germans were from a special paratroop unit, he was certain they were raw troops and would not dare to carry out their threat unless they were authorized to do so from above. Nevertheless, it was an uncomfortable period. The men put their blankets on the stone floor and tried to sleep. A while later, they were given a little soup and bread.

Stirling and McDermott bedded down next to each other and deliberated over their situation in low voices. There were at least ten guards in the room. Some sat on a bench in the far corner; others were clumped near the door. The window was too high to attempt an escape and there was no obvious way to steal away. They decided that the best thing to do was act like submissive prisoners and try to trick the Germans into lowering their guard. He knew that Hitler had issued personal instructions that all sabotage troops were to be shot upon capture, but that Rommel was ignoring these orders by refusing to comply with such unchivalrous conduct in direct violation of the Hague and Geneva Conventions.

The next day passed slowly. The SAS lolled about in groups on the floor, and Stirling methodically studied the German soldiers who clomped in and out, searching for potential weaknesses. Ten guards seemed to be the permanent sentries, for there were never less and often more. He and his men were given only bread for breakfast, and the same soup ration for lunch as the night before. However, there was no more talk about firing squads. Indeed, there seemed to be a subtle change in the attitude of the captors. Their jubilation was now tinged with pride, which meant that they had been congratulated by their superiors for their accomplishment of capturing the much-sought-after Phantom Major and his desert commandos.

By evening, Stirling had made up his mind that an opportunity to escape in which skill or craftiness could be employed was unlikely. If he and McDermott wanted to get away, they would have to make a run for it.

"You really think we can pull it off?" asked the Irishman.

"Absolutely," he replied. "So far, we've been allowed out to relieve ourselves. But it's always one at a time with three guards."

"So what do you propose?"

"The guards are on continuous duty, but they're always posted in the immediate area of the garage door or inside with us. Our best chance is a simple cut-and-run."

"Yes, but how?"

"After I've had been escorted just after dark by the guards to the farthest point they'll allow me to go, I'll give a shout and run. At that precise moment, you must jostle the guard at the door and break out yourself."

"It sounds like in the movies."

"Yes well, let's just hope it turns out happily like in the pictures. Because it's all we've bloody got."

CHAPTER 63

MEDINA, TUNISIA

JANUARY 23-24, 1943

AT PRECISELY 22:00, Stirling motioned to the guard and asked to be taken outside to relieve himself. All his senses were on high alert. The guard nodded for him to come forward and motioned for another guard to join him. McDermott had already moved near the door and stood against the wall casually smoking.

Serving up his most pleasant smile as if giving thanks, Stirling walked up to the two young guards. The soldiers escorted him twenty yards from the garage. He noted that they were relaxed and unsuspecting. When one of them took out a cigarette and asked the other for a light, Stirling prepared to make his move, his heart fluttering in his chest in anticipation of escape. He pretended to start to unzip his fly, keeping an eye on the Germans. When the second one transferred his rifle to his left hand and fumbled in his pocket for a match, Stirling made his move.

Giving a blood curdling yell, he dashed for the scraggly brush as fast as he could, heading south. All of his pent-up frustration and anger went into the demonic scream and he almost frightened himself. Fortunately yesterday, when he had been dropped off under armed guard at the garage with the other prisoners, he had been able to take a quick bearing with his hidden compass before disembarking from the truck, so he knew which way to go.

The soldiers fired furiously into the blackness and one of them ran blindly after him, but even though the moon was a brightly lit gibbous orb it was masked partially by clouds in the winter sky.

At the sound of the shots, more German guards came running out of the garage. With all the commotion, McDermott slipped through the door and also disappeared into the night.

Meanwhile, Stirling descended quickly into a shallow dry channel, downstream from the garage, and kept running south.

Reaching a section of gravelly outwash, he cranked into another gear. He could hear the Germans shouting and running after him, but fought back the temptation to glance over his shoulder. His eyes were fixed on an outcrop ahead, silhouetted against a thin ray of moonlight. He passed the rocky protuberance and spurred down a gently sloped gulch, gobbling up ground as more blind shots echoed across the dark, barren desert.

But soon he grew tired and was forced to slow his pace to a jog. The fact was his health had deteriorated significantly in the past six months. Though he had received treatment for his desert sores in October, they were still infected and he had not completely rid himself of the migraines that had plagued him. In the fall, he had also come down with a bad case of solar conjunctivitis, an eye infection caused by a combination of flying sand and blazing sun. Stirling had taken to wearing sunglasses to protect his eyes, which he was pleased to note gave him an oddly gangsterish appearance, but he had not followed Dr. Pleydell's medical advice to bathe his eyes on a regular basis. He was also dangerously thin, worn down by his multiplying responsibilities over the past three months, which had included the creation of a parallel SAS regiment commanded by his older brother Bill.

With adrenaline now coursing through his body in a steady torrent, he forced himself to pick up his pace and run on. But with little food in his stomach and his body a physical wreck, he knew he could not last much longer. More shots rang out, but in the darkness the sentries were still firing blind. He realized that his escape plan to head south was based almost entirely on wishful thinking since he had no idea where he was. Worse yet, a single exceptionally tall, pale-faced foreigner was certain to be spotted.

A half mile from the garage, he took cover in a clump of bushes and paused to catch his breath. He could hear shots still being fired but the enemy obviously had no idea where he was.

Trying to control his heavy breathing, he took stock of his position. He was on the outskirts of a town. Normally in his experience, the towns along the North African coast gave way to wilderness almost immediately, but this part of Tunisia was built up, and he would have to walk rapidly to get into rough country by first light. He would head for the rendezvous at Bir Soltane, which he reckoned was about fifty miles away.

But first, he would like to find McDermott. He had no way of knowing whether the corporal had managed to get free. They had arranged a special whistle and Stirling cautiously sounded the notes.

But there was no response. With dread, he wondered if the young Irishman had been shot.

Taking a bearing with his button compass, he began to walk again, continuing south. Soon the German shouting disappeared altogether. Every ten or fifteen minutes he gave the whistle, but after an hour had passed he abandoned hope of rejoining McDermott.

He covered fifteen miles during the night. He passed over large sections of cultivated land, skirting in and out of farmyards. Twice he caused an ear-splitting commotion, begun by barking dogs and picked up by braying donkeys and frightened sheep.

As dawn broke, he found himself on a well-kept, prosperous-looking farm of some sort. The house was bigger than the normal Arab farmhouse and there was a light in the kitchen. David knew that the natives were apt to be hostile in this part of North Africa, but he was so hungry and thirsty he decided to risk it. He knocked on the door, and to his surprise it was opened almost immediately by a portly Tunisian man. He wore a beige *burnous*, a long cloak of coarse woollen fabric with a hood in the manner of a Berber, and several shiny gold rings, attesting to his affluence. His wife was bending over the stove and a small child played in the corner. The farmer smiled, bowed graciously, and welcomed him into his home.

You've lucked out, old boy, he told himself. *Get some water, grab a bite, and be on your merry way. Or perhaps you could hole up here for the day?*

The man spoke passable English and it soon transpired that he had a grievance against the Germans. He said they had taken a piece of his land to use as a rifle range, and had not given him adequate compensation. After they had spoken for a few minutes, the Arab gave him bread, tea, dates, and cold meat, and informed him that it was not the first time he had helped a British "airman." As it turned out, three others had been his guests in the last year. Stirling did not alter the farmer's conjectures about who he was and muttered something about his plane catching fire and having to bail out. With much ceremony, the farmer produced cigarettes and sticky sweets, and settled down to hear how the war was going.

In the course of the conversation, Stirling learned that there was a large German aerodrome only five miles away; it had often been bombed by the British, which explained the farmer's contact with pilots. The farmer then asked if he wanted to hide out for the day. When Stirling agreed, he was led to a barn a hundred yards away and showed a safe hiding place where the grain was stored. The refuge had been used by the previous airmen. He spent the rest of the day in hiding there.

Once the sun went down, the Arab came out with more dates and water and sent him on his way.

"Thank you—I won't forget this," said Stirling to the Tunisian, and he meant it.

"Go in peace, my friend. And win this war against the Germans and Italians. They are not friendly people like you and me. I think they have sticks up their asses."

"That is yet another thing we can agree on, my friend. Thank you once again."

They shook hands and he started once again on his way. He reckoned that the Bir Soltane rendezvous was only thirty miles away now. If he could cover twenty miles during the night, he could reach it by late tomorrow evening.

But he had not gone a hundred feet when he thought of the German aerodrome the prosperous Arab farmer had described. Should he recce it? *No, you bloody fool,* he told himself. *You should move with all possible haste towards the RV.*

But he found he couldn't resist checking to see whether the aerodrome would be a worthwhile op for the SAS. It lay not far off his southward course, and at this point in the war airfields were his second nature.

An hour and a half later, he saw a small light flickering in the distance and knew he was near the edge of a tarmac. As he approached, he was surprised to see that there was no perimeter wire and only a single guard post. He crept up to the edge of the airfield and studied the layout. He could see the shapes of a large number of Junkers 52s; they would be an easy target from his recon of the weak defenses. He walked down the whole length of the field, which was about a mile long. He took note of hangars, administrative buildings, and repair shops. There were muffled lights but all was quiet. He made up his mind that when he reached Bir Soltane, he would bring a team back with him to raid the airfield as a final operation before making contact with First Army.

He looked at his watch, which thankfully the Germans hadn't stolen from him. It was now half-past ten. Damn, his reconnaissance had taken nearly two hours, which meant that he had only six and a half hours of darkness left. He reckoned he could walk three miles an hour and should not be far short of his twenty miles by first light.

He walked on. But two miles after leaving the field the ground became unbelievably rocky. His progress turned agonizingly slow. Just before first light, he took cover in a small depression and hauled bits of scrub and grass to camouflage his lengthy frame as best he could. To his dismay, he estimated that he had only covered around ten miles. Then he went to sleep. He was so exhausted that he was out cold until late afternoon when he awoke to hunger pains. He decided to get moving again.

Shaking the foliage covering off him, he stood up and brushed off his clothes. To his surprise, a voice posed in broken English, "You sleep good?"

He wheeled around to see an Arab grinning at him. He was a young man in rags and he leaned on a crook.

Stirling smiled pleasantly to show that he posed no danger.

"If you desire food and water, I show you."

He decided there was no harm in going a short way with the man to see if he meant what he said. He nodded in assent and followed him along the wadi. They had walked half a mile when the Arab motioned to a track leading to the top of a hill. Halfway up, he complained about his foot and fell behind. Stirling strode ahead, and as he reached the top, the sight that greeted him made his jaw drop.

There, only fifty yards away, were four or five Italian lorries. On both sides of the dirt road patrols with machine guns were fanning out. Swiveling his head, he quickly saw that another patrol had approached from the other direction and was descending into the wadi to cut him off from behind.

Feeling a wave of desperation, he looked back at the Arab that was supposed to be helping him. Having closed the distance between them, the man now pulled out a pistol and pointed it menacingly at him.

You sneaky bastard! I shouldn't have trusted you!

He looked back at the Italian soldiers. Now it was clear: the Arab had been keeping watch over him while he slept and had sent a comrade to alert the enemy, in order to collect the cash award which was paid for British soldiers and airmen.

Coming up swiftly behind him, the Arab pressed his revolver into Stirling's ribs and motioned him forward to meet the enemy. Now he had no option but to keep walking. The Italian soldiers came cautiously but threateningly towards him, grim-faced and pointing their guns. Among them was a second Arab—obviously the man who had gone to fetch the patrol. Excitedly, he pointed to Stirling to make sure there would be no argument about the reward.

It was then the traitor made his fatal mistake.

As Stirling was handed over to the Italians, the Arab came within arm's length of him. The Phantom Major did not hesitate. Feeling a blinding anger, he reached down and grabbed the Arab by the ankles with what seemed like superhuman strength, whirled the hapless man around his head, and proceeded to bash him into the rocky ground to the amazement of the Italians. The Arab screamed. Stirling tried to knock him again, but the soldiers dashed forward and pinioned his arms before he could cause further damage.

This time his captors were taking no chances: he was quickly bound and taken under heavy guard to the village of El Hama, and then on to the Italian headquarters at Menzel for interrogation. Throughout his journey, they kept him under a heavy guard. The Italians were overjoyed to have captured the notorious desert raider whom the Germans had clumsily allowed to slip through their fingers.

Stirling couldn't believe that he was once again back in captivity. But it was the timing that bothered him most. In only the last three months, he had taken what had begun as a small, semiprivate army and built it into the most powerful Allied special forces unit of the war, a multicultural and ever-expanding family that didn't just include Brits, Scots, and Irishmen but now included large numbers of French troops, a unit of tough Greek fighters known as the Greek Sacred Squadron, and a special boat squadron. It was a pity he would be sent to a POW camp for the duration of the war just when the SAS idea he had worked so arduously to make a part of the regular order of battle was finally bearing fruit. It seemed unthinkable that it was all coming to an end just when the freemasonry of mediocrity that had once pooh-poohed him and his unit was now singing his praises.

At Menzel, he was given a fresh pack of *Sigarette Nazionali* and interrogated by Colonel Mario Revetria, the chief of Italian military intelligence in North Africa. Revetria was so excited to have captured the notorious Phantom Major and SAS leader that he could not resist showing off, and instead of pumping Stirling for information he described everything he knew about the SAS—although not how he had come to know it.

Unbeknownst to Stirling, the wily Revetria had planted an English fascist spy who went by the name of Captain John Richards as a stool pigeon in the POW camp at Benghazi and at other contact points in North Africa. Practicing the oldest and nastiest form of espionage, Richards had been able to cleverly extract sufficient information from captured SAS prisoners for Revetria to build an accurate profile of the mysterious British raiders who emerged from the desert, often hundreds of miles behind the front lines, to attack airfields and ambush convoys. Rumors had abounded about this unit, but there had been very little in the way of hard intelligence until Revetria's prized informant told the Italian officer everything he needed to know about the unit's leader, size, training, and tactics. The stool pigeon's real name was Theodore John William Schurch, a pre-war accountant by trade, private in the British Army, and committed fascist born in London to an English mother and Swiss father.

By the time the exquisitely polite Revetria was finished, Stirling had to admit that he was duly impressed. "Why, Colonel," he said silkily, "it would appear you know as much as I do about my own organization."

The Italian smiled chivalrously and puffed on his cigarette. "I must confess," he said, "a part of me is sad to see it end for you like this, *Signore* Phantom Major. For me, the hunt has ended."

"Well, I wouldn't worry about it too much if I were you. You won't be in Africa more than a couple months before the Allies drive you out—and then take Sicily and Italy. I imagine that you, being in the intelligence business for the losing side, will have some serious explaining to do at that point."

Revetria's smile dropped instantly.

A few hours later, Stirling was taken to the Tunisian airfield he had reconnoitered and flown to Sicily in one of the Junkers 52s he had planned to blow up. Here he was interrogated once more, in a cavalry barracks, first by the Italians, and then by a German staff officer.

Once again, he gave only his name and rank.

CHAPTER 64

MARETH LINE, SOUTHEASTERN TUNISIA

FEBRUARY 2, 1943

ROMMEL PEERED through his field glasses at the rocky ridges of the Matmata Hills and the semiarid, scrub-covered Tunisian coastal plain. Across the plain in a line extending southwest to northeast stretched the Mareth Line, the antiquated fortifications built by the French where he and his *Panzerarmee* had set up a defensive position following the long retreat from El Alamein.

The dissected coastal plain was the only route north for Montgomery and his Eighth Army. It was blocked by both the Mareth Line and the Wadi Zigzaou, a natural tank obstacle with steep banks rising up to 70 feet. The northwest side had been reinforced by the Desert Fox, but he was still not satisfied with it as a defensive position. He would have preferred to have formed his defensive line at Gabès Gap, but was regrettably overruled by his superiors. Wadi Zigzaou crossed the coastal plain from Zarat to Toujane and into the Matmata Hills beyond and could be penetrated by experienced Allied tank crews, he felt.

With dusk approaching, the sun was a fading yellow ball on the horizon. The desert was still and peaceful, the winter air pleasantly cool but not cold. With the Matmata Hills forming a majestic backdrop, what spread before him was an awe-inspiring sight. The serenity of the Tunisian desert had put him in a reflective mood. All he had ever wanted was to be was a field commander leading great armies to victory in battle. But now, it seemed he couldn't even do that anymore. He was as low as he had ever been in his life, and there were whispers and outright accusations that he was a loser, a defeatist.

How had it come to this?

Angrily, he remembered back to his last meeting with Hitler. The trip had proved a crushing blow. On November 28, after his defeat at Alamein, he had flown to Rastenburg and appealed directly to the Führer. He was convinced that overly optimistic reports from the Italians and Kesselring lay behind Hitler's failure to grasp the true situation in North Africa. He informed him that victory in the theater of operations was hopeless and the abandonment of North Africa should be accepted as long-term strategic policy. Hitler exploded. For the first time Rommel was treated to one of his infamous tantrums. Red in the face, spewing saliva, and pounding his fist into the table like a child throwing a fit, the leader of Nazi Germany called the Desert Fox a defeatist and accused his men of being cowards. Generals who had made the same sort of suggestions in Russia had been shot, he bellowed. He would not yet do this to Rommel, but the field marshal had better be careful. Never one to be cowed into submission, Rommel tried to explain the reasons for his defeat at Alamein and why he felt North Africa was a lost cause. He was continually interrupted by *Reichsmarschall* Göring, who played the role of Hitler's mouthpiece. At the end of Hitler's tirade, the Führer shouted, "North Africa will be defended and not evacuated! That is an order, *Herr Feldmarschall!*"

Rommel was stunned: Hitler was beyond control. He raved on and on about how his decision to hold on at all costs had saved the Eastern Front in the winter of 1941-42. He expected his orders to be ruthlessly obeyed in Africa as well. Rommel interrupted, and asked him whether it was better to lose Tripoli or the *Afrika Korps*. Hitler replied that the lives of soldiers were unimportant and Rommel would have to fight to the bitter end. The Desert Fox, also angry now and unmoved by Hitler's tantrum, asked if the Führer or some of his entourage would come to North Africa and show them how to do it. At this, Hitler became completely unglued, "Go!" he screamed. "I have other things to do than to talk to you!"

Rommel saluted, turned on his heel, and walked out. Less than a week later he was back in North Africa.

Once again with his troops, he realized that his initial reaction to Hitler's "victory or death" order at El Alamein, along with the conclusions which he had drawn from it, could not be dismissed as angry outbursts born of the stress and chaos of a desperate war. The conference of November 28 had established once and for all for Rommel that Hitler's orders could no longer be treated as rational, and hence could no longer be regarded as inviolate. In the past the Desert Fox had defied, evaded, and interpreted orders to fit his own needs when he felt that the superior authority issuing them was lacking either sufficient information or the requisite judgment. But he had never anticipated that he would be given orders by the Führer himself revealing a leader who had lost touch with military reality. Nevertheless, that was precisely what had happened.

He realized that his gravest mistake was his long-held belief that while Hitler was good for Germany, the Nazis were bad, never recognizing how the two were inseparable. But now—as he stood staring at the prewar French fortifications that had been built to hold off the Italians but would now be used to turn back Montgomery—he understood. For almost a decade, Rommel had never found reason to differentiate between loyalty to Hitler and loyalty to Germany. Suddenly, in just the past few months, all of that had changed. The realization was as profound as it was inevitable: suddenly he understood that the current conflict would never bring greater glory and security for Germany, or provide restitution for the one-sided and patently unfair Treaty of Versailles. Hitler's war was exactly that—Hitler's war, its aim nothing more than the aggrandizement of Adolf Hitler. Rommel could never again fully support his Führer, not because Germany was losing the war, or that Hitler was losing it for Germany, but because of how Hitler was forcing it to be lost through his own ruthless narcissism and myopia. Rommel refused to become Hitler's vassal and Goebbels's propaganda piece at the cost of his duty to the Fatherland.

He watched as a triumvirate of his soldiers stepped out from behind his *Mammut* Moritz and the other parked command vehicles of his *Kampfstaffel* to watch the sunset. After climbing a little knoll, they locked arms and began to sing. The faint strains of *Lili Marlene* rose up in the light desert breeze, and Rommel couldn't help but smile. The song about a lovesick German soldier drifted up and hung there in the desert-scented air, and he felt a great lonesomeness inside. *Lili Marlene* made him think of how much he missed Lucie and their "wonderful time" together with Manfred in Semmering. That was the thing about his Lucie. Whether she was right there beside him or he was thinking of her a continent away, she never failed to reach down and tug at his soul like nothing else in the world.

He looked up at the sky. The ball of sun was leaning into the Matmata Hills in a pastel burst of pinkish-purple. The majestic scenery reached down and touched his soul. Even though the anger hadn't completely vanished inside him over his ill treatment at the hands of Hitler and Göring, he couldn't help but feel the power of the land, the infinity of it all and the feeling of oneness inside as the tender notes of *Lili Marlene* filled his head. The desert was a reassuring presence, like an old friend.

The desert itself was eternal. This barren but spectacularly beautiful place North Africa and his beloved *Afrika Korps* were eternal. Deep in his soul, he felt the anguish of the more than 25,000 German and Italian graves left behind in Egypt and Libya when Panzer Army Africa had crossed into Tunisia days earlier.

He was interrupted by a voice.

"Pardon me, *Herr Feldmarschall*, but I have important news."

He turned to see his chief of staff, Colonel Bayerlein. "Hopefully, some good news, Fritz."

"A little of both, I'm afraid. However, even the bad news I believe will interest you. But I shall start with the good news first. The British SAS commander, David Stirling, has been captured."

"The Phantom Major? Really?"

"Yes, sir, and the Phantom Major is no longer a major—he is a lieutenant colonel. He and eleven of his men were caught north of Gabès Gap by one of our patrols. Unfortunately, Stirling was insufficiently guarded and managed to escape, but he was later recaptured."

"By us?"

"No, by some Arabs. Apparently, Stirling offered them a reward if they would help get him back to British lines. But his bid must have been too small, for the Arabs, with their usual eye to business, offered him to the Italians for eleven pounds of tea. A bargain which the Italians soon clinched, I am told."

"So the Italians got him back? Well, that has to be a first. Where is he being held?"

"After being interrogated by Colonel Revetria, he was flown to Sicily and interrogated again before being sent to the Caserma Castro Pretorio POW Camp outside Rome."

"I hate to admit it, but I shall miss young Stirling. The British have lost a very able and adaptable desert commander. You know that he and his men have caused us more damage than any other British unit of equal strength? By far."

"Yes, *Feldmarschall*, I am aware of that."

"Then you also know that if *he* were leading the Eighth Army instead of the ponderous Montgomery, *we* wouldn't still be here in North Africa."

"Lucky for us he has been captured then."

"Indeed. Now what is the bad news?"

Bayerlein cleared his throat. "As I said, I wouldn't call it bad news. But I do have important information on the outcome of Operation Condor."

The Desert Fox's interest was instantly piqued. "You don't say? What news do you have?"

"From our contacts in the Egyptian government and the Swiss Legation in Cairo, we've finally learned the full details of Almasy's operation."

"Go on."

Bayerlein withdrew a three-page long intelligence report and began summarizing it. "The Abwehr Lieutenants Eppler and Sandstette—Max and Moritz—made it safely to Cairo in late May."

"Quite an extraordinary feat by Almasy, I must say."

"Yes, it was. Soon after reaching the city, they found lodgings on a houseboat and tried to establish wireless contact with our forward listening post in the agreed-upon manner. But they could never establish contact. They were arrested in late July along with a number of their contacts in the city who lent them assistance. The trial was held in late August and all of those arrested were tried and convicted. Several of those found guilty were interned, but I am told no one received a death sentence. According to our government contacts, they were arrested by one Major A.W. Sansom of British Field Security and interrogated by a Major Dunstan at the Maadi Interrogation Center outside Cairo. The two Brits later sat in on the court proceedings."

"So we had trained spies in Cairo for two months from late May to late July, but we didn't have enough fuel or tanks to break through the Alamein Line and make proper use of them? That's what you're telling me?"

"I know, it's painful. The plan could have worked."

Rommel couldn't believe he had been that close to both victory on the battlefield *and* an intelligence coup. *My God,* he thought with a sense of missed opportunity, *we were close enough to taste the whiskey on the breath of the British officers at Shepheard's! It was all within our grasp! Cairo, the Suez, Palestine—all of it!"*

Bayerlein was shaking his head. "It would be funny, sir, if it weren't so tragic."

"No, it is beyond tragic," said Rommel stiffly, and he, too, shook his head in disgust. "So if Eppler and Sandstette weren't put before a firing squad, where are they now?"

"The Court of Inquiry set up by the Egyptian government decided on August 25 how those arrested should be dealt with. Eppler and Sandstette escaped its jurisdiction."

"What do you mean escaped?"

"From the start they were treated as prisoners of war rather than spies, and were handed over to the British. Major Dunstan and other officers interrogated them thoroughly, and then incarcerated them in a POW camp. We have not yet learned which one."

"And the other conspirators?"

Bayerlein looked over his type-written intelligence report. "As I said, many others were implicated in Operation Condor. On August 13, Eppler was brought in and he quickly identified two Egyptian officers who had helped him."

"Who were they?"

"Flight-Lieutenant Ezzet and Signals Unit Captain Anwar el Sadat. Eppler identified them as two of his fellow conspirators. Later Sandstette and Eppler's Egyptian stepbrother Hassan Gaafar were brought in. He identified Ezzet and Sadat too, but the stubborn Egyptians continued to deny any knowledge of events."

"The British obviously threatened Eppler and Sandstette and they cut a deal to save their own skins."

"Our contacts have not yet been able to confirm that, but it does appear likely. Almasy and his Abwehr colleagues believe that Eppler and Sandstette are being treated by the British as prisoners of war so that they can be kept away from the Egyptian authorities. Apparently, the British don't want the details of the Condor case to get out and run the risk of jeopardizing their relationship with the Egyptian government. In his testimony on August 5, Sadat stated that he believed Eppler and Sandstette were lying to spare them from the hangman's noose. But he and Ezzet soon began to crumble under the weight of evidence and finally admitted knowledge of Operation Condor. Soon thereafter, General el Masri appeared in court."

"El Masri Pasha was involved in the plot?"

"He, too, denied ever knowing Eppler, again claiming that the two spies were accusing him to gain favor with the British."

"So instead of being shot or hung, Eppler and Sandstette are being kept as political prisoners for the rest of the war? Thus avoiding the usual fate of spies?"

"It appears so. Sadat and Ezzet also avoided execution—even though the British Ambassador, Sir Miles Lampson, wanted them to be put before a firing squad. The Egyptian military refused to put them to death. They were cashiered from the armed forces and are now in an Egyptian prison."

"And el Masri?"

"He has been interned."

"Interesting." They fell silent for a moment as they listened to the singing soldiers. The Desert Fox's expression turned thoughtful. People thought that he was just a skilled technician of war, with no horizons outside of strategy and tactics, no sense of a future that held anything but yet another battle. But he felt the power, inspiration, and beauty of the singers' voices and couldn't help but wonder what the world would be like, one day, when the fighting stopped.

The world could be so beautiful for all men. Such infinite possibilities exist to make them contented and happy. There is so much to be done here in Africa with its wide-open spaces.

After reflecting a moment longer, he turned back towards his subordinate. "What about the others arrested?"

"The Austrian woman Frau Amer, her Egyptian relative Abdel Salama, and Eppler's brother Hassan Gaafar were interned. They will spend the rest of the war behind bars. The Hungarian priest Father Demetriou, the friend of Almasy's, has been deported to Palestine. And there were two other low-level Egyptians let off with a warning."

"Is that everyone then?"

"No, there is one more: the famous Egyptian belly dancer and film star Hekmat Fahmy."

"I have heard of her. She is said to be much admired by British officers."

"Yes, that is what the reports say as well. She has danced before Hitler and Mussolini, amongst others."

"How was she involved?"

"That's just it—she wasn't. She was no Mata Hari at all. Apparently, all she did was put Eppler and Sandstette up for one night on her houseboat on the Nile and find their own boat to rent—without even knowing that they were spies."

"That sounds like bad luck to me. What happened to her?"

Bayerlein again consulted his intelligence report. "She was let off with a warning. Apparently, she was Eppler's old girlfriend and she was simply doing him a favor."

"Poor woman, she got caught up with the wrong man. It wouldn't be the first time something like that has happened. Is there anything else?"

"No, that's it. I thought you would want to know."

"Thank you, Fritz. This has been most interesting, though completely secondary to our current predicament."

"Montgomery."

"No, right now, he is of little interest to me. It is the Americans I am talking about."

"What are your plans to deal with them?"

"For starters, I shall deliver a lightning-quick blow to knock them back on their heels, perhaps even push them farther westward. Then my *Panzerarmee* will swing back to the Mareth Line to meet any counterstroke by the Eighth Army before the overly cautious Monty can finish amassing his troops and supplies."

"That sounds like a good plan, *Herr Feldmarschall*. But I doubt Tunisia can hold out indefinitely against the Allies. As you have said yourself, the overwhelming industrial capacity of the United States assures an eventual Allied victory in any theater where its output can be properly brought to bear."

"That is true. Between them, the Americans and the British are bringing not just superior numbers to war, but a more intelligent and sophisticated application of their resources than either the mindless brute Soviets—or us. But the Americans have no practical battle experience yet—and it is up to us to install in them from the outset an inferiority complex of no small order."

"But how can we do that?"

"By exploiting our interior lines. We are now in a position to concentrate the mass of our motorized forces for an attack on the British and Americans in Western Tunisia, and possibly force them to withdraw."

"That is a bold plan."

"Yes, it is bold. But it is what our friend Lieutenant Colonel Stirling would do if he was a general. I tell you, that man never lacked for boldness. He is a Lion of the Desert."

"A Lion of the Desert?"

"Yes, that is how I shall always remember him. You know the SAS motto: *Who Dares Wins*."

"If I may say so, *Feldmarschall*, that is as much a motto for you as it is him."

"Yes, and that is why I like him. I am proud to have fought against such a warrior. He—far more than Montgomery, who is not only sluggish in pursuit but has an absolute mania for always bringing up deep reserves and risking as little as possible—was truly a force to be reckoned with."

"If Stirling is a Lion of the Desert then so, too, are you, sir."

Rommel shook his head. "No, I'm afraid I'm just a tired old man who has seen the error of his ways. I should have seen the madness of our Führer much earlier. I just hope now it is not too late."

And with that, the Desert Fox leaned down and picked up a clump of desert soil, sifting it through his fingers and watching the caliche-bearing dust blow off in the crisp breeze along the resurrected Mareth Line where he would make his final stand in North Africa. He would always remember this somber little moment in history: the lonesome tug he felt inside as he gazed out at the sweeping desert landscape and took in the homesick voices of his *Afrika Korps* soldiers singing about the loved ones they had left behind.

Bundling himself in his greatcoat against the coming evening chill, he thought again of the Phantom Major, Colonel Stirling.

Perhaps Bayerlein is right. Perhaps we are both Lions of the Desert. In any case, I shall miss such an able and imaginative adversary.

He turned his gaze to the dusky desert sky above the singing soldiers—bold paint strokes of brilliant pink with purple rims fringing the clouds, like spring flowers bursting into bloom.

Tonight...tonight I shall listen to Lili Marlene *on the radio for you, Colonel Stirling. And I will salute you.*

AFTERWORD

Lions of the Desert: A True Story of WWII Heroes in North Africa was conceived and written by the author as a work of historical fiction. Although the novel takes place during the Second World War and is a true story based upon actual historical figures, events, and locales, the novel is still ultimately a work of the imagination and entertainment and should be read as nothing more. Though I have strived for historical accuracy and there is not a single primary or secondary character in the book that is not an actual historical figure, the names, characters, places, government entities, armed forces, religious and political groups, and incidents, as portrayed in the novel, are products of the author's imagination and are not to be construed as one-hundred-percent accurate depictions. With that said, the story is based primarily upon known and reasonably well-documented historical events and real people.

With respect to the events portrayed in the novel, I have tried to place the actual historical figures where they physically were during a given event and have used their actual words based on journals, case files, contemporary transcripts, trial documents, memoirs, and other quoted materials. Like Michael Shaara in his Pulitzer-prize-winning historical novel about the Battle of Gettysburg, *The Killer Angels*, I have not "consciously changed any fact" nor have I "knowingly violated the action." Most of the scenes in the book are based on known events with specific historical figures present, but a minority are based on incidents that are generally accepted to have taken place but have unfortunately not been documented by history, or that I believe happened under similar circumstances to those described in the book but for which there is no historical record. In these cases, the interpretations of character and motivation are mine and mine alone. Thus, the book's characters are ultimately a part of my overall imaginative landscape and are, therefore, the fictitious creations of the author, reflecting my personal research interests and biases.

Below I present the true historical legacy and ultimate fate of the four primary point-of-view characters and three major secondary historical figures of the book: David Stirling, Erwin Rommel, Hekmat Fahmy, A.W. "Sammy" Sansom, Johannes Eppler (Hussein Gaafar), Bonner Fellers, and László Almasy. I also provide a comparison between the traditional representations of several of the major historical figures and the new, more historically accurate interpretations based on the latest declassified materials and up-to-date research as presented in this work, so that readers of the Condor story can finally separate fact from fiction.

DAVID STIRLING

Soon after his interrogation at the hands of Colonel Revetria, chief of Italian military intelligence in North Africa, Stirling was imprisoned at Caserma Castro Pretorio outside Rome. He found the Allied POW camp "well equipped and comfortable," but after fifteen months of dangerous and exciting raids on German aerodromes and military targets, he found the inertia boring beyond description. When the Desert Fox learned of the Phantom Major's capture, he wrote his wife Lucie describing how the twenty-seven-year-old Scotsman who had made so much trouble for him, for so long, was finally in captivity: "The British lost the very able and adaptable commander of the desert group which has caused us more damage than any other British unit of equal size." Rommel knew a kindred spirit and innovative tactician when he saw one.

At Stirling's new camp, prisoners were required to remain in their cells throughout the day, but in the evening they were allowed out to eat together and socialize. The man in the next cell, another officer undergoing interrogation, introduced himself as Captain John Richards of the Royal Army Service Corps and explained that he had been captured in Tobruk in November 1942. Richards was, in fact, the British fascist and stool pigeon Teddy Schurch who had already obtained "all the necessary information regarding the SAS" and was now under orders from his Italian handlers "to obtain the name of Colonel Stirling's successor." There was really only one person capable of taking over the regiment—Paddy Mayne—and Stirling revealed as much to Schurch. The information was then passed on to the Abwehr and, in an amusing twist, the Germans knew he would be taking over the SAS before Mayne knew himself.

Stirling was awarded the Distinguished Service Order in recognition of gallant and distinguished service in the Middle East on February 24, 1942. He most certainly deserved it. In the fifteen months before Stirling's capture, the SAS in North Africa destroyed over 250 aircraft on the ground and dozens of supply dumps, wrecked railways and telecommunications, and put hundreds of enemy vehicles out of action. When his men learned of his capture, there were widespread fears that the unit would be disbanded or not up to its former standards without his leadership, which, given the crucial role he had played in the SAS since the beginning, was not unreasonable. But the rumors proved unfounded, and the SAS went on to enjoy continued success under the hard-drinking and hard-fighting Paddy Mayne, while the Phantom Major's brother, Lieutenant Colonel William Stirling, established the 2nd SAS Regiment in Algeria.

Still, without the soft-spoken and humble yet occasionally "pomposo" Scot's long-range vision and nurturing, the group was never quite the same. At the time of his capture, the Desert War was drawing to an end, and with victory in sight in Tunisia, the role, location, and very nature of the SAS would change once again. By the invasion of Sicily in July 1943, the unit had already been altered beyond recognition from the handful of soldiers dropped into the desert in Operation Squatter. Many of the "Originals," as the first recruits described themselves, were gone. But, of course, the heavily bearded commandos in the Arab headdresses that the Desert Fox himself found time to write home to his wife about would never be forgotten.

Since its inception, the SAS has proved itself as one the most capable military forces in the world, ready to take the fight to the enemy when and where they least expect it. Stirling's SAS motto *Who Dares Wins* is still the official moniker of the Special Air Service to this day.

According to Ben Macintyre in *Rogue Heroes: The History of the SAS, Britain's Secret Special Forces Unit That Sabotaged the Nazis and Changed the Nature of War*, Stirling made multiple escape attempts from 1943-1944 as a POW that eventually led to him being imprisoned at Colditz Castle for the remainder of the war. When he was transferred to the notorious and supposedly escape-proof German

POW camp in Germany, he was reunited with Georges Berge and Augustin Jordan, the French SAS commanders captured earlier. The link between the Special Air Service's acclaimed desert taxi service, the Long Range Desert Group, and SAS was also continued behind the barbed wire. Prior to Stirling's extended stay at Colditz, he and Pat Clayton, a pre-war desert explorer who had worked with the famous adventurer, mapper, and sand-dune expert Ralph Bagnold as well as Count László Almasy, continued the fight behind enemy lines by serving on the Escape Committee of the *Oflag* 79 POW camp at Querum near Brunswick, Germany.

As Macintyre states, following the war Stirling's unconventional tactics and disdain for traditional military culture would see him eventually commit to several unusual business ventures. But first, on November 14, 1946, he was appointed an Officer of the Order of the British Empire in recognition of gallant and distinguished service in the field. He settled in Rhodesia, where he became president of the newly founded Capricorn Society, an idealistic venture to unite Africans without regard to racial, political, and religious divisions. When that failed, he first blamed the Colonial Office then returned to the United Kingdom and set up a series of television stations around the world, mostly in developing countries, another project that was as imaginative as it was unprofitable. "I had the biggest collection of the most bankrupt television stations in the world," he proclaimed. Later he ran Watchguard (International) Ltd., a secretive company through which he helped train security units for Arab and African countries. He later became associated with several instances of covert military action in the Middle East. In the aftermath of the 1974 miners' strike, he set up GB75, "an organization of apprehensive patriots" who would help keep essential services, such as power stations, running in the event of a general strike. In 1984, he gave his name to the Hereford headquarters of the SAS, the Stirling Lines.

In September 1967, former British officer and espionage author Len Deighton wrote an article in the Sunday *London Times Magazine* about Operation Snowdrop, the ill-fated SAS raid on the harbor and storage facilities at Benghazi and at Benina airfield in Libya in September 1942. Deighton, considered one of the top three British spy novelists of his time along with Ian Fleming and John le Carré, is the author of the bestseller *City of Gold* (1992)—one of the many highly fictionalized accounts of the Operation Condor story. The following year, in 1968, Stirling was awarded "substantial damages" in a libel action about Deighton's article. The passage complained of states "Stirling himself had insisted upon talking about the raid at two social gatherings at the British Embassy in Cairo although warned not to do so." Stirling made the point that Winston Churchill had been at both gatherings and the issue had been raised in a private discussion with the Prime Minister.

In 1990, he was appointed a Knight Bachelor in the New Year Honors for services to the military. Later that year he passed away at the age of 74. Stirling would have found his knighthood ironic and probably chuckled. After all, here was a man who had made a name for himself and his regiment by flouting British military tradition. The irony is that if Stirling had never broken the rules and thumbed his nose at the military hierarchy, the SAS may never have been born. The privileged Scot was an iconoclast to the core—and yet due to his privileged upbringing a part of him would always remain a traditionalist like his father,

Brigadier General Archibald Stirling.

In 2002, the official SAS memorial, a statue of Stirling standing on a rock, was unveiled on the Hill of Row near his family's estate at Park of Keir near Doune, Scotland. The magnificent life-size bronze shows him wearing his long wind-blown desert jacket, officer's peaked visor cap, trademark tie, and lengthy military trousers. The statue is quite fitting. During the Desert War, whether lounging around in Cairo or fighting in battle in the inhospitable desert, Stirling never failed to be dapperly dressed in his immaculate military uniform and tie.

ERWIN ROMMEL

In February 1943, shortly after his 1,300-mile retreat into Tunisia, the Desert Fox led his rebuilt *Panzerarmee* in his last battle on North African soil at Kasserine Pass. The battle was the first major engagement between American and Axis forces in WWII. Despite once again facing a superior force, Rommel crushed the inexperienced and poorly led American troops, inflicting 6,500 casualties and pushing the Allies back over 50 miles from their forward position. But the victory parade was short-lived as in the same month the German Sixth Army was annihilated at Stalingrad. Germany was now retreating on all fronts, and the days of the Third Reich and a unified Germany were numbered.

In March, due to continuing poor health, Rommel handed over command of *Armeegruppe Afrika* to General Von Arnim and left for Germany, never to return to Africa. Von Arnim and more than a quarter million Axis troops were forced to surrender to the Allies in May 1943, and, as Rommel predicted, there was nothing left with which to defend Sicily. The island fell in August 1943, but not before Mussolini was overthrown and replaced by an anti-Nazi government. Rommel, who had been assigned to command Army Group E to defend Greece against possible Allied landings, was swiftly transferred to Italy to command Army Group B. When Kesselring took command in Italy, Rommel was sent to France with Group B to prepare the defense against the much-anticipated Allied invasion across the English Channel.

Although most of the German commanders, including Hitler, believed that the Allies would land at Pas-de-Calais, Rommel thought it more likely they would attack Normandy. His view was that the invasion should be stopped on the beaches, because Allied air superiority would expose large movements of troops and armor to heavy bombing. In contrast, Field Marshal Gerd Von Rundstedt believed the German mobile reserves should be held further back in a position from where a more traditional counterattack could be launched. Hitler vacillated between the two plans but picked neither, instead placing the reserves farther forward, but not close enough for Rommel or far enough back for Von Rundstedt. The war would be over less than a year after the Americans and their British and Canadian Allies took the beaches of Normandy.

Although the Desert Fox soldiered on following his Africa campaign, he had increasing misgivings about Hitler and a deep and growing distrust of the Nazis and the German High Command. Finally, by mid-1944 he became convinced that they were betraying the German people, as they had betrayed the *Afrika Korps*. He then took what was for him a difficult step: he joined the conspiracy to dispose of the dictator and stop the slaughter, despite the risk to his own life. However, he himself held the view that Hitler should not be assassinated but rather imprisoned.

On July 17, 1944, he was commanding German forces in Normandy when his staff car was strafed by a British Spitfire and machine-gun bullets shattered his skull. Three days later, while the Desert Fox lay in a coma in a French hospital, Colonel Count Claus von Stauffenberg planted a bomb under Adolf Hitler's feet during a conference at his Wolf's Lair field headquarters near Rastenburg, East Prussia. The July 20 plot was known as Operation Valkyrie. Unfortunately, the Führer was merely wounded in the subsequent explosion. Enraged and out of control, Hitler ordered the Gestapo to track down everyone associated with the plot, along with their families. The conspirators were to be hung with piano wire; their loved ones were to be sent to concentration camps.

Soon Rommel's closest officers were implicated in the conspiracy and were broken under interrogation, and his complicity was discovered. On October 14, 1944, he was offered the choice of suicide or a trial by the People's Court, where the verdict was already decided. If he killed himself, Hitler's SS messengers said, none of the customary actions against his family would be taken. Knowing that the former almost certainly meant execution and that his family would be badly treated, he opted to commit suicide and was given an hour to explain his decision to his wife Lucie and fifteen-year-old son Manfred. Then, wearing his *Afrika Korps* jacket and carrying his field marshal's baton, he was driven by the SS men out of his village and took a cyanide capsule to end his life.

Ten minutes later, the group telephoned Rommel's wife to inform her of his death. Witnesses were struck by the smile of deep contempt on the dead man's face, never seen in life, and his widow Lucie thought it was for Hitler. The official Nazi line was that he had died of a heart attack brought on by his wounds. He was buried, against his wishes, with all the pomp the Führer and Nazi state could muster. The fact that his state funeral was held in Ulm instead of Berlin had, according to Manfred, been stipulated by his father. Rommel had also specified that no political paraphernalia be displayed on his corpse, but the Nazis made sure his coffin was festooned with swastikas. The body was then cremated so no incriminating evidence would be left. The truth behind Rommel's death did not become known to the Allies until after the war, when German-speaking U.S. intelligence officer Charles Marshall interviewed Lucie and a letter by Manfred was uncovered in April 1945.

Rommel's grave is located in Herrlingen, a short distance west of Ulm. For decades after the war on the anniversary of his death, veterans of the North African Desert War, including former opponents, would gather at his tomb in Herrlingen.

What should the Desert Fox's legacy be? For his unabashed critics, if Erwin Rommel is to be remembered, "it should also be remembered that each of his victories helped secure Hitler's agenda of genocide, mass murder, and exploitation. It should be remembered that the weight of evidence shows that Rommel did nothing to oppose the crimes of the Nazi regime. Ultimately, if Erwin Rommel is to be remembered, then it is just as important to remember that being a hero should not be based so much on daring exploits or unique skill as what side someone was ultimately on."

For those who see more nuance in the man, the words of British historian Daniel

Allen Butler, the author of *Field Marshal: The Life and Death of Erwin Rommel (2017)*, probably strike closer to home: "Erwin Rommel was a complex man: a born leader, a brilliant soldier, a devoted husband, a proud father; intelligent, instinctive, brave, compassionate, vain, egotistical, and arrogant. In France in 1940, then for two years in North Africa, then finally back in France once again, in Normandy in 1944, he proved himself a master of armored warfare, running rings around a succession of Allied generals who never got his measure and could only resort to overwhelming numbers to bring about his defeat. And yet he was also naïve, a man who could admire Adolf Hitler at the same time that he despised the Nazis, dazzled by a Führer whose successes blinded him to the true nature of the Third Reich. Above all, though, he was the quintessential German patriot, who would still fight for Germany even as he abandoned his oath of allegiance to the Führer, when he came to realize that Adolf Hitler had morphed into nothing more than an agent of death and destruction, and in that moment he chose to speak Truth to Power. In the end, Erwin Rommel was forced to die by his own hand, not because, as some would claim, he had dabbled in tyrannicidal conspiracy, but because he had committed a far greater crime—he dared to tell Adolf Hitler the truth."

In Charles Messenger's biography *Rommel: Leadership Lessons from the Desert Fox*, the author praised Rommel's skill on the battlefield, and in the foreword to the book, written by U.S. General Wesley Clark, the former NATO commander remarked that "no foreign general has ever quite inspired as much passion, curiosity and respect among Americans as German Field Marshal Erwin Rommel." In the harrowing summer of 1942, when the Desert Fox appeared poised to take Cairo and the Suez, Churchill hysterically exclaimed, "Rommel, Rommel, Rommel! What else matters but beating him?" Like most of history's conspicuously successful commanders, he had an uncanny ability to dominate the minds of his adversaries.

Today, Rommel is recognized for his military prowess while acknowledging his political naiveté and ugly association with Hitler and the Nazis. On the one hand, he is seen as a master battlefield tactician, chivalrous practitioner of fair play in warfare, and a loving and devoted husband who never joined the National Socialist party, was firmly aware of the plot to kill Hitler and yet did nothing to stop it, and did not learn of the Holocaust until mid- to late-1944 shortly before his death. On the other hand, he is considered to have been a less than stellar military strategist who too often blamed the German High Command and Italians for his failures, a brusque and stubborn prima donna and publicity hound (just like his rivals Patton and Montgomery), and a political neophyte who willingly fought for the most despicable leader and cause of all time.

It should be remembered, however, that all Rommel ever wanted to be was a simple soldier. Which is why perhaps Winston Churchill has summed up the Desert Fox's legacy best of all. In his 1942 speech to the Houses of Parliament, he declared: "We have a very daring and skilful opponent against us, and, may I say across the havoc of war, a great general." And after the war, his praise was just as fulsome: "In the height of the war, I paid tribute to General Rommel's outstanding military gifts, and I am bound to say now, in time of peace, that I also regard his resistance to the Hitler tyranny, which cost him his life, as an additional distinction to his memory."

But there's another Rommel anecdote that I think illuminates the true Desert

Fox. In May 1944, Captain Roy Wooldridge of the British Royal Engineers was taken prisoner during a covert nighttime mission to examine submerged mines along the Normandy beaches prior to the D-Day landings. He was not wearing his Army uniform, nor carrying identification, due to the intense secrecy surrounding D-Day. Under Hitler's "Commando Order," all Allied commandos encountered in Europe and Africa were to be handed over to the SS and killed immediately without trial, even if in proper uniforms or if they attempted to surrender. But instead Captain Woolridge was brought before Rommel. The Desert Fox asked the Briton if there was anything he needed, to which the captain replied, rather cheekily, that he would like "a good meal, a pint of beer, and a packet of cigarettes." Then he was dismissed.

Shortly afterwards, he was taken to the mess hall and a waiter delivered him a stein of beer, cigarettes, and a plate of food. Woolridge couldn't believe his eyes.

"Hitler had issued orders that commandos were to be shot but Rommel declined to obey that instruction," said the captain years later. "Rommel saved my life. He was a very fine German and a clean fighter."

Novelists, Hollywood filmmakers, and others have been attracted to the legend of the Desert Fox and the heroic and chivalrous nature of the Desert War on both sides. British Army Brigadier Desmond Young, captured by German forces in North Africa during World War II, met Rommel and became enthralled by him. Young wrote the seminal 1950 biography of the Field Marshal, *Rommel: The Desert Fox*, which served as the basis of the 1951 movie, *The Desert Fox*, starring James Mason in an "utterly convincing" performance as Rommel. Mason reprised his role as Rommel two years later in the movie sequel entitled *The Desert Rats*.

Rommel's war in North Africa was not, however, quite as glamorous as portrayed by Hollywood. The fortunes of war left the Desert Fox—perhaps coincidentally, perhaps not—once his precious "little fellers" went off the air, Captain Seebohm was killed and his 621st Radio Intercept Company and all its codes were captured, Aberle and Weber were taken prisoner, and Operation Condor was thwarted. Some claimed Rommel had lost his "sixth sense"—but being outmanned and outgunned by the British at El Alamein and relinquishing air superiority to the enemy, what he truly lost was the ability to take chances and fight the type of offensive battle where he could outflank and defeat the British.

HEKMAT FAHMY

On August 25, 1942, the court of inquiry set up by the Egyptian government ruled that Hekmat Fahmy should be let off with merely a warning for her admittedly peripheral involvement in the Operation Condor affair. Mohamed Abdel Rahman Ahmad (the chauffeur of car no. 14060 used by Eppler and Sandstette) and Albert Wahda (the money changer) were also set free by the court with a simple warning. The British agreed with the Egyptian court findings—except in the case of Hekmat Fahmy.

Sir Miles Lampson, the British ambassador, had a reservation about the wildly popular entertainer. "Ought the dancer Hekmat to be let out again?" he sniffed. "To consort (as in the past) with erotic young British officers? I should have thought surely not?" Though it is doubtful that his recommendation prevailed, there is disagreement on exactly what sentence Hekmat Fahmy ultimately received. Saul

Kelly, author of the well-researched *The Lost Oasis: The True Story Behind the English Patient*, states that, despite Lampson's wishes, she was set free with only a warning just like the other minor players Ahmad and Wahda. The newly declassified British Security Service files in KV-2-1467 make no mention of whether Hekmat's sentencing was altered based on Lampson's recommendation. Former Middle East MI5 officer H.O. Covey, author of *Operation Condor, Intelligence and National Security*, regarded as the most accurate British account based on War Office and Foreign Office files, also states that Hekmat was let off with a warning by the Egyptian court of inquiry but acknowledges that Lampson's "view may have prevailed: though the file says nothing."

According to Leonard Mosley—the British war correspondent for *The Sunday Times* and author of *The Cat and the Mice*, who first came across Eppler and the Condor story while serving as a journalist in the Middle East—Hekmat served a prison term of one year before retiring to Upper Egypt. But Mosley, as explained in detail below, has been shown to be an unreliable narrator with regards to the Condor story. Mark Simmons, author of the excellent *The Rebecca Code: Rommel's Spy in North Africa and Operation Condor*, also says that she was "released after a year," but his reference is apparently Mosley. Other (mostly Internet) resources give sentences served of between one to a whopping five years, but none of these appear to be credible given Hekmat Fahmy's negligible involvement in Operation Condor.

The false but unfortunately nearly ubiquitous image of Hekmat Fahmy as a Nazi spy akin to Mata Hari was started by Eppler and Mosley and has been shamelessly regurgitated by dozens of chroniclers in history books, novels, the Internet, and on the silver screen. In this fanciful scenario, the gorgeous and irresistible Hekmat plays the role of dark-skinned Oriental seductress and master Abwehr spy. Deep down, she is a rabid Egyptian nationalist and British-hater, who uses her sexual powers to lure top secrets out of one or more gallant, unsuspecting British officers. To accomplish her Machiavellian ends, not only does she put Eppler and Sandstette up on her houseboat and find them their own accommodations on the Nile knowing that they are German spies, but she puts her old lover in contact with two anti-British-officers, Ezzet and Sadat, and drugs the drinks of her infatuated British lover, a mysterious man called "Major Smith." She performs these diabolical deeds masterfully, of course, allowing Eppler to read the high-level dispatches while she keeps Major Smith preoccupied, and later the clever German spy is able to send word of Allied reinforcements and supplies back to Rommel along with information on Auchinleck's defensive positions. There's just one problem: almost none of it is true and there never was a Major Smith.

As shown in British Security Service file KV-2-1467 and in this book, Hekmat's real British live-in lover was one Captain Guy Bellairs. The detailed British interrogation records make it clear that Captain Bellairs, not Major Smith, was the owner of the superannuated map of the Tobruk fortifications and the other belongings in the spare bedroom on her houseboat taken into evidence by Major Sansom during Hekmat's arrest. Perhaps Captain Bellairs was at some point promoted to major during the Condor affair, but his name was not Smith. Whoever the mystery man was, he was apparently never punished and his involvement in the Condor affair was kept hush-hush. As Kelly states, "There is no evidence that

Hekmat's British lover was ever reprimanded for his admittedly peripheral involvement in the Condor affair." This is echoed by Covey: "There is nothing in the file to suggest that Hekmat's English officer lover was penalized for the company she kept while he was in the Desert."

Based on the most reliable sources (KV-2-1467, Saul Kelly, H.O. Covey, and Mark Simmons), Hekmat Fahmy was not even close to being a spy, which is why I haven't made her one in this book. In the 16-page enclosure dated August 24, 1942 to a letter from Colonel G.L. Jenkins of the Defense Security Office, Egypt, dated August 29, 1942, Hekmat is not even listed on the "Index of Principal Persons Involved in the German Spy Case." In addition to Eppler and Sandstette, the list includes the principal conspirators Hassan Gaafar, Victor Hauer, Frau Doktor Fatma Amer, Abdel Salama, Hassan Ezzet, Anwar el Sadat, and Aziz el Masri—but Hekmat Fahmy is conspicuously absent along with the other minor players, the chauffeur Ahmad and the money changer Wahda. As Kelly states, "There is no evidence for the feats of espionage or of help to the agents that Hekmat Fahmy has since been credited with by many authors. She was no Mata Hari. Though she found another *dahabia* for them to live on at Agouza near the Egyptian Benevolent Hospital, that was all she did."

The MI5 man Covey also neatly debunks Hekmat's mythical role in the Condor story based on the British intelligence records. "Against these new characters and old ones with bigger roles, Hekmat Fahmy stands out in contrast. There is no suggestion in the records that she did anything to help the Germans other than putting them up for one night and then finding a houseboat for them to live on. There is no hint of the feats of espionage or of the help to the agents that Mosley, Carell, Brown, Mure, and Eppler himself credit her with. And as her Mata Hari role disappears so does her lover, Major 'Smith', in both his guises: Mosley's devoted wooer, assuaged by Hekmat on one night only, and Brown's more frequently gratified afternoon visitor—in neither case aware as he lay in the dancer's bed that Eppler was reading the contents of his briefcase in the adjoining room." Simmons puts a slightly different spin on the renowned belly dancer and socialite: "Hekmat herself denied having anything to do with Eppler and Sandy's espionage activities, or even showing them her lover's papers. No doubt she was willing to pass on any pillow talk gleaned from British officers, much as her colleagues on the belly dancing circuit did for a financial consideration, but she was no Mara Hari."

So how, without a shred of evidence, did Hekmat Fahmy become Mata Hari 2.0 with dozens of book, movie, and Internet references claiming she was a German spy who lured her British victims to her bedchambers on the Nile? The tall tales spun by Eppler to Mosley, who had yet to write *The Cat and the Mice* (1957), the first book to cover the Condor story, and the gross exaggerations put forth by Eppler in his own book (*Rommel Ruft Cairo*, 1960, later translated as *Operation Condor: Rommel's Spy*, 1977) had a great deal to do with it. Eppler pulled one over on Mosley and then pulled the wool over everyone's eyes again with his own wildly embroidered account three years later. As Simmons states, "Mosley was in Cairo at the same time the events took place" and he interviewed Eppler and Sandstette in prison. "He also kept in touch with Eppler after the war. However, in view of the later accounts, one written by Eppler, and later firm evidence, it is certain that Eppler strung him along to a degree in order to embellish his own image as some sort of James Bond."

At the same time, Eppler embellished Hekmat's role as well, turning her into the Mata Hari *femme fatale* that has permeated the Condor narrative for decades. But to his credit, during his interrogation by the British at Maadi he claimed vehemently that she had not helped him, except to put her up platonically for the night on her *dahabia* and to help him and Sandstette rent a houseboat of their own. Thus, it is only in his books after the war that he made Hekmat into his master accomplice. As shown in KV-2-1467, "Both P.W. (prisoners of war) deny strenuously that Hekmat obtained or ever offered to obtain any military information for them...Eppler stressed the fact that Hekmat is a very ignorant girl who knows nothing outside of dancing, drinking and the etc., who speaks no other language but Arabic and cannot possibly understand any conversation relating to military matters." That Eppler was protecting his former girlfriend is obvious since the historical record has firmly established that Hekmat Fahmy was a cultured socialite who spoke English well with her legion of British officer fans at the Kit Kat Club and Continental Hotel.

It was, therefore, only later when it came time to write his book and juice up the spy story that Eppler changed the Hekmat narrative: "I discussed everything with Hekmat during the remainder of the night in her fabulously furnished houseboat," he claims in *Operation Condor: Rommel's Spy*, sounding more like James Bond than the bumbling Abwehr agent he truly was, "while we lay in her wide sensuous bed under its silken mosquito net. We perfected our plans to the last detail." And then later in the same chapter: "Hekmat was something special. She fitted well into undercover work....She gave me proof of her faithfulness later, during some very unpleasant hours she spent in the hands of the Secret Intelligence Service." Again, there's just one problem: she was never a spy or accomplice, although at some point it is likely that Eppler did confide in her, given their romantic history together. But possessing information in wartime Cairo was hardly a crime as many Cairenes at the time gossiped and peddled information to both sides.

In *The Key to Rebecca* (1980), Ken Follett's fictionalized recreation of the Condor story based on Mosley, Eppler, and Anthony Cave Brown's inaccurate original rendering, the Welsh author has taken it a step further: he has turned Hekmat into a sexual deviant that reads like the twisted fantasy of Sir Miles Lampson. Like the real-life Hekmat, Follett's Sonja el-Aram is an alluring belly dancer, lives on a houseboat on the Nile, and is the former lover of the book's main villain Alex Wolff, the "brilliant, handsome, daring and ruthless Nazi master agent" based on Eppler—but this time she is an unlikable, bisexual, masochistic, Anglo-loathing Egyptian nationalist. Together with Wolff (Eppler), Sonja (Hekmat) repeatedly lures a wimpy British major into feverish liaisons on her houseboat while the German agent steals secret papers from the unsuspecting officer's briefcase. Hekmat would, of course, roll over in her grave at Follett's characterization, for not only has she been unfairly turned into a willing Nazi spy but she is now a pouty little slut who can't stand up to Eppler (as Wolff) and is coerced into having sex with a British officer she despises to gain military secrets for her former lover. In fairness to Follett, he at least changed Hekmat's name to disguise her true identity, and the critical British intelligence files on Operation Condor available to writers today were not available to the public at the time he penned his novel in the late 1970s, which was why he relied upon the Mosley, Eppler, and Anthony Cave Brown accounts of the Condor saga.

What became of the real Hekmat after her one-month (if she was, in fact, released on August 25, 1942, as Kelly claims) to one-year (if Mosley and Simmons are somehow correct) incarceration and the end of the war? What we know for certain is that, at the time of her arrest, she was the most sought-after dancer in Cairo, with a fame that rivaled Madame Badia's. From the mid-1930s until her arrest, she moved in high-class circles, danced for the rich and famous of many countries, and was the most well-known dancer in Europe and Africa. And then, when she was imprisoned and British fortunes in Egypt turned around with Montgomery's victory at El Alamein, her popularity declined and she became something of a *persona non grata* in her own hometown. Though still employed as a dancer, she no longer moved in the elite circles she had in the past or had access to socialites, politicians, and army officers. Soon, the new crop of younger talented dancers that had arrived on the scene like Samia Gamal and Tahia Carioca who were in their twenties began to eclipse her and she could no longer compete at her previous level.

She appeared in six films in her career, including the successful *El Azima* (The Will, 1939) and *Rabab* in 1942. In 1947, she made a movie called *El Moutasharida*, which flopped miserably at the box office. In the movie, she lip-synched the singing scenes and another actress performed the voice-overs. She apparently retired after this failure to Upper Egypt. According to Mosley, at this point in her life, "Her body has thickened and the fire has gone out of her eyes and her limbs. She will never be the exotic and exciting dancer that so many Eighth Army officers knew in 1942."

She died in Egypt in 1974, at 66 years old. In 1994, the Egyptian movie *Hekmat Fahmy The Spy*, directed by famous film director Hossam El Dine Mostafa, was released. In a final twist of irony, the synopsis for the 128-minute thriller could have been written by Eppler, Mosley, or Follett: "The true story of the Egyptian belly dancer Hekmat Fahmy who served as a spy for the Germans during WWII."

Poor Hekmat—even after her death she couldn't get a fair shake. But as history now informs us, she was no Mata Hari.

ALFRED W. "SAMMY" SANSOM

Following his arrest of Eppler and Sandstette on July 25, 1942—the zenith of Sansom's career—the major continued to work in Cairo as a senior security officer. After serving as chief of security during Churchill's visit to Cairo in August 1942, his duties as the war progressed westward away from Egypt increased in the area of protection for VIPs, as the City Victorious became a favorite place for conferences.

He dealt with a variety of factions, from Egyptian nationalists wishing to cast off the British imperialist yoke, to mutinies within the Greek forces then serving in Egypt that heralded the civil war in Greece. He was also faced with the machinations of various Zionist groups who had their eye on Palestine.

According to Mark Simmons in *The Rebecca Code: Rommel's Spy in North Africa and Operation Condor*, the assassination of Lord Mayne, the British Minister of State in the Middle East, in November 1944 deeply affected Sansom. He had warned Lord Moyne that he was a likely target: "He only laughed. But I still blame myself for having let it happen." Sansom was first told of the plot by Yvette of the Zionist Stern Gang, whom he had first met during the Condor case. Seeking him out in a nightclub, she informed him that an assassination was likely. Lord Mayne proved unwilling to accept protection, not wanting his private life to be intruded upon by security men. After having dismissed his guard detail in the morning, later that day he was gunned down by two Jewish youths with submachine guns as he arrived to his house. His driver tried to come to his aid and was also murdered.

Sansom was furious that the report by the guards of their dismissal that morning had not been passed on to him; two hours had passed between their leaving and the assassination. The fact that within minutes the security forces caught the assassins crossing the Boulac Bridge was a hollow victory. At the trial, the accused freely admitted they had killed Lord Moyne and were found guilty and condemned to death. Selected to be present at the execution in March 1945, Sansom found the hanging to be "an unpleasant job if ever there was one." He was however impressed by the dignified way the two Jewish freedom-fighters met their end. As they were positioned on the scaffold they both sang the *Hatikvah*, the Jewish national anthem. Neither finished it. One moment their voices filled the execution chamber, the next, there was absolute silence.

According to Simmons, by February 1947, Sansom had swapped his army peak cap for a civilian bowler hat, when he was transferred to the Foreign Office and was appointed as security officer at the British Embassy, Cairo. In July 1952, the Egyptian Army took over the government by force. The former Egyptian Army signals officer Anwar el Sadat became the First Minister of State in the revolutionary Egyptian government and King Farouk was deposed as head of state. Sansom had to leave in a hurry, given his background of having arrested most of the leading nationalists in the Egyptian Army during the war years, who had openly vowed revenge.

He returned home to England, a country he had spent hardly any time in and scarcely knew. He had to learn to live without his luxury flat and servants in an austere postwar Britain, but his service to the nation was recognized with his award as a Member of the Most Excellent Order of the British Empire (MBE) recorded in the New Year's honors list for 1953.

In 1960, Sansom met Eppler again in London at a reception for the premiere of the film *Foxhole in Cairo*. The movie was based on Leonard Mosley's famously inaccurate 1958 book *The Cat and the Mice*. The film poster called it "the greatest spy story of the desert war." That is, of course, true though it must be said that the real-life spies Eppler and Sandstette, and their pro-Axis supporters who served prison sentences for helping them, were about as competent as the Three Stooges. In the film, James Robertson Justice plays the British intelligence officer, a naval commander, tasked with catching the spies, while Eppler and Sandstette are portrayed respectively by Lee Montague and Michael Caine, appearing in one of his early roles as the German wireless operator.

In 1965, Sansom published his memoir, *I Spied Spies*. Unlike Mosley's book, Sansom's book is mostly accurate in the details, which is why it was used extensively in the writing of this book. What Sansom doesn't get quite right is the chronology of events and the way in which the Operation Condor case was ultimately solved. Old Sammy just couldn't resist placing himself at the center of the events in the case and skewing the timeline to make himself look important, when from the declassified British files we know how the investigation and capture of the German spies really occurred.

As the ever-reliable Kelly states, "Successive writers and filmmakers have claimed that the arrest of Rommel's spies was due to the tracing of the sterling notes to them by...Major Sansom, the efforts of the mysterious Yvette, the beautiful Jewish Agency spy, and the monitoring of the signals sent by Eppler and Sandstette from Cairo. However, a Security Intelligence Middle East report of October 1942 states that the Condor agents 'were never able to make contact with their distant station, and spent most of their time and money in riotous living. It was partly through their own carelessness, together with the converging on them of information derived from several independent channels, including the statements of POW's, and reports of secret agents, that they were arrested.' The reckless use of sterling by Eppler and Sandstette in Cairo's nightclubs, bars and brothels no doubt aroused the interest of Major Sansom and Field Security, who kept a watch on the 'mysterious happenings' at the houseboat on the Nile. But the actual arrest of Rommel's spies, and their contacts, was due to the receipt of information as to the presence of the two Germans on the *dahabia* from the recaptured German civilian escapee, Siegel. It was not until two days after the capture and interrogation of Eppler and Sandstette that British Counter-Intelligence in Cairo realized [for certain] that they were the two spies that had been brought across the desert by Almasy, as revealed by Aberle and Weber, the two Abwehr operatives captured by the LRDG." The reliable historical sleuths Covey and Simmons echo these sentiments.

In *The Rebecca Code: Rommel's Spy in North Africa and Operation Condor*, Simmons states that the details of Sansom's last days are not clear. There is an Alfred William Sansom, apparently born in Egypt, buried at the Ta' Braxia cemetery in Malta with a date of death given as February 19, 1973. "Did Sansom spend his last years on the sunny island of Malta?" Simmons asks rhetorically. "It is to be hoped, for if there is one hero in this story surely it is 'Sammy' Sansom." Yes, Old Sammy was certainly a heroic figure in the Condor saga, but the chap did regrettably fudge the facts a wee bit in his book (or not get his facts straight due to faulty memory), which has inadvertently led to the continued misrepresentation of the Operation Condor affair by a succession of writers and filmmakers.

JOHANNES EPPLER (HUSSEIN GAAFAR)

After Eppler and his accomplice Sandstette were arrested on July 25, 1942, they were treated as prisoners of war rather than spies, and were handed over to the British rather than face an Egyptian Court of Inquiry. They were thoroughly interrogated, put through a court martial, and sentenced to death, the fate awaiting most spies. However, in view of the volatile political situation in Egypt, their willing cooperation with their captors, and the fact that Eppler was the son of prominent pro-British judge Salah Gaafar, both Eppler and Sandstette were treated as political prisoners and given leniency. After being tried and convicted, they were incarcerated in a POW camp for the duration of the war rather than executed as spies. According to Mosley, Sandstette was distraught at being imprisoned and tried to cut his own throat with a knife, but ended up botching the attempt and merely spent several weeks in the hospital.

In the end, the two German operatives that have been portrayed as virtuoso master spies in books and the silver screen for several decades emerge with little credit from the Condor affair. There is no sign that they ever had any worthwhile information to transmit, even if they had been able to do so. As Kelly states, "Their bogus diary entries and Eppler's desperate plans to get back to Rommel do not speak well for their morals or their morale." It is, therefore, not surprising that during their interrogation following their arrest, they came completely clean to save their own skins even though they incriminated many of those who gave them assistance. But according to Covey, not all the blame can be placed on their shoulders: "In mitigation it must be said that their Abwehr masters let them down badly, first by providing them with the conspicuous English currency, then by allowing Aberle and Weber to be moved so far forward in the desert that they were taken prisoner, and finally by making no attempt to contact the Condor men in Cairo once radio communication had become unsafe. The cross-desert journey to the Nile (for which the credit goes mainly to Almasy) was a fine achievement, but the rest of the mission was an anti-climax and nothing for the Abwehr to be proud of."

After the arrests of the spies and their contacts, Colonel G.J. Jenkins, British Defense Security Officer (DSO), Egypt, reported that, "Their transmitter, their codes and their diaries are in our hands." But as Covey makes clear in *Operation Condor, Intelligence and National Security*, there is nothing in the official British records about "the counterespionage work which preceded this satisfactory result, nothing to confirm the highlights of the books." These highlights include the tracing of the sterling notes by Sansom and his team, the discovery of the Rebecca cipher, the monitoring of the signals, the role of the enterprising Jewish underground figure Yvette, the raid on Eppler's and Sandstette's houseboat and Hekmat Fahmy's houseboat, and the rolled-up socks simulating hand grenades. "Instead," says Covey, "we have only the surveillance of car 14660 and its chauffeur Mohammed and the detection of 'mysterious happenings' on the houseboat. But for all the surveillance, it was not until Siegel the escapee was recaptured and yielded up his information that the DSO had what he needed to make some arrests. It is not difficult to guess what that information might have been: his compatriot Hauer had told Siegel that he might find shelter on the houseboat—because two Germans were living there."

So in the words of Covey, "the end of the affair had a curious symmetry with the beginning." Captain Almasy's activities as they appeared in the British intelligence reports were no more than "mysterious happenings" in the desert until Aberle and Weber were captured and interrogated and revealed that the Hungarian explorer's task was to shepherd two spies into Egypt equipped with the same ciphers and signals plan as the two prisoners. That was all the two Abwehr wireless operators knew—more alarming than useful, and all too little to guide DSO Jenkins or Sansom in the search for the spies. Furthermore, the British authorities did not know for certain that there was a link between Aberle and Weber and the Germans living on the houseboat, or that Eppler and Sandstette were Almasy's spies, until the two Abwehr operatives had been thoroughly interrogated and divulged virtually everything about Operations Salam and Condor. MI6's mystery man Bob and Sansom had suspicions, but confirmation had to wait until full disclosure by the spies was secured under interrogation.

Eppler was held in prison until the autumn of 1946, when he was flown to Germany. There he was mistakenly transferred to and interned at Hamburg-Neuengame in a camp for war criminals, but MI6 intervened and he was released. He then began working in the black market, at which time, according to Eppler himself, the Russian KGB contacted him to spy for them, but he turned them down. Life became too "hot" so he moved to the rural south of Germany to Saarland, where his mother had come from, and started a book business. Sandstette, too, was flown back to Germany at the end of the war and imprisoned as a war criminal, but was also able to secure his release and returned to East Africa to take up farming.

In 1957, Eppler moved to France and became a resident. The German film *Rommel Ruft Kairo* (*Rommel Calls Cairo*) came out in 1959 and was based upon the subsequently released book of the same name published in German one year later in 1960. In the film, Eppler is portrayed by Adrian Hoven. In a 1960 photograph of Eppler and Sansom meeting again for the first time since Eppler's arrest, the two old foes can be seen smiling together in their dapper suits and ties. The reunion was a reception for the premiere of the film *Foxhole in Cairo* based on Mosley's *The Cat and the Mice*. Eppler, seated next to his wife and daughter, smiles at Sansom and his wife across a bar table covered with cocktail glasses, looking as though the war the two fought in was a distant memory or perhaps never even happened. In 1970, in an ironic twist, Eppler went on to portray Field Marshal Erwin Rommel in the French film *Le Mur de l'Atlantique*.

In 1974, he wrote a more extensive version of his memoirs, again in German, while living in a flat in Paris on the banks of the Seine. The end result was *Geheimagent im Zweiten Weltkrieg: Zwischen Berlin, Kabul und Kairo* (*Secret Agent in World War II: Between Berlin, Kabul and Cairo*). In 1977, the wildly exaggerated book making himself out to be a German James Bond was translated into English as *Operation Condor: Rommel's Spy*. Despite Eppler's penchant for embellishment, when one reads his account of the Condor affair and examines his photographs from the 1940s-1970s, one cannot help but smile as Eppler comes across as a lovable rogue. As Sansom said of him, "You couldn't help liking him, you know. Even though he was a German and a spy, he had something about him. He knew how to enjoy himself. He liked people. And he was never afraid. But he was damned lucky, you know. I'm glad we didn't shoot him!" As stated previously and made clear by Sansom, perhaps the most important reason the two spies were treated as political prisoners and weren't shot was because Eppler's stepfather, Judge Saleh Gaafar, was a prominent and influential supporter of the British in Egypt.

During his time in France in the 1960s, 1970s, and 1980s, Eppler went into construction and became wealthy building factories around the globe. Traveling from Budapest to Amman to Helsinki to Rio supervising projects, he prided himself on his fluent command of German, English, French, Italian, and Swahili, as well as five dialects of Arabic. "Money can be lost overnight," he said more than thirty years after the Condor affair, "but no one can take languages from you." During the course of his life, he was married five times, including to a Danish ballet dancer, a Hungarian countess, and a French engineer.

In 1980, journalist Pamela Andriotakis interviewed Eppler for *People* magazine in connection with the release of Ken Follett's *The Key to Rebecca*. Then 66 years old, Eppler was a millionaire businessman living outside Paris in an apartment near Versailles. At the time, the WWII government documents on the Condor affair were still classified and most people at the time—including Follett himself—believed the book was for the most part a true story and not the wild imaginings of Eppler, Mosley, and a host of others who simply embellished their stories. The title of the *People* article is ironic itself: *The Real Spy's Story Reads Like Fiction and 40 Years Later Inspires a Best-Seller*. As we now know, there's a good reason Eppler's account reads like fiction: most of it is.

Johannes Eppler died on August 15, 1999 at the ripe old age of 85, probably with a smile on his face at the preposterous legend of Operation Condor he had helped create.

BONNER FELLERS

After Rommel's Good Source was recalled from Cairo to Washington in mid-July 1942, he was assigned for temporary duty in the British Empire branch of the Military Intelligence Division. The U.S. military did not in any way fault Fellers or discipline him for the fact that his reports were intercepted by the Germans; instead, he was decorated with the Distinguished Service Medal and made a brigadier general. His successor simply replaced the Black Code with the M-138 strip cipher, a military code which the Germans were unable to penetrate throughout the war.

The truth was that President Roosevelt and the top military brass knew that the U.S. Government was ultimately responsible for the Black Code intelligence fiasco—not a military attaché simply following orders. Fellers was not responsible for the security of U.S. Foreign Service Encryption Code 11; his mission was simply to write comprehensive intelligence reports and send them to Washington using the officially designated code. It was not in his control what code was used nor his fault that he was not provided with a secure system. Furthermore, as Christian Jennings, author of *The Third Reich Is Listening: Inside German Codebreaking 1939-45*, states, "Although it would seem tempting to blame Colonel Fellers for appalling lack of radio discretion and discipline, in his defense he did protest to the American State Department about the insecure codes he was made to use. In one of his own telegrams, on 2 February 1942, he stated that '[I] believe that code-compromised', but Washington insisted the code was secure." Thus, he objected to the code in writing, but his concerns were dismissed by the U.S. Government.

However, some historians do point out that Fellers was guilty of at least complacency in failing to safeguard the integrity of his messages, for the Germans found it easy to locate his reports amidst the electronic traffic. As John Bierman and Colin Smith state in *The Battle of Alamein: Turning Point of World War II*, throughout his tour in Cairo, Fellers obligingly coded them and marked them for MILID WASH (Military Intelligence Division, Washington) or AGWAR WASH (Adjutant General, War Department, Washington), and signed them FELLERS. Had he been more security conscious and varied the way he prefaced and signed off his dispatches to Washington, the authors claim, they would not have been so easy to pick out from the hundreds of messages going through the Germans' main radio intercept station every day, and not so easy to decode quickly. Thus Rommel, each day at lunch, knew exactly where the Allied troops were standing the evening before.

The British analysis of Enigma decrypts through Ultra cumulatively made it apparent that the U.S. legation in Cairo was the source of the leaks. Once the British were in no doubt that Fellers's office was the reason for the steady intelligence leakage, they made their case to the U.S. military attaché's superiors in Washington and he was sent home. However, the British were probably more upset at how accurately his detailed first-hand accounts had captured their ineptitude in the face of Rommel and his *Panzerarmee*—and were terrified that the robust American aid they were generously being given through Lend-Lease would cease and the U.S. would give its own troops the much-needed Sherman tanks, Priest guns, and aircraft that had thus far done nothing but barely hold Rommel at bay.

No reason was given for Fellers's coming "home for consultations" other than the flimsy one that "with the reorganization of the Middle East Command it appears that Colonel Fellers's usefulness...has ceased." But the Black Code affair was acutely embarrassing for some time to Anglo-U.S. relations in the Middle East. However, the British could not make a public fuss; they were deeply beholden to the Americans for all kinds of arms assistance, in particular tanks. And according to Bierman and Smith, "even in confidential internal memos, the American top brass would continue to fudge the reasons for Fellers's abrupt removal from Cairo to a non-job in Washington."

British-American intelligence managed the Fellers affair on a need-to-know basis. Only a very few U.S. commanders held sufficient Ultra clearance to know the disturbing truth behind Fellers's recall from Cairo. Chief of Staff Marshall and General Eisenhower were two of the elite handful who were briefed on the intelligence snafu; however, there is no record that they were informed officially in writing, so it appears that they were only told verbally. Word must also have filtered down to a select few from the chief of staff's office. Lady Ranfurly recalls that when she mentioned Fellers's name approvingly to Eisenhower at a Cairo dinner party in November 1943, he cut her off dead. "Any friend of Bonner Fellers is no friend of mine," he snarled, and turned his back to resume a conversation with Kay Summersby, his driver and paramour. Fellers's pessimistic yet highly accurate assessment of British performance in the Desert War and his prescient forecast that there would be friction in future combined U.S.-U.K. operations was unacceptable to the Anglophile Eisenhower. However, he apologized to Lady Ranfurly the next day for his rudeness. Purportedly, his dislike of Fellers had begun at the time the two were serving under MacArthur, who had strained his relationship with Eisenhower in 1936-1937 while in the Philippines.

Eisenhower's extreme antipathy towards Fellers was largely because the North Africa leaks had strained British relations, which he found unacceptable in any U.S. officer; and because Fellers had been instrumental in getting presidential approval of increased support for the British in North Africa, which included Operation Torch. This was at odds with how the Joint Chiefs of Staff and the U.S. European

Command wanted the war to proceed. The U.S. military policy at the time was that saving the British in North Africa was not strategically required, and especially not through a North Africa invasion (Operation Torch) as that would divert focus from Operation Bolero, the plan for an early European cross-Channel invasion.

The most important outcome of Fellers's pessimistic but accurate reports was to ensure that more American supplies, troops, and aid were given to the wobbly British in North Africa. Throughout his tenure in North Africa, Fellers advocated for increased American support for the British in Libya and Egypt. This included both weapons and a commitment of American troops. President Roosevelt admired Fellers's reports and was influenced by them enough so that on June 29 General George Marshall wrote the President that "Fellers is a very valuable observer but his responsibilities are not those of a strategist and his views are in opposition to mine and those of the entire Operations Division." When the President invited Fellers to the White House on July 30, 1942 following his return from Cairo, Fellers persuasively argued for "robust and expeditious reinforcement of British forces in the Middle East." Thus, despite Fellers's blunt criticism, his analysis of the Middle East's strategic importance was instrumental in Roosevelt's decisions to massively reinforce the Eighth Army for Montgomery's forthcoming Second Battle of El Alamein and to support Operation Torch.

When Roosevelt awarded Fellers the Distinguished Service Medal, he did so in recognition of the maverick colonel's "uncanny ability to foresee military developments" in the Middle East and for the "clarity, brevity and accuracy" of his dispatches. The citation further reads: "Colonel Fellers, by personal observation of the battlefields, contributed materially to the tactical and technical development of our armed forces." The president cared little about Fellers's *persona non grata* status among the fussy British in Cairo or his blunt criticism that had obviously ruffled overly sensitive British feathers. America was a waxing world power, the British a great ally but a waning power on the global stage, and he wasn't about to admit that the U.S. had made a huge blunder by not being more diligent in handling its diplomatic code. He also seemed to like Fellers. As British historian C.J. Jenner notes, "Possibly the brilliant military attaché's notoriety appealed to Roosevelt's appetite for eccentric cloak and-dagger escapades. Certainly, Fellers's putative anticolonialism would have attracted the president."

Following his return to Washington, one of his colleagues in the Office of Strategic Services claimed he was the "most violent Anglophobe I have ever encountered." Soon thereafter, Fellers left his job in the OSS, where he played a role in planning psychological warfare, and returned to the Southwest Pacific to resume working for General MacArthur. Now promoted to brigadier general, he served as military secretary to the general, whom he greatly admired. While serving as a senior officer on MacArthur's Pacific Command staff, where his military career had commenced, he was psychological operations chief. During the liberation of the Philippines from the Japanese, Fellers had several assignments, including Director of Civil Affairs for the Philippines. For these efforts, he received a second Philippine Distinguished Service Star.

After the war, Fellers played a major role in the occupation of Japan. Tasked with investigating Emperor Hirohito's war responsibility, Fellers conducted hearings on Japanese government officials and advised MacArthur that it would be advantageous for the occupation, reconstruction of Japan, and U.S. long-range interests to keep Hirohito in place if he was not clearly responsible for war crimes. Thus, he played a major role in absolving the emperor of responsibility for Japan's wartime aggression across Asia. In a memo to MacArthur, now the Supreme Commander for the Allied Powers (SCAP), he wrote that the emperor had no authority and that if he was convicted as a war criminal, a general uprising would be inevitable. The emperor's name was subsequently stricken from the list of men to be charged as war criminals.

In October 1946, after returning from a postwar speaking tour in the United States, Fellers reverted to the rank of colonel as part of a reduction in rank of 212 generals. Retiring from the military in the same year, he became a prominent and active member of the hard-right John Birch Society and served as the national director of the Citizens Foreign Aid Committee. In 1948, his retirement rank was reinstated as brigadier general, and in 1953, he wrote a book entitled *Wings for Peace: A Primer for a New Defense*. He was also involved in promoting Republican Barry Goldwater for the presidency during the 1964 campaign.

In 1971, Emperor Hirohito conferred on Fellers the Second Order of the Sacred Treasure "in recognition of your long-standing contribution to promoting friendship between Japan and the United States." Fellers passed away two years later in 1973 at age 77.

Fellers's role in exonerating Hirohito is the main subject of the 2012 film *Emperor*. In the film, Tommy Lee Jones and Matthew Fox star in lead roles as General Douglas MacArthur and Brigadier General Bonner Fellers, respectively. The movie portrays Fellers, the main character, as a kind person who was sympathetic towards Japan. But Haruo Iguchi, a professor of international politics at Nagoya University's Graduate School of Environmental Studies, describes Fellers as a "tremendously ambitious man who posed some danger to both Japanese and American governments." Dangerous and a right-wing extremist he may have been, but what is most important is that he showed his mettle at the very center of dramatic events in WWII Egypt and Japan between 1941 and 1946. And the resourceful and charming Lady Ranfurly—who worked secretly for the British Secret Intelligence Service and was a good judge of character who mingled with the likes of Patton, Montgomery, Auchinleck, actor Douglas Fairbanks Jr., all three Stirling brothers, and kings Peter II of Yugoslavia, Farouk of Egypt, and the future Paul of Greece—certainly got a kick out of her close friend the outspoken American colonel during their time together in Egypt.

COUNT LÁSZLÓ ALMASY

Who was the real Captain Count László Almasy—the Hungarian adventurer, flight instructor, and Abwehr agent who the Bedouins reverently called *Abu Romia*, Father of the Sands?

In the 1992 novel *The English Patient* by Michael Ondaatje and the 1996 film of the same name, Almasy reluctantly gives the Germans his desert maps in return for the loan of a light aircraft in order to recover the body of his mistress from a cave. In real life, Almasy was an enthusiastic supporter of the German war effort and the architect of Operation Salam—and quite possibly an Axis spy well before the conflict. In the 1996 film version, Almasy, played by a Ralph Fiennes, is a disfigured patient in an Italian hospital who had been the handsome young heterosexual lover of an Englishwoman (Kristin Scott Thomas) in pre-war Cairo. In real life, Almasy was a "very ugly and shabbily dressed" man "with a fat and pendulous nose, drooping shoulders and a nervous tic." Photographs clearly show he looked far more like a gangly, beardless Geoffrey Rush than a strapping Ralph Fiennes. And, as revealed by John Bierman in *The Secret Life of Laszlo Almasy: The Real English Patient*, he was also a homosexual, counting a young German soldier named Hans Entholt amongst his lovers.

"How far a novelist is justified in bending the facts about a historical personage—even a little-known one like Almasy—to fit a work of fiction is, of course, a subject for hoary debate," say historians Bierman and Smith in *The Battle of Alamein: Turning Point of World War II*. "But Michael Ondaatje, the author of *The English Patient*, might easily have avoided any suggestion of misrepresentation by giving his protagonist a fictitious name." True enough. So, to separate fact from fiction, who then was the real Almasy, what did he do before the war, and why was he important?

László Almasy was born into a noble family at a castle in what is now Bernstein in Eastern Austria but in 1895 was Borostyanko, Hungary. Like the sons of many well-to-do Hungarian families at the time, he was sent to an English school. Almasy joined the 11th Hussars Regiment during the First World War and saw action against the Serbians and Russians. Showing an early aptitude for flying, in 1916 at the age of 20 he served as a pilot in the Austro-Hungarian Air Force. He was shot down over northern Italy in 1918 and became a flight instructor for the rest of the war.

Following the signing of the Treaty of Versailles, Almasy became a representative of the Steyr Automobile Company. In 1926, while demonstrating vehicles in Egypt and Sudan, he developed a lifelong love of the desert. In 1932, he took part in an expedition with three Englishmen, Sir Robert Clayton, Squadron Leader H.W.G.J. Penderel, and Patrick Clayton to find the legendary Zerzura Oasis—"The Oasis of the Birds." Instead, they found rock art sites in the "Cave of the Swimmers" of the Gilf Kebir. In 1933, Almasy claimed he had found the third valley of Zerzura. At the outbreak of the Second World War, he returned to Hungary and joined the Hungarian Air Force. In 1941, he was recruited by the Abwehr for his extensive desert knowledge, and in the spring of 1942 he took part in Operation Salam, successfully transporting Eppler and Sandstette from Jalo Oasis to the outskirts of Cairo.

According to Simmons in *The Rebecca Code: Rommel's Spy in North Africa and Operation Condor*, Almasy left North Africa in August 1942 for Athens to get treatment for amoebic dysentery, which he had picked up on Operation Salam. At this time, his friend and lover Hans Entholt returned to the *Afrika Korps* to serve on Rommel's staff. He was despondent that they couldn't be together. After treatment in Athens, Almasy decided to go home to Hungary via Italy and Germany.

In Italy, he looked up his old friend Pat Clayton, who was imprisoned in the Sulmona POW camp in the Abruzzi region. The camp commandant allowed Almasy to take Clayton out of the camp to a bar and they fondly reminisced about their old desert exploration days in Egypt before the war. There, he told Clayton that he had outwitted the LRDG during Operation Salam, showing him photographs of the Ford V8 he had used and its modifications. Following their reunion, Almasy was later able to help him by blocking Clayton's transfer to the notorious Campo Cinque, the Italian high security POW camp equivalent of Colditz, and arrange instead for him to go to Campo 29 Veano in Northern Italy. This act was very much appreciated by his English friend and former desert exploring colleague.

From Abruzzi, Almasy went on to Germany and reported to his Abwehr commander Major Seubert. He requested to be put on the reserve due to his ill health. In Hungary, he wrote his memoirs—*With Rommel's Army in Libya*—published in 1943. The book became a bestseller. It was vetted by the Abwehr and "doctored" by the Nazi Propaganda Ministry, so that there was no direct mention of Operation Salam or Condor. However, in chapter eight, "Desert Patrol," dated May 1942, he describes episodes straight out of Salam.

According to Simmons, Almasy was still on the Abwehr books and in the winter of 1943-1944 he was sent to Istanbul, Turkey—then a hotbed of intrigue and spies—to work with the pro-German Egyptians there. Abwehr agents in the city had run Father Demetriou in Cairo and installed the wireless set concealed by the priest in his church for use during Operation El Masri, the failed attempt to fly the Egyptian Army chief of staff out of Egypt. Even after the Allied invasion of Sicily in July 1943, Operation Husky, the Germans were still worried about the possible Allied invasion of the Balkans and sought to plant spies in Egypt, the likely starting point for an invasion. Soon thereafter, Almasy got further involved with Operation Dora and the top secret Luftwaffe unit KG 200 *Kampfgeschunder*. KG 200 was to set up secret bases in the North African desert to enable aircraft to refuel on long flights behind Allied lines to drop agents.

By this time the Abwehr was losing its independence, coming more under the control of the fanatical SS. Almasy was gravely worried about the German occupation of Hungary in March 1944. The Germans had learned that Admiral Miklos Horthy, the Hungarian dictator, had been making secret peace overtures to the Russians as the Red Army neared the borders of Hungary. At this stage of the war Hungary had become a refuge for Jews; 750,000 of them had taken up residence in the country, many having fled Poland. As the German Army poured across the border, they were followed by the SS, who swiftly began rounding up the Jews and deporting them to concentration camps. To his credit, Almasy saved the lives of several Jewish families, using his rank and reputation as a war hero to bluff his way through thorny situations, and sheltering them at great risk to himself.

In early 1945, Budapest fell to the Red Army in an orgy of rape and looting. Thousands of Hungarians were sent to labor camps in Siberia, and Almasy was arrested and imprisoned by the Soviets as "an enemy of the people." His book *With Rommel's Army in Libya*, heavily edited by the Nazis, had come back to haunt him, making him appear as if he was in line with National Socialist ideology. He was subjected by the Russians to a series of long, brutal interrogations at notorious 60 Androssy Boulevard in Budapest, the same building that had been used by the Hungarian Fascist Police. After being questioned for eight straight months, he was finally put on trial. Many people spoke on his behalf, the charges against him were dropped by the Peoples Court, and he was released. However, in January 1947 he was arrested again, this time by the Hungarian Secret Police, and questioned about his links with western intelligence. At this point, Alaeddin Moukhton, a cousin of King Farouk, paid a substantial bribe to Almasy's jailers to obtain his release and he made his way through a circuitous route to Cairo. This was done with the help of MI6, with whom Almasy was in touch with during the Soviet invasion, sending the British details of Red Army movements. As Simmons states, Almasy must have been a British agent at some point and of some importance—even a double agent while still apparently serving the Germans—for MI6 to have gone to such lengths to save his life.

Alaeddin Moukhton and men from British intelligence picked him up at Cairo airport. After years of desert hardship and months of abuse by the Soviet and Hungarian Secret Police, he was a physical wreck and walked with a stoop. He was set up in a flat in the fashionable Zamalek district of Cairo and was paid a small allowance, thankful to be back in his beloved Egypt. King Farouk soon made him Technical Director of the Desert Research Institute. According to Bierman and Simmons, he was still obsessed with the prospect of finding Zerzura and the lost army of Cambyses, who according to Herodotus had taken his Persian Army into the desert and promptly disappeared in a sandstorm somewhere between the Farafra Oasis and Bahrein in the Great Sand Sea. However, the Hungarian adventurer's health was failing badly and he was found to be suffering from hepatitis and amoebic dysentery, which he had first contracted on Operation Salam. At the expense of Farouk, he was invalided to Austria for treatment near Salzburg. The doctors found that his liver was seriously damaged and little could be done medically to improve his condition. He had no visitors and was barely conscious, rambling on about Zerzura and King Cambyses and his lost army.

The Father of the Sands died on March 22, 1951 and was buried in the Salzburg municipal cemetery. The only mourners were his doctor, a priest, and his brother Janos Almasy and his wife. It would be more than forty years later that he would receive posthumous, albeit somewhat spurious and distorted, international celebrity as the romantic protagonist of the Booker Prize-winning novel and multiple Oscar-winning film, *The English Patient*, which propelled the desert adventurer once again into the limelight. The epitaph on his grave, erected by Hungarian aviation and desert enthusiasts in 1995 three years after the book's publication, honors him as a "Pilot, Sahara Explorer, and Discoverer of the Zerzura Oasis."

A bronze bust of Almasy is now displayed in the grounds of the Hungarian National Geographical Museum at Erd near Budapest. The verdict of his old Zerzura Club colleagues on his desert explorations and war record was summed up by George Murray of the Egyptian Desert Survey: "A Nazi but a sportsman!"

Almasy was unquestionably a man of changing loyalties but he was hardly a Nazi. While he did fight for the Reich as a captain in the Abwehr, he also rescued Jews, lent aid to his English desert explorer friend Clayton, plied his anti-Soviet tradecraft secretly for the British Secret Service after the war, and didn't look or act anything like Ralph Fiennes. That, as history tells us, was the real Almasy.

SOURCES AND ACKNOWLEDGEMENTS

To develop the story line, characters, and scenes for *Lions of the Desert: A True Story of WWII Heroes in North Africa*, I consulted over a hundred archival materials, non-fiction books, magazine and newspaper articles, blogs, Web sites, and numerous individuals, and I visited many of the historical locations in the novel. There are too many resources and locations to name here. However, I would be remiss if I didn't give credit to the key historical references upon which this novel is based, as well as the critical individuals who dramatically improved the quality of the manuscript from its initial to its final stage. Any technical mistakes in the historical facts underpinning the novel, typographical errors, or examples of overreach due to artistic license, however, are the fault of me and me alone.

In addition to the primary reference materials from British and United States archives listed below, I relied heavily upon fourteen reliable primary and secondary sources dealing specifically with the North African Desert Campaign, the Special Air Service and Long Range Desert Group, Operations Salam and Condor, the British Occupation of Egypt, and the major historical figures in the novel. These references were invaluable and included the following for those interested in further reading about the historical events and personalities presented in the book: *Operation Condor, Intelligence and National Security* (1989) by H.O. Covey; *The Lost Oasis: The True Story Behind the English Patient* (2002) by Saul Kelly; *The Rebecca Code: Rommel's Spy in North Africa and Operation Condor* (2012) by Mark Simmons; *The Battle of Alamein: Turning Point, World War II* (2002) by John Bierman and Colin Smith; *The Rommel Papers* (1953) by B.H. Liddell Hart (ed.); *Field Marshal: the Life and Death of Erwin Rommel* (2017) by Daniel Allen Butler; *Monty and Rommel: Parallel Lives* (2012) by Peter Caddick-Adams; *The Phantom Major* (1958) by Virginia Cowles; *David Stirling: The Authorised Biography of the Creator of the SAS* (1992) by Alan Hoe; *Rogue Heroes: The History of the SAS, Britain's Secret Special Forces Unit That Sabotaged the Nazis and Changed the Nature of War* (2016) by Ben Macintyre; *I Spied Spies* (1965) by A.E.W. Sansom; *The Third Reich Is Listening: Inside German Codebreaking 1939-1945* (2018) by Christian Jennings; *Turning the Hinge of Fate: Good Source and the UK-U.S. Intelligence Alliance, 1940-1942* (2008) by C.J. Jenner; and *Cairo in the War 1939-1945* (1989) by Artemis Cooper.

In writing the novel, there were many excellent historical books and articles in addition to those listed above from which I drew facts and inspiration to flesh out the story of the Desert War in 1941-1942 and the major historical figures presented in the book. The interested reader is referred to the following additional sources used to write the true story presented herein.

North African Desert Campaign, General WWII, Rommel, and Montgomery: *Rommel's Intelligence in the Desert Campaign* (1985) by Hans-Otto Behrendt; *Rommel: The Desert Fox* (1955) by Desmond Young; *The Imperial War Museum Book of the Desert War, 1940-42* (1992) by Adrian Gilbert (ed.); *Patton, Montgomery, Rommel: Masters of War* (2008) by Terry Brighton; *Alamein: Great*

Battles (2016) by Simon Ball; *Monty: Master of the Battlefield 1942-1944* (1983) by Nigel Hamilton; *Pendulum of War: Three Battles at El Alamein* (2005) by Niall Barr; *The Memoirs of Field Marshal The Viscount Montgomery of Alamein* (1959) by Bernard Law Montgomery; *Knight's Cross: A Life of Field Marshal Erwin Rommel* (1994) by David Fraser; *Rommel: In His Own Words* (2015) by John Pimlott (ed.); *The Rommel Myth* (2003) by Maurice Philip Remy; *The Phantom Army of Alamein: How the Camouflage Unit and Operation Bertram Hoodwinked Rommel* (2012) by Rick Stroud; *An Army at Dawn: The War in North Africa, 1942–1943* (2002), *The Day of Battle: The War in Sicily and Italy, 1943–1944* (2007), and *The Guns at Last Light: The War in Western Europe, 1944–1945* (2013) by Rick Atkinson; *The Second World War* (2005) by John Keegan; *El Alamein: The Battle that Turned the Tide of the Second World War* (2012) by Bryn Hammond; *Tobruk* (2016) by Peter FitzSimons; *The Desert War: The Classic Trilogy on the North African Campaign 1940-1943* (2017) by Alan Moorehead; *Montgomery and the Eighth Army: A Selection from the Diaries, Correspondence and Other Papers of Field Marshal the Viscount Montgomery of Alamein* (1991) by Stephen Brooks (ed.); *Rommel's Desert War: The Life and Death of the Afrika Korps* (2007) and *Rommel's Desert Commanders: The Men Who Served the Desert Fox, North Africa, 1941-42* (2008) by Samuel W. Mitcham Jr.; *Rommel in North Africa: Quest for the Nile* (2017) and *With Rommel in the Desert: Tripoli to El Alamein* (2017) by David Mitchelhill-Green; *The Day Rommel Was Stopped: The Battle of Ruweisat Ridge, 2 July 1942* (2017) by F. R. Jephson and Chris Jephson; *The Allies Strike Back, 1941-1943: The War in the West* (2017) by James Holland; *Joint by Design: The Western Desert Campaign* (2015) by Major Kathryn Gaetke; *The Real Rommel: A Gentleman German Officer* (2014) and *Soldier Roy Wooldridge's Life Saved by Erwin Rommel* (2014) by BBC; *The Mirage of the Desert Fox: Erwin Rommel and the Whitewashing of the Nazi Past* (2017) by Will Greer; *Drive to Nowhere: The Myth of the Afrika Korps, 1941-43* (2018) by Robert Citino; *North Africa: The War of Logistics* (2017) by Allyn Vannoy; and *How Hitler's Most Dangerous General Met His Match* (2018) by Harold E. Raugh Jr.

David Stirling, Special Air Service, and Long Range Desert Group: *Stirling's Men: The Inside History of the SAS in World War II* (2006), *The SAS in World War II* (2011), *The Daring Dozen: 12 Special Forces Legends of World War II* (2012), *Stirling's Desert Triumph: The SAS Egyptian Airfield Raids 1942* (2015), and *The Long Range Desert Group in World War II* (2017) by Gavin Mortimer; *Wind and War: Memoirs of a Desert Explorer* (1990) by R.A. Bagnold; *The Originals: The Secret History of the Birth of the SAS: In Their Own Words* (2006) by Gordon Stevens; *Eastern Approaches* (1991) by Fitzroy Maclean; *Popski's Private Army* (1950) by Vladimir Peniakoff; *Killing Rommel: A Novel* (2008) by Steven Pressfield; *Rogue Warrior of the SAS: The Blair Mayne Legend* (2011) by Martin Dillon and Roy Bradford; *Paddy Mayne: Lt Col Blair 'Paddy' Mayne, 1 SAS Regiment* (2004) by Hamish Ross; *Desert Raiders: Axis and Allied Special Forces 1940–43* (2007) by Andrea Molinari.

Operations Salam and Condor, British, U.S., and German Intelligence Services, and Bonner Fellers: British MI6 files about Johannes Eppler, Agent Condor: *Public Records of The British National Archives, Kew, London: KV 2/1467*; U.S.

Government Records on Bonner Feller's Reports to Washington and Service Record: *Records of the U.S. War Department General and Special Staffs, G-2 Regional File, 1933-1944, Record Group 165 Entry (NM-84); Records of the U.S. Army Staff, Military Intelligence Division, Project Decimal Files, 1941–1945, Record Group 319 Entry (NM3); Records of the Army Staff. Office of the Assistant Chief of Staff for Intelligence. Dispatches and Cables, 1941–1964, Record Group 319 Entry (NM3); U.S. Army Center of Military History, Bonner Frank Fellers U.S. Army Service Record; Rommel Ruft Cairo* (1960) and *Operation Condor: Rommel's Spy* (1977) by John Eppler; *With Rommel's Army in Libya* (2001) by László Almasy (Author) and Gabriel Francis Horchler (Translator); *The Lost Keys to El Alamein* (1993) by Wilhelm F. Flicke; *MI6* (1983) and *Double Cross in Cairo: The True Story of the Spy Who Turned the Tide of War in the Middle East* (2015) by Nigel West; *The Foxes of the Desert* (1953) by Paul Carell; *Rommel and the Secret War in North Africa: Secret Intelligence in the North African Campaign 1941-43* (2004) by Janusz Piekalkiewicz; *The Cat and the Mice* (1958) by Leonard Mosley; *Intercepted Communications, A Secret Ear for the Desert Fox* (1996) by Wil Deac; *Bodyguard of Lies* (1976) by Anthony Cave Brown; *'C': A Biography of Sir Maurice Oldfield* (1985) by Richard Deacon; *The Key to Rebecca* (1980) by Ken Follett; *The City of Gold* (1992) by Len Deighton; *Practice to Deceive* (1977) and *Master of Deception* (1980) by David Mure; *The English Patient* (1992) by Michael Ondaatje, screenplay (1996) by Anthony Minghella; *Hitler's Spies: German Military Intelligence in World War II* (2000) and *How I Discovered World War II's Greatest Spy and Other Stories of Intelligence and Code* (2014) by David Kahn; *Deceiving Hitler: Double Cross and Deception in World War II* (2008) by Terry Crowdy; *The Deceivers: Allied Military Deception in the Second World War* (2007) by Thaddeus Holt; *Wild Bill Donovan: The Spymaster Who Created the OSS and Modern American Espionage* (2011) by Douglas Waller; *Into the Lion's Mouth: The True Story of Dusko Popov: World War II Spy, Patriot, and the Real-Life Inspiration for James Bond* (2016) by Larry Loftis; *Defend the Realm: The Authorized History of MI5* (2009) by Christopher Andrew; *The Real Spy's Story Reads Like Fiction and 40 Years Later Inspires a Best-Seller* (1980) by Pamela Andriotakis.

Cairo in the War: *Cairo: The City Victorious* (2000) by Max Rodenbeck; *The War of the Weak Nations: Egypt in World War II 1939-1945* (2018) by Israel Gershoni; *Revolt on the Nile* (1957) by Anwar el Sadat; *Egypt Didn't Shill for the Nazis in World War II* (2018) by Orit Bashkin; *To War with Whitaker: The Wartime Diaries of the Countess of Ranfurly, 1939-45* (1995) by Hermione Ranfurly; *Cairo: A Thousand Years of the City Victorious* (1971) by Janet Abu Lughod; *Sergeant Kennedy's World War II Diary* (2010) by William M. Kennedy; *Cairo* (2001) by André Raymond; *Cairo: Histories of a City* (2013) by Nezar AlSayyad; *Shepheard's Hotel: British Base in Cairo* (2012), *The Hotel That History Forgot* (2012), and *Shepheard's in Photographs* (2016) on Egypt in the Golden Age of Travel website; *Tiki Expert Recounts Amazing Life of Joe Scialom* (2012) by Todd A. Price; *Joe Scialom & the Suffering Bastard* (2014) by Morgan Hamilton-Griffin; *The Fox Behind the Desert Fox—Hekmat Fahmy* (2017) by Piper Bayard; *Rabab: Hekmat Fahmy Egyptian Bellydancer* (2018) Film Bio; *Hekmat Fahmy: Profile of a Spy* (2018) by Priscilla Adum.

I would also personally like to thank the following for their support and assistance. First and foremost, I would like to thank my wife Christine, an exceptional and highly professional book editor, who painstakingly reviewed and copy-edited the novel. Any mistakes that remain are my fault, of course.

Second, I would like to thank my literary agent, Cherry Weiner of the Cherry Weiner Literary Agency, for thoroughly reviewing, vetting, and copy-editing the manuscript, and for making countless improvements to the finished novel.

Third, I would like to thank Stephen King's former editor, Patrick LoBrutto, for thoroughly copy-editing the various drafts of the novel and providing detailed reviews.

I would also like to thank the late Austin and Anne Marquis, Governor Roy Romer, Ambassador Marc Grossman, Betsy and Steve Hall, Rik Hall, Christian Fuenfhausen, Bill and Doug Eberhart, Fred Taylor, David Boyles, Mo Shafroth, Peter Brooke, Tim and Carey Romer, Peter and Lorrie Frautschi, Deirdre Grant Mercurio, Dawn Ezzo Roseman, Joe Tallman, John Welch, Link Nicoll, Toni Conte Augusta Francis, Brigid Donnelly Hughes, John and Ellen Aisenbrey, Margot Patterson, Cathy and Jon Jenkins, Danny Bilello and Elena Diaz-Bilello, Charlie and Kay Fial, Vincent Bilello, Elizabeth Gardner, Robin McGehee, and the other book reviewers and professional contributors large and small who have given generously of their time over the years, as well as to those who have given me loyal support as I have ventured on this incredible odyssey of historical fiction writing.

Lastly, I want to thank anyone and everyone who bought this book and my loyal fans and supporters who helped promote this work. You know who you are and I salute you.

ABOUT THE AUTHOR

The ninth great-grandson of legendary privateer Captain William Kidd, Samuel Marquis is the bestselling, award-winning author of a World War Two Series, the Nick Lassiter-Skyler International Espionage Series, and historical American fiction. His novels have been #1 *Denver Post* bestsellers and received multiple national book awards (Kirkus Reviews and Foreword Reviews Book of the Year, American Book Fest and USA Best Book, Readers' Favorite, Beverly Hills, Independent Publisher, National Indie Excellence, Next Generation Indie, and Colorado Book Awards). His books have also garnered glowing reviews from #1 bestseller James Patterson, Kirkus, and Foreword Reviews (5 Stars). Critics and book reviewers have compared the books of his WWII Series to the epic historical novels of Tom Clancy, John le Carré, Ken Follett, Herman Wouk, Daniel Silva, Len Deighton, and Alan Furst.

Below is a list of Samuel Marquis novels along with their release dates and book awards.

THE WORLD WAR TWO SERIES
Bodyguard of Deception – March 2016 – Winner Foreword Reviews' Book of the Year Awards; Award-Winning Finalist USA Best Book Awards

Altar of Resistance – January 2017 – Award-Winning Finalist Foreword Reviews' Book of the Year Awards, American Book Fest Best Book Awards, and Beverly Hills Book Awards

Spies of the Midnight Sun: A True Story of WWII Heroes – May 2018 – Winner Independent Publisher Book Awards

Lions of the Desert: A True Story of WWII Heroes in North Africa – February 2019 – Winner Readers' Favorite, National Indie Excellence, and Beverly Hills Book Awards; Award-Winning Finalist Foreword Reviews' Book of the Year and American Fiction Best Book Awards

Soldiers of Freedom: The WWII Story of Patton's Panthers and the Edelweiss Pirates – March 2020

THE NICK LASSITER – SKYLER INTERNATIONAL ESPIONAGE SERIES
The Devil's Brigade – September 2015 – #1 Denver Post Bestseller; Award-Winning Finalist Beverly Hills Book Awards

The Coalition – January 2016 – Winner Beverly Hills Book Awards; Award-Winning Finalist USA Best Book Awards and Colorado Book Awards

The Fourth Pularchek – June 2017 – Winner Independent Publisher Book Awards; Award-Winning Finalist American Book Fest Best Book Awards and Beverly Hills Book Awards

HISTORICAL PIRATE FICTION
Blackbeard: The Birth of America – February 2018 – Winner Kirkus Reviews Book of the Year and Beverly Hills Book Awards; Award-Winning Finalist American Book Fest Best Book Awards

THE JOE HIGHEAGLE ENVIRONMENTAL SLEUTH SERIES
Blind Thrust – October 2015 – #1 Denver Post Bestseller; Winner Foreword Reviews' Book of the Year and Next Generation Indie Book Awards; Award-Winning Finalist USA Best Book Awards, Beverly Hills Book Awards, and Next Generation Indie Book Awards

Cluster of Lies – September 2016 – Winner Beverly Hills Book Awards; Award-Winning Finalist USA Best Book Awards and Foreword Reviews Book of the Year Awards

Thank You for Your Support!

If you can lend a helping hand, please post a review on Amazon (https://amzn.to/2yr3M0q**), Bookbub (**https://bit.ly/2RVxukV**), and/or Goodreads (**https://bit.ly/2KlfpbQ**). Thanks in advance!**

To Order Samuel Marquis Books and Contact Samuel:

Visit Samuel Marquis's website, join his mailing list, learn about his forthcoming historical fiction novels and book events, and order his books at www.samuelmarquisbooks.com. **Please send all fan mail (including criticism) to** samuelmarquisbooks@gmail.com.

Made in United States
Troutdale, OR
05/26/2025